THE AUTOBIOGRAPHY OF
JEAN-LUC PICARD

THE STORY OF ONE OF STARFLEET'S MOST INSPIRATIONAL CAPTAINS

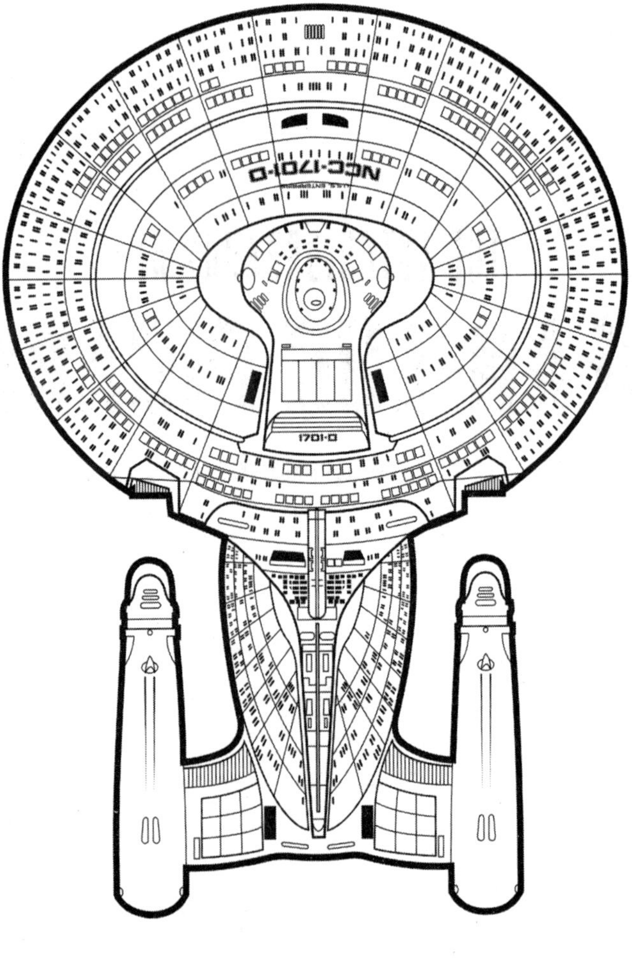
NCC-1701-D
1701-D

THE AUTOBIOGRAPHY OF
JEAN-LUC PICARD

THE STORY OF ONE OF STARFLEET'S MOST INSPIRATIONAL CAPTAINS

BY
JEAN-LUC PICARD

EDITED BY DAVID A. GOODMAN

TITAN BOOKS

The Autobiography of Jean-Luc Picard
Print Edition ISBN: 9781785659409
E-Book Edition ISBN: 9781785656637

Published by Titan Books
A division of Titan Publishing Group Ltd.
144 Southwark Street, London SE1 0UP

First edition: October 2017
10 9 8 7 6 5 4 3 2 1

TM ® & © 2017 by CBS Studios Inc. © 2017 Paramount Pictures Corporation. STAR TREK and related marks and logos are trademarks of CBS Studios Inc. All Rights Reserved.

All rights reserved. No part of this publication may be reproduced, stored in a retrieval system, or transmitted, in any form or by any means, electronic, mechanical, photocopying, recording, or otherwise, without prior written permission from the publisher.

Illustrations: Russell Walks
Editor: Simon Ward
Interior design: Tim Scrivens

A CIP catalogue record for this title is available from the British Library.

Printed and bound in India by Thomson Press India Ltd.

Did you enjoy this book? We love to hear from our readers. Please e-mail us at: readerfeedback@titanemail.com or write to Reader Feedback at the above address.

To receive advance information, news, competitions, and exclusive offers online, please sign up for the Titan newsletter on our website: www.titanbooks.com.

CONTENTS

FOREWORD BY BEVERLY CRUSHER PICARD, M.D., STARFLEET CAPTAIN 1

PROLOGUE 3

CHAPTER ONE 7

CHAPTER TWO 29

CHAPTER THREE 57

CHAPTER FOUR 83

CHAPTER FIVE.. 99

CHAPTER SIX..127

CHAPTER SEVEN 155

CHAPTER EIGHT..177

CHAPTER NINE 213

CHAPTER TEN... 243

CHAPTER ELEVEN 269

For my father.

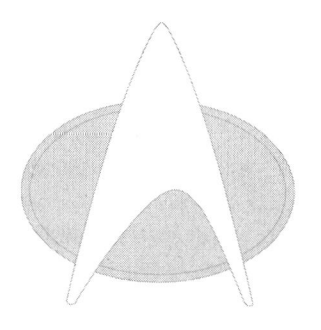

FOREWORD
BY BEVERLY CRUSHER PICARD, M.D., STARFLEET CAPTAIN

WHEN JEAN-LUC ASKED ME TO WRITE THIS INTRODUCTION, I was overtaken by a flood of emotions. I've been through so much with this man, how could I put into words what he means to me, but more importantly, what he means to the history of the Galaxy? He single-handedly prevented wars, saved civilizations, as well as expanded the boundaries of knowledge—

OH, WHAT DRIVEL! I am the Q. You may have heard of me, I'm somewhat all-powerful and I am rewriting this dull essay by Dr. Beverly. Don't ask how—I have the ability to be in all places and times at once, and I'm improving the introduction as you read it. You know they were in love? We all knew it and it took them years to do something about it. I think Picard talks about that in this book—I assume he does, I haven't read it. Maybe I'll read it right now.

Okay, I just read it.

It's spectacularly mundane, filled with all those dull human tropes of triumphing over adversity and learning from your mistakes. Oh, and the importance of love and friendship. Humans are so predictable. I don't know why I'm even bothering with this, but I am. Maybe it's because next to Picard I am a god, and yet he has been able to get in my way. I could've destroyed him years ago, wiped him from existence. In fact, I still could.

I just did.

And I just brought him back. That's how easy it is.

But as much as I hate to say it, Picard gives my life meaning. I've toyed with many of his species throughout the ages; most end up in insane asylums, but not Picard. He is the perfect human: he strives, he achieves, he wrestles with problems until he finds his solutions, and as often as he's right, he's wrong. But, unlike most of you, he admits when he's wrong. You have no idea how rare that is in your species. Maybe that's why you like him. And maybe, pathetic human, you'll like this book. Now back to poor Dr. Beverly.

—it is a testimony to his achievements, but also to the man himself. I hope you enjoy it as much as I did.

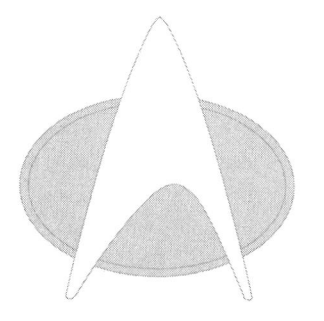

PROLOGUE

THE CORRIDOR WAS BOTH OPPRESSIVELY WARM AND HARSHLY COLD. The warmth was the literal temperature; the chill came from a profound lack of emotion. This was the end of my freedom.

"To facilitate our introduction to your societies, it has been decided that a human voice will speak for us in all communications. You have been chosen to be that voice."

I was flanked by two guards, silent man-machine hybrids, in a modern catacomb three kilometers on either side. Starkly white and gray figures, just like the ones standing next to me, stood in rows on stacked floors of a vast metal superstructure. I searched for the source of the voice. There was none, yet it surrounded me. It seemed to come from all the figures, yet their mouths never moved.

This was the Borg. An alien race of cybernetic beings, part-organic and part-machine, linked together into a hive mind. They scooped whole cities off the face of planets, absorbing the people and technology, homogenizing them as part of the collective. And now they wanted me to speak for them to help accelerate the absorption of my people.

This was a fight for civilization. I was in command of the Federation flagship, the *U.S.S. Enterprise*, a *Galaxy*-class starship with a crew of over a thousand. We had been the first to engage the Borg cube, the huge 27-cubic-kilometer starship that had penetrated our sector of space. It had already destroyed the New Providence colony on Jouret IV.

Our first engagement with the Borg cube had not been completely successful. Once I realized we wouldn't be able to stop it, my hope was to at least delay its progress so that Starfleet would have time to gather a superior force to destroy it. This ended up playing into their plans, as the Borg had shown specific interest in me, and when my delay tactics eventually were exhausted, they kidnapped me from the bridge of my own ship.

Now I had discovered why they were interested in me. They said our "archaic civilization" was authority driven and that they needed one voice to talk to it. I wouldn't let myself be used. I was scared, but I remembered that courage is not the absence of fear, but the triumph over it. I had to fight. I had faced many adversaries in my career; my life had been at mortal risk numerous times. I had a wealth of experience to draw from in the coming fight; I was determined to hang on.

I was foolishly naïve.

Without warning, my two guards grabbed me, their grip around my arms like a metal vise. They lifted me off the ground and dropped me on a nearby table. While one held me down by the throat, the other removed my tunic and trousers. I lay naked and helpless.

I looked at the one who held me by the throat. He'd been human once. His right eye was completely covered by a cybernetic implant, tubes and conduit connecting his head to his chest, and his face a ghostly white. He looked at me with the empty gaze of a dead man. Lifting his free hand, three tubules extended from it and pierced my neck. They injected something and everything changed.

I heard voices, softly at first, then like a cresting wave I couldn't escape, they overtook me and I was submerged. Disparate, deafening noise, languages I didn't understand… and then suddenly I understood them all. Hundreds of thousands of minds on this Borg ship alone, connected to billions more, each working individually and together. And it felt like all of them wanted to pry open my mind.

I tried to block them out, but I had no defense; they were already in there. Like a billion hands rooting through a used-clothing bin in an ancient thrift shop, picking and examining what they wanted, tossing aside what they didn't. In my memories they jumped around in time: my first haircut; a laugh shared with a childhood friend; a similar laugh shared with my first officer; my final exam at the academy; my brother pushing me down in the mud; the first woman I was ever intimate with.

Then the search became more discerning and focused on what they were looking for: my casual memory of a starbase commander telling me how his defense shield worked; operating the phaser bank on a *Constellation*-class ship in battle until it was drained; my crew apprising me of their plans for counteracting the Borg weapons.

It didn't stop. The collective now wanted my mind to work: it wasn't just pilfering memories, it wanted my opinion on how to attack my compatriots. I concentrated, trying to present false information, but my deception was ripped away like a paper Halloween mask. My experience and judgment belonged to them. I had an image of myself, it was still there, but I had no control over my mind anymore. It was part of the collective, which used my thoughts and experiences and created a new identity. The morality and ethics and loyalty and affection of Jean-Luc Picard dropped away, a small puddle this new identity stood over.

They called it Locutus. It had access to everything I was. It was me, but it wasn't. I had no strength against it.

And what was left of me watched as Locutus made his plans with the Borg, using what I gave them. I could see it all, how it would all happen. The *Enterprise* would be first; the plan to destroy the Borg cube was laid bare for the enemy now, and the collective had begun work on a defense. And in just a moment, the work would be finished. The *Enterprise* would fail.

I was nothing. A puddle on the floor. I wanted to die. And the collective knew it, heard my plea for death. For a moment, the voices went silent, as if ordered to be quiet. And then came the quiet laughter, malevolent and mirthless.

"Oh, we won't let you die, Jean-Luc," she said. "Not yet."

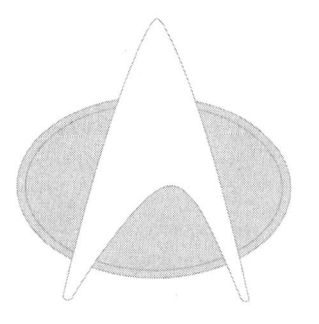

CHAPTER ONE

THE DOOR TO THE BASEMENT WAS OAK, with five thick vertical slats and two crossbeams, and always locked. The lock had a large, ancient key, which was attached to an oversized metal ring and kept on a hook just inside the hall closet. I had seen my father go through that basement door only a few times. He'd take the key from the closet, turn the lock, enter, and quickly close the door behind him; I could hear the creaky wooden stairs beyond. Eventually, he'd emerge, lock the door, and replace the key.

It is difficult to describe how tantalizing that locked door was to my younger self. Our house was several centuries old, so there were locks on many of the doors, all unused. On 24th-century planet Earth there was no crime, no intruders, no theft or vandalism; there was no need for locks on most of our world, especially in the small, sleepy village of La Barre, France.

Yet *this* door my father locked.

Once, when I was around five, he caught me jiggling the handle to see if it would open. He pulled me back by the shoulder and gave me a stern look.

"You are not allowed in there," he said. His tone was quiet but threatening, and I was so scared I burst into tears and ran to my room.

By the time I reached the age of seven, however, fear of my father's wrath was overtaken, or at least obscured, by the ever-growing curiosity about what lay beyond the wooden barrier. It was the first week of September, the harvest had begun, and I'd been out in the vineyard with my father, mother, and brother sorting grapes. My father had decided the grapes had reached their desired ripeness, and we'd take the bunches from the vines, then separate the fruit from the stems. For a seven-year-old, this was endless, tiring work. There were plenty of machines that could've done the work for us, but my father refused (more on that later). The work held no interest for me, but, like all the work the family did in making our wine, it went without saying that I had to participate. Making matters worse for me, the first harvest's work was always done at night. The heat of the days made the work too straining, and since we were picking grapes, in the daytime the sugar from the fruit attracted all manner of hungry insects.

I had come into the house for one of my frequent trips to the bathroom, many of which were just an attempt to avoid some of the work. On my way back outside, a plan suddenly took shape in my mind. The family was engaged in the harvest; I would have the house to myself for a while before anyone came looking for me. I went to the hall closet and, after a quick look outside, grabbed the ring with the key.

And immediately dropped it.

The loud clatter of the iron against the wooden floor froze me in panic. I slowly moved to the front window (somehow equating that making more noise with my footsteps might be the tipping point in my mission's failure), and saw that no one appeared to be approaching the house. I then went back to the key ring and picked it up. It was much heavier than I imagined.

I went to the basement door and inserted the key. It took both of my small hands to turn the weighty lock. After some struggle, it opened with a satisfying thunk.

I turned the knob, and the door creaked open. The staircase beyond was only partially illuminated by the light from the doorway—after the fifth or sixth step there was complete darkness.

I moved into the unknown. The handrail was very high up for my seven-year-old height, and after two steps I decided to throw caution to the wind and let go of it. When I reached the barrier of blackness on the sixth step, I paused. My eyes adjusted to the darkness beyond, and I could make out the bottom of the stairs. I was sure there had to be a light switch on the wall down there, though I couldn't see one from where I was standing. Excitement overcame nervousness; I proceeded. As I lifted my foot to keep going, however, I was interrupted.

"What are you doing?!"

THE STORY OF ONE OF STARFLEET'S MOST INSPIRATIONAL CAPTAINS

The voice was behind me. I turned toward it and lost my footing, slipping on the next step. I reached for the handrail in vain and tumbled down the staircase. Though it was perhaps only another six or seven steps, it seemed endless. I landed backwards, slamming my head onto the basement's concrete floor. I howled, then tried to move, but was overwhelmed by an intense pain in my leg. More torture than I'd ever felt, I couldn't catch my breath; it was too much to process. I looked up in panic.

At the top of the stairs my thirteen-year-old brother Robert stood in the doorway, stiff and unsure. He was caught in an unsolvable dilemma: he knew he should come to my aid, but to do so would break our father's strict rule about not going into the basement. At the time I could not appreciate his position, I only saw him staring at me then running off, abandoning me in distress.

Again, I tried to move, gingerly, but the pain was unbelievable. I looked around, overcome with fear, weeping helplessly.

My eyes adjusted to the darkness, and I saw something that momentarily made me forget my agony.

There were faces. They surrounded me, staring. Large ghosts floating in the shadows. I couldn't understand what I was looking at.

"Jean-Luc?!" The voice of my rescuer, my mother, as she ran down the steps. Even in her work boots and overalls, an elegant angel of mercy. She immediately examined my leg.

"Oh, dear, what have you done?" she said. "Maurice, bring the first aid kit…"

"I have the damn kit, calm down," he said as he came down the stairs at his usual unhurried pace, carrying the small black case. Behind him, at the top of the stairs, Robert had returned, and from his expression was clearly now jealous of the attention I was receiving.

My father handed the kit to my mother, who removed a hypo and injected it into my arm. The pain in my leg and head suddenly abated. She replaced the hypo, then took out a small gray device: a bone knitter.

"Maman," I said, whispering, still scared but comforted by her presence. "There are people in the dark…"

"Shhh, I know," she said, as she activated the device and applied it to my leg. "Turn on the lights, Maurice. They're scaring the boy…"

"What doesn't scare the boy?" he said.

"Maurice," my mother said, a snap of condemnation.

Whether the judgment of my mother's tone affected him, his expression didn't reveal, but he went to the wall switch, and the room was illuminated. I could see now the staircase ended in the center of a long hallway dug from the stone beneath the house, three meters high, a hundred meters long. On both sides, the faces became clear; framed paintings and photographs, all portraits, lined the walls. There were dozens. Some of the paintings depicted scenes of ancient Earth, while some of the photographs were more recent. It was a museum of some sort. I turned to my father.

"Who are those people?"

"That," my father said, with grave import, "is the family."

✦

I have to say, the discovery that the secret of the basement was a portrait museum was something of a disappointment. My father had kept the room locked for the mundane reason of keeping the portraiture safe from his often rambunctious sons. However, once my brother and I were in on the "secret," my father began our education of its importance in his life, and, by extension, ours. He wanted us to know the Picards mattered.

This, as it turned out, was not without justification.

The name Picard has a long heritage on Earth that began in ancient Brittany; the line can be traced back all way to the 9th century AD, when Charlemagne, King of the Franks, was uniting Europe. For several centuries, the Picards would hold a family seat in the fiefdom of Vieille Ville in Brittany, where they were elevated to *Vicomtes* (Viscounts), a title of nobility. The name spread throughout France, and by the 14th century there were Picards in Normandy, Lyonnais, and Champagne.

Over time, I would become aware and eventually awed by the important work of my ancestors: Pierre Picard arrived in Quebec in 1629, one of the earliest French settlers in North America; Bernard Picart (an ancestor despite the variant spelling) was a famous French engraver known for his book illustrations of the popular Christian religious text, the Bible, in the 18th century; noted astronomer Jean-Félix Picard, for whom the Picard crater on Earth's moon is named; Joseph-Denis Picard, a divisional general during the French Revolution of the late 18th century; Frank Picard, who won the Nobel

THE STORY OF ONE OF STARFLEET'S MOST INSPIRATIONAL CAPTAINS

Prize in Chemistry in 2028, and later Louise Picard, who helped found the Martian colony. All of their likenesses were in the basement family shrine, maintained for centuries by their relatives who lived in the vineyard.

The specific history of the Picard vineyard began during the Napoleonic Wars of the 1800s. Henri Picard, a captain in Napoleon's navy, purchased the land in the small village of La Barre, in the eastern French region of Bourgogne-Franche-Comté. The gently rolling hills and sleepy way of life appealed to a man who had spent his life at sea; it was a great tragedy that he never got to enjoy it. The purchase was made shortly before his death in 1805 commanding the French ship *Saturne* at the Battle of Trafalgar.[*]

His brother, Louis, decided to plant pinot noir grapes on about a half-acre of the 20-acre parcel. The winery took years to produce that first vintage of Chateau Picard, 1815; then it was a very low-yielding vineyard, producing a paltry four hundred bottles. Over time more acreage was planted and the winemaking improved so that by the end of the 20th century each acre of grapes produced six thousand bottles of wine.

In that pre-industrial age of the first vintages, the winemaking methods were determined by the limited technology; grapes were harvested and pressed either by hand or primitive machines. For better or worse, these crude methods became tradition. My family ignored advances in winemaking technology, and, as a result, Chateau Picard has been made the same way for the last five hundred years. This would end up being an unforeseen advantage during the World War in the 22nd century. When John Ericsson, the genetically engineered ruler of Europe, invaded France, he destroyed the country's technological base. So, even during this dark period of the world's history, Chateau Picard survived.[**]

---

[*] **EDITOR'S NOTE:** There is no official historical record of a Henri Picard or a ship named Saturne at the Battle of Trafalgar. However, it is well known that record keeping of the time was not always accurate; private family histories often contain precise details lost in the more official histories.

[**] **EDITOR'S NOTE:** Destroying the technological base was not the only legacy of Ericsson's invasion. Though of Nordic descent, Ericsson was raised in the United Kingdom, and sought to remake Europe as a reborn British Empire. One of the remaining monuments to the success of his efforts is the fact that, even in the 24th century, many French people have British accents.

This first refusal of technology became dismissiveness, and eventually disdain. By the time my father, Maurice, was born in 2270, it had seeped into the bones of our familial culture. Father grew up in a home that reveled in the primitive. We worked our vineyard, food was cooked by hand. His leisure time, what there was of it, was spent reading. He developed a love of Shakespeare, which he passed on to his sons, as well as a fondness for Earl Grey tea.*

Modern society changed how people consumed and produced wine, the invention of the replicator radically altering the economics of food production. By the 23rd century, anyone manufacturing wine was doing it for the art of it, and my paternal grandparents, François and Genevieve, were experts. They produced some of our most memorable vintages, including the renowned 2247. My father reveled in this reputation, and threw himself into this life, taking over as the winery's cellarmaster at the relatively young age of 29, even though my grandfather was still alive and living at the vineyard.

"He was single-minded," my mother once told me. "Even François [his father] recognized Maurice's passion and determination to make great wine surpassed his own." I suppose if I inherited a character trait from my father it was his single-mindedness, his drive to do something, or create something, great and memorable. In one conversation with my mother she admitted to me that she felt my father lacked some imagination; he not only never physically left La Barre, his mind never did either. He decided to only imagine himself running the family winery. "Of course," she said with a wry smile, "some found this dedication and single-mindedness attractive."

My mother, born Yvette Gessard in 2274, was also from La Barre. She met my father in secondary school, where they began a romance. When she left for university (at the renowned École Polytechnique), he had already proposed marriage, and she had accepted. She was interested in the sciences, but she tailored her education to give her a place on our family vineyard.

"My professors were quite frustrated with my desire to become an enologist," she said. "They felt I was wasting my potential." An enologist is a scientist whose background includes chemistry, microbiology, geology, meteorology, and soil science. Of course, the enologist's only concern with

---

*EDITOR'S NOTE: A French father passing along a love of the Bard and a very British tea seems to confirm the previous note.

these varied subjects is their intersection with regard to grapes, wine, and especially fermentation. Whether or not my mother agreed with her professors or had any regrets about this decision she never revealed. She always gave the impression of being very content with her life, which consisted of her husband, children, and the work of the family vineyard.

My brother Robert was born in 2299. By the time I was born on July 13, 2305, he was already a dedicated assistant to my parents. Growing up, I became keenly aware of a stifling dynamic; Robert did everything he could to seek my father's approval by imitation. There was no way for me to compete. Robert had six years of wine education and experience ahead of mine. But that wasn't the chief resource he used to dominate me.

"Idiot, you're doing it wrong," he said as I tried to help tie vines, or, "You're as dumb as the moon," as I struggled at using pruning shears to cut stems. It was a cascade of abuse whispered in my ear or shouted aloud at every opportunity, to the point that I grew to disdain our family occupation. It reached a pinnacle one July afternoon. We were standing among the vines as my father gave us one of his many lectures on how to tell when the grapes were ready to be harvested. I asked why we didn't use a computer, which would tell us exactly when they were ready.

"A computer cannot taste a grape," he said, "or tell if the skins are about to burst, or if the heat has eaten the acidity in them." From my little knowledge of computers (I was only eight) I imagined that a computer could probably do all those things. Instead, I decided on a less mature argument.

"Wine is boring," I said.

My father showed no visible reaction, but from the look on my brother's face it appeared as if I'd committed murder.

"Go inside then," my father said. "Robert and I have work to do."

As I turned away, I expected to see pleasure on Robert's face, but instead I saw contempt and judgment. I suppose he was emoting in my father's stead.

I went inside. It may sound like an exaggeration, but this was one of the most important moments of my life. I'd just declared my independence. I wasn't fully conscious of the ramifications, the rift I'd cemented with my father and brother, and the implied decision I'd made about my future—that I wouldn't stay at the vineyard. But the fear and exhilaration made clear to my young self that I was at a crossroads, and that I'd broken free of what felt like a trap. Even at eight, I knew the vineyard and winery would someday be Robert's. He'd guaranteed that path for himself long before I was even born. And the fact was I had no passion for making wine. It seemed so trivial to me. I knew I was on the road to somewhere else, I just didn't know where.

I needed to do *something*. Our computer time was strictly limited to schoolwork. I supposed I could sneak off to my friend Louis's house; his family was not nearly as technology adverse as mine was, and there was an assortment of modern entertainments for children's play. But I sensed from my father that I was being punished, and one rebellion per day seemed enough. Reading was out, I was too restless, so I wandered the house. I eventually found myself in the basement.

This was no longer a forbidden zone. Since my invasion of a year before, my father decided to make use of it. With a natural inclination to take the fun out of everything, he began our rigorous education of the family. We had to learn, by rote, all our ancestors and their achievements. This schooling in our family history had a subtle effect on me. We had a complete family history—a handwritten tome charting every blood relative on the tree and where they lived and what they did—but the forebears in the gallery were all people of great accomplishment: scientists, great writers, explorers. To my young mind it was these people I needed to emulate.

As I strolled through the hall of portraits, I realized I had to do something to distinguish myself, to guarantee my place in this gallery of the skilled and gifted.

I got to the photo of Louise Picard. She was in a spacesuit, standing with several other people on the surface of Mars. They were settlers, jovially holding shovels, as if they would literally be breaking ground on what would be the first human Martian city. Louise was the only photo on the wall of an ancestor who'd gone to space, and though there were others, Louise was the first. As I looked at the picture, I went through in my head my relatives who'd left Earth. There weren't that many… and then a thought occurred to me.

I ran upstairs to our library, and went to the small dais where my father kept the handwritten family history. I scoured the passages of the generations who came of age during space travel, and after a few minutes was able to confirm the hunch I'd had in the basement.

No Picard had ever left the solar system, had ever gone to the stars.

I was eight years old, and I'd found my path.

THE STORY OF ONE OF STARFLEET'S MOST INSPIRATIONAL CAPTAINS

✦

I began work immediately. However, since I was a child and had limited understanding of what that work should actually be, my goal "to leave the solar system" was as vague as it was grand. I didn't want to ask my parents for guidance for fear of giving away my plan to escape the vineyard. So I devoured whatever books I could find on the technology of space travel and the history of the Galaxy. There were few of these in our home, so most of that reading took place either at school or my friend Louis's house, much to his chagrin (Louis, like most boys our age, wasn't in love with reading). I already had a keen interest in the ancient Age of Sail, when men explored the world in wooden ships, and my study of space travel was a natural extension. I also began building and collecting model spaceships and attempted to become an expert on each one.

My mother indulged this interest, helping me acquire an extensive model collection, and for my ninth birthday we took a trip to the Smithsonian Institution in Washington, North America. I was in awe at the many spaceships on display, including Zefram Cochrane's faster-than-light *Phoenix*, and the first starship *Enterprise*. It was on that day that I acquired a model of that ship, and when we got home I immediately set about its construction. One of the reasons I was interested specifically in the NX-01: my brother Robert had a model of it when I was little, which he never let me play with. He had long since dispensed with such toys, but it had stayed in my memory.

When it was finished, I showed it to my mother, who asked me what I knew about it.

"First ship to go warp 5," I said. "Its helmsman was Travis Mayweather." Like most boys at that age, the most important thing about a ship was how fast it went and who drove it.

"Is that who you want to be?" my mother said. "The helmsman?"

"Yes," I said, "he's the one who flies the ship."

"But he takes orders from the captain, who is the true pilot."

I had never thought about it before. "How do you get to be the captain?"

"You have to go to Starfleet Academy," she said, "and do very well." She left me to a new fantasy. I had of course heard of Starfleet Academy, but this was really the first time I considered that it would be a place that I might go. As I stared at my collection of spaceship models, a different fantasy of the future began to emerge.

That night at dinner, I announced my intention to go to Starfleet Academy. I was met with a derisive laugh from Robert.

"They'll never accept you," he said. "They don't want idiots." He was as predictable as a damp, cold wind in November, yet in my childlike naïveté I still wandered into every interaction with my brother hoping for some wisp of friendship, or at least politeness.

"Robert…" At my mother's warning, Robert withheld his next taunt. Whatever it was, I was certain I would hear it later.

"I'll get in," I said. "I'm not stupid."

"You're not," Mother said. "But it will take a lot of work."

"I'm going to do it," I said.

"Waste of time." This was my father. He was into his second bottle of wine, and had settled into one of his occasional dark moods.

"Well, I think he will," Mother said.

"What do you know about it?" My father snapped this at my mother.

"Obviously," she said, "I couldn't hope to know as much as you. Eat your dinner." Her condescension trumped his, and we sat in silence and finished our meal, though I was just about bursting with plans and determination.

The next day I came home from school. The night before, I'd been dying to research more about the academy, but I had to wait for my free periods in school to gather up all the information I could. There was more than my nine-year-old brain could comprehend, but I was on my way. I had taken copious notes, and was so anxious to go over them that I almost didn't notice the tragedy that was waiting for me.

My new NX-01 model was broken on the floor. At first I thought it had just fallen off the table, but on closer inspection I saw a bit of mud on the broken engine. Someone had stepped on it. Probably a year before I would've burst into tears, but not on this day. I got angry.

I stormed downstairs, the pieces of my new favorite model in my hand, and pushed the front door open. On my way back from school, I'd seen Robert in the vineyard tying off a vine, and made a beeline for him. He didn't see me coming, and just as he turned I got one good shove in. He lost his balance and fell to the ground. He was shocked, but up on his feet and on top of me before I could react.

"You piddly piece of trash," he said. He was enraged that I'd gotten the upper hand on him, even for just a second. He punched me repeatedly, and it was only the sound of my father's voice that put a stop to it.

"What the hell is this?"

My father stood over us, glaring. He pulled Robert off of me.

"He knocked me down," Robert said.

"Because he broke my spaceship!" I said it as I held out the broken pieces as incontrovertible proof of Robert's crime.

"I did no such thing!"

"You're lying!" I lunged at Robert again, but this time my father grabbed me. He took the pieces of the spaceship out of my hand and threw them in the dirt.

"Why did you do that..."

"Get in the house, Jean-Luc! I don't have time for your childish nonsense. There's work to be done."

I had no idea what to say. I had a childhood sense of justice, and I expected my father to enforce it, but he didn't. Tears in my eyes, I gathered up the broken pieces and went back to the house. I was even more determined to escape these bullies who dominated my world.

✦

From that day forward, I took a much more serious attitude to my schoolwork. Acceptance into Starfleet Academy was extremely competitive; less than two percent of applicants were admitted so I was determined to win high marks. I also focused on sports, including track and field, boxing, and fencing. Though I was driven by a desire to both make my mark on the universe and escape the vineyard, the attention I got from my successes was like a drug. My mother was openly delighted by each of my academic achievements. Even my father was impressed, giving me a crisp "very good" for each triumph. Of course, each accomplishment brought a scowl from Robert, which at the time gave me nothing but pleasure. I let myself believe that though he was older and stronger, he wasn't as smart as I was. This was of course not true; he focused his efforts on the winery, and as a result his studies suffered. But feeling the victim of his oppression, I reveled in the pain I was causing him. Looking back, I regret this youthful arrogance, as it cost me a relationship with perhaps the one person who knew me best, and a person I would not fully understand until I was an adult, when it was too late. At the time, however, we were engaged in a battle of wills, and though I gave him no explicit explanation of my escape plans, he seemed to intuit them. From my perspective, he did everything he could to get in the way.

I remember once, I was eleven, in my room, reading a book. It was one of the many biographies of Starfleet Captain James T. Kirk. As I'd begun to study the history of Starfleet, his name kept coming up. He was a swashbuckling hero of a simpler time, and his adventures captured my imagination at that age.

"Father wants you to mix the grapes," Robert said. Lost in the outer space exploits of the book, I hadn't noticed my brother standing in my doorway until he spoke.

I looked up at him. I couldn't be sure that Robert was being truthful. It was quite possible my father had sent him. But the only way to find out would require questioning my father, and I knew that even if he hadn't sent Robert, he'd be annoyed that I would be trying to get out of work, so I'd have to do it anyway.

I put my book away and trudged outside to the barn where we kept our fermentation tanks. This is where the grapes, after they were picked and had their stems removed, would spend about a week fermenting. During this process, the skins separated from the grape, and formed a cap or crust at the top. It was necessary to regularly punch down on that crust, extracting more juice from the skins. To do this, one had to stand above the tank, using a paddle. It was one of many laborious chores that took me away from my new passions.

That day, I climbed up onto the eight-foot-tall tanks, and stood on the gangplank which crossed over it. I grabbed my paddle and began pressing down on the grapes, but my mind was still caught up in the adventure I'd been reading: Captain Kirk, disguised as an enemy Romulan, sneaking aboard their vessel to steal a cloaking device right out from under them... Anxious to get back to my book, I began pressing too hard and fast on the crust, hoping to move my task along quickly. The paddle wouldn't move at the speed I wanted it to, and I slipped.

I fell off the gangplank and landed with a splat and splash into the fermenting wine. The smell, unpleasant enough when standing above it, was truly overpowering. I tried to find my footing, but couldn't touch the bottom; I was around five feet tall, and the fermenting grapes rose to a level higher than that. I stretched for the gangplank, but it was out of reach; I couldn't get high enough to grab it. I tried to move to the side of the tank; the mix of liquid and grape pulp had a consistency closer to quicksand than water. I sank. I took liquid into my mouth; the mixture of juice, alcohol and yeast burned my throat and stung my eyes. I tried to scream, which only made me gulp more of the vile liquid. Every effort I made failed, and panic took over.

"Grab it!"

I looked up. Robert was kneeling on the gangplank. He had retrieved my paddle, and held it out to me. I grabbed onto it, and he pulled. Once I came up out of the muck, he reached down and grabbed my arm. He pulled me up over the gangplank, where I caught my breath and calmed down.

"You're as stupid as the moon," he said. I felt embarrassed, and would soon face punishment for ruining several hundred bottles of wine, along with the added humiliation of having purple skin that lasted several days.

It was only with the gift of hindsight that I realized the only way Robert was there so quickly was that he had to have been watching me. The same was true when I fell down the stairs in the basement, and who knows how many other times. Whatever my brother's feelings for me at the time, he also felt responsible, and for that I owed him my life.

I would eventually leave home and Robert behind; it would take years for me to repent my ingratitude.

✦

"Congratulations," the computer voice said, "your application for entry to the Starfleet Academy Class of 2326 has been approved for final testing. Please report to Starfleet Headquarters, San Francisco, on September 28, 2322 at 0900."

I smiled at the news, and found it in no way surprising. I couldn't wait; my academic achievements led me to expect that I would gain entrance to the academy, and that this was almost a formality. I was 17, and had grown from a quiet, bookish child to a bold, arrogant teen, well past cocky. My life outside in the world was active and social, but things with the family were very different.

I'd become almost a boarder in my own home. Given my size and athletic ability, Robert could no longer effectively bully me physically or mentally, and now that he was in his twenties he had little interest. He was well on his way to becoming the winery's next cellarmaster. He had also gotten what he always wanted—he'd become my father's best friend. They spent most of their time together, talking about their wine, their grapes, their soil, and other people's wines, other people's grapes, and other people's soil. It was an endless wine symposium that they both enjoyed as it fueled my brother's need for approval and my father's need for admiration.

As far as I was concerned, though my father had complimented my academic and athletic achievements, he made no secret that he thought it a waste to use them to gain entrance to the academy. The closer I got to the age of admission, the harsher his disdain for the service and the people in it; it seemed to actually anger him, that somehow my decision was a personal betrayal. This only reinforced my desire to go.

The only person in my family I still had a good relationship with was my mother. I sensed her conflict as a loving parent and a loving wife. And she wanted to encourage my interests but knew that those interests would take me away from her. When I brought her the news of the final step in my application, I could see she was ambivalent.

"That's wonderful, Jean-Luc," she said, "but please keep this to yourself for the moment."

"Why?"

"I want to delay upsetting your father for as long as I can," she said. This was, of course, exactly the opposite of what I wanted to do, but I decided to accede to her request, especially since I needed her help to get to San Francisco.

I would be staying in San Francisco in a dormitory for the three days of testing, so I packed a small bag and we set out early on the morning of the 28th. The day happened to coincide with Robert and my father shipping out a new vintage, so they were properly distracted; we didn't have to say goodbye. We took an air tram from La Barre to Paris, and then my mother surprised me with an energy matter transport to San Francisco. I'd never gone through the process before, and hid my excitement for fear of looking like a child.

The municipal transporter in Paris was outside, a small pad near Notre Dame on the Île de la Cité. The weather was warm and humid, and a technician

THE STORY OF ONE OF STARFLEET'S MOST INSPIRATIONAL CAPTAINS

led us onto the pad. I looked down at it, which was unfortunate, because a moment passed and I was looking down at an almost identical pad. I looked up to see I was now standing in San Francisco near Fisherman's Wharf. The city was covered in fog and a good twenty degrees cooler. I was furious with myself; I'd missed the transposition between cities because I had been looking at my feet.

I'd been to the North American continent several times before, but never to San Francisco. The home of Starfleet Command and Starfleet Academy, this city was the largest spaceport on planet Earth. The crisscrossing of shuttles and trams over the Golden Gate Bridge and ultra-modern skyline was stunning and exciting, and it was impossible to maintain my façade of teenage indifference. Walking the streets was a spectrum of alien life unlike any I'd ever seen. This was the world where I wanted to be, away from what I felt was the primitive, stultifying environment I'd grown up in.

We found our way to Starfleet Headquarters; the testing took place in the Archer Building, one of the older structures, named for Jonathan Archer, captain of the NX-01 *Enterprise*.* After I signed in, my mother gave me a hug as she handed me off to a young female ensign.

"Right this way, Mr. Picard," she said, as she led me to a turbolift.

"Call me Jean-Luc," I said. At this young age, I fancied myself a ladies' man, most days greatly overestimating my appeal.

"No, thank you," she said. She led me to the testing room and gave me a curt goodbye. I entered the room. There were four computer stations arranged in a square each with a chair facing away from the others. Two people were there already, a human male around my age, and a humanoid alien of a species I'd never met in person before, blue-skinned with a ridge running down the center of his face. The human stood and gave me a friendly smile.

"Robert DeSoto," he said as we shook hands.

"Jean-Luc Picard," I said.

"*Parlez-vous francais?*" he responded. I smiled and we had a short conversation in French, which DeSoto seemed to delight in speaking. He told me his mother had been raised in France and taught the language to her

---

*EDITOR'S NOTE: It is a regrettably common mistake Picard makes here: the Archer Building was in fact named for Jonathan Archer's father, Henry, who designed the warp 5 engine.

children. I broke off our conversation to introduce myself to the other occupant of the room.

"Fras Jeslik," he said.

"Are you a Bolian?" I said.

"Yes," he said. He seemed surprised. "I have to admit, you're one of the first humans who didn't think I was an Andorian who'd had his antenna chopped off." We began chatting, all of us a little nervous at being there, all immediately recognizing that some of us would not make it through this round of testing. We were soon joined by a young woman, also human. She held out her hand to me.

"Marta Batanides," she said. She was attractive, with brown hair and an appealing smile. I took her hand. In my immature, adolescent mind I decided she must be attracted to me, and depending on how things went over the next few days I thought I might take advantage of it. (It is with embarrassment and a small amount of nausea that I relate my thinking regarding women at this age, but I feel honesty is an essential part of capturing my younger self truthfully.) The four of us engaged in a lively discussion until an officer entered and we immediately fell silent.

"I'm Tac Officer Tichenor," he said. He was tall with curly blond hair that seemed to match his wry, puckish demeanor. "You're here for three days of testing. Right now there are only a few open spots left in next year's class, and there are testing rooms like this all over the Galaxy. If you can't do the math on your chances, you're probably not going to get in." If this was meant to discourage me, it had the opposite effect.

Tichenor showed each of us to a computer console, and we began the tests. Over the course of the three days, the tests covered a variety of subjects ranging from Galactic history, warp physics, and astrobiology. The four of us would finish our testing for the day, go to dinner, then go to sleep. As young and energetic as I was, this was the most stress I'd ever been under, and I was exhausted at the end of each day.

At the end of the third day of testing, Tac Officer Tichenor informed us that we had two tests left, the tactical simulation and the psychological exam. Tichenor told me I was first, and took me out of the room. He led me down a corridor toward an area marked BRIDGE SIMULATOR. I entered and found a detailed recreation of the bridge of an *Excelsior*-class starship. I'd seen pictures of them and

THE STORY OF ONE OF STARFLEET'S MOST INSPIRATIONAL CAPTAINS

had studied the systems with an almost obsessive interest. I was convinced I could operate any of the control panels. I couldn't wait to show off my abilities—I was certain I would impress whoever from the academy was watching us.

Sitting casually in the simulator room were three other students in civilian clothes, all about my age. I assumed they were from another testing group, but before I could introduce myself, Tichenor left, shutting the door behind him. The room was bathed in red light as a klaxon blared.

"Red alert," the computer voice said. I was momentarily startled; this tactical simulation felt very real. I looked at my fellow "crewmen," all of whom seemed genuinely flummoxed. I took this as an opportunity.

"You," I said, pointing to a rotund fellow, "take the science station, activate sensors."

"Where is it?" he said. I realized that my years of studying spaceships probably put me ahead of a lot of my peers. I pointed out the science station just behind the captain's chair, then turned to a young woman.

"Can you get the viewscreen on?"

"I think so," she said, and sat down at the helm station. I turned to the last crewman, a thin reed of a man.

"Man the weapons console," I said, indicating the corner station by the viewscreen. He went over to the console, and tentatively sat down. I then turned to the rotund boy.

"We have anything on sensors?"

"I don't know. I don't know what I'm looking at." He was staring helplessly at the science station control panel. Annoyed, I ran up and activated the sensors. I saw three images of ships closing in on us. Sensors said they had weapons locked on.

"Shields up!" As I yelled, my voice cracked.

"Who are you talking to?" the woman said.

"And what are 'shields'?" Thin Guy said. Unbelievable, I thought. These people think they deserve to be in Starfleet?

Frustrated, I ran to the weapons console and threw the switch to activate the shields. I was too late; the simulator registered a hit and the weapons console shorted out. I looked at the indicators; we now had no weapons. I turned to look at the viewscreen; it was still off.

"Turn on the viewscreen!" I was getting very angry. "We've got to get out of here!"

"I thought I knew how to do it, but I guess I don't..." the woman said. This was insane. Did I have to do everything? I ran down to the helm station.

"Get out of the chair," I said, and the woman got up. I sat down, activated the viewscreen, just in time to see three old Romulan birds-of-prey firing their energy plasma weapons. I keyed the control for warp speed; the simulator recorded another hit. The engineering console shorted out, and the lights dimmed. I looked over and saw that we had no engine power.

"Simulation ended," the computer voice said. Anger overflowed, but I kept my mouth shut. Then someone had to speak and ruin it.

"Sorry," the rotund boy said. The weakness I sensed in his apology set me on edge, and I lost it.

"Sorry?! You're sorry?! Why are you even applying to the academy?!" I'm not sure I'd ever heard myself yell that loudly, but I'd worked so hard to get here, and in my mind these three strangers just ruined it.

"We did the best we could," Thin Guy said.

"Imbecile! Your 'best' would've gotten us killed!" I was making so much noise that I hadn't noticed the sound of the door opening.

"Now, now," Tichenor said, "let's all take a breath." I wheeled to face him; his dry tone made me realize I'd lost control, and I fell into silent embarrassment.

"Picard, I'll take you back," Tichenor said. "The rest wait here."

He led me out of the control room. We walked in silence back to the classroom, where my other three classmates waited. They could immediately see I was upset.

"Hey, Picard, what's wrong?" DeSoto said.

"Tactical simulation went badly," I said.

"It couldn't be as bad as all that," Marta said. I noticed she looked at Tichenor, whose half smile did nothing to confirm or deny Marta's supposition.

"Mr. Picard, you're done for the day," Tichenor said, and then turned to DeSoto. "You're next, come with me." DeSoto followed him out, and I stayed behind and told Marta and Fras what happened.

"I just don't know how that could be considered a tactical simulation," I said.

"Maybe it wasn't," Marta said. "Maybe that was the psych test." That thought hadn't occurred to me, mostly because I couldn't see how it made sense.

THE STORY OF ONE OF STARFLEET'S MOST INSPIRATIONAL CAPTAINS

"What were they testing?" I said. "How fast I would get annoyed at incompetence?"

"I don't know," Marta said. "Did Tichenor *say* it was the tactical simulation?" I realized that he hadn't said anything; if it was the psych test, I had a sinking feeling I'd failed it spectacularly. And I wasn't even sure what they were testing. Since I was done for the day, I decided to go back to my room and sulk.

The next day, I showed up in the classroom. I hadn't seen my classmates the previous evening, and they all looked somewhat nervous as Tac Officer Tichenor addressed us. He informed us that, of our group, only Robert DeSoto had gained entrance to the academy. DeSoto and I had become friends, but I was also so overcome with jealousy and confusion that it was a struggle to offer him congratulations. He saw through it instantly, reading my expression.

"Yeah, I agree," Robert said. "It should've been you." I was embarrassed at my self-centeredness.

"I'm sorry," I said. "I really am happy for you."

"*Ce n'est pas grave*," he said. "I'll see you there next year."

Marta and I walked out of the building. I was so lost in thought, it was a moment before I noticed Marta was laughing at me.

"What's so funny?"

"You," she said. "You're so arrogant it's unbelievable."

"Look," I said, "I worked really hard for this..."

"And I didn't?" she said. "In case you hadn't noticed, you weren't the only one whose dreams were postponed." She of course was right, but I couldn't let it go. "Did you even find out whether that was the psych test?"

"No," I said. I had been too humiliated to ask. I didn't want to admit to Tichenor that I didn't know what I was being tested on. This of course was ego, and self-defeating; if I came back next year, I would be no closer to understanding what I needed to do to gain acceptance.

Marta and I said our goodbyes, and made what would turn out to be empty promises to stay in touch. My mother wanted to come pick me up, but I had talked her out of it. This meant I had to take an air tram first to Paris, and then one to La Barre. It was a couple of hours traveling, more time for me to bathe in my own self-pity.

I arrived in La Barre, threw my duffel bag over my shoulder, and walked home from the station. As I passed the familiar trees, I was overcome with a feeling of dread. I knew Robert would take great pleasure in my failure, and I'd been so arrogant in the time leading up to the test, on some level I knew I deserved it. I had no clue as to what my father would do, but I imagined the two of them would share some hearty laughter about it.

I approached the door to our home, which suddenly opened and my mother was there to greet me. She gave me a warm hug.

"It's all right, Jean-Luc," she said softly, and I started to cry. I thought myself such a man, but I was still a child, and my mother's maternal sympathy broke down the false construct of masculinity. She brought me inside and I quickly wiped away my tears.

"Where's Father and Robert?"

"In the barn, still packing wine," she said. "Don't worry, we have a few moments. I want to hear what happened." I told her in some detail, including the mystery of what that last test was.

"It's no mystery," she said. "It was the psych test."

"How can you be sure?"

"You want to leave here and make your mark on the world," she said. "You have for years, and at some point you decided that Starfleet was the way you wanted to do it." My mother could see me so clearly; my youthful arrogance had convinced me that my motivations for self-aggrandizement were well hidden to everyone.

"What does that have to do with it?"

"You were presented with a test that you thought you were quite ready for. Yet there were three incompetent people standing in your way," she said. "Your biggest fear." Realization dawned on me.

"My fear, that I won't have control," I said. And then Marta's comment came back to me. "And that it's all about me." What worried me was that, even with this knowledge, I didn't know what the right way to handle that test was.

"So he's home," Robert said. He and Father had come in from outside. Robert's tone was what I expected, full of derision. They sat down as they removed their dirty boots.

"I'm home," I said.

"And when do you leave again?" Robert said. "Off to the stars, I suppose?" I was confused by this, and looked at my mother, whose expression said that she had not told them.

THE STORY OF ONE OF STARFLEET'S MOST INSPIRATIONAL CAPTAINS

"I didn't get in," I said. I saw Robert and my father exchange a look, and fully braced myself for an onslaught of ruthless snickering at my expense.

"Oh," Robert said. He didn't laugh. He in fact seemed uncomfortable.

"Well, that's a bit of luck for us," my father said.

"Really? Why is that?"

"We could use your help with the shipment tomorrow," my father said. "If you're available." This last comment had a slight sarcastic bite, but only slight. It has taken me a lifetime to understand that in that moment my father and brother felt bad for me. They took no pleasure in my failure. The next day I helped them pack shipments of wine. It was in some way cathartic for me, helping me move past my failure.

Soon, however, things returned to normal around our house. Robert went back to demeaning me at every opportunity, and I in turn dismissed him with a condescending arrogance. My father continued his loud contempt for my goals, which I pursued with even more fervor. The next year, I succeeded at getting another chance for admission. I went through the testing again, this time with a new group of applicants, still supervised by Tichenor. As with the first time, I did well on the computer monitor testing. On the final day, Tichenor again escorted me to the bridge simulator.

The same three students were there again. Tichenor shut the door and the red alert klaxon sounded.

I was momentarily confused. I had spent the last year going over this situation in my head, preparing what I would do if confronted with a similar test. I had decided that I would take the helm control myself, turn on the viewscreen, and immediately try to pilot the "ship" out of danger, since one man couldn't properly take the three ships on in a battle. But what I hadn't considered was the possibility that the situation would be *exactly* the same, with the same three people. My instinct was to ignore that, take the helm and proceed with the plan, but those other three applicants convinced me that their presence was part of the test.

And then I realized: they weren't applicants. They couldn't be. I decided to ask an obvious question.

"Are the three of you now any more experienced operating this simulator than you were last year?"

"Yes," the rotund boy said. "We've received complete training." I smiled, feeling victorious. I could start giving orders with a fair amount of confidence that they'd be able to carry them out.

Then I hesitated.

The rotund boy's phrase "complete training" stuck in my head. I hadn't received *any* training, I'd just read and studied on my own. I decided on a new strategy.

"If you're all completely trained," I said, "maybe you should take charge."

The thin guy smiled.

"All right," he said, "you take the helm and activate the viewscreen…"

✦

I wish I could say that was the moment I stopped being a cocky bastard, that I learned to show humility and a modest sense of inquisitiveness, but all I did was pat myself on the back for beating the test. I didn't have any real insight into why, and it would cost me dearly.

But right then, all that concerned me was that I passed, and was going to the academy.

A few months later, I left for school. I got up at 4:30am. I had hoped to leave the house without saying goodbye to my family. I knew that, given modern modes of travel, I wouldn't really be that far from home, and convinced myself that I didn't want to deal with my mother's emotionalism. In truth I think I was probably afraid of my own. I gathered my belongings in my duffel and headed downstairs. As I did, I noticed a light in the family room.

"So, you're leaving," my father said. He was sitting in a chair, illuminated by a small table lamp.

"Yes," I said. He didn't have a book or a drink, he was just sitting there. It was impossible for me to believe it at the time, but I think he was waiting for me.

"It is a dangerous path you're on," he said. "Don't do anything stupid." From another man, this might have sounded like a joke, but from my father there was not a hint of humor. At the time, all I read in my father's face was disparagement and rejection, but I see now it was actual concern he didn't know how to express. I regret that at that moment, I turned and left without saying goodbye.

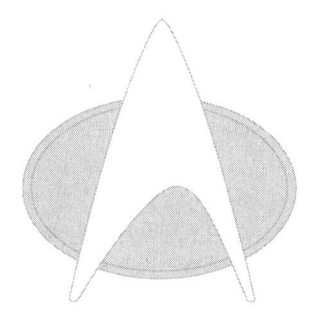

CHAPTER TWO

I WAS ABOUT TWO AND A HALF HOURS INTO THE MARATHON, the last hill just ahead of me. It was almost 30 degrees Celsius, and I hadn't had a drink for almost five miles: the last time people on the route handed out cups of water I didn't take one, I didn't want to risk slowing my pace. My focus was paying off—most of the other runners had fallen behind. There were five of us who'd opened up a lead from the rest of the pack of academy students. The four runners, all ahead of me, were upperclassmen. Cadet Captain Sussman and Cadet Lieutenant Matalas, both fourth-years, were in the lead, followed closely by Cadets Black and Strong. The four were competing against each other; they didn't even realize I was there.

But they would. I decided on my first day at the academy that everybody would.

When I entered in 2323, Starfleet Academy was over 150 years old. Generations of its graduates had helped shaped the events of the last century, and for that reason it was one of the most revered educational institutions in the Galaxy. This fed my own desire for respect and achievement—by being associated with such an admired institution, I assumed I would also be admired. (This belief would lead to one of many rude awakenings.)

The first day at the academy is a trial in and of itself. After being signed in, you are given a large red bag, and sent on an organized scavenger hunt to acquire your needed supplies. In the old days I am told that you would face an angry upperclassman around every corner telling you how worthless you were. This was a leftover tradition from the military academies of old Earth, which had to create soldiers from children, ready to respond to orders on instinct. Over the decades Starfleet was able to chip away at the more barbaric traditions; the individuals of our evolved society respected the chain of command without the need of vicious discipline. Still, that didn't eliminate the difficulties involved in interpersonal relationships.

After I'd gathered my belongings on that first day, I found my way to my room in one of the older dormitories from the original campus, Mayweather House. My roommate lay on his bed, his feet up, the bag of his belongings still packed.

"Jean-Luc Picard," I said. "You must be Cortan."

"I prefer Corey, Corey Zweller," he said. "Pleasure to meet you, Johnny."

We were off to a bad start. No one had ever referred to me by that nickname; I hated it at once, and Corey along with it. I gave him a thin smile, and turned to put my belongings away. As I did, Corey started asking questions about where I was from, to which he received curt responses. Corey himself was from the American continent, the city of St. Louis. He was friendly and outgoing, but I couldn't forgive the nickname.

"So what classes have you registered for? Maybe we've got a few together..." Corey said.

"I haven't registered yet," I said. I had assumed that registration for classes would take place once we got to school, but I could tell from the expression on Corey's face that I was mistaken.

"You better get on it," Corey said. He showed me his computer screen where he had signed in and registered for his classes. I turned to the computer monitor allocated to me; this was a first, I'd never had my own computer. And I was also face to face with how the Luddism of my upbringing disadvantaged me. Unlike every other academy student, who was used to having unlimited access to a computer, I not only hadn't registered for classes ahead of time, I was unaware that I could.

"You never see a computer before, Johnny?" Corey said. He was joking, but I was so embarrassed I could only ignore him by staring intently at my computer as I stumbled through class registration. Corey chuckled to himself, I thought somewhat derisively, then left the room, as I faced the realization that I was already behind.

The education at Starfleet Academy was wide-ranging, with a heavy load of requirements for its cadets in science and engineering, as well as a plethora of courses in the social sciences and humanities, all with a bent to better a cadet's understanding of the Galaxy. There were some courses a student had to take (starship engineering, galactic law, etc.) and some requirements could be filled with one of several courses. I had planned to take a survey course to fulfill my galactic history requirement, but the class was full, and the only history course still open was Xenoarchaeology, a subject I had no interest in because I didn't really know what it was. Nevertheless, I breathed somewhat easier in that at least I'd completed my registration. I was certain that once I started classes things would fall into place.

I was of course completely wrong. The first summer at the academy, before the academic semester begins, cadets face a grueling series of athletic challenges. Starfleet requires students maintain a high level of physical abilities, and the "Plebe Summer" ritual is meant to weed out any cadet who isn't up to the challenge. I had succeeded in school sports, but I grew up on a vineyard; I'd never been through survival training, never carried a hundred-pound pack on a run, never climbed a real mountain. I got through the summer with a barely passing grade.

The feeling of physical superiority I had as a teenager vanished during that summer, and now the surety that I was smarter than everybody else disappeared on the first day of the fall academic semester. Though at the top of my class in my village school, everyone else who was at the academy was also at the top of *their* class. Many of my fellow cadets had been through a much more rigorous education; next to the several Vulcans in my advanced mathematics seminar, I felt like a shambling Neanderthal watching a Cro-Magnon make fire.

After the first day of classes, I sat in my room alone after dinner. Corey had invited me on excursions to find women and drink for the first few weeks, but my standard "no, thank you" eventually led him to stop, even to the point where he dropped his usual "see you later." I sat at my computer console pretending to work, but in fact wondering if I'd made the right choice. I hadn't made any friends, I felt intellectually and physically inferior. I never thought I'd be homesick, but I longed for the soothing voice of my mother, who had made Herculean efforts to stay connected to me, calling and writing at every opportunity. But I kept our conversations short, too proud to reveal to her (and then, by extension, my father and Robert) that the academy might be too much for me. The dreams of going into space and becoming a starship captain seemed very out of reach.

The second day of classes it wasn't much better, especially when I showed up for my first session of Xenoarchaeology. When I arrived, the classroom was empty, and I double-checked to see if I was in the right place. As I did, I was joined by another student, a young man of African-American descent, named Donald Varley.

"Did you get shut out of all the history sections too?" I asked.

"Uh, no," he said, with a smile. "I actually am interested in this. Is it possible there's only two of us?"

"That is my average class size," a man said. We turned to see a man in his seventies, wearing a worn safari vest and carrying a satchel. We assumed correctly that he was Professor Galen. He was a rare breed. Most academy instructors were Starfleet personnel of one form or another; older cadets who'd stayed on after graduation, or officers on leave or retired. Professor Galen however was strictly an academic of the pipe-smoking, tweed-jacket variety.

"Which of you is Varley and which is Picard?" he said as he made his way to the lectern in the front of the room. We identified ourselves, and he motioned us to sit right in front of him.

"The Federation has been in existence for almost two centuries," he said. "It is considered by many of its inhabitants as the greatest civilization in history. The work we will review here will prove the inanity of such a judgment…"

I settled in for what I expected would be a lot of dull photos of potshards and fossils. Instead, Professor Galen took two objects out of his satchel and handed one to each of us. They were small figurines, what appeared to be the torso of some kind of humanoid, perhaps in armor.

"Any idea what you're holding?" Neither of us knew. "That is a figurine from the Kurlan civilization."

This seemed to peak Varley's interest, and he began to examine his very carefully.

"They were created in a workshop by a Kurlan who is now only known as the Master of Tarquin Hill. He used materials and tools several centuries ahead of his time to create those pieces. Any idea of their age?"

"Well," Varley said, "the Kurlan civilization disappeared over ten thousand years ago…"

"Yes," Galen said. "In fact, the objects you hold in your hand are over twelve thousand years old." I now considered the object a lot less casually.

"Because of his artistic eye," Galen said, "and the advanced techniques he used, those objects have survived. Can we make an assumption as to why?"

Varley didn't have an answer, but as I stared at the small object in my hand, I pictured a lonely artist using primitive tools and materials in some ancient workshop. He was focused on his work, and he had only one goal in mind.

"He wanted to be remembered," he said.

"If that's the case," Galen said, "why not inscribe his name on his work?"

"The work is what was important to him," I said. "He left his mark."

"Rather impressively I would say," Galen said. "But, as my old professor said, archaeology is the search for facts, not truth. So we will stick to the facts…" But I wasn't listening. I felt in some way Galen was telepathic; like an archaeologist in my head, he'd uncovered for me my true motivation, which had gotten lost in the insecurity of Plebe Summer and the first day of classes.

I wanted to leave my mark.

It was childish, to be sure. I wasn't interested in accomplishing anything other than my own aggrandizement. I wanted immediate gratification of my desire to make the people here remember me. I saw my answer on my way across campus as I passed a viewscreen with a list of upcoming academy events:

ACADEMY MARATHON REGISTRATION OPENS TODAY.

I'd never run more than ten kilometers at a stretch, and that was during Plebe Summer; I came in almost last, just ahead of a Tellarite cadet, the large, slow-moving porcine species. But the academy marathon was one of the most visible contests the academy sponsored; it was broadcast via subspace, so much of the Federation had a chance to watch it. If I could do well in this, they would have to notice me. I signed up immediately. Now all I needed to do was figure out how to run a marathon.

I did some research, and began my training immediately. I ran five times a week, and quickly got up to a long run once a week, increasing to 20 kilometers in less than two months. Adding this extra challenge further isolated me from my classmates. I suppose in retrospect I was in a kind of hiding; it was easier for me to focus my energies on physical and intellectual activities, rather than face the emotional insecurity I felt. But I rationalized I was happier alone.

One night after a run, I returned to my room to find a surprise. A woman lay on my bed, relaxed with a small bottle in her hand. It took me only a second to recognize her.

"Marta!" I said. I hadn't seen Marta Batanides since our final testing together. I wasn't even aware that she'd gotten into the academy but was very pleased to see her, and that surprised me as well. "How did you find me?"

"Oh my god, Jean-Luc," she said. "Is—is this your room?" She hurried off the bed and stood awkwardly, and I immediately realized she wasn't there to see me.

"Hey, Johnny," Corey said. He came in behind me, having returned, I assume, from the bathroom. "Do you know Marta?"

"Yes," I said.

"We failed our first set of entrance exams together," Marta said. This added to my discomfort—in my constant insecure state, I would never have volunteered to Corey that I'd failed anything. "I'm really sorry. Corey kept saying his roommate's name was 'Johnny,' I didn't know that was your nickname…"

"It's fine," I said, and moved to get my toiletries and towel for a shower.

"Corey and I are going out for a drink," Marta said. "You should come…"

"Don't bother, Marta," Corey said. "Even if Johnny wasn't prepping for the marathon, he wouldn't have a drink."

"You're going to do the marathon?" Marta said. "That's terrific." I gave her a curt smile. Though I had a brief flash of delight upon seeing her, I forcibly suppressed it. In a bit of juvenile pique, I decided I wasn't going to let myself show even friendly interest in someone who'd be friends with Corey. (Looking back I am amazed and ashamed at the extent of my infantile behavior.)

"You're going to win that thing, Johnny," Corey said, as I gave a quick goodbye and headed to the showers. Though Corey's tone seemed sincere, I wouldn't let myself trust it or him. He was taunting me, I was sure of it; no freshman had ever won the academy marathon. When I entered, all I hoped for was a respectable finish, perhaps breaking the standing freshman record. That night, because I was so disappointed that Marta was there to see Corey and not me, I became determined to do the impossible.

The marathon was part of a three-day-long biannual Academy Olympics that took place on Danula II, a planet several light-years from Earth. When it came to the marathon, upperclassmen had a distinct advantage: aside from having more of the academy's physical training under their belt, if they had participated as a freshman or sophomore they had familiarity with the course and could train accordingly. I'd received a superficial description of the terrain when I signed up for the event, but if I was going to win I couldn't let myself be satisfied with such minimal information.

With only a little bit of trouble, I was able to get ahold of the survey Starfleet Academy personnel had done of Danula II in preparation for the athletic events. Their description of the course was a lot more detailed than the one given to the runners, and I saw actual data on the road surface and the incline of the hills. It appeared that the steepest hill was the last one leading to the finish line, and had an incline of 18.1 degrees. I knew I had to design my training runs in San Francisco to imitate it as closely as I could. There was a hill not too far from the academy on Filbert Street, which had an incline of 17.5 degrees, so from then on I always ended my runs there, and practiced holding a little energy in reserve for that final leg.

The day we left for the Olympics was actually a momentous one for me: it was my first trip into space. I was excited to board the shuttle that would take us to a starship in orbit. I crowded in with the other two hundred or so cadets participating in the Olympics; the remaining 12,000 stayed behind and watched the event via subspace. As I strapped myself in, I scanned the small craft looking for a familiar face, but recognized no one, or at least no one I'd had more than a passing contact with. It re-emphasized for me the isolation I'd constructed for myself. I'd been lonely when I arrived at the academy, and all my efforts in my first year only exacerbated that feeling.

"Stand by to launch," the pilot said over a speaker. Shortly we were moving, but I could barely tell. The inertial dampeners on the shuttle kept me from feeling any G-force, and I was seated in the center of the shuttle, meaning my view to the portholes was blocked as other cadets leaned in, as eager as I was to get a look outside. So my first trip into space felt like the equivalent of sitting in a waiting room at a doctor's office, except with a seatbelt.

The shuttle landed in the shuttlebay of the starship that was going to transport us to Danula II. We filed off the craft and were immediately greeted by a yeoman, a man not much older than any of us.

"Tennn hut..." the yeoman said. "Captain on deck."

We stood at attention, as a burly man of about forty, receding hairline, looked us over with a scowl.

"Welcome to the *Enterprise*," he said. "I'm Captain Hanson." We hadn't been told that we were being transported aboard the *U.S.S. Enterprise*, NCC-1701-C, one of the new *Ambassador*-class vessels. Hanson himself was well known to the cadet corps. He'd had a distinguished career already, making captain before he was thirty. I thought for a moment that this said a lot about our status.

"You should all know, I didn't want this assignment," Hanson said, immediately deflating my sense of self-importance. "The *U.S.S. Hood* was supposed to take you children to your reindeer games, but they had to put in for unexpected repairs, so I got stuck with it. This ship is brand new. If any of you do anything to mess it up, I find a scratch on a wall or a crumb on the carpet, I will make sure none of you ever see the inside of a starship again. Is that clear?"

"Yes, sir!" we all said in unison.

"Dismissed." He walked off, giving the impression that we mattered to him not one whit. Later, in my quarters, I tried to discover the meaning of the phrase "reindeer games" but all I could find was an unremarkable movie from the early 21st century.[*]

The three-day trip to Danula II was almost as unexciting as the shuttle ride. The two hundred of us were confined to our rooms on one deck. We had access to an exercise facility, and a recreation room where we also took our

---

[*]**EDITOR'S NOTE:** The phrase refers to a lyric in an archaic song, "Rudolph the Red-Nosed Reindeer," written by Johnny Marks. It remains a mystery as to whether Hanson was familiar with the song,

meals. Security men and women kept a strict guard on us; Hanson was serious that we weren't going to interfere with the running of his ship. One of the cadets, a member of the Parrises squares team, tried to sneak past security and get to the bridge. He was quickly caught and confined to the brig for the remainder of the voyage.

When we finally arrived at our destination, I made a concerted effort to get a seat in the shuttle by the window. When we left the shuttle bay, I was overcome with a strange sense of vertigo: I was sitting upright, but had the overall sensation that I was looking down. Out the porthole was a blue-green Class-M planet, easily mistaken for Earth in my mind. I knew Danula II was a good deal smaller than Earth, and expected that I would be able to tell, but all I saw was a giant world. Then suddenly we were in the cloud layer and heading toward a landing. We flew over a large ocean, heading to the small northern continent.

The planet's sports complex sprawled across my view; the Danulans built it as a gift to the Federation upon its admittance, and Starfleet Command was under some political pressure from the Federation Council to use it for its Olympics, even though it was far from convenient. We were taken to a modern dormitory, spartan but clean.

The marathon was the last event of the Olympics, so I spent most of my time continuing my training. One day, however, I decided to watch the events. The Academy Olympics drew a large in-person audience. As I watched them cheering the cadets, I realized many were family members—excited, proud parents and siblings showing their pride and affection. I hadn't even considered telling my family that I was participating. I found myself jealous of all the goodwill of those friends and families, and I quietly returned to my solitary training.

The day of the marathon was warm, even as early as I got up—I was one of the first to arrive at the starting line. The road we would run on was a wide dirt path, lined with trees that seemed similar to Earth's oak trees but with a purple tint to their trunks and leaves. Eventually my competitors joined me; over a hundred cadets were participating in the marathon, while the others watched. The crowd of onlookers was larger than the events I'd gone to. The marathon was the big event.

The chief judge of the event was the commandant of the academy, Devinoni Grax. He held up a phaser and fired a burst. We were off.

I gave myself an early lead from most of the pack, but the four lead runners quickly passed me, and I let them. Sussman, Matalas, Black, and Strong all ran together, with Sussman out in the lead. They had all run the course before, and the only competitors they were worried about were each other. Over the course of the first thirty kilometers, I slowly closed the distance to them; in the last ten kilometers I knew I wouldn't have the energy to make up a large distance, but also wanted them unaware of me for as long as possible.

Now I saw the final hill coming up. I knew that I was within two kilometers of the finish line. The hill itself was half a kilometer in length, and it looked a lot steeper to me than Filbert Street. I could see Matalas start to kick and pass Sussman as they hit the bottom of the hill. Once he was comfortably out ahead, I saw his pace steady. Now was my time.

I increased my pace, and as I passed Black and Strong first I heard a gasp of frustration. They were not expecting this since they probably didn't even recognize me. My training was paying off; the pain I'd suffered running up Filbert Street was familiar, and I pushed through it. I passed Sussman and closed on Matalas. He was several inches taller than me so his stride was longer. I was less than a meter behind him as I saw the finish line at the top of the hill. (It was often said that whoever designed a marathon course with the finish line at the top of a hill was a unique kind of sadist.) Several dozen officers and academy personnel waited beyond, cheering us on. I pushed up next to Matalas. He turned and looked at me, surprised, annoyed. I'd broken his concentration and that gave me the advantage I needed to get out a centimeter ahead as we crossed the finish line.

I ran only a few feet and collapsed on the other side. There was applause and cheers, and one of the athletic directors came over to help me up. As I stood I saw the ovations came from faculty and staff. Most of the cadets and their families were ignoring me, and congratulating the upperclassmen who'd just crossed the finish line. A few gave me cold stares. I'd just broken a record: I was the first freshman to win the academy marathon. I don't know what I was expecting, but I seemed to have further alienated myself from my colleagues. Or so I thought.

"Johnny!" Startled, I looked up to see Corey and Marta jostle their way through the crowd. "That was amazing!"

"What… how did…" I said. I could barely breathe and I couldn't process the fact that they were there. Neither of them were participating in the Olympics. They grabbed me and took me through the crowd to a table with refreshments.

"Congratulations, Johnny, you're the pride of the class," Corey said.

"It was really amazing," Marta said. She handed me a cup of water, which I gulped down, most of it spilling over me.

"How did the two of you…" I said.

"Commandant Grax, before he left, asked for volunteers to serve as stewards," Marta said. "We've been serving drinks and hors d'oeuvres for the last three days."

"I spilled champagne all over some Vulcan captain," Corey said. "A little on purpose, to see if I could get him mad. But he didn't."

"Why…" I said. I still wouldn't let myself believe they were there to see me.

"Because," Corey said, "what would be the point of winning the marathon if you didn't have any friends to see it?" I'd underestimated him. I wasn't used to this type of person, someone outgoing and personable, someone willing to bend over backwards to be my friend. I had greeted it with suspicion; he hadn't been insulting me by saying I was going to win, he had taken my measure and realized my goal. And I was thrilled. He'd given the race I'd just won a little more meaning.

"Thank you," I said.

"Cadet…" I looked up to see Captain Hanson. We stood at attention. I was shocked; the last time I'd seen him was on his ship.

"Yes, sir," I said.

"At ease," he said, but we didn't. He looked me up and down, and gave a hint of a smile. "Well done." And with that, he turned and left.

"Jean-Luc," Marta said, "looks like you're on the scoreboard."

"Call me… Johnny," I said, and meant it.

✦

"What is ex parte communication?" Rodney Leyton said. He was a recent graduate who'd stayed on as an instructor, and taught my Introduction to Federation Law class. He was a little full of himself but was widely acknowledged to be going places in his career. I wasn't really paying any attention to him anyway, but to the person who answered his question.

"It's an archaic term referring to communication between a judge or juror and a party to a legal proceeding outside of the presence of the opposing party," she said. She was slim, confident, and assertive, and I'd been trying to make eye contact with her for the entire class. Her name was Phillipa Louvois. She was around my age but had already graduated from law school.

"And can you tell me why it's archaic?" said Leyton.

"Though many of the laws guiding the Federation and Starfleet find their origin in ancient British and American jurisprudence," Phillipa said, "some have fallen away."

"For instance?" This was an example where the instructor probably knew less than the cadet; Leyton was using the cadet's knowledge to not only teach the class but himself.

"Well," Phillipa said, "there have been many instances where Federation law has been decided by a Starship captain, without a judge, jury, prosecutor, or defense lawyer."

"And why are those no longer necessary?"

"Trust," I said. They both looked at me, along with the rest of the class, which hadn't really been part of the discussion. At the time it felt like a bold move. It wasn't, but it got her attention.

"What does trust have to do with it?" Phillipa said.

"Something like ex parte communication," I said, "implies that the judge, prosecutor, and defense lawyer cannot be trusted to have communication without all parties present. That implies that either might not follow the law. It appears that our system now trusts that all involved will obey it. It speaks to our evolution as a species."

"Perhaps it does," Phillipa said, "or perhaps it leaves us open to someone waiting to take advantage of it."

"Vigilance, Mr. Picard," Leyton said. "Freedom requires vigilance." He checked the wall chronometer. "That's it for today…"

As the class broke up, I made sure to intercept Phillipa on her way out.

THE STORY OF ONE OF STARFLEET'S MOST INSPIRATIONAL CAPTAINS

"Do you really think that?" I said.

"What?" She looked at me curiously.

"That someone is waiting to take advantage of us?"

"Why else have lawyers?" She gave me a smile that was at once suggestive and condescending.

"I'd like to talk to you more about the necessity of lawyers," I said, rather awkwardly. But it had its intended effect.

"I take my lunch outside the library every day," she said. "Perhaps I'll see you there sometime…"

This was my second year at the academy, and it was going much more smoothly.

Winning the academy marathon the year before had done a lot for my confidence, and, though the upperclassmen weren't thrilled, my class celebrated me as a hero. I roomed with Corey again, and he and Marta became my closest friends, though the beginning of the year I was still primarily focused on my studies, and begged off on some of their more daring adventures.

But despite my social and athletic successes, the study of archaeology with Professor Galen had taken a dominant role, becoming an unexpected tributary of my ambitions. Growing up, my desire to be a starship captain was unique; it set me apart from my surroundings. Now, at the academy, a large portion of the cadets I met had the same ambition, and I saw that I had come to miss my uniqueness. Galen's mentorship led me to see the potential rewards of being an academic. It appealed to the intellectual side of my personality, and yet was also a form of exploration and achievement. The many discoveries made in the excavations of ancient civilizations on other worlds had led to modern advancements in medicine, agriculture, and terraforming that had changed the face of the Galaxy. Professor Galen had also become something of a surrogate father—a man who understood my inner self in a way my real father never did.

On the last day of the first academic quarter Galen asked me to stay after class. He pulled up an image on the viewscreen at the head of the room.

"You're looking at two paintings; one is Vedalan, the other from Trexia," Professor Galen said. "What do you notice about them?"

There were two ancient paintings side by side. They'd withered with extreme age, but the images were still not difficult to make out. They each represented completely different media and style: the Trexian painting on the right used something similar to oils and was in an almost impressionistic style, with short brush strokes and no sharp edges. The Vedalan painting, on the left, was hyper realistic, almost looked like a photograph. The paintings were from two civilizations that were long dead, and what was interesting was the shared subject.

"They're showing the same scene," I said. The scene showed a scared group of natives, cowering as creatures stepped out of a doorway in the sky. The natives were different; in the Trexian painting they were Trexians, and in the Vedalan painting Vedalans. But the creatures, even though drawn in different styles, on different planets light-years away, were basically the same: lean figures, large-eyed with antenna, and no apparent clothing. And they were both painted gray.

"Yes," Galen said, "should this be of interest to us? We've seen similar myths on different worlds; in fact, Hodgkin's Law of Parallel Planetary Development guarantees that there would be. Are we just looking at two primitive minds expressing their superstitions and fears?" I knew he was testing me, and I enjoyed the challenge. There was another clue in the painting.

"The clothes," I said. "They're different." The natives in the Vedalan painting were cave people; the Trexians depicted were much more advanced, perhaps from a 12th-century Earth equivalent.

"So?" Galen smiled when he said it. I knew I was on to something, but he wasn't going to hand it to me.

"If the paintings were from the same period of time," I said, "they may represent actual events, rather than a depiction of a common myth."

"An archaeologist *did* quantum date the paintings," Galen said, "and they do come from the same period, both created 200,753 years ago."

"That can't be coincidental," I said.

"No," Galen said, "so the archaeologist looked for more clues. For pieces of art to survive the death of these two civilizations meant they themselves must have been considered important. But there were no other clues on either of these planets as to what this scene depicted. So he looked elsewhere." As Galen went to his satchel, I knew that "the archaeologist" he referred to was Galen himself. It was no surprise; I'd come to learn that he was the foremost in his field, having spent the last sixty years of his life uncovering the most famous historical finds of the Galaxy. He had acquired more knowledge in the field than any other living person, and his experience unlocking the mysteries of ancient artifacts was of enormous value to the Federation.

From his satchel, Galen produced a pottery shard.

"This is from a piece of Dinasian pottery from the same time period," Galen said. "And as you can see, a similar depiction of the invader, with the inscription 'the Creature of Air and Darkness.'"

"That's from the legend of Iconia," I said. Up to that point in time, the Iconian civilization was thought to be a myth, conquerors that ruled the Galaxy over a quarter of a million years ago. "You've proved they existed…"

"I haven't proven anything yet," Galen said. "But I have made a proposal to the Federation Archaeology Council to begin a dig on Dinasia; if all goes as planned we will begin next year."

"Wait," I said, "we?"

"I will need help," Galen said.

✦

"That's an amazing opportunity," Phillipa said. "You're not going to turn it down…"

We were outside the academy library. Soon after Phillipa mentioned she regularly had lunch there, I found her and made a point of returning every day with a different culinary delight, which wasn't difficult given the abundance of food replicators on campus. Still, I was making creative choices unfamiliar to her. Today we ate a lamb *vindaloo*. It was the kind of romantic gesture that I've long since abandoned.

"Of course not," I said, and meant it. I was being offered the opportunity to be the protégé of the Federation's greatest archaeologist, putting me in a position to possibly inherit that title myself.

"That's a relief," Phillipa said. "We will be quite a couple." She smiled and I leaned to kiss her. For a while she had playfully discouraged my more assertive romantic overtures, but recently I'd worn her down. Phillipa was ambitious; she saw Starfleet as an opportunity to put her own stamp on galactic law. She took pride in her unusual track of law school and then the academy, and there was something that appealed to her about the road I was on that might lead me to chase archaeology at the expense of an academy career.

That evening, I returned to my room with Phillipa to find Corey and Marta there.

"Pack your bags, Johnny," Corey said.

"What are you talking about?" I said.

"We've got into the flight school on Morikin VII," Marta said. "The three of us." Several weeks previously Corey and Marta had convinced me to apply for training on Morikin VII. It was an elective the academy offered, a ten-week elite flight instruction on a remote world.

"I didn't know you'd applied to Elite Flight," Phillipa said. I had actually forgotten about it, assuming that among the 12,000 cadets in the academy, there was little chance that I would get in. I had a feeling that Corey must have had something to do with our acceptance. It was too much of a coincidence.

"What are you looking at me for?" Corey read the suspicion in my expression. Corey had gotten very good at breaking rules and not getting caught.

"You're not going, are you?" Phillipa said, less as a question than a demand.

I was conflicted. I was half a step from leaving the academy altogether, and I certainly didn't see myself on a path as an elite pilot. And yet, the idea of getting a chance to be stationed on a faraway planet with my two good friends, learning how to fly state-of-the-art ships...

"Have a nice time," Phillipa said, and left the room. I had gotten lost in a bit of a reverie, and hadn't noticed that I'd hurt her feelings. I ran out after her.

"Phillipa, please stop." I caught up to her outside the building and grabbed her arm.

"Let go of me," she said.

"Let's just talk..."

"There's nothing to talk about. I don't want to get in the way of your little jaunt with your drinking buddies."

"It's just ten weeks..."

"Ten weeks with Marta..." Phillipa said, and this was the heart of it. She wasn't comfortable with me having such a close friend who was a woman. The fact was, I thought Marta was very attractive, but I was in love with Phillipa, or at least I thought I was, and I'd told her as much.

"You have to trust me," I said.

THE STORY OF ONE OF STARFLEET'S MOST INSPIRATIONAL CAPTAINS

"I will," she said. "If you don't go." I don't know what it was about this request, but it rankled me. It showed that Phillipa didn't trust me. I couldn't accede to it.

"I'm sorry," I said. "I want to go." I saw in her reaction a flash of hurt and vulnerability, but only a flash.

"Fine, go," she said. "I'm going to go, too." She turned and walked off. I didn't quite know how it happened, but our relationship was over. I wandered back to my room, a mass of confusion. Corey and Marta were still there. I told them what happened.

"I'm really going to miss her," Corey said.

"Corey," Marta said. Corey, admonished, gave me an apologetic look.

"It's all right," I said. "It probably wasn't meant to be." I was hurt, but also a little angry. It would be a while before I let myself miss her.

"We're going to have the time of our lives," Corey said. I smiled. His enthusiasm was infectious enough that I momentarily forgot my rejection. It was exciting; I was about to go to a new world. And I wouldn't see Phillipa again for over twenty years.

✦

"Probably don't want to unpack your clothes until I fix the moisture problem," the captain said. Marta, Corey, and I were crammed into one of the small shelters on Morikin VII. There were three cots, three dressers, and one closet. And it was raining inside. There was something wrong with the environmental controls and moisture was dripping off the ceiling. "Maybe one of you can give me a hand…"

We had just arrived after a two-week flight on the *U.S.S. Rhode Island*, an antique class J freighter resupplying the flight school. It was my second trip into space and it was only marginally more exciting than my first. My cabin, such as it was, at least had a porthole, and the captain, a jovial man named Griffin who ran the ship with his family, had no problem with giving the three of us the run of his vessel.

It turned out the ship was a lot more pleasant than our destination. Morikin VII was not a very hospitable place. The atmosphere was a combination of carbon dioxide, nitrogen, and sulfuric acid, and the winds often reached hundreds of kilometers an hour. When we arrived we expected to find a state-of-the-art facility; instead we found quite the opposite. We were beamed into a darkened cargo storage warehouse, one of several domed structures connected to each other by underground tunnels. There was a man about sixty, waiting for us alone. As he approached, I was surprised to notice that he was wearing the rank of captain. We stood at attention.

"At ease," the man said with a smile. We relaxed somewhat. "I'm Captain Kirk." Captain Kirk? The same name as the famous starship captain? It was impossible of course; he was much too young, and James T. Kirk had been dead for decades. I decided it must just be a coincidence.

We introduced ourselves, and he led us out of the warehouse on a short tour of the facility, which was only made up of five domes: the warehouse, his quarters, our quarters, a common area for meals and recreation, and a hangar. Corey and I had speculated on the journey what kind of cutting-edge craft we would get to fly. What we saw in the hangar deck surprised us.

"These are class F shuttlecraft," the captain said. We were looking at two dilapidated transports, showing signs of age and wear.

"They're like fifty years old," Corey said.

"More like seventy," Kirk said, with a wry smile. I think we weren't the first disappointed cadets to be under his charge. He then took us to our waterlogged quarters. Marta and I helped him repair the reclamation controls, the source of the problem. He then served us a simple meal of some kind of broiled meat with mashed potato, which he prepared himself. He plated our food, showed us where to clean up when we were done, then went to his quarters and left us alone.

"No replicator?" Corey said. "This has to be some kind of joke."

"I feel that we've done something wrong," I said. Marta looked at us; she seemed to know more than we did.

"You guys know who that is, right?" she said. "That's Peter Kirk, James Kirk's nephew." I'd forgotten that the famous Captain Kirk had a nephew; though he'd entered Starfleet, his career had not been as notable as that of his famous relation.

"That can't be," Corey said. "Did he commit some crime we don't know about? Sleep with the Federation president's daughter or something?"

"No," Marta said. "He started this school. It was his idea."

"His idea," I said, "to create a terrible place for cadets to spend ten weeks?"

THE STORY OF ONE OF STARFLEET'S MOST INSPIRATIONAL CAPTAINS

"Every cadet who has gone through the program has gotten a prime starship posting upon graduation," Marta said. "He must be teaching something."

The next day he went through a thorough maintenance check of one of the shuttlecraft, then took us for a flight. It was a rough ride leaving the atmosphere; once we got into space it became quite boring. Kirk did not engage us in much conversation beyond familiarizing us with the shuttle controls. He had us take turns flying the ship; it was a leisurely flight to some outlying asteroids. Kirk indicated one of the larger ones.

"There's a Nausicaan mining base there," he said. "Probably want to avoid it." The natives of the planet Nausicaa had been a surly species, historically pirates, only recently reaching an uneasy peace with the Federation. Corey, Marta, and I tried to get a look at the base; it was built into the side of the asteroid. Extending from it were two docking arms with Nausicaan fighters docked.

"They have a base in Federation space?" I said.

"It's been here for over a hundred years," Kirk said. "I think they have a claim." He then turned a ship around to return to Morikin VII, taking back the controls to re-enter the atmosphere. Once back in the hangar, Kirk ordered us to complete another maintenance check on the ship, even though we'd done that before we took off. But as we examined the aged craft, we saw that flying in Morikin VII's atmosphere had caused a lot of damage; the ship needed quite a bit of attention. This ended up being our daily routine: maintenance session, a flight into space, then another maintenance session. Despite all our preparations, we often faced mechanical and electrical failures while flying, and Kirk insisted on letting us fix them ourselves.

Kirk himself seemed something of an enigma. He didn't talk to us much outside of his lessons, and he cooked for us every night, always some kind of food native to his homeland Iowa. We tried to ask him questions about his career, but he didn't seem that interested in talking about it. And though I was filled with curiosity about the man who was his uncle, it seemed impolitic to ask.

Eventually, he began taking us up one at a time, to see how much we could do on our own. On my first solo flight, I successfully piloted the shuttle out of the atmosphere. Once in orbit, however, I noticed an imbalance in one of the engines. In order to check it out, I needed to leave the helm.

"Pretend I'm not here," Kirk said. "What would you do?" I realized he wasn't going to help me, so I put the ship on automatic pilot and headed to the engine compartment in the rear of the ship. Before I reached it, there was a small explosion.

I turned. Kirk was slumped back in his chair, and the control panel was on fire.

I grabbed the fire extinguisher and doused the flame, then went to Kirk. He was unconscious, his face slightly burned. I pressed my finger against his neck and thankfully, there was a pulse.

I would have to tend to him later. I looked at the console; the automatic pilot must have shorted out. The control readouts indicated the main engines were off. The short must have triggered an automatic shutdown. I hit the emergency restart for the engines; the cycle would take two minutes. That's when I noticed our position.

The shuttle was being pulled down to Morikin VII. I would burn up in the atmosphere long before I could restart the engines. The only power I had was in the attitude jets, which were separate from the engines, but they wouldn't give me nearly enough power to escape the pull of the planet. I clicked on the communicator.

"Mayday! Mayday! This is shuttlecraft one. Morikin base, do you read?" It was a futile effort—the communication system was out—and frankly I didn't really believe that Corey or Marta would have any suggestions for me about how to handle this. I looked out the porthole: Morikin VII was filling the view. I would be entering the atmosphere in seconds. I was lost.

"Bounce…" It was Kirk. He was fighting his way to consciousness.

"What, sir?"

"Aim toward the planet…" he said. His voice was weak. "Bounce… off…" He fell back into unconsciousness.

Bounce off what? The planet? That didn't seem likely. Then I remembered something from my studies of ancient spacecraft, about how they used to skip off the atmosphere to slow their descent. It was just a matter of hitting it at the proper angle. I took the controls, and turned the craft directly down into Morikin VII.

The shuttle started to rock, buffeted by atmospheric turbulence. The temperature inside rose as the outer skin began to heat. I pulled the shuttle up hard.

At first the turbulence didn't stop, and I thought I had miscalculated, but then saw the planet begin to fall away out the porthole. The shuttle steadied, and I was in a low orbit.

The engines' restart sequence completed; I had power again. I pushed the throttle forward to move out into a higher orbit, then grabbed the emergency medical kit and tended to Kirk's wounds. He was not seriously injured, and came round after a bit.

"It worked?"

"Yes, sir," I said.

"My uncle taught me that," he said. I took this as permission to say something about his famous relative; I had missed the wistfulness in the way he said it.

"He was one of my heroes growing up," I said.

"Mine too."

"What was he like?"

"You probably know him as well as I did," Kirk said. The heartbreak apparent in his voice spoke volumes, and I decided this would be the last conversation we would have on the subject.

✦

After almost ten weeks on Morikin VII, we felt changed. The mundane routine combined with the poor living conditions and the moments of true terror dealing with old, unreliable equipment had given Corey, Marta, and I a strength and confidence that we'd never had before. It made us all a little cocky (although, in Corey's case, it just made him more so) and led to an incident which would have dire ramifications for me.

Eventually, Kirk let us take the shuttles up by ourselves, and one day I was flying out toward the asteroid field. I wanted to get a closer look at the Nausicaan station. We'd had no contact with the Nausicaans, and I'd never met one face to face, though the images I'd seen made me very curious.

I'd brought my shuttle to within a few hundred kilometers when my communication panel lit up.

"Alien vessel! State your purpose!" The voice was rough and intimidating. I should have just turned the ship around and fled back to Morikin VII, but I was too curious and overconfident.

"Cadet Picard," I said. "I'm stationed on Morikin VII. My vessel is in need of repairs. Request permission to dock." I wanted to get a look inside that base.

"Request denied!"

"Your base is inside Federation space," I said, "and Federation law requires that you help ships in distress." There was a long pause; I didn't know why the Federation let the Nausicaans, who were not part of the Federation, keep a base in our territory, but I made the assumption that they wouldn't want to do anything overt to disrupt that.

"You may dock," the voice said.

I pulled the shuttle up to one of the empty docking arms, and a mooring tube extended to my hatch. I opened it and entered the base. I walked through a cold, dank corridor lined with piping, leading to a catwalk overlooking an ore mining and processing facility. The interior of the asteroid had been carved out; conveyers carrying buckets of ore moved slowly out of a massive cave. Miners, presumably Nausicaans, in environmental suits oversaw the dumping of the ore into a giant fusion furnace, where it was melted. It was both primitive and impressive. Before I could admire it for too long, I was confronted by two Nausicaans.

"Hello," I said.

They were both much taller than me, had ashen skin, large manes of hair, and small tusks surrounding their mouths. They were very intimidating, an obviously predatory species.

"What is wrong with your ship?" the lead Nausicaan said.

"Just a problem with the guidance control," I said. "Shouldn't take too long to fix. I was wondering if I could use your bathroom?"

"Bathroom?" The lead Nausicaan looked like he would kill me without a second thought. "No, you will not use our bathroom."

"Federation law requires that you provide sanitary facilities to ships in distress." I was now lying, there was no such law, but I didn't think these two would know. I tried to walk past them, but the leader grabbed me by the collar.

"Get your ship repaired and get out!"

"Let go of me," I said. I looked him hard in the eye. He laughed, and brought his hand up to strike me.

THE STORY OF ONE OF STARFLEET'S MOST INSPIRATIONAL CAPTAINS

"Puny human," he said.

I immediately hit him in the center of his chest. The move surprised him, and he was momentarily winded. The other turned to pull out a knife, but I kicked it out of his hand and hit him in the throat.

I turned on the lead Nausicaan, who had gotten his breath back. He swung his large fist at me, but I grabbed it and threw him over my shoulder. He landed on the other Nausicaan, and they both flew back onto the floor of the catwalk. I had clearly overstayed my welcome.

"On second thought, I don't need the bathroom," I said, and ran back through the mooring tunnel to my shuttle, closing the hatch behind me. I started the engines, and disconnected from the docking arm, flying away from the base at full speed. I was initially concerned about being pursued but no craft followed me. The two Nausicaans probably wouldn't make a fuss, I'd just embarrassed them, and as I headed back to Morikin I laughed heartily, exhilarated by my daring.

Soon after, Corey, Marta, and I left Morikin and returned to the academy. I quickly found that I had a new problem. The classroom had very little appeal to me. I'd survived an adventure, and found myself more easily distracted from my studies. I also discovered a new confidence with women, one that is often excused in men as "youthful indiscretion," but was really an insensitive indulgence. I was self-centered, unconcerned with the feelings of the women I pursued. I would pursue them with abandon and cast them aside without a second thought. It was shamefully superficial, and I often find myself mortified by my memories.

"*Vous êtes une femme très attirante.*" I was sitting with a young woman near a large elm tree on the academy grounds. I prefer not to say her name, as I have not seen her since those days and am unsure how she felt about what went on between us.

"What did you say?"

"That you're a very attractive female..."

"Stop it," she said.

"It's the truth. Here, I'll put it in writing," I said. I took out my pocketknife and carved in the tree. When I was done, she looked at it curiously.

"'A.F.' aren't my initials..." she said.

"It stands for 'Attractive Female,'" I said. She laughed and I was moving in to kiss her when we were interrupted.

"What the hell are you doing?" We looked over to see an elderly man in work boots and overalls, wielding pruning shears rather threateningly. It was the groundskeeper, who I'd occasionally noticed since I'd arrived, but had given no mind to.

"I'm sorry..." I said, stumbling to my feet. My confident masculinity quickly evaporated.

"Don't apologize to me," he said. "Apologize to the tree."

"You... want me to apologize..." I said. I wasn't looking at her, but I could hear my companion quietly giggling at my embarrassment.

"What did that poor elm tree ever do to you?" the groundskeeper said. "Nothing! And you take a knife to it. It's a living thing!" He stood there glaring at me. After a long moment, I turned to the tree.

"I'm sorry..." I said, then turned back to him. "Will that do?"

"It will not. I need help with weeding," the groundskeeper said. "You'll report to me here every morning at six o'clock for the next two months."

"With all due respect, I don't know why..."

"Defacing the academy is grounds for expulsion," he said. He turned and walked off. I sat back down.

"Do you think he'd really get me expelled?"

"I wouldn't mess with Boothby," she said, which is how I learned his name.

For the next two months I met Boothby on the academy grounds every morning and helped him with weeding, pruning, and general maintenance. He didn't talk to me at all except to give me instructions. My childhood on the vineyard made this more natural work for me than it might have been for others, but I didn't enjoy it. And between this and my new romantic adventure with "A.F.," my studies faltered and I actually failed organic chemistry. But that, as it turned out, was the least of my concerns.

One afternoon I received word to report to Professor Galen in his office. It was a cramped room, filled with artifacts from his expeditions. Galen sat at his desk.

"Mr. Picard," Professor Galen said. "The dig on Dinasia has been approved. We leave in two weeks."

"That's wonderful, Professor," I said. I had been dreading this moment since my return from Morikin VII; my recent adventures had muted my desire

THE STORY OF ONE OF STARFLEET'S MOST INSPIRATIONAL CAPTAINS

to be an archaeologist, but I hadn't had the courage to talk to the professor about it.

"You will have to tender your resignation to the academy immediately," he said. I was very conflicted. Professor Galen was very important to me. I decided at that moment that I wouldn't disappoint him.

"Yes, sir," I said.

✦

The next morning I joined Boothby again, this time helping plant a new row of mophead hydrangeas.

"You failed organic chemistry?" Boothby said. This shocked me. It was the first time he'd spoken to me about something personal. I had no idea how he'd found out.

"It doesn't matter," I said. "I'm leaving the academy."

"To spend the rest of your life digging in the dirt," Boothby said. He was showing an almost supernatural clairvoyance.

"How did you know…"

"People talk," he said. "They don't seem to notice I'm listening. Or maybe they don't care."

"Archaeology is important work," I said. "This is an opportunity of a lifetime…"

"Keep saying it," Boothby said. "You may convince yourself." His comments were making me face something I didn't want to face. And I lashed out.

"Look, I don't need career advice from a gardener."

Boothby didn't respond. I should've been thanking this man for understanding me better than I knew myself, but I was too immature, and worked in petulant silence for the rest of the morning. Then, after planting the last of the hydrangeas, he turned to me.

"You're finished," Boothby said. "Your debt to the garden is paid." And he went about the rest of his work. It would be years before I apologized to Boothby, and thanked him for putting me on the right path.

I walked the academy grounds the rest of the day, lost in thought, eventually finding myself at Galen's classroom. He had just finished up a lecture, and there were a few artifacts on his desk. He picked one up and handed it to me.

"Mr. Picard," he said, "can you tell me what this is?" He enjoyed testing me, probably partially because he knew I enjoyed it. I examined the artifact, a stick carved out of stone.

"The images are from Gorlan mythology," I said. "This is a Gorlan prayer stick."

"The ancient Gorlans believed these prayer sticks had the power to grant the owner whatever they desired," Galen said. "I usually would dismiss such superstition, but I acquired this one shortly before my Dinasian dig was approved…"

"I'm not going." I blurted it out. It was tactless and a little cruel.

"What?"

"I've decided to stay at the academy," I said. Galen nodded, then slowly packed up the artifacts into his bag.

"You must decide what's best for you," he said. "If you change your mind, a career in archaeology will always be there." He shook my hand and left the room. I stood there alone, muddled. I had expected him to be angry with me, but he wasn't, or at least didn't seem to be. Looking back, I now know he'd protected my feelings by covering his own. Like a father would.

✦

"And so, Class of 2327, today you are fully-fledged ensigns," announced the president of the Federation. We sat in our dress uniforms, wearing caps for the first time during our enrollment. We were out on the main lawn, a rapt audience for the elderly statesman. The graduating class at the academy didn't always receive an address from the Federation president, except if the current office holder was a Starfleet veteran, as Nyota Uhura was.

"Four short years ago," she said, "you assembled here from all parts of the Galaxy, from all walks of life. Each of you knew what the service meant, or you wouldn't have volunteered. Each of you knew the Federation needs to be cherished and protected, and that sometimes our way of life may require the sacrifice of life itself. From here on, your education must continue in the more demanding school of actual service. Wearing the gold pin of Starfleet, you go

THE STORY OF ONE OF STARFLEET'S MOST INSPIRATIONAL CAPTAINS

out into space to face the great challenges of our final frontier. Your fellow citizens share my confidence that you will serve Starfleet and the Federation with honor and distinction. Good luck."

We stood up and cheered, throwing our caps in the air, continuing a tradition that went back to the early years of the academy when caps were part of the dress uniform. There was backslapping and hugging—we were a joyous crowd. The tumult died down as we broke up to look for loved ones in the crowd.

I found my mother. She gave me a warm embrace.

"It was difficult for your father and brother to get away," she said, responding to a question I didn't ask. I knew that spring was a challenging time of year at home. In the vineyard a time of vigilance for diseases among the grapes, and at the winery removing yeasts and perhaps returning wines to barrels for a second fermentation. But my mother worked just as hard as her husband and son, and she managed to get away.

I'd seen very little of my family and even less of the vineyard since starting at the academy, but my mother wouldn't let me go easily. She made as many trips as she could to San Francisco, and I could tell that the stress of the chasm between me and the other men in my family weighed heavily upon her. But, where my father was concerned, I couldn't consider softening the resolve of my animosity.

"It's all right, Maman," I said. "Let's go get some lunch." As we headed off, an officer intercepted us. I immediately stood at attention.

"At ease, Ensign," Captain Hanson said.

"Captain Hanson, may I introduce my mother," I said. "Yvette Picard."

"A pleasure, madam," he said as he took my mother's hand.

"You are Jean-Luc's new commanding officer," she said. I had told my mother when Captain Hanson had chosen me for a flight controller position on the *U.S.S. New Orleans*. This wasn't just a new ship, it was the first of a new *class* of ship; this would be the third time Hanson would take out the first ship in a new class. I had tried to explain to her why earning a spot with someone considered such an important captain was prestigious, but I could tell she didn't fully understand.

"You should be very proud of your son," Hanson said. "He has already accomplished a great deal." It was a very paternal gesture, though Hanson was only about fifteen years older than I was. He then turned to me. "See you at Starbase Earhart, Ensign." He shook my hand and smiled, then turned to leave.

"He seems very fond of you, Jean-Luc," my mother said. I had always been so nervous around him I don't think I could see that objectively, but it made sense. When I look back on my academy years, the time I spent there was looking for fathers. I hungered for mentors, and found them in both expected and unexpected places. Hanson had been a surprise, showing interest in my career from the moment I won the marathon. Of course, this was all an attempt to fill a hole in my life left by my upbringing.

"Why don't we go home for lunch, Jean-Luc?" my mother said. I had transporter privileges, so we could beam to La Barre. We could be back at the vineyard in less than an hour. I looked at her and smiled.

"I'm sorry," I said. "I'd prefer to eat here."

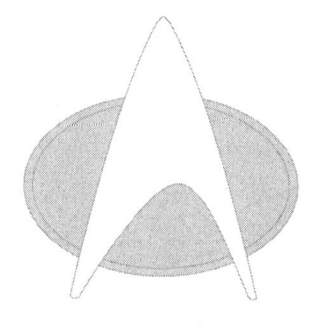

CHAPTER THREE

"WE GOTTA GET EVEN," Corey said.

Marta, Corey, and I were in my room at Starbase Earhart. It was late, and we'd just come back from an evening at the Bonestell Recreation Center. It had been almost a month since graduation. The three of us, still happily joined at the hip, would all be leaving on our separate missions from this starbase. During our time off, Corey had engaged in games of chance, and I had indulged in some more superficial romantic entanglements that I still regret. In fact, earlier that evening a woman I had successfully pursued the night before discovered that I had a date with her roommate for this evening. My cheek still stung from her slap.

"What did you have in mind?" Marta said. She and I had witnessed Corey losing a game of dom-jot* to a Nausicaan, which had cost him several slips of gold-pressed latinum. This surprised all of us as Corey was well-practiced at the game, and the Nausicaan's victory had been suspiciously quick.

"Well, we can do to him what he did to us," Corey said. "Cheat." Corey had earlier conjectured to us that the Nausicaan had some kind of magnetic device in his belt that allowed him to control the metal ball's path on the table. "Only this time, we rig the table so his device will backfire on him."

---

*EDITOR'S NOTE: Dom-jot is a game with some similarities to both the ancient games of billiards and pinball.

"I know just the thing," I said. My confidence at taking down Nausicaans was still fresh in my mind from my experience back at Morikin. I wasn't really worried about getting caught; in fact, I think I was looking forward to it.

It was a last hurrah for the three of us. We'd spent four years together, and now our respective careers would separate us. We were looking to cause some trouble, and in retrospect it was juvenile, and very dangerous.

But we went ahead.

Late that night, when the recreation center was closed, Corey, Marta, and I snuck in. While Marta dealt with the security systems, Corey and I adjusted the electrical setup that controlled the bumpers on the table to create interference that would block any nearby magnetic device. We got out of there without being detected.

The next evening, we went to the recreation center. I had arranged a date with an older woman who worked as a receptionist in the personnel office. I think she could tell that my mind wasn't on her when I noticed that the Nausicaan had returned with two friends; she soon left me, saying she had to get up early. This was disappointing, but wouldn't be the worst moment of the evening.

"Play dom-jot, human," the Nausicaan said to Corey. "Give you a better chance." Corey happily obliged. Less than thirty seconds into the game, the Nausicaan threw down his cue in frustration; whatever device he'd been using was no longer working.

"Human cheat!"

"I'm cheating?" Corey said. "I don't think so. But if you want to forfeit the game..."

"I do not forfeit to a human," the Nausicaan said. "Humans have no *guramba*." The three of us stood toe-to-toe with the Nausicaans, who towered over us.

"What did you say?" I said, stepping up to the Nausicaan, flanked by Marta and Corey.

"Humans have no *guramba*," he said. I actually had no idea what the Nausicaan had said, since the universal translators wouldn't translate "guramba," but I assumed from context that it was particularly insulting.[*]

---

[*] **EDITOR'S NOTE:** *Guramba* is Nausicaan slang for male genitalia.

"That's what I thought you said." I hit the Nausicaan in the chest, and suddenly the three of us were involved in a melee. I was the only one with experience fighting a Nausicaan, and relied on my previous encounter, which served me well; I had taken out my first opponent with a blow to the chest and neck, and turned to help with the one who was wrestling with Marta. As I did, I felt a sharp pain in my back. It forced me to my knees.

I looked down. A serrated blade, covered with blood, protruded from my chest. I wasn't feeling any pain, and the last thing I remembered was the sound of laughing. My own.

✦

"Ensign?" The voice was distant and unfamiliar. I was in a deep sleep, but was confused. I didn't remember going to bed. I didn't remember anything. I opened my eyes, and it was difficult to focus. There was a doctor, a Vulcan woman, standing over me.

"How are you feeling?" the Vulcan doctor said.

"I'm not sure," I said. Hearing my voice, I realized my mouth was covered by a respirator. "How long…"

"You have been unconscious for three point seven nine weeks," the doctor said, with the usual Vulcan bedside manner. Almost a month?

"The damage to your original organ was too extensive," the Vulcan doctor said. "You were placed in suspended animation until a doctor of sufficient skill and experience could arrive here to perform the necessary surgery." It was clear that the Vulcan was talking about herself. I was so annoyed at her arrogance that I almost missed the meat of what she was saying.

"Original organ? You mean… my heart?"

"Yes," the doctor said. "It has been substituted with an artificial mechanism. It will last many years without having to be replaced." It was too much to take in; I had a mechanical heart?

"When can I get out of here?" I said. I wanted to make a big show that I was ready to leave, but I didn't even have the strength to lift my head off the pillow.

"You will need at least two point four more weeks of observation and physical therapy," the doctor said.

"But my ship…" I said, already knowing the answer.

"You have been temporarily reassigned," the doctor said. "To this hospital bed. You will rest now." She left the room. I lay there thinking about what I had done. That fight had changed everything. No doubt Hanson, leaving on a deep space mission, wasn't waiting months for a relief flight controller to get out of the hospital. What had I done? Had I shattered my whole life trying to cheat a Nausicaan in a game of dom-jot? I felt such a fool. Tears fell from my eyes as I drifted back to sleep.

✦

Within a few days, I had mostly recovered, and was able to review several messages that were left for me. The first was from Corey.

"The doctors assure me you're going to be fine, Johnny. I hope so," Corey said. He was bruised and bandaged, having recorded the message shortly after the bar fight. "I'm sorry I can't stay around; the *Ajax* is leaving. Right after you got stabbed, the security boys showed up and stunned the Nausicaans. They got arrested, and were extradited back to their homeworld. Starfleet security had some questions for me and Marta, but they didn't dig too deep about what exactly happened, which I guess is good." That was something of a relief, since I don't think Starfleet would've looked kindly on three officers riggings a dom-jot table to cheat someone, even if it was a Nausicaan. I looked at Corey on my viewscreen: his usual bravado was gone. I could see he was very remorseful. "I'll check in as often as I can to see how you're doing, but the *Ajax* is headed out to the Romulan Neutral Zone, and Captain North is pretty strict about using subspace for personal communications. Sorry I… sorry I got you into all this. Take care of yourself." Corey signed off.

Marta's message was much more emotional. She had obviously been crying before she made it.

"The *Kyushu* is leaving today, and I don't want to go," Marta said. "It's very difficult leaving while you're unconscious. The doctors say you'll be all right… I just wish I could stay." She broke down again. "I should've stopped you guys," she said. "It was so stupid…" She wiped her eyes, and composed herself. "I love you, Jean-Luc. Please be well…" She signed off. Jean-Luc. She hadn't called me that in years. I watched it again, and regretted that Marta and I never took the time to explore how we felt about each other. Perhaps one day.

I also got a short written message from Captain Hanson, wishing me a speedy recovery. I couldn't help but interpret it as disappointment in my rash actions. I promised myself I would never be so foolhardy again.

During my convalescence I devoted a lot of time to looking for a new posting. I was anxious to make up for lost time, so I rearranged my priorities. My hope to be a flight controller on a ship whose assignment was deep space exploration would have to wait, as there were no postings available. So instead, I looked at the openings on ships assigned to Starbase Earhart's sector; a vessel close by would at least get me on active duty sooner. I found one on the *Reliant*, an opening for a junior science officer. The ship was a small one, assigned to routine patrol in this sector of space. It wasn't really what I wanted, but I was qualified—though I'd failed organic chemistry, I had high marks in astrosciences and archaeology. I submitted my application, and received a call via subspace from the ship's commander.

"Ensign," Captain Quinn said, "I don't like troublemakers." Gregory Quinn was a large man, with a soft, intimidating voice.

"I understand, Captain," I said. I tried to think of what I could say to convince him that I was no longer a firebrand, and decided instead to stay mum. Despite my recent indiscretion, my transcripts had been adequate enough for him to seriously consider me.

"I don't know Captain Hanson, or why he wanted you," Quinn said. "But this isn't that job. Are you sure being a junior science officer is going to be exciting enough for you?"

"I'm not looking for excitement, sir," I said. "I'm looking to serve." On the viewscreen, I could see that Quinn was studying me, trying to tell if I was being sincere. I honestly didn't know if I was, I just knew that was the only appropriate answer to give. It seemed to be enough for him.

"I need to fill this opening, so you've got the job. I'm not sure if I'm happy about it, but it's the situation we're in. *Reliant* will be docked at Earhart by 0800. Report to Lieutenant Nakamura then," he said, and signed off.

✦

"Welcome aboard," Nakamura said as I stepped off the transporter, my duffel in tow. "Captain wants you to have a stem-to-stern tour." Nakamura was the senior science officer, friendly if a little officious. He had me drop my belongings in my quarters and then led me through the small, clean ship. There were only thirty-four crewmembers, and by the end of the first few hours on board I'd met a good number of them. The only part of the ship I didn't get to see was the bridge.

"You only go there if you're reporting for your shift, or if you're called," Nakamura said. "Captain Quinn doesn't like extra people up there." After our tour, Nakamura took me to a room about the size of a large closet, just large enough for a computer console, table and chair.

"Welcome to the science lab," Nakamura said, with a smile.

"This is it?"

"This is it." Nakamura showed me what I would be doing as a junior science officer. There was no real research on a ship this small; most of what the science officers did was take in data. The ship ran on four six-hour shifts; I would be serving on two: 1900 to 0100 in the science lab, and 0100 to 0700 on the bridge. While on the bridge, the science officer, aside from providing information to his commanding officers, coordinated whatever scientific information was coming into the ship, whether significant or trivial: sensor data, reports from planetary surveys, communications from Starfleet or Federation planets. The officer serving in the lab, when not assigned to an away team, was to make sure the information routed from the bridge was properly categorized and catalogued, and reported to Starfleet Command. This was one of the pillars of our civilization: ships all over the quadrant were taking in information and sending it to Starfleet Command, where it became part of the collective knowledge of the Federation.

It was also very tedious work. My first shift in the lab was spent sorting data and preparing reports to be approved later by Nakamura before being sent off. Whatever fantasy I had of serving aboard a starship, six hours sitting alone in a room staring at a computer screen wasn't part of it. But what got me through the tedium and disappointment of that first day was my anticipation of reporting to the bridge. At the end of my shift in the lab, I closed it up and went there.

Like most starships, the *Reliant* duplicated Earth conditions of day and night, so I was reporting on what would be considered 1am; the lighting in the corridors was low, as it was on the bridge. It was the familiar layout, though smaller than what I expected. I was a few minutes early for my shift change, and reported to the commanding officer in the captain's chair, a woman in her thirties: Commander Shanthi, the ship's first officer.

THE STORY OF ONE OF STARFLEET'S MOST INSPIRATIONAL CAPTAINS

"Ensign Picard, reporting for duty," I said. She turned and looked at me.

"You are early, Ensign," she said. She had a thick East Indian accent, and a formality that I found a little intimidating. "Report to your station." I went to the science station, and met the other junior science officer, a man about my age. He stood up; I was surprised how much taller he was.

"Walker Keel," he said. He smiled and held out his hand. I shook it. He looked familiar.

"Jean-Luc Picard," I said. "Have we met?"

"Yeah," he said. "You and your friends almost started a fight with me and mine at a bar on Tau Ceti III." I remembered the incident: Corey, Marta, and I were on our way home from Morikin, and had had a little too much to drink.

"Sorry about that," I said.

"No apology necessary," Walker said. "We were all a little full of ourselves." I was relieved there were no hard feelings, as it turned out he was my roommate; we hadn't seen each other yet due to the staggered shifts.

"I relieve you, sir," I said, indulging with full seriousness the ceremony of my first duty shift on the bridge. Walker chuckled.

"I stand relieved," he said, amused at my obvious pleasure. I took the science station, as the other crewmen were relieved by their graveyard shift replacements. This shift was a young one. The ship's second officer, Lieutenant Commander Altman, who was only a few years older than me, relieved Commander Shanthi. I looked out the large viewscreen. The beautiful blue-green planet that was home to Starbase Earhart filled the bottom quarter of the screen. The rest was stars.

It wasn't exactly what I wanted, but it was close enough.

✦

"Sir, I want to make a proposal," I said. It was during one of my duty shifts in the science lab. Lieutenant Nakamura had stopped by to review a few reports I'd completed for approval.

"Proposal?" he said. I could tell he just wanted to get through his work and sign out for the day, but I had to make my pitch now or it would be too late.

"Yes," I said. "Since we'll be in orbit of Milika III for one more day, there's an archaeological site that we should investigate." We'd come to Milika III delivering the new Federation ambassador and his staff to the planet. It was an arid planet, home to an advanced species of humanoids. The Milikans until quite recently had been a culture ripped apart by religious differences, but in the last few decades had united under one government and quickly gone into space. There were still pockets of religious dogmatists on the world, but the Federation had determined that the planet fit enough of the guidelines for admission to the Federation, and the government began the process of opening diplomatic relations. *Reliant* had been assigned to set up a Federation embassy on this planet. It had been a stressful time for Quinn and the crew, as the ambassador, an elderly man named William Smithie, had been exacting in his demands. I, on the other hand, had very little to do so I'd been reading everything I could about the planet and stumbled upon a native archeologist's research paper on a recently discovered site.

"What is so important about this site?" he asked. I could see Nakamura was getting a little annoyed, but I had to push on.

"It contains Vulcan artifacts," I said. "A local archeologist discovered them last month, and the Federation has not confirmed the find yet. If they are authentic, it might mean the ancient Vulcans had an unknown colony on this world."

"I don't know if we have anyone on board qualified in the procedures to authenticate a site like this," he said.

"Actually, I'm qualified, sir," I said. My years of study with Professor Galen had left me prepared for this opportunity. I could tell, however, that Nakamura's annoyance had now grown to frustration. "If I authenticate the find, it would save the Federation Archaeology Council from having to task another ship."

"Give me the proposal," Nakamura said, "and I'll take it to the captain." I was ready for this and handed him a PADD with my proposal on it. He wasn't happy. No one on this ship would care about Vulcan artifacts, especially the captain. But I'd presented him with an opportunity that he had to take up the chain of command. The Federation Archaeology Council would certainly ask for the site to be authenticated before sending a team to explore it further. The efficiency of my proposal was compelling, even if it was also a little annoying. Because Nakamura knew that the main reason for my suggesting it had nothing to do with science.

I wanted to go on an away mission.

THE STORY OF ONE OF STARFLEET'S MOST INSPIRATIONAL CAPTAINS

My eighteen months on the *Reliant* had been pleasant. I'd begun to make friends among the crew, and the work was rarely demanding. It was also rarely interesting. I wasn't going to let that affect my performance, and I completed all my duties quickly and effectively. I didn't see much of the captain: he came on bridge duty just as I was signing out. My vague impression was that my work ethic had done a lot to ease his initial concerns about offering me the posting.

But I hadn't left the confines of the ship. If there was an away mission that required a science officer, Nakamura usually went, and if he didn't go, he sent Walker. I was getting the shipboard equivalent of "cabin fever" and was looking for some way to justify walking on solid ground. The obscure archaeology journal I'd found in the database from Milika III gave me my opportunity.

As the day went on, and I hadn't heard anything, my hope began to dim. We were due to leave orbit the next morning at 0900, and by the time I reported for my duty shift on the bridge, I assumed that my proposal had either been turned down or ignored. When Nakamura relieved me at 0700, he said the captain wanted to talk to me. I stepped down into the well of the bridge near the captain's chair. Quinn, having just taken over from Altman, was reading his shift report. He didn't look up.

"Archaeology, huh? Was never that interested in it myself," he said.

"Yes, sir," I said.

"How long would you need?"

"Once at the site, the scans would take less than thirty minutes," I said. It would actually take a lot less than that, but I didn't want whoever was leading the away mission to rush me. Turns out that wouldn't be a problem.

"You will be leading the away mission," Quinn said. "Pick an assistant and a security officer, report back to the ship in one hour. Dismissed." Quinn never looked up from his report, but I'm sure he could tell I was dumbfounded. *Leading?* I was leading an away mission? I'd never even been *on* one. Quinn finally looked at me.

"I gave you an order," he said.

"Yes, sir!" I stumbled out of the bridge, eager and queasy.

✦

"Thanks a lot," Walker said. We had just beamed down to Milika III with a security officer. It was like being shoved into an oven: it was over 43 degrees Celsius, an intense dry heat. We were a few kilometers outside the capital city, near a small congregation of ruins many thousands of years old. I'd assigned Walker to come, for the simple reason that, though I was in charge of the mission, every officer on the ship outranked me. Although he wasn't pleased that I'd conscripted him during his off-duty shift, I was at least assured he wouldn't be challenging my already shaky authority.

The security officer, Ensign Cheva (her full Thai name was Chevapravatdumrong, but she used the shortened version), examined her tricorder.

"Vehicle approaching," she said. We turned to see a floating vehicle, an air raft, open with four seats but only one occupant. It slowed as it got near, and settled softly to the ground. Its driver, a squat, brown-faced figure with ridges above his eyebrows, climbed out. He ran up to us, his flowing tan robes fluttering behind him, and excitedly held up his hands in the traditional Milika greeting. As was customary, I placed my palms against his, briefly.

"You must be Picard," the Milika said. "I am Mantz. I'm so delighted you read my paper."

"It was my pleasure," I said. I introduced the rest of the away team. Mantz started talking about how he had been working this dig site for over a decade, and went into what would be a lengthy lecture about its history. After several moments, Walker gave me a look, and I took the hint.

"You should probably show us the artifacts," I said. "We are somewhat pressed for time." Mantz apologized much too profusely, and led us down into the dig site to an excavated room. He took us to a sealed case which he opened; it contained catalogued artifacts. He indicated a broken sculpture inside. I kneeled down and scanned the pieces with my tricorder.

"Pottery?" Walker said. "We're baking in this heat for some pottery?"

"It's not just pottery," I said. I picked up part of the sculpture; it was a head with pointed ears, and the base had a symbol on it. "This is a *katric* ark."

"Is it authentic?" Mantz was very excited. I completed my scan.

"It was made out of native materials, but the design and age would indicate that it is," I said.

"What's a *katric* ark?" It was Cheva who asked the question, but it was also apparent from Walker's expression that he didn't know either.

THE STORY OF ONE OF STARFLEET'S MOST INSPIRATIONAL CAPTAINS

"Upon death," I said, "a Vulcan's 'living spirit' is transferred to a *katric* ark."

"Transferred?" Walker said.

"Telepathically," I said. "Supposedly, the spirit exists there indefinitely."

"Come on," Walker said.

"I'm being serious. Captain Jonathan Archer supposedly had the *katra* of Surak in his head..."

"This confirms my theory," Mantz said. "There was a Vulcan colony on this planet."

"We would need more evidence to reach that conclusion," I said. "But this artifact is at least authentic. The Federation Archeology Council will certainly send a team." We were interrupted by a call from the ship. I opened my communicator.

"*Reliant* to Picard," Nakamura said. "We're beaming you up immediately."

"Yes, sir." I could hear the red alert klaxon over the speaker. I turned to Mantz. "We'll have to come back later."

"But what's the matter? I have more to show you..." Mantz looked apoplectic.

"I know, I apologize, but we must go," I said. Walker, Cheva, and I stepped away from him. "Picard to *Reliant*, we're ready to beam up."

"Stand by," Nakamura said. "Belay that, transporter not functioning." I turned to Cheva, who had her tricorder out.

"There's a particle-scattering field," she said. "It wasn't there before."

"Someone doesn't want us to beam up," Walker said.

"Picard to *Reliant*, we're detecting a particle scattering field. Do you read that as well?"

"Affirmative, stand by," Nakamura said. His tone was unusually taut.

"What is going on?" Mantz said.

"Please, sir, I need you to be quiet," I said. "You're safe with us." That of course was a lie. If we were the object of the scattering field, then he was completely unsafe with us, but I needed information.

"Picard, this is the captain," Quinn said. "The Federation ambassador has been kidnapped. The scattering field was set up so we can't beam him up, or beam anyone down."

"Who kidnapped him?"

"Religious extremists," Quinn said. "They've demanded the removal of the embassy, and want the Federation off their planet by tomorrow, or they'll kill the ambassador." I noticed Mantz listening to this, registering understanding. "Stay out of sight until we resolve this. They're hiding somewhere in the old section of the capital city. It's unlikely the extremists even know you're there. *Reliant* out." I turned to Mantz.

"You know who these extremists are?" I said. Mantz nodded.

"They call themselves the Xaalas. They continue to adhere to the old beliefs. You must understand they represent only a small minority of our people." He seemed embarrassed and worried by the act of his fellow natives. I decided to use that to our advantage.

"Mantz, can you take us into the city?" I said.

"Captain told us to lay low," Walker said.

"Because they don't know we're here," I replied. "Which is exactly the reason we should try to ascertain the situation." Walker smiled, and nodded.

✦

We waited until nightfall, and then flew to the city in Mantz's air raft. Mantz picked up clothing at his home for us, and in a short time Walker, Cheva, and I were covered in the flowing robes the natives wore. We then headed for the old section; unlike the modern glass and steel constructions of the capital, the buildings in the old section were made of brick and mortar. The streets narrowed to alleys, and the air raft became too conspicuous, so Mantz parked it, and the four of us moved through on foot. Cheva was on her tricorder, tracking the ambassador's life signs.

She stopped us two streets away from the ambassador's location. She indicated down an alley to a three-story building. We could see several Milikans with weapons patrolling the streets around it. I gave Cheva permission to leave us to perform a closer scout. Walker and I were a bit taller than the average Milika, but Cheva was an appropriate height, and could move among them unnoticed, especially at night. After she left, I turned to Mantz.

"Mantz, you should go," I said. "Thank you for your help."

"I am not leaving," he said.

"I don't want to put your life in danger…"

"*They* are the ones putting us in danger," Mantz said, referring to the guards. "I want to help." I was surprised and impressed by how personally

Mantz was taking the actions of his fellow Milikans. This was a man who was standing up for progress.

"All right," I said. I handed him a communicator and showed him how it worked. "Go back to your air raft. I may need you to come in a hurry." Mantz nodded and left, just as Cheva returned.

"They're on the third floor," she said, showing us the scans she'd taken with her tricorder. "In a central room with no windows. Two guards on the street, one on the roof, one at that third-floor window, and one in the room with the ambassador."

"Too many for us to make a frontal assault," Walker said. "Or even one by stealth." Walker was saying what I was thinking. Any attack might give the extremists enough time to kill the ambassador.

"We might be able to get him if they had to move him," I said. I looked around and saw, two blocks away from our target, a ruined structure, destroyed in some kind of fire or attack. It had been a three-story building like the ones surrounding it, but less than half of it was left. "Cheva, scan that building. Any life signs?"

"No, sir," she said.

"Get on the other side of it and wait for my signal," I said. "When I tell you, blow it up." Cheva nodded and disappeared into the dark. Walker and I then headed to a spot in an alley opposite the entrance to the building the extremists were in, and crouched behind a refuse receptacle. We had a view of the only door to the building; Smithie was too old to climb out a window, if they were going to escape with him it would be from here. I took Walker's communicator. "Picard to Mantz…"

"I hear you," Mantz said.

"In a few moments, you will hear an explosion. When you do, take the air raft and head to the alley directly south of the building where they're holding the ambassador."

"Directly south, I understand," Mantz said. I then switched frequencies on the communicator.

"Picard to Cheva, report," I said.

"In position," came her voice.

"Wait for my signal," I said, then switched the frequency once more. "Picard to *Reliant*."

"This is *Reliant*." It was Quinn.

"Captain, I've found the ambassador," I said. "And I have a plan to rescue him, but I won't carry it out without your order." There was an excruciatingly long pause.

"All right, let's hear it."

I laid out the situation and what I had in mind.

"What if they decide to just kill the ambassador?" Quinn said.

"It seems unlikely, unless they feel they have no way out," I replied. "They will try to escape." I don't know why I was so sure of myself, but it appeared Quinn agreed with me.

"Make it so," Quinn said. This was the first time I'd heard Quinn use this expression, and it wasn't until he added, "Good luck," that I realized he'd given me permission. I turned to Walker.

"Set phaser for stun, widest possible beam," I said. Walker nodded. I opened my communicator. "Picard to Cheva: go, repeat, go."

After a short moment, the ruined building down the alley exploded. The vibration shook the nearby structures; the guards on the street turned and immediately started shouting. We heard responses from the guard up in the window, who ran inside. The guards on the street took up positions near the door. We watched as two more Milikans came out of the door, dragging the ambassador.

"Fire," I ordered. Walker and I shot at the group. They were all clustered together; the Milikans and the ambassador were bathed in a red glow, and then fell to the ground unconscious. We moved out of the alley and headed for them.

"Wait," I said. "There's one missing…" We both looked up to see the Milikan on the roof, aiming his weapon at us. He was hit with a red beam, and fell backward. We turned to see the source of the shot was Cheva, running to join us, phaser in hand.

"We gotta move," Cheva said. "They could have friends in the neighborhood…"

We grabbed the still unconscious ambassador, and carried him, just as Mantz's air raft landed at the end of the alley south of the building. We got on board and flew off.

In the air raft, Cheva took position in the rear to watch for pursuit. Walker patted me on the back.

THE STORY OF ONE OF STARFLEET'S MOST INSPIRATIONAL CAPTAINS

"Good job, Jean-Luc," he said. I smiled. I noticed that Ambassador Smithie was slowly regaining consciousness. He looked up at us, frightened and confused.

"It's all right, Ambassador," I said. "You're safe."

✦

"Come in, Picard," Quinn said. He was sitting at his desk in his quarters, which I had never seen. They were simple and efficient, like the man himself. I entered; he indicated a chair across his desk, so I sat.

"Good work down there," Quinn said. Thanks to my actions, the extremists had been rounded up, the Milikan government had apologized, and the embassy had been established.

"Thank you, sir."

"You know, it's rare that I have to apologize to one of my officers," he said.

"Sir?"

"When I was unable to beam you up, my first order to you should've been to reconnoiter and get me more information. That's what the book says, but..." Quinn paused. "But I didn't have enough faith in you. So you did my job for me, and now I will get credit for saving the ambassador."

"Sir," I said, "you don't owe me any..."

"You showed better command judgment than I did," he said. "You saved a man's life, at great risk to your own. And there was no loss of life on the other side, which helped repair a delicate diplomatic situation." He took out a small wooden box, and set it on the desk.

"You're wasted as a science officer," he said. "You need to be on a command track. Flight controller, right? That's what you originally wanted?"

"Yes, sir," I said.

"Unfortunately, there's no room for you on this ship in that position," he said. "My flight controllers are good at their job, and I don't have any reason to transfer them. Same goes for all my command track positions, at least for the time being." He slid the small wooden box over to me. "Open it."

I did. Inside were lieutenant bars.

"You're promoted," he said. "A 23-year-old lieutenant is going to get noticed, and you deserve it."

"But, sir," I said. "I'd like to stay..." I was truly stunned. I had felt a bit of victory saving the ambassador, but it was all in an effort to solidify my place on this ship. I had no intention of leaving.

"You need to be on a bridge, and not at the science station," he said. "And even if it was this ship, puttering around a safe sector like this one, it's going to take you too long to do the work you were born to do. Get out to the edge. Dismissed."

I left Quinn's quarters in a bit of a daze, and wandered back to my quarters. Walker was there, and saw my new rank.

"You just lapped me," Walker said, as he pinned the lieutenant bars on my uniform. "How did that happen?"

"He wants me to transfer," I said.

"You bastard, you're ruining my day." Walker and I spent the next hour looking at the available postings. There were a few on bigger ships, more prestigious names, but there was only one opening that appealed to me.

"You ever hear of the *Stargazer*?" I said.

"No," Walker said.

"*Constellation*-class ship," I said. "It's got an opening for a relief flight controller." We both looked at the record; the ship had just returned from a five-year exploration of the unexplored mass of the Galaxy, and it was about to be sent out again.

"Do you know Captain Humphrey Laughton?" Walker said. I didn't. We did a quick search: he had a very impressive record of exploration.

"Wow," Walker said. "That's a lot of new worlds. Are you going to apply?"

"I just did."

✦

"Starbase 74, this is *Reliant*," Altman said. "Request permission to assume standard orbit."

We arrived at Starbase 74 during the gamma shift, my shift on the bridge. Though I now outranked Walker, I didn't see a need to take his shift, since I was leaving the ship so soon. Altman was in command, and on the viewscreen the massive space station hung in orbit around another blue-green world.

"*Reliant*, this is Starbase 74," a female voice said. "You are cleared for orbit."

"Thank you, Starbase 74." Altman said, "We have one passenger for transfer."

Altman gave the order to put the ship in standard orbit near the station. Normally, a ship would enter the massive doors and berth inside the cavernous interior dock, which could hold several large starships. However, *Reliant* was only there to drop me off.

I had submitted my application to the *Stargazer* and got an almost immediate reply offering me the post. The *Stargazer* had a maintenance overhaul scheduled at Starbase 74, which was not too far off the *Reliant*'s course. Captain Quinn agreed to drop me off here, and I would only have to wait a little over a week for the arrival of my new ship.

But now that I was here, I faced a problem: I hadn't said goodbye to anyone. There were over thirty people on the ship; I had come to know some of them very well, but not nearly all. Do I go to every department and say goodbye? Since this was the gamma shift, a lot of them were still asleep. Do I wake them up? That seemed presumptuous. On the other hand, if I didn't make that effort, would they think me arrogant? The way Starfleet operated I could easily find myself serving with some of them again, and I didn't want to leave anyone with a bad impression. And yet still, the idea of walking through the entire ship looking to say goodbye to people… it seemed an unsolvable dilemma.

I finally decided that I would send a group message to the crew saying what an honor it was to serve with them. I wrote that first: "It was an honor serving with you all," and looked at it on the screen. It seemed a little perfunctory, but I couldn't figure out what else to say. It was then that I noticed Lieutenant Nakamura was standing next to me, quite a bit early for his shift. He looked at me, smiling.

"Attention on deck," he said, quite loudly. I had been so focused on how I was going to say goodbye, I hadn't noticed that a good portion of the crew had squeezed onto the bridge, including Walker, first officer Shanthi, and the captain. They were all standing at attention. I hurriedly stood up, stunned by the courtesy.

"Thank you," I said. "It's… been an honor serving with you all." Somehow saying it out loud seemed to convey a little more weight than writing it. Or at least I hoped so. Captain Quinn stepped forward and shook my hand.

"Good luck, Lieutenant," Quinn said.

"Thank you, sir," I said. I stood there awkwardly for a moment.

"Crew dismissed," Quinn said. "Back to work." I had the distinct impression he sensed my discomfort. He turned to Walker. "Ensign, get this man off my ship."

"Right away, sir," Walker said, and we got on the turbolift and took it to the transporter room. My packed duffel was already there. Walker shook my hand.

"Maybe with you gone, I can finally get a promotion around here," Walker said. I laughed. I got up on the pad, and Walker operated the controls. The hum of the transporter beam coincided with Walker and the *Reliant* fading from view.

✦

I had guest quarters on Starbase 74, and it ended up being a relatively quiet first few days as I waited for the *Stargazer* to arrive. The station was well equipped and pleasant, and I spent the time reviewing what I could about the *Stargazer*'s systems, as well as practicing navigation in one of the station's simulators. I was getting used to the relaxed schedule when early one morning I was awakened by a voice on the intercom.

"Lieutenant Picard," the voice said. It was one I didn't recognize.

"Yes," I said. My voice was more of a croak, as I was fast asleep when the voice came through.

"Report to Shuttle Bay One in fifteen minutes," the voice said. "In your dress uniform." I sputtered a response but whoever it was had ceased communications. It sounded like an order. Could the *Stargazer* be early? It seemed unlikely. And why wear a dress uniform? I didn't have any time to figure it out, so I cleaned up, got dressed, and reported to the shuttle bay. When I got there, I found about a dozen officers, all in their dress uniforms, and a waiting shuttlecraft. None of them had any more information pertaining as to why we'd been called. We didn't have a long wait to find out.

An elderly man, also in a Starfleet dress uniform, approached us. I silently guessed he was about 100 years old. As he got closer I noticed three more things: he was an admiral, he wore the insignia of the medical branch of the service, and he seemed annoyed at all of us.

"What are you all waiting for? Get in the damn shuttle."

"Excuse me, sir," I said. "May I ask where we're going?"

THE STORY OF ONE OF STARFLEET'S MOST INSPIRATIONAL CAPTAINS

"Nobody told you?" He seemed even more annoyed. "We're going to down to the planet for Spock's wedding. You're going to be the honor guard. He doesn't want an honor guard—too bad, he's getting one. Now get a move on, we're going to be late. That's a blasted order."

We all quickly filed onto the shuttle, and as soon as we were settled on board, it launched. Starbase 74 was in orbit around Tarsas III; the planet itself was the site of an old Earth colony that had terraformed the planet.

But to a man and woman on the shuttle, no one was interested in the *where*, but the *why*. We all knew who Spock was, probably one of the most well-known veterans of Starfleet, as well as a distinguished ambassador to the Federation. And he was getting married, and this doctor, whoever he was, had decided to provide an honor guard made up of any officer he could find.

Doctor. I stared at him as he pulled a small flask from his jacket pocket and took a healthy swig. I felt like such an idiot. This was *McCoy*. For the short ride, I tried my best to get a look at him without letting him know. I was not successful.

"Something I can do for you, Lieutenant?" he said, after catching me.

"No, sir," I said. "But it's an honor to meet you…"

"Stow it," he said, sat back in his chair, and closed his eyes. After a few minutes he was snoring peacefully. The rest of us exchanged amused excitement.

"Who is the senior officer here," I said, "besides the admiral?" A woman, a lieutenant commander, realized she was, and immediately understood why I asked.

"Let's all figure out what we're going to do once we get there," she said. "I imagine we're all a little rusty at marching drills…"

✦

We landed on Tarsas III, at the spaceport a few kilometers outside the main city. Since its inception, Tarsas III had undergone a stark transformation thanks to modern terraforming techniques, and where once natural growth was confined to a small area around the city, it was now over the entire continent. We were taken by hovercraft to the city. It was made up of twelve boulevards that radiated out from a town square. When we got to the square, we saw that preparations were made for a sizable event. There were chairs set up around an altar. It surprised me as the whole thing had a very human flavor. This was not, from what I understood, how Vulcans got married. Our hovercraft stopped, and McCoy turned to us.

"Don't embarrass me," he said, and got off first. There were fourteen officers, so, with the lieutenant commander leading, we formed two lines of seven, and marched out of the hovercraft. We stayed in formation until we reached the altar, then split so there was seven on each side. We stood there at attention as the guests trickled in.

And what a guest list it was. The president of the Federation, the commander-in-chief of Starfleet, members of the Federation Council and dignitaries from dozens of worlds. There was nothing "Vulcan" about this event. Which probably meant the bride was not a Vulcan.

"Lieutenant," a man said, "I have a query." I was at the end of the line on the left side of the altar, and kept my movement to a minimum so as not to break formation. I glanced sideways at the person talking to me.

It was Sarek. Sarek of Vulcan. One of the greatest figures in history, a man who helped shape the modern Federation. I hadn't forgotten he was Spock's father, but the whole human flavor of the event made me forget he would probably be here.

"Um..." was all I could get out in response.

"I am unfamiliar with human wedding traditions. Is there a specific section for the blood relations of the groom?"

I just stood there, grinning like an idiot. The lieutenant standing next to me leaned in to answer, telling Sarek that it would be first row, whatever side the groom was on. Sarek nodded in acknowledgment, looked at me briefly, and sat down.

The ceremony began shortly thereafter. The president of the Federation stood under the altar to officiate, and Dr. McCoy walked in with Spock. Spock did not seem nearly as old as McCoy, and had the quiet power that came from the inner peace his species enjoyed. They stood only a few inches from me, and I heard a quiet conversation.

"I distinctly requested no honor guard, Doctor," Spock said.

"It's not for you," McCoy said. "It's for her. Now shut up, you're getting married." A string quartet began to play Vivaldi's "The Four Seasons," and the bride walked down the aisle. She was human, but wore a veil; it was impossible to get a good look at her. When she approached the altar, Spock lifted the veil. From where I was standing, I couldn't turn to look and see who she was.

"Dearly beloved," President Uhura began, "we are gathered here today to join in the bonds of matrimony, Spock and..." At the moment President Uhura said the bride's name, an elderly guest in the front row coughed loudly, so I missed it. The wedding continued in a very human tradition, ending with President Uhura giving Spock permission to kiss the bride. He did so, and when he did I happened to have a direct line of sight to Sarek, in the front row. He wore an expression that I could only describe as disgust. At the intermarriage? No, that couldn't be, Sarek himself had married an Earth woman. Maybe the display of affection? It was impossible to know.

The wedding ended, and I and the rest of the honor guard returned to Starbase 74. The whole trip back I was in a daze at the company I'd just been in. Once I returned to my quarters, I looked for information on the wedding on the Federation news services, but I couldn't find anything. Some of the biggest names in the Federation had just come to a private affair that had no publicity. And I had been there too.

✦

I sat in the lounge of Starbase 74, with a book on the history of the Federation, reading about the people that a few days ago I'd actually been around. I'd chosen this spot to settle in and wait for my new ship, scheduled to arrive sometime that day. Through the bay windows in front of me was the cavernous interior docking compartment of the station. There were several starships berthed inside, undergoing various degrees of repair and maintenance. I was interrupted from my reading by an announcement over the public address system.

"*U.S.S. Stargazer* arriving Bay 3." I looked up; after a brief moment, the *Stargazer* slowly came into view directly in front of the windows. In the pictures I'd seen it had seemed much smaller than it actually was. That was probably due to its squatness. It was much less sleek than the modern starship design. I remembered the ancient American naval officers used to refer to their ships as "tin cans," and somehow that moniker fit this vessel.

I loved it.

I practically ran back to my quarters, picked up my packed belongings and made my way to Bay 3. I'd spent weeks brushing up on my navigation skills and couldn't wait to sit at my new station on the bridge. I had very poetic thoughts that I was "plotting the course to my future." I found myself standing at the doorway to the airlock to Bay 3, pausing dramatically at the control pad that would open the hatch. As I keyed the panel, I said quietly to myself...

"On the other side, destiny awaits..."

The door opened and something hit me. It went splat across my chest, and dropped to the floor. An egg. Somebody had just hit me with an egg. As the slime of the white and yolk slid down my tunic, there were squeals of delighted laughter. I saw two boys—one around twelve, the other a little younger. They seemed to have been waiting for someone to open the airlock door. I stood there stunned. They stuck their tongues out at me and ran off, just as an officer came up from inside the ship.

"Anthony! David! Get back here," the officer said, but the boys were gone. The officer turned to me. He was in his thirties and had commander bars.

"Lieutenant Jean-Luc Picard," I said, a little lost. "Reporting for duty."

"Glad to meet you, Lieutenant, I'm Commander Frank Mazzara," he said. "I'm the exec. Let's get you cleaned up, and then I'll take you to the captain." He led me into the ship, and I was too confused as to what had just happened to even be aware of my surroundings.

"Who..." I said, "who were those boys?"

"Oh, those are my sons," he said. "Great kids."

"They're on the ship?" I'd never heard of children being allowed on board a starship.

"Yeah," he said, with genuine enthusiasm. "You will love them once you get to know them."

About that, he would end up being wrong.

Commander Mazzara took me to my quarters, where I quickly changed into a clean tunic, and then he took me to the captain. Along the way I was able to refocus on where I was. The ship was bigger than *Reliant*; just on the walk from the airlock to my quarters and then up to the captain's quarters I saw more crewmen than I served with on my old ship. Mazzara was affable, and filled me in on how the ship ran and what would be expected of me. There were three shifts instead of four, and I would serve on the bridge as second shift flight controller—a great improvement over the graveyard shift on *Reliant*. I began to relax and regain my enthusiasm for my new position. We reached the captain's quarters, buzzed the door chime and were ordered in.

The captain's quarters were larger than Quinn's on *Reliant*, but seemed much tighter. Wall space was completely filled with art. There were shelves groaning with books and knick-knacks, as well as stacks of PADDs and piles of papers. Paper had never been used for record keeping in Starfleet, so I couldn't imagine what it all was. It seemed less a captain's quarters and more a family attic.

In the center was Captain Laughton, naked except for a towel around his waist, sitting in the chair at his desk, which was piled high with much of the same debris that was spread throughout the room. Laughton was a large man, very overweight by Starfleet standards. Directly in front of him a small space had been cleared for a plate of food: a half-eaten meal of curried chicken with rice, which I identified by the pungent odor. I stood at attention.

"Lieutenant Jean-Luc Picard, reporting for duty, sir."

"Our new junior flight controller," Laughton said. "You can stand at ease, Lieutenant, we don't go in for all that." That clearly went without saying. "So, the hero of Milika III. Made quite a name for yourself already." His air was subtly taunting.

"Thank you, sir," I said, doing my best to ignore his tone.

"We could use a few more heroes around here, right, Mazzara?"

"Yes, sir," Mazzara said.

"Well, just so you know," Laughton said, "I like people to pitch in even if it isn't in their job description. I hope you don't have a problem with that."

"No, sir," I said, having no idea what he meant.

"Good, welcome aboard." He took a healthy forkful of chicken curry, and as he chewed said: "Mazzara, put him to work." Laughton fully engaged with his meal as Mazzara led me out.

"The captain's something else, isn't he?" Mazzara said, once we were in the corridor. I might have said the same thing, except not with Mazzara's admiring tone.

Mazzara had to return to duty on the bridge, so he took me with him. As we walked through the corridors, maintenance workers from the station had already begun to stream on board the ship. We would be in spacedock for at least a week for repairs and upgrades.

"Truth be told, the old lady could probably use a month," Mazzara said. We arrived on the bridge, where the second shift was on duty, and the person sitting in the captain's chair was a bit troubling.

"Anthony, get out of the chair," Mazzara said to the older of the two boys who had egged me. "Where's your brother?"

"Don't know. Said he was going to play in the warp core," Anthony said, still sitting in the captain's chair.

"I want you to apologize to Lieutenant Picard," Mazzara said.

"For what? We didn't do anything. It was David who threw it…"

"Anthony," Mazzara said

"It's fine, no need," I said. The other bridge officers were watching this, their first impression of me, and I just wanted it to end.

"All right," Mazzara said. Anthony continued to sit in the captain's chair, as Mazzara took me around to meet the other officers on the bridge. I wasn't a parent, but I knew terrible parenting when I saw it.

The next week I threw myself into helping with the ship's repairs and upgrades, and it quickly became apparent to me the *Stargazer* was in terrible shape. Some of the systems were very outdated, and regular maintenance had not been performed on everything from the engines to the hull to the coffee cups, so everything felt worn and dilapidated. This went for the crew as well. Lieutenant Christoph Black, who'd been one of the cadets I'd passed in the academy marathon, was a communications officer. One day I joined him for lunch in the ship's wardroom and asked him tactful questions about Mazzara and his children.

"He's a single dad," Black said, "and Laughton wanted him, so this was a condition of him coming on board." Black was also being politic; neither one of us was going to reveal how we felt about the two boys. He then asked me how I ended up on the *Stargazer*. I told him I applied for the open position, and the derisiveness of his laugh cut me like a razor.

"Probably should've done a little more due diligence," Black said. I didn't need to ask him why he thought that.

Finally, it was time to leave spacedock. The ship was scheduled to depart in the middle of my shift. I was at the flight controller station and Mazzara sat in the captain's chair, in command for this shift. I was nervous; I was about to fly a starship for the first time. Every free minute I'd had I'd practiced in the

THE STORY OF ONE OF STARFLEET'S MOST INSPIRATIONAL CAPTAINS

simulator, but I still wasn't sure I was ready to handle a ship this large with an engine this powerful. Black turned to Mazzara.

"Dock command signaling clear," he said.

"Inform the captain we're ready to depart," Mazzara said.

"Captain acknowledges and is coming to the bridge," Black said. Mazzara moved from the captain's chair.

"Conn," he said to me,* "Captain might want to take a look at the final maintenance report. Have it ready." I nodded and went to the science station to get a PADD, then downloaded the report onto it to give the captain. When I finished, I headed back to my chair, only to find someone was in it.

"I'm going to fly the ship," David said, the younger of the two Mazzara children.

"That's my job," I said. I looked for Mazzara, who was nowhere to be found. I assumed he must be in the washroom behind the viewscreen.

"No, it's my job," David said. This was a true no-win scenario. I had to get this child out of my chair before the captain arrived, which would be any second. I looked around helplessly, but every bridge officer was avoiding my silent plea. All of them had been veterans of the *Stargazer*, some if not all had probably been victims of the tyranny of these imps.

"Well," I said, "how about I let you have a turn when I'm done?"

"It's my ship, I'll do what I want." He spun back and forth in my chair. He knew he had power. Absolute power corrupting absolutely. I was hoping Mazzara would return before Laughton arrived, but I couldn't risk it. I wanted to tell the spoiled rodent that I would wring his neck if he didn't get up, but threatening my superior officer's child seemed ill-advised. I wracked my brain for another plan, and then realized I was over-thinking it. I looked over David's shoulder to the empty captain's chair.

"Were you sitting in the captain's chair?"

"No."

"Oh," I said, and walked over to the chair. "I guess finders keepers..." I pretended to reach for something in the chair, and David immediately got up from the conn station and ran over.

"My dad was sitting there, whatever it is it's mine..."

---
*EDITOR'S NOTE: Conn is shipboard parlance for the officer manning the flight controller station.

With a quick step I was back in the conn chair, just as the turbolift doors opened and Laughton strode onto the bridge. David, realizing he'd been fooled, ran back to me.

"Hey, I was sitting there…"

By then, Mazzara was out of the washroom.

"David," Mazzara said. "Go to our quarters."

"But I was sitting…"

"Go now," Mazzara said. He gave a slightly worried glance to Laughton, who didn't seem interested. David looked me in the eye—I'd made an enemy today. He then shuffled off the bridge.

"All right, Mr. Picard," Laughton said. "Take us out. And try not to sideswipe the door jamb." After what I'd just been through, getting to handle the ship seemed a relief. I also decided when I became a captain, children wouldn't be allowed anywhere near my ship, let alone the bridge.

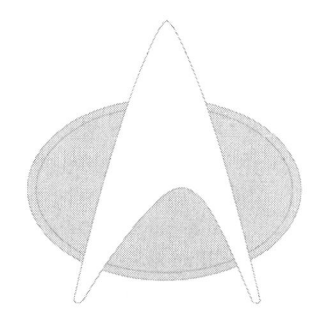

CHAPTER FOUR

"**SET COURSE FOR THE NORTH STAR COLONY**," Mazzara said. "Maximum warp." The order, like many I'd carried out, made little sense, but after four years on this ship I'd learned to accept such things.

"Course set," I said. "Engaging at warp factor 7." The ship shook a little as we went into warp; the inertial dampeners were old and always in need of adjustment. We'd just been examining the Kobliad system, a binary star system with one sparsely populated planet. We were about to make contact with its inhabitants when the captain gave the order to change course and go to the North Star colony. This almost certainly didn't come from Starfleet Command. I knew this because we hadn't heard from Starfleet in weeks.

Laughton had crafted his image at Starfleet as a great explorer. In the first part of his career on the *Stargazer* he'd catalogued a record number of new worlds for a shipmaster. He was now living off that reputation, and had been for some time. He was still making new discoveries, charting new systems, meeting new species, but not nearly as rapidly. However, the *Stargazer*'s age and condition meant it had little use anywhere else, so even if the reports of new systems were down to a trickle, the Admiralty still felt it was getting its "money's worth" from the old bucket.

But because they gave him such a long leash, Laughton took ridiculous privileges. The current situation was a perfect example: one more day and we could've finished the survey of the Kobliad system, but instead, we were heading off at high warp for some unknown reason that was almost certainly frivolous. Whatever it was, we would have to turn around and come right back to finish the survey. It was inefficient, indulgent, and an infuriating waste of time and resources. And it would invariably involve me doing something I didn't want to do. As he mentioned on my first day, Laughton liked officers to "pitch in" outside their job description.

When we reached colony a few days later, I got a call from the captain to come to his quarters.

"I need you to take a shuttle to the surface," Laughton said. He was in a bathrobe, which was better than the towel. "You're to pick up a piece of equipment from a man in the main city; I'll give you his contact information. You'll pay for the equipment with one of our power converters."

"Yes, sir," I said. "What kind of equipment am I picking up?"

"You'll find out when you get there," he said. "Oh, also, have someone come in here and take out this desk."

So he bought a new desk.

This was his modus operandi; he was a collector and spent all his free time scouring subspace marketplaces for things that struck his fancy. It wasn't just his quarters that were filled with his acquisitions: storage spaces all over the ship were stocked with objets d'art, books, furniture, and rare documents. Now he found a desk he wanted and had taken his ship and crew away from its duties to pick it up. He could just have it beamed into the cargo bay, but in his mind that would be too conspicuous. Somehow, by tasking me with this, he thought only I would know about it, not taking into account all the people I would have to deal with on the way. But I'd learned there was no point in trying to explain this to him.

I took the information from him and went to engineering. The chief engineer, Lieutenant Commander Scully, a large, usually affable man, looked annoyed when I asked him for a power converter.

"They don't grow on trees, son," he said.

"The captain..."

"All right, all right..." he said and walked off to retrieve one. He handed it over, and I then went to the shuttle bay and informed the bridge that I was taking a shuttle to the surface on orders from the captain. Nobody questioned anything, no one asked for any more detail. They all knew what was going on.

THE STORY OF ONE OF STARFLEET'S MOST INSPIRATIONAL CAPTAINS

I took the shuttle down to the surface. The North Star colony (not to be confused with Polaris, the "North Star" in the Earth's nighttime sky) was a pleasant throwback. Some time in the 19th century on Earth a wagon train had been abducted by aliens called the Skagaran, who used the humans for slaves on this planet. Eventually the humans rose up and took over the planet, and when they were rediscovered in the 22nd century by the first starship *Enterprise*, they'd built an entire town that looked like it was from the 19th-century North American West, complete with horses and buggies and gunslingers. It still exists to this day, but now with many modern conveniences.

I landed at the starport and then made my way to the address the captain had given me. It was a small adobe-like home. I knocked on the door. A hunched, wizened old man named MacReady answered.

"I'm here from the *Stargazer*," I said. I gave him the power converter. The old man nodded and led me into his home.

He was a woodworker, and the whole house was set up as a workshop. The old man gestured toward a wooden desk. It was quite stunning, polished dark wood, and very large. Troublingly large. Larger than any desk I'd ever seen on a starship.

I took out my tricorder and did a quick scan of its measurements; it wouldn't even fit through a turbolift's doors. Again, there would be no point in trying to explain this to the captain, so I just decided to get it back to the ship and deal with it there.

"Do you have an anti-grav unit?" I said. The old man shook his head, then handed me four pieces of wood attached as a square, with wheels on the bottom. It appeared to be a primitive device called a "dolly," used to move heavy objects. With some difficulty, I got the desk up on the dolly, and slowly pushed it out the door and down the street, back to the starport. It was a difficult trek, as the desk was much larger than the dolly, and it took some effort to keep it balanced as I pushed. I used my time on this excursion to ponder, as I often did, how I might extricate myself from this ship, but every attempt I made to get transferred was denied by the captain. He seemed to understand that he was getting in my way, which is why the previous year he had promoted me to lieutenant commander. The new rank did nothing to help me haul this giant piece of wood.

I finally reached the shuttle, and realized I had another problem: there was no hatch on the shuttle big enough for the desk. The only solution seemed to be to beam it up, but I wasn't going to do that. A few weeks earlier, the captain had me on a similar errand to pick up a statue of Kahless, the ancient Klingon leader. The most efficient way to get it back on the ship was to transport it, but when he found out that's what I did he was furious and threatened to demote me. Black had quietly explained to me that transporter logs were very detailed, and Laughton didn't want an official record of all the cargo he was bringing up. I didn't want to risk his ire again, so I had to come up with another plan.

There was a life-support belt in the shuttle; it projected a low-level force field around the user, providing oxygen in case of emergency. I adjusted the field so that it would surround the desk, and attached it. Then I secured several magnetic clasps to the surface.

I got in the shuttle and lifted off, hovering a few feet off the ground, and then maneuvered the shuttle over the desk. I slowly lowered the shuttle until I heard a thunk as the magnetic clasps attached themselves to the belly of the craft, and then I began a slow ascent into space. I hadn't had a lot of time to calculate how much acceleration those clasps could take, but as long as we took it slow I figured I should be all right.

That was when the captain called.

"Laughton to Picard," he said. "What the hell is taking so long?"

"Uh, sir, there was some difficulty…" I said.

"We've just received a distress call, get back to the ship immediately," he said. This was a problem. I was pulling out of the atmosphere but still inside the planet's gravity well. If I increased my acceleration, I wasn't sure the clasps would hold against even the limited air resistance.

"Picard, acknowledge!" Laughton was a little panicked, for good reason. If the *Stargazer* failed to acknowledge a distress call because we were busy getting him a new desk, he could lose his command.

"Acknowledged, sir," I said, and pushed the throttle forward. It seemed to be all right for a moment, and then there was a slight jolt. I checked my scanner; the desk was tumbling back toward the planet. I switched on the communicator.

"Picard to Transporter Room," I said. "Emergency."

THE STORY OF ONE OF STARFLEET'S MOST INSPIRATIONAL CAPTAINS

"Transporter Room, this is Chief Mazzara," the voice said. Wonderful. Anthony Mazzara, now 16, had been made a transporter chief petty officer. He had not matured in the least since throwing an egg at me four years ago.

"There's an object falling away from my shuttle," I said. "You need to lock onto it and beam it aboard."

"What is it? Is it dangerous…"

"I'm giving you a direct order!"

"Okay, okay. Calm down…" I was fast approaching the shuttle bay of the *Stargazer* and had to deal with my approach and landing, so I couldn't monitor what was happening with my cargo. As I settled onto the landing pad, I heard from the transporter room.

"It's a desk. What am I supposed to do with it?" It was a very good question.

I informed Chief Mazzara to just get it off the transporter pad and wait for instructions. I then raced to the bridge, where his father was at ops and Captain Laughton was in command. I took over the conn and hoped that I would have time later to properly explain to the captain why I had to use the transporter to retrieve his "equipment."

The ship had gone to maximum impulse power soon after I'd landed and we were headed to the inner part of the system. The planet closest to the sun had a large mining operation. One of the miner's ships had lost engine power and was now being pulled into the star. By the time I assumed my post, the magnificent orb was growing in the center of the viewscreen. The mining ship wasn't even visible against the orange conflagration.

"Are we in transporter range?" Laughton said.

"Not yet, sir," Mazzara said. I silently hoped his son had gotten the desk off of the transporter pad.

"Try to raise them," Laughton said. Black, who was at communications, said there was no response. It didn't mean they were dead—there were still three life signs on the mining ship, and this close to a star's magnetic field older communications systems had a tendency not to work well. Or at all.

"How long until we're in transporter range?" Laughton said. I checked my board.

"Eleven seconds," I said. Though Laughton was often a strange man with deplorable priorities, he also knew how to be a captain when necessary. He sounded cool and confident, which, with a sun growing on the viewscreen, went a long way in keeping the rest of us calm.

"Transporter Room," Laughton said. "Stand by to lock onto the crew of that ship." I had a moment of fear over what the response would be.

"Acknowledged," Anthony said. "Standing by." Good, he must have moved the desk out of the way. I again looked down at my panel. We were a few seconds from transporter range when an alarm flashed.

"Sir," I said. "We've got an ion surge in helm control..."

Before I could finish my sentence, my panel erupted. The force of the blast sent me tumbling backwards out of my chair. I looked up, and saw that my console was on fire. The ship's fire control system immediately doused it. The sound of the blast caused me to momentarily lose my hearing; there was silent chaos around me. I tried to get to my feet, and saw Frank Mazzara standing by the captain's chair.

Laughton was slumped back, and his eyes were open; a piece of debris from my panel was lodged in his head. He was dead. Mazzara looked stunned, then turned to the bridge crew. My hearing was returning, and I took over Mazzara's post at the ops panel—the conn was a charred mess.

"Status," he said. Even with my impaired hearing, Mazzara sounded shaky.

"We're in transporter range," I said. "We've got no helm control up here."

Mazzara turned to Black.

"Inform the transporter room to beam the miners on board," he said. "Bridge to Engineering—"

"All impulse and warp control circuits completely burned out," Scully said. "We must have had a build-up of ions on the hull, and it induced transients..."

"It doesn't matter what happened," Mazzara said. "We need to get control of the ship back."

"I don't know what to tell you," Scully said. "The engines have shut down, but we're still traveling at close to the speed of light. All I've got is maneuvering thrusters, they won't slow us down. I need some time to rig something up..."

"Transporter Room reports the miners are on board," Black said. But Mazzara wasn't listening. He was staring at the viewscreen, where the sun was growing in size.

"Distance from the star," Mazzara said.

THE STORY OF ONE OF STARFLEET'S MOST INSPIRATIONAL CAPTAINS

"One point five million kilometers," I said. Our shields were still protecting us, but with no engines to escape the sun's gravity, they wouldn't help us if we ended up inside. There was one possibility as long as we did it before we got too close. I started a quick calculation, when I was interrupted by Mazzara's order.

"All hands abandon ship," Mazzara said. He'd also been doing a calculation: at this distance, shuttles and escape pods would still escape the sun's gravity.

"Sir, I think we can—" I said, but Mazzara cut me off.

"Get to your assigned evacuation stations," Mazzara said. I could see his mind was somewhere else—his family, his children. He was playing it safe for them. Then he did something truly startling.

He left the bridge.

This act left the bridge crew momentarily stunned. I wanted to explain my plan to everyone who remained, hoping to convince them we had a chance, but I was out of time. The other members of the bridge immediately began shutting down their stations, preparing to evacuate. There was no time to explain. I had to act.

"Belay that order," I said. The remaining crewmen turned and looked at me. By abandoning the bridge, Mazzara had left me in command even though he hadn't stated it explicitly. I could see doubt in the faces of most everyone, especially Black, who until a short time ago had outranked me. But they obeyed and didn't leave their posts. Mazzara hadn't just abandoned the bridge, he had abandoned *them*, and, with their captain lying there dead, they wanted some hope. Black signaled a cancellation of the abandon ship signal. I leaned into the intercom.

"Bridge to Engineering, Scully, fire all port thrusters," I said.

"Aye, sir," Scully said. "They won't last long…"

"They won't have to," I said.

"Mazzara to Bridge, what the hell's going on up there? Who countermanded my order?"

"One moment, sir," I said. I checked our position; as long as we started the maneuver before we reached the distance from the star equal to its diameter, we still had a chance. The star was eight hundred and seventy-five thousand miles across—I'd fired the port thrusters at over a million kilometers out. It would work.

"Mazzara to Bridge, answer me!" On the viewscreen, the sun started to slowly move to the left.

"Sir, this is Picard—the thrusters, our momentum, and the sun's gravity are moving us into a high orbit around the star. This should buy Engineer Scully enough time to make repairs." There was a long pause.

"Shield status?"

"Sixty-five percent," I said, which would give us plenty of protection for the time being. Though I'd saved the ship, I took no pleasure in the fact that Mazzara was humiliated. I needed to change the subject. "Your orders, sir?"

"Have damage control teams make reports. I'll be right up," he said. "Inform sickbay to make arrangements for the captain."

"Aye, sir," I said. I looked at Laughton. He'd done so much to define life on the *Stargazer*, it was hard to imagine what this ship would be like without him. I stood over him and closed his eyes.

✦

"Laughton had an ex-wife," Captain Mazzara said. "She lives on the New Paris colony, and he left instructions to bring his belongings to her in the event of his death. Once there, I want you to handle it personally, Number One." Since I'd become his first officer, Mazzara had referred to me as "Number One," an ancient Earth term for the first officer on naval vessels. I assumed it was something he learned on a previous posting, because Laughton never used it. But I didn't mind it.

"Yes, sir," I said. Mazzara was behind his desk in his quarters, which he shared with one of his sons, David, who was now 14. Anthony, now a crewman, was quartered with another engineer. Though he'd been promoted, Mazzara had not moved into the captain's quarters because of the sheer amount of Laughton's possessions. (With the giant desk in there, it was now almost impossible to get inside.)

"Don't bring an away team," Mazzara said. "Go see her yourself first. She's not human, and I don't know anything about her species. I would go, but…"

"Yes, sir," I said. "Better for you to stay on board." A first officer's duty was to protect the life of his captain, even if he didn't have any respect for him. Mazzara didn't like leaving his sons. As a father it was admirable, as an officer, disgraceful.

THE STORY OF ONE OF STARFLEET'S MOST INSPIRATIONAL CAPTAINS

"That'll be all," Mazzara said.

"You heard him—get lost," David said. David had been sitting in the back of the room, playing a game on a PADD and looking at us intermittently. Mazzara snapped an admonishment at his son for his rudeness but as usual it did little good. From the first day I came aboard this ship, David had decided to be my personal nuisance. I'd long since learned to take pride in the fact that he couldn't faze me, which only provoked him more. My new position undoubtedly made things worse. I smiled at the captain and left.

In the wake of Laughton's death a month before, Mazzara had promoted me to First Officer. Mazzara never mentioned my countermanding his order. I'd committed a court martial offense, but in order for him to press charges he would have had to mention to Starfleet Command that he'd left the bridge in a moment of crisis. His first act as interim captain, preceding the rest of the bridge crew in an evacuation, did not violate any regulation, but went in the face of thousands of years of heroic tradition: the last man off a sinking ship is always its captain. Starfleet Command would've frowned on his behavior, and it might have kept Mazzara from getting the captaincy.

So though he had the rank, Mazzara had completely undermined his authority. Crewmen snickered about his cowardice. I was in the rec room having dinner with Black, Chief Engineer Scully, and two other officers one evening when I discovered just how bad things had gotten. Black was relaying a story about showing up late for his shift.

"...I'm pulling on my clothes as I run to the bridge, get on the turbolift with my shirt over my head, and when I pull it down, there's Captain Quitter who must've gotten on before me..." The other officers laughed at the story, but I had a different reaction. The nonchalance that greeted the moniker troubled me.

"'Captain Quitter'?" I said. "Where did that come from?"

"Oh," Black said, realizing that as first officer I might not have been privy to it. "Yeah, someone nicknamed him that, I don't know who..."

"It was me," Scully said. Scully was so vital to his job that he knew it wouldn't cost him anything to admit responsibility. He was also old enough that he didn't care if it did.

"I don't want to hear it again," I said. "Next person who says it in front of me goes on report." I got up from the table and took my tray to the recycler.

"What's the big deal?" Black said.

"The big deal is he's the captain," I said, "and even if he wasn't, he has two sons on board." I then walked out, and considered that it might seem puzzling that two boys who were such irritants to me could arouse this level of compassion. I suppose, looking back, I might have been jealous that they had a father who was so devoted to them he had essentially destroyed his own career to prioritize their safety.

✦

New Paris was one of Earth's oldest and largest colonies, dating back before the founding of the Federation. It had a population of over three million, and the planet had a wide variety of populated ecosystems. When we arrived, Mazzara provided me with exact coordinates of the home where Laughton's ex-wife lived.

"Shouldn't we try to call first?" I said. "It seems strange to go in unannounced."

"Laughton's instructions were to do just that," Mazzara said. "She doesn't have a communicator. Wants her privacy." Me showing up with no warning seemed to fly in the face of that desire, but I decided to follow orders.

I went to the transporter room. Anthony Mazzara was on duty. I gave him the coordinates.

"Kind of hard picturing fat Captain Laughton finding a wife," he said.

"Belay that," I said, and got on the transporter pad. There was no bottom to the depths the Mazzara boys would dive.

I beamed down to find myself in a lush thicket of trees and vines. I could hear a soft rain high above, but the canopy of leaves kept much of it from reaching me. It was a serene and beautiful environment.

I took out my tricorder and detected a structure not far away. There were no life-form readings, however. I moved through the thicket and in a few moments found a house, one story high, set in amongst the forest, made of indigenous wood and stone. It had a natural camouflage making it impossible to see until I was almost upon it. But my scanning for life-forms was still unsuccessful.

THE STORY OF ONE OF STARFLEET'S MOST INSPIRATIONAL CAPTAINS

"Hands in the air," a woman's voice said, behind me. I did as she told me. The woman circled around me. She wore a long gown and a wide-brimmed hat, and held a large, formidable-looking rifle, aimed right at me.

"How did you find me? I know it wasn't that tricorder, I can fool those stupid things."

"Um... I'm from the *Stargazer*. Captain Humphrey Laughton..."

"Figured that loser would come bothering me," she said. "What does he want?"

"I'm very sorry to inform you..."

"Wait a minute..." she said, breaking out into an infectious smile. "You're Jean-Luc Picard... Oh my, it's been such a long time, and I didn't recognize you with all that hair." This caught me off guard. I'd never seen this woman before. But she obviously knew me. She lowered her rifle, so I dropped my hands.

"I'm sorry, you have me at a disadvantage," I said. "You know me?" Her demeanor suddenly changed. She seemed slightly awkward with the situation, but also amused.

"Oh... no... sorry, I thought you were someone else."

"Someone else named Jean-Luc Picard?"

"Yes, strange coincidence, he's a bald guy, lot older," she said. "I'm Guinan, nice to meet you. Sorry about the 'hands up' thing." She shook my hand, her grin filled with Cheshire cat irony. "So you're in Humphrey's crew?"

"Well, yes, in a way. On behalf of Starfleet and the Federation, I want to express my condolences on his death."

"Oh, that's very nice, but Humphrey was three husbands ago," she said. "It's been thirty years since I've even seen him." Thirty years? She already seemed quite a bit younger than the captain, but that was in human terms. The mysteries were multiplying. "Now, I'm going to need you to get me out of here. They've known I was on the planet for some time, and they were probably keeping track of your ship because they knew Humphrey was one of my husbands."

"Wait..."

"I don't have time to wait; if they detected your transporter beam..."

"Who are we talking about?"

We were interrupted by a blast from a pulse weapon, which knocked the bark off a tree right next to me.

"Them," she said, taking my hand and leading me off in a run. More blasts, each just missing us. We reached a large stone, and she had us hide behind it. I tried to get a look at our assailant. He had taken up a position about twenty meters away.

"Who's shooting at us?"

"Some mercenary or bounty hunter," she said "And he's not shooting at me, he's shooting at *you*—he wants me alive." Every answer she gave led to more questions, but I had had enough. I took out my communicator.

"Picard to *Stargazer*, two to beam up…" There was no answer.

"He's probably jamming you," Guinan said. "I'm worth a lot." She held up her rifle. "If you make a run for that big tree over there, it'll draw him out and I can get a clean shot." I looked to where she was indicating; it was a distance.

"Don't take too long to aim…"

"Don't worry," she said. Her confidence was reassuring.

"Ready?" I said. She nodded. I took off. After about three steps I heard a blast that didn't sound like our assailant's.

"You can stop running," Guinan said. I turned and saw a prone figure on the ground. I went over to him. It was a species I didn't recognize in camouflage clothing, with a ridge bisecting his forehead. I took his weapon, found a device on his belt that was jamming communicator transmissions, and shut it off.

"I'll take him back to the ship and turn him over to the New Paris authorities," I said.

"You're taking me too," she said. "I can't stay here anymore."

"But…"

"No buts; I had a perfectly good hiding place till you showed up. Where are you guys going?"

"Well, our command base is Starbase 32…"

"That sounds fine," she said. She smiled. "Besides, aren't you interested in getting to know me?"

In truth, I was.

✦

Captain Mazzara wasn't happy about our new passenger, but was at least relieved that she let us store Laughton's cargo in her home on New Paris. After

I had enlisted several crewmembers to transfer our former captain's extensive collection of artifacts and memorabilia, we left for Starbase 32.

During the week-long trip, I spent a fair amount of my free time talking to Guinan. I did not learn much about her, however. She was an El-Aurian, a species I knew nothing about, and she gave me almost no details other than there were very few of them left in the Galaxy, and that they lived extremely long lives. This led to rumors about their blood being a source of immortality, which made them the victims of unscrupulous bounty hunters.

Though I couldn't draw much more information out of her, I unexpectedly found myself quite comfortable sharing my personal details. She was a compelling listener, and with very few questions I opened up about my history and feelings quite easily. I disclosed thoughts and ambitions that I had never mentioned to anyone. I quickly formed a connection with this woman, but there was nothing romantic about it. She just wanted to be my friend. I didn't know why, but it was comforting nevertheless.

It was, however, difficult for me to imagine her married to Captain Laughton, and she laughed when I mentioned that.

"You should've seen Humphrey at 28," she said. "Full of drive and ambition. He was going to explore the universe and make it his own." I didn't know whether it was a coincidence that the age she picked to mention just happened to be mine.

"He had quite a career," I said.

"In the beginning," Guinan said. "He started out as an explorer, but over time he decided the self-aggrandizement was more important to him, and he lost sight of his goals. His life became empty. And so did he. So he started collecting."

"I think it's easy to lose sight of your goals," I said. "It happens to me all the time."

"You have responsibilities, they can distract you."

"Yes, they can," I said. I was verbalizing something that had been in the back of my mind since Laughton's death. Out of a sense of loyalty, I had not broached the subject of a transfer to Captain Mazzara. I thought he would be more open to it than Laughton was, but I also knew that to ask too soon after Laughton's death was inappropriate. Now, however, a month had gone by and the ship was running as smooth as it ever had.

"You look like a man with a mission," Guinan said. I had become preoccupied by my own thoughts. I smiled and excused myself, and called the captain on the intercom. He was in his quarters, and I requested to see him.

On my way there, I let myself enjoy the possibility of finally leaving this ship. I was so energized and preoccupied that I walked into the captain's quarters without buzzing. He was playing a game of three-dimensional chess with David.

"What, you don't knock anymore?" David said.

"Sorry, sir," I said.

"It's all right, Number One," the captain said.

"You should call him Number Two," David said. I knew that this was some kind of insult, since David said it all the time, but I never learned what it meant.

"David, please," Mazzara said. "Give us a minute." David begrudgingly got up and left.

"What can I do for you, Jean-Luc," Mazzara said. "You want a drink?" Mazzara went and got a bottle of green liquid that I later discovered was Aldebaran whiskey. I didn't feel like drinking, but I also didn't feel like saying no, so I took a glass. Mazzara indicated a seat in front of him. He seemed to have forgotten that I was the one who asked to see him; there was a lot on his mind.

"I've been thinking a lot about the captain," he said.

"Yes, sir," I said. "A tragedy."

"I know he wasn't popular," Mazzara said. "And now, I feel a lot of sympathy for him. You can't understand command till you've had it. It's the loneliest, most oppressive job in the whole universe. It's a nightmare."

"Sir," I said, "you've been quite good at it…"

"Yeah, as soon as I got it I ran right off the bridge," he said. "I'm sure the crew has come up with plenty of nicknames for me by now…" I had not considered until then what must be going on in Mazzara's mind. Of course, a moment of bad judgment would haunt him, as it would any of us.

"Sir, I think everyone has forgotten about it," I said.

"I doubt that," he said. "In any case, I haven't. I'll remember it till the day I die. Everyone's life turns on a few crucial moments, and mine turned that day on the bridge." He took a long pull on his drink and placed the glass down on the desk. "I'll be resigning my commission."

THE STORY OF ONE OF STARFLEET'S MOST INSPIRATIONAL CAPTAINS

"Sir, you should reconsider." This was, in my mind, tragic. Mazzara was letting one mistake define the rest of his life. "You're a good officer…"

"That's very kind, but I've already informed Starfleet Command. When we arrive at Starbase 32, this ship will have a new captain." Oh, wonderful, I thought. What broken-down failure had they found to take this ship? I couldn't risk staying around to find out. I had to get Mazzara to approve my transfer immediately.

"Sir, with all due respect to your situation, I came to talk to you about something. I would like a transfer…"

"Jean-Luc, I think you'll be needed here…"

"I understand, but I have my own career to think about, and I just don't think my future is on the *Stargazer*."

"Really? Even as its captain?"

"Yes… wait… what?" The word "yes" was already on the way out of my mouth when I processed what he had said. "Me?"

"You," Mazzara said. "It was my suggestion, and frankly I don't think command had any captains they wanted to spare. Or no one wanted it. *Stargazer*'s class is too large to be commanded by a commander, so you'll skip a rank and be promoted to full captain. Or I can approve your transfer."

"No, sir," I said. "I mean, yes, sir. I'll happily accept. Thank you, sir."

"Congratulations," Mazzara said. He picked up the bottle and poured himself another drink. "Dismissed."

I'd arrived at his cabin determined and excited to leave the *Stargazer*, and now I left having inherited it.

I had no idea what to do. Do I tell everybody? There was no one I really wanted to tell, so I wandered the ship for hours and I found myself alone in the observation lounge. It was at the top of the primary hull and faced the stern of the ship. I stood there for a long time, watching the stars streak away at warp speed.

"Good news?" It was Guinan. I hadn't heard her come in.

"What? Oh, yes… wait, how did you know?"

"You were smiling," she said. "Can you tell me?"

"I'm… I'm the new captain." Saying it out loud, I had to laugh. I felt joy over this news. I was 28 years old and was a captain. I'd only graduated from the academy six years ago.

"That's wonderful," Guinan said. "Some childhood dreams do come true." She already knew me well enough to know this, as well as a lot of other things. "What's going to be your first act as shipmaster?"

"I'm going to make a sign," I said. " 'No children allowed.' "

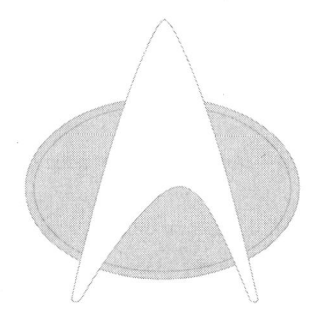

CHAPTER FIVE

"TO CAPTAIN FRANK MAZZARA, COMMANDING OFFICER, *U.S.S. Stargazer*, stardate 13209.2, you are hereby requested and required to relinquish command to Captain Jean-Luc Picard as of this date…"

I stood on the deck of the main shuttlebay next to Captain Mazzara as he read the order off the PADD, in front of a good portion of the four hundred people who made up the crew. Mazzara turned to look at me. I played my part.

"I relieve you, sir," I said.

"I stand relieved," Mazzara said, then looked up and addressed the ship's computer. "Computer, transfer all command codes to Captain Jean-Luc Picard, authorization Mazzara Beta Alpha 2." The computer immediately responded.

"*U.S.S. Stargazer* now in command of Jean-Luc Picard…" It was an amazing thing to hear. A computer voice had just made it official. I looked around at all the faces of the crew. I had fantasized my whole life about what this would feel like, and my imagination had never gotten it right. Because, as I stood and looked at all those expectant faces waiting for my first command, I realized in a flash that I was responsible for all of them.

"If you don't mind, I'd like to leave right away." It was Mazzara, in a hurry to get off the ship. I hadn't been fully aware of his embarrassment until he relayed it to me in his quarters, but since then it was all I could see. He didn't make eye contact with the rest of the crew, and he certainly wasn't staying around to say goodbye.

"Of course," I said. I turned to the crew. Here it was, my first order as captain. It was going to be nothing special. "All standing orders to remain in force until further notice. Prepare shuttlebay for launch. Dismissed." I then escorted Mazzara to the shuttle, where his two sons awaited him.

"It was a pleasure serving with you, sir," I said. I held out my hand and Mazzara shook it perfunctorily. I then turned to Anthony and David. "Good luck to you both."

David ignored me and followed Mazzara onto the shuttle. It probably wasn't David's best day that I, the officer whom he seemed the most disdainful of, now had his father's job. Anthony, however, hesitated a moment. His father, before I assumed command, had had his son transferred off the ship. It was only then that I realized that perhaps Anthony didn't want to go.

"Um… sorry about the egg," he said. "I hope I can serve with you again." I smiled, nodded, and he boarded the shuttle. As the hatch shut, I thought to myself: *Over my dead body.*

✦

We were circling Starbase 32, a planetary facility on Tagan III. There were limited dry dock services in orbit, but I planned to make use of them as much as I could. I had one goal in mind: get as many repairs and upgrades done as possible to the *Stargazer* before my replacement crew arrived. I needed a new conn officer (to replace me) as well as a new ops officer, security chief, and doctor. And one of those positions would also be my first officer.

I headed back to my cabin and passed a lot of crewmen in the corridors, exchanging friendly nods. I had enough relationships on the *Stargazer* that I felt there was plenty of goodwill at my promotion. Still, there were some officers who I knew did not take the news well. One of them intercepted me outside my cabin.

"May I speak with you a moment… sir?" It was Lieutenant Commander Black, the communications officer. I noticed that the "sir" took an extra moment; he wasn't comfortable with the change in our relative status. I ushered him inside.

"I would like to make a request," Black said. Undoubtedly, he wanted a transfer, which I would grant. Though he would actually be a big loss to the

THE STORY OF ONE OF STARFLEET'S MOST INSPIRATIONAL CAPTAINS

ship—it was doubtful I could find anyone with his experience—I didn't want to stand in the way of anyone who didn't want to be here.

"Go ahead."

"I'd like to throw my hat in the ring for first officer."

"Oh." This I did not expect. I was all set to offer to give him a recommendation to another ship. "I've already offered the position to someone else. I'm sorry." I'd only just assumed command, but had made arrangements for a new first officer a few days before.

"I see," he said. "That's disappointing. You're not… you're not replacing me are you?"

"No."

"Good, thanks," he said. "I'm really looking forward to serving under your command." With that, he left. This came as a considerable surprise to me. Somehow, despite Black's obvious jealousy of my promotions over him, I'd earned his respect. Just that bit of amity made me think if I hadn't already had someone else ready to take that post, I might have considered him.

A few minutes later, I had put on my new rank pin, and headed "upstairs." I wanted to sit in my new chair.

"Captain on the bridge," Black said, as I entered. This was a leftover protocol from the days of the Earth navies; when a captain entered the bridge, it was carefully noted in a written log so that if there was a grounding or collision, the captain's presence was a matter of formal record. On a starship, the sensor logs placed me and every other member of the ship at all hours. Black indulging in it was a show of respect, one he'd never shown to Laughton or Mazzara.

I looked around the room: the overall impression was of anarchy. Half the control panels in the room were open; maintenance crews were either scanning underneath them with tricorders or ripping out and replacing the innards with new parts. I went toward the captain's chair and stopped. An engineer stood on a small anti-grav platform and rewired optical cabling in the ceiling. The small floating disk was almost directly over the captain's chair. I would have to ask him to move to sit down. I decided against it, and instead walked past the captain's chair to the ops station, where Engineer Scully worked underneath the control panel. He noticed me as I approached.

"Hey there, sir," he said. He managed to walk the line between informality and respect, and I had to accept him as he was. Forty years older than me, and having served on the ship since before I was born, it was a lot more his than mine.

"How go the upgrades?"

"The ship's systems weren't really designed to handle a lot of this new stuff, but we're doing the best we can," he said. The technology of the *Stargazer* was years out of date, and the best I could hope for, barring a complete refit, was patchwork repairs. The ship would never be top of the line again, but as I stood there on that mess of a bridge, it didn't matter. The old lady was mine, and I loved it.

"Sir, Starbase 32 signals crew replacements standing by to beam aboard," Black said. This was sooner than I expected. I just had to hope there might be a delay in getting my orders so that most of the work I'd had started could be completed. I left the bridge and headed down to the transporter room.

As soon as I found out I was getting command, I knew I wanted a friend as my first officer. I thought of Corey and Marta, but knew they were both already up the chain of command on much better ships than the *Stargazer*: Corey was chief of security on the *Ajax*, and Marta was already the first officer of the *Kyushu*. Maybe I didn't want to put them in an awkward position, or maybe I didn't want to face rejection, but I didn't ask either of them. The only person I asked gave me an immediate yes, because for him it was a big step up.

"Request permission to come aboard, sir," Walker Keel said, as he stepped off the transporter. I warmly shook his hand. We hadn't been in touch that much since I left *Reliant*, but I knew he was ready to move on. With him on the pad were my new security chief, conn officer, and doctor. Three humans and one Edosian.

"Lieutenant Cheva reporting for duty, sir," Cheva said. I'd gotten her a promotion and was happy to have her as my chief of security. I hadn't forgotten the vital role she'd played on Milika, and how that had changed my career. Behind her, the new medical officer stepped forward.

"Commander Ailat," I said. "Welcome aboard." I'd never seen an Edosian in person before. Her orange skin, three arms and three legs fascinated me. Walking seemed impossible—as each leg took a step forward, her lower half rotated; three steps was a full circle.

THE STORY OF ONE OF STARFLEET'S MOST INSPIRATIONAL CAPTAINS

"Thank you, Captain," Ailat said. Her voice was high-pitched, with a staccato speech pattern.

"And let me introduce your new conn officer," Walker said. I'd been so riveted by Ailat I'd ignored the young man standing toward the back. Walker had recommended him; he knew his family and had helped him get into the academy, which he'd just graduated from a couple of years before. Despite his slightly awkward bearing, he had an affable smile.

"Ensign Jack Crusher, reporting for duty, sir," he said.

✦

"You have all your crew replacements," Admiral Sulu said, "so I'm hoping you're ready to leave." I was in my quarters, and she was on my desk viewscreen, speaking from her office on Starbase 32. Though she was the commanding officer for this entire sector, she was sociable and engaging, and seemed very young for someone in her sixties. I never wanted to disappoint a superior officer, and Demora Sulu's casual authority heightened that need.

"Yes, ma'am, we're ready," I said. That was pretty far from the truth; I'd begun too many repairs and upgrades, gambling they'd be finished before *Stargazer* might be sent into action.

"Good," she said. "We've lost contact with a scientific research facility in system L-374. We'd like you to check it out."

"Can you tell me what the nature of their research is?"

"It's all in the briefing packet I'm sending now," Admiral Sulu said. "It's an old research facility that's been studying an ancient derelict spaceship. You're to depart as soon as possible."

"Right away, Admiral," I said, again not really sure if I could leave.

"Sulu out," the admiral said, and the picture went off. I then called Scully on the intercom.

"Scully here," he said.

"How much longer to complete all the repairs and upgrades?" I said.

"We're done with some stuff, but there's still more I'd like to do. How much time do I have?"

"About ten minutes," I said. "Sorry."

"All right," he said, with a heavy sigh. "I can do some of it on the fly after we go, but before we leave I'm going to have to reconnect the conn and op controls. And I won't be able to do anything about the engine circuit upgrades, so don't make me go too fast. Scully out." It was clear that this was a large inconvenience, but Scully never complained. I was about to read the briefing packet when the door chimed. I opened it to find Guinan.

"Guinan, I'm a little busy…"

"I won't take too much of your time," she said. "I just wanted to say goodbye." This shouldn't have come as a surprise; she wasn't a member of the crew, and all she had asked of me was to take her to the starbase. Still, I was very disappointed.

"Are you sure? You are welcome to stay aboard."

"Thanks, but I don't really have a job here," she said. "And there isn't one I really want."

"What would you like to do?"

"I don't know, tend bar?" I smiled at the joke.

"Well," I said, "in that case, I have something for you." I pulled out a bottle of Aldebaran whiskey. "For the bar you eventually tend."

"Where'd you get this?"

"Mazzara gave it to me," I said. "But it was from a case that I think he stole from Laughton, so it belongs to you anyway."

"Thanks."

"Where will you go?"

"Oh, I'll be here and there. Don't worry, you and I will run into each other again." She smiled, and, just like on that first day I met her, it seemed like she was engaging in some private joke. She gave me a hug. "Thanks again for saving my life."

"You're welcome," I said, and she left. I sat back down.

She was probably one of the most unique personalities I'd ever met. Her presence had a strange calming effect on me, and I was sorry that there wasn't a place for her in my crew. I was sorry we didn't have a bar on the ship.

I looked back at the briefing packet on my viewscreen to familiarize myself with the mission ahead, as I tapped the button for the intercom.

"Picard to Bridge," I said, "stand by to leave orbit."

"Dock command signaling clear, sir," Black said.

I was in my chair, but that was about the only thing considerably different from the previous day. A lot of control panels were still open, and a lot of crewmen had their heads inside them. But we had to leave. Jack Crusher was at the conn, Walker at ops, and Engineer Scully was lying on the floor between them, working underneath their stations.

"Set course for system L-374, Mr. Crusher," I said.

"Uh, sir, I don't have any helm or navigation control…"

"Just one more second, sir," Scully said. "Okay, try it now…" Crusher operated his controls.

"Still nothing, sir," Crusher said. My first moments on the bridge as captain were off to a terrible start.

"Oh, okay, got it now," Scully said. "You're good to go…" Crusher tried the controls again.

"Course plotted, sir," Crusher said.

"Engage," I said. On the viewscreen, Tagan III fell away, and we leapt to warp. The stars streamed by. And then the inertial dampeners strained, and we all were pulled forward as the ship came to a sudden stop.

"Report!" I said.

"We're no longer at warp," Crusher said.

"That much is clear," I said.

"That was me, that was me," Scully said. "Sorry, okay, here we go…" The screen changed again as we went back to warp. I held my breath, waiting for another breakdown, but it didn't come.

"On course for system L-374," Crusher said. "ETA 47.9 hours."

"Communications," I said. "Put the image I sent to you up on the main screen."

"Aye, sir," Black said. On the main viewscreen the image of a kilometers-long structure hung in space, a dark tube with an immense mouth on one end, tapering to a point on the other. Its immense size was apparent by how it dwarfed the three starship tugs hanging near it. I got out of my chair and walked near the screen.

"What is that?" Walker said. I was about to answer when someone did it for me.

"That's the planet-killer, isn't it?" It was Jack Crusher. I was impressed that he recognized it.

"Yes," I said. "About eighty years ago that machine entered Federation space and destroyed four solar systems."

"How?" Walker said. I turned to Crusher.

"Ensign?"

"It used an anti-proton beam to destroy planets and ingest the debris from those planets for fuel. It was very difficult to destroy because its hull is solid neutronium." Once Crusher said that, there were sounds of recognition from the rest of the bridge crew. This object, made out of the ultra-dense matter that exists in the center of a neutron star, was part of academy legends.

"Okay, this is coming back to me," Walker said. "Kirk stopped it, right?" I nodded. The planet-killer had all but destroyed the starship *Constellation*, though it had left its impulse engines functional. Kirk himself had driven the wrecked ship inside the deadly machine and beamed off just before blowing up the *Constellation*'s impulse engines. It was one of the many swashbuckling stories of Starfleet's most famous captain that had inspired generations of cadets.

"The object was immobilized," I said. "And for the last eighty years Federation scientists had been studying it in system L-374, trying to unlock the secrets of its construction. Yesterday, Starfleet lost contact with the science team, and now there's heavy subspace interference in the area."

"The neutronium itself is the cause of the interference," Crusher said. "The science team used signal boosters to counter it. They must be malfunctioning."

"Or destroyed," Scully said. I'd forgotten about him, still lying on the deck with his head under the conn and ops consoles. But he had hit Starfleet's concern—that someone had decided to steal the planet-killer. Still, there was no proof of that.

"The *Stargazer* is the closest ship available," I said. "We're going to see what's going on, so let's not jump to conclusions. However, Number One, schedule some battle drills."

"Who's 'Number One'?" Walker said. He was serious and I realized I'd unconsciously adopted Mazzara's penchant for that nickname. It was an interesting lesson to me; you could cherry-pick aspects of someone's command style even if you disdained them as a whole. I enjoyed that Mazzara had called me "Number One," a charming relic of the days of sail.

THE STORY OF ONE OF STARFLEET'S MOST INSPIRATIONAL CAPTAINS

"That's you," I said.

It would take two days to reach our destination, so I tried to give Scully as much help to complete the repairs and upgrades as possible without compromising other ship's functions. However, it would turn out we wouldn't have the full two days; about ten hours from our destination, sensors picked up the planet-killer, moving at warp speed.

"How is that possible?" I said.

"I don't know," Walker said. "I thought Kirk destroyed its engines."

"It's on a course away from us," Crusher said.

"Heading?"

"It's a precise heading for the planet Romulus." That gave me pause. The Romulans? The Federation had not heard from them in decades. Had they snuck into Federation space to steal this artifact? It seemed unlikely. But I had a more pressing problem.

"We need to intercept it before it enters the Neutral Zone,'"* I said.

"Its speed is warp 5.9," Crusher said. "To catch it before it reaches the Neutral Zone, we'll have to go to warp 8.3." Engineer Scully would not be pleased, but I didn't see that I had a choice. I couldn't risk pursuing it into Romulan space, even if they were the ones stealing it.

We changed course, and after a few hours we closed in on the behemoth. When we were in visual range, we were able to determine how it was able to travel at warp: it had a large girdle built around it, with two warp engines attached.

"That's Starfleet equipment," Walker said. "The Federation science team must have had the Corps of Engineers build it so they could move the thing." I noticed an engineering compartment at the base of the engines.

"Scan for life signs," I said.

"One human, very faint," Walker said.

"All right," I said. "We'll have to beam aboard and try to ascertain what is going on."

---

*EDITOR'S NOTE: Picard's concern about entering the Neutral Zone dates back to the treaty negotiated at the end of the Romulan War in 2160. The Neutral Zone was a border area between the Federation and Romulan Empire. The treaty states that entry into it by either Federation or Romulan ships constituted an act of war.

"If the Romulans are responsible," Walker said, "it's possible there's a cloaked ship nearby that we can't detect." The Romulans, the last time Starfleet had seen them, had perfected their ability to "cloak" their ships from Starfleet detection devices. No doubt in the intervening years their technology had continued to improve.

"I'm still not sure why the Romulans would risk this," I said.

"Even with no power," Crusher said, "it is a formidable weapon. Send it into a system at warp speed and it might be difficult to stop before it crashes into an adversary's planet. The destruction from such an impact would be catastrophic." I wasn't that impressed with Crusher's theory, because it neglected the obvious.

"Stealing it and taking it back to their homeworld?" I said. "We would know they had stolen it. What do they gain from such a bold move?" I needed more answers.

"Scully to Bridge," Scully said on the intercom. I knew what this was about.

"Yes, Engineer," I said, anticipating his demand, "I know we've got to slow down…"

"And soon," he said, "or we're all going to be a big pile of scrap metal."

"I understand, Picard out." I checked our distance from the Neutral Zone; we had maybe twenty minutes. I turned to Walker. "We need to regain control of that ship. Mr. Crusher, you're with me." It was a difficult thing, after acquiring a ship of my own, to then leave it in someone else's hands. But I felt like I had to solve this problem myself.

"You have the bridge, Number One," I said.

With Security Chief Cheva and Dr. Ailat, Mr. Crusher and I beamed into the engineering compartment. It was clean and efficient, a series of control panels surrounding a warp reactor. Dr. Ailat took out her tricorder.

"The life sign is over here," Ailat said. Cheva and Ailat led the way and we found a human in a Starfleet engineer's uniform. He was unconscious, lying in a pool of his own blood.

"He's been stabbed repeatedly," Ailat said. She immediately got to work, using her three hands to treat and close the wounds.

"Stabbed?" I said. "With what?" Cheva had her phaser out. Crusher meanwhile was checking the control panels. Ailat's hands glided from her patient to her medical bag and back; she spoke to me without looking up.

"Difficult to determine at this stage," Ailat said. "I will have to do more study at a later time." I went over to Crusher.

"Sir, the controls are locked out," he said. "I can't shut down the engines or adjust the course or speed."

"*Stargazer* to Picard," came Walker's voice over my communicator.

"Go ahead," I said.

"Engineer Scully apologizes, but he reports we have about ten seconds before he has to take us out of warp, or the engines will overload." This was not very convenient. If the *Stargazer* dropped out of warp, the planet-killer would leave it behind, and it would be almost impossible for it to catch up. I quickly went through my options, and decided I had to stay on board.

"Beam back the rest of the away team and Dr. Ailat's patient."

"Request permission to stay on board," Cheva and Crusher said in unison.

"Denied," I said.

"Sir, I think I can stop this thing," Crusher said. He had a very earnest look, and since the only idea I had was firing my phaser into the warp core and possibly blowing myself up, I decided he was worth the gamble.

"All right," I said. "*Stargazer*, beam back Cheva, Ailat, and her patient." After a moment, the three of them disappeared.

"Picard to *Stargazer*, do you have them?" There was no answer. I assumed, hoped, they had made it before my ship had to drop out of warp. In any event, Crusher and I were by ourselves.

"Enlighten me, Ensign. What is your plan?"

"I've done some calculations," he said, "and I think the reason this thing is going warp 5.9 is that the structural integrity of the girdle pushing such a large mass won't handle a higher speed."

"You said we couldn't adjust the course or speed."

"Not with these controls, but we could use our phasers to open up the plasma injectors to increase our speed. I estimate at warp 6.2 the girdle will crack and we'll drop out of warp drive." What he was proposing was very dangerous.

"Did you do all these calculations in your head?"

"Yes," he said. Now I was starting to be impressed.

After a brief conversation about our procedure, we took our phasers, and each went into a Jefferies tube leading to each of the two engines. I found the plasma injectors, and programmed my phaser to fire automatically for one nanosecond on an extremely tight beam. I had to fire several pinprick shots to put extra holes in the injector so that more plasma could flow out of it, but if my phaser stayed on a millisecond too long, the beam would hit the plasma and ignite it, and I'd be consumed in a radioactive fire. I took careful aim, and fired the shots. The phaser went on and off automatically; there were now three almost microscopic openings in the injector. More plasma started to flow out of it, and after a brief moment the Jefferies tube began to vibrate. I climbed out and rejoined Crusher in the engineering compartment, who was already at the controls.

"It's working," he said. "Our speed's increased to warp 6.1... 6.2..." We heard the creaking and groaning of straining metal. Crusher checked his board. "Structural integrity at forty-three percent... twenty-eight..."

"Hang on..."

There was a loud crack that reverberated through the room. The room went dark and we were thrown forward over the console to the deck. I hit my head on something, and in my mind I saw myself on the floor of my family's basement all those years before...

✦

"Captain... Captain..." My vision cleared and I was looking up at Ailat. Emergency lighting was on, and her orange skin was bathed in red, making a color I couldn't quite recognize.

"Crusher?" I said.

"I'm fine, sir," he said. I looked to see he was standing with Cheva and Walker.

"You did it, sir," Walker said. "The planet-killer dropped out of warp just short of the Neutral Zone."

"Crusher's idea," I said, and pulled myself up. I looked hard at Walker.

"You all right, sir?"

"Yes, I'm just wondering who the hell is in command of my ship?"

Later, back on the *Stargazer*, the crewman we rescued, an engineer by the name of Lounsbery, had recovered. Walker and I interviewed him in sickbay, but unfortunately he had little information to offer.

"I didn't see whoever it was," Lounsbery said from his sickbed. "I was alone on the graveyard shift. I'd received word from our base that our long-range

THE STORY OF ONE OF STARFLEET'S MOST INSPIRATIONAL CAPTAINS

communication array had been sabotaged. Then someone stabbed me and the next thing I knew I was here." I told him to get some rest then went to talk to Ailat in her small office attached to the exam room.

"Any more indication of what the weapon was?"

"It was an efficient blade designed to cause a great deal of damage," Ailat said.

"Could it be a *d'k tahg*?" I said.

"The wounds are consistent with such a weapon," Ailat said.

"A Klingon weapon?" Walker seemed dubious. "They stole the planet-killer for the Romulans? Why would they bother?"

"They weren't stealing it," I said. "They were doing what Ensign Crusher proposed it might be used for, sending it at high warp on a collision course to Romulus." I could see that Walker was putting it together.

"And making it look like we did it," he said.

"Even if the Romulans had been able to stop it," I said, "they would've responded with an attack on the Federation."

"And even though *we* stopped it," Walker said, "we don't have any evidence that the Klingons are responsible."

"Lounsbery's stab wounds. Hardly conclusive." I would make a report to Starfleet, but there was little to be done. The Federation had been engaged in peace talks with the Klingons for sixty years. The alliance was never a solid one, always on the verge of falling into conflict. And it was becoming clear that the Klingons weren't really interested in peace. It appeared that they were looking to ignite a deadly Galactic war. They would even resort to subterfuge to gain an early advantage—putting the Federation in conflict with the Romulans would do that quite nicely.

"At least one good thing that came out of this," Walker said.

"What's that?"

"You gotta like that Crusher kid," he said.

He was right, I did.

✦

Out of the blocks on that first mission, I learned some very important lessons. 1) Lean on your officers. If I hadn't had Crusher with me, I'm not sure I would have come up with a solution that left me alive. And 2) Don't lie to your admiral about the condition of your ship. I was fortunate that our next assignment was a general star-mapping mission of an unexplored region so we had breathing room for Scully to finish a good portion of the upgrades and repairs. I settled into a routine and soon found myself exploring what kind of commanding officer I wanted to be.

There are many different types of captains. Some find it most effective to govern their ships with a god-like detachment. But given my age and relative inexperience, I found myself approaching my role less a master and more a servant. The needs of the crew were foremost on my mind, and the best way to learn about those needs was through conversation. I enjoyed walking my ship from stem to stern for at least an hour, if not longer, every day. During these walking tours I'd talk to fifty or so crewmembers, giving me an up-to-date snapshot of what was occurring below decks. Unfortunately, my daily walkabouts led to an increasing pile of administrative work left undone, which I eventually left in the hands of my first officer. Walker complained sarcastically, though I rationalized he was getting his own education on the requirements of being a captain.

As time went on, I learned whose opinions I could rely on and constructed a web of crewmen throughout the *Stargazer* who gave me a good gauge of where problems might arise. Along with Walker, Scully, Crusher, and Cheva, I relied on a junior officer working in the torpedo bay named Ensign Vigo, who seemed to trade in the most intimate levels of gossip and helped me avoid management difficulties with his extensive knowledge of the state of the crew. Ironically, the ship's designated personnel officer, Lieutenant Felson, was too formal with me and seemed uncomfortable sharing what she considered unseemly personal details. The walkabouts also let me know where there were technological challenges, which we had in abundance.

I became increasingly comfortable as captain of the ship, which in turn, made my crew more comfortable. With Laughton and Mazzara gone, the vessel was alive with a new atmosphere—I could see it as the crew went about their duties. I soon allowed myself the luxury of friendships. A trio of sorts formed: Walker Keel, myself, and, surprisingly, Jack Crusher. I began to identify with him; he was like a different version of me, as if the bookish intellectual I'd been in my youth had been encouraged, and I'd avoided becoming the ego-driven teenager whose arrogance almost got him killed.

THE STORY OF ONE OF STARFLEET'S MOST INSPIRATIONAL CAPTAINS

Stargazer moved into an unexplored region of the Alpha Quadrant. Much of our time was spent exploring systems with no sign of advanced technology, and over the next year or two we catalogued dozens of planets and countless forms of life. The ship, unlike the *Reliant*, had better scientific facilities, which Walker oversaw as part of his operations duties. I became quite proud of the work I was doing, and it went to my head. I fell into the trap early on that some starship captains had: I began to see myself as infallible.

"The asteroid is 3.2 kilometers in diameter," Crusher said. "It will strike the planet in less than a day." We were in an uncharted system, formerly designated HD 150248, and discovered an asteroid on course to impact the fifth planet in orbit, Class M. I ordered a scan of the planet.

✦

"That asteroid…" I didn't have to finish the question. Everyone knew what I was asking.

"It will exterminate all life on the planet," Crusher said.

"The poor inhabitants won't even know what hit them," Walker said.

"Can we divert it?"

"It's too late," Walker said. "Too close to the planet."

"Any signs of civilization?" I said.

"Yes, primitive, fifth-century Earth equivalent, agrarian. Spread across the northern continent," Walker said.

"I want to take a look." I could see that some of the bridge crew were uneasy at this suggestion. Walker stepped over to me.

"Jean-Luc, it's too dangerous," he whispered.

"We should have some record of this," I said. "Some memory of who these people are." Walker wasn't happy, but he wasn't going to disobey an order.

✦

I had the transporter put me and the away team down on a hill overlooking a village and some surrounding farms. It was me, Cheva, and Jack Crusher. We hid at the edge of a vast forest, over 4,000 kilometers square, out of sight of the natives. Cheva scanned for possible approaches by native life, while Crusher and I used our recording binoculars to film some evidence of this civilization that was about to die.

"They're bipeds," Crusher said. "The village seems to be some kind of fortress."

"No doubt," I said, "providing temporary shelter in case of approaching enemy hordes."

"I think I found a farmer," Crusher said. I looked where he was pointing and could see a stocky creature tilling the soil with some sort of plow.

"Captain," Cheva said, "picking up life signs approaching. We should go."

"Hey," Crusher said, "he's got an assistant." I watched as the stocky creature was joined by another that looked very similar, only a good deal smaller.

"Not an assistant," I said. "A son."

"Assuming they're male," Cheva said. Her point was well taken, but I was lost in a memory. I was a child, following my father out in the vineyard, helping him plant the grapes. A few brief minutes, just my father and me—no Robert. I had forgotten there were such moments…

"Sir," Cheva said, "they're closing in…" She indicated to the left of us a group of four of the local inhabitants, about 100 meters away. They carried spears, and moved cautiously toward us.

"All right, let's go," I said. We stepped into the forest, and as Cheva had us beamed up, I watched through our recording binoculars as the farmer placed his child up on his shoulders.

"We've got to do something," I said. I could see from his expression that Walker had now decided I was certifiable.

"Jean-Luc, it's about to enter the atmosphere…"

"We have a responsibility to try," I said.

"Sir," Crusher said. "The Prime Directive specifically states we can't interfere with the natural evolution of a society…"

"It's a captain's prerogative to interpret the Prime Directive," I said. "I don't think it applies here. This society should have a chance to survive to evolve naturally."

"Mass extinctions play a large role in evolution," Crusher said.

"We're not going to discuss this further," I said. "I want to try to cut the asteroid into smaller pieces."

"If we'd gotten here a week ago, we might've had a shot. But now…"

THE STORY OF ONE OF STARFLEET'S MOST INSPIRATIONAL CAPTAINS

"Walker," I said, "that's an order." I ordered an analysis of the asteroid and its possible weak spots and found myself growing optimistic that we would succeed. Crusher and Cheva targeted phasers and photon torpedoes.

"Weapons locked," Cheva said.

"Fire," I said. We watched on screen as *Stargazer*'s weapons tore into the large rock, breaking it up. Cheva aimed the weapons, slicing pieces into smaller and smaller chunks. Dust from the debris filled our view.

"The debris is interfering with our targeting sensors," Cheva said. "I can't maintain a lock anymore…"

We hadn't done nearly enough to reduce the size of the asteroid. There were still too many large pieces that would cause catastrophic damage. If they hit land they would bring up enormous amounts of ash and dust, blocking out radiation from the sun and causing an "impact winter." The global temperature would drop, causing a mass extinction. I stepped over to the weapons console.

"Let me take over," I said. Cheva quickly got up, and I sat at the console. I switched the targeting sensor off, brought up a real-time view of the debris, then opened the switch to fire the phasers and held it open. It was an excessive use of phaser power; I used it like a knife, slicing back and forth through the remaining pieces. Eventually, the *Stargazer*'s phasers powered down; I'd completely drained them.

"You've done it, sir," Crusher said. I went back to the captain's chair and watched as the hundreds of pieces of asteroid began their descent through the atmosphere. There were some larger pieces, but nothing that would cause the catastrophic damage that the original would have. I was feeling quite proud of myself. I could see that Walker, however, wasn't sharing my optimism.

"The forest…" he said. I didn't initially understand what he was implying. Walker then changed the viewscreen to feature this grand stretch of trees, and it dawned on me.

From even a high orbit I could see flaming debris striking across the length and breadth of the 4,000 square kilometer woodland. Within minutes, a wall of flame stretched across and kept growing. I realized that it would have the same effect as if the asteroid had impacted whole: soot and ash from a fire that was impossible to extinguish would fill the atmosphere and block out the sun. The mass extinction would happen anyway.

A species would die that I'd felt I had gotten to know through one moment of joy between a father and son.

✦

"Sensors are picking up a ship," Walker said.

"Let's see it," I said. On the viewer, a small, scout-sized craft. Its engines were forward of the ship, and the general shape of it reminded me of a hammerhead shark. It was drifting, plasma leaking from one of its engines.

"Two life signs," Walker said. "Unknown species, but if they're oxygen breathers they're in trouble. I'm reading minimal life support."

"Hail them," I said.

"No response, sir," Black said. I did not have a lot of experience dealing with adversarial situations, but I was on guard. Despite the apparent helplessness of the vessel, its design appeared predatory.

"Shields up, Mr. Crusher," I said. "Then move us in closer." The *Stargazer* moved within a few hundred meters. There was no change in the other ship. I told Black to put me on a hailing frequency.

"Unidentified ship, this is Captain Jean-Luc Picard of the *U.S.S. Stargazer*, we stand ready to assist." I waited, still no answer.

"Sir, it's possible they don't understand us," said Crusher. "Our universal translator works by comparing frequencies of brainwave patterns, or by processing language that it's hearing. If the aliens are unconscious, it's possible the universal translator doesn't have enough information to translate your hail."

"And if they haven't developed the universal translator yet," I said, continuing his thought, "they're hearing gibberish." There was, however, no way to prove this was what was happening. The ship could still be laying some sort of trap.

"I advise caution, sir," Cheva said. "The damage and radiation signatures seem consistent with the ship being in proximity to an exploding impulse engine. I'd say they've seen some action." Though she echoed my concern, I was still left with no choice.

"Bridge to Dr. Ailat, report to the transporter room." I couldn't bring the survivors on board without knowing who they were, but I also couldn't ignore people possibly in distress. "Cheva, Crusher, you're with me. Number One, drop shields long enough to beam us over."

"Sir, may I remind the captain..."

"I know, I'm not supposed to go on away missions," I said. "But I'm going." Walker had given up fighting me on this. The captain was supposed to stay on the bridge, and the first officer was supposed to lead the away missions. But I had only served as a first officer for a little over a month, so I still enjoyed the hands-on experience.

Dr. Ailat, Cheva, Crusher, and I beamed over to the small scout vessel. We found the two crewmen, both unconscious, with lacerations and burns. They had pronounced ridges on their heads and neck, giving them an almost reptilian look. They wore matching armor; they were definitely part of a military. Ailat scanned them.

"They are alive, though their internal systems are unfamiliar," she said.

"Can you help them?"

"I believe so," Ailat said. "Their unconsciousness seems to have been caused by severe concussions."

"That would be consistent with the damage to the craft," Cheva said.

"Very well," I said. I had Dr. Ailat beamed back with the two survivors, while Crusher, Cheva, and I continued to examine the ship. It was very small; there was only one crew quarter, presumably for the commander—it had framed medals on the wall. There was a bridge and an engineering compartment. Every other available bit of space was used for storage.

We then set out to understand the workings of their machinery. The language of the control panels was unfamiliar, but our scans of the systems told us they were consistent with a level of technology close to our own. This is where my background in archaeology was helpful; I'd been taught by Professor Galen how to translate ancient languages of lost civilizations by finding a key. If said civilization had a developed understanding of mathematics and science, all you needed was to find some written example of a constant, like pi or the speed of light, or even better the periodic table of elements, and with the help of a computer the whole language could be deciphered. This was much simpler on a spaceship with advanced equipment scanning the heavens around it.

"Sir, I think I found something." Crusher was looking at a display. "This is measuring radiation... see, there's the *Stargazer*'s engines, and that graph there must be background radiation." He was right, and we were able to use this as a basis for our language key. Once we could translate the displays, we would be able to make a determination of damage to the ship. Cheva, meanwhile, was taking stock of the armaments and defensive capabilities, as well as examining their handguns. Their energy weapons were less technologically advanced but quite durable and probably very deadly (there didn't seem to be a stun setting).

We then returned to the *Stargazer*. Walker met us at the transporter room, and the two of us then went to sickbay to see to our guests, who were awake. Two security guards stood by the door.

"I am Glinn Hovat," one of them said. The universal translator had had enough time to translate their spoken language. The posture and bearing of this being told me he was in command; what helped to confirm it was that his companion did not attempt to speak. What I'd seen on the other ship—their weapons and medals indicating a martial philosophy—made me suitably wary of them.

"I'm Captain Jean-Luc Picard," I said. "You're aboard the Federation ship *Stargazer*."

"I demand you release us immediately," Glinn Hovat said, "or you will face serious consequences."

"You are not our prisoners," I said.

"Oh?" Glinn Hovat said. "The presence of the guards would indicate otherwise." I smiled; this was a shrewd man. I could tell from the aggressiveness of his remarks that he was testing me and my resolve.

"Glinn Hovat, forgive me," I said, "but I am forced to take precautions. That includes not letting strangers have free run of my ship."

"What is the status of my vessel?"

"Life support is still operational," I said. "But our unfamiliarity with your systems and language make it difficult to tell the extent of the damage." I was lying to him, in an effort to gain some advantage. But it was clear I was failing; this man didn't believe a word I was saying. "Can you tell me what happened to it?"

"Captain… Picard was it? You are strangers to us, and you understand I am forced to take precautions. That includes not telling you events that may be classified." He was throwing my cautious attitude back at me, and I would now get nowhere with him. I had begun badly, and now there was no way back.

"Well, yes, but…" I fumbled, trying to find some way to keep him talking, but he wasn't interested.

THE STORY OF ONE OF STARFLEET'S MOST INSPIRATIONAL CAPTAINS

"Thank you for rescuing us, but if you will allow us to leave, we must return to our ship." I turned to Ailat, hoping the plea in my expression would tell her I wanted them to stay longer, but she either didn't read it or didn't care.

"I would recommend rest," Ailat said, "but they appear to have recovered from their wounds."

"Very well," I said. "Are you sure there isn't anything else I can do for you?"

"Yes," he said, after a brief pause, "I'd like a glass of water."

"A… glass of…?"

"Your doctor was kind enough to give me one earlier, and I'd like another." I don't know why this seemed like a very strange request, but it was. There was no reason to refuse. Dr. Ailat didn't wait for my permission; she went to the wall replicator, made the request, and a glass of water appeared. I noticed Hovat watching intently as Ailat brought it back to him. He took a healthy sip, and then asked to be taken back to his ship.

A few hours later on the bridge, we watched on the viewscreen as the small ship's engines came back online.

"Those guys must have been working nonstop," Walker said. "The damage report you brought back was pretty extensive."

"The place was packed with spare parts," Cheva said.

"Why would they carry so many spare parts?" Walker said. "If they had replicators, much of what they'd need…"

"Wait," I said. "Did you notice a replicator?"

"Oh," Cheva said. "No, you're right, I didn't." We'd missed an important piece of information in taking stock of that ship. Then I looked at Walker.

"You remember the glass of water?" Walker realized what I was getting at.

"He wasn't thirsty, he wanted to see the replicator in action again." We turned and looked at the screen. The ship moved away and leapt to warp.

"If that's the case," Crusher said, "then they're very dangerous."

"What do you mean, Mr. Crusher?"

"Replicator technology eliminated need on planet Earth," Crusher said. "A lot of exploration previous to the invention of the replicator was about the hunt for resources. That invention more than any other helped make us a peaceful society."

"And without one," I said, "a society might be more aggressive."

"They'd have to be," Crusher said. "Without replicators, space travel is very expensive. And resources are never freely given by anyone." The message was clear to everyone in the room. We may just have discovered a new adversary. I was constantly impressed with Jack Crusher's view of the Galaxy. It challenged me to be more thoughtful. I was lucky to have him in my crew.

"Did they ever tell us the name of their species?" Walker said. We never asked them because Crusher had discovered it while searching the ship.

"Those medals framed on a wall in the quarters," Crusher said. "I translated the inscriptions. They all read: 'For the glory of Cardassia.' They're Cardassians."

✦

"Go and talk to her," I said to Jack Crusher. He, Walker, and I sat at a bar on Sigma Iotia II. Across the room was a young woman around Crusher's age, sipping an elaborate cocktail and occasionally looking our way. The bar was called The Feds, and the woman, as well as everyone else in the place, was in a 23rd-century Starfleet uniform, or a close approximation of one. In fact, just about everyone on the planet was dressed that way. And none of them were actually in Starfleet.

"I think Jean-Luc is right," Walker said. "She looks interested."

"They're always interested in the real ones," Crusher said. He was a little insecure when it came to women, although in this case, he was right: actual Starfleet officers were considered something of celebrities on this world, which was one reason why it was such a popular shore leave destination.

"How did this place get like this?" Crusher said.

"Oh, no," Walker said. "Why are you going to bring that up? Now we're going to have to listen to another Starfleet legend…"

"It's an amazing tale," I said. "A starship discovers the planet, which, a century earlier, had been contaminated by its exposure to the history of 20th-century Earth. Everyone on the planet acting like Al Capone…"

"Who's Al Capone?" Crusher said.

"This is going to take forever…" Walker said.

"It's not," I said, though I'd had a few drinks and was having a little trouble staying succinct. This was true alcohol, and though I'd been raised on it, I hadn't had much since I'd left home. "Now, where was I… oh, yes, so, the starship shows up and tries to fix the contamination, but all that happened was that he *altered* the contamination… but he saved these people by doing that…"

"So instead of pretending they're El Cabone…"

"Al Capone."

"Al Cabone, instead everyone pretends they're in Starfleet," Crusher said. "That's better?"

"It is," I said. "Much better. They used to kill each other every day; now their focus is on education, diversity, and a brighter future. That's what a captain's supposed to do, fix things…" I'd had too much to drink, but I was enjoying myself. During my lecture however, I'd failed to notice the woman making her way over until she was already talking to Jack.

"I was wondering if we could have a drink," she said, looking him in the eye. He smiled.

"I'm here with my friends," he said. "Sorry." She shrugged and walked off. Walker slapped his palm into his forehead.

"What the hell, Jack?"

"Guys," Crusher said, "I'm not going to meet the woman I want to spend the rest of my life with in a fake Starfleet bar on some nutty planet." Through my liquored haze, I admired this grounded but also romantic view of the world. He did not need womanizing conquests to buttress his self-esteem. It made me think that perhaps I was the insecure one. The thought faded, and I decided to resume my good time.

"Another round!" I shouted to the bartender.

✦

"The government of Tzenketh is accusing us of spying on them," Admiral Sulu said. "They say they've captured a Federation insertion team, and that they're going to execute them."

"*Are* we spying on them?" It was an obvious question, though it seemed to catch Admiral Sulu off guard. She was tightly framed on the viewscreen in my quarters, and I noticed that she glanced away; there must be someone else in her office. She quickly looked back at me.

"Whoever they have captured are not Federation spies," she said. She hadn't quite answered the question, but there was no need for me to pursue it.

"We need you to go there immediately, Jean-Luc. They've specifically asked for *Stargazer* to parlay for their release."

"Really? Do we know why?"

"*Stargazer* made first contact ten years ago, that might have something to do with it. Check your former captain's logs. But above all, you need to get those hostages out safely."

"I understand, Admiral."

"I'm not sure you do," she said. "You've got to get them out *with* the permission of the Tzenkethi government. No rescues—we need to keep the peace."

"Yes, Admiral," I said, and then we signed off. I called the bridge and ordered Walker to set a course for Tzenketh, while I stayed in my quarters and did some research.

Captain Laughton's logs contained some information on the Tzenkethi, all of which was now part of the Federation database. They had an unusual appearance for bipeds: they had four arms—two for strength and two smaller ones for more meticulous work. Their skin resembled a rhinoceros hide and their heads were similar to that of a hadrosaur, with a large duckbill sweeping back behind them. They were fierce creatures who had managed to venture out into space and achieved warp drive shortly before *Stargazer*'s encounter with them. But on the subject of the events of the actual first contact, Laughton's logs were disappointingly sparse. There were no clues as to why the Tzenkethi would ask for the *Stargazer*.

I went to the bridge and informed the command crew of our mission. We were still an hour away from the Tzenkethi system when Crusher picked up three of their ships closing in on our position.

"Their speed is warp 6," he said. I turned to Walker.

"When *Stargazer* discovered them ten years ago, they were only capable of warp 2," I said. I'd just read that in Laughton's log.

"Maybe we *should* be spying," Walker said.

"Captain," Cheva said, "they're locking weapons. Looks like they've got disruptor cannons…"

"Shields up," I said.

"Their ships had projectile weapons back then, too," Walker said.

"Curiouser and curiouser," I said. I got a strange look from Crusher. "It's from *Alice in Wonderland*." His expression told me he'd never heard of it.

THE STORY OF ONE OF STARFLEET'S MOST INSPIRATIONAL CAPTAINS

"Receiving a message, sir," Black said. "Audio only. They're ordering us to follow them to orbit."

"Acknowledge the message," I said. "Crusher, follow them in. Lieutenant Cheva, conduct a discreet scan of those ships. I want as much information as you can get."

We followed the ships into a standard orbit, and I was almost immediately talking to the leader of their world, called the Autarch, named Sulick. His large head nearly filled the viewscreen. He wore a gold helmet that fit over the duckbill on top of his skull. The image was both frightening and comical.

"We have your spies, Federation," Sulick said.

"I can assure you, Autarch Sulick, they are not spies."

"They were digging a secret base to carry out attacks on us. They thought by choosing a forgotten part of our land we wouldn't detect them." Digging a base? This didn't provide me any clues as to who the prisoners might be.

"What did they say they were doing when you caught them?"

"Their lies matter not," Sulick said. I had to cut to the meat of things.

"Sulick, what can I do to secure their release?"

"We will trade the spies for Laughton," Sulick said. I exchanged a look with Walker. That's why they asked for *Stargazer*, and they didn't know that Laughton was dead.

"Why do you want Laughton?"

"I was commander of the ship that met Laughton when he was here. He will know why I want him," Sulick said. "Once he is here, you may have your hostages."

"And if Laughton cannot come to you?"

"Then they are dead."

"I will get back to you shortly." I gave Black the cut sign, and Sulick disappeared from the screen.

"You can't lie to them," Walker said.

"I know," I said. "But if I tell the truth, that Laughton's dead, there's a good chance they'll think I'm lying and kill whoever it is they have down there." I needed more information about what happened when the *Stargazer* visited the first time. It was then I remembered that there was one crewmember on board who might be able to fill in some of the blanks. I ordered Scully to come to the bridge.

"Stupid, mean creatures," Scully said. "How they ever got into space is beyond me. Their ship was two hundred years behind ours, but they came at us guns blazing."

"What did the captain do?" I said.

"Laughed at 'em," Scully said. "He let them fire off all their projectile weapons, and once they bounced off our shields, he figured they'd be more willing to talk."

"Were they?" I said. Scully laughed.

"Nope," Scully said. "So the captain decided to have a little fun with them. He locked onto the ship with a tractor beam and took it for a ride. See, their ships were maybe capable of warp 2—that day they broke the warp 5 barrier." It was unlikely that a primitive warp ship could internally handle that speed; the crew was undoubtedly bounced around, if not worse. I'd come to accept that Laughton lived by a different set of rules than most starship captains yet was also always surprised how far he'd taken things.

"Fun with them?" Walker said. "He completely humiliated them."

"And unlucky for us, the captain of that ship is now in charge," I said. There was a lot going on here: hostages being accused as spies, a considerable technological leap by a hostile species, and a mess left by my predecessor. It seemed an unwinnable situation. And then a thought occurred to me.

"Cheva, what's their sensor capability?"

"Not as advanced as ours," she said. "They can detect life signs and species. Roughly equivalent to our 22nd-century technology." That was what I needed to hear.

"Poker faces everyone," I said. "Black, open a hailing frequency." Sulick was back on the screen.

"Well, human, what is your decision?"

"Captain Laughton has agreed to turn himself over to you," I said. "In exchange for the hostages." Despite my order that everyone put on their poker faces, Walker glanced at me with some surprise. Fortunately, I don't think the Tzenkethi had the ability to read human expressions.

"Very well," Sulick said. "Have him use your transporter to beam down, then we will give you coordinates—"

"I'm afraid we need a little more of a guarantee," I said. "So Captain Laughton will board one of our shuttlecraft and leave the *Stargazer*. Once he does, you must give us the coordinates for the hostages, or he will return to the ship." I saw Sulick consider this proposal.

"Agreed," Sulick said. I had Black cut off the transmission, and briefed everyone on my plan.

Thirty minutes later, we watched a shuttlecraft leave the hangar deck and hold station a few hundred meters from *Stargazer*.

"*Shuttlecraft Tyson* to *Stargazer*, I've cleared the hangar deck." It was Laughton's voice on the intercom; it was a simple program Crusher had put into the shuttle's main computer. It duplicated Laughton's voice and gave programmed responses. There was also a transmitter on board that was fooling the Tzenkethi sensor into believing they detected a human male at the helm. Cheva reported that the Tzenkethi were scanning the shuttlecraft.

"Acknowledged," I said. "Tzenkethi vessel, transmit the hostage coordinates." There was a pause, and then Black nodded that he'd received the transmission. I had him send the coordinates to the transporter room. A short time later, Scully called from there to report the hostages were aboard.

"*Stargazer* to shuttlecraft *Tyson*," I said. "The hostages have been recovered."

"Acknowledged," Laughton's voice said.

The shuttle started to move toward the lead Tzenkethi ship, and then suddenly took a sharp turn away.

"*Shuttlecraft Tyson*," I said, "return to your course immediately, acknowledge." Then for a little more drama, "Acknowledge, damn you!" I watched as the Tzenkethi craft moved in pursuit of the shuttle, and had Black turn off the speaker.

"Make it look good, Mr. Crusher," I said. Crusher nodded. He had control of the shuttle from his console, and put the shuttle through a series of evasive maneuvers, eventually taking it out of orbit. I signaled Black to put me back on hailing frequency.

"Laughton, you'll never make it!" After Black cut me off again, I turned to Walker. "Too much?"

"We're about to see..." he said. We watched the screen as the Tzenkethi ship fired on the shuttle. It was destroyed in a single blast. After what I determined to be a pause that would convey confusion on my ship, I had Black connect us. Sulick came back on the screen.

"Sulick, I must protest this attack," I said.

"We have what we wanted, Picard," he said. "And you have what you wanted. Now withdraw." He disappeared from the screen. I smiled at my crew. "Well done, everyone. Mr. Crusher, set a course for Starbase 32."

I left the bridge to find out who the hostages were. I was very proud of myself. I'd pulled off a clever ruse that had saved innocent lives and done it with a bit of flare, like my heroes had done before me. I was becoming the kind of captain I wanted to be.

I found the hostages in sickbay, getting a physical from Ailat, and was in for another surprise.

"Mr. Picard," Professor Galen said. He was sitting on a diagnostic bed as Ailat scanned him with a medical tricorder. Three other people were there, one Vulcan female and two human men, all much younger than him.

"Professor Galen," I said. "It's a pleasure to see you." I offered a warm handshake; his response was cold and perfunctory.

"I suppose we have you to thank for our lives," he said. There was no gratitude in his voice.

"Yes," I said. I was about to tell him how we'd done it, but could see he wasn't interested, so I decided instead to satisfy my own curiosity. "What were you doing on Tzenketh?"

"During my Dinasian dig, I discovered an ancient text with a star map that, once I compensated for stellar drift, led to Tzenketh. There was an Iconian base on this planet. My team and I would have found it before we were captured by the natives."

"Did you ask for permission…?"

"Permission? For what? I wasn't coming to steal anything; I would've shared everything I discovered. I'm not Starfleet, barging in with phasers blasting." That last remark was directed at me. I realized that when I had turned down his offer all those years ago, though he hadn't shown any resentment over my decision, it was clear it had been there.

"Well," I said, "I'm glad you're all right. We'll do our best to make you comfortable while you're here."

"Thank you, Mr. Picard." I wanted to tell him it was Captain Picard but decided against it. I nodded and walked out, leaving him, and that piece of my past, behind.

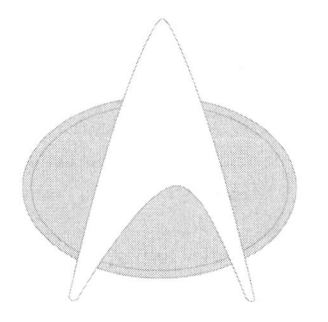

CHAPTER SIX

"MOTHER IS VERY ILL," ROBERT SAID. "She may die soon."

He stared at me from the viewscreen, locked up with grief. I was in shock. She was only 68.

"What's happened?" I stared at Robert. Hard physical labor in the sunlight had caused him to age quite a bit in the fifteen years since I'd left Earth.

"Something called Irumodic Syndrome," he said. "She hasn't been herself for some time. You wouldn't know that, of course." Though his physical appearance was different, his bitterness toward me had not diminished. I also felt a pang of guilt; I had been diligent in staying in contact with Mother, but the last few months had been busy and I hadn't spoken to her.

"Fortunately, we are on our way back," I said. "I should be there in a few days."

"Very convenient for you," he said.

"How is Father?"

"How do you think? His wife is dying." I saw now that Robert had no interest in talking to me, but that familial obligation required that he call to tell me of our mother's condition. I decided to put him out of his misery.

"I will let you know when I achieve orbit," I said. "Please update me if her condition worsens." Robert nodded and the transmission ended. I then called Dr. Ailat, and asked her what she knew about Irumodic Syndrome.

"It is a neurological disorder," Ailat said. "It can have varying symptoms as it deteriorates the synaptic pathways."

"Is it always fatal?"

"Yes, though there are many cases where humans survive for many years with it. Do you know someone who has it?"

"Yes," I said, but decided not to reveal my personal reasons for asking, and signed off. I went to the bridge.

"Status?"

"On course, Captain," Walker said, "Holding at warp 6, ETA to the Sol system in 97.1 hours."

"Increase speed to warp 8," I said. Walker stared at me briefly, then gave the order. Nine years as my first officer, he knew me well enough not to ask why Robert had called, and why we were increasing speed.

Almost a decade of exploration, and we were finally heading back to Earth. The *Stargazer* under my command had been a success, and we'd been ordered home, though I wasn't exactly sure why. The ship would be in dry dock for several weeks to finally receive upgrades that had been put off since the day I took over. My hope was that I would be moving on to a new ship. I loved the *Stargazer*—it held a special place as my first command—but I was also looking forward to piloting something that wasn't always on the verge of breaking down.

A day and a half later, as we passed Saturn's familiar rings, I was reminded how much I missed Earth. I'd seen many wonders out on the Galactic rim, but the familiar planets of our home solar system offered a strange kind of comfort.

"Passing Luna," Crusher said. We passed the moon, and Earth filled our view. There was an audible sigh from the bridge crew. Home.

Spacedock gave us clearance, and we entered the huge bay. Inside, I saw something that made me gape with envy.

"Will you look at that," Black said.

"That's the *Horatio*," I said. "*Ambassador*-class vessel, fresh off the assembly line." The clean blue lines, grand saucer, and sleek engines made the *Stargazer* look like the jalopy it was. I secretly hoped that I'd be offered command of that ship.

We docked at the bay, and I knew that everyone who had relatives on Earth were anxious to disembark—given Earth's centrality in the Federation, this went for many of the non-human crew as well. Once all the ship's systems were shut down, I granted everyone but a skeleton crew shore leave.

Before he left, Walker asked to see me in private.

Top: Jean-Luc at 7 with his brother Robert, age 10.
A rare pleasant shot of Robert, who was enjoying the new gift of a toy spaceship.
Bottom: Picard with Jack Crusher, shortly after Crusher was promoted to First Officer of the *Stargazer*.

Picard upon graduating from Starfleet Academy.

Top: The *U.S.S. Stargazer*, Picard's ship for over 20 years.
Bottom: The command crew of the *U.S.S. Enterprise, 1701-D*.
Clockwise from upper left: Worf, Geordi LaForge, William Riker, Picard, Deanna Troi, Beverley Crusher, Data.

This picture was found in 1962 among the personal letters of Samuel Clemens bequeathed to the University of California/Berkley. Picard would remain unidentified by historians for over 400 years. The inscription from Picard reads: "A great man once said 'Truth is stranger than fiction, but it is because fiction is obliged to stick to possibilities. Truth isn't.' Thanks for the possibilities! J.L.P." In quoting Clemens himself, Picard created a conundrum: He met Clemens in 1893, four years before Clemens would publish that quote.

An unused poster created by Commander Data for Picard's lectures on his experiences on Kataan.
Data suggested hanging them in the corridors, but Picard denied him permission.

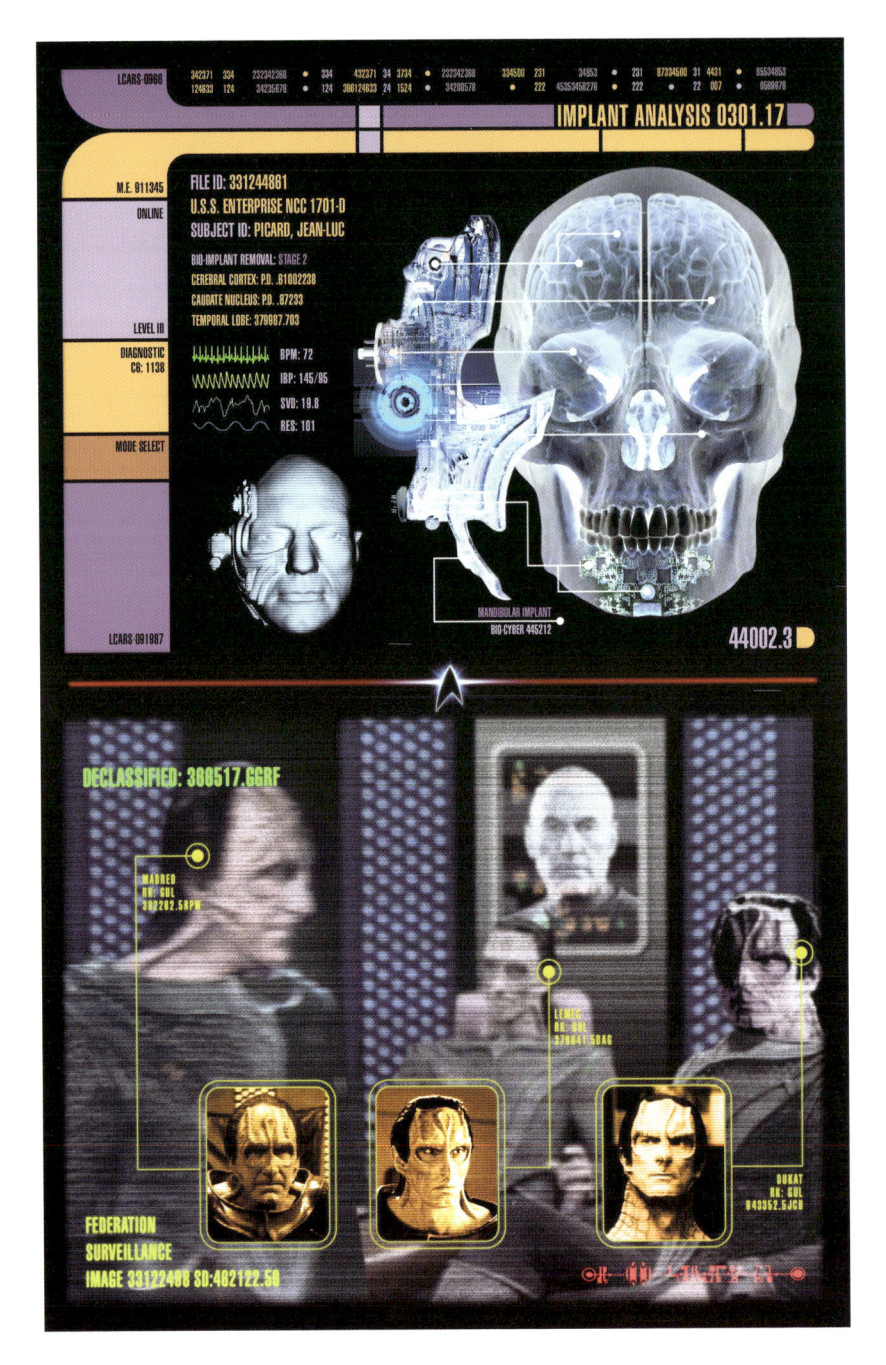

Top: A scan Beverly Crusher took of Picard's skull when he was assimilated by the Borg.
Bottom: Part of a transmission obtained by Starfleet Intelligence of three Cardassians: Gul Madred, Gul Lemec and Gul Dukat, discussing Picard, shortly before his capture and torture at the hands of Madred.

Captain Beverly Crusher, M.D.
Starfleet
and
Captain Jean-Luc Picard
Starfleet (Retired)

Request the pleasure & honor
of your company at their wedding

Saturday, October 8, 2383
Picard Family Vineyard
LaBarre, France
Seven o'clock in the evening
Reception to follow

The betrothed respectfully request no gifts

Picard and Beverly Crusher's wedding invitation.

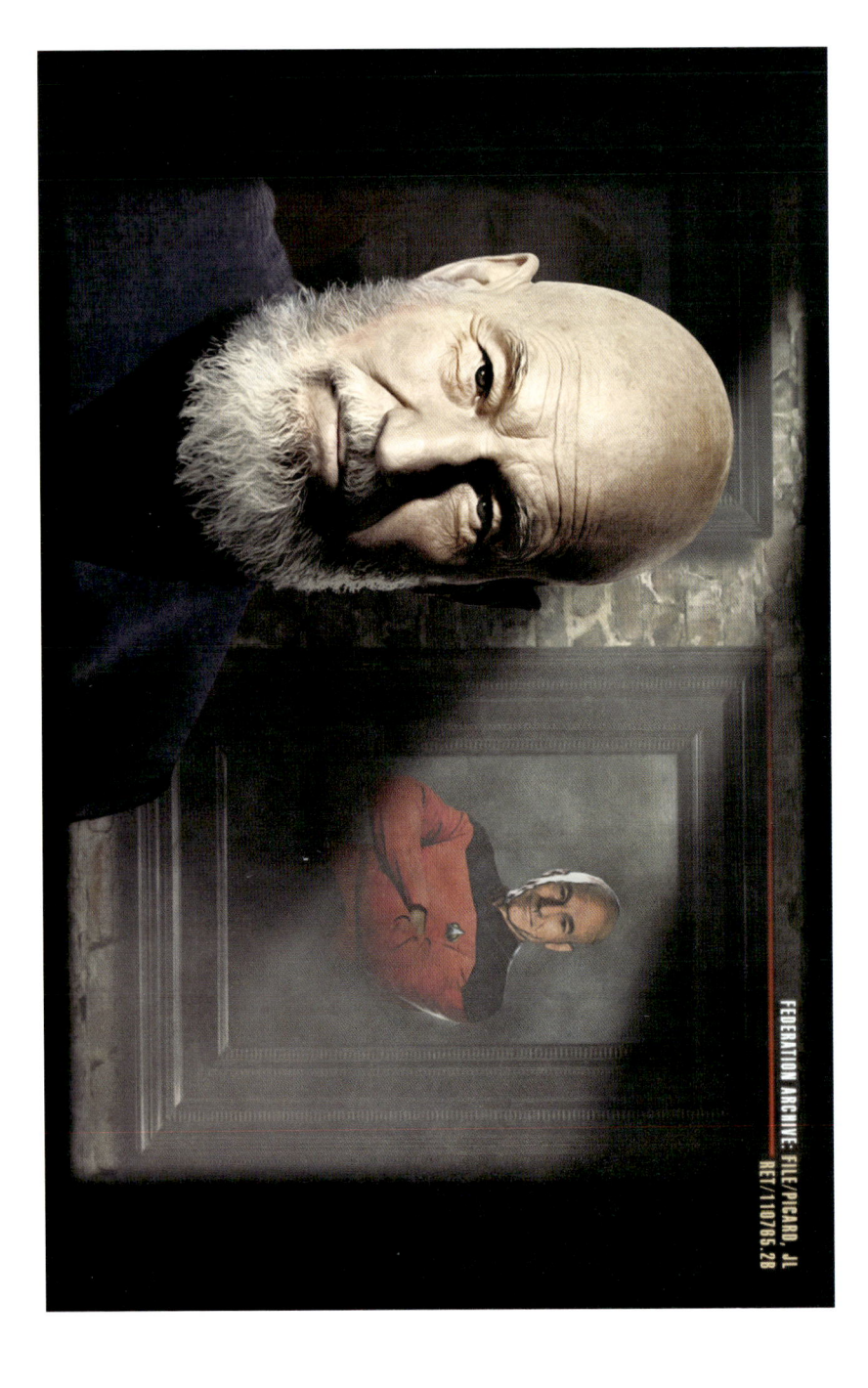

A recent photo of Picard in front of his portrait in the gallery beneath his home.

"I'm leaving the *Stargazer*," he said. "I've been offered a ship." He was sitting across from me in my quarters, and I was thrilled. I hadn't actually told him my plans, since I didn't know what they were, but there was no doubt in my mind that Walker deserved his own command.

"Wonderful," I said. "What ship?"

"The *Horatio*," he said. The shock must've registered on my face, and he reacted to it. "You don't think I deserve it?"

"No," I said. "Of course you do. I'll be honest, I'm envious." I was having trouble processing this; if the newest ship off the assembly line was going to my first officer, what ship would I get?

"When are you due to leave?"

"I haven't even begun to put the crew together, so I'll be here for a while," Walker said. "I won't poach anyone from *Stargazer* without checking with you first."

"Thanks," I said. "If I have to come back to this bucket, I'm going to need all the help I can get."

"I wouldn't worry. They must have big plans for you," Walker said. I supposed he was right, but given that he'd just gotten what I wanted, I couldn't imagine what those plans could be. "Now, how about joining me and Jack for a drink? There's a woman I'm going to introduce him to."

"No, thanks," I said. "I'd better get home."

I had just enough time to get to the vineyard and see my mother; the next morning I had an appointment with Admiral Hanson, who'd been promoted the year before and put in charge of Starfleet Operations. I assumed he would be giving me a new assignment.

Beaming into the La Barre station was not the sentimental experience I thought it might be. It was night in France, and as I approached the vineyard I was overcome with dread. Somehow my fifteen years out in space, all those experiences, adventures, and the maturing that came with them—or that I thought came with them—were wiped away. I was a child again.

By the time I reached the house it was one o' clock; all the lights were off except one downstairs. I entered as quietly as I could.

"You look tense, Jean-Luc," my mother said. I turned and saw her in the living room. She was fully dressed, in a bright purple and silver blouse, wearing silver earrings, her ghostly white hair perfectly coiffed up.

"Maman," I said. It was a strange tableau: one lamp on, her sitting at a table with a silver tea set.

"Come and have a cup of tea. I'll make it good and strong the way you like it. We can have a nice, long talk." She started to pour some tea into a cup. I walked over and gave her a kiss.

"Maman," I said, "how are you feeling?"

"Oh, I'm fine," she said. "Now, tell me about school."

"School?"

"Yes, school is very important to your future…" I'd read about the confusion this disease caused, but I didn't expect it. I was at a loss as to what to say.

"He's not in school," my father said. He was in his dressing gown, standing in the hallway. He looked exhausted, but I don't think he'd been asleep. "Yvette, what are you doing up?"

"I wanted to have some tea with Jean-Luc when he came home from school."

"I just said, he's not in school anymore." Father was very aggravated, impatient with what must have been a tragic situation for him. "He's a grown man."

"I know, you don't have to tell me," mother said, but her voice wavered. Then it looked like she'd started to remember. "You were in space."

"Yes, Maman," I said.

"You're the pilot… you always wanted to be the pilot…"

"Come to bed," Father said.

"I'm having tea with Jean-Luc…"

"I said come to bed!"

"We'll have tea in the morning, Maman," I said. I helped her to her feet, and my father took her hand and walked her out of the room. I sat alone in the room.

Nothing I'd seen in my years of command prepared me for this.

✦

I slept in my childhood room that night, unchanged since my departure for the academy. When I woke the next morning, I looked over my spaceship collection, and the carefully repaired NX-01, still there among the rest. I picked up a *Constellation*-class ship I'd built when I was nine, identical to the vessel

THE STORY OF ONE OF STARFLEET'S MOST INSPIRATIONAL CAPTAINS

I'd been commanding for almost a decade. I had been living the dreams of my childhood, dreams that I had used to escape the unhappiness of my years in my father's house. And now I'd come home to an even harsher reality: the one person who I knew loved me was fading away.

I dressed in my uniform and went out into the kitchen to find my father and brother eating breakfast in silence.

"So, you're home," Robert said.

"Yes," I said. "Where's Mother?"

"Asleep," my father said. There was a baguette and a few wedges of cheese on a cutting board in front of them. I sat down and helped myself.

"That service of yours requires you wear a uniform to breakfast?" Robert said.

"I have to go to headquarters," I said. We continued to eat in silence. It was a strange experience. I hadn't seen either of them in 15 years. Even if there hadn't been a pall hanging over our home, they still would have had no interest in the life I had been leading. I certainly wasn't in a mood to share it.

"I'm going to request a leave of absence," I said. "I will be around more." Robert looked unaffected by this.

"Your mother will be pleased," my father said. I could forgive that he said this without the least bit of indication that it would please him as well.

"What do the doctors say about the progression of the illness?"

"It has progressed very quickly," Robert said. "They have not been optimistic." We ate in silence for a few more minutes, and then I got up.

"I will be home by dinner." Neither one said anything, and I left.

The problem with instantaneous travel by transporter on a planet is the time difference, so I arrived in San Francisco the night before, and had time to kill before my morning meeting with the Admiral. I wandered the city for a few hours, then headed to Starfleet Headquarters. Entering the Archer Building in my uniform, surrounded by members of my service, I was more at home than I had been at breakfast at home. I found my way to the top floor of the building, occupied by the offices of the Admiralty, where a yeoman escorted me to Admiral Hanson's office. When he saw me he practically bounded from the other side of his desk.

"Jean-Luc, get yourself in here," he said, shaking my hand. "How 'bout some coffee?" I said yes, and the yeoman brought in a tray with coffee and sandwiches. The admiral dismissed the yeoman and poured the coffee himself. I was a little taken aback by the attentiveness. It had all the warmth that had been missing from my own father.

"I've been keeping tabs on you," Hanson said, as he handed me a cup. "I'm just sorry you weren't able to serve under my command so I could take more credit for all your accomplishments."

"Thank you, sir," I said. "And congratulations on your promotion."

"Well, I enjoyed being in the center seat," Hanson said, "but they need me here. I probably don't have to tell you we're facing a potentially devastating conflict…"

"The Klingons?"

Hanson nodded.

"They've increased ship production two hundred and fifty percent, and we'd had some hope of negotiating a new, more far reaching Khitomer Accord*, but they're more interested in trying to surround us with enemies. Your work has given us valuable information. Aside from that incident with the planet-killer, we have a fair amount of circumstantial evidence that they're the ones arming the Tzenkethi. And they've reaffirmed their alliance with the Romulans. The Federation could be facing a war on three fronts."

"The Romulans don't know about the incident with the planet-killer?"

"Oh, they do," Hanson said. "The Klingons told them, said rogue elements in the Federation were responsible. We were never able to find more conclusive proof of Klingon involvement, so we couldn't counter their misinformation."

This was a troublesome turn of events. I had studied war my whole life but had not experienced it. War on a galactic scale could cost billions of lives. Even Earth itself might be threatened in such a conflict.

"How does Starfleet plan to deal with this situation?"

"You're going to find all that out soon enough," Hanson said. "You have a big role in this." I had come to the office with the purpose of asking for a leave of

---

*EDITOR'S NOTE: The First Khitomer Accords, signed in 2293, established peace between the Klingon Empire and the Federation. The Second Khitomer Accords established a permanent alliance between the two governments. As of 2342 (the year Picard is writing about) negotiations had not begun.

absence to spend some more time with my mother in what might be her final year, yet the obligations of service were pulling me in another direction.

"Yes, sir," I said. "Whatever you need." How could I ask the admiral to put my own priorities above those of the Federation? The answer was, I couldn't.

"Good," he said. "I want you to be my chief of staff."

"What?"

"You'll be stationed here, and help me whip the fleet into shape. We've got a lot of work to do, and I think your experience out there will be of immeasurable help. What do you say?" My head was a mass of confusion. Hanson was offering me a compelling opportunity, the chance to help prepare Starfleet and protect the entire Federation. This work could end up shaping the quadrant for the next two decades. It also meant that I could be home for my mother.

"Of course, sir," I said. "I'd be honored."

"Great," he said. "I'd like you to start as soon as possible."

"Yes, sir," I said. I knew that this was the moment I should let him know about my personal situation, but I could not bring myself to say the words. "I still have a few things to wrap up on the *Stargazer*."

"Yes, of course," he said. "Also, I understand your mother is facing some difficult challenges. Please send her my regards. I remember meeting her at your graduation. Lovely woman."

He really had been keeping tabs on me.

We said our goodbyes, and Hanson then had the yeoman show me my new office. It had a window with a stunning view of San Francisco. I could see the academy and the Golden Gate Bridge. I'd just spent fifteen years crammed into an outdated ship, and now I was literally on top of the world. Yet something at the edges of my mind gnawed at me. I didn't want to be a deskbound officer, I wanted a captaincy. But I consciously pushed these thoughts away. This is where it was decided I was needed. It implied respect and esteem, not just by Hanson but by Starfleet itself. Whatever my personal desires were, I tried to let this cascade of approval overwrite them.

I left the office, and had myself beamed up to *Stargazer*. There was, as typical when the old lady was in spacedock, a lot of maintenance work underway. On the bridge, I found Jack Crusher supervising all of it. As he took me through the repair and upgrade schedule, I realized I probably wouldn't be serving with him much longer. I would however make sure that Starfleet was aware that *Stargazer* had a good replacement for Walker as XO. When we finished, I decided to indulge my curiosity.

"I heard Walker fixed you up last night," I said. Crusher brightened.

"She's nova," Crusher said. "Medical student, really smart… beautiful." His expression revealed a lot more than his words.

"Not someone you'd meet in a bar," I said.

"Well, maybe," he said, "but not someone who'd go home with me if I was drunk." I laughed. It appeared Walker had hit the mark.

I took a short tour of the ship, and, satisfied that Crusher had things well in hand, told him to call me if there were any difficulties.

When I returned home, I had another surprise waiting for me. There was a woman in the kitchen I'd never seen before, cooking. She met me with a smile. She was fair-haired with blue eyes, a stunner in a plain dress and apron.

"You must be Jean-Luc," she said. Her hands were deeply involved in kneading dough, but she quickly wiped them off to shake mine. "I'm Jenice."

"I'm sorry," I said. "Do you work here?"

"Your father didn't tell you?" she said. I shook my head. "Oh, well, since your father and brother have to spend their days in the vineyard, they requested an aid from the Federation Health Service, who sent me. I've been helping take care of your mother."

"I see," I said. "Thank you."

"Have you had a chance to see her?"

"Yes, last night." She read my expression very well.

"She has good days and bad," Jenice said. "It's a very difficult time. She's sitting out back. I'm sure she'd love to see you." Jenice indicated the window in front of her, and I could see my mother in one of the wooden chairs that overlooked the vineyard in the back of the house. I thanked Jenice again and went outside.

Mother sat staring at the vineyard. She was in a heavy bathrobe, and her hair was ill kept. It was a stark contrast to the well-presented image she'd had the previous night. As I approached, she looked up at me.

"Hello, Maman," I said. She smiled at me.

"Hello," she said. I could see she was confused, but trying to hide it. Her "hello" had no recognition in it.

"I'm Jean-Luc," I said. She nodded, still smiling. I didn't know whether she didn't recognize me, or just didn't have the words. "I'm just going to sit here awhile, if that's all right?" She nodded, and looked back out at the vineyard. I sat in the chair next to her. She held her hand up, indicating the long stretch of vines.

"Look how pretty," she said.

"Yes," I said.

✦

She passed away two weeks later. There had been flashes of lucidity, but the disease progressed very rapidly, and in her last days she was lost in a private world none of us could see. We buried her in the local cemetery, in a plot surrounded by Picard ancestors. The service was small: my brother and father, Jenice, as well as Walker and Jack, whom I hadn't told about my mother's sickness but had managed to find out anyway. There were also a few people from the town who knew her, including my childhood friend Louis. My father said a few words: about how my mother would not have wanted us to fuss about her death, about what a strong person she was, and how much her sons meant to her.

Afterward, I thanked my friends for coming, said goodbye to them and Jenice, and went home with my father and Robert. When we arrived, my father went to his room. My brother and I exchanged few words, and then I suggested we open a bottle of wine. I thought we might find a way to speak about our loss, but the dialogue never came. We drank in silence.

A short time later, my father appeared. He'd changed into his work clothes.

"Come," he said to Robert, "we have things to do." Even Robert was surprised by this, but, after only a brief pause he stood up and went to change. My anger, however, boiled over.

"Do you really think it's appropriate," I said, "on the day of our mother's burial…"

"I don't expect you to do anything," he said. "Stay here and wallow in wine and self-pity…"

"I don't have to listen to this."

"No, you don't," he said. "Fly away on your toy spaceship, the men have work to do." He walked outside. Furious, I threw my wine glass and it shattered against the wall, the red juice dripping down to the floor.

I went to my room, packed my bag, and left without saying goodbye. I don't remember the walk to the transporter station, I was so engulfed in white-hot rage. There was a short line of people waiting to use the transporter pad, and I got in line to wait my turn.

"Jean-Luc," Jenice said. "What are you doing here?" She was standing right in front of me, but I'd been so lost in my fury I hadn't noticed her.

"I'm going back to San Francisco," I said.

"I see." She seemed to understand, which shouldn't have surprised me, since she'd spent time with my family. Her presence made me suddenly ashamed of my display of anger. I tried to hide what I was feeling in a forced gentility.

"Where are you headed?" I said.

"Home to Paris." I nodded. She stared at me, gave me an empathetic smile.

"Thank you… for everything you did," I said. The line of people in front of us had disappeared; it was now just the two of us waiting for the pad.

"I wish I'd known your mother longer," she said. "She was a lovely person." She placed her hand on my arm. The fugue of rage I was in dissipated, overcome by a wave of sorrow.

"Yes." I wanted to run past Jenice and get on the pad, escape before it overcame me.

"She loved you very much. You made her very proud," Jenice said. The ire I felt toward my father was spent, and all I could think about was my mother, and that she was gone. Tears welled; I wanted to say something else to try to fight it off, but I had no words. I soon found myself in Jenice's embrace, crying softly.

✦

I was in deep mourning, and I wouldn't leave it for several months. I tried to distract myself with work, and this would have a temporary effect, but being on Earth brought my mother to mind often. Eventually, the pain of her death became dulled, though there are still days where it comes back at me full force. She taught me more about compassion, love, and learning than any one person in my life, and I owe so much of who I am to her.

But as she went on in her life, I went on in mine. Though still grieving, I returned to San Francisco and forced myself to focus on my role as Hanson's chief of staff. He put me to work organizing fleet construction, trying to remove logjams that had slowed down new ships coming off the assembly line, and making sure that ships already in service were properly equipped for potential conflict. Hanson also tasked me with personnel recommendations for captain and first officer postings, with an eye to shoring up command teams with at least one command-level officer who had combat experience. Ironically, my first assignment in this area was finding my replacement for the *Stargazer*.

Despite the intensity of the work, I started to lead a very different life. The work days could be long, but it was nothing like being on *Stargazer*. When you're serving on a ship, you are always occupied; the life never allows you to truly relax. You lose some of your personal identity to your responsibility to the people you serve with. This is especially true when you're captain. The lives of the people under your command depend on you being fully attuned at all hours of the day and night.

So however busy life as Hanson's chief of staff was, I still found myself with time to relax. After a long day of work, I would often meet Jack Crusher and Walker Keel for drinks. I also began a relationship with Jenice, beaming over to Paris for dinner or a weekend. (Serving on ships, weekends are irrelevant.) The emotional vulnerability that I'd revealed to her opened me up to an intimacy I'd never had before. She and I became very close, very quickly. We spent many days and evenings together. It was unlike any connection I'd ever had with a woman. She was intelligent and lovely, and though our bond was still very new, the pull I felt toward her was compelling. I could easily lose myself to her.

I was having a good, happy life. And it was beginning to drive me mad.

It wasn't happening consciously, there were just snippets of annoyance over trivial things that I couldn't explain: restless sleep, slight indigestion, having to wait a moment too long for a transporter. The moment I became aware something was wrong was in a meeting with Admiral Hanson. The maintenance on *Stargazer* was almost complete, and I was going over my recommendation for my replacement.

"Edward Jellico has been first officer of the *Cairo* for five years," I said. "Relatively young for a captain, but an exemplary record. He would make a fine captain of the *Stargazer*."

"Milano won't like losing him," Hanson said, referring to Dan Milano, the captain of the *Cairo*.

"Captain Milano has forty years experience in command, and will undoubtedly be adept at training a replacement."

"You recommended Crusher for XO of the *Stargazer*," he said. "A good mix with Jellico?"

"I've never served with Jellico, but Crusher knows *Stargazer* almost as well as I do, and Jellico will need that expertise. I've also left him an experienced command crew."

"Okay, done. I'll recommend that Jellico gets *Stargazer* at the Admiralty meeting tomorrow," Hanson said. There was something about the finality of this that left me uneasy. Hanson read my expression, and smiled.

"Hard to give up your first girl to another guy," Hanson said. "Even if she isn't the prettiest one on the block."

"Yes, sir," I said. I smiled, but in truth his anachronistic, and rather offensive, metaphor did not make me feel better. I felt a great sense of loss, and it stayed with me the rest of the day.

That evening, as I routinely did, I met Jack and Walker for a drink in the 602 Club.* I told them about the new captain of the *Stargazer*. We all were a bit wistful.

"Hard to imagine the ship going on without you," Walker said.

"Jack'll have to carry the flag for the three of us," I said. I had another piece of news for Crusher. "And assuming the Admiralty approves Jellico, *Stargazer* could ship out as early as tomorrow."

"Is the *Cairo* here?" Crusher said.

"No, it's at Starbase 11," I said. "So, you have to take *Stargazer* and rendezvous with him there." I thought Jack would be thrilled at this news; though I'd left him in charge of the bridge from time to time, he'd never been in command for that length of voyage. His reaction, however, wasn't what I expected: he looked forlorn.

"I thought you'd be more excited," I said.

---

*__EDITOR'S NOTE:__ The 602 Club was a famous watering hole frequented by Starfleet officers since the 22nd century. It was unfortunately destroyed in 2375 during the Dominion war when the Breen attacked Earth.

THE STORY OF ONE OF STARFLEET'S MOST INSPIRATIONAL CAPTAINS

"No, I am," Jack said. "And I really appreciate what you've done, Jean-Luc... but I've got to go." He hurriedly finished his drink and left. Walker laughed.

"Our boy's in love," Walker said. "He didn't expect he'd have to say goodbye to Beverly so soon." I hadn't met Jack's girlfriend yet but he was clearly enraptured.

"Another drink?" I said, but Walker shook his head.

"I should probably get going, too. Still have some work to do tonight if *Horatio* is going to ship out on time." He left and I found myself alone in the bar, ignoring the other patrons. I was supposed to see Jenice the next afternoon in Paris and had the thought I could call her tonight. But instead, I just stared at the walls.

I wasn't staring at nothing. The walls of the 602 Club were adorned with pictures and souvenirs of past Starfleet heroism. Directly in front of me was a photo of A.G. Robinson, the first man to break the warp 2 barrier. To the left of that was the famous Captain Garth of Izar. On the right, two young captains, Matt Decker and Jose Mendez, who'd brought a superior Klingon force to a stalemate in the Battle of Donatu V. Looking at the past, I felt my future was slipping away.

"Can I get you something else?" The voice was familiar. I looked over and was surprised to see a new bartender on duty.

"Guinan," I said. "What... what are you..."

"I wanted to tend bar," she said. "They had an opening." I hadn't seen her in nine years, and she didn't look a day older.

"Finally started losing your hair," she said. My hair had been thinning lately, and this, again, seemed to be some kind of private joke between her and me, except I didn't know what it meant.

She had been living on Earth for over a year but was rather mysterious about how she'd come here or what she'd been doing in the intervening years. As she had done in the past, her listening skills effortlessly shifted the focus to me. I filled her in on what I'd been doing since coming to Earth. She looked at me with a slightly sardonic expression.

"What?" I said.

"Nothing," she said. "You sound very happy. Working in an office, helping out an admiral."

"It's a little more important than that," I said.

"Of course it is," she said. As she poured me another drink, she referenced a picture on the wall of a middle-aged Starfleet officer receiving a medal. "You know this guy?"

"Yes, of course," I said.

"To work here, you're supposed to memorize every picture. You know what he got the medal for?"

"Was it for bringing the humpback whale forward in time to save the Earth?"

"No," Guinan said, "I don't think he got a medal for that. I think this was when he saved the president's life at Camp Khitomer... or maybe it was after stopping the V'Ger probe..."

"Can't be," I said, "the uniforms were different then."

"You're right," she said. "Who knows, the guy did so much."

"I feel like you're trying to make a point," I said.

"I am? What point would that be?" I didn't answer her question, because it was obvious. I finished my drink and left the bar. Emboldened by alcohol, I decided to visit Admiral Hanson at home.

This was not a short trip; Admiral Hanson had his own personal transporter, so he could live anywhere in the world. He chose to live in a small home on Cape Kidnappers, on the east coast of New Zealand's North Island. It was daytime when I arrived there. A yeoman took me to the admiral, who was seated outside, overlooking the rocky coast and a beautiful blue ocean. When he saw me, he looked concerned.

"Jean-Luc? What's the matter?"

"Sorry to disturb you, Admiral," I said. "I was wondering if I could have a word." He looked at me curiously, then offered me the empty chair next to him, and dismissed the yeoman.

"What can I do for you?" Hanson said.

"I appreciate all you've done for me," I said, "but I'd like to return as captain of the *Stargazer*."

"Why?" He was clearly disappointed, but I couldn't say he looked surprised.

"I feel I can do more good out there."

"You're doing a lot of good down here," Hanson said. "You've already made yourself invaluable to me, and as Starfleet officers we unfortunately don't always get to choose our postings."

THE STORY OF ONE OF STARFLEET'S MOST INSPIRATIONAL CAPTAINS

"I know, sir," I said. "I can only make the request; if you decide not to grant it, I understand."

"If you wait just a little longer," Hanson said, "the *Melbourne* or the *Yamaguchi* will be off the assembly line, I'll make sure you get one of those. That way I'd get a few more months out of you." As attractive as a brand-new ship might be, they didn't interest me. I felt a need to *get out*.

"Yes, sir," I said, "but if it's important to have experienced captains out there now, the right choice is to put me back on *Stargazer*. The old lady is temperamental, and anyone else in that chair may not have time to get used to her before we need to put her in action."

Hanson considered me for a long while, then sighed. I knew he was worried about the situation with the Klingons, and my appeal went to the heart of those concerns. He wanted people he could rely on in positions of command. He looked out at the ocean. A flock of gannets flew over.

"Beautiful, isn't it?"

"Yes, sir," I said. "It's paradise."

"What we're trying to protect," he said.

I could see I'd made my point. Though I was making his job easier on Earth, he wouldn't let his own privileges get in the way of his commitment to the service.

"All right," Hanson said. "You ship out tomorrow."

"Thank you, sir," I said.

I left his home, momentarily pleased. This was what I wanted, to be out on the edge, in charge, and participating in the making of history. I still had this overwhelming desire to make my mark, and being the captain of a ship, even an old tin can like the *Stargazer*, fulfilled that desire.

The only remaining problem, of course, was Jenice. My desire to get back on a ship right away was fueled in part by my fear that saying goodbye to her would only become more difficult, if not impossible. Right then, I thought I could walk away; a few more weeks, I wasn't sure. We were set to meet at the Café des Artistes in Paris the very next day. I would tell her then. It would be a difficult parting, but I knew it was best for me. If I didn't say goodbye then, I might never.

✦

"Captain on the bridge," Commander Black said, as I walked on.

It was the next morning, and Black had received my transfer of command order, so by the time I beamed up the whole crew knew. I'd gotten warm greetings and handshakes all the way from the transporter room to the bridge.

Crusher was there at the conn, Cheva was at ops. Vigo, who'd been down in the torpedo room, was now the bridge weapons and security officer, and Scully was at the engineering console. And though I'd skipped over Black again to be first officer, I'd gotten him a grade promotion, and he seemed happy to stay.

As I stepped off the turbolift, they all applauded, and I couldn't help but laugh. I looked around; the maintenance the ship had undergone had breathed new life into it. Or maybe I was seeing it with new eyes, I didn't know.

"Status report, Number One," I said.

"Dock command has signaled we're clear for departure," Crusher said. "All stations report ready." This caught me a little by surprise. I was supposed to meet Jenice at noon in Paris; it was ten o'clock Paris time then. I could have delayed our departure three hours. No one would know why or even question it.

I was going to order a delay, and stopped myself. I pictured seeing her, saying goodbye. She would understand, she'd let me go. I had to go see her, but if I did…

"Orders, sir?" Crusher said.

I was at war with myself. I felt a pull, a need, to delay our departure so I could go see Jenice. And, in that moment, I was overcome with a new perspective: I thought I wanted to be back here, on this bridge, but Jenice's smile, her eyes, her presence in my mind diminished the desire for this ship to a shadow. We'd only just started our romance, but Jenice embodied love, affection, and desire. This machine, the "old lady," couldn't compete. If I went to see her, Jenice might let me go, but I was suddenly unsure, face to face, that I could leave her.

"Stand by to depart," I said. I couldn't say goodbye. I wanted my career. I was a coward.

✦

"The raiders came in the middle of the night," Governor Harriman said. "They were in a small scout ship. They wore armor…"

"Take your time," I said. He was lying on a cot in the infirmary on Hakton VII.

About 80 years old, he'd been the governor since its founding a decade before. Dr. Ailat tended to a gash on his forehead, as other members of the *Stargazer*'s medical team worked with colony doctors administering care to the rest of the patients, victims of a recent attack by persons unknown.

"They were very aggressive," Harriman said.

"They weren't Klingons," I said.

Harriman shook his head. "They were more civilized in one way, but there was an arrogance about them," he said. "They landed, we went to greet them, and they came out firing. I immediately surrendered; they were better armed than we were. They rounded up most of us, picking just a few to load equipment into their ship. And then they left."

"You acted properly," I said. "You probably saved a lot of lives by cooperating."

"I hope so, because it just felt like cowardice."

I tried to look reassuring, then excused myself and went outside. The infirmary was in the center of the colony. The colony itself was an orderly collection of single-story buildings made of stone in a unified architectural style, designed to coexist with the natural surroundings.

We'd received the distress call less than an hour before. Fortunately, we were already on our way to Hakton VII, delivering supplies from Starbase 32. But we hadn't made it in time to stop the raid. I was immediately met by Cheva and Vigo, returning from their scout of the area.

"I examined the blast marks from their weapons," Vigo said. "Some kind of disruptor."

"What did they steal?"

"That's the strange thing," Cheva said. "They didn't take any of the colony's weapons, they were only interested in replicators." The jigsaw was slowly coming together in my head when Crusher called from the ship.

"*Stargazer* to Picard," he said. "I've picked up an ionization trail. We can track that ship."

"Beam everyone up but the medical team," I said. "Go to red alert."

We were lucky: the small scout vessel was slower than *Stargazer*, and it didn't take long before we were closing in on them. The unmarked ship's hammerhead design was very similar to one I'd seen before. I had Black open a hailing frequency.

"This is Captain Jean-Luc Picard, of the Federation ship *Stargazer*. We are investigating an attack on the Federation colony on Hakton VII. Please secure from warp drive…"

I was cut off as the ship rocked, the result of an impact by a torpedo on our shields.

"Vigo, report on their weapons," I said.

"Standard photon torpedo," Vigo said. "We can take 'em, sir."

"Lock phasers," I said. "Target their engines and weapons." Vigo complied and the *Stargazer* fired on the unknown ship.

"Sensors report we've knocked out their torpedo launcher," Cheva said. "But they haven't slowed down."

"Reading an overload building in their warp reactor," Crusher said. "We damaged them, but they're trying to ignore it." I checked the scan of the ship; its reactor was reaching critical mass.

"Transporter Room, lock onto that ship, and beam—"

I was cut off again, this time by the ship exploding. Whatever their mission was, they didn't want to get caught. I had Crusher extrapolate their destination based on the course they were on, and ordered him to stay on that course. I thought that perhaps by finding their destination, we might gather some clue as to their purpose.

We soon found ourselves entering an uncharted system with fourteen planets. The raider's course led us to the largest one, the eleventh planet—a Class-M world. Sensors showed an extensive and ancient humanoid civilization. A formidable-looking space station was in orbit. It was a strange design, dark, almost skeletal, like a giant incomplete gyroscope. Arms curved up and down from the hub of the station, where spaceships were docked.

"That station is heavily armed," Vigo said. "Photon torpedoes, disruptor cannons, some other weapons I can't identify. And their shields just went up."

"I'm also detecting a lot of active machinery," Cheva said. "Some kind of ore refinery operating there."

"We're being hailed," Black said.

"On screen," I said. A member of a species I'd met only once before appeared on the viewscreen. He gave me a smile that I can only describe as malevolent.

"Unidentified ship," he said. "I am Gul Dukat, commander of the station Terok Nor, and Cardassian prefect of Bajor. Please state the nature of your business."

"Captain Jean-Luc Picard, Federation ship *Stargazer*. We were pursuing raiders who attacked one of our colonies. They were heading to this system."

"Really? How terrible," Dukat said, with oily sincerity. "And what happened to the raiders?"

"Their ship was destroyed," I said. I decided to be as vague as possible regarding my role in the ship's destruction. Dukat, however, could see through my deception.

"Well, whoever they were," he said, "I'm sure they won't be missed."

"So you can't provide us with any information about them?"

"I'm afraid not. As governor of this system, I have much more important things to concern myself with."

"Forgive my ignorance," I said. "We've never visited this system before. You said it was called… Bajor?"

"Yes," Dukat said. "It is a protectorate of the Cardassian empire. We defend the peaceful Bajorans from a hostile universe, and in exchange we only ask for a modest payment from their abundant planetary resources. It is an equitable exchange." Though he wasn't being explicit, I felt Dukat's meaning was clear: they had enslaved the Bajorans, and they didn't plan to stop there.

"We are explorers," I said. "We would enjoy the opportunity to perhaps learn more about the Cardassian–Bajoran relationship."

"As I mentioned," Dukat said, "I'm quite busy. Perhaps another time. But if you do return, I will happily demonstrate how we protect Bajor from unwanted intruders."

Cheva reacted to something on her board, and she leaned in to me. "Sir," she said, "they've locked weapons on us." I knew *Stargazer* would not last long in a battle with that station, and Dukat knew it too.

"Well," I said, "thank you for your time." Dukat smiled that terrible smile, and his face disappeared from the viewscreen. I had Crusher set a course out of the system, back to Hakton VII, to pick up our medical personnel.

"He was lying," Crusher said, very matter-of-factly. "He probably ordered the raid."

"Yes, but why?" Cheva said.

I asked Cheva to give me the inventory of what had been stolen from the colony. "They want a replicator," I said. I referenced the list of stolen items. "They ripped three replicators out of the walls of several structures, leaving potentially more valuable technology alone."

"This is a dangerous situation," Crusher said. "They want that technology and are willing to sacrifice the lives of their own soldiers to steal it."

"Why don't they just ask us to trade for it?" Vigo said.

"A sign of weakness," I said. "They wouldn't want to reveal their position to a potential adversary."

"And I bet they think they could get more by just taking it," Crusher said.

As we went on our way, I realized Starfleet had a lot more to worry about than the Klingons.

✦

It was in 2346, two years into returning as captain of the *Stargazer*, and I began to understand why "you can't go home again" is an enduring cliché. I was happy to be back but it wasn't nearly the same. Many of my officers remained, but they had all grown over time. I also came to the captain's chair with more experience and a little less wonder and enthusiasm. And of course, Walker Keel was gone. I still had my friendship with Jack Crusher, but he had also changed. He'd taken to the responsibilities of first officer very naturally and his boyish eagerness was gone. In fact, he was often quiet, and sometimes even despondent. I had been blind to the cause, so I asked him about it.

"Oh, sorry, Captain," he said, one day at lunch. "I'm just a lovesick fool." His relationship had gotten very serious, and since we'd left Earth almost two years before, he'd only seen her by subspace communication. She was a student in the Starfleet medical program. Because of the separation caused by their respective careers, they had been having discussions about the reality of the future of their relationship. It would be years before they could be together, and that was only if they were posted to the same ship.

"How many years at the academy does she have left?"

"Two," Crusher said, "and then another four of medical school." Starfleet Medical Training had become that much more complicated as more and more species fell into the Federation's sphere of influence. A Starfleet doctor had to have working knowledge of the physiologies of hundreds of species, and an even larger number of medical ailments. I couldn't do anything about the medical training, but the academy education was another matter.

"What if Beverly completed her academy years aboard the *Stargazer*?"

"Really? Could we get approval for that?"

"I would think so," I said. "As first officer, it would be your job to make sure she completed the curriculum. And if she worked in sickbay I would imagine she might be able to gain medical credit as well."

"Jean-Luc... are you sure?"

"Absolutely," I said. "Though I have to insist on separate cabins until you're married."

Crusher laughed. "Thank you."

"Don't thank me yet," I said. "We're not due to go back to Earth for some time; you'll have to figure out some way to get her out to us."

"That," Crusher said, "I can handle."

He was a man determined. We shortly received orders to rendezvous with a squadron near the Federation–Klingon Neutral Zone, and Crusher found out that one ship assigned to the squadron, the *Hood*, was coming from Earth. He was able to not only get approval for Beverly to complete her academy degree aboard the *Stargazer*, he also got her passage aboard the *Hood* within three hours of the ship's departure from Earth. Watching Jack receive the news that Beverly was winging her way to him, I saw some of his youthful zeal return.

When we reached the rendezvous, ten ships had gathered, and I had to face some of my own decisions. Among the ships were the *Melbourne* and the *Yamaguchi*, still relatively new, both of which had been offered to me by Hanson. The *Stargazer*, twelve years after I'd taken command of her, was worse off than ever, and, as I looked at the clean lines and powerful grace of those new ships, I had to wonder what it would've been like if I'd had a little more patience.

The lead ship, the *U.S.S. Ambassador*, signaled for me and my first officer to beam over immediately. Crusher and I headed to the transporter room, and when we arrived, Transporter Chief Youlin informed me that someone was beaming over from the *Hood*. A woman materialized on the transporter pad, and it appeared that Crusher was embracing her before the process was even complete. She had red hair; the rest of her face was momentarily obscured as they were locked in a passionate kiss. I exchanged an awkward glance with Youlin, who stifled a laugh. I finally cleared my throat, and Crusher broke from his embrace.

"Captain Jean-Luc Picard," Crusher said, still quite flushed, "may I introduce Cadet Beverly Howard." She smiled and gently pulled her hand from Crusher's, who hadn't realized he was holding it.

"An honor to meet you, Captain," Beverly said.

"Welcome aboard, Cadet," I said. "Unfortunately, Mr. Crusher and I are late for a meeting." She quickly stepped off the transporter platform, and as Crusher and I beamed off the ship, she blew him a kiss.

✦

The captains of the squadron and their execs gathered in the enviably spacious conference room of the *Ambassador*, which easily held us all. Out of the large view ports we could see all the ships lined up aft of the lead ship. *Stargazer* was the runt of the litter. I knew most of the men and women in the room, if not personally, then from my work as Hanson's chief of staff. Only two were more than an acquaintance: Robert DeSoto, the friend I'd made on my first academy testing day, now captain of the *Hood*. He greeted me with a hearty "Bonjour, mon ami!"

The other friend was a lovely surprise: Marta Batanides. She had been promoted to captain of the *Kyushu*. We got to say a brief hello before the meeting. She gave me a hug, which made me a little self-conscious in such august company.

"It's been too long," she said. I studied her face: the youthful woman was still there, behind a touch of gray. She then leaned in closer to me. "I heard about your mother; I'm so sorry." I thanked her. I'd forgotten what a close friend she had been, and I wanted to talk to her more, but then we noticed our leader was at the table, and we all took our seats.

THE STORY OF ONE OF STARFLEET'S MOST INSPIRATIONAL CAPTAINS

We didn't need to be told to come to order, because no one in the room was as impressive as the person at the head of it: Andrea Brand, shipmaster of the *Ambassador*, the Federation flagship. Even without saying a word, she was a formidable presence.

"The Klingons are planning a surprise attack," Brand said. "We can't stop them, but we can track their ships." This statement was counter-intuitive: the Klingons still had cloaking devices, so their ships could gather in secret, within striking distance of their target, and we wouldn't be any the wiser until they launched their attack. But, as I looked at Captain Brand, I knew she must have the answer to such an obvious question.

She stood up and activated the viewscreen on the wall behind her. A star map appeared, and, at every star, groups of red markings.

"These symbols on the map represent every Klingon ship in existence," she said. "Starfleet Intelligence has kept close watch on Klingon ship movements and construction, and thanks to their diligence, we now have a complete inventory of their entire fleet, as well as each ship's current whereabouts."

There was a murmured response of disbelief.

"Captain Brand, how do we know they don't already have a mass of ships under cloak?" This came from Owen Paris, a few years ahead of me at the academy, and the captain of the *Al-Batani*.

"For the simple reason," Brand said, "that this project started over sixty years ago. After the first Khitomer Accords allowed Klingons access to Federation space, Starfleet Intelligence began a clandestine cataloguing initiative, monitoring individual ship movements as well as construction projects." It was so simple, and yet brilliant: even if the Klingons knew we were monitoring them, a Klingon ship couldn't stay under cloak that long. Eventually it would appear and be tracked.

Brand continued, pointing out an area along the Klingon–Federation border.

"As you can see, they've concentrated the bulk of their ships in this area, in easy striking distance to Starbase 24 and Starbase 343." It would be the right move to attack those bases, since they were the closest Federation outposts to Klingon space. If they were destroyed, it would limit Starfleet's ability to repair and resupply ships in an extended conflict.

Brand then adjusted the controls under the viewscreen. Blue markings appeared on the map.

"Our plan is simple," Brand said. "Each of your ships will proceed to a preassigned route. Using long-range sensors, and without crossing the border, you will surreptitiously monitor the Klingon ships on your patrol station. If you lose contact with any of them, we will assume they've cloaked, and you will report to the command ship immediately. Where they launch their ships from should give us some information as to what the Klingons plans are."

It was very clever. I must have been smiling.

"Something amusing, Captain Picard?" It was Brand; because I'd been lost in thought, I didn't notice her looking at me. I decided to be honest.

"Not at all, Captain," I said. "It's brilliant. It reminds me of a blockade from the age of sail, when a frigate would be assigned to keep enemy ships bottled up in harbor."

Now it was Brand's turn to smile.

"Can you tell me," Brand said, "the one problem with that comparison?"

"Sometimes the enemy ships slipped through," I said.

✦

The ten ships left the rendezvous and moved to their assigned routes. I regretted that I didn't have more time to spend with my friends, but duty called. Our patrol station was near the Federation outpost on Ajilon. We pretended we were on leisurely patrols, training all our sensors on the Klingon outposts on the other side of the border. *Stargazer* was responsible for monitoring twenty-five ships of various sizes. It was apparent to me that I'd been given what was considered a low-risk patrol sector; we were the furthest away of any of the ships from Starbase 24 or Starbase 343. If the Klingons were going to attack those two bases, they would certainly launch from a closer location. But we kept a careful watch nevertheless.

During the two weeks we were on patrol, I was beginning to get to know the love of Jack's life. She was young and soft-spoken, but I soon learned her manner hid a passionate intellect. Crusher himself was also different around her, a little more brash as well as occasionally, well… silly. He seemed to enjoy making her laugh.

THE STORY OF ONE OF STARFLEET'S MOST INSPIRATIONAL CAPTAINS

"…and he was sitting in your chair?" Beverly said. The three of us were in the rec room having dinner. Crusher had prompted me to tell her why I didn't approve of children on my ship.

"That's nothing," Crusher said. "Tell her about the egg." I suppose some captains might think such informality would undermine their authority, but I'd learned I could trust Jack with these confidences, and now that trust seemed to naturally extend to the woman he loved.

"You can tell her," I said. "I want to check in with the bridge."

"They'll call if they detect anything," Crusher said. "What are you worried about? I don't think the Klingons are going to attack here, do you?"

"What we think doesn't matter," I said. "We have our duty."

"Excuse me for asking, but aren't we near Archanis?" Beverly said. "That might be a prime target for them."

"It's not the most strategically valuable," Crusher said.

"No," Beverly said. "But the loss of Archanis in 2272 was a humiliation for them. Warfare for the Klingons is as much about honor as it is about strategy." Crusher and I exchanged a look. She had insight into the current situation because academy lessons were fresh in her mind. And as if to confirm it, Cheva called from the bridge.

"Red alert," she said. "Captain Picard to the bridge." I clicked the intercom. "Bridge, this is Picard, report…"

"All the Klingon ships, sir," she said. "They're gone."

✦

A few hours later, we were at Archanis. I'd contacted Brand, and she agreed with my analysis (really Beverly's), that the Klingons were headed there. Brand would be coming with the rest of her squadron to buttress Archanis's defenses. There were three Class-M planets in the system, several orbital facilities, but currently no starships. Until help arrived, *Stargazer* would be alone.

The situation of our patrol had gone from dull to dire. It seemed unlikely we would survive the day.

But all we could do was wait. I paced the bridge, occasionally staring at the starfield. I remember reading that the original Klingon cloaks caused a slight distortion of the stars, and so I searched, vainly hoping for some forewarning before those ships appeared. I looked around at the faces of the bridge crew: they wore expressions of determination, but fear was just below the surface.

"There's a spike in neutrino emissions," Cheva said. "Could be cloaked ships."

"Bearing, Mr. Crusher?"

"Directly ahead of our position," Crusher said. I looked back at the viewscreen. The stars began to shimmer...

"Shields up," I said. "Stand by all weapons."

Twenty-five Klingon ships solidified into reality, filling my screen, blotting out the stars. Their forward torpedo launchers were all trained on us, all glowing red.

"They've all locked onto us," Cheva said. We would not survive that onslaught.

"Phasers, lock onto the lead ship," I said. "Fire..."

And then suddenly, the ships shimmered again, dissolved, and disappeared. All of them.

"Sensors, report!"

"They're gone, sir," Cheva said. "I've got nothing."

"Stay sharp," I said. We remained at the ready. I glanced at the chronometer; thirty seconds passed. I checked our boards: no neutrino emissions, no sensor contacts, nothing. I looked back at the chronometer. Now a minute had passed.

"They had us," Crusher said. "What happened?"

"Sir, message coming in from Captain Brand," Black said.

"On screen," I said, and turned to see Brand on the spacious bridge of the *Ambassador*.

"Captain," I said, "the Klingons were here, but they... left."

"I don't think they're coming back," Brand said. "They're needed elsewhere. There's been an attack on two Klingon colonies." This seemed unbelievable; the Federation had never initiated a war. She immediately read the confusion in my expression. "The Romulans have attacked Narendra III and Khitomer. The Klingons have another war to worry about."

It turned out that the Romulans had not believed the Klingons regarding the event with the planet-killer, and had been planning their own military action in retaliation. They were both warlike societies, and I suppose the

Federation was lucky that they turned their hostility to one another. However, the war between Romulus and Qo'noS* was not without casualties for Starfleet. When the Romulans attacked Narendra III, the inhabitants sent a distress call. The only ship to answer it was the *U.S.S. Enterprise*-C, the first ship that had taken me into space. The vessel, under the command of a woman named Rachel Garrett, engaged four Romulan warships in an attempt to stop the attack. The efforts of Captain Garrett and her crew of 700 were unsuccessful. The ship was lost with all hands, and the Klingon outpost destroyed. I was discussing the tragedy the next evening at dinner with Jack and Beverly—meals with them were quickly becoming a regular event. Crusher was going over the crew list of the *Enterprise*-C. He found the name of someone he knew, the ship's helmsman.

"I knew Richard Castillo at the academy," Crusher said. "Good guy, very earnest. Sad that he had to die for nothing."

"Maybe not for nothing," Beverly said.

"What do you mean?" I said.

"There's been an intense focus on Klingon culture in my classes at the academy," Beverly said. "I think the commandant knew war was coming. In any event, one Klingon warrior sacrificing himself to protect other Klingons is a very meaningful act of honor, even if he or she fails. It guarantees them a place in the warrior's afterlife."

"I don't understand what you're getting at," Crusher said.

"Well, seven hundred Federation 'warriors' on the *Enterprise*-C sacrificed themselves to save Narendra III…" Beverly said. "If they are true to their own customs, there may just be the possibility of real peace between our two societies."

Beverly would turn out to be right, and as the days went on I became more impressed at this person who'd come into my friend Jack Crusher's life. And as we sat down to eat, and I watched how she looked at my best friend, I found myself envious that she hadn't come into mine.

---

*EDITOR'S NOTE: Qo'noS (pronounced "KRO-nus") is the homeworld of the Klingon Empire.

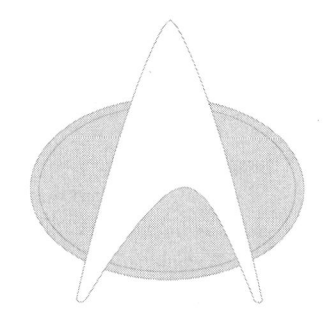

CHAPTER SEVEN

"**AND SO, IT IS MY HONOR TO UNITE YOU,** Jack Crusher, and you, Beverly Howard, in the bonds of matrimony…"

It was a sunny, humid spring day in the small village of Cornwall, in the state the ancient Americans called "Connecticut." Jack said that his family went back several centuries in this town: his maternal grandmother, Clara Sedgwick, who officiated the wedding, had regaled the visitors the night before about her ancestor who served in the United States Civil War.[*]

The village had remained almost as rural as when it was founded. The wedding took place at Jack's family home, set amongst a stretch of woods. It was the second wedding I would attend in my dress uniform, this one however as best man. I stood next to Jack, who faced Beverly. Though still a cadet, she eschewed a uniform and instead wore a white dress and veil in the ancient Earth tradition. She wore it with grace and splendor, and stared soulfully into my best friend's eyes, never noticing my rapt gaze.

Clara had them say their vows and exchange rings. Jack lifted Beverly's veil and they kissed. The audience of about a hundred people broke out into

---

[*] **EDITOR'S NOTE:** The ancestor was John Sedgwick, born in Cornwall Hollow, Connecticut, who served as a general in the Union Army, and was killed at the Battle of Spotsylvania Court House in 1864. Upon viewing the placement of Confederate sharpshooters, his famous last words were "They couldn't hit an elephant at this dist—."

spontaneous applause, and I joined in. The joy I felt for my friends was tempered by the feelings I'd developed for Beverly over the past two years.

After the service, Jack was thanking his grandmother, when Beverly stepped over to me.

"I hope you don't mind, Captain," she said. She leaned in and gave me a soft kiss on the cheek. "It means so much to us that you're here."

"I wouldn't have missed it," I said, returning her smile. I felt my face flush. Uncomfortable with our closeness, I stepped back. "You're both very special to me." Jack came back over and shook my hand warmly.

"Thank you, Captain," he said.

"None of that 'Captain' business today," I said. We joined the other guests, including several members of the crew. I noticed Scully already with a drink in his hand. I did my best to engage with the merriment. When I felt I'd given an appropriate amount of time to the party, I made my excuses and said my goodbyes. My last image was of Jack and Beverly absorbed in a lively dance, sharing their joy, surrounded by loved ones. I withdrew, headed to the center of town, alone.

My thoughts went to my own family. I reached the Cornwall transporter station, very reminiscent of the one in my hometown. I'd been avoiding going back to the vineyard, but there was unfinished business waiting for me there. I stepped forward to the technician at the control panel.

"Destination?" he said.

"La Barre, France," I said.

An hour or so later I was standing in the barn that held the wine tanks.

"So, you're home," Robert said—his standard greeting. He stood on the gangplank over one of the wine tanks, pressing down the skins with the large paddle.

"I can't stay long," I said.

"I didn't expect you would," he said. Robert was infuriating. He continued on, pressing the paddle into the sloshing purple mess. He wasn't going to make this easy for me.

"How was the funeral?"

"Very simple," Robert said. "Just me and some people from town. Smaller than Mother's."

"I am sorry I wasn't here," I said. "I was several hundred light-years away when I found out." This was the truth; I was out at the Cardassian border when

I'd received word of my father's death. It would've taken me weeks to get back home. And the truth was, upon hearing of my father's passing, the memory of his coldness toward me when Mother died was still fresh in my mind. It left no room for sorrow.

"He wouldn't have wanted a fuss," Robert said. He stopped what he was doing; I felt like I'd passed some test by bringing up the awkward subject of my father's death. Robert took the paddle and laid it across the gangplank, then made his way to the ladder on the side and climbed down.

"Come with me."

He led me into the house and into the kitchen. There was a small lockbox on the table.

"Father left you that," Robert said. This was a surprise; I hadn't expected him to leave me anything. And I was correct not to; I opened the box, and took a quick glance inside. There was a PADD, and on it was a letter from Starfleet Academy. It began "Dear Mr. Picard: we are sorry to inform you…" It was my rejection letter from when I first applied.

"What is this about?"

"I don't know," Robert said. "It was the only thing he left in his will to you."

I didn't understand it. It seemed to be an insult from the grave, but the purpose of which I couldn't comprehend. A reminder of a failure? I looked at Robert. I could see he wasn't interested in this. He had another agenda, and I immediately knew what it was.

"This was all he left me," I said. "That's what you want me to know."

Robert stood still, unable to meet my gaze. I had no expectation that my father would leave me anything, but Robert's concern was the vineyard. It was his now, and he wanted me to know it. I looked at him. He was almost 50, and though he would probably live a lot longer, he'd devoted his whole life to the family business. It was his entire past, and the only possibility of a future. I didn't know what Robert's plans were, though I assumed he would want a family to pass the vineyard onto as my father had to him. Yet, I was stung by Robert's lack of generosity. He didn't want to risk sharing any of it with me. We'd lost both our parents, and though that might have brought some brothers closer together, in our case, it only cemented our distance. We were both victims in a sense; my father hadn't dealt with this situation with respect for either of us.

"Good luck," I said. I shook his hand. He wouldn't look me in the eye. When I left, I expected this would be the last time I would see him. I walked back to the transport station in La Barre, and beamed back to the *Stargazer*.

✦

"Beverly's pregnant," Crusher said.

"Congratulations," I said, giving him a warm handshake. He had just returned from his honeymoon and found me in engineering, where Scully and I were reviewing the completed maintenance we'd done while in Earth orbit.

"That was fast," Scully said. "Wedding was only two weeks ago." Crusher and I exchanged a glance and laughed.

"Yeah," Crusher said. "I guess you didn't notice the shotgun her father was holding." This was of course a joke. Jack told me that his and Beverly's families had known that Beverly was pregnant before the wedding. It was a fait accompli that they were going to marry, and humans were beyond such narrow-mindedness that said they *had to* because the woman had got pregnant.

Crusher and I left Scully and headed up to the bridge. I asked him where his new bride was.

"Actually, that's something I wanted to mention to you," Crusher said. "She's decided to finish her studies on Earth. With your approval, of course."

"Why?" This news caught me off guard. I'd been steeling myself for her return, and now I was sincerely disappointed not to be seeing her again. "I certainly hope she didn't think I would have trouble with a pregnant crewman."

"She wasn't worried about the pregnancy," Crusher said. "She was worried about what would happen afterward."

"I don't understand."

"Come on, you're not exactly a fan of having children aboard your ship," Crusher said. "And since we weren't sure where *Stargazer* would be seven months from now, she decided she wanted to avoid the potential awkwardness of that situation."

"That was very thoughtful," I said. But this revelation had left me embarrassed and a little somber. That my stories of difficult children on board the *Stargazer* had been the deciding factor in Beverly not returning upset me. I somehow felt I'd hurt her, which I knew was ridiculous.

"Well," I said, "when she's through with the academy, I hope she'll consider a posting on this ship."

"I hope we're not still here." As we got on the turbolift to the bridge, I could see beneath his good cheer was a sadness.

"Was it difficult to leave her?" I said.

"Leave *them*," he said. "I have a family now."

"I'll get you back to them," I said. He smiled, and we exited to the bridge.

✦

"The Cardassians have destroyed the colony on Setlik III," Captain Ross said. He was on the viewscreen, calling from the bridge of his ship the *Crazy Horse*. Over the past few years, incidents of Cardassian raids on ships and colonies had escalated, so Starfleet sent a task force commanded by Ross to the border with Cardassian space. This was supposed to prevent a conflict, but it had in fact seemed to ignite one, as now the Cardassians had wiped out a Federation colony.

"Code One?" I said. Ross nodded.

Code One. We were at war.

"I have new orders for you, Captain," Ross said. "The *Stargazer* has been detailed to my task force, while we await further reinforcements."

"Yes, Captain," I said. I looked at Ross. A beefy man with a hangdog expression, he was still several years younger than me. I'd often been in the position of giving orders to older people, and now I would find myself on the opposite end of that awkward relationship.

"You are to proceed to Starbase 32 and pick up a shipment of supplies that will arrive there tomorrow from Earth," Ross said. "I'm sending the manifest now. We're about to find ourselves in a shooting war, and we're going to need those supplies as soon as possible."

"Acknowledged," I said. "We won't let you down." I signed off and Ross left the screen. "Mr. Crusher, set course for Starbase 32, warp 6, engage." As we entered warp, I noticed the crew looked uneasy. We'd engaged in the occasional skirmish and had faced down a fleet of Klingon ships, but none of the crew had ever fought in an actual war. That, unfortunately, was also true for their captain. Still, I had to find some words of comfort and encouragement.

"War is something to be avoided at all costs," I said. "But when circumstances don't allow you to, then all you can do is your best. This ship has survived a long time and accomplished a great deal, because its crew understood where its duty lay. This war will be no different. We will do our duty, and we will succeed."

As it turned out, I was right, but not quite in the way that I thought.

I assumed that once we picked up the supplies at Starbase 32, *Stargazer* would join Ross's task force. But Ross had a string of newer, faster, better-armed ships than mine, and the "milk run" became our chief duty. We transported supplies and personnel back and forth between Starbase 32, other starships and the ships on the front line. During the first two years of the war, the *Stargazer* participated in no battles. It gave one the ambivalent feeling that you were both safe and somehow not doing enough.

A few months into our third year of war, however, one person aboard got something out of the situation. We were in the recreation room one evening playing poker (I had started a regular game with Jack Crusher, Dr. Ailat, Scully, and Cheva). We had just delivered dilithium and photon torpedoes to Ross's task force. The game helped relieve the monotony on these long trips back and forth. I was dealing five-card stud when Jack told us the news.

"Beverly and Wesley are on Starbase 32," Jack said. I was overcome with a wave of anticipation. I had not seen Beverly since she'd left the ship, and she had faded from my mind. I'd seen photos of her and their young son, but having her far away made me forget the feelings I'd had for her. Now that I might be seeing her again, they came flooding back. I focused intently on the game, and let the others ask the questions that were on my mind.

"That's wonderful," Cheva said. "Just visiting?"

"No," Jack said. "She's finished with the academy, and is going to complete her medical training at the starbase hospital."

"It is an exceptional teaching facility," Ailat said.

"You're going to get to see a lot of them," Cheva said, and Jack smiled. He hadn't met his son face-to-face yet, only over subspace communications. It had been weighing on him, and he told me he'd even been toying with the idea of resigning his commission. I had encouraged him to find another solution, and it seemed he had.

THE STORY OF ONE OF STARFLEET'S MOST INSPIRATIONAL CAPTAINS

"Could we focus on the game, please?" Scully said. "Looks like the captain's dealt himself a straight draw." Scully read my hand well: I had a two, four, five showing, and my hold card was a three.

I dealt everyone's last card. I got a six of spades, completing my straight, a very difficult hand to get in this game. The betting started. Jack had two kings, a nine and ten up: his best possible hand was three of a kind, which wouldn't beat me. He bet heavily and Cheva, Ailat and Scully folded. The betting got to me and I raised; I knew I had a better hand than Jack. Jack, however, didn't seem to care, or thought I was bluffing. He raised me.

I looked at my hole card, then his hand, playing coy because I knew I had him beat.

"Well, Jean-Luc," Crusher said. "Raise, call, or fold." If I raised, he would probably raise as well, and I would take all his chips. But I looked at this man, my friend. I thought of his anticipation of the warm embrace of family, one that I'd never really experienced. I don't know why I did what I did next.

"Fold," I said, flipping the cards over, and pushing them into the center with the other folded hands, so no one could see what I had.

"Funny," Jack said. "I thought you had me beat."

"No," I said. "You had the better hand."

✦

"This is Captain Picard," Jack said. He held his toddler son, Wesley, who hid his face in his father's neck when I tried to say hello. Beverly gave me a hug. She looked lovely. We had arrived at Starbase 32 and were standing at the airlock hatch. I'd come to greet Jack's family, which in some ways I regarded as my own.

"Please come have dinner with us, Captain," Beverly said.

"Thank you," I said. "But I have some work to finish up." Seeing the three of them together, I felt the connection that I wasn't a part of, and certainly didn't want to be in the way. I watched them leave and headed back to the bridge.

After over two years of coming to this base, the shore facilities held little interest for me, so after completing my shift on the bridge, I retired to my cabin for dinner.

I sat down at my desk for a meal of soup and bread. I intended to read some dispatches, but I couldn't focus. My mind wandered to Jack holding his young son, and I tried to recall being held by my own father. He must have picked me up at some point, I just didn't remember.

I hadn't thought about my father since I had returned home, but now I was distracted with the one unsolved mystery of his death: the PADD he had left for me with my rejection letter from the academy. I hadn't looked at it since Robert had given it to me.

I dug out the PADD from the storage container that I'd tossed it in. Why would my father leave this for me? I started to read it, which I realized I hadn't really done when I first got it from Robert, and immediately noticed something. The date was wrong.

March 13, 2287. My first application to the academy was in 2321. I kept reading. It was the same letter. Except for the "Dear Mr. Picard" it was a form letter. And then I saw and understood—I wasn't the "Mr. Picard" it was addressed to.

It was addressed to Maurice Picard.

My father.

I couldn't believe what I was reading. My father, at 17, had applied to the academy and been rejected. He'd kept this a secret, maybe even from my mother, and decided before he died to let me know.

There was so much to process. For my entire adult life he had denigrated my ambitions; in my hand was the key to understanding why. He resented not just that I was living my dream, I was living *his* dream, which had been denied to him. What had looked to me like disapproval had actually been jealousy. It brought back so many memories, placing them all in a different context, and it raised as many questions as it answered. When I was rejected the first time, he couldn't express any empathy in a situation *that he himself had experienced*. It was hard for me even as an adult to see how small a man my father was.

And the broken ship model, the NX-01, which I blamed on Robert, who claimed innocence. I remembered how angry my father got when I accused my brother. I was suddenly sure that Robert *was* innocent; the boot that had stepped on it had in fact belonged to my father.

The anger dissipated, replaced by loss and regret for a connection that could have been—if he'd been a different man, a man who could communicate with his son, share his dreams, who didn't let his envy and frustration get in his way. And then I felt envy, envy of that young boy I'd just met who had a father to hold him.

✦

"We have read your report," Admiral Blackwell said. "I'm sorry to say we weren't convinced." I was in a large conference room on Starbase 32. At the table were two admirals, senior members of the Admiralty, and a third watching from a viewscreen. I knew none of them personally. This was a large gamble, one I had to take, not just for the war effort, but for everyone close to me.

The duty *Stargazer* drew was taking its toll on the ship and crew. Everyone understood the importance of keeping our ships supplied with those valuable assets that our replicators couldn't make, but as news of Starfleet's losses reached us, my ship's crew (and its captain) desired a more important role. I contacted Admiral Hanson, and made my pitch. Hanson arranged the meeting for me, though he couldn't be there; he was still on Earth. His task of keeping fleet production on its vigorous pace was even more vital.

The day-to-day operations of the war effort were in the hands of a few admirals, two of which were in this room and the third was sitting in a darkened room from an undisclosed location somewhere in the Galaxy. He was the important one, the one that I was counting on. The eldest of the three, at least 100 years old, didn't introduce himself, and seemed to be willing to leave me to the other two. But I was hoping when the moment came he would speak. Only he might have the information that would sell my plan. He in fact was the one admiral I'd asked Hanson to get in the meeting.

"I understand, Admiral Blackwell," I said. "But I have new information to add. I will keep it brief." I directed most of my presentation to Margaret Blackwell, a reserved woman in her fifties, as she at least offered some courtesy or the pretense of it.

I went to the viewscreen on the wall and brought up my chart.

"As I pointed out in my report," I said. "All the raids on Federation shipping and colonies before the Setlik III massacre were focused on specific technology. Technology related to our replicators."

"Yes, yes," Admiral Janeway said. "We told you we read your report already." This was Edward Janeway, clearly a man who wanted to be anywhere else. And I really couldn't blame him. Starfleet crews were losing their lives daily, and he was responsible for them.

"Captain Picard," Admiral Blackwell said, "your theory that the Cardassians became interested in Federation technology after having observed the replicator aboard your ship is interesting. But to suggest they went to war over it…"

"That's not what I'm suggesting," I said. "The raids were about the technology. The war is about us settling on Setlik III and establishing Starbase 211." Starbase 211 was the newest Federation outpost, built only a few light-years from the Cardassian border.

"Those were completely separate events," Janeway said. "The Starbase began construction long before the raids started, and the Federation colony on Setlik was not a Starfleet operation."

"There is no way the Cardassians could be sure of either of those facts," I said. "It is easier for them to believe that we knew of their lower technological level, and assume that we planned on taking advantage of it by invading from two new outposts."

"That is not the Federation way," Janeway said.

"No, but it is the Cardassian way," I said. "They projected their own motivations upon us." I could see that I wasn't making any progress. This was all in my original report; I was repeating a case I'd already argued unsuccessfully. But I had to keep going. "There is a way to end this conflict. We offer them the technology they were trying to steal before the war started."

"If, as you say," Admiral Blackwell said, "the raids are about replicator technology, then surely by now they've got it."

"Exactly," Janeway said. "We've lost several ships and bases. They must have salvaged something by now."

This was the moment I was waiting for, the reason I had stuck my neck out to make my case. I knew that Starfleet had intelligence operations behind the lines, operations that I didn't have clearance for. But one person in this meeting did. Now I looked over at him.

He was old, and gray. He had been a Starfleet officer since he was 22 and was now in charge of Starfleet Intelligence. I would love to have spent a day with him and learned about his incredible career, serving on two ships named *Enterprise*. But right now I just needed him to answer Blackwell's query.

He looked up and cracked a smile. The other two turned, sensing that their older companion was about to speak.

"The Cardassians haven't got it," he said, his voice thick with a Slavic accent. "Or they haven't figured out how to make it work. Their people are starving, and the military continues to promise that victory will feed their children."

This was what I needed. Blackwell and Janeway exchanged a look. "Wouldn't giving them replicator technology," Blackwell said, "violate the Prime Directive?"

"Do you think if it ended the war," Admiral Chekov said, "anybody would care?"

"The ends do not justify the means," Janeway said.

"Do what you want," Chekov said. "The kid's idea deserves a shot." He disappeared from the viewscreen. It took me a moment to realize that, at the age of 48, I was the "kid." Blackwell and Janeway exchanged a silent glance. Janeway sighed, resigned, and was the first to speak.

"Walk us through your plan once more."

✦

It took us five days to reach the Cardassian border. I'd chosen an area that was known to be well patrolled; it was important that I get their attention, but not be so close to their homeworld as to appear a threat.

"Approaching Sector 21503," Crusher said, from the conn.

"Hold station," I said, then turned to Black, and had him open a hailing frequency. I sent a general message to any Cardassian ship in the area that I was there to parlay for a truce.

It wasn't long before I received a response.

"Ship closing," Cheva said. "*Galor* class." This was the newest type of Cardassian vessel, and I'd suggested this area specifically because several of these newer class of ships had been encountered here. The *Stargazer* was no match for it, and that was the point. I wanted the Cardassians to believe my intentions were sincere. To get them to agree to a parlay, I would be offering a replicator. I was certain that it would show our good faith, and the relative weakness of my ship would show I was no threat.

The vessel hung in front of us.

"Sensors detect they've locked weapons," Vigo said. "Should I do the same?"

"Negative," I said. "We will take no provocative action." I had Black open another hailing frequency.

"Cardassian vessel, please respond," I said. "I bring greetings from the United Federation of Planets, who wishes to negotiate a ceasefire."

Still no response. I could tell them what I had to offer, but with them not responding I was doubtful they would believe me. They were aggressive and suspicious, and I expected they would think I was setting some kind of trap. I needed something to change the game.

"As a gesture of goodwill," I said. "I will lower my shields." Crusher turned and looked at me.

"Captain," he said, "I think we should give it a few more minutes." I thought about his suggestion; I suppose it had some merit. But I had already told the Cardassians what I was going to do, and so I was committed.

"Carry out my order," I said. Crusher turned back to his console, and Cheva lowered the shields. "Cardassian vessel, as you can see—"

I was thrown off my feet as a Cardassian disrupter ripped into the saucer section of the ship. Consoles exploded on the bridge.

"Direct hit," Cheva said. "Weapons systems damaged…"

"Shields up," I said, pulling myself off the deck.

"Shields non-responsive," Vigo said.

"Get us out of here…"

The Cardassian ship fired. I watched as the engineering console caught fire.

"Impulse engines off-line," Crusher said. I leaned over him. There was a course plotted away from the Cardassian ship, and I saw the warp engines were still online. I threw the switch to engage them, and we jumped to warp speed.

"Report!"

"We're at warp 2…warp 3…" Crusher said.

"Cardassian ship pursuing… they're at warp 4… warp 5…" Cheva said.

"Engineering," I said, talking into the intercom, "Scully, we need more speed…"

"I can give you warp 6," Scully said, "but we won't be able to hold it for long… it's a mess down here. Why did we lower the shields?"

THE STORY OF ONE OF STARFLEET'S MOST INSPIRATIONAL CAPTAINS

"Just give me what you can," I said, ignoring his question. I was slammed forward—the Cardassian had hit us again with a torpedo. It looked like there was no salvaging this peace mission.

"Weapons status," I said.

"Forward and aft torpedo bays damaged, phasers inoperative," Cheva said.

The only reason we were still alive is the Cardassians had focused on taking out our weapons first. They'd been certain I was laying a trap.

"Black, send out a distress call," I said.

"They're jamming transmission," Black said. I checked the status of the Cardassian ship; it was overtaking us. This was bad and getting worse.

"Ship coming in," Cheva said. "It's the *U.S.S. Crazy Horse*." The "cavalry" had arrived, ironically named after a Native American. The *Crazy Horse* raced past us, and opened fire on the Cardassian ship, who turned and ran.

"Subspace interference is fading," Black said. "Captain Ross calling." Captain Ross appeared on the viewscreen, smiling at me from the bridge of the *Crazy Horse*.

"Nice try, Jean-Luc," Ross said. "We'll get this guy off your back." I thanked him and headed for the barn. My "big swing" was a complete failure. We would stay on supply duty for the foreseeable future.

A few months later, the *U.S.S. Cairo*, under the command of the newly promoted Edward Jellico, took three ships, surrounded a *Galor*-class vessel and demanded a parlay. They respected the strength he showed and agreed to a temporary ceasefire… in exchange for a replicator and the instructions on how to build one. Jellico and Starfleet Command had seen the truth in my proposal, but I got no credit for it because my method almost lost me my ship. I wasn't sure my situation could get much worse.

How wrong I was.

✦

"They're called the Chalnoth," Ailat said. "My people have avoided them."

We had entered the Chalna system, which had one habitable world. The system was uncharted, but we'd entered an area of space not far from the Edosian homeworld, so I had called Dr. Ailat to the bridge to see if she could provide us with any information that wasn't in our computer memory.

"Do they have warp capability?" I asked.

"They did," Ailat said. "Their society fell victim to narcissistic leaders, and has since devolved into anarchy. Such unrest makes maintaining a space-going infrastructure impossible. Which, I would say, is fortunate for its neighboring systems."

"Put us in a standard orbit," I said. I watched on the viewscreen as we approached the brown and yellow planet.

"I'm detecting orbital structures and ships," Cheva said. On the screen, a large space station floated toward us. "No power signatures or life signs."

As we got closer, it was very clear that the station had been abandoned for a long time. There were signs of battle damage, breaches to its hull caused by energy weapons and projectiles. A number of ships of various sizes were drifting nearby, all dead. The scene was foreboding.

"Scan the planet," I said.

"Heavily populated, signs of some advanced technology," Cheva said.

"Have they scanned us?"

"No, sir," Vigo said. "No sign of scanners or advanced ground-to-space weapons systems."

"There's a lot of dilithium down there," Cheva said. I looked over at her scanner. There was a highlighted section on the planet, a rich vein over a hundred kilometers square. It was very tantalizing. Starfleet had no source of the valuable substance—responsible for powering starships—in this section of the Galaxy. Having a mining treaty in this sector that could supply Starfleet with dilithium would be a vital resource given the current political situation. We had a ceasefire with the Cardassians that could break down at any moment, and though the Klingons were no longer threatening the Federation, they had armed the Tzenkethi, who were making aggressive moves. The possibility of war was never far off.

"What does the Prime Directive say about a planet like this?" Cheva said.

"They had warp drive once," Crusher said. "And those ships aren't that old. They're aware of other worlds and other cultures."

I looked over at Ailat, who nodded.

"The Chalnoth have been in space in my lifetime," Ailat said. "It is unlikely they've forgotten that other worlds exist." The Prime Directive specifically stated that any contact with a primitive society with no knowledge of the other

THE STORY OF ONE OF STARFLEET'S MOST INSPIRATIONAL CAPTAINS

star-faring species meant that could not be revealed to them. However, if they were already aware, the Federation could trade with them.

"And we've got to have something they want," Crusher said. I smiled, knowing what was behind Jack pushing this mission. He'd recently gotten other offers to be first officer on better ships than this one, and turned them all down. He maintained he was only going to leave for a ship of his own. But I knew he was staying out of loyalty to me, and I also knew it would only be a matter of time before someone gave him a captain's chair. Until that happened, he'd taken it upon himself to get me out of my career purgatory. A treaty to mine dilithium on Chalna might do the trick.

"Still," I said, "it seems dangerous to beam down without knowing more."

"We can't beam down near the dilithium vein anyway," Cheva said. "There's too much interference."

"All right," I said. "Cheva, you, Vigo, and Dr. Ailat take a shuttle, scout the area and report back." I stared at the derelict spaceships hanging in front of me. They felt like a warning. One I didn't heed.

✦

"*Shuttlecraft Erickson*, do you read?" Black said. There was no response.

We'd lost contact with the shuttle just as it cleared the cloud layer. They were flying low over the area when Cheva reported they'd been hit by an energy weapon and lost engine control.

"I've got them," Crusher said. "They've crashed."

"Life signs?"

"Faint," he said. "Difficult to read with all the interference."

"Transporter Room," I said, into the intercom, "can we lock onto them and beam them up?"

"Negative," Transporter Chief Youlin said. "All that interference from the dilithium is disrupting their patterns."

"What about the emergency transporter in the shuttle?" Crusher said.

"It's not powerful enough to reach the ship at this distance," Youlin said.

"It doesn't have to be," Crusher said. "We can operate it remotely to act as a pattern enhancer so we can beam down to *them*." Transporter-to-transporter beaming was always much safer; Crusher's idea was brilliant. Once there, the shuttle's transporter could be used to enhance our lock on the survivors.

"If it's still operational," Youlin said, "that should work, but we can only send one person at a time. More than that is too risky."

"All right," I said. I had decided it was my responsibility to rescue Cheva and the landing party. I had ignored the danger signs, and now they might die because of it. "Mr. Crusher, you have the bridge…"

As I reached the turbolift, Crusher moved to intercept me.

"Request permission…" he said.

"Denied," I said.

"With all due respect, sir," Crusher said, "we have no knowledge of who shot the shuttle down, no knowledge of the damage it has sustained. It is reckless for you to beam in there with so little information." I looked at him; he felt responsible too. And, as much as I hated to admit it, he was right. As cowardly as I felt staying behind, it was irresponsible of me to beam myself into an obviously dangerous situation with absolutely no knowledge of the conditions awaiting me.

"Very well, Mr. Crusher," I said. "Proceed." I watched him leave the bridge, wishing I'd had another choice.

A few minutes later, Crusher had beamed into the shuttle, and immediately managed to activate the onboard communicator. We had a visual image of the interior of the damaged craft. Cheva, Ailat, and Vigo were all unconscious, bleeding from head wounds.

Crusher scanned them with a medical tricorder.

"They've got concussions," Crusher said. "Looks like it was a pretty rough ride."

"Is the shuttle operational?" I said.

"Negative," he said. "But we should be able to beam everybody up, one at a time." He picked up Cheva and brought her to lay under the shuttle's emergency transporter.

"Youlin, one to beam up."

"Picking up life signs closing in on the shuttle," Black said, sitting at ops. I looked at the readout: five life-forms were closing on the shuttle from all directions.

"Did you hear that, Jack?"

THE STORY OF ONE OF STARFLEET'S MOST INSPIRATIONAL CAPTAINS

"Affirmative," Crusher said. We watched as Cheva energized and disappeared. Crusher then picked up Ailat and put her in the same spot. The shuttle was suddenly rocked. Someone or something was trying to get in from outside. Crusher braced himself as the craft slid back and forth. "Youlin, you've got another one, energize!"

"Can we fire weapons from here? Stun those intruders?"

"We won't have an exact lock," Black said. "And if we hit the shuttle, even on the stun setting, it might negatively affect the transport." We watched Ailat disappear. Crusher was already hauling Vigo out of his seat and bringing him to the transporter.

A gash suddenly appeared on the shuttle wall, which looked to be caused, incredibly, by a *knife*. It must have been made of a fantastically hard metal. And whoever was wielding it tore through the bulkhead like it was tin.

And then another knife sliced another part of the hull. And another.

"Looks like I've got company," Crusher said, as he dragged Vigo, a head taller than him, achingly slowly. I wanted to get down there and help him, but there would be no use, it would just slow down his escape. So all I could do was watch.

He finally laid Vigo into place. "Youlin, go!" Crusher said, as he stepped away and drew his phaser. The first intruder had now opened a hole in the shuttle revealing his face: a mane of red hair and small tusks around the mouth reminiscent of a Nausicaan but with a wild-eyed fierceness. It cut away an entrance big enough to move through.

Jack fired his phaser, and the creature fell back, only to be replaced by another. Vigo finally energized, and disappeared. Crusher went to the transport area.

"Beam him up!" I said. I watched as two more Chalnoth forced their way into the shuttle. Jack fired again. One went down as the other moved across the craft, slashing his formidable blade across Jack's neck, just before he disappeared in the transporter beam.

I ran down to the transporter room. A medical team was wheeling out Vigo as I raced inside. Two medics were standing over Jack, who lay on the pad. Blood flowed freely from a laceration that went across his neck and up to the top of his head. The medics worked on closing the gaping wound as I kneeled down beside him.

"Jack," I said. "We got you…"

He looked up at me, in pleading disbelief. A gurgling sound came from his neck. The medics closed the wound, placed him on a waiting gurney, and hurried out with him. I stayed where I was, kneeling in a wide pool of my friend's blood.

✦

"It's good of you to come," Beverly said. It was overly formal; she was struggling to hold back her emotions.

"It's the least I could do," I said. We walked slowly through the corridor of Starbase 32 heading to the morgue. I had arrived with the *Stargazer* to bring Jack back to his family. We were withdrawn, both mourning the loss of the most important person in our lives. Jack had died because he was protecting me. He was my friend, my family. I felt a loss that was immeasurable. And yet I knew it was nothing next to the loss Beverly was experiencing.

We entered the morgue and approached the table where Jack's body lay, covered with a sheet. I knew what was under the sheet. I'd watched as Dr. Ailat, still recovering from her own injuries, worked with her medical team to try and save Jack's life. The image of my dead friend was branded in my memory. I turned to Beverly.

"You shouldn't remember him like this." She looked down at the sheet, stoic.

"It's important to me," she said. "I have to face the fact that he's gone."

I nodded and reached for the sheet. It seemed to take all my strength to lift it up. Jack lay there, white and still. Beverly took a moment, leaned in, and kissed his forehead. Her tears began. I covered Jack and held her a moment. She forced herself to recover.

"I've got to go find Wesley," she said.

"He doesn't know?" I said. She shook her head.

I went with her back out into the corridor, and we made our way to one of the station's schoolrooms. Wesley, now five years old, sat at a table, playing with geometric toys. The teacher in the room had obviously been informed; she ushered the other children to another part of the room as we knelt down next to him.

"Wesley," Beverly said. "You remember Captain Picard." He looked at me, unsure. We'd only met a couple of times, and I'd kept my visits short. He held up the geometric toys.

"I'm building a model of the atomic structure of dikironium," he said. I looked at the toys and realized that he had indeed made them to resemble an atomic diagram. "It's an element that can only be created in a laboratory."

"That's very clever," I said.

"Wesley," Beverly said, "I have something to tell you. Dad… is… he's been hurt. I'm sorry… he died."

"Did he go to the doctor?"

"He did, but the doctor couldn't help him." Beverly was holding back her tears, her arm gently around the little boy's shoulder.

"Oh," he said. "Can I finish my model now?"

Beverly smiled and nodded. "Sure," she said, kissed his forehead.

"Can we stay and watch you?" I said. Wesley nodded, and I sat down with Beverly and watched as he worked on his remarkably complex model.

Later, I said goodbye to Beverly, and told her that if there was anything she needed I hoped she would contact me. But I knew that she wouldn't; I was an unpleasant reminder of how the man she loved was taken away from her. I had given the orders that led to his death. I expected I would never see her again.

The love I felt for her could never be returned.

I returned to the *Stargazer*, lost and empty, about to embark on what would be my last mission as its captain.

✦

"Phasers coming to full charge, sir," Black said. "Torpedoes armed."

Smoke was filling the bridge. I stared at the strange wedge-shaped ship on the viewscreen, circling away from us.

"Who are they?" I said to Black, but he had no answer. I couldn't expect my new first officer to know any more than I did. We had been charting the Maxia Zeta star system, and were near a moon near the seventh planet. We'd passed over a large crater, and then suddenly we were hit. Our adversary must have been lying in wait for us deep inside, shielded from our sensors by the moon's mineral deposits. Our shields were down, and the first attack took out our impulse drive and shield generator. The second attack destroyed our life-support systems, including fire suppression. Fires broke out on the bridge.

"They're turning for another pass, sir," Black said.

"We can't take another hit, Captain," Vigo said. It was clear their intention was to destroy us. Sensors indicated they had a weapons lock. I had to fool that lock…

"Set course 7-7, mark 20," I said. This course would move us to within a few hundred meters of the enemy. It was a risky maneuver, one that would not work against a more experienced captain.

"Ready phasers and lock," I said. "Stand by on warp 9." My conn officer, Lieutenant Lee, still relatively new to the job, keyed in the course, despite his obvious confusion about what I was doing. By jumping to warp, we would appear to this enemy ship to be in two places at once; for a brief moment, their weapons lock would be on our former position. I would only have a second…

I watched as the adversary turned full on to face us.

"Engage!" The enemy ship zoomed in; the underside of its hull filled our viewscreen. "Fire!"

Torpedoes and phasers overwhelmed the enemy's shields and cut through the hull. There was a cascade of explosions, and then it was gone. I considered myself lucky; it was entirely possible that his shields might have held against that attack, and then we'd be finished. As it was, my ship was in deep trouble.

"Engineering to Bridge," Cheva said. After the first attack, we'd lost contact with engineering and I'd sent Cheva down to take stock of the situation. "I can't get the system back online, and the fire control teams have more than they can handle. It's spreading out of control."

"What about the life-support system?"

"Completely fused, sir, can't be repaired," she said. With fires throughout the ship, and a failed life-support system, the air would be gone in a matter of minutes.

"Where's Scully?" I said.

"Chief Engineer Scully… is dead, sir," Cheva said. "Killed in the first attack." I was stunned. Scully had survived so long, *Stargazer* was more his than mine. And now he was dead, and our ship along with it. A brutal and merciless enemy had just attacked us.

There might be more of them. I had to try to get the crew to safety.

"All hands, abandon ship," I said, then turned to the bridge crew. "Get to your evacuation stations."

✦

I was crammed inside a shuttle with about twenty crewmen. Cheva was at the piloting controls. I took the seat next to her, and watched out the view port as the rest of the shuttles left the bay.

"We're the last, sir," Cheva said. "Ready to depart."

"Make it so," I said. I'd never used that phrase before; it had belonged to Captain Quinn, my first commander. It took me only a little while to understand why.

We flew out of the ship, and joined a string of shuttlecraft and escape pods, all moving in formation away from *Stargazer*; a flotilla, limping away from our dead home. I had sent a distress signal to Starfleet before we evacuated, laying out the course our ships would be taking. The crew was under strict orders to maintain radio silence on their shuttles and escape pods. I knew it was a futile gesture—if an enemy ship was nearby and looking for us, they would find us long before help from Starfleet arrived.

Ailat and her medical team were on three medical shuttles tending to the injured. We'd had twenty-three deaths in the attack—I made sure Black kept a record. If we were to survive I had to inform their families. Was it my fault they were dead? I couldn't let myself think about that, I had to make sure I concentrated on the survival of the rest of the crew. I focused on protocol: I had to mark the time and date that I'd left the ship. A captain abandoning his vessel was an act Starfleet would scrutinize.

I looked back at the old lady, wrecked and lifeless. A fount of so many memories: Laughton, Mazzara and his children… becoming a captain, Walker and Jack coming on board… Beverly…

I couldn't let myself get lost in sentiment. I had work to do. I opened the log. That's when I noticed the date.

I remembered the first time I heard Captain Quinn say, "Make it so": he was giving me the order to save the ambassador on Milika III. That had imprinted on me as the defining moment of my career. Unconsciously, I must have known abandoning my own ship was one, too. I looked at the date again.

July 13, 2355.

My 50th birthday. And I'd just lost everything.

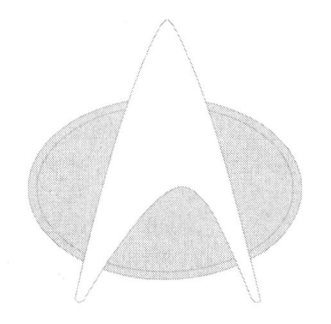

CHAPTER EIGHT

"THIS COURT-MARTIAL IS NOW IN SESSION," Admiral Milano said. Six other officers, captains and admirals, joined him on the court-martial board. I sat opposite their table in courtroom #3 of the Bormenus Building, headquarters of the JAG* at Starfleet Command. The clerk, on a nod from Milano, activated the computer, and the familiar female voice read the charges against me.

"Charge: Culpable Negligence and Dereliction of Duty. Specifications: In that on stardate 33994.5, by such negligence and dereliction of duty, Captain Picard, Jean-Luc, did cause both loss of life and destruction of *U.S.S. Stargazer*, NCC-2893…"

I sat with my defense counsel in a bit of a daze. Across from us was the prosecutor. The whole event was surreal. Only two months ago I was still in space, limping along with shuttles and escape pods with the remainder of my *Stargazer* crew. We had been traveling for weeks when we were rescued by the hospital ship *U.S.S. Caine*. They saw to our needs; Dr. Ailat had done a superb job keeping the wounded alive, but many of them needed further treatment. The rest of us were suffering from fatigue and post-traumatic stress.

---

*EDITOR'S NOTE: The Starfleet Judge Advocate General's Corps (JAG) is the branch concerned with Starfleet law and justice. The building was named after Bormenus, an Andorian, who, before serving as president of the Federation in the 23rd century, was one of the first Starfleet Judge Advocate Generals.

We arrived back at Earth, the *Caine* moored in the orbital dockyard. I received word to report to Starfleet Headquarters to give a debriefing. As I was leaving the ship, I found many of the survivors of the *Stargazer* crowded in the corridor by the airlock. At the front of the pack were Cheva, Ailat, Vigo and Black.

"Everything all right?" I said.

"Yes, sir," Black said. "The crew and I just wanted to say goodbye."

I realized, as they must have, that, given the vicissitudes of the service, it was quite possible I might never see them again.

"I hope we can serve together again," Cheva said.

"I hope so, too," I said. I then turned to the crowd.

"We owe you our lives," Vigo said.

"Oh, no," I said. "We all owe our lives to that ship who protected us longer than anyone ever expected her to, and the crew who sacrificed their lives so that we could survive. And now, it's up to us to keep the memory of our fellow crewmen, and the old lady herself, alive by continuing to serve as you all have done, and as they did, with integrity and distinction."

"Hear, hear!" Black shouted, and the rest joined in, cheering and applauding. I smiled at them all, and waved goodbye, wondering when I'd see them again. It turned out for some, it was sooner than I could imagine.

✦

I had been told to report to Admiral Quinn's office. I was looking forward to seeing him. He was now in charge of Starfleet's Operational Support Services. When I arrived in his office, he wasn't alone.

"Jean-Luc, good to see you," Quinn said. "Glad you made it back in one piece." He then turned to introduce me to his guest. I was too stunned upon seeing her to tell him we'd already met. "This is Commander Phillipa Louvois of the Judge Advocate General."

I hadn't seen her in over 25 years. Her hair was short, but other than that she looked much the same as she did at the academy. I was filled with a nostalgic affection for that more innocent time. I walked over to greet her and was met with a metaphoric wall of ice.

THE STORY OF ONE OF STARFLEET'S MOST INSPIRATIONAL CAPTAINS

"Captain Picard and I know each other from the Academy," she said. She couldn't have been clearer if she'd been a telepath: Quinn wasn't to know about our former relationship. I held back; I could certainly respect her position.

"Nice to see you again, Commander," I said. If Quinn picked up on anything between us, he didn't let on. He made a gesture for me to sit down. I took the chair next to Phillipa as Quinn went back behind his desk.

"Captain," he said, "the commander has informed me that the Judge Advocate General is convening a court-martial regarding your loss of the *Stargazer*."

"On what charge?" I said.

"There is no charge as of yet," Phillipa said. "It's routine. A court-martial is standard procedure when a ship is lost. My preliminary findings don't indicate any other charges. As of yet."

"*Your* preliminary findings?"

"I am prosecuting this case, yes," she said. "Someone in my office will be contacting you to serve as your defense counsel. Now, I hope you'll excuse me, I have another appointment." Phillipa got up and left the room.

"Jean-Luc," Quinn said, "I've read your report. I don't think you have anything to worry about. She's just doing her job."

I thought about telling him about our past, and that I thought she was pursuing an old grudge, but that seemed silly, and I couldn't tell him without it looking like I was unfairly trying to impugn her motives. So I let it lie.

Admiral Quinn invited me to join him for dinner, but I declined. I was assigned quarters in San Francisco and went back there that evening to think about my situation. A court martial? I hadn't even considered that was a possibility. I'd been mourning the crew that had died and the ship I'd lost. And now I found myself concerned about Phillipa. We'd had a brief romance, I wondered if that would affect her prosecution of my case. Would it lead her to be vindictive? I couldn't imagine that it would.

My brooding was interrupted by the doorbell. I went to answer it and found a Starfleet lieutenant commander in his thirties. He was overweight, balding, and somehow familiar. He carried a briefcase.

"Hello, Captain Picard," he said.

"Hello," I said. I felt I knew him, but I couldn't figure out from where. He saw my confusion.

"My apologies, sir," he said. "I'm Lieutenant Commander Anthony Mazzara. I look a lot different than when we last met."

A strange surprise. I hadn't seen him since he left the *Stargazer* when he was 17. Between seeing Phillipa in Quinn's office and now Anthony showing up at my door, it felt like an aphorism about chickens returning to roost was appropriate. I had a fair amount of questions about what he was doing there, but I had too many things on my mind at that moment to indulge my curiosity.

"Anthony," I said, "it's nice to see you, but you're really catching me at a bad time..."

"I'm sorry again, sir," he said. "This isn't a social visit. I've been assigned as your defense counsel by the JAG office."

"You've been assigned..."

"Yes, I'm sorry no one informed you," he said. "May I come in?"

In a bit of a daze, I gestured for him to come inside. This felt like a terrible practical joke, but there was no one alive who would know to play it. With little choice, I joined him at the table.

"You're a lawyer?"

"Yes, sir, I've been in the JAG corps for seven years. I'll do my best to help you."

I knew Phillipa, and I knew him; I thought she would eat him alive.

"Seems like quite a coincidence, you getting assigned to me."

"Truth be told," he said, "when I heard you were being court-martialed, I asked to be made defense counsel."

"Really? Why?"

"I felt like I still need to make up for the egg."

I couldn't help but laugh. I had no choice but to embrace the absurdity of the situation.

"All right, Mr. Mazzara," I said. "What do we do?"

✦

He spent the next two weeks asking me questions about my service aboard the *Stargazer*, as well as the specific events leading up to the exodus from it. Though I might have been initially reticent about being defended by Anthony Mazzara, those concerns quickly vanished. He had grown up on the *Stargazer*,

THE STORY OF ONE OF STARFLEET'S MOST INSPIRATIONAL CAPTAINS

and he knew much about the specific challenges of serving on and commanding that ship. There was so much I didn't have to explain to him; we saved a great deal of time. And I felt I had a sympathetic ear.

But, as the trial date approached, I became more concerned about Phillipa. Anthony knew her, and said that the staff in the JAG office had never seen her so driven on a case. My worries were confirmed the day before the trial when Mazzara came to my quarters, looking grave.

"She's charging you with culpable negligence and dereliction of duty," he said.

"On what grounds?"

"That I don't know," he said. "She has the same evidence I have. I don't think she has a case."

The next morning, Anthony met me at the courtroom, and as we headed inside, I saw Phillipa approaching. I asked Anthony to let me talk to her alone.

"As your counsel, I have to strongly advise against that."

"I'll be all right," I said.

"Watch what you say." Anthony went inside. I intercepted Phillipa before she reached the courtroom.

"May I have a moment?"

"I don't think that's a good idea," she said.

"Phillipa, why are you doing this?"

"What I'm doing is my job," she said. "I don't know who you told about us…"

"I haven't told anyone…"

"Whether you have or not, I can't afford to let people think I'd make it easy on an old boyfriend. Now, if you'll excuse me." She walked past me into the courtroom, and I realized she still cared about me. But she was going to prove that her feelings wouldn't get in the way of her work. I thought, as I walked into the courtroom, this made her a lot more dangerous.

✦

After the reading of the charges, Phillipa called her first witness.

"Please state your name and rank for the record," Phillipa said.

"My full name is Tcheri Chevapravatdumrong, Lieutenant Commander," Cheva said. "I use the last name 'Cheva' for short." I could see that Cheva was nervous on the stand. She was concerned that something she might say would get me in trouble. Phillipa began asking general questions about how long she served with me, and then got into the specifics about the events leading to my order to abandon ship.

"We'd suffered catastrophic damage. The impulse drive was inoperative, the shield generator destroyed, the life-support system was fused and the fire suppression system was offline, among other things."

"That seems like an awful lot of damage," Phillipa said.

"They hit us with our shields down."

"As operations officer, making sure *Stargazer* is up to date on its scheduled maintenance is part of your duties?"

"Yes," Cheva said.

"And was it?"

"I'm sorry?"

"Did *Stargazer* adhere to the Starfleet schedule of maintenance?"

"No…" Cheva said. The trial board looked surprised by this response, but I knew what she was going to say. "*Stargazer* was over sixty years old. Starfleet's maintenance schedule wasn't strict enough, so the captain had the chief engineer devise a more rigorous one."

"Thank you, Commander," Phillipa said. "No further questions." Unlike the board, Phillipa wasn't surprised by Cheva's answer. It appeared that this was the answer she expected, even wanted. It was Anthony's turn to ask questions.

"Lieutenant Commander Cheva," Anthony said, "in your opinion, as an officer experienced in space combat, was there any action Captain Picard took that you would characterize as being directly responsible for the disabling of the *Stargazer*?"

"Absolutely not, sir," Cheva said. "In fact, Captain Picard's actions saved the lives of the surviving crew."

"Thank you, Commander," Anthony said. "No further questions."

Over the next two days, Phillipa interviewed other crewmembers. They all confirmed Cheva's version of events. But Phillipa always continued questioning with some aspect of their work that indicated the difficulty of working on a ship as old as the *Stargazer*. She'd done her research: she had Black recount my first day taking the *Stargazer* out, with Scully repairing the helm as we did; Vigo relayed our disastrous encounter with the Cardassian

THE STORY OF ONE OF STARFLEET'S MOST INSPIRATIONAL CAPTAINS

ship; Dr. Ailat spoke of the difficult stress the crew was constantly under because the ship was often on the verge of breaking down. Anthony always cross-examined them, emphasizing the ship's achievements. Toward the end of the second day, Phillipa called one last witness.

"Prosecution calls Captain Jean-Luc Picard to the stand."

Anthony reacted immediately.

"Objection, Your Honor," he said. "Starfleet and Federation law plainly state that Captain Picard is not required to testify as a witness for his own prosecution."

"Prosecution concedes this," Phillipa said. "Captain Picard is free to decline."

"I need a moment to confer with my client," Anthony said. He leaned into me and spoke very softly. "You don't have to do this. If you don't take the stand I think I can get a dismissal. She hasn't come close to making a case for culpable negligence or dereliction of duty."

"She's hoping I make the case for her," I said. Anthony nodded. I looked over at Phillipa, back at her table, giving me a challenging stare. I then scanned the faces of the trial board. The men and women were impassive, difficult to read. I knew that if I didn't take the stand, there might be some of those captains and admirals who'd assume I had something to hide. Phillipa knew how much my reputation meant to me, and she assumed that it would compel me to put myself in a vulnerable position. And, of course, she was right, I had no choice. I stood up, and walked over to the witness stand. I saw Phillipa smile.

✦

"...we moved into position, and fired everything we had," I said. Phillipa had made me go through the battle, and my account bore little difference from the other witnesses.

"Very clever," Phillipa said. "Please tell the court, were you surprised at the amount of damage your adversary caused the ship?"

"No," I said, "the fact that the shields were down, combined with the *Stargazer*'s age..."

"So you think that the ship's age played a role in it being so easily disabled?"

"I don't know for certain..."

"Do you know what the average life of a ship is in Starfleet, Captain?"

"I do not," I said.

She immediately walked over with a PADD in hand. "I would like to offer into evidence Starfleet Exhibit 2, the Starfleet Ship Inventory," she said. She handed me the PADD. On the screen was a spreadsheet of all the types of ships currently in active duty in Starfleet, along with their ages.

"Please read me the average ship age of all the ships in the fleet, Captain." At the bottom of the sheet, the average ship age had been calculated.

"16.2 years," I said.

"And, as has been previously testified, *Stargazer* was over 60 years old. Is that correct?"

"Yes," I said. "63.7 years in fact."

"Thank you. Did you ever consider that *Stargazer* was too old to be in service?"

"That was not my decision to make," I said. But I began to understand where Phillipa was headed.

"Did you ever consider recommending to the Admiralty that they take *Stargazer* out of service?"

"No," I said.

"Why not? If, as has been testified, the ship's age caused it to be plagued with difficulties, required a much stricter than average maintenance schedule, caused undue stress on its crew, and made it more vulnerable to catastrophic failure after an attack, wasn't it your duty to inform Starfleet that the ship was unsafe?"

I glanced at the faces of the court-martial board. They looked annoyed. One of them, Admiral Dougherty, shook his head slightly in frustration. It appeared that Phillipa's line of attack was working. I looked back at her waiting for my answer; she knew my weakness. If I'd informed Starfleet that *Stargazer* was unfit for service, I'd have been potentially giving up my command, with no guarantee of another. And perhaps that pride and ambition had kept me from seeing the danger I was putting the crew in.

"Court will direct the witness to answer the question," Phillipa said.

"It may have been my duty," I said.

"No more questions," she said, and sat down.

Admiral Milano, the court-martial board chair, turned to Anthony. Anthony, however, wasn't paying attention; he was furiously typing into another PADD.

"Defense counsel," Milano said, a little annoyed. "Any questions for the witness?"

"No questions," Anthony said without looking up from the work he was doing. I could see this surprised Phillipa.

"Defendant may step down," Milano said. I went and rejoined Anthony at the table. "Does the prosecution wish to call any more witnesses?"

"No, sir," Phillipa said. "Prosecution rests."

"If defense has no objection," Milano said, "the court suggests we adjourn till tomorrow, and defense can begin its case."

"Actually, Your Honor," Anthony said, looking up from his PADD, "defense moves all the charges and specifications in this matter be dismissed. The prosecution has failed to make her case for culpable negligence or dereliction of duty."

"Objection, Your Honor," Phillipa said. "I have shown that Captain Picard ignored the condition of his craft and unnecessarily put his crew's life at risk."

"In fact, Your Honor," Anthony said, "she has not. Captain Picard did not ignore the condition of his craft. He worked to make sure that it was in proper working order. And, for twenty years, he succeeded, until it was brutally and mercilessly attacked. The prosecution, having never served as part of a crew, does not understand if a vessel is space-worthy; the requirements of the service necessitate the captain 'make do,' which Captain Picard did. Historical precedent is on the side of the defense."

"What historical precedent?" Phillipa said.

"I just did a record search," he said, holding up his PADD. "No captain in the history of Starfleet has ever suggested to the admiralty they decommission their own ship. I submit this as Defense Exhibit 1." Anthony brought the PADD over to Milano, and then he stood in front of the board.

"Captain Picard never hid the condition of his ship from the admiralty. His maintenance and repair reports were quite thorough in their description of the *Stargazer*'s deficiencies. He did his job. It was up to the admiralty to decide whether the ship should be decommissioned, not its captain."

"The board will consider defense's motion," Milano said. "Court stands adjourned until tomorrow."

Phillipa, annoyed, left the courtroom. I turned to Anthony.

"I'm not sure this will work," I said. "She made a very convincing case."

"Not to them," Anthony said, referring to the board as it filed out of the room. "Did you see their faces?"

"Yes," I said, "they looked angry."

"At *her*, not you. Almost all those officers have been in command of a ship, and I bet they've all had to live with substandard equipment at one time or another. None of them would want to have been held to the standard Louvois is trying to hold you to."

I considered Anthony's point. The fact was Phillipa's argument had landed with me. But I appreciated this man's passion in my defense.

"How about some dinner?" he said.

"Sure," I said. "I'm in the mood for eggs."

Anthony looked at me and laughed.

✦

"Congratulations, Jean-Luc," Quinn said. I was back in his office three days later. Two days before, the trial board had ruled in favor of Anthony's motion and dismissed the charges, clearing me of any wrongdoing. I had tried to talk to Phillipa, but as soon as the court was adjourned, she was gone. It turns out my exoneration had ramifications for her as well.

"You'll be happy to know your prosecutor resigned," Quinn said.

"What? Why?"

"Judge Advocate General thought her prosecution was unnecessarily aggressive from the start, but against his advice she went full steam ahead anyway. The fact that the trial board ruled against her only confirmed her superior's opinion, so she drew a reprimand. I heard she quit on the spot."

That was unfortunate. I was never sure what was behind Phillipa's uncompromising prosecution of my court martial. The romantic egotist in me wanted to believe that it was an attempt at retribution for a broken heart, but I think it was simply that she liked to win. I was sorry to hear that it had ended her career.

"So, now that you're a free man," Quinn said, "what are your plans?"

"Well," I said, "I'm hoping for a new command."

"I'm going to be straight with you, my friend," Quinn said. "That's not going to be possible for a while."

"Why not?"

"Phillipa did land a few punches, mostly on the admiralty. She made us look bad by implying we left *Stargazer* in service too long. A complete re-evaluation of the fleet is underway. We're going to be pulling a lot of ships off the line and getting new ones going. I need to put you on a desk for a while."

This was far from what I wanted to hear, and I also knew he was leaving out the most important fact: I had lost a ship. There were some ways Starfleet was still quite traditional, and, no matter the circumstance, losing a ship was not something that was going to be rewarded. Which also meant I wouldn't be seeing a promotion anytime soon.

"All right," I said. "What did you have in mind?"

"If you come work for me," he said, "I promise to get you back on a bridge, and it'll be the right ship, I assure you."

"It would be my honor to serve with you, Admiral," I said. He shook my hand and had a yeoman show me to an office. It was much like the one I'd had when I was Hanson's chief of staff, but unlike that job, I would see little of this room.

Though Quinn had described this as a "desk job," he and the admiralty had an agenda that required I be dispatched to starbases and shipyards to deal with a variety of issues regarding construction, upgrades and personnel. But before I left, I made sure to see to a couple of important loose ends.

I used my influence with Quinn to try to find the crewmen and women of the *Stargazer* prominent positions throughout the fleet. Cheva, after twenty years serving with me, deserved her own command, and Quinn approved her posting to command of the *U.S.S. Roosevelt*. Ironically, it was much easier to get her a ship than to get one for myself. Black also deserved his own vessel, and with some prodding Quinn was able to get him posted as captain of the science vessel *Bonestell*. Dr. Ailat took a leave of absence from Starfleet, but I secured her promise to return if I ever had a command again. I found positions for many others as well, and felt good that, despite my difficulties, my crew wouldn't be tarred with the same brush as me.

Soon after, Quinn briefed me on my specific agenda. Our department was working with Starfleet Tactical to move ships and personnel so that there would be a strike force ready at a moment's notice near Sector 003. Quinn couldn't fully brief me on why; that would have to wait until I arrived at Starbase 3, the last stop on my journey. I accepted the secrecy without question. Nothing I knew about the major civilizations in that sector—Tellar, the Vega Colony and Denobula Triaxa—made me think that any of them would provide a threat.

The first leg of my trip was a short one: the Utopia Planitia shipyards in orbit of Mars. I requisitioned a shuttle and flew there myself. The trip took less than an hour, but it was still pleasant being back at the helm of a ship. When I entered orbit of Mars, I took a leisurely tour of the web-like dry docks arranged above the red planet. A diverse assortment of ships were in various stages of completion. I had a specific ship to visit and headed for its coordinates. The vessel was the first of a new class of starship Starfleet was developing and was still under construction. I was there to prod the captain and chief engineer along, in the hopes that the ship might be of use in the upcoming mission. But as I approached, I knew this was an impossibility: much of the saucer section of the ship was still just a skeleton. Still, I'd been sent by Quinn to try to move things along, so that's what I would do. I received permission to berth the shuttle at the dry dock's center of operations and disembarked.

The center of operations was a buzz of activity, monitoring all the teams of crewmen in spaceships working on the hull through the large windows of the operations center. Two people greeted me: a gray-haired captain and a young woman.

"Welcome aboard, Captain Picard," the captain said. "I'm Tom Halloway, this is Chief Engineer Sarah MacDougal." Halloway was in command of the ship under construction. "Can we show you around?"

"That would be splendid," I said.

"He doesn't want a tour, Tom," MacDougal said. "He wants to know why we're so far behind."

I have to say that despite her rather rude manner, I appreciated her cutting to the point.

"Well, Admiral Quinn did want me to get an update on your current schedule," I said.

THE STORY OF ONE OF STARFLEET'S MOST INSPIRATIONAL CAPTAINS

"It's the damned holodecks," MacDougal said. "It's impossible to get one of them working properly, let alone *seven*."

"Holodecks?" I said. "What's a holodeck?"

"Oh crap, are you cleared for this?" MacDougal said.

"My god, Sarah, what have you done?" Halloway said, in mock dismay. He clearly enjoyed teasing her.

"I have level 10 security clearance," I said. "Now, what's a holodeck?"

"We'll show you," Halloway said, then turned to MacDougal. "It's on the tour."

They led me out of the operations center down to a docking tunnel to a docked support vessel. We walked through a corridor over to a control panel near a large hatch.

"This holovessel was designed specifically to test the holodeck in space," MacDougal said.

"I still don't know…"

"You from Paris, Jean-Luc?" Halloway said.

"Actually, a small village named La Barre," I said. Seemed a strange question to ask at that moment.

"Well, I don't know if that's in the memory banks, but let's see," Halloway said. He leaned into the computer panel, "Computer, location, La Barre, France, Earth, Picard home, nice autumn afternoon." I couldn't imagine what he was doing.

"Program complete," the computer said, and Halloway led me to the hatch; it opened automatically.

I almost fainted.

I was standing in front of my childhood home, with the large wooden wine barrels next to the front door. I felt the slight breeze, the smell of fermented grapes. It was impossible. I was seeing my whole vineyard—the area took up an area larger than the ship itself. I bent down and grabbed a handful of the gravel beneath my feet. I stood back up and let it roll around in my hand. It was real. I was back at home. I half expected Robert to walk by.

And then he did.

Robert exited the barn, wearing an apron covered in wine stains, wiping his hand with a dirty cloth. I knew it was a computer simulation, but he still conjured an adverse reaction. Until he gave me a big smile.

"Good morning," he said. "Welcome to my humble home."

I reached out and gently touched his shoulder. He was *there*; it wasn't a hologram.

"Are you quite all right?" he said.

"Computer, freeze program," Halloway said. Robert froze in position with that ridiculous and unnatural smile. "Pretty good, huh?" I looked back and saw Halloway and MacDougal standing in an archway by the door leading to the ship's corridors, which bluntly interrupted the view down our path to the village.

"It's unbelievable," I said. "How does it…?"

"It combines transporter and replicator technology for the simpler forms like plants, trees, buildings," Halloway said, "and holograms and force fields to create the people and animals." Almost before I could finish, the scene disappeared. As it did, the walls seemed to move in; the winery and the horizon along with it were an illusion. Now I was standing in a large black box, segmented by a grid of yellow lines on the walls, floor, and ceiling. MacDougal went to the archway control panel.

"It shorted out again," MacDougal said. "This is why we're behind; this holodeck is actually hooked up through the dry dock to *Enterprise*'s power grid, but it keeps overloading it."

"We'll solve it," Halloway said, "but you've got to tell Quinn it's going to take time."

"Understood," I said. I was still processing the experience, and what it meant for starship travel. Such a convenience would be an amazing advantage: it would reduce the need for shore leave, as well as providing a multitude of training and technical simulations.

"Was it nice going home?" Halloway said.

"Oh, it was wonderful," I said. I decided quite rightly that, in this case, the truth was completely unnecessary. I would never be using a holodeck to go home again. Still, the *Enterprise* was going to be quite impressive when they were done.

✦

I left Utopia Planitia as a passenger on the *U.S.S. Saratoga*, which was under the command of a Vulcan captain named Storil. It was a small ship, similar to the *Reliant. Saratoga* was going to take me to Starbase 2, and then I would get other transportation to Starbase 3.

I was surprised to discover that there were children aboard the ship. A few officers and crew had their families with them. One night, Captain Storil invited me to join him for dinner in his cabin. We were enjoying a vegetarian meal, though mostly in silence, when I decided to ask him about it.

"It is Starfleet policy that having families aboard is a captain's discretion," Storil said. "It is logical that if Starfleet personnel have made the decision to have families, they will perform their duties more efficiently if they are not separated from them."

"Still," I said, "aren't children a disruption?"

"If rules are properly enforced," Storil said, "children follow them." I couldn't really mount an argument to this, but I also couldn't imagine inconveniencing myself to this level.

I thought I would enjoy being back on a ship, but the week I spent on the *Saratoga* ended up being far from relaxing. My first few nights I was restless and unable to sleep. I took to getting up and wandering the corridors, hoping some exercise would relax me. This ended up being useless, and by the third day I was a physical wreck. I didn't understand what the problem was; I'd spent my adult life on starships and I'd never had any trouble sleeping. But every time I lay down in bed, I had a strange and unsettling impression of danger lurking nearby. I'd get out of bed and stare out a porthole for hours, trying to see if I could make out if some enemy ship or undiscovered anomaly was threatening the vessel. All I saw were the stars. I came to know that my feeling, whatever it was, was unfounded, but I couldn't shake it.

On the fourth night, having reached my limit, I went to sickbay in the hope of receiving some medical help to get to sleep. When I got there, it was empty except for one young cadet, a woman who couldn't have been much older than 20. I had trouble believing that this woman in a cadet uniform was also a doctor, but I'd learned never to presume anything.

"May I help you, Captain?"

"Yes," I said. "I'm having trouble sleeping and was hoping you could give me something."

"I'm not allowed to prescribe medicine," the cadet said. "The *Saratoga* medical staff is short-handed, so they have me serving the graveyard shift, but I'm to wake one of the doctors if they're needed."

"No," I said, "it's not necessary…"

"You seem very anxious," she said. This bit of insight surprised me. And then I noticed her deep black eyes.

"Are you Betazoid?" I said. The Betazoids were natural telepaths; it was possible this woman was reading my mind.

"I'm half-Betazoid, on my mother's side," she said, then held out her hand. "Deanna Troi."

"Jean-Luc Picard," I said, shaking her hand. "Serving part of your academy time on the *Saratoga*?"

"Yes, I'm training in Starfleet's new ship counselor program."

I was vaguely aware of it: Starfleet had decided that on larger starships it was preferable to have a trained psychologist who was separate from the ship's doctor.

"Well, good luck," I said. I suddenly felt a strong desire to leave. I certainly didn't feel like I needed to have my head examined. I moved toward the door.

"I do think your insomnia is related to your anxiety," she said.

"I do not need to be psychoanalyzed by a cadet," I said. My tone was unnecessarily sharp, and I immediately regretted it.

"Forgive me, Captain," she said. "I didn't mean to pry."

"No, no," I said. "My fault." I stood there. I wanted to leave, but there was something comforting about this young woman that kept me there.

"Would you like to sit down for a moment?" she said. She sat at a small table near one of the bio beds. I paused, and, not quite understanding why, I joined her. We sat in silence for a moment.

"How did you know I was anxious? Did you read my mind?"

"I'm not a true telepath," she said. "My father was human. But I can read strong emotions. Do you know what it is you're anxious about?"

"No."

"I see." She considered me for a moment. "Is this your first time on a starship?"

"Hardly," I said. "I just finished twenty years as captain of the *Stargazer*."

"Oh," she said. "What made you decide to leave?"

"I didn't decide to leave," I said. "The ship was disabled in an attack, we had to abandon it."

"I'm sorry," she said. She appeared genuinely saddened. "Did you lose any of your crew?"

"Yes." The images of the people who'd died on that ship that I left behind came forward in my mind. What kept me from sleeping suddenly made sense. I'd made some association with being on this ship and their deaths on *Stargazer*; my mind had tried to push them away. But they had lurked there, an "impending danger."

"That's terrible," she said. "I can feel they meant a lot to you." I was resentful that this woman was prying into my emotions. I wanted to escape, but I couldn't. Somehow, by sitting down with her in the first place, I had consented to her meddling. Her questions made me uncomfortable, but I wanted them.

She waited a few more moments; it might have just been seconds, but it felt a lot longer.

"Do you think being on the *Saratoga* is reminding you of their deaths?"

I didn't answer her. I couldn't. But she properly read that as affirmation.

"It's not uncommon," Deanna said, "for someone to feel they've done something wrong surviving a traumatic event that others did not."

"I was the captain," I said. "It was my responsibility to protect them."

"You were the captain. You are also just a man. Some situations are out of your control." We again sat there in silence for a few moments. The feeling that had held me there initially eased. I knew I could get up. But now I wasn't sure I wanted to.

"What do I do?" I said.

"There's a voice inside of you telling you to avoid the memory," she said. "But there's also a part of you that wants to remember them. They meant a lot to you. I think you should try to listen to that part of yourself."

I nodded, and got up.

"Thank you, Cadet," I said. She smiled, and I left the room.

I went back to my quarters and lay down on the bed. I thought of my late friend Scully, underneath the bridge helm controls of the *Stargazer* trying to reconnect them so the ship could leave spacedock. I smiled a sad smile and drifted off to sleep.

THE AUTOBIOGRAPHY OF JEAN-LUC PICARD

✦

A few weeks later, I'd finished the final leg of my journey and reached Starbase 3. One of the oldest of the Starfleet outposts, it was a planetary facility built on the smaller of two M-Class worlds circling Barnard's Star. The architectural style of the starbase reflected the fact that Starfleet, in its original inception, was an Earth-based service and the facilities were built to resemble something that felt familiar to humans. Space travel took much longer back then, and the designers of the early Starbase program wanted personnel posted there to feel like it could be home. It was effective; when I beamed down to the main administration building, I felt like I'd arrived in the Earth city of Denver, despite the orange sky.

A yeoman ran out of the building to greet me and escorted me to the administrator's office. The man behind the desk was about my age with gray in his beard and stood up to greet me.

"Good to see you, Jean-Luc," Admiral Leyton said. "Been a long time."

"Introduction to Federation Law class," I said. "Right?" Leyton laughed. I had seen him at the academy after that class, but not since graduating. He'd recently received the promotion to vice admiral and this posting. Though he was more than deserving of the rank, when renewing acquaintances with old colleagues I was often left with the feeling that my career was standing still.

The yeoman left us alone, and I made my report to Leyton regarding the readiness of ships to be moved to this sector. I could see that the news I'd brought wasn't what he wanted to hear.

"Fifteen ships ready now," Leyton said. "That's all?"

"Another twenty will be available in three weeks," I said, but this didn't seem to make him feel better. "Perhaps if I knew what this was about..."

"I'm sorry you had to be kept in the dark, Jean-Luc," Leyton said. He then tapped the communicator on his chest. "Leyton to Lieutenant Data, please report to my office."

"Acknowledged," the voice said. A moment later, a Starfleet lieutenant from a race I'd never seen entered the room. He seemed human except for his golden-white skin and yellow eyes. His demeanor was simultaneously pleasant and distant.

"Lieutenant Data," he said.

THE STORY OF ONE OF STARFLEET'S MOST INSPIRATIONAL CAPTAINS

"Captain Jean-Luc Picard." I extended my hand. He looked at it curiously for a strange beat, then shook it. There was something inorganic and forced about his touch, like an expert imitation of a human handshake. It was then that I realized who this was.

"You're the android," I said. The words came out of my mouth involuntarily.

"Yes," Data said. It was a matter of some note that an android, created by noted cyberneticist Dr. Noonian Soong, had graduated from Starfleet Academy, but I was in no way prepared to meet it and quickly realized I'd been rude.

"Forgive me for calling you 'the android.'"

"There is no offense," Data said. "As I am the only android in Starfleet, referring to me as 'the android' is an accurate description."

"Lieutenant," Leyton said, "please brief Captain Picard on the situation related to his mission."

"Yes, Admiral," Data said, walking to the large computer interface on the wall. He brought up an image of a planet. "This is an image of the planet Denobula taken with long-range sensors."

"As you know," Leyton said, "Denobula withdrew from Galactic affairs after the Romulan War when the enemy fleet killed three million of their people…"

"Three million, seven hundred sixty-three thousand, two hundred seventy-one," Data said.

"Just show him what you found," Leyton said.

I could see that the android lieutenant had not picked up on Leyton's annoyance at the pointless correction. Data adjusted the image, which magnified to reveal another globe in orbit of the planet.

"Is that a small moon?" I said.

"Negative," Data said. "It is an artificial construct, perhaps a space station."

"It's larger than any space station I've ever seen," I said. "Are we able to determine its purpose?"

"That's the difficulty," Leyton said. "It's projecting an enormous amount of subspace interference that disrupts our long-range scans. Starfleet Tactical is concerned it's a weapon of some kind."

"The Denobulans were allies," I said.

"Who we haven't heard from in two hundred years," Leyton said.

"The Denobulans do have a long history of war in their culture," Data said.

I was fascinated by this creation. His delivery of information somehow immediately engendered trust in me.

"There is also the message," Leyton said.

"Message?"

"Starfleet Intelligence intercepted a coded message sent throughout the Alpha and Beta Quadrants," Data said.

"A message," Leyton said, "which only Data was able to decode."

"The code was based on a Denobulan lullaby," Data said, "which was commonly known in Denobulan culture, but virtually unknown anywhere else. This led me to hypothesize that the message was meant only for Denobulans, perhaps some who might still be residing on other planets."

"What did the message say?"

"Two words: 'Come home.' Along with a date." Data indicated a date on the screen.

"That's about two weeks from now," I said. "Is that a deadline?"

"It would appear so," Leyton said. "Starfleet Tactical is concerned that that globe is a first strike weapon, and that's the date they plan to use it. We have to destroy it."

"We're going to attack? The Federation has never committed a first strike…"

"There is no better alternative," Leyton said. "The Denobulans won't respond to our attempts to communicate."

"Have you told them you plan to attack?"

"How can we do that, Jean-Luc?" Leyton said. "If it really is a weapon, we'd be giving them another advantage. We have no choice. I need you to find me more ships. Lieutenant Data will help you."

I had my orders, but I didn't like them. This situation was very troubling. The idea that Starfleet might make a first strike was a terrible precedent and undermined the philosophy of peace that the Federation had lived under for centuries.

But the one positive in this mission was Data. As I spent the next two days with this artificial man, I went from fascinated to awed. He had an amazing ability to process a wide variety of information from multiple sources, as well as having a veritable encyclopedia of knowledge in his own brain. And though he claimed to have no emotions, he had a cheerful desire for learning and acceptance. I soon looked to him as an indispensable resource.

One day while we were going over the repair schedules of ships in the sector, I hit on an idea.

"Data," I said, "what do Denobulans look like?"

"There are twenty-three thousand, one hundred seven images in the Federation database," Data said.

"Choose one," I said. Data pulled a picture up on the viewscreen in his small office. I was only vaguely familiar with the species I was looking at: it had a prominent forehead, outlined with ridges that extended down to its cheekbones. Though I'd learned about Denobulans in history, I don't think I'd ever seen one in person.

"Now, cross-reference this photo with facial recognition software and see if any resident of a Starfleet or Federation facility has similar features." I thought that if there were still Denobulans living in the Federation, they might be living incognito.

"I have found one," Data said. He brought the picture up. It was a similar being to the one we'd just looked at, although a great deal older. "His name is Sim; he is a resident of Starbase 12 where he has run a facility since the year 2314." There was something familiar about Sim, but I couldn't put my finger on it.

"Facility? What kind of facility?"

"A bar. It is named 'Feezal's.'"

"Check and see if he's still there."

"He has left. He filed a flight plan yesterday… for Denobula." Data looked up at me; he seemed impressed that I'd been able to track down a Denobulan in the Federation. "Intriguing. This person may be a source of valuable information."

"He almost certainly knows why he's going home," I said. "His course will take him fairly close to Starbase 3, correct?"

"Yes, sir," Data said. "In six point seven days. But it would seem unlikely that he would voluntarily provide us with the information we seek."

"He won't have to," I said. A plan was forming in my mind. One that I hoped would avoid a military incursion that would stain Starfleet for generations.

"Let's go see Admiral Leyton," I said.

✦

One week later, Data and I were in a small, somewhat ancient Tellarite scout vessel, floating in space without engine power. Our warp reactor had been sabotaged. By us.

Also, we were disguised as Denobulans.

The prosthetics we wore were quite convincing, and small devices that Lieutenant Data had created made us read to any scanner as being Denobulan. I hoped our deception would succeed. Leyton had recognized that this was a good intelligence-gathering opportunity, but had given me a strict time limit: if he didn't hear from me in four days he was going to proceed with his attack.

"I'm detecting the transport," Data said.

"Send the distress signal," I said. I needed to wait until the last possible moment. I couldn't risk another ship answering our faux plea for help, but it had to be general enough to avoid looking suspicious.

"The transport is responding," Data said.

"On screen," I said.

On the small viewscreen, an elderly Denobulan appeared. It was Sim. This was a particularly long-lived species, so the fact that Sim appeared elderly meant he must be of a considerably advanced age.

"What have we here?" the old Denobulan said. Despite his age, he had a youthful bearing.

"I am Phlogen," Data said. "This is Mettus." Data and I had agreed ahead of time that I would let him do most of the talking. He had in his head more information about the Denobulans than anyone, which was how I was able to sell Admiral Leyton on this spy mission.

"How interesting," he said. "I named one of my children Mettus. I am Sim. What seems to be the trouble?"

"Our engines have failed," Data said. "We do not possess the necessary tools or expertise to fix them." I realized that there was a downside to letting Data speak: he was overly formal. I hoped that our friend wouldn't notice.

"I don't know that I can help you, I don't really have much mechanical expertise," he said. "Were you heading home?"

I nodded.

"Well, if you're willing to abandon your ship, I can, as the humans say, 'give you a lift.'"

"That would be greatly appreciated," Data said.

Sim docked with us, and we boarded his ship. It was a small craft, crammed with cages holding all manner of creatures and plants.

"Forgive my menagerie," he said. "And I suggest you keep your hands free of the cages." He led us to two seats behind his at the control panel. He took the helm, disconnected from our derelict craft, and headed off to Denobula.

A bat in a cage near me tittered noisily.

"What kind of bat is that?" I said.

"Pyrithian," he said. "Careful, she enjoys the taste of fingers."

"You have quite a collection."

"I was a doctor in a previous life, back when practicing space medicine relied on live animals and plants for cures, so I would collect flora and fauna from whatever planet I visited. Medical technology has long since made this kind of thing obsolete, so I stopped practicing medicine, but I haven't been able to cure myself of the habit of collecting."

"How long have you been away from Denobula?" I said.

"Oh, I haven't lived there in over two hundred years," he said. "But I've been back to visit. What about you? What took you away from home?"

I glanced at Data. I wanted him to answer this question.

"We are geologists," Data said, "exploring other planets looking for solutions to the seismic problems on Denobula."

"A worthy effort," Sim said.

I was relieved but not surprised. I'd spent enough time with Data to know that he could tap into the historical database in his head to reference Denobulans who'd left their homeworld and use the information to craft a believable answer. What interested me about Data as a creation was that, if instructed, he had the ability to lie. And he did it very convincingly.

We had to travel several hours to Denobula, and Sim chatted with us the entire time. Data did an incredible job maintaining our cover, while I waited for an opportunity to find out what Sim knew. I had to be careful and wait for the subject to come up naturally. Eventually it did.

"I have to say," Sim said, "I was surprised they were able to complete the project so quickly."

"Yes," I said, "it's quite an accomplishment."

"Hmmm," Sim said.

"You seem conflicted," I said. "Do you think we're making the wrong decision?"

"No," he said. "But I have made a lot of friends in the Federation. I will miss them."

I glanced at Data—this had an ominous ring to it. I was afraid that Leyton might be right. But, as I had been spending time with Sim, memories started to nag at me. His face was still familiar. I decided to try to figure out why. I got him talking about his bar on Starbase 12.

"Why did you decide to settle there?"

"I don't talk about it very often," he said. "I served in Starfleet. I still enjoy the company of their officers."

"When did you serve in Starfleet?" Some lost piece of memory was fighting its way forward to the front of my brain…

"Oh, before they founded their Federation. I was part of something called the Interspecies Medical Exchange, and served on one of their starships."

I remembered, and a split second before I could stop him, Data did too.

"The name of that Denobulan," Data said, "was Phlox."

"Yes, I changed my name a while back," Sim said. "I knew that I had gained some notoriety in the Federation, and was looking to live out a quieter life. You've heard of me?"

Heard of him! When I realized who he was, I had to stifle a gasp of recognition. Phlox was the doctor on the NX-01, the original *U.S.S. Enterprise*. But I'd momentarily forgotten that I was disguised as a Denobulan, and that a Denobulan might not be so well versed in the personnel on humanity's first starship.

"Yes," I said, "you're well known among scientists like us. You blazed a lot of trails."

"Oh, I think you exaggerate," Phlox said. "But it's nice to know I'm remembered back home."

I had so many questions I wanted to ask but held back—Data and I had almost blown our cover. Still, our companion's identity only made the situation harder to accept. Everything I knew about Phlox, his compassion and scientific integrity, made it impossible for me to believe he would accept his people launching some kind of attack against the Federation. Yet if he did accept it, I couldn't take the risk to reveal ourselves. I had to see the plan through.

We arrived at the Denobulan system, and this was where my plan to be picked up by Phlox paid its greatest dividend: Phlox had a clearance code for his ship, and they let us enter the system with no difficulty. We approached the planet, passing the large artificial globe that hung in a wide orbit. It was a monstrosity. Its dark metal skin and vibrant internal energy seemed to confirm a malevolent purpose.

Phlox took his ship to a landing pad on the planet. The entire Denobulan population was on one continent, and when we landed the population density was startling, even at the spaceport. The Denobulans themselves seemed very comfortable with close physical proximity. It seemed many were returning home, receiving enthusiastic greetings from friends and family.

"It was a pleasure meeting you," Phlox said. "I'm sure I'll see you again."

"I hope so," I said.

"We greatly appreciate you 'giving us a lift,'" Data said. His inflection was stiff and unnatural, but Phlox laughed—he seemed to take it as a bit of humor. We went our separate ways.

Data and I journeyed into the main city off the starport. In the sky above the city, even in daylight, the giant artificial globe was visible. It was incongruous to the sight of the city itself. The homes and buildings were close together, and Denobulans seemed in the midst of an extended celebration, singing, drinking, and enjoying each other's company.

"Is this what a warlike species looks like?" Data said.

"Hardly, Mr. Data," I said. "We have to get more information about what that device is. How much time do we have?"

"The date the Denobulans originally gave is now three point seven three five days away."

Leyton would stick to the timeline he'd given me—he wasn't going to wait past the deadline. It was imperative for him to destroy that device rather than risk it being used on the Federation. So Data and I had two days to get into our roles as Denobulans and hopefully find out something useful, and then get off the planet to intercept Leyton and his fleet.

I was immediately overwhelmed by the general hospitality and openness of this species. The Denobulan culture was focused on family; they gave freely of shelter and food, and celebrated familial relations in a way I hadn't seen on any other world. Men and women had multiple wives and husbands, and there were many children from those connections. It felt like a vibrant, advanced society where individuals were firmly connected to one another. My companion agreed with me.

"It would seem," Data said, "that Starfleet's concern that the Denobulans have returned to their historic warlike period is unfounded." We had just left a large meal with a Denobulan family, who had invited us in off the street.

"Then why build a giant weapon?" I said. "And if it's not a weapon, why hide its purpose with subspace interference?"

"There is one possibility we have not considered," Data said. "Perhaps the subspace interference is not intended to hide its function, but is just a necessary aspect *of* its function."

"A giant subspace transmitter? What would it be used for?"

"You don't know what it is?" The voice surprised both of us, and we turned to find ourselves facing a young Denobulan, probably ten years old. He had been at the dinner that we'd just enjoyed, and must have followed us out. Not sure what to do, I paused. Data did not.

"No, we do not. Can you tell us?"

"It's a subspace engine," he said. "Everybody knows that." With that, the child scampered off.

"A subspace engine?" I said. "Have you ever heard of such a thing?"

"They are theoretical," Data said. "It has often been postulated that since we use subspace to send faster than light communication, it might also be used to transfer objects."

"We need more information," I said, "and I'm afraid we're going to have to take a bigger risk."

We set out, with the help of a directory, to find our way to Phlox's home. When he answered the door, he looked genuinely pleased to see us. His home was filled with children and adults, and Phlox seemed intent on introducing us to all of them, including his son named Mettus. Eventually, I found a moment to take Phlox aside.

"We need to talk to you alone about a matter of some urgency," I said. He could see I was concerned and took us to a more private room.

"What is the problem, Mettus?"

I looked at Data, and I knew he had no idea what I was planning to do. Nor would he know how to give me any support for it even if he did.

"I'm not Denobulan. I'm human. Captain Jean-Luc Picard from Starfleet."

"Really?" He started looking over my disguise. "Quite convincing…"

"We came here to find out why your people have built a subspace engine," I said. "Starfleet is greatly concerned."

"They have no need to worry," Phlox said. "It was built to take Denobula and its sun away."

" 'Away'?"

"Yes," he said. "In a few days, it will generate a subspace field that will remove this entire system from our Galaxy, and transfer it into subspace."

It sounded incredible. I looked at Data, who nodded.

"That is theoretically possible," he said.

I turned back to Phlox. "Why are you doing this?"

"My people never recovered from the deaths caused by the great attack," he said. He was referring to the attack on the planet that had occurred two hundred years before. "Three million Denobulans were killed; those deaths touched every family on the planet. We've seen the hostilities Starfleet has recently engaged in, with the Cardassians and the Tzenkethi, there was almost a war with the Klingons, and the Romulans still loom large. It is only a matter of time before our world is pulled into conflict again."

I couldn't tell him how correct he was: Starfleet itself was planning an attack as we spoke.

"So we are pulling ourselves from the Galaxy. Replicators give us everything we need. The effective radius of the engine will include our sun and the other bodies in the system. The invention has been tested; our scientists assure us our star system will survive in subspace. And we will survive in peace. But you, my friends, must leave, unless you wish to spend the rest of your lives here."

"That would be most intriguing," Data said.

"But not preferable," I said. "Can you help us?"

✦

"I don't know that I can afford to trust this, Jean-Luc," Leyton said. It was a day later, and I was on the bridge of the *U.S.S. Excalibur*, the lead ship in the fleet

Leyton had assembled. We were a few light-years out from the Denobulan system, and Data and I were still in our disguises. Phlox had been able to get us to a spaceship, and we'd intercepted the fleet.

"You have to trust this, Admiral," I said.

"It is not a weapon, sir," Data said. Leyton looked at him; it was hard to argue with Data. "They have no harmful intent."

"Sir," the ops officer said, "I'm reading a massive build-up in subspace interference."

Leyton looked at us, annoyed. We'd delayed him, and, in his mind, perhaps doomed him.

"Shields up, red alert," Leyton said. "All ships, stand by to—"

Before he could finish, the ship was hit with a shockwave that knocked us all off our feet. Leyton and his conn officer crawled back to right the ship. Data helped me up. When we looked on the screen, I knew it was all over.

"Message to all ships," Leyton said. "Engage course to Denobula."

"Sir," the conn officer said. "I can't. It's gone."

"What?"

"The star, the planet, they're not there."

I looked at Data and smiled. The Denobulans had got what they wanted, a universe without war. And as I watched Leyton, simmering with frustration that events hadn't played out the way he'd expected, I knew such a universe would escape the rest of us—at least for a while.

✦

Over the next few years, I found satisfaction in my job as a troubleshooter for Quinn. The work I was doing was active and engaging, and the desire to command a ship began to fade. Quinn seemed to have forgotten his promise to put me back in command, and in any event I felt I had made a transition to another career, maybe one I would find as satisfying as being a starship captain. I also took delight in being free from the confines of one ship; I'd been on the *Stargazer* for so long, I felt like I was discovering a whole new generation of people who'd come out of the academy and begun to make their mark on

THE STORY OF ONE OF STARFLEET'S MOST INSPIRATIONAL CAPTAINS

Starfleet and the Federation. And I found satisfaction in sharing my experience with them, acting as a kind of elder statesman.

One such person I met while I was serving as interim commanding officer of Starbase 23. The old commander had unexpectedly passed away, and a new commander was en route, and since I was the most senior officer in the area, Quinn had me take over running the facility. Starbase 23 was a space station in a system with no Class-M planets, but one that did have an abundance of asteroids, on which the Starfleet Corps of Engineers had built mining facilities. Part of my duties were regular inspections of those asteroid facilities. One day, leaving for a round of these inspections, I had the shuttlebay officer of the deck assign me a pilot.

When I showed up in the shuttle bay, the young officer greeted me. He wore an unusual device over his eyes, a gold visor made of a light metal. I introduced myself, and we shook hands.

"Lieutenant Geordi La Forge," he said.

We were on a tight schedule, so I refrained from indulging my curiosity about his eyewear and we got on board. La Forge took the controls, and went down a complete checklist of all the shuttle's systems. (I would've usually dispensed with this protocol, but this was a young officer trying to make an impression, so I let him go through with it.)

On our short trip out to the asteroid, I found out a little bit about him. He was from Earth, had served on the *Victory* and was between assignments, so he volunteered for shuttle pilot duty. I decided to ask about his accessory.

"It detects electromagnetic signals and transmits them to my brain," Geordi said.

"That sounds like a useful device," I said.

"Especially when you're blind," he said.

"Excuse me?"

"Oh, I'm sorry, sir, I assumed you knew. I was born blind. The visor lets me 'see,' kind of."

The man piloting my shuttle was blind. It was at times like this I marveled at the age in which I lived that such a thing was in no way worrisome.

We returned from the inspection of the first asteroid mining facility and parted company for the evening. I returned to the shuttlebay the next morning for my tour of the next asteroid facility. La Forge was already there, working on the shuttle. He looked very tired, and I asked him what he'd been doing.

"I refitted the fusion initiators, sir," he said. "Just finished."

"That must have taken all night," I said.

"Yes, well, I thought I should do something about it when you commented on the engine efficiency…"

This was strange; I had no recollection of saying anything about the engine efficiency.

"I think you must be mistaken…" I said.

"When I went down the launch checklist and reported the shuttle's engine efficiency was 87 percent, you said: 'Probably not what it should be.' They should be up over 95 percent now."

If he'd done it to impress me, he'd succeeded, but I could tell that it wasn't his motivation. He sincerely just wanted to make a piece of equipment work better. A short time after, La Forge received a posting on the *Hood*, but I knew this was someone I was going to remember.

✦

"*U.S.S. Constellation* arriving Bay 2," the announcer said.

I was packing up my office at the starbase, which looked out on the internal bay. As I looked up and saw the ship pulling in, I had a moment of déjà vu. The *U.S.S. Constellation* was the same class as the *Stargazer* and looked virtually identical. When I had first seen that old ship of mine, it was pulling into the bay of a starbase; now it felt like I was reliving that moment 25 years later. My temporary assignment was over, and I would be leaving on the *Constellation*. In command, if only for a little while.

Cliff Kennelly, shipmaster of the *Constellation*, had just been promoted to vice admiral and would be taking command of Starbase 23. Since Kennelly was taking much of his command crew with him to the starbase, and much of the rest of the crew was being reassigned, someone had to get the *Constellation* back to the Sol system, where it would be decommissioned and its parts recycled. I was ambivalent about the mission, but Quinn needed me back on Earth, and this was a very efficient way to get me there.

THE STORY OF ONE OF STARFLEET'S MOST INSPIRATIONAL CAPTAINS

Kennelly reported to my office, and I released the starbase command codes to him. Though I'd read his reports on the condition of his ship, he gave me a quick briefing on its handling. He was an ambitious man, at least ten years my junior. Just a few years earlier I would've been jealous of his success, but I had found some peace in the intervening years of not being in command, or I thought I had.

Later, after I'd gathered my belongings, I went to the *Constellation*. The ship was as old as the *Stargazer*, and on the inside looked much the same. I walked along the corridors with a little sense of nostalgia, mournful for the friends who'd died, accepting of the loss. My interaction with Deanna Troi years earlier had helped me to fully process that terrible tragedy.

When I got to the bridge, an unusual sight greeted me.

There was only one officer there, an ensign. Who was a Klingon.

"Captain on the bridge," the Klingon said. The fact that he was announcing it to no one made the situation that much more strange.

"You must be Ensign Worf," I said. I had read the records of the crew of the *Constellation*, and had learned a little about this unique officer.

"An honor to meet you, Captain Picard," he said. Like many of his species, he was large and intimidating, with an almost animal growl under every word out of his mouth. I'd met a few Klingons over the years, but had never found common ground with any of them. This one, however, had an amazing story: he was one of the last survivors of the Romulan attack on Khitomer. He spent much of his childhood on the farming colony on Gault, raised by human foster parents of Russian origin, and was the first Klingon to graduate from Starfleet Academy.

"Glad to be aboard, Ensign," I said.

"I studied your battle at Maxia when I was a cadet at the academy," Worf said. "Your victory was worthy of a Klingon warrior."

I hadn't heard anyone put the event quite that way. I looked at this young officer. No matter where he was from, I decided it was my responsibility to contribute to his education.

"Did you also study the Duke of Wellington?" I said. Worf looked at me confused.

"Duke of...?"

"I'd like you to tell me why I might not see it as a victory, and use the Duke of Wellington as your guide."

"Yes, sir," Worf said. "Now, sir?"

"On your first free shift," I said. "Now I'd like you to make preparations to get underway." He turned and recalled the bridge crew to duty. While he did, I took the command chair.

We left orbit a few hours later. About half the crew had disembarked at Starbase 23 for other assignments. The ship's maximum speed was warp 6, but I kept it at warp 4—Kennelly had warned me it wasn't up to specs. For the entire trip back, there were only four of us on the bridge: Ensign Worf at the ops station, Ensign Tania Lotia at the helm, and doing double duty of engineering and communications was Lieutenant Lexi Turner.

It was going very smoothly. We were only a few days from Sol and it felt as if it would be a very dull trip. During my one shift off, I spent the time alone in my quarters. Off of Worf's remark that he'd studied "The Battle of Maxia" at the academy, I decided to investigate what exactly it was that was being taught. I found in the database the academy text "Strategies and Tactics of Starship Combat" and was startled to discover something called the "Picard Maneuver." My last-ditch tactic on the *Stargazer* of jumping to warp against my unknown enemy had made it into a text.

I watched a computer simulation of the event linked to the text: the ships moved in a dance that looked choreographed. It was horrifying to me. The text had taken out all the desperation and risk. This wasn't a game—people had died. I turned off the screen.

I began writing a formal complaint to the academy commandant. This seemed like a terrible way to teach students. Halfway through, I took a pause. Yes, my experience had been fraught and difficult, but because of what I'd had to go through, perhaps some future captain in a similar position might benefit from my experience. I deleted my letter. My reverie was interrupted by the door chime.

"Come," I said.

The door opened revealing Worf.

"May I come in, sir?"

"Certainly, Ensign." I offered him a chair, which he declined.

"I've completed my assignment," Worf said, handing me a PADD. "I have studied the career of Arthur Wellesley, the First Duke of Wellington. Perhaps one of Earth's greatest warriors."

"Is that why I had you study him?"

Worf took a long pause.

"No," Worf said, "I believe it was because of a quote he was well known for. In an ancient correspondence he was reflecting on the loss of comrades, and wrote: 'Nothing except a battle lost can be half as melancholy as a battle won.' You take no joy in your victory; it is only slightly less sad for you than defeat. You do not celebrate your victory at Maxia for this reason."

"Yes," I said. This young officer had passed the test with flying colors. "Do you agree with me and the Duke of Wellington on this?"

"The honor is to serve," Worf said. "If they died well, in service, there is no reason for... melancholy."

"And yet you understood what I wanted you to glean from it."

"If you'll forgive me, sir," Worf said, "I have lived with humans my whole life. I understand their proclivities." This was an interesting man; straddling two worlds and doing it quite well.

My little seminar on war was interrupted by a call from the bridge.

"Receiving a distress call from the Federation colony on Carnellia IV," Turner said. "Several of the colonists have accidentally crossed into an old minefield. There are severe injuries. The *U.S.S. Roosevelt* has also responded."

"Set course, maximum warp," I said. "Inform the *Roosevelt* we will stand by to assist." Worf and I left for the bridge in a hurry. Without a full crew compliment or dedicated medical staff, I wasn't sure we would be that much help, but, as Worf said, the honor was to serve.

When we arrived at Carnellia IV, the *Roosevelt* was already in orbit. The colony was very new; about one hundred people had settled on the planet after it was charted. Soon after they arrived, the colonists found evidence the original inhabitants of the planet had died out long ago. I beamed down with Worf and every crewmember who had any sort of medical training.

A field hospital had been set up near the minefield; it was a nightmare of injured people, some missing limbs. The *Roosevelt*'s doctors were already hard at work treating the victims. I instructed our medics to lend a hand, while Worf and I headed to the scene of the accident.

We followed the sound of a man howling in pain, and found the ship's captain at the edge of the minefield. There was evidence that several mines had exploded—blood and body parts were scattered around. It was horrific, but that wasn't what I was focused on.

In the middle of the carnage, a Starfleet ensign was looking intently at the ground as she slowly but steadily walked through it. A few feet in front of her, the source of the unnerving screams was a middle-aged man, his left leg blown off at the knee.

I approached the captain, who didn't take her eyes off her officer.

"Captain Cheva," I said. She turned and glanced at me.

"Captain Picard," she said, "I wish we were meeting under better circumstances." Her focus was on her officer, a young woman who was no more than 25. I watched as she slowly picked up her foot, and gently placed it forward. Another step.

"Can't we just beam the man up?" Worf said.

"We don't know anything about these mines," Cheva said. "The energy from the transporter, or even a scanner, might set them off."

"Your ensign is very brave," I said.

Cheva nodded. "Natasha Yar," she said.

"How is she determining where to walk?" I said.

"She's making judgments based on her own experience planting mines," Cheva said. "Inexact to be sure. Tasha's from the Turkana colony." That was a violent, unforgiving place, and if this woman had survived it and made it through the academy she was special indeed.

We watched as Tasha took another careful step. She was now inches from the injured man, whose howling was unnerving us all. Tasha carefully knelt down, and injected the man with a hypo. He fell into unconsciousness. She then lifted him up over her shoulder and slowly stood up. Blood from his wounds soaked her uniform as she slowly retraced each of her steps out of the minefield.

"Warrior," said Worf, quietly. I couldn't have agreed more.

✦

THE STORY OF ONE OF STARFLEET'S MOST INSPIRATIONAL CAPTAINS

It quickly became clear that *Constellation*'s presence on Carnellia was superfluous. Cheva and her crew of the *Roosevelt* were quite able to take care of the injured, as well as determining how to deactivate the minefield. So with Cheva's permission, I left. It was quite a thing to see my former officer now in command, and I felt in some sense the torch had been passed. It was the next generation's turn to take over.

I returned the *Constellation* to Utopia Planitia, and on my way, I reflected on the terrible effect of war: the close brush with Denobula, the carnage on Carnellia IV. I'd had my fill of it. It wasn't enough to just be a Starfleet officer, one had to commit oneself to peace. I decided as I ended what I thought would be my last command that I had new purpose.

We reached Utopia Planitia, and the crew disembarked without fanfare. I turned all the necessary paperwork over to the yard commander, then requisitioned a shuttle to take me to Earth. But before I got very far away from Mars, I received a call from Tom Halloway, who asked me to come meet him back on Utopia Planitia. I turned the shuttle around, and headed to the dry dock where the *Enterprise* was still being built, now almost complete.

As I closed in on the all but complete ship, I took it in. It cut a grand profile, the largest Starfleet vessel in history. I docked, and Halloway met me in the operations center.

"A beauty, isn't she?" he said. We were looking again at the *Enterprise*, this time through the bay windows of the operations center. "They've designated her the Federation flagship." This was quite an honor; in the absence of an admiral, the flagship's captain would have implicit seniority over other captains and ships in the fleet.

"You've done an amazing job," I said. "Almost ready to launch?"

"Yeah, taking her on a three-week shakedown cruise on Monday," Halloway said. "Then after that, to Earth where she'll be someone else's problem."

"You're not going to stay her captain?"

"I'm a 'first captain,'" Halloway said. He was making reference to the old naval tradition of the United States Navy where the first captain of a ship was only responsible for building it; it was the second captain who took her out.

"Well, someone is very lucky then," I said.

"That's actually what I wanted to talk to you about," someone said. I turned to see that Admiral Quinn had just walked in.

"Admiral," I said. "What are you doing here?"

"I wanted to hear who you thought should be captain of our new ship," Quinn said. "Halloway, can I borrow your office?"

Quinn and I went to a small office off the operations center.

"So," Quinn said. "Who do you recommend?"

"Well, Andrea Brand…"

"She's only a couple of years away from being promoted to Admiral," Quinn said. "I want someone who is going to stay a while."

"There's Jellico, DeSoto, Bill Ross…" Quinn dismissed all of them with a wave of his hand. I was finding this little game, whatever it was, quite annoying.

"We had someone else in mind," Quinn said.

"Who?"

"You," Quinn said. "Unless you just want to stay in your current job."

This took me by surprise for a lot of reasons. In that moment, I realized how much I had been protecting myself from disappointment. I'd wanted a captain's chair again, but had rationalized that that part of my career was over because I didn't think it was possible.

"You've done excellent work the last few years," Quinn said. "Your mission to Denobula alone was enough to rehabilitate you in the eyes of the Admiralty. I could've put you on a ship before this, but it felt like the *Enterprise* was the right one, so I held you back. I hope that's all right." He'd made me captain of the Federation flagship, the highest honor a captain could achieve.

"Thank you, Admiral."

"Don't let anyone ever say I don't keep my promises," Quinn said.

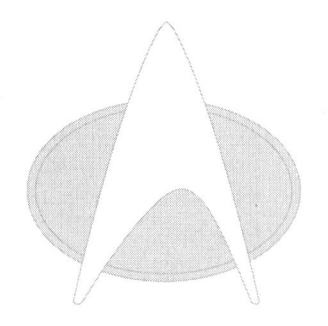

CHAPTER NINE

"**CAPTAIN'S LOG: STARDATE 41153.7.** Our destination is the planet Deneb IV, beyond which lies the great unexplored mass of the Galaxy. My orders are to examine Farpoint, a starbase built there by the inhabitants of Deneb IV. Meanwhile, I'm becoming better acquainted with my new command, this *Galaxy*-class *U.S.S. Enterprise*. I'm still somewhat in awe of its size and complexity…"

I was in my new quarters, grand, plush, and comfortable, staring at the stars distorted by warp speed. I'd put a lot of thought into what I was going to say in that first log entry. I was recording a moment for posterity, and my words were carefully crafted to disguise the mass of chaotic feelings that threatened to overwhelm me. I had a new ship, a new crew, a new life. And I was surrounded by strangers, there were children all over my ship, and I was on my way to see the one woman in my life I'd ever truly loved.

Several weeks previous, while Halloway was still "shaking down" the *Enterprise*, I was in my rooms at Starfleet Headquarters going over personnel choices. There were over a thousand crewmen tasked to this ship, almost a complete city in space, and I wouldn't choose them all; I picked department heads and they in turn staffed their sections, though I could certainly make strong "suggestions" if there was a junior officer I liked. Because the *Enterprise* was the Federation flagship, Quinn had made it clear that I had my choice of any officer I wanted. Though this was a boon for me, it had a downside as I would be taking talented people away from captains I knew, many of whom were my friends.

I had spent hours reviewing the service records of all the candidates I was considering for first officer. It was becoming impossible to tell them apart. They were all very much the same: accomplished young men and women from countless species, all with glowing letters of recommendation and spotless records. It was telling that the one that caught my eye was the one whose record had a "spot."

William Thomas Riker, first officer for my friend Robert DeSoto on the *Hood*. He'd disobeyed a direct order from his captain and refused to let DeSoto beam down to Altair III, because Riker deemed it unsafe. He risked a general court-martial to, in his mind, protect the captain and the ship. I decided to look into this one.

"Bonjour, mon ami," DeSoto said, from the monitor in my quarters; I'd contacted him via subspace. "You going to steal my first officer?"

"It is a possibility," I said. "I'm assuming your letter of recommendation was honest?"

"Not entirely," DeSoto said. "He's got a sense of humor; I left that out because some captains don't like that."

"Good to know," I said. "Was he joking when he wouldn't let you beam down to Altair III?"

DeSoto smiled. He knew what I was getting at.

"Anybody who's had this job, Jean-Luc," he said, "knows you're alone in a thousand decisions, and a bad one can cost lives. Do I need to tell you that you need people who will stand up to you when they think you're making a bad call?"

"No, you don't," I said. This was the heart of it. I knew how hard it must have been for this young officer to stand up to his captain, because I had been in that position myself. I had disobeyed Mazzara's order to abandon ship, risked my own court-martial because I thought the captain was wrong. It was a lonely, scary moment, and an important one.

"Anything else?" DeSoto said.

"Yes," I said. "If I were you, I'd start looking for a new first officer."

After picking my XO, there were other key positions I already had people in mind for. I contacted Cheva and asked her if she'd mind giving up Natasha Yar, whom I wanted for my chief of security. Cheva chuckled at the idea that she would turn down a request from the man who'd gotten her a command.

THE STORY OF ONE OF STARFLEET'S MOST INSPIRATIONAL CAPTAINS

The *Enterprise* was also one of the first vessels to have a ship's counselor, and Deanna Troi, the young woman I'd met several years before on the *Saratoga*, was my only choice.

I also had to get Data away from Leyton. I offered Data a promotion to lieutenant commander, but Leyton didn't want to let him go—he knew how lucky he was to have him. I had Quinn put in a call and it was done. I hired my blind pilot Geordi La Forge as my conn officer, and gave Ensign Worf a promotion to lieutenant, and suggested him to Yar as a security officer.

When it came time to choose a chief medical officer, I thought my decision had been made. Dr. Ailat had been on Earth at Starfleet Medical Headquarters since her time on the *Stargazer*. I'd told her years ago that if I got another command, I would be asking her back. I didn't question this course of action until I came across a resume I didn't expect.

Beverly Crusher. She had put in for duty in the *Galaxy*-class program because it made room for families; she had never remarried and had raised Wesley on her own. When Quinn had given me the news that the *Enterprise* would have families aboard, I was aghast—children on my ship. I was in no position to argue, I wasn't going to give up the post, but it rankled me. Until, that is, the moment I realized it might mean I'd see Beverly again.

It occurred to me that she might not know I was captain, and if I offered her the position she might turn it down. And then there was the problem that Ailat might be expecting the position. It seemed irresponsible to alter my decision for such personal reasons. Beverly, though competent and skilled, wasn't nearly as experienced as Ailat was. I decided to call Ailat; perhaps she wasn't expecting me to make the offer. She was in her office at Starfleet Medical; I spoke to her via my computer monitor.

"You've heard I've been made captain of the *Enterprise*," I said.

"Yes," Ailat said. "Congratulations. You will need a chief medical officer."

"Yes," I said. "I would love for you to accept the post." I realized that I had to, in good conscience, offer her the job. She was the most qualified, and I'd had a long, comfortable working relationship with her. But my heart ached at what I was giving up.

"I am honored," Ailat said. "But are you aware that Beverly Crusher is also available?"

"Wh-what?" I sputtered, confused, embarrassed. "No... I mean, yes, her service record came my way... but..." Why was she bringing up Beverly? Were Edosians telepathic?

"Captain," Ailat said, "I served with you a long time." Her tone was as flat as it always was. She looked at me with those strange Edosian eyes set apart in that giant orange skull. Edosians didn't smile the way humans did, and certainly didn't seem warm or friendly. But Ailat was taking care of me.

"I owe you, Ailat," I said. I disconnected from her and immediately sent a request for Beverly Crusher to be posted to the *Enterprise* as chief medical officer. I stared at my computer console waiting for a response. There was still a lot of service records to look over, other posts to fill, but I couldn't concentrate.

Finally, a message. A simple moment of joy.

"Position: Chief Medical Officer. Candidate: Beverly Crusher. Candidate accepted."

✦

"Here are your orders, Captain," Quinn said, handing me a PADD. I was in the Admiralty Meeting Room with him and Admiral Norah Satie. Satie was one of Starfleet's most senior admirals. Her presence was a testimony to the prestige of the command I was being given. I was set to take command later that afternoon; Halloway had finished his shakedown cruise, and brought the *Enterprise* to McKinley Station for final adjustments.

"Anything I should be aware of?" I said. Admiral Satie sat silently for a moment; her stare was penetrating, and it unsettled me.

"After you've solved the mystery of Farpoint Station, your mission is chiefly exploration," Satie said. "You are headed into an area of space that we still have very little information about. And of course, there are security concerns."

"And, Captain Picard," Satie said, "command of the Federation flagship is a vital responsibility. We're giving it to you because we trust you to protect us from our enemies without and within."

"'Within'?" I said. "I'm sorry, Admiral, I'm not sure what that means."

"It means, Captain, be vigilant." There was definitely more to this than what she was saying, but she wasn't going to elucidate any further. I took my leave and headed to the main San Francisco starport. I was surprised to see Tasha Yar waiting for me by a shuttle.

"Security Chief Natasha Yar, reporting for duty. It's a pleasure to meet you." I found her formality unusual; she seemed to think she needed to introduce herself.

"Yes, Lieutenant, we met on Carnellia IV," I said.

"I wasn't sure you'd remember me," she said. I was incredulous.

"I watched you walk through a minefield. I chose you to be my chief of security because of it."

"Sorry, sir," she said. Her unique strength seemed to hide a bit of insecurity, at least around me.

"No apologies necessary," I said. "Shall we go?"

We boarded the shuttle, and flew over San Francisco as I'd done many times before. Tasha however appeared amazed at the views.

"It's so beautiful," she said.

"You went to the academy, surely you've seen it before."

"Yes," she said. "I've never gotten used to it. And I don't want to." I remembered then that Tasha came from Turkana IV, a truly violent world, a place where civilization had fallen apart.

"I understand," I said. "I guess I take paradise for granted."

"You've earned it, sir," she said. "The example you've set in your career has raised the bar for the rest of us."

I wasn't used to hero worship, and my instinct was to put a stop to it. But her feeling seemed so genuine, I think I would've regretted discouraging it.

Tasha piloted us toward the *Enterprise*. McKinley Station looked like a giant metal crab that was gripping the ship from above. We went into one of the smaller shuttle bays, and Tasha led me out.

There was a relatively small group of crewmembers in the bay. As there was still plenty of work to be done so we could launch, both Captain Halloway and I had agreed to dispense with a grand "transfer of command" ceremony.

"Commanding Officer *Enterprise*, arriving," Tasha said. The group stood at attention. I went to a small lectern that had been set up in the bay and read my orders aloud.

"To Captain Jean-Luc Picard, stardate 41148.0, you are hereby requested and required to take command as of this date. Signed Rear Admiral Norah Satie, Starfleet Command." I nodded to Tasha.

"Crew dismissed," Tasha said.

I walked over to Deanna Troi and Lieutenant Worf. "Welcome aboard, Captain," she said.

"It's an honor once again to serve with you, sir," Worf said.

"Thank you," I said. I noticed that not only Worf but the rest of the crew present looked at me with a kind of reverence I hadn't before experienced. It was both satisfying and unnerving. "Resume your posts, stand by to get underway." I left the shuttle bay and headed to my quarters.

As I walked the corridors, I was struck by the ship's beauty. Even with the activity the ship had an inherent tranquility. It felt like the pinnacle of civilization. For a moment at least…

"Ow!"

I'd come around the corner, and something had hit me in the shins. It took all my willpower to regain my composure. I looked down to see what had collided with me: a boy.

A child. On my ship.

Merde.

"Harry!" A man in a science uniform ran over to us and helped the boy up. He then saw who his son had run into and looked genuinely horrified. "I'm so sorry, Captain…"

"It's quite all right," I said, lying.

"I'm Dr. Bernard, sir," the man said. "This is Harry. Harry, apologize to the captain."

"No," Harry said.

"It's quite all right," I said, again lying. I left them quickly and headed to the turbolift. Once on it, I thought of my first day on the *Stargazer*, the frustration I felt at having to deal with Mazzara's children. And now there were about seventy-five on this ship. I tapped the communicator on my chest.

"Picard to Lieutenant Yar," I said.

"Yar here, sir," she said.

"From this point forward, no children allowed above Deck Two," I said. This, at least, was something I could do to limit my exposure.

THE STORY OF ONE OF STARFLEET'S MOST INSPIRATIONAL CAPTAINS

"Aye aye, sir," she said. I could hear a little confusion in her voice, but I didn't mind.

I'd just posted a sign: NO CHILDREN ON THE BRIDGE.

✦

"Captain on the bridge," Data said as I stepped off the turbolift.

My first view of the bridge was quite startling. It was large and comfortable. I initially felt ill at ease walking in such a large room; bridges in my mind were compact and efficient. This almost felt like a living room.

Data was at the ops station, Lieutenant Torres at the conn, serving there temporarily. Tasha was on the upper level at the security and communication station. Worf stood behind her, operating the defensive systems. I stopped by Data at ops.

"Good to see you, Mr. Data," I said.

"It is… good to see you too, sir," he said, as if unsure he was understanding what he was saying.

"For the future, you won't need to announce my presence on the bridge," I said.

"Aye, sir," Data said. I felt the formality didn't go with the setting. This place was to be our home. I then sat down next to Counselor Troi. She looked at me and smiled. There was something behind it.

"Something wrong, Counselor?"

"Nothing at all, sir." She leaned in closer. "Your enthusiasm is infectious."

I smiled, a little awkwardly; it would take a little getting used to being around an officer who could read my emotions so clearly.

"McKinley Station reports we're clear to depart," Yar said.

"Take us out," I said.

McKinley Station's crab-like claws lifted away, and the ship moved out of orbit. As I gave the orders for us to set a course for Deneb IV, I took in the room; we had the most up-to-date technology and an accomplished and gifted crew. I felt a great deal of anticipation for what awaited us. I was confident I was ready. My first encounter on Deneb IV brought home that my youth was long behind me.

Shortly after arriving in orbit, I stood on the deck of the hangar as a small shuttle came through the forcefield and landed. I stepped forward to greet its esteemed passenger, Starfleet's most senior physician who was going to inspect our medical layout. I hadn't seen him in a very long time, and was looking forward to our reunion.

"Admiral McCoy," I said, "Nice to see you again."

"Have we met?" He was much older, over 130 years old, white haired and stooped, but had lost none of his irascibility.

"Yes, I was in the honor guard, in Ambassador Spock's wedding."

McCoy grunted. I felt foolish; of course he wouldn't remember me.

"I was quite a bit younger," I said.

"Did you have hair?"

"I did," I said. We stood for a moment in self-conscious silence. I realized he had no interest in talking to me.

"Someone going to take me around? I'm not getting any younger."

"Of course sir." I decided to assign Lieutenant Data to the task, and returned to my duties. A few years earlier I would've felt obliged to take such an esteemed man around myself, and suffer through an awkward interaction out of a feeling of obligation. Now, however, I spared myself the indignity.

Thinking back, some of my strongest memories of that first mission center around what the circumstance revealed about members of my new crew.

Commander Riker came on board, and immediately and enthusiastically fell into his role as my first officer. He was a man of action, reminding me of my younger self, and we quickly fell into a rhythm that was efficient and complementary. I also gave him the unenviable task of trying to make me look genial with children. Geordi La Forge took his place at the conn, and my bridge crew was complete.

My first encounter with Beverly, however, was a little less satisfying. Within days of assuming command, I was on the bridge when I noticed the turbolift doors open. A teenager was standing there.

"What the hell?" I said. "Children are not allowed on the bridge."

Then Beverly stepped out of the turbolift. My breath left me. I remembered this feeling before. It was as if I was always surprised at how beautiful she was, that I couldn't hold her true beauty in my memory.

"Permission to report to the captain," she said. She was strained—this was difficult for her, too.

"Dr. Crusher," I said. I suddenly felt I'd made a terrible mistake. As her captain, any hopes for a relationship with Beverly would be impossible. I had created a new purgatory for myself.

"Captain," she said. "Sir, my son is not on the bridge, he just accompanied me on the turbolift."

"Your son?" I said. I felt a fool. I knew Wesley had aged, yet locked in my mind was the image of him as a toddler.

"His name is Wesley," she said. Of course I knew his name. How could she think I'd forget his name? Then I realized she didn't know I'd been thinking about her since the day we parted. I felt the urge to apologize for my initial coldness, so I broke my own brand-new rule, and invited Wesley on the bridge.

As he left the turbolift, I had a moment of intense déjà vu. I remembered his father, stepping off the transporter back on the *Stargazer*. This boy had the same awkwardness. The more I looked at him, the more I saw my friend.

Jack was back from the dead. I hoped I wouldn't have to see a lot of him.

✦

"Thou art directed," Q said, "to return to thine own solar system immediately."

He strutted around my ship dressed as Christopher Columbus. His primitive costume belied his virtually limitless power; he'd stopped my ship with an energy force field that stretch to every horizon of space. He changed his appearance in a flash of light and was suddenly a marine from the ancient United States, expounding about the need for "a few good men." A flash, and then he was a soldier from World War III, in battle armor sniffing amphetamines before he went into combat. All very dramatic, meant to intimidate us. Q had the power to do to us whatever he wanted. But he didn't want to destroy us, he wanted to sit in judgment.

Any student of Starfleet history knows of the extraordinarily advanced beings in the Galaxy. The Organians, the Excalbians, the Metrons—all very much like Q, judging "lesser" beings, sometimes for what they considered the greater good, sometimes just for their own amusement.

THE AUTOBIOGRAPHY OF JEAN-LUC PICARD

On that first mission, Q promised that if we failed in discovering the truth about Farpoint Station, we would all be sent back to our home planets, confined for eternity. I had a lot of questions as to whether he could and would have carried out his threat if we hadn't solved that mystery;* as I look back, I'm convinced he would've regretted it. He's enjoyed toying with me and my crew too much.

✦

"Captain," Riker said, "I'd like to talk to you about Wesley Crusher." I had a regular morning meeting with Riker in my ready room. Though we would go over a wide variety of issues involved in running such a huge ship, I never expected Wesley to make the agenda.

"What about him?"

"He's shown remarkable aptitude at understanding the ship's systems, with very little training," Riker said. "I tested him on the flight simulator, and he's as good a pilot as I am."

"Please don't exaggerate," I said. Riker's record as a pilot was exemplary—he literally had the best ratings of the entire crew.

"I'm not," Riker said. "His score on the flight simulator was higher than mine." I could tell that Riker was serious. "I think we should take him under our wing. He'd be an incredible resource."

"Why is it necessary? We have a full crew compliment." I was resisting the idea, although at that moment I didn't understand why.

"Well, sir, one of the arguments for having families on board was the opportunity for Starship captains to identify potential academy candidates among the relatives of the crew. This appears to be one of those opportunities." I envied Riker, his ability to get along so easily with everyone, while also not losing his authority. And I knew he'd formed a bond with Wesley. I was pleased

---

*EDITOR'S NOTE: Farpoint Station was in fact not a building, but an unusual energy creature that had the power to alter matter. It had been captured and enslaved by the inhabitants of Deneb IV, and forced to assume the shape of a ground facility that the inhabitants wanted to allow Starfleet to use, in exchange for payment. Once Picard discovered the truth, the creature was released and never seen again.

THE STORY OF ONE OF STARFLEET'S MOST INSPIRATIONAL CAPTAINS

about that, as the fact that Wesley was without a father was something that I took as my responsibility.

"I will think about it," I said.

✦

"Captain's log, stardate 41263.4. For outstanding performance in the best of Starfleet tradition, Wesley Crusher is made Acting Ensign, with the duties and privileges of that rank."

It was only a few weeks later. The young man had played major roles in a number of missions, and Riker's suggestion stuck in my mind. I had Riker put him on a strict course of study, with the idea he would tender an application to the academy. And since he was now an acting ensign, he was allowed on the bridge. Riker gave him a lot of time at various duty stations, serving in a support capacity. Sometimes he would take ops. I soon forgot my initial resistance to training him, until one morning, when we were on our way to Starbase 74, and La Forge excused himself from his conn position momentarily. A crewman stood by to take his place, when Riker leaned into me.

"Might be a good opportunity for Wesley to get some flying time," he said.

Something about Riker suggesting Wesley take the conn overwhelmed me with fear. What was I afraid of? It only took me a moment to realize… I had to control myself; I could feel Deanna's eyes on me.

"Make it so," I said. There was no reason not to agree.

Wesley took the conn.

Over the years, some who have reviewed my career as captain of the Enterprise have questioned my decision, specifically how I could let a teenager who'd never gone to the academy take the conn of the Federation flagship. My answer is I trusted my first officer, who had trained the young man, and our experiences proved him to be correct: Wesley was an excellent navigator and helmsman. But that wasn't the true reason I did it. The reason that I acceded to it was much more personal.

I enjoyed having Wesley at his father's post.

✦

When we left Earth, I'd been certain, based on Starfleet's reports, that the Ferengi would be the biggest new challenge we would face. It turned out that these concerns were unwarranted; they were not the dangerous adversaries we thought they would be. They were more an annoyance than a threat, a greedy, opportunistic culture whose sole motive appeared to be profit. Our most important encounter with them, however, solved a mystery that had haunted me for a long time.

DaiMon Bok commanded* a Ferengi ship, which had sought us out. He'd made overtures of friendship, wanting to give me a gift: the Stargazer. He'd found it and had it repaired.

I learned quickly that this was a ruse; Ferengi don't give gifts. It is against their religious and cultural beliefs. Bok's true motive was revenge. When he returned my ship to me, we spoke of the "unknown" ship that had attacked the Stargazer, and Bok spat out the answer of who my assailant was.

"That proud ship was Ferengi!" The vessel that had attacked Stargazer was commanded by Bok's son. Bok gave no reason why his son had attacked me, and his revenge plot failed.**

The result was I got my old ship back. We would rendezvous with a Starfleet towing vessel that would take it back to the Fleet Museum in the Sol system. I was surprised at how interested my crew was in it, and during the two days leading up to the rendezvous with the towing vessel, several of them asked permission to tour it.

"What is the crew's preoccupation with my old ship?" I said this to Riker during one of our morning meetings.

"You're kidding, right?"

"I am not kidding," I said.

"Sir, it's Columbus's Santa María, Cook's Endeavour, Armstrong's Eagle, Archer's Enterprise…" Riker said. "Your mission was required reading at the academy. Forgive me if this embarrasses you, but…"

---

*EDITOR'S NOTE: DaiMon" is a Ferengi equivalent of a starship captain, although in their culture a more accurate parallel would be to a chief executive officer of an old Earth corporation.

**EDITOR'S NOTE: Bok had acquired an illegal mind control device, which he used on Picard to get him to pilot his old ship to attack his new one. Bok was unsuccessful, and since there was no "profit" in revenge, his own people removed him from command.

"But what?"

"We all wanted to be you."

It was ironic; those years where I'd felt unknown and forgotten were now the cause of reverence from the crew. It sent me down a different road in terms of my command style. I remembered the choices I'd made as captain of the Stargazer, seeing my role as captain as less a master and more a servant, putting the needs of the crew first. Now I was falling into that god-like detachment. Part of that was the natural outgrowth of the crew's esteem, and part of it was self-protection. I'd lost a lot of friends on the Stargazer, and subconsciously at least I was probably reticent to let myself get too close to anyone.

Still, I wanted to get to know these young people I was working with, and I began to host each one of them for dinner in the observation lounge. When it was Tasha's turn, I had a meal prepared with dishes in the style of French country cooking: roasted chicken with spring onions, tomato tart, mustard-roasted poussin, butternut gratin. She looked at it all in wonder.

"These are the foods of my childhood," I said.

"It smells delicious," she said. I served her a healthy portion, and she began eating. I then offered her a glass of wine.

"I'm sorry, sir," she said. "I don't drink."

"Oh, I'm sorry," I said. "Do you not enjoy it, or is there a medical issue."

"Where I'm from, sir, alcohol and other drugs are abused. People were easier to take advantage of if they were under the influence. I found it was easier to just stay away from them."

"It must have been a very difficult place to grow up. It's an achievement that you were able to escape."

"You never really escape," she said. "You're taught from a young age that you're worthless… that's not something you ever really let go of." I began to understand her bravery; she could risk her life because on some level she didn't think it was worth anything.

"You're worth quite a bit to me, and to this ship." I could see that she was touched by the remark. But it was but a drop of water in a very dark well. I was determined after this conversation to do everything I could to make sure that Tasha felt her life was worthwhile.

I wouldn't get the chance.

"We are here together to honour our friend and comrade, Lieutenant Natasha Yar."

I was with the command crew on the holodeck, in a recreation of a green field, and a burial plot. Tasha had been killed in the line of duty, callously murdered by a malevolent life-form.* It was a profound loss for our crew, and a great failure for me. This was her memorial service, and we watched a holographic recording she'd made; she knew her job put her life at risk, and she felt such a connection to the crew that she'd left this message to be played in the event of her death. She spoke to each of her close friends; I wasn't surprised at the connections she'd formed with them. But I was taken aback at what she recorded for me.

"Captain Jean-Luc Picard," she said. "I wish I could say you've been like a father to me, but I've never had one, so I don't know what it feels like. But if there was someone in this universe I could choose to be like, someone who I would want to make proud of me, it's you."

This touched me deeply. In some sense, I could relate to not having a father, and though I never got over the tragedy of this bright young person's death, I felt some satisfaction that I'd given her something of value while she was alive.

But Tasha's death began a bleak period that would mark the end of my first year as captain of the *Enterprise*. It seemed many chapters of my past suddenly came to a close at that time, and what had been a bright period in my life and career turned into a grim interval. It began with a reunion I'd been avoiding for a long time.

"I waited all day," Jenice said. We were in the observation lounge of my ship. Even so many years later she was still lovely. She was on board with her husband, the well-known physicist Paul Manheim. While I wasn't hiding, I'd avoided being alone with her since she'd come on board. We were finally having the difficult conversation that I had long owed her.

"I went to Starfleet Headquarters to look for you," she said. "But you'd already shipped out." She was composed, but the hurt and anger were coming through

---

*EDITOR'S NOTE: Tasha Yar was murdered by Armus, a strange being who was created when the inhabitants of Vagra II developed a means of ridding themselves of all that was "evil" within themselves. This "evil" formed itself into Armus, a bitter and lonely creature who took amusement in Yar's death.

even after all these years. She tamped it down with an order that sounded a little playful. "So come on, Jean-Luc, let's hear the truth."

"It was fear," I said. "Fear of seeing you, losing my resolve. Fear of staying." She smiled.

"I've thought a lot about this over the years," she said, "and perhaps you're leaving out your greatest fear. The real reason you couldn't stay."

"Which was?"

"That life with me would have somehow made you ordinary." I laughed a little at this, though the brutal truth of it was cutting.

"Am I that transparent?"

"Only to me," she said. Shortly after, we parted amicably, but what she had said stuck with me. Enough time had passed that she'd moved on and was with someone she loved. But I'd given up the chance of a happy life with someone I loved—someone who understood me. And for what? Achievement and recognition? It seemed very shallow.

✦

"You know, I always wanted to own a bar," Riker said.

It was a few days later, and I was sitting outside at the Blue Parrot Café enjoying a drink with Riker and Deanna. The ship was taking shore leave on Sarona VIII, and we were in capital city of Kel. Kel was set on the northern tip of one of the planet's largest continents, at the edge of a vast desert. It had an Earth-like feel; its low buildings and narrow streets resembled ancient French Morocco. As we sipped our elaborate cocktails, we watched the active street life of species from across the quadrant.

"Too bad we can't have one on the ship," I said.

"Where would we put it?" Deanna said.

"Forward station one is just an empty lounge," Riker said. "We could put it there."

"Make it so!" I said. "But we'll need a good bartender."

"I'll start gathering resumes," Riker said.

Just then, Beverly and Wesley came by. I invited them to join us.

"Isn't this great? So many different species." Wesley directed his comments to Commander Riker; he was still a little intimidated by me. "Mom and I just saw the local police break up a fight between a Klingon and a Nausicaan."

"That must have been something else," Riker said. "Hey, Wes, have you seen the amusement center?"

"Not yet," Wesley said. "Mom, can we go?"

"I just got my drink, Wesley," she said.

"Deanna and I will take him," Riker said, with a glance toward me for my approval. I gave him a nod; the atmosphere and the cocktail had me very at ease. The three of them left, leaving me alone with Beverly. We drank and chatted casually, and for the most part superficially. The conversation shifted to our recent encounter with Jenice and her husband.

"She's a lovely woman," Beverly said. "How did you meet her?"

"She cared for my mother," I said. "We were involved briefly." I wasn't comfortable with talking about one old love with another, though I couldn't tell Beverly that.

"Revisiting the past can be difficult," she said.

"Yes, it can," I said. I could see that there was more she wanted to say. The liquor had perhaps made me a little too brave. "Was there something you wanted to tell me?"

"Yes… there's a senior position at Starfleet Medical," she said. "I would like to put in for it."

"You're leaving?" I said. This wasn't at all what I was expecting, and I knew my plaintiveness was too apparent.

"Not yet," she said. "Only if I get it."

"Are you unhappy?"

"Not at all," she said. "The ship, the crew… you… it's been wonderful. It's just that…"

"Jack…"

She nodded.

"Too many memories. I wasn't ready for it."

"It would be a big loss for me," I said. "A loss for the ship, I mean." The Blue Parrot used real alcohol, and it made me a little too honest.

"Thank you," she said.

"Obviously you have my support." I meant that professionally; personally, I was crushed, and as we finished our drinks and waited for the others to return, I fell into a dark silence. I didn't want her to leave.

✦

"Hello, Jean-Luc," Walker Keel said. "It's been a long time."

"Too long, old friend," I said. I'd been asleep in my quarters when the emergency message from him came through. Looking at him on the viewscreen told the story; he was gray, but beyond superficial aging, something was very wrong. Walker had none of the youthful vigor and humor I associated with him. He was very solemn.

"We need to talk, face to face," he said. There was an undercurrent of panic in his voice. "I want you to meet me on Dytallix B."

This would take me off our course and violate my orders, and he knew that. He persisted—I felt I had to agree.

"Something is beginning," he said. "Don't trust anyone."

✦

On Dytallix B, in an abandoned mining facility, I was confronted by three Starfleet captains: Rixx, a Bolian; Tryla Scott, a young woman famous for being the youngest captain in Starfleet history; and Walker. Rixx and Scott held phasers on me as Walker peppered me with strange questions.

"Do you recall the night you introduced Jack Crusher to Beverly?" Walker said. I paused to consider this. A giant lie embedded in the question. Did he think I was an imposter?

"You know full well," I said, "I hadn't even met Beverly then. You introduced them."

"My brother introduced them," he said. This was ridiculous.

"You don't have a brother," I said. "Two sisters, Anne and Melissa. What the hell is all this about?" I was losing patience, but this seemed to be enough for them. Walker nodded to his two companions, who put their weapons away.

"We all came secretly, Picard," Rixx said. "To discuss the threat."

"What threat?"

"Have you noticed anything about Starfleet Command lately?" Scott said. I said I hadn't, though we hadn't had much contact with command.

"Some of us have seen strange patterns emerging," Walker said. "Unusual orders."

They went down a list of strange coincidences, accidental deaths, limited communications. It sounded like a paranoid conspiracy theory. Tryla Scott read the distrust in my face.

"He doesn't believe us," she said.

"You've given me nothing to believe in," I said.

"I think it's spread to my own ship," Walker said. "My first officer hasn't been the same since we stopped off at Earth. Our medical officer says he's perfectly normal, but I don't think I trust him either…"

"Walker!" He was almost raving. I couldn't believe this was the same man. I left the three of them, agreeing to keep in touch, but not at all believing anything they were saying.

I regretted my skepticism. Walker's ship was soon destroyed under mysterious circumstances. I realized they'd been telling the truth: something sinister was going on.

My friend was dead, and I had to do something about it.

✦

"You've done well, Captain Picard," Admiral Satie said. We stood in a communication room in Starfleet Headquarters over the dead body of a Starfleet lieutenant named Remmick. Riker and I had just killed him and the unknown alien that had taken up residence in his body.

Our investigation into the circumstances around the death of Walker Keel led us back to Earth, where we discovered crab-like parasitic aliens had entered the bodies of Starfleet officers, taking over their cognitive brain functions. They were only a few short steps away from conquering the Federation.

"It was some kind of 'mother alien,' " Riker said.

Satie had arrived with several officers shortly after we'd killed the creature. It turned out she was the first to become suspicious of a conspiracy within Starfleet Command, as far back as when she gave me command of the *Enterprise*. She was also the one who sent Walker to me before she herself went into hiding. She had instructed Walker not to tell me she had sent him, in case I myself fell victim to the aliens

I looked down at the remains of Remmick. I'd been taught to cherish life in the universe, I took no pleasure in taking it.

"Once you killed the mother," Satie said, "the others fled the bodies they occupied and died."

"I didn't believe Walker," I said. "If I'd moved more quickly…"

"We all bear the responsibility, Captain," she said. "We must be vigilant."

A few days later, there was a memorial service for Walker on Earth. Beverly and I attended it. It was in the city of Chicago, in an ancient religious church called Rockefeller Chapel. As I listened to the speakers at the service talking about Walker, I felt the loss of my old friend. He'd been such an important part of my life, a person I'd relied on for many years for advice and comradeship. I took for granted he would always be there.

After the service, Beverly, who was very close to Walker's sisters, stayed behind, and I left the chapel alone. As I walked out onto the street, I didn't notice as someone came up behind me.

"Sorry for your loss, Jean-Luc," Guinan said. She was in her usual wide-brimmed hat and long robes, but all in black. I embraced her; I felt such a sense of comfort from her presence.

"It's wonderful to see you," I said. "Where have you been?" She'd long since left the 602 Club, and I'd lost track of her. She seemed to move through the universe with nary a care.

"Here and there," she said. "You ever figure out how to put a bar on your ship?"

"You know," I said, "I just did…" I felt, after the loss of my friend, I had a small reason to be happy.

✦

"Dr. Pulaski of the *Repulse* seems the best option," Riker said. We were going over the resumes of possible replacements for Beverly. She had gotten the position at Starfleet Medical and was leaving that afternoon, as soon as we arrived at Starbase 57. The only person I had in mind for the position was Dr. Ailat, but she'd retired to her homeworld, and I had put off making a firm decision on finding someone else, secretly hoping Beverly would change her mind. But she hadn't. I looked over Pulaski's service record.

"Pulaski is very qualified," I said.

"Is that your decision?" Riker was gently nudging me along. He could tell I was dragging this out unnecessarily, although I'm not sure he knew why.

"Make it so," I said.

"Yes, sir. Now, I think I've got a solution to our problem in engineering." I'd been frustrated with the command structure in that department. The ship was a complicated piece of technology, and the designers had decided on several chief engineers, each with their own area of expertise. But every time we had a problem I was talking to someone different: MacDougal, Argyle, Lynch, Logan. I wanted a more traditional captain-engineer dynamic like the one I'd had with Scully. I needed one person in charge of everybody.

"Let's hear it," I said.

"Geordi," Riker said. "Lot of engineering experience, comes up with creative solutions, and already has a strong working relationship with you."

"He's shown he knows how to take command," I said, "but it could raise some hackles with others who have seniority in that department."

"That's his problem," Riker said, with a smile. "Seriously, he'll figure it out. That just leaves the question of who takes over his spot at conn."

"My preference would be Wesley," I said. "Too bad he's going with his mother."

"You've come a long way," Riker said. I had: I'd come to appreciate the young man, my old friend's son, who'd taken the role of relief conn officer. He would be leaving the ship to accompany his mother to her new posting, after he finished his school term in a few weeks.

"Bridge to Captain Picard," Geordi said, over the intercom. "We're arriving at Starbase 57."

"Very well, assume standard orbit," I said, "and inform Dr. Crusher." I hoped Will hadn't noticed that my voice cracked when I said this. If he had, he gave no indication.

A few minutes before she was scheduled to depart the ship, I excused myself from the bridge, saying I would return momentarily, and went down to sickbay. I don't know that I expected to say anything significant to Beverly; I just wanted one last moment alone with her.

When I got to sickbay, her office was empty.

"Can I help you, sir?" It was Nurse Ogawa, a young ensign who'd just joined the staff.

"I was looking for Dr. Crusher."

"Oh, I'm afraid she left," Ogawa said. This set off a bit of a panic, but I controlled myself, nodded to Ogawa, and left as quickly as I could without looking rushed. I headed to Transporter Room 1. When the corridor was empty, I increased my pace to almost a run, then returned to a walk if someone appeared. I arrived at the transporter room. Chief O'Brien was alone in the room.

"Has Dr. Crusher beamed down yet?"

"No, sir. Not yet." I nodded and left the room. I was short of breath, beginning to sweat. This was no good, and I realized in my tizzy that I'd avoided the most obvious solution to the problem.

"Computer," I said, "locate Dr. Crusher."

"Dr. Crusher," the computer said, "is in the captain's ready room."

I was such a fool. She was of course coming to request permission to leave the ship. I took a deep breath, and leisurely made my way back to the bridge. As I headed for the ready room, Beverly stepped out.

"Oh, I was waiting for you," she said.

"Yes," I said. "My apologies. I was called away." That was a stupid lie; the entire bridge crew was watching us, and they knew I hadn't been called anywhere. I quickly led her back into the room.

"So," I said. "You're ready to depart."

"Yes. Thank you again for letting Wesley stay a few more weeks."

"It is my pleasure. He's a valued member of the crew."

We stared at each other, smiling a bit uneasily.

"I want to thank you," I said. "Your presence here was of enormous help to me."

"I'm sorry I can't stay."

"If you ever want to come back…"

"That might be difficult if you have another chief medical officer."

"I will make it work," I said. She reached out and took my hand, then leaned in to kiss me on the cheek.

"Request permission to depart," she said.

"Granted," I said. She turned and left. Again, I let a moment pass where I could have told her how I really felt about her. I didn't want her to leave, but hadn't the strength to risk stopping her.

Two weeks later, it was time for Wesley to leave, and he came to see me in my ready room.

"Captain Picard, I've thought about this a lot," Wesley said. "I want to remain on the *Enterprise*." I looked at the young man. He was on his way to becoming a Starfleet officer, but he was still young, he needed parenting, and I was afraid of assuming those responsibilities. I gave him an indication that I wasn't sure.

"Captain," he said, "this is where I want to be. This is where I feel I belong." I listened in silence, then dismissed him without giving him an answer. He had started me thinking of my own youth, the feeling of disconnection from my family and home. And here we'd given this young man a place that he felt a connection to. I thought of the father he'd been denied. Nothing could make up for that, but perhaps the *Enterprise* could come close. I decided to let him stay.

It was also a way to guarantee that I would never fully lose contact with Beverly.

✦

"Q set a series of events into motion," Guinan said, "bringing contact with the Borg much sooner than it should have come." We were playing three-dimensional chess in Ten-Forward, the bar that Riker had converted from forward station one. It was a wild success. In a short time, it had become second nature for the crew to gather in this room to relax, socialize, or even work. I was spending time with Guinan after a traumatic encounter with Q, who had introduced us to what would become the Federation's most dangerous adversary. The Borg.

"You're just raw material to them," Guinan said. The Borg are a cybernetic species that assimilated other cultures. They literally scooped cities off of worlds, taking their inhabitants. They would then alter them with cybernetic implants. The minds of the species they assimilate become one with the Borg collective consciousness. This one mind allowed them to work together with deadly efficiency. Guinan spoke from experience: her people, the El-Aurians, were victims of such an assimilation. "Since they are aware of your existence..."

THE STORY OF ONE OF STARFLEET'S MOST INSPIRATIONAL CAPTAINS

She let her sentence hang unfinished; it was clear what she was implying.

"They will be coming," I said.

"You can bet on it," Guinan said.

"Maybe Q did the right thing for the wrong reason," I said. Q had used his immense power to transport my ship 7000 light-years away in an instant, where we encountered a Borg cube, one of their giant ships. We were no match for them and were only able to escape when I begged Q to save us.

"How so?" Guinan said.

"Well, perhaps what we most needed was a kick in our complacency, to prepare us for what lies ahead." I made my last move on our chessboard, and Guinan saw that I'd beaten her. She smiled, but then it faded as someone else came into the room. I turned to see Mr. Worf, carrying a PADD.

"Here is the list of the missing, sir," Worf said. When the Borg had attacked, they had sliced out a section of the ship. Eighteen people had been in that section and were now missing, presumed dead. I looked at the names on the list, many of which I recognized. Logan, Torres, Whalen, Solis, T'su... young people at the start of their careers. Gone.

A terrible cost for this encounter. I had been too cavalier to refer to this as a "kick" in our complacency.

"Excuse me, Guinan," I said. "I have to go write to their families."

✦

"Dr. Pulaski," I said, "I'm afraid I don't think this is working out." Katherine Pulaski had been chief medical officer for about a year when I decided I'd had enough. She was exceedingly competent in her job,* but she had taken to openly disagreeing with me one too many times, even at certain points insulting me. The news I was giving her didn't seem to be much of a surprise.

"I was going to ask for a transfer," she said. "Because, with all due respect, from the minute I came on board, it was clear to me you didn't want me to succeed in this job."

---

*EDITOR'S NOTE: Indeed, Dr. Pulaski actually replaced Captain Picard's artificial heart in emergency surgery, saving his life.

"I'm not sure that's quite fair," I said, though in a way I knew she was right. "What actions can you point to that support that?"

"I'm afraid I can't point to a single incident," Pulaski said. "It's just a feeling that I had from you that I was unwelcome."

"I'm sorry you felt that way," I said. I couldn't argue with her impressions. I'd kept my distance from Pulaski, and recently had begun silently compiling a list of minor offenses in my mind to justify my dissatisfaction. It was an incident a week before where something happened on the bridge that led me to make up my mind and let her go.

Data sang a song.

I had been sitting on the bridge, flanked by Deanna and Riker. Wesley was at the conn, Data at ops. Worf behind me.

"I spoke to Beverly," Deanna said. I was focused on the keypad on the arm of my chair, pretending to review a duty roster Riker had given me to approve.

"How is she?" Riker said.

"She's well," Deanna said. "Though I think she misses us."

"She definitely does," Wesley said. "I can tell."

"It would appear," Data said, "that she made an incorrect decision accepting that post."

"Sometimes, Data," Deanna said, "you don't know what you've got till it's gone."

"They paved paradise and put up a parking lot," Data said.

"What does that mean?" Worf said.

"It is from an old Earth song," Data said. "I assumed that is what Counselor Troi was referencing, since 'You don't know what you've got till it's gone' is the lyric that precedes it." Everyone laughed.

"I wasn't, Data," Troi said. "It was just a coincidence."

"Sing it for us, Data," Riker said. Data looked to me, and I pretended to be taking note of the situation for the first time, and nodded. As Data began to sing the unusual but sweet song, I fantasized about the future. It led me to contact Beverley directly. I spoke to her via subspace a few hours later.

"What a delightful surprise," she said. We chatted for a while about her job, and how things were on the ship. I then mentioned my troubles with Dr. Pulaski, and that I thought she would be leaving soon.

THE STORY OF ONE OF STARFLEET'S MOST INSPIRATIONAL CAPTAINS

"So there will be an opening for a new Chief Medical Officer," I said. "I was hoping to get someone with the appropriate experience..." Beverley smiled. She saw right through me.

"I can't keep secrets from Deanna," she said.

"I don't know what you're talking about," I said. "Counselor Troi is not telepathic. In any event, are you aware of any potential candidates?"

"Candidly, Jean-Luc," she said, "I thought being on the *Enterprise* was too difficult, but I'm finding that being away is worse. I miss everyone too much."

"Then come home," I said. "The feeling is mutual." A short while later, Pulaski left, and Beverley returned.

✦

"We've been ordered to Vulcan," I said. "We're going to take Ambassador Sarek to meet the Legarans to negotiate the treaty." I was on the bridge, and had just received the orders. Everyone reacted as I expected. Sarek was a legend, and he had been attempting to negotiate a treaty with the Legarans, an advanced and enigmatic species, for a long time. They'd been discovered by a starship many years ago.* The Legarans were a species that lived in liquid; they looked like large blue lobsters, and had a very advanced technology and culture. They also had no interest in joining the Federation. Sarek had taken them on as a personal project, and spent the last *93 years* attempting to get them to the negotiating table. If this treaty negotiation were successful, it would go down in history as the crowning achievement of his career. And we were going to be a part of it.

I felt that third year on the *Enterprise* was in some ways the true beginning of my captaincy. I was comfortable, I had the crew that I wanted, and we began playing an unprecedented role in galactic affairs. And this, for me, was a personal triumph—a chance to talk with the man I'd been unable to speak to out of nervousness all those years ago, and get his insight into all the history he had made. It would happen, though not how I expected.

---

*EDITOR'S NOTE: It seems that Captain Picard has forgotten that the Legarans were first encountered by James Kirk during his second five-year mission on his starship *Enterprise*. For reference, see *The Autobiography of James T. Kirk*.

"I will not be spoken to in this manner!" It was a few days after Sarek had come aboard, and he was shouting at me. *A Vulcan was shouting at me.*

"Do I hear anger in your voice?" I said. I was baiting him, trying to get him to admit to the truth of the situation. I'd learned of a conspiracy among his aides to hide the fact that Sarek was suffering from a degenerative disease called Bendii syndrome. It made him unable to control his emotions, and through his own telepathic ability he was spreading his emotional outbursts into the minds of people throughout the ship.

"It would be illogical for a Vulcan to show anger! It would be illogical! Illogical! Illogical! Illogical!" He had completely lost control of himself. It was sad to have to force him into this, but I had no choice.

I left him in his quarters to try to regain his composure and went to my ready room. The only option I had was to contact the Legarans and cancel the conference. If the Legarans were to come on the ship with Sarek in this condition, the negotiations would be a disaster. All Sarek's work over the past nine decades would be thrown away. As I faced this unsolvable dilemma, his wife came to see me.

"I must speak with you, Captain," Perrin said. Sarek's wife was human, the second human that he'd married. I found it interesting that a Vulcan, whose entire philosophy was based on controlling his emotions, had chosen for companionship women who culturally were taught to express theirs. She pleaded with me to let the conference continue to save her husband's reputation and legacy.

"The mission can be saved," Perrin said.

"I don't understand," I said.

"If you mind-meld with him," Perrin said, "he will be able to regain control of his emotions."

"I don't see how that would work," I said. "I don't know that I have the mental discipline to control his emotions." Vulcan emotions were known to be even more raw and disturbing than those of a human, another testimony to their culture's success in restraining them.

"You won't need to control them," Perrin said. "You will be a receptacle for his feelings, physically separated from him, allowing him to conduct the negotiations." I looked at Perrin. She had no doubt that I would accede to this request. How did she know? We'd only met a few days ago, and yet somehow she knew that this offer, as dangerous as it was, would be irresistible to me. She smiled knowingly.

My answer: "I can't turn this down."

"Sharing thoughts with one of the greatest men in history? I would think not."

✦

Sarek was in my quarters, facing me. He placed his hands on my face, and I could feel him in my mind... and then his mind *was* my mind. I became vaguely aware that he'd physically left the room, but we were still joined in our minds. Beverly sat close by as the emotions, the memories, flooded in.

"Bedlam!" I said. I could hear myself screaming, but it didn't feel like me. "I am so old! There is nothing left but dry bones and dead friends..." The memories took me over...

"I'm Amanda Grayson," Amanda said to me. She was a teacher, taking human children on a tour of the Vulcan embassy on Earth. I had come out into the hallway, and saw the warm smile and bright eyes, and had let this attraction sweep the logic aside and push me toward her to introduce myself...

My baby son, newly born, crying... I showed outward disapproval for the infant's unrestrained emotion, as inside I felt joy, an overpowering emotional need to protect this innocent, vulnerable creature from a harsh, unforgiving world...

Visions of the aftermath of an explosion. Fire and rubble everywhere while the panicked voice of Amanda implored me to save her...

"I will attend Starfleet Academy..." Spock said to me. He was a teenager, and chose a different path than the one I took. An insult! Was he saying the life I led wasn't good enough for him? I couldn't show him how much it hurt me, I couldn't show him that, even though he was the child, how much I wanted his approval...

"Sarek..." Amanda said, withered, frail, in our bed, her human lifespan so much shorter than mine. I took her hand, and for the first time, showed her emotion. I said the words...

"I love you," I said. But her eyes were closed. She was gone. Had she heard me? Did she know?

"It's an honor to meet you, Ambassador," Perrin said. She was so young, her expression of interest sparkled at me, and I felt that same attraction, but also guilt. Horrible guilt. Amanda had been dead for decades, yet she was the one person I had told that I loved. The feelings I had for Perrin were a betrayal of that love, but yet I pursued those feelings...

Sarek's memories, they consumed me. I fell into Beverly's arms, weeping uncontrollably.

Soon it was over. Sarek had been successful. The Federation had a treaty with the Legarans. Sarek left, and through our connection, I understood the weaknesses of the great men of history, the ambitions, the loves, the loneliness. I could relate to Sarek; I was, in fact, trying to *be* him, to make a difference in the world in which I lived, spreading culture and law in the hopes of being remembered as a force for good. As emotionally wrenching as the experience was, I'd succeeded. It gave me confidence; I was a living instrument of civilization.

As I was often reminded when I described my lofty ambitions, I was also a fool.

✦

"Resistance is futile," I said. I was on the Borg cube, communicating with forty Federation starships. They had gathered in the system Wolf 359 to stop our advance to Earth. The Borg's plan was to assimilate the entire Federation, starting with humanity's homeworld and moving out from there. When I said "resistance is futile," I was speaking as both Locutus and Picard. From Locutus it was a statement of fact: the Borg collective mind did not accept the possibility that any resistance would succeed.

From Picard, "resistance is futile" was a howl of despair. I had been trying so hard to break through, to regain control of myself, but I was pushed aside.

I looked out at the forty ships; the companion beside me spoke.

"They are going to resist," the Queen said.

"Yes," I said. Though she spoke out loud, she also spoke through the collective; all the billions of voices were in my head. The Queen's was the loudest.

We hadn't known the Borg had a queen. She oversaw the organization of the collective, supervised the assimilation of countless species. She was in fact the creator of the Borg; thousands of years old, in her previous life she was a cyberneticist. She created nanoprobes that could enter cells and cure diseases. The nanoprobes also worked in conjunction with cybernetic implants, allowing direct mind-to-mind connection with computers on their world. The nanoprobes evolved, and became a kind of virus that at first infected other members of her species, and then other species they came into contact with. As the collective grew, there was soon a hunger for more species, and they became the Borg.

From the beginning, the Queen seemed interested in me. I knew I was some kind of plaything. Soon after the Borg had taken me, we had disabled the *Enterprise* in battle. But we had stopped short of destroying it. She left them alive to tease me. The collective responded to her control, and she had convinced it that the *Enterprise* wasn't a threat. But there was something else. She had complete control of me, yet she wanted something more. She wanted me to give myself to her. I thought that I had lost myself to the Borg, but the fact that the Queen wanted me in a way she wasn't experiencing meant that some part of Picard had managed to hold himself back. At the time, however, I felt I'd lost. Especially as she took me further apart, forcing me to fight, to defeat my own people.

I saw the ships spreading out around the cube from several different angles. It was a strategy I recognized from both my Starfleet training and my recent briefings. They would attack on multiple fronts, searching for signs of weakness. The lead ship, coordinating the attack, would determine where the weak spots were and move ships to concentrate fire in that area.

"We will counter this strategy," the collective said. I couldn't keep anything from them. They were both reading my mind and they *were* my mind.

I turned to the viewscreen. I was being seen by all the starships who were now closing in. And, in turn, I was looking into the bridges of all those ships as their captains and crews stared at the man they once knew as Jean-Luc Picard.

Admiral Hanson on the bridge of the *Fearless*... He looked determined, hiding his sadness that he was about to try to kill me. The Vulcan captain Storil on the bridge of the *Saratoga*, passionless, ready to do his duty. My old communications officer Chris Black, in command of the *Bonestell*. He looked confused, far from certain that he was doing the right thing.

Robert DeSoto, on the *Hood*, his affability gone.

Marta Batanides in command of the *Kyushu*. Heartbroken.

Corey Zweller, on the *Melbourne*. I hadn't seen him in so long; no longer the young man I had known. Aged, rugged, tired.

Cheva on the *Roosevelt*. Tears in her eyes as she gave the order to fire all weapons.

"Destroy them," the Queen said.

I did. All eleven thousand.

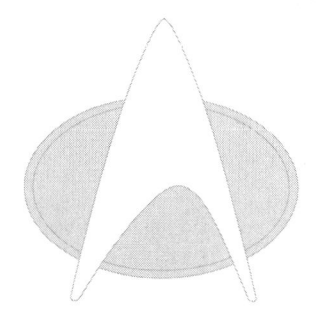

CHAPTER TEN

"HOW MUCH DO YOU REMEMBER?" Riker said.

"Everything," I said. "Including some rather unorthodox strategies from a former first officer of mine."

Riker smiled. I was in Data's lab, naked and infested with Borg implants. Riker had rescued me from the Borg cube. Through me, Data had been able to access the collective, and destroy the cube before it could attack Earth. But I still remembered all the destruction I'd caused, and all of the friends I'd killed. Joking with Riker was an attempt to avoid my pain, which was too much to bear.

I was taken to sickbay, where over the next several hours Beverly removed every trace of Borg technology from my body. Guinan came to see me while I recovered.

"How are you feeling?"

"Almost myself," I said. "Riker says you were of enormous help to him."

"I knew he'd rescue you," Guinan said. "You and I have a date."

"We do? When?"

"I'm not sure," she said with a cryptic smile. "Get some rest." And with that, she left. I didn't know what she meant—Guinan had an air of the unexplained about her, which she enjoyed cultivating.

I was back on duty in a day. I was tired but human again. The *Enterprise* returned to McKinley Station for repairs, which would take six weeks.

Crewmen were free to go to Earth for shore leave. I stayed aboard, however, meeting with Counselor Troi regularly for the first few weeks.

"Did you have another nightmare last night?" she said, as we began one of our sessions.

"Yes."

"Do you remember it?"

"Some of it," I said. The nightmares I'd been having were stark remembrances of recent events, with only a little bit of the usual dream confusion. "The *U.S.S. Roosevelt* was crippled and drifting toward the cube. The collective sent drones to assimilate the survivors."

"Did you know anyone on the *Roosevelt*?"

"Its captain, Cheva..."

"She served with you on the *Stargazer*."

"Yes," I said. "I watched in the dream as the drones took her off the bridge and injected her with nanoprobes."

"Do you remember that really happening?"

"I believe so," I said. "Although in the dream I was physically next to her. She looked at me and asked me to help her. And I put my hand on her shoulder and said something."

"What did you say?"

"'Resistance is futile,'" I said. "I whispered it, it was gentle, like I was trying to tell her not to fight. And then two dead hands pulled her away from me."

"Did you see who the hands belonged to?"

"They were mine," I said. "I was staring at myself as a Borg."

The nightmares were all like this, some obvious imagery tied in with the traumatic events I'd experienced. We talked through these dreams every day, and it helped; the nightmares eventually ended. I felt more rested. Deanna suggested that I consider taking a little shore leave on Earth. I thought I didn't have anywhere I wanted to go.

Then I got a note from my brother's wife, Marie. Robert had married her almost ten years before, and she would periodically write to me. I had given her perfunctory responses, but this had not stopped her from writing. She had told me about Robert, and the son they had. She'd been spurred to write the most recent note when she heard about the *Enterprise* staying in orbit for repairs. She was inviting me to come visit. I decided to accept.

THE STORY OF ONE OF STARFLEET'S MOST INSPIRATIONAL CAPTAINS

A few days later, I was walking from the village toward the vineyard. It was a beautiful spring day. Along the path, I was met by the vision of my brother at seven; it was my nephew René. He, however, seemed much more pleasant than Robert ever was.

"You know," he said, after we'd walked and chatted for a minute, "you don't seem so arrow... arrow... you know..."

"Arrogant?" I said.

"Yes, arrogant. You don't seem that way to me. What does it mean anyway, arrogant son of a—"

"Let's talk about that later, shall we?"

René led me to his mother, Marie, a beautiful, elegant woman who gave me a heartfelt welcome. She stood in front of the family home, unchanged in all these years.

"Robert can't wait to see you," she said.

"So René tells me," I said. "Where is he?"

I found Robert in the vineyard, tending to his grapes. As his son was the image of him, Robert was the image of his father... our father. Even down to the hat he wore to protect him from the sun. He sensed me approaching.

"So, you arrived all right," he said. "Welcome home, Captain." It was cold and distant. What I expected, and yet, still not what I was hoping for.

I stayed a few days at the vineyard. Though Robert was his critical self, I found myself not wanting to leave; Marie and René were the warm familial embrace that had been missing for me since my mother's death. I was beginning to think that I didn't need to return to the *Enterprise*. Marie made several overtures to me moving back home, and I began to think I could finally have that simple life that had always eluded me. Looking back, it was obvious I was hiding from my feelings. On some level I knew that.

I also, unfortunately, took the opportunity to indulge in the family wine. For the recent years I'd been in Starfleet, most of the cocktails I consumed were made of synthehol, which did not have the deleterious effects of alcohol—you could always stay in control. Not so with the family wine. I had gotten through a bottle one afternoon, when Robert came in. He joined me in a glass.

"What did they do to you?" he asked. I didn't want to tell him about what I'd been through. I got up and went outside.

"Why do you walk away? That isn't your style," he said. He had followed me; he seemed to be looking for a fight. I realized later the truth of it: he *was* looking for a fight, but to help me. I was in a drunken fugue, barely maintaining my control.

I really don't remember exactly what happened. He taunted me, called me the great hero who'd fallen to Earth. I heard his jealousy and resentment towards his responsibility to look after me. But I scoffed at it; to me he'd always been a bully, and now, my years of anger combined with alcohol took over.

I hit him.

We fell through the vines and wrestled in the muddy irrigation ditches. The fight did not last long, not because either of us prevailed, but because we both quickly realized the ridiculousness of two grown men rolling around in the mud. We started laughing at our immaturity. I couldn't ever remember laughing with Robert. The laughter died down.

"You've been terribly hard on yourself, you know," he said. In that moment, I saw Robert understood me, like no one had. The sorrow and guilt poured out of me. The Borg had shown what a fraud I was.

"So, my brother is a human being after all," he said. "This is going to be with you a long time, Jean-Luc. A long time." In that moment, I realized how much I missed Robert. *I missed Robert.*

We got up out of the mud, and he put his arm around me.

"There's something I want to show you," he said. He led me into the house, and went to the hall closet. He took the giant metal key ring that opened the door to the basement, and I followed him down into our family museum.

We walked along the hallway of the famous relatives, until we got to what had been the end. Now there was a portrait of Robert.

And next to it, a portrait of me in my uniform, smiling, arms folded.

"Where did you get this?"

"I had it made," he said. "The first Picard to leave the solar system. I think Father would've approved."

I soon returned to the repaired *Enterprise*, fully repaired myself. Robert had become the brother I'd wanted. Maybe even the father. I realized that I needed Robert; he was the only one left in the world who knew me before I'd become "Captain Jean-Luc Picard," the only person I could show true weakness to.

THE STORY OF ONE OF STARFLEET'S MOST INSPIRATIONAL CAPTAINS

A few years later, Robert would die. It was a profound tragedy: Robert had maintained the primitiveness of the family home, a primitiveness that made it dangerous, and he and René were killed in a fire in the barn. It is the greatest regret in my life that I took so long to try to fix our relationship. I'd stayed a child too long, angry at how he treated me, and missed out on getting to know him, truly getting to thank him for all the times he was there looking after me. He was the last connection to my childhood, to my family, and he was gone.

✦

A few weeks later, Wesley was finally leaving to attend the academy. Various circumstances had kept him from joining, and in the intervening years I'd given him a full promotion to ensign. But now was the time. On his last day on the ship, there was a goodbye party for him in Ten-Forward.

I noticed Beverly standing alone, watching the proceedings. I went over to her.

"Sad to see him go?"

"It's difficult," she said. "He's so clearly a young man, but for me it's as if my five-year-old Wesley is leaving me."

"He'll be back," I said, although I wasn't sure that was true. I looked over at Wesley standing with Riker, La Forge, and Worf. La Forge was telling some story that they were all enjoying.

"I want to thank you, Jean-Luc," she said.

"Thank me? For what?"

"He didn't have his father," she said. "But thanks to you, he's had a family, filled with love. You helped me raise him." The group with Wesley shared a loud laugh. Beverly gestured toward them. "And he's had the most incredible role models."

"He was born to the best one," I said. "His mother." She looked at me and smiled, tears welling in her eyes. Though it was in public, I gave in to the urge to hug her.

There was something about that moment that changed our relationship; we began to spend more time together. We began a morning ritual of breakfast. It wasn't in any way romantic, but our past had slipped behind us, and we could enjoy the present together.

✦

"Indeed, you've found him, Captain Picard."

I stood in a cave with Data. We were on another undercover mission, disguised as Romulans, on the planet Romulus. In front of me was a man I hadn't seen in 40 years, and though I was at his wedding, we'd never actually spoken.

Spock.

"What are you doing on Romulus?" he said.

"That was to have been my question of you, sir." Spock, now a Federation ambassador, had disappeared four weeks earlier, and then shown up on one of Starfleet Intelligence's long-range scans of Romulus. Command was concerned that he might actually be defecting, and Data and I had been sent on a mission to find him. Our excursion to Denobula all those years before had not been forgotten by the Admiralty.

We were successful in tracking him down, but he initially refused to reveal his reasons for coming to Romulus. Yet, I also had to deliver some profound news to him. News he seemed to anticipate before I could tell him.

"Sarek," he said. "Sarek is dead."

Sarek had died shortly before our arrival on Romulus. At the news of his father's passing, Spock opened up to me: he revealed he was trying to facilitate a reunification of Romulus with its ancient homeworld of Vulcan. It was a mission that had incredible ramifications for the Federation—it would literally redraw the quadrant.

Spock wanted Data and I to leave, but I refused. We could not depart in the midst of such a delicate mission, one that the Federation had in no way approved. On top of which, Ambassador Spock was one of the single most important individuals in the Federation; I had to do my best to protect him. So we stayed to assist him.

As we spent time with him, I learned we had much in common. Despite the philosophy of logic that Spock followed, he was also ambitious—he was now the most famous Vulcan in the Federation, even surpassing his father. But, ironically, he had sought approval from that father who would not, or could not, provide it.

Spock's mission did not succeed while we were there, but he wanted to stay on Romulus and continue his work. As we parted, we talked about his

THE STORY OF ONE OF STARFLEET'S MOST INSPIRATIONAL CAPTAINS

father, and he told me something that I already knew: he and Sarek had never chosen to mind-meld. I offered him a chance to meld with me, and touch what Sarek had shared.

He placed his hand on my face. I felt our minds drawn together...

I saw events from a shared past. It was a strange experience, like two different cameras filming the same scene. A young Vulcan boy, crying after being bullied, his father standing by impassive, and the father's internal struggle to maintain composure, while feeling fear for his son, worry, sadness.

The father's pride as his son helped rescue the Federation president from assassination.

The son, standing at his own wedding, looking out at his father in the audience; the father's secret joy at his son's happiness in that same moment.

Then I saw Spock in the cave, melding with me, closing his eyes in emotion. I was giving this son a profound gift, a gift I'd never had.

✦

"Dad, what's a 'dollar'?" Meribor said. She was my daughter, ten years old.

"It's a unit of currency," I said.

"And what's a 'big yellow taxi'?" Batai said. He was my son, four.

"It's like the carriages that we use to get to other towns," I said. They were referencing song lyrics I'd written out for them. Lyrics I remembered from my previous life. Data had sung it once on the bridge. I had found it quite affecting, so I had looked it up in the ship's database, and had learned the lyrics. In my new life, I had taught myself to play the tune on my flute, and was now teaching the song to my children.

My children.

Years before, I'd found myself on this planet that the natives called Kataan. I had no idea how I got there, and there had been no sign of the *Enterprise*. To make matters more complicated, everyone on this world saw me as someone named Kamin. I thought I'd somehow been transported and looked for any way to return to my ship. For five years, I studied the night sky looking for some clue as to where this planet was. I was living with a woman named Eline, who claimed to be my wife. She loved me despite my insistence that I came from somewhere else. I did my best to hang on to Picard, but the world I was on and the day-to-day experiences of this peaceful, friendly people, who showed me love and respect, pushed Starfleet from my mind. I gave in to Eline's love and forgot my old life.

Except for songs. It was the one thing I'd hung on to, the final link to the life that I had before. I had learned the songs of Kataan but also played songs from distant Earth.

"Mother, we're ready!" Meribor shouted. Eline came from the other room.

"Ready for what?"

"For the concert," Meribor said.

"Not the 'Skye Boat Song' again," Eline said. Eline knew they were left over from something she didn't understand, but she didn't seem to mind. It was only a token, it didn't take me away from her.

"No, we've learned the lyrics to a new one," Meribor said.

"It's my favorite," Batai said. As I played the song and the children sang along, Eline and I caught each other's eyes. The joy of children was something I'd never experienced in my other life—I'd kept my distance from the ones on the *Enterprise*. But now it *was* my life, and their unrestrained enthusiasm and unconditional love delighted me. Watching them grow from tiny helpless creatures, almost immediately developing their own personalities… seeing how they were similar to each of their parents, yet their own people almost from birth.

There were struggles in this life, to be sure. The world I was on was dying, and I couldn't convince anyone to do anything about it. It was frustrating to stand by while I watched this lovely place begin to decline. But it was ultimately a gift, this life that someone had decided to give me, a life in another society, as another man. The simple life that had eluded me as Picard was mine as Kamin. True happiness: children, grandchildren.

And then I woke up from it.

The *Enterprise* had encountered a probe that had linked to my mind; the probe was from Kataan, a world that knew it was dying. They had given me this gift so I would teach the rest of the Galaxy about them.

It was a difficult adjustment to make. On the *Enterprise* I'd been linked to the probe for only twenty-five minutes. But I'd lived a whole life, a whole life where I was happy.

And it was now gone.

I went back to my quarters, lonely, depressed. Riker came to see me. He'd examined the probe, and handed me a small box.

"We found this inside," he said. Riker left me. I opened the box; it was my flute. Or the flute of the real Kamin. I didn't know. I held it to my chest, then realized I knew how to play it. I had never been able to play the flute before. I began to play the "Skye Boat Song." I then played "Big Yellow Taxi" and heard Meribor and Batai singing the lyrics.

"Don't it always seem to go,
That you don't know what you've got till it's gone…"

✦

When we arrived in 19th-century San Francisco, we were all almost overcome by the smell.

"Oh my god, it's awful," Deanna said.

"Is that sewage?" Beverly said.

"Yes, and horse manure," I said.

"Maybe a little burning coal," Riker said.

"I think I might throw up," Geordi said.

I, however, had other concerns. We were standing in the middle of a cobbled street, in our Starfleet uniforms. Passersby were looking at us, aghast at our strangeness. Riker noticed it too.

"We need to get some clothes in the local style," he said.

"We'll need money," I said. Geordi took his comm badge off his tunic.

"There's some gold in this," he said. "Should be worth something."

We were able to trade a few of our comm badges (with the circuitry removed) for about ten dollars, which, in this time period, was almost a king's ransom. We used it to purchase some clothing. I didn't know how long we would have to stay, so we would also need food and shelter.

"Look, sir," Geordi said, indicating a sign that read "Rooms for Rent." I knocked on the door. An elderly woman answered.

"Yes?"

"We were hoping to rent a room," I said.

"All of you?"

"Yes," I said. "We don't have a lot of money, so we're going to share."

"You're a strange lot," the woman said. "Who are you?" She seemed put off by us.

"Well, I'm Jean-Luc Picard, and this is... my acting troupe." It was the only lie I could think of that could explain what a group of men and women who bore no resemblance to each other would be doing together.

The woman, Mrs. Carmichael, reluctantly let us a room. And from there we began our search for Data, who'd already preceded us to this time period. He'd followed the Devidians, a strange species from the 24th century, who were using a time portal of their own design to go back to old Earth. They were stealing the life forces from cholera victims, which their people fed on.

I was initially not going to come on this mission, until I received some "encouragement" from a special member of my crew: Guinan pressed me to go. We spent several days tracking the Devidians as well as looking for Data. When we found him, it seemed he'd already done a fair job of tracking the Devidians himself, with some help from people who lived in the period, including the famous author Samuel Clemens, better known by his pen name, Mark Twain. There was, however, one other person there who was also helping him, one I expected to meet. She came to his rented room soon after we were reunited.

"Do I know you?" Guinan said. She was wearing period clothing that somehow still evoked the outfits she wore in our century.

"Not yet," I said. "But you will."

Now everything about my relationship with Guinan was explained; why she seemed to know me when we first met. Her interest in me. I realized that I was also now a part of that unique aspect of time travel that no one has ever been able to properly explain: the temporal causality loop. I was meeting Guinan five hundred years in the past. For her, it was our first meeting, for me, I'd known her for decades. Because of this first meeting, she would recognize me five hundred years in the future. We would form a bond that would lead her to send me into the past to meet her for the first time. Our relationship had no true beginning.

After we defeated the Devidians and returned to the 24th century, I went to see Guinan in Ten-Forward.

"So, what did you think of old San Francisco?" she said.

"The smell was awful," I said. "You're very patient to have kept that from me all these years."

"I didn't want to screw it up," she said.

"It does raise a question in my mind," I said.

"Yes?"

"When I was taken by the Borg," I said, "Will said you were instrumental in getting him to save me…"

"I never told him to save you," she said. "I said he had to let you go."

"But did you know he was going to rescue me?"

"I hoped he would," she said, "or we never would have been friends. Face it, Jean-Luc, we're eternal." I laughed. I felt we were.

✦

"I'm here to relieve you of command of the *Enterprise*," Alynna Nechayev said. She was my new commanding admiral. We'd never met before she came into my ready room to take away my ship.

"I don't understand," I said.

"I need you for a mission," she said. "We believe the Cardassians are developing a metagenic weapon." This was a frightening prospect: a metagenic weapon could destroy an entire ecosystem, releasing a toxin into a planet's atmosphere where it mutates, seeking out and destroying all forms of DNA it encounters. Within a few days, everything is dead.

"Have they solved the delivery problem?"

"We believe they are experimenting with using a theta-band subspace carrier wave," she said. I had experimented with such a device while captain of the *Stargazer*. "There's evidence they're conducting these experiments on Celtris III. I want you to lead a strike team to take out their laboratory."

"Why relieve me of my command? Certainly I could supervise the mission."

"I need the *Enterprise* somewhere else. It looks like the Cardassians are planning an incursion into Federation space. I'm sending the *Enterprise* to engage them in talks."

"I still don't understand," I said. "Shouldn't I be the one…"

"You are an expert on theta-band carrier waves. I want you on the mission."

"I see," I said. It was becoming clear that it wasn't *just* that she wanted me on the mission. "Who will command the *Enterprise*?"

"Edward Jellico," she said. "He brought the Cardassians to the table before, I need him to do it again." I understood it now; there were other officers who could've commanded the mission, and I certainly didn't need to give up command of the *Enterprise*. But Nechayev wanted me to go because she wanted Jellico in my chair on the Federation flagship. He'd gotten a lot of credit for bringing the Cardassian war to a close, perhaps justified, perhaps not. But Nechayev wanted his CV. So I would lead a strike team and lose my ship. She was willing to put my life in danger because she actually had someone else she preferred to be in command of the *Enterprise*.

✦

"What are the Federation's defense plans for Minos Korva?" Gul Madred said.

I was hanging by my wrists, naked in a cold room.

It turned out the mission Nechayev had assigned me was all part of the Cardassians' plans. They weren't preparing to launch a metagenic weapon, they were trying to lure *me* to Celtris III.

I had been captured, held as a prisoner, and tortured by the Cardassians. Nechayev was correct, they were planning to invade Federation space and capture Minos Korva, a system with over two million Federation colonists. The Cardassians were under the misapprehension that I, as previous captain of the *Enterprise*, had been briefed on potential defense plans. They were wrong.

My torturer, Gul Madred, didn't really care. He toyed with me: he was unpredictable and harsh one moment, then kind the next. Making empty promises, then depriving me of food and water. They took me down from my shackles and implanted a device inside me.

"What are the Federation's defense plans for Minos Korva?" he repeated. We'd been through this before, several times over several days. He held up the keypad he'd used to activate the device inside me. I remembered the excruciating pain of it. It felt as if there was no source, no way to stop it, as if all my skin was being pulled off with a white-hot blade. I couldn't bear it. So I begged.

"Not again," I said. "Please..."

"Tell me," he said. I had to say something, but I didn't have an answer to his question. I didn't know. So I lied.

"The Federation will... deploy four starships... led by the *Enterprise*..." I was trying to think of something to make it sound plausible.

"Really? We heard it was seven."

Had they heard? Was he lying? Seven was also plausible.

I didn't know.

"It's seven," I said. "You're right..."

"You're lying. We'd heard three."

"I'm not lying. It's the truth... it's seven..."

"Is it?" He held up the control pad, and turned it on. I screamed.

It went on like this for days.

I woke up one morning to the smell of food. My head lay on his desk. I looked up to see Gul Madred cracking open a large boiled egg. There were two plates of food. Was one for me? I didn't dare ask; I'd learned the decision was not mine. Every decision was his.

"Oh, you're awake. Have something to eat. I insist." He handed me the food, but first only a raw egg with what looked like some kind of pulsating reptilian mass inside that smelled like sulfur. There was also a plate of cooked food, but he wasn't handing me that. I wanted the cooked food, but I couldn't ask for it. The only food he'd given me was the raw egg, so I ate it. This was the learned helplessness of torture. This was different than my experience with the Borg. Madred made the pain he inflicted personal; the lack of predictability forced me to give up. It was a battle of wills in which I could not compete; he controlled my environment, and wanted to control my perceptions as well.

"How many lights do you see there?"

There were four lights over his head, but he told me there were five. He came back to this "game" day after day, dispensing excruciating pain if I did not accept the untruth. I resisted, but Madred had an accomplice: my unconscious mind. It wanted to protect me from the pain. Eventually, I actually thought I saw a fifth light. Madred had altered my reality.

The uselessness of torture as a means of gaining information; I not only would have said anything to end the torment, my mind would convince me it was true.

I was kept in captivity, but it turned out to be pointless. Jellico stopped the Cardassians' invasion plans and successfully demanded my release. It wouldn't end so easily for me.

✦

"We're ready to leave orbit, sir," Riker said over the intercom. We were at Starbase 310, picking up crew and cargo. I was in my ready room. Since returning from my captivity, I had chosen to spend less time on the bridge.

"Very well," I said. I sat in silence.

"We're due at Deep Space 9 tomorrow," Riker said. Deep Space 9 used to be the space station Terok Nor, run by the Cardassians, which I'd visited on the *Stargazer*. The Cardassians had withdrawn, and the Bajoran government had invited the Federation to administer the station. The *Enterprise* would be delivering crewmen picked up from Starbase 310, as well as three runabouts to supply the station.

But I didn't want to go. I did not want to run into Cardassians.

"Sir?"

He needed me to make the decision, the very simple and obvious decision to leave orbit. It was a small decision, inconsequential really. But my captivity had taken away my ability to make decisions. I'd been taught they belonged to Gul Madred. I had to force the words out.

"Make it so," I said.

When we arrived at Deep Space 9, I was on the bridge.

The incomplete gyroscope with dangerous-looking claws reached out for us. When I was last here, the scans showed it was heavily armed. Now, the Cardassians in their exit had stripped it of everything. Still, it took all my self-control to order the conn officer to dock with one of those unpleasant-looking metal arms.

"See," Deanna said, "nothing to worry about." She'd been sitting next to me, monitoring my progress since I'd returned. I smiled. As scared as I was, I did feel I was regaining control.

"Should I begin offloading our cargo?" Riker said. I nodded.

"Has the station commander arrived yet?" I was due to brief him, and then I was to leave.

"No, sir," Data said. "Commander Sisko is scheduled to arrive in two days."

Two days. It sounded like forever.

"I'll be in my ready room," I said, and left.

The two days passed, and eventually, Commander Sisko arrived. He was an imposing man, and I immediately sensed a ferocity about him as he walked into the observation lounge.

"It's been a long time, Captain," he said as we shook hands. There was no warmth in the remark, and I didn't recognize him.

"Have we met before?"

"Yes, sir. We met in battle. I was on the *Saratoga* at Wolf 359."

I felt suddenly nauseous. This was a completely inappropriate thing for him to say, but I should have been ready for it—I'd been so preoccupied with my own recovery, I had somehow missed this on his record. I tried to continue the briefing, tried to find a connection, but this man wouldn't allow it. He had obviously lost people who meant something to him when the Borg… when I… destroyed his ship. We finished, and soon after I left him and his station behind.

As I thought about Sisko, who was still so clearly locked in the tragedy of that attack, it suddenly gave me perspective. I connected my recent imprisonment with the Cardassians to my abduction by the Borg. In both instances I'd been stripped of the most basic human right of self-determination. Linking them in my mind, I was able to step outside of the fear. I was able to let it go. The fear of the Cardassians did not rule me.

I wondered at my fortune over being able to mend my psyche. I certainly had to credit my ship's counselor, Deanna Troi, whose patience, kindness, and professionalism helped me to face the truth of the situations.

But I'm certain I also owed the two mind melds I'd had with Vulcans. I'd transferred to my own mind certain mental disciplines that allowed me to conquer the emotional responses. I suppose the other advantage I'd had was that, over time in my life, I'd become emotionally detached. I hadn't let myself be close to anyone for a very long time. This made the disciplines I'd learned from my contact with the Vulcans that much more natural. It helped me recover, but didn't help in my own pursuit of personal happiness.

✦

"Jean-Luc," Professor Galen said. "I was too harsh." He was lying on a bed in sickbay, his chest burned by a disrupter wound. It was remarkable that he was still alive; he was well over 100 years old, and such a wound would have killed a much younger man. These were his last words.

Three weeks before, he'd come to the ship. It had been over thirty years since I'd seen him, and recently I'd begun to worry about him; for the last several years he'd stopped publishing works in his field. But when I saw him again, he'd lost none of his astuteness or self-assurance. He also still had not acquired any respect for the career I'd chosen. His first evening aboard ship, I took him to Ten-Forward, and asked him why he'd gone so silent.

"I made a discovery so profound in its implications," Galen said, "that silence seemed the wisest course." I asked him to tell me what it was all about, but he shook his head.

"That information comes with a price. Your agreement to join me on the final leg of this expedition."

"For how long?"

"Three months, perhaps a year," he said. It was absurd—I couldn't leave the *Enterprise* for such a length of time. I had to refuse, and when I finally told him, he was furious. His anger at me for my decision all those years ago came flooding out.

"I gave you the opportunity to become the finest archaeologist of your generation. Your achievements could have outstripped even my own, but no, you decided to reject a life of profound discovery. You walked out on me."

He left on his ship. I had hurt him, again. He had been like a father to me; perhaps because I'd been rejected by my own father, I had rejected Galen, but I prefer to think that I just wanted another path.

Soon after, we received a distress signal from him. Yridians boarded his small craft, and they killed him. I never did learn what his discovery was, and knowing the man as I did, I'm sure it would live up to his description as "profound." But I will always live with a little doubt that if I'd gone with him, I might have saved his life.

It was another overwhelming loss for me, one of thousands of deaths that had occurred since I'd become Captain of the *Enterprise*. Many would wonder how I could keep all the losses from being too much for me, yet it was those deaths that kept me going; only by committing myself to the work of Starfleet and the Federation could I justify in my own mind the sacrifices of others. I had made mistakes, some of which had resulted in casualties, but I did not,

---

*EDITOR'S NOTE: I feel Captain Picard is in fact telling us he *does* know what Galen had discovered. I don't know why he would keep it a secret, unless it might still be classified by Starfleet or the Federation.

THE STORY OF ONE OF STARFLEET'S MOST INSPIRATIONAL CAPTAINS

would not, let regrets consume me. I had a bargain with the dead; I would keep working, and they would remain quiet. I owed them.

✦

"It was… fun…" James Kirk said. His expression changed. He seemed to see something in his mind's eye that scared him. "Oh my…" he said, and then he was gone.

I'd only just met him, a man history had believed to be dead for 80 years, returning like King Arthur to save us. Unfortunately, our efforts to defeat Dr. Soran[*] led to Kirk's second death.

I had been inside a temporal Nexus, a strange parallel reality that provided the image of a contented life. My own experience was a Christmas I had never had: family, wife, children, gifts, a tree… It was warm and wonderful, and I knew it wasn't right. I wanted to stay, but the voices of the dead would not let me.

"This isn't real," I said.

"It's as real as you want it to be." It was Guinan, or an echo of Guinan who had been in the Nexus once. The mysteries surrounding her never ceased, and, like so many times in my past, she was there to guide me, like a mythical guardian angel. She led me to Kirk, who was also in the Nexus. Though he wasn't easy to convince, he agreed to leave with me, and help my mission. I would not have succeeded without him.

We were on hard, rocky terrain on the planet Veridian III. It would be impossible to dig him a grave, so I gathered large rocks and placed them around and on top of his body. He and I had worked together to defeat a common enemy, and I felt I was a part of the adventures I'd read about as a child. But it was so brief, it only served to make me want to get to know him

---

[*] **EDITOR'S NOTE:** In 2293, on the maiden voyage of the *U.S.S. Enterprise*-B, Kirk had been caught in a temporal nexus, a "ribbon" of energy of unknown origin, which traveled through the Galaxy. People who'd entered it relayed accounts of having their fantasies fulfilled. A man named Dr. Tolian Soran had wanted to enter the nexus, but the only way to do that was by being on a planet that it passed over. He had to change the ribbon's course, and had determined the only way to do that was by destroying the star in the Veridian system. Picard and Kirk defeated his plans.

more. In my short time with him, I didn't find anything unusual about his intellect or personality beyond a kind of boyish energy. Our plan to defeat Soran wasn't clever or complicated. More than anything, the experience showed me that I'd come into my own as a starship captain. Though I had held Kirk up as a hero, I had as much to contribute to the situation as he did. We were equals.

When I'd beamed down to Veridian III, the *Enterprise* had been in orbit and a Klingon warship was nearby. After we had defeated Soran, and I'd buried Kirk, I signaled the *Enterprise*, and they sent a shuttle to pick me up.

I was surprised to see Riker piloting the shuttle.

"Didn't I leave you in command?"

"You did," he said. "I have some bad news. I felt I should bring it to you myself, since I'm responsible."

"The *Enterprise*?"

"It's gone," he said. "The Klingons penetrated our shields. We had a warp core breach. I was able to separate the saucer section, but it crashed on the planet."

"Casualties?"

"A lot of injuries, no deaths."

"We can be thankful for that," I said. I'd just lost another ship, and some of the same insecurities invaded: did I make a mistake? Was there anything else I could've done? This time, the answer came back quickly: no. I then looked over at Riker. I could see he was troubled—I realized I'd gone through this before, but he hadn't. I had a dozen questions as to what exactly happened, but I decided they could wait.

"You can give me a full report later; I'm sure you did everything you could," I said.

"I'm not so sure," he said. I could hear the self-recrimination in his tone.

"Will," I said, "they put us in charge of these vessels, they train us as best they can to be emissaries of peace, to avoid conflict... but there will always be those who look to war and violence for their solution, who operate out of greed and self-interest. We can't blame ourselves for their occasional success. Just be certain the moral arc of history is on our side."

"Very philosophical for a man whose first officer just wrecked his ship," he said.

THE STORY OF ONE OF STARFLEET'S MOST INSPIRATIONAL CAPTAINS

"It's all right," I said. "I spent the afternoon saving the Galaxy with James T. Kirk. It balances out."

I wish I had a photograph of Will's expression.

✦

"There she is, Captain," Commander Shelby said. Shelby and I stood in the operations center of a dry dock at Utopia Planitia, looking out over a new ship that was almost completed. She'd originally been designated as the *U.S.S. Sentinel*—one of the new *Sovereign* class—but in the wake of my ship's destruction, they renamed her the *Enterprise*.

And they were giving it to me. This time I wasn't court-martialed for losing the ship. By stopping Soran, we'd prevented the deaths of millions, and that seemed to be enough for the Judge Advocate General.

"It's lovely," I said, although I wasn't sure I meant it. The ship was larger and sleeker than my *Enterprise*, but in my personal assessment it was missing some of the charm. I'm sure that was my own sense of nostalgia for something I'd lost, and kept it to myself, as I didn't want to insult Shelby. A few years earlier Shelby had served on the *Enterprise*, and had come back to Starfleet Command to supervise ship design and construction in the wake of the conflict with the Borg. The *Sovereign*-class ship had been one of her projects.

I gave the crew the option of coming with me, since some of the senior staff were certainly eligible for their own command. All but one decided to wait for the *Enterprise*-E to be completed. It was a surprise when Mr. Worf turned down my offer to be chief of security, even with a promotion in rank. I decided to go to see him at his parents' home in Kiev.

"I told him to take the offer," Sergey Rozhenko said. "Why would you leave Starfleet?" We drank hot tea in glass cups, having just finished a meal of beet soup and roasted potatoes.

"Father, please," Worf said. "I didn't say I was leaving Starfleet."

"Then why not go with the captain to his new ship?"

"Sergey," Helena said, "perhaps we should leave them alone to talk." She got up and began to pull Sergey out of the room with her.

"I just asked a question," Sergey said. "Is it so hard to answer a question?" When they left the room, I smiled at Worf.

"They love you very much," I said.

"I am very fortunate," Worf said.

"Whereas I am not," I said. "I would like to hear the answer to your father's question."

"I owe you that," Worf said. He got up and went to the window. "For my whole life, I've looked for a home. Khitomer and my birth parents were taken from me. I've never been fully comfortable in either the human world or the Klingon world. I sought to find my place in the universe. I finally found it… and it was taken from me again."

I didn't realize how profound the loss of the ship would be to someone like Worf. He was in mourning.

"We may be able to rebuild that place on a new ship," I said.

"Forgive me, Captain, but there is a Klingon saying," Worf said. "*Pagh yijach Soch jatqua.*"

I laughed. I had studied enough Klingon to translate it.

"I believe the Klingons have appropriated 'You can't go home again' from the Earth author Thomas Wolfe."

"Impossible," Worf said. "Kahless said it when he returned to Quin'lat after the battle with the Fek'lhri…"

"Point taken, Mr. Worf," I said. "But if you ever want to come back, there will always be a place for you." I soon took my leave and began my walk back to the transporter station in town. I thought about how Worf felt: the *Enterprise*-D had been my home too, and I wondered whether what I said was true, whether I could recreate the same sense of home on a new ship. I remembered going back for my second tour on *Stargazer* and not being able to recapture the feeling of the first. This would be different, I thought.

As I contemplated the nature of home, I fancied I heard a voice. It belonged to a woman, very faint.

"You've only had one home," she said. I searched the area for the source of the voice, but couldn't find it. It spoke again, and I realized the voice was in my head.

"Stop looking for me, I'm not there, Locutus…"

I subconsciously recognized the voice, but I pushed it away: I did not want to remember. It was the voice of the Borg queen. The memories of her had been repressed, the trauma of how she'd used me too difficult for me to face. The Borg were on their way.

A year later, they would return. My crew on my new ship were tested as they never had been before. But we defeated them, and it would lead to my favorite captain's log:

Captain's Log, April 5, 2063. The voyage of the *Phoenix* was a success... again.

This is, as every child knows, First Contact Day, the day Zefram Cochrane flew his own spaceship, the *Phoenix*, past the speed of light, and caught the attention of a passing Vulcan spacecraft. Humans and Vulcans met for the first time, and it would eventually bring humanity to the stars, where they would help found the United Federation of Planets.

And I got to witness it.

And it also almost never happened.

The Borg attacked Earth by going into the past. The *Enterprise* followed them, to stop their plan to assimilate Earth in a more vulnerable period, thus preventing First Contact. They were trying to erase the Federation from history. I began to understand their obsession with us: we were the only people who'd slowed their previously relentless success in assimilating other species.

"Destroy them," the Borg queen said. This time, she wasn't saying it to me; I was strapped to a table in engineering, where she planned on turning me into a drone. She was giving the order to Data, whom she had apparently seduced by grafting human skin on to his body. We were watching the *Phoenix* about to go to warp. Data fired a volley of quantum torpedoes. They headed right for the primitive ship.

"Watch your future's end," the Queen said.

The torpedoes closed in... and missed. Data had fooled her; resistance hadn't been futile. Data smashed a plasma coolant conduit, and the green super-hot gas swamped engineering, killing the Queen and all her drones. We had won, again.

Data and I left engineering, and headed toward the transporter room to reunite with our crew on the surface.

"Captain," Data said. "You had not mentioned the Borg queen in your report on the Borg from your previous assimilation."

"Yes," I said, "I think I repressed my memory of her. But she was on that original cube."

"Which was destroyed," Data said. I knew what he was getting at.

"Yes," I said. "She survived. And she may survive again."

"This time," Data said, "we must remember to include her in our report."

Later, we waited at the Montana missile silo with the rest of the crew and the hero of the day, Zefram Cochrane. He'd just returned in his warp spaceship. His support crew had consisted of Riker and La Forge. He wasn't quite what we expected.

"Now, you're saying this is going to be in the history books," Cochrane said. "How do you spell your names?"

"R-I-K..." Riker said, then, catching a disapproving glance from me, he smiled. "Just joking. If anybody asks you don't remember our names."

"What are your plans now that you've completed this trip?" I said.

"You said the aliens were coming, do you think they'll pay me a lot of money for my ship?"

"I do not," I said. "The Vulcans aren't interested in money."

"Oh," said Cochrane. "That puts a little crimp in my plans. What do the history books say I do next?"

"It's a little vague," Riker said. "Best play it by ear."

"I don't think these aliens are going to show," Cochrane said. "I'm going to bed."

"Just hold on," Riker said. He indicated the sky as the familiar design of a Vulcan scout ship broke through the clouds.

"Holy shit,"—this from Cochrane.

✦

"So Shinzon, the Praetor of the Romulan Empire," Admiral Janeway said, "was your *clone*?" She sat in my ready room, having come aboard the *Enterprise* to receive my report after we'd returned to Earth from Romulus. It was an interesting experience reporting to her; several decades ago I'd had to report to her father. She was much more affable.

"Yes," I said. "It would appear someone in the empire got hold of my DNA and embarked on a project to replace me." I understood her disbelief.

I myself had confronted this younger copy of myself, and I still had trouble accepting it.

"Wouldn't it take some 50-odd years to grow a clone that could be mistaken for you?"

"They were able to accelerate his age," I said. "But there was a change in government, and the project was discarded. They exiled him to the dilithium mines on Remus."

"And yet from there he was able to rise to power and overthrow the Romulan government."

I nodded.

"I suppose he had the advantage of good genes," Janeway said. I smiled, but the encounter had disgusted me. I had seen some of myself in Shinzon's ambition, but his upbringing had led him to be sadistic and Machiavellian. He had successfully conspired to kill the entire Romulan Senate, and start a war with the Federation. In our conflict, he'd killed a good portion of my crew, including one of my closest friends. Janeway read my expression, and regretted her remark.

"Sorry, Jean-Luc. You are not responsible for his actions."

"I appreciate that."

"You've suffered terrible losses," she said. "It must be especially difficult given the death of Commander Data." Difficult did not cover it; it had been traumatic. Data had rescued me from Shinzon, and in doing so sacrificed his life. I had always taken comfort in the fact that Data would outlive us all, and become a living witness to the history we all shared. He had been my companion for a very long time, and I wouldn't let him go so easily.

"He left us a remembrance," I said. I tapped my communicator. "Picard to Bridge, please send in B-4."

A moment later, B-4 entered. B-4 was a prototype of Data that we'd discovered on the mission. Before Data had died, he had downloaded all his memories into this avatar.

"Hello," B-4 said.

Janeway stood up and shook B-4's hand. "It is nice to meet you."

"Why?" B-4 said.

"His positronic brain is not as advanced as Data's," I said. "He may never be at the level Data was…"

"Oh my goodness, this is pathetic."

I turned; it wasn't Janeway. In her place was Q.

"Q, what the hell are you doing? Where's Admiral Janeway?"

"I sent her to a Kazon prison camp in the Delta Quadrant. I'm kidding, take a joke. She's fine."

"What are you doing here?"

"I'm here to express my condolences," Q said. B-4 held out his hand to him.

"Hello," B-4 said. Q looked him over with disgust, then turned to me.

"Are you really willing to put up with this?"

"Q…" I stepped forward, raised my hand. "Don't."

"Don't what?" He stared at me and smiled that Q smile. I knew what he intended, and it seemed wrong. I had to try to stop him.

"I respect Data's sacrifice," are the words that came from me but I didn't mean them. Q had the power, and I was tempted. Very tempted.

"You know, normally I would force you to ask me to use my power," Q said. "But I'm not doing this for you… I'm doing this for me. I miss him."

"Why?"

"Shhhhh…" Q snapped his fingers. He was gone in a flash, and Janeway returned.

"Jean-Luc," Janeway said. "What happened?" But I wasn't looking at her. I was focused on B-4. The android's childlike expression was gone, in its place a much more familiar, confident bearing.

"Data, is it you?"

"I believe it is, sir," said Data.

Data was back, and very much himself. There was something about this event that put my entire life in perspective. Q knew this was what I wanted, and I had not protested forcefully enough to stop him. Usually, my moral compass was clear on issues like this, but I'd lost some of my bearing. I couldn't see what was wrong with this, because I didn't want to have to accept the loss of Data as I had had to accept the loss of so many loved ones before.

The ship continued on, but it wasn't the same. Worf had been right, I had to relearn the lesson that I couldn't go home again. Riker and Deanna had married soon after he'd been offered his own command, and they left. Geordi and Data had stayed behind I think out of loyalty to me, and I felt I was holding them both back; they both could have had their own ships.

I had been in space too long. It was time to step down, it was time to move on.

One morning I was telling all this to Beverly over our regular breakfast, as we sat together on the couch in my quarters.

"What are you going to do?"

"I don't know," I said.

"Well, this makes what I have to tell you a little easier. I'm leaving the *Enterprise* as well. I've been offered command of the medical ship *Pasteur*." This shouldn't have been a surprise; Beverly had in the last few years shown an interest and ability in command. But I was surprised nonetheless, and a little panicked.

"That's wonderful," I said. "I'm very happy for you."

"You don't really sound happy for me."

"I'm sorry. Somehow, when I decided to leave the *Enterprise*, I didn't think I'd be leaving you. I'll miss you."

"I'll miss you, too."

What happened next surprised the both of us. I kissed her, and we were caught in a passionate embrace. We broke, and I looked at her, the woman who'd been in my life for so long, but always at arm's length. The moment I had decided to be free from my ship, I realized I didn't have to deprive myself of her any longer.

"Beverly," I said, "will you marry me?"

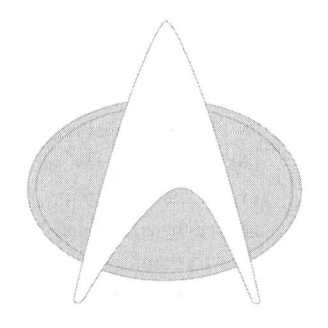

CHAPTER ELEVEN

"WELCOME TO VULCAN, AMBASSADOR PICARD," T'Pring said. She was one of the members of the High Council, striking and statuesque and 154 years old. She greeted me at T'Plana-Hath spaceport in the city of ShiKahr. With her was a small entourage of Vulcan diplomats, who welcomed me to their world. ShiKahr was a beautiful ancient city, surrounded by desert and the characteristic Vulcan red rock mountains. It was home to the Federation embassy.

I was led to a waiting hover transport, and our driver took me and the other diplomats to the embassy. We sat in silence for the entire trip—there was no small talk on Vulcan. Most humans would find this awkward, but my preparations for this assignment convinced me not to give in to the impulse to "chat." It was important that I have the respect of the Vulcans I would be dealing with, and showing human insecurities would not help. I felt ready for this new chapter.

When I informed Starfleet Command that I wanted to resign my commission, there was a flurry of protestations from every admiral that I knew. Many of them wanted me to stay, guaranteeing me a promotion, but I turned them down. I was marrying Beverly—that was my priority.

After leaving the *Enterprise*, Beverly and I had moved into temporary accommodations at Starfleet Headquarters, and from there we had to move quickly on our wedding plans, as she would be assuming command of her ship in a matter of weeks. We put our invitation list together. There was one name

I put on the list that worried Beverly, but she finally agreed. We planned the ceremony for a few days before Beverly was to ship out.

The wedding was at my family home. Marie no longer lived there, having left after the tragedy she faced when my brother and nephew died. I didn't expect she would return for the wedding, but she sent us a lovely note. We arrived there a few days before the wedding took place.

"It's beautiful," Beverly said. "Is it sad for you to be here?"

" 'Things without all remedy should be without regard,' " I said. " 'What's done is done.' "

"Those are Shakespeare's words," she said. "What would you say?"

"I'd say let's have a grand wedding."

It was a very large affair, and I was touched at the number of crewmates and friends who made the effort to return to Earth to be a part of it. Guinan officiated; at some point in her long past, she had been a clergy, although I wasn't sure where or for what religion. Wesley was my best man, the image of his father, which made it a little strange for both me and Beverly, but we didn't discuss it, we just had a wonderful time, dancing and drinking. It was a truly magical day for me. I don't know that I ever felt joy as complete and unrestrained as that day. I looked at Beverly, so happy and beautiful. I could hardly believe we would finally be together. I was 79 years old, and felt that my life was just beginning.

At the end of the reception, an elderly man I didn't recognize walked over to me.

"It was a beautiful affair, Jean-Luc," he said.

"I'm sorry," I said. "Have we met?" He smiled. For a brief flash, his face changed, and I was staring at Q. Another flash, and the old man returned.

"Thanks for inviting me," he said.

"I wasn't sure how to get you an invitation," I said. "But I figured you always seem to be looking over my shoulder, so putting it on the list was enough. Why the disguise?"

"Guinan hates me," Q said. "As do a few of your other friends. I didn't want to cause a stir."

"Thank you for coming," I said. "And for what you did for Data."

He smiled, and with a flash, was gone. Some might ask why I would've invited someone who'd been such a nuisance to me over the years. I would

THE STORY OF ONE OF STARFLEET'S MOST INSPIRATIONAL CAPTAINS

respond with an old aphorism: you can choose your friends, but you can't choose your family. And Q was, unfortunately, family. In some sense, I owed him. He had tested and tempted me; in our encounters, I was pushed to my limits, I had to be the best person I could be. It would always verify my ethics and morality, but I also had to confront some of my very serious flaws.

There were several dignitaries there, and we were honored to have the Federation president as a guest. Andrea Brand had retired from Starfleet several years before and had been elected to the Federation Council. She had the year before been elected president.

"Congratulations, Jean-Luc," she said to me. "I was wondering if I could have a word with you in private before I leave?"

"It is my wedding, Madam President."

"It won't take long," she said. We took a short walk away from the festivities. "What are your plans?"

"I haven't made any," I said, which was the truth. I had decided to throw myself into building a life with Beverly, and for the first time in my life was not really thinking about the future.

"I would like to appoint you Federation Ambassador to Vulcan," she said. "There is concern that the Vulcans and the Romulans have begun secret talks regarding reunification. Your knowledge of the Vulcans would make you invaluable." I had never considered a career in politics, but President Brand's argument was compelling. I told her I would think it over.

The next day, I raised the subject with Beverly over breakfast.

"You're a wonderful diplomat," she said. "I can think of no one better for the job."

"The problem is… we just got married."

"I think I can arrange to be in the vicinity of Vulcan now and again," she said. "After all, I'm the captain."

"Already planning on abusing your authority."

"We can't all be as selfless as Captain Jean-Luc Picard."

"Thank god," I said.

I called President Brand and accepted her offer. I received a briefing and certification, and Brand arranged for Beverly to take me to Vulcan on the *Pasteur*.

When it was time for us to leave, I insisted on piloting the shuttle myself, just so Beverly and I could have a few more minutes alone. We landed in the

Pasteur's shuttlebay. As the rear door of the shuttle opened, I saw a large number of the crew waiting.

"Commanding officer *Pasteur* arriving," I said, and the crew stood to attention. Beverly looked at me and smiled; she leaned in and gave me a kiss, then moved to the lectern to read her orders.

"To Captain Beverly Picard, stardate 60768.1, you are hereby requested and required to take command of *U.S.S. Pasteur* as of this date. Signed Rear Admiral Kathryn Janeway, Starfleet Command."

I smiled in awe and pride.

The few days it took to get to Vulcan were an interesting experience for me. The crew seemed to want to cater to my every need, and I couldn't figure out whether it was because I was an ambassador or because I was married to the captain.

We made it to Vulcan, and she took me to the shuttle bay. Seeing her in command of her own ship was revelatory. She had always been a forceful presence in sickbay, but the ease with which she transferred that to the bridge was impressive. She was a remarkable woman, and I was consumed with love for her.

"Goodbye, dear," she said. "I'll be back soon."

"I'll hold you to that," I said.

✦

T'Pring and her diplomats took me to the Federation embassy. There was a large gathering of staff waiting to welcome me. I wasn't used to this level of pomp and circumstance, but did my best with the introductions. T'Pring said whatever I might need, I shouldn't hesitate to ask, that all of Vulcan welcomed me. She then left with her entourage. I let out a silent sigh of relief; I don't think T'Pring knew that I'd mind-melded with Spock, the man she'd left at the altar.

I quickly got myself into the day-to-day routines of being an ambassador. It was complicated, bureaucratic work. I was representing the president of the Federation on this world, and Vulcan's unique role in that Federation was more delicate than I thought. I was fortunately spared the usual ceremonies and parties that ambassadors typically had to attend—Vulcans found them "illogical." But there were a number of other situations that would require a great deal of tact. I often found myself stuck between Federation members who wanted Vulcan help in a specific area of study or technology, and the Vulcans, who were not the most collaborative of species. There was also the Romulan-Vulcan situation, and trying to get information out of the High Council was proving to be a challenge.

I spent the most time dealing with individuals from other planets of the Federation wanting to visit Vulcan and helping them navigate Vulcan's strict visitation and immigration laws. After a few months on the planet, I came to understand the reason for these laws: it was the most peaceful society I'd ever seen. There seemed to be no fear, no anger, no sadness. Just calm. Outsiders often proved problematic.

"I was taking my morning walk," I said to Beverly, during one of our evening talks via subspace, "and I saw a Tellarite talking to a Vulcan woman."

"Oh, they're such pigs," Beverly said.

"This may not be a secure channel, Captain. We need to be diplomatic."

"Yes, Ambassador."

"So the Tellarite is yelling, 'Hey, I just want to buy you a drink.' The Vulcan woman says she's not thirsty. The Tellarite then says, 'Come on, you know what I mean,' to which the Vulcan responds, 'If you're inferring you wanted to use a drink to initiate a mating ritual, Vulcans mate only once every seven years.'"

"Did he buy it?" Beverly said.

"No, he said she was lying, to which she gave the usual, 'Vulcans never lie.'"

"Which in and of itself is a lie. Was the Vulcan pretty?"

"Not as pretty as you."

"I was just curious." I laughed, and we ended our conversation with a promise to see each other soon. We didn't. I didn't blame her; she was a starship captain, and her duties kept her from any personal priorities she might have. Over the next three years, Beverly and I were together for no more than four weeks. It was an irony that we'd spent all those years together on the *Enterprise*, and now that we were married we barely saw each other. I didn't have an expectation she would sacrifice her career for our marriage, but it hurt nevertheless.

My job as an ambassador settled into routine, and I found the emotional distance of the society I was in familiar; I decided I would have made a pretty good Vulcan. But I also started to get restless. Even at my advancing age I wanted a little more action in my life.

I was about to get it.

I was in my office trying to expedite passport applications for some children of an Andorian on the Federation Council, when I received a subspace call from an old friend.

"Captain Data," I said. "To what do I owe the pleasure?" He was in my old ready room on the *Enterprise*-E.

"Sorry to disturb you, Ambassador," Data said. "I'm sending you some information attached to this transmission. Please look it over."

On my screen, a long-range scan of a star system appeared along with a familiar-looking device emitting high levels of subspace interference.

"What system is that?"

"The Hobus system," Data said. "It is in Romulan territory."

"It has the characteristics of the subspace engine the Denobulans built."

"That was my supposition as well."

"Do the Romulans have something to do with it?"

"Negative. They are in fact sending a strike force to the Hobus system."

"The people of the Hobus system have been periodically subjugated by the Romulans," I said.

"Perhaps they heard about the Denobulans and were looking for a means of escape."

"But the Romulans probably assume it's a weapon…"

"Starfleet has tried to warn them," Data said. "The Romulans will not respond. Their strike force will be there in a matter of hours."

"There is one person I can call," I said. "Meanwhile, please come to Vulcan, we may need you."

"Yes, Ambassador," Data said. "That was my thought as well. We are already on our way."

I left the Federation embassy. Over the years, I had been forced to develop a small intelligence network on Vulcan to gather whatever snippets of information I could on the reunification talks. I also kept tabs on the movement of the diplomat who was spearheading the discussions with Romulus, and, if my information was accurate, he was currently at the headquarters of the Vulcan High Council.

I entered the building and went right up to the receptionist.

"I want to see Ambassador Spock," I said. The receptionist just stared at me.

THE STORY OF ONE OF STARFLEET'S MOST INSPIRATIONAL CAPTAINS

"I am unaware of an Ambassador Spock…"

"Vulcans do not lie," I said. "He's upstairs negotiating Romulan–Vulcan reunification." The receptionist stared at me for a while longer, then went to get help. A few minutes later, I was led into a conference room.

"Ambassador Picard," Spock said. He stood with T'Pring. Neither one of them looked pleased to see me, but then again, that's always hard to tell with Vulcans.

I apologized for the intrusion, then explained the situation.

"The Romulan government is still quite paranoid," Spock said. "I sincerely doubt I can talk them out of their attack. But I will try."

I wanted to go with him, to add my voice to his, but he didn't invite me. I think he was probably right not to, as frustrating as it was. I went back to my office, where the passport applications were still on my desk.

When the *Enterprise* arrived in orbit, things picked up again. Data brought me aboard and took me to the stellar cartography room. Spock was already there, along with the ship's first officer, Geordi.

"I was unable to convince the Romulans," Spock said. "We will now have to pursue other options, as the situation has deteriorated."

They showed me a map of Romulan territory. On it, a spreading mass of light was expanding from the Hobus system.

"Is that a supernova? That's impossible, the Hobus star wasn't nearly that old."

"You are correct, sir," Data said. "The Romulans attempted to destroy the subspace engine, but appear to only have damaged it. It was accidentally set off."

"The damaged subspace engine caused the Hobus star to go supernova," Geordi said. "A supernova that exists in both normal space and subspace."

"Because it exists in subspace as well, the supernova will spread far beyond the Hobus system," Spock said. "It will consume Romulus in a matter of days."

"And then move on to Vulcan and the rest of the Alpha Quadrant," Geordi said.

"We must stop it." I turned to Spock, "I remember from our meld you had an invention called 'red matter' which you could use…"

"Ambassador," Data said, "we have already taken steps to carry out that plan."

"You can't take a Federation ship into Romulan territory," I said. "Perhaps Geordi…"

"Already have my engineers on it," Geordi said.

275

Data and Geordi had things well in hand; they had just included me out of courtesy. Data helped Spock build his red matter device, which he would use to consume the supernova. Geordi's unmarked vessel would allow Spock to enter Romulan space without causing an interstellar incident.

On the day Spock left, I went to see him off.

"Good luck, Ambassador," I said.

"You are aware, Picard," Spock said, "that I do not believe in luck."

"You are also aware," I said, "that I know that's not true."

I never saw him again.

✦

"I'm afraid, Jean-Luc," President Brand said, "I'm recalling you."

Spock did stop the subspace supernova, but he had failed to do so before it reached Romulus. The Romulan homeworld was destroyed, and Spock was now missing, presumed dead. The Vulcan High Council blamed me; I had ignored protocol.

"I understand," I said.

"I could've made a case for you ignoring protocol if Romulus had been saved," Brand said. "But as it is, you're to leave immediately."

Data was still in orbit and offered to take me back to Earth. On the way, I communicated with Beverly.

"I'm so sorry," she said. "What do you think happened to Ambassador Spock?"

"I don't know," I said. "But I think he's alive somewhere."

"How do you know?"

"You always retain a bit of a person you've mind-melded with, and you feel it when they die. I felt it when Sarek died. But the piece of Spock is still alive in my mind."

"I guess you weren't cut out to be an ambassador," she said.

"I guess not."

"I'll get back to Earth as soon as I can," she said.

"You take your time. You have a ship, and a job to do."

"But what about us?"

"There's time for us," I said. I wasn't sure there was, but I would wait for her.

THE STORY OF ONE OF STARFLEET'S MOST INSPIRATIONAL CAPTAINS

✦

I stood on the plank on top of the tanks, punching down the crusts of the fermenting grapes. It was getting more difficult for me to do this work myself, but I had no choice; there weren't many people on Earth interested in producing wine. The year before, a Klingon had answered my advertisement that I was looking for help, but I turned her down. I didn't think a Klingon and I would work well together.

But I was excited. This would be my third vintage since coming back to the vineyard. For the first vintage I'd harvested the grapes two years ago. They would be bottled soon. I had high hopes for the Picard vintage of 2393. As difficult as the work was, I'd learned to enjoy it, finally.

I finished mixing the tanks, and got down. The sun was setting, and I decided to go in and fix myself some dinner. I might try Beverly on subspace tonight, although it was sometimes difficult to reach her. She had promised to be home for my birthday, and I was very much looking forward to that; it would be my ninetieth. I imagined she might arrange for some of our other friends to be there as well. It would be lovely to see some of the old crew again, and hear about their new adventures. And then they would leave, and that would be fine as well.

After dinner, I settled down with a cup of Earl Grey tea, and took one last look at this volume I've written. It reminds me that I've really lived my life alone, for better or worse. But that's who I am, and I feel lucky to have the life I've had. I've seen more of the Galaxy than one man is owed, and met more than my share of the great men and women of our time. I feel proud of whatever small role in our civilization that I've played. But now, it's up to others to make the history.

For me, I'm happy making my father's wine.

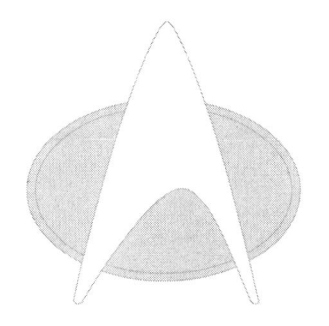

EDITOR GOODMAN'S ACKNOWLEDGMENTS

Thanks to everybody at Titan Books, especially Laura Price and my editors Andy Jones and Simon Ward, for all your patience and hard work, and, again, patience; Dana Youlin for whipping the manuscript into shape; Russell Walks, a wonderful artist, for your collaboration and for lending your talents to creating all the amazing photos; Dave Rossi, again, for making me an author; John Van Citters, for listening to Dave Rossi the first time, and then continuing to let me do this.

André Bormanis, for all those questions you answer promptly, completely, and with good humor; Mike and Denise Okuda, for all your work that makes this book possible; Mike Sussman, who suggested why Picard put Wesley at the helm; Admiral James Stavridis, for his memoir *Destroyer Captain: Lessons of a First Command*; Steve Kane, who recommended I read *Destroyer Captain: Lessons of a First Command* by Admiral James Stavridis; Bryan Wolf and Brian Lazarus, great lawyers; Brannon Braga and Rick Berman, who made me a *Star Trek* writer.

Patrick Stewart, for obvious reasons; Seth MacFarlane, without whom I wouldn't get to do any number of amazing things, including working with Patrick Stewart; my friends Mark Altman, Adam-Troy Castro, Howie Kaplan, Anne Lounsbery, Scott Mantz, Glen Mazzara, Dan Milano and Austin Tichenor, because you read the last book; my family: Fred, Phyllis, Bill, Jason, Rafael, Crystal, Anthony, Steven, Julia, Emma and Steve; my sisters Ann and Naomi, carrying on our mom's legacy with me; and Talia, Jacob and especially Wendy, for your love, attention, humor and care, despite my annoying work habits.

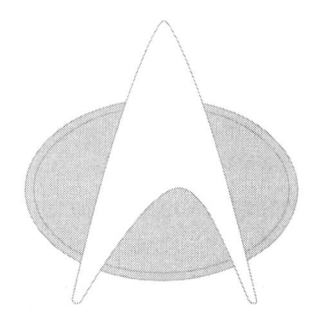

ABOUT THE EDITOR

David A. Goodman began his writing career in 1988 as a staff writer on *The Golden Girls*. After getting fired from that job, he worked on over 20 other television series, among the more relevant: *Star Trek: Enterprise*, *American Dad*, and *Futurama*, where he penned the *Star Trek* homage "Where No Fan Has Gone Before." He is best known for his work on *Family Guy*, where he served as executive producer and head writer for over 100 episodes. As of this writing, he is working with Seth MacFarlane on the new show *The Orville*. He lives in Pacific Palisades, California with his family.

THE AUTOBIOGRAPHY OF
KATHRYN JANEWAY

THE HISTORY OF THE CAPTAIN WHO WENT FURTHER THAN ANY HAD BEFORE

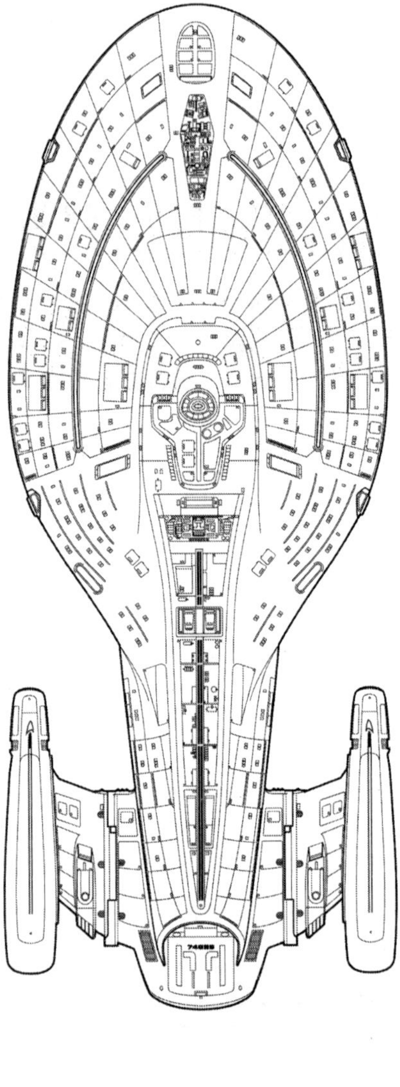

THE AUTOBIOGRAPHY OF
KATHRYN JANEWAY

THE HISTORY OF THE CAPTAIN WHO WENT FURTHER THAN ANY HAD BEFORE

BY
KATHRYN M. JANEWAY

EDITED BY UNA McCORMACK

TITAN BOOKS

The Autobiography of Kathryn Janeway
Paperback Edition ISBN: 9781789095333
Hardback Edition ISBN: 9781789094794
E-Book Edition ISBN: 9781789094800

Published by Titan Books
A division of Titan Publishing Group Ltd.
144 Southwark Street, London SE1 0UP.

First paperback edition: October 2021
10 9 8 7 6 5 4 3 2 1

TM ® & © 2020, 2021 by CBS Studios Inc. © 2020, 2021 Paramount Pictures Corporation. STAR TREK and related marks and logos are trademarks of CBS Studios Inc. All Rights Reserved.

All rights reserved. No part of this publication may be reproduced, stored in a retrieval system, or transmitted, in any form or by any means, electronic, mechanical, photocopying, recording, or otherwise, without prior written permission from the publisher.

Illustrations: Russell Walks
Editor: Cat Camacho
Interior design: Rosanna Brockley/Adrian McLaughlin

A CIP catalogue record for this title is available from the British Library.

Printed and bound in India by Thomson Press India Ltd.

Did you enjoy this book? We love to hear from our readers. Please e-mail us at: readerfeedback@titanemail.com or write to Reader Feedback at the above address.

To receive advance information, news, competitions, and exclusive offers online, please sign up for the Titan newsletter on our website: www.titanbooks.com.

CONTENTS

INTRODUCTION BY COMMANDER NAOMI WILDMAN 1

CHAPTER ONE 3

CHAPTER TWO 19

CHAPTER THREE 37

CHAPTER FOUR 53

CHAPTER FIVE 71

CHAPTER SIX 89

CHAPTER SEVEN 107

CHAPTER EIGHT 125

CHAPTER NINE 141

CHAPTER TEN 155

CHAPTER ELEVEN 171

CHAPTER TWELVE 191

For Daniel, for years of fun conversation, and the best ideas

INTRODUCTION

BY COMMANDER NAOMI WILDMAN

WHEN I WAS A LITTLE GIRL, I WANTED TO BE THE CAPTAIN OF A STARSHIP. I know lots of kids have the same ambition, but I wasn't planning to be the captain of any starship. Oh no, I had a very specific ship in mind. I was going to be captain of the *U.S.S. Voyager*.

The thing about this ambition of mine is that it wasn't so outlandish. Because I was born in the Delta Quadrant, and I spent most of my childhood on board *Voyager*, and as far as I was concerned, our captain was the best person in the entire Galaxy. I wanted to be her when I grew up. And in the meantime, I'd settle for being her assistant.

Most people my age grew up following the story of *Voyager*—lost in the Delta Quadrant, seventy thousand light-years away from home, trying to get back to family and friends. For me, this was everyday life. You may have thrilled to hear the news that *Voyager* had been found, or two-way communication had been established, or, most excitingly of all, that after only seven years, a Borg transwarp conduit had brought our ship home.

This might have been an amazing adventure for you, but for me it was—well, it was home. My mom, Sam Wildman, was serving as an ensign when *Voyager* was whisked away—and then found out she was pregnant. My birth story is one amongst many strange tales of those years, but it meant that growing up I knew no other life. Home was a little ship,

1

a long way from where it had started, full of Starfleet and Maquis and all sorts of other interesting people, which most of the time sailed quietly through space—and some of the time came under attack from Vidiians or Hirogen or Kazon. My childhood friends were a Talaxian, an Ocampan, and two decommissioned Borg drones learning to be individuals. I learned logic games from a thoughtful Vulcan, and how to fix anything in front of me from a half-human, half-Klingon. I played the *Captain Proton* holodrama before most people had ever heard of it. And I learned courage, and wisdom, and grace under fire from the very best captain of all—Kathryn M. Janeway.

Admiral Janeway, as she is now known, has been an inspiration to so many throughout the years. Who else could have held that crew together? Who else, through intelligence and sheer force of personality, could have made a group of Starfleet officers and Maquis fighters pull together and set course for home? Who else could have battled the Borg Queen, fought off the Hirogen—or played with such aplomb the part of holographic Arachnia, Queen of the Spider People, nemesis of Captain Proton? Who else would have taken time out of most days to check on her youngest crew member, Naomi, who loved her and admired her so much? Who else would have made that little girl her assistant?

When I was that little girl, I wanted to grow up to be Kathryn Janeway. But the truth is, nobody could replace her—and Kathryn's great skill is to persuade people to be the very best they could be. So many of us owe her so much. Thank you, Admiral, for bringing us home—but thank you, most of all, for the faith you showed us, and the way you brought out the best in us. There can only ever be one captain of *Voyager*—Kathryn Janeway.

Naomi Wildman
Executive Officer, Deep Space K-7

CHAPTER ONE
NO PLACE LIKE HOME—2336-2347

WHEN I WAS A LITTLE GIRL, MY MOTHER MADE POP-UP BOOKS. Do you recall the kind I mean? You turn a page and a whole scene springs up before your eyes. Even now, at this late stage of my life, I think these creations are miraculous. I guess it's something to do with the craft, the careful construction and—yes—the engineering that's involved. My mother's creations were sheer marvels.

My little sister and I each had our favorite. For Phoebe, three years my junior, it was *Alice in Wonderland*: an appropriate choice for a creative and artistic little girl, who seemed to inhabit a world of wonders. I loved that book as well: there was a little tunnel that my mother had constructed from card and clear paper, into which you had to peer to see Alice and the White Rabbit tumbling down. There was the house that sprang up with Alice's huge arms and legs sticking out that never failed to make us laugh. Most beautiful of all, however, was the grand display of playing cards flying up into the air when we—joining in with Alice—would say, "You're nothing but a pack of *cards!*"

Yes, I loved Wonderland, but my real passion was for *The Wonderful Wizard of Oz*. The story of Dorothy Gale, caught up in a tornado and torn away from her family to a strange land where she had to live by her brains, her heart, and her courage, making new friends, and finding her way home, appealed to me profoundly for some reason. My first glimpse of adventure. Safe at home, among my loving family, I dreamed of flying away to Oz. Mom's version of the book was cunningly designed, from the cyclone that swept open on the first page, to the little pair of green glasses tucked into an envelope that you opened to explore the Emerald City, to the very last page where—most thrillingly, to my mind my mother's most elaborate creation was to be found: a cardboard balloon that lay flat between the pages, until lifted on a string between two straws and pressed out, to leave the tiny basket dangling below. I sat with that book for many hours as a small child, enchanted not only by the story, but by working out how my mother had put all the elements together. Mom used to say that Daddy was the one who gave me the flying bug, the desire to take wing and soar off into space. But a huge part was played by her most wonderful, wizardly, cardboard balloon, travelling all the way from Oz.

Looking back on my childhood, I see now that these books were the place where all our family's interests came together. My mother, born Gretchen Williams, was an artist. She was always experimenting with new forms, but illustration was her true talent. You most likely know her as the author of over two dozen books and holodramas for children. Two or three generations of children have taken her stories to heart. Phoebe followed in her footsteps by having an artistic bent: I have a holopicture of them standing next to each other, Mom with a brush in her hand and a dollop of paint on her nose; Phoebe, beside her, exactly the same. I was no artist: my houses leaned sideways; my cute furry creatures looked savage; my human beings something from a horror holo. I can, however, hand draw very clear schematics.

I was the scientist, the engineer, the practical one, the one who worked in numbers. I was the one who stared at the stars and mapped them, who wanted machines, who wanted to fly. In this, I followed my father Edward—Ted to friends, Teddy to my mother—who was an enthusiastic amateur pilot and astronomer. He was also a Starfleet flag officer, and this fact—which shaped our childhood through the sadness of his inevitable absences, and, at least as importantly, through the joy and intensity of his presence—was surely the defining feature of my life. More than anything, I wanted my brave, cheerful, wonderful father to be proud of me. More than anything, I wanted him to see me become the captain of a starship, exactly like him. It's one of the great regrets of my life that this didn't come to pass. Daddy saw me enter the Academy, but he didn't see me captain a ship, let alone bring one safely home from the furthest journey a ship has ever made. But I get ahead of myself. Let's go back to the beginning, back to a small country farm, in the Midwest, in the northern part of the continent of America, on Earth.

✦

Our family home was a small farm outside Bloomington, Indiana. My mother's family had been settled in the region for several generations—Midwesterners through and through. We knew the Williams family story (pioneers, settlers—the traditional covered wagons), and both my maternal grandparents and my mother herself made sure we knew the full history of this land that we lived on and not the partial account that had once been taught, in the old days of nation-states and manifest destiny. One of the peoples who lived here before my ancestors arrived were the Potawatomi, Native Americans of the Great Plains, forced out in the nineteenth century. They call themselves the Neshnabé, the original people. My mother made sure that both Phoebe and I understand that the land that we called home had been the home of many people before us and will be the home of many after us. We learned stories from other people too. A particular favorite of mine was a Cherokee story about the Water Spider; one of my mother's friends wrote and illustrated a book about it that I loved. The Water Spider goes on a long journey to find fire to help the other animals survive. The other animals boast that they will find it and laugh at her when she promises them that she will. But she weaves a boat from her own webs and sails across the water, carrying back with her a hot coal, and she is celebrated for her courage and her honor. I often thought of the Water Spider, on my journey home.

My maternal grandparents, Hector and Ellen Williams, lived on their own farm on land adjacent to ours, and Phoebe and I were often there. One of my earliest memories is of an old oak tree that stood on my grandparents' farm. I learned to climb on that old tree, and Grandpa built a swing for me on its boughs. It was a favorite playmate. One very hot summer afternoon, when the grown-ups were sitting sweltering in the shade, my demands for a playmate were rebuffed; after a tantrum, I took my grievances off to the swing, which I punished for a good hour or so. It's testament to Grandpa's skill as a carpenter that I didn't bring the whole thing down on my own head. When I got tired of that, I climbed up the tree, and sulked for a while. Eventually, still cross but now tired and hot, I repented, and went back indoors, where Grandma cheered everyone's spirits with slushes. An hour later, the inevitable storm started, and I watched from the window as the rains hammered down. The thunder started, then the light show, and I counted between lightning and rumble to see how close the storm was coming. And then—I can still see this in my mind's eye—a strike of lightning hit the oak tree, splitting it right down the middle.

The scream I let out brought the whole household running. Grandpa was there first, but he couldn't get any sense out of me. When I pointed out to the tree, however, he understood. He put his big arm around my shoulder and pulled me into a hug.

"Scary, huh, Katy? One minute a tree's there, tall and strong, and the next it's gone."

Yes, he understood. Lightning strikes so suddenly, so unexpectedly. An old tree that had been supporting you that afternoon could be gone by evening. Looking back now I see that this was my first sense that misfortune can hit even in the safest of places, that we cannot prepare ourselves for every eventuality that life throws at us. I can see too that it was my first brush with mortality, the realization that even old, strong things might suddenly be felled in their prime.

That night the house rattled in the storm, but the next morning was sunny and bright. Grandpa and I went out together and had a good look at our poor old stricken tree. I shed a tear or two, until Grandpa distracted me by saying we were here to find a present for my mother. And we did find a present, a good big piece of burned wood, and brought it back home for her, like proud hunters: a fine piece of charcoal for Mommy to draw me pictures with.

✦

THE HISTORY OF THE CAPTAIN WHO WENT FURTHER THAN ANY HAD BEFORE

My father's family, the Janeways, whose roots ultimately went back to the west of Ireland, were considerably more peripatetic than the Williams clan, but Portage Creek, Indiana was their base from at least the early years of the twentieth century. My paternal grandparents came back to Bloomington when my paternal grandmother, Caitlin Janeway, took up a professorship at the university: she was an aeronautics engineer, a materials scientist specializing in alloys for use in deep space, one of a long tradition of women in our family to devote themselves to exploring the stars, a tradition which it has been my honor to continue. My paternal grandfather, Cody Janeway, was Starfleet, reaching the rank of commander and serving as chief science officer on various vessels. Family legend has it that he once turned down the chance to serve with a certain Captain Kirk, but I have not been able to find any evidence to prove this, and Grandpa, the old rogue, would never tell the story past a nod and a wink. I'd love to find out the truth of things: family legends do have a tendency to exaggerate! Granddad took up a teaching post at the university when my grandmother took up her chair, and both seemed content to have put down roots at last, allowing their teenage children to attend the same school for several years in succession. Since they lived in the big city of Bloomington, Phoebe and I called our paternal grandparents Granny-in-town and Granddad-in-town, the Grands-in-town for short. They weren't daily presences in the same way as my mother's parents, Grandpa and Grandma, but they were still significant influences in our lives.

My mother and father, despite growing up so close to each other, did not meet at high school, nor were they even introduced to each other by mutual friends (and there were several, or so it turned out). No, they met in Geneva, of all places. How did that happen, when my mother did not willingly go further than Bloomington, and even then complained about having to leave her art and the farm behind? Well, shortly before graduating high school, my mother became deeply concerned with humanitarian issues: I think she had seen footage of the refugee crisis on Koltaari. Somehow, a teacher at school persuaded her to attend a youth conference being held at the old United Nations buildings in Geneva, where young people from across the Federation were gathering to learn more about how the Federation and Starfleet could assist in bringing aid to the refugees. My mother was not sure: the event lasted a whole month. But her passion won out over her domesticity, and she duly went along. Even my mother, a true home bird, had to admit that this trip—the longest she ever spent away from home—had been worth it. She brought home a young man, a Starfleet cadet, starry-eyed with love for this quiet and talented girl. They married the year they both turned twenty-two, when my father graduated from Starfleet Academy.

Knowing that my father's career meant that he would by necessity be away for long periods of time, but not wanting to delay starting their family, my mother and father decided that they would make their home close to my mother's parents. Mom was well supported when we were small, and able to carry on with her own work as an artist and illustrator. Grandpa and Grandma were therefore very strong presences in our lives; their wedding gift to my parents was the land next to their own farm, and there my parents built their family home, and established their own small farm. I know that many people are anxious to get away from their families as quickly as possible on reaching maturity, but this was not the case with my mother. She simply did not have the wanderlust of her husband and elder child. She was happy in the land where she had been born; she had everything she needed there. One of many ways in which we never quite understood each other—but I guess that this is the definition of true love, isn't it? It doesn't try to change; it accepts the other for what she is. Still, children are sensitive creatures. I knew that this gap in her understanding of me existed, and when I thought about that, it made me sad.

Don't let me leave you with the wrong impression! Most of all you should imagine a very happy, very loved little girl, who lived—in many ways—an idyllic childhood. The great grief of my early childhood—and Phoebe will forgive me for saying this, I know—was the arrival of The Baby. I was three years old, and had, until then, been the absolute center of attention for all the adults in my immediate vicinity. With Grandpa I dug in the garden and ate Welsh rarebit. With Grandma I baked cookies and other treats. As for Mommy and Daddy, they had surely been put on Earth to do my bidding. And then… Well, I knew something wasn't right when Mommy started to have naps all the time, just when I was giving up on them, and wasn't as eager to get down on the floor and play with me as usual. Then she started to get bigger and bigger... People said things like, "Are you looking forward to The Baby, Katy?" and "You'll have a playmate when The Baby arrives, won't you, Katy?" and "Do you want a brother or a sister, Katy?"

Well, I am here to tell you that I was not sold on the idea of The Baby: not one little bit. I was a bright kid, and I think I guessed what the score would be. Everyone would be fussing around the new arrival; nobody would want to play any longer with Katy. And when the darned thing arrived... Well, this was no playmate, was it? A tiny red screeching thing—Jeez! What a con! A noisy, troublesome, demanding con!

"Here you are, Kathryn," Mommy said, holding the creature in her arms. "Meet your baby sister. Little Phoebe."

I eyed the new scrap of life suspiciously. "Mommy," I said, "can we swap it for a puppy?"

I have never been allowed to forget this. But I did get the puppy: Jess, a border collie of such perfection that even now I get a tear in my eye thinking about her. She came to me at ten weeks old, a warm little bundle of energy and love, and Grandpa helped me train her. We were devoted to each other. Jess trotted everywhere with me, and she snuck into my room at nights, despite stern warnings from Grandpa that spoiling her would ruin her as a working dog. (It never did.) In the holopictures that we have of that time, we are always together, and I loved her with all my heart. But in some ways, I knew that Jess was a consolation prize, and that with Phoebe's arrival, I had lost some little part of Mommy. My beautiful and elusive mother, always the first object of my devotion, was now shared. I was not wholly the center of her life any longer, and never could be again.

✦

This was my early childhood. We were a very happy, close-knit family, in which two little girls basked in the love of their various devoted adults and were encouraged to follow their own paths. Phoebe soon showed the artistic bent that rivaled even my mother's, permanently smudged with paints and modeling clays. My mother, around the time of Phoebe's arrival, started to grow roses, firstly for pleasure, but increasingly she became very competitive. This was most unlike my mother, although, as in all her endeavors, she excelled. There is a rose named after each one of her daughters. I recall one morning, not long after The Baby landed, when I was outside helping her, proud in my little blue overalls and my tiny spade and glad to be spending time with Mommy, when a man walked past the gate and stopped to watch me work. Mom came over to say hello, and he nodded at me and said, "Nice to see a boy helping his mom."

A boy?! This was intolerable. This was not to be permitted. By all accounts I gave that man the fiercest of stares—*skewered* him, as my mother tells it—and delivered the memorable putdown, "Katy not boy! Katy *girl*!"

"I've never seen a man move so fast," Mom said. "She more or less ran him out of town." I loved it when she told this story. I basked in the glow that came to her eye. Mommy was proud of me, and that was everything.

Let me describe my mother as she was in these years. A free spirit—but quiet, solitary. Still waters ran very deep in my mother; it was as if some kind of spirit of the natural world had been temporarily caught in a mortal body. By the sea, she would surely have been a selkie; here on the plains she was a genie of the river, perhaps, or of the lakes, some kind of spirit drawn to live among us ordinary mortals. She was outdoors as much as she could be—in the garden, or else working on the long porch at the back of the house. She had a shed which she used as a studio in bad weather, but rain did not daunt her and, in fact, often she would go out to meet it, walking around the farm and coming home drenched, her eyes shining. She was sweet-natured, funny, often absent in that way that very creative people can be, and endlessly creative with her two small children. Need it be said that I adored her?

People often ask me what it was like, having a writer of children's books as a mother. Truth be told, both Phoebe and I took it largely for granted. She had so many stories she wanted to share! Phoebe leaned toward fantasy: Wonderland, of course; later, she loved Meg Murry's journeys through the universe by means of the tesseract, Binti's career at Oomza Uni, Awinita Foster's slipstream adventures along the shining way.

THE HISTORY OF THE CAPTAIN WHO WENT FURTHER THAN ANY HAD BEFORE

I tended toward more realistic stories: the Melendy children making a new home in the countryside, exploring the land and the people around them; Omakayas and her family of the Birchbark House, growing up near Lake Superior; Cassie Logan's struggles under Jim Crow; the stories of Mildred Jones and her friends, rebuilding the post-atomic world in the 2080s. Even my beloved Dorothy Gale was in many ways a practical child, focused on returning to her home at least as much as on the marvels she encountered.

There was one case I recall when Mommy did share her stories with us, and that was when she was invited to write for the well-known children's holoprogram, *The Adventures of Flotter*. I think it was a new direction for her—she hadn't written for holos before, although many followed afterward—but she was naturally drawn to a river creature. She was keen, too, to try out her ideas. Well, I loved them! Mommy had a flair for story, and an eye for detail. What a wonderful world that was: a truly magical space, a first encounter, for most children, of the possibilities of the holosuite: part play, part drama, all imagination. At first, this was something that only Mommy and I did: Phoebe was deemed still a little young even for the gentle perils of the Forest of Forever. Mommy and I wandered through the Forest with Flotter and Trevis, and built parts of the world together. It wasn't long before Phoebe wanted to take part though, and I have to confess I wasn't happy about that. But I swear, Phoebe, that flood was an *accident*.

Many people have told me how much they loved Flotter as a child (I think the only person I have encountered who didn't was a former CMO of the *Enterprise*, who called it 'that damn tree nonsense'), and many of them recall specific adventures that my mother wrote, such as the encounter with the fireflies, and the pebble house by the river. It was a delight to see the young captain's assistant on *Voyager*, the inimitable Naomi Wildman, take to the stories so much; yet another generation enchanted by them. So when people ask what it was like having a children's writer as a mother— well, here you are! But some part of my mother—a crucial part—remained forever elusive, out of reach. As a child, you try to bridge that gap; perhaps the definition of adulthood is accepting that some of the gap between you and your parents might well be forever unbridgeable.

Aged seven, and always eager to win her approval, I leapt at my mother's suggestion that I take ballet classes. Let me be the first to say that ballet did not play to my strengths. I was a strong and energetic child, and had a certain amount of athleticism, but not the kind that makes a prima ballerina. What I lacked in natural skill, however, I made up for in enthusiasm and hard work. My "Dying Swan" has become a family legend. I grasped at the time that it wasn't entirely for the right reasons, and I realized that if I were ever to become a star of the stage, it would be for comedy rather than tragedy. I kept up my dancing lessons for many years—less ballet and more ballroom and character dances—and I even picked up a bronze medal once for my Charleston, but let's just say that if ever I needed a new career, this wouldn't be the skillset I'd draw on. Phoebe refused point blank to learn ballet, and for this I am eternally grateful, since I'm pretty sure she would have been superb, outclassing me artistically once again.

Both Phoebe and I spent a lot of time out in the garden, not least because my mother—who felt such a strong connection to this place—encouraged us in this. I have to confess that I didn't appreciate this much as a kid: I'd rather have been building a model airplane, but Mom wanted it, so Mom got it. One summer, when I was nine and Phoebe six, Mom decided that we were old enough to look after our own little plots of land. She told us that if we cultivated them, we could choose where to visit next time Dad was back home. This was a big deal for us, to be given such a responsibility in Mom's beloved garden. I dutifully turned the earth and planted vegetables, many hours of solid back-breaking labor. Phoebe—clever girl—threw seeds in the air and told Mom she was growing a meadow. Given the hours she spent there, lying on her stomach staring at the flowers that bloomed, and the insects and wildlife that came to her wild garden, and the careful drawings that she made of them, Mom had to admit that she had kept her side of the bargain. We made biryani from the vegetables I'd grown and Grandma's special recipe, and we made postcards from the pictures that Phoebe had drawn. I earned my trip to the Smithsonian Air and Space Museum, and Phoebe her trip to the Van Gogh Museum. Boy, though, did I envy Phoebe her smarts!

Daddy, on his arrival home, was not the outraged ally that I had expected. When I told him the story, brimming over with indignation at

Phoebe's cheating, he laughed out loud. "Work smarter, Katy, not harder!" he said. Not bad advice, and advice I took to heart—I am aware that sometimes I can be a little rigid in my thinking (not allowing deviations from Starfleet uniform regulations when you're seventy years' flight away from the nearest Starfleet base, for example), and I do try my best not to get overly set in my ways. I must say, however—since it is possible that some Starfleet cadets may well be reading this memoir—that hard work never did me any harm and those rules kept us together during some tough times.

I still have one of the postcards that Phoebe made. It shows *Dodecatheon meadia*, a type of primrose, native to our part of America, known more commonly as the shooting star. It's beautiful work for a six-year-old: she has captured the nodding petals with a sharp eye and painted them a delicate shade of lavender. Granny-in-town showed her how to imbue the card with the scent of the flower it depicted; this being Granny-in-town's work, it sure lasted. Phoebe and I joked about it, but the day came when I was grateful for Granny-in-town's skill.

Because that card went everywhere with me. It went to Starfleet Academy, and then onto the *Al-Batani*, and the *Billings*. And naturally it came with me on *Voyager*, and therefore all the way to the Delta Quadrant, and back again. I had it tucked away in my desk for safekeeping, but I brought it out very often, when I was alone and feeling bereft, and I would just catch the very last of the scent (it had mostly gone by the third or fourth year of our journey). Often, I would flip it over to read the message my sister had written. Just before I left for the Academy, she dug the card out, and wrote: "To my big sister Katy, may she always shoot for the stars." Those words kept me going through many a long dark night among unfamiliar stars, looking for the one that would lead me home to my beloved family: to Phoebe, to the grandparents in the country, and the grandparents in town, and, most of all, to Mom.

✦

Given that this account is about my early years, it's perhaps natural that I have written a great deal about my mother, but now let me tell you about my father. He was, after all, the great hero of my early life. Edward Janeway was Starfleet to the core: a first-rate cadet who became an officer of distinction, and who earned rapid promotion until, shortly before I went to high school, he became a vice admiral. As a child, like many who enter Starfleet, he had looked to the stars: he was an enthusiastic amateur astronomer, and he loved to fly. He began as a test pilot in his early Starfleet career, although, after Phoebe's arrival, listened to my mother's concerns about his safety, and agreed to move toward command posts. This, naturally, took him away a great deal, often to Starfleet Command, which wasn't so bad, as we could follow him there during school holidays for a week or so. But more often than not he was away from Earth entirely. Children accept what they are given, and both Phoebe and I accepted that Daddy would be away for long periods of time. Still, we didn't have to like it. Since Daddy was incapable of doing anything wrong, we needed to have someone else to blame —and blame fell squarely on the shoulders of the Cardassians.

Cardassians were the great ogres of our childhood, as I suspect they were for many of our generation, and given that the ongoing border skirmishes of the '40s and '50s eventually led to full-scale conflict, one perhaps can be sympathetic to that opinion. Much has changed since the Dominion War, of course, but to my sister and me the Cardassians—these aggressive, seemingly monstrous aliens—were also the entire reason that Daddy was so often away from home. It took me a long time to recognize the root of my hostility toward the Cardassians, and even longer to shake this off and reach a better understanding of them.

A little context is surely helpful here. First contact between the Federation and the Cardassians was many years in the past, but from the start of the twenty-fourth century, the Cardassian Union had become markedly more aggressive in its imperial ambitions, most notably its expansion into Bajor during the 2310s. We know now that conditions on Cardassia Prime were becoming increasingly difficult: intensive industrial farming on an already dry world was leading rapidly to soil exhaustion. The Cardassians were on the hunt for the resources of other worlds; this expansion led, ultimately, to the formal annexation of Bajor in 2328 (eight years before my birth). For my father, moving up the ranks, Cardassian ambitions and incursions into Federation space were his chief source of concern, as they would continue to be the concern of his daughter years later, at the start of her career. Starfleet Command, at the time, was chiefly trying to prevent the outbreak of full-scale war, while at the same time protecting our border worlds, and supporting the Bajorans without violating our principles of nonintervention. At this age, before high school, these issues meant little to me, but they created the condition of my father's continuing absences, shaping my early years and providing the backdrop for my own eventual decision to enter Starfleet.

When Daddy was at home, Mommy was happy, and when Mommy was happy, we could all be happy. Like everything else that he did, Daddy approached fatherhood with dedication, bringing his fullest attention to the task. He might not have been there all the time, but when he was, he was there completely. I see now how he must have been awake until the early hours of the morning to get through reports and messages before turning his complete attention to his girls. And when he was with us—oh, the fun we had! He combined the authority of a father with the mischief of an uncle, the curiosity of a child, and the instinct for guidance of a born teacher. Do I sound as if I idolized him? Well, of course I did. He was my wonderful Daddy, Starfleet captain and all-around hero. More and more, I wanted to be the apple of his eye.

Whenever he was home, he would devise some new project or excursion for the whole family. He would take us all camping—making sure we knew how to live in the wild, be self-sufficient, show us how to forage and find fresh water. He encouraged Phoebe in her interest in the natural world and helped me to understand what to look for, too, and why I should care about the environment around me. He saw that my eyes turned upward, and on inkblot nights beneath the heavens, he taught me the names of constellations. My first voyages into the stars, with him. Phoebe learned them too: he realized that that mythological names captured her imagination. We learned the name of Mars in different languages, some still living, some long lost. Mars, Huoxing, Nergal, Wahram… This, I realized, was a kind of different world that I could get behind: not made-up fantasy worlds, but real planets that I might visit one day. And indeed Daddy took us to Mars, when Phoebe got to high school.

Here's a typical project of Daddy's, from when I was about eight years old. He decided that what our farm lacked was a telescope. Well, of course! He was Starfleet, after all, he said. He always had to be keeping an eye on things, even when he was on leave. So we made one. The whole Janeway-Williams clan got together and built the darned thing. And not some small instrument, but the kind of telescope that would have been the envy of an Edwardian gentleman. Granny-in-town was brought on board, of course, this being something of a specialty for her, and I think she was pivotal in replicating the parts we needed. Granddad-in-town came in handy too, bringing along a couple of graduate students to help renovate the old pig shed that was to be the telescope's new home. Grandpa made them work for their supper: sawing and hammering, fetching and carrying. I hope they got extra credit for this, those kids; what a flagrant abuse of power!

We girls oversaw the process from start to finish: the tooling of the parts, the grinding of the lenses, the construction of the outhouse, the assembly of the device itself. Good lord, it was magical—no, better than that. It was *science*. There was no mystique to this, no trick. This was something that could be built, crafted, made—and yet once it was assembled, it could show the beauty and majesty, the awe-inducing grandeur, of the stars. Out on the porch, Mom lay out long sheets of black paper, and together she and Phoebe and I created star charts. At last we were done, and we went out late one night—well past our bedtimes—and Daddy showed us the stars. I spent many nights in there, learning the names of the constellations, much later than perhaps my parents realized, sneaking past their room to my own bed, head full of the wonder of space.

On my ninth birthday, Dad took me over to the local flying club, and took me up in a little plane. The thrill of this. At last I was in flight! We were up for about twenty minutes, and Dad flew us over the land that I knew so well. I saw my home, all these places that I knew intimately and up close—our farm, Grandpa and Grandma's farm, our school, the road to the city—but from up above, like a map, but real. This little trip changed my perspective on the world entirely. Earth was never going to be enough for me now.

✦

THE HISTORY OF THE CAPTAIN WHO WENT FURTHER THAN ANY HAD BEFORE

As we grew older, my father continued this new tradition of taking me and Phoebe on separate excursions. Good tactic for anyone in a parenting or mentorship role, I think; give someone your undivided attention. Phoebe, in general, asked for cultural visits: ticking off one by one all the major galleries on Earth, Luna, or Mars. Me being me, I skipped culture and ran for the hills. I wanted to be outdoors. I wanted to hike and climb and ski and whitewater raft and in general feel myself moving or—best of all—in flight. I nearly got him to agree to bungee jumping (he didn't take much persuading, if I'm being honest) until Mom got wind of my plans and absolutely, categorically forbade it, on the grounds that I should at least reach double digits before risking my life (I guess she had a point).

I still haven't tried bungee jumping. I should go and book a trip to Queenstown now, leap from a bridge and feel the air rushing past, and shout, "This one's for you, Dad!" as I head toward the water. One benefit of getting older is that you no longer care how eccentric you look. I have embraced this in recent years, and I intend to avail myself of this freedom indefinitely.

Such freedoms were not available to me in my tenth year, however, and after my father and I were thwarted in our plans to throw ourselves off a bridge, he suggested we go to the Grand Canyon instead—the biggest ditch on Earth, as Dad called it. While my first impressions were of a big, dusty hole in the ground, this fortnight proved to be one of the defining periods of my life. We transported to Flagstaff, Arizona, and then took a small flyer out to the north rim. We hiked a few miles every day and camped at night. When we were done cooking and washing up, Dad and I would lie on our backs and look up at the stars. Sometimes he would tell me stories of worlds that he had seen; sometimes we just lay there peacefully, quietly enjoying each other's company. I thought of what it had been like, flying high above my home, and wondered what other worlds might look like from a great height.

"I'd like to go there one day," I said.

"Where, Kitten?" he said. I think I hated and loved that nickname at the same time.

"Up there."

He looked up at the heavens. "What? Luna? Mars?"

"Dad!"

"Oh," he said. "I see. Starfleet."

"What's it like?" I said. "Not the stories. I mean *really*."

I watched a smile pass over his face. He seemed... transported is the only word for it. "Kitten," he said. "It's like nothing else. It's *wonderful*."

I looked back up at the stars. I have never felt so happy in my life. I thought about leaving home, going to the Academy. I imagined myself on the bridge of a starship, people calling me "Captain," being the one in charge. But then a cold feeling washed over me. "Do you think Mom will mind?"

"Why would Mom mind?"

"It's a long way from home... You know how she is. There's no place like home..."

I watched him from the corner of my eye, and I could see that he understood. "You know," he said, "all that Mom and I want is for you to discover your own way. Find what it is you were born to do. It might take you to places that you or I or Mom can't even begin to imagine, but that's the deal you sign up for when you become parents. You want to keep your kids safe, close by—but in the end you have to set them sailing off, wherever they want to go. You just have to show them how to keep their ship afloat." He smiled at me. "Wherever you choose to go, Kathryn—we'll support you."

Do I need to say how much I loved him? Do I need to say how much I loved them all: my clever, curious, excellent family; my beautiful, sensitive mother; my gifted, creative sister; my brave and brilliant father? When I think back to this time, I picture them like this: Phoebe lying on her stomach among the flowers, her sharp eye catching everything about the world around her; Dad gazing wide-eyed at the stars, longing for adventure, longing to see whatever was out there; and Mom, lying on the bed beside me, reading from my favorite book, and whispering to me softly: *"There's no place like home... There's no place like home..."*

CHAPTER TWO
REACH FOR THE SKY—2348-2353

IN MY EARLIEST YEARS, I ATTENDED A SMALL COUNTRY SCHOOL very close to the house, with a dozen other children of varying ages from the local area. Phoebe and I were able to walk there, and, later, we cycled along the country lanes. At the end of the school day, Phoebe and I would take our time coming home, stopping to walk our bicycles along back lanes, while Phoebe collected samples, or I explored a new patch of land. The school itself was down a long lane: a white wooden building in its own grounds, with a flower garden and a vegetable plot and a huge wooden treehouse and climbing frame, and even its own stage. There were three little classrooms where we split off into age groups after assembly, before gathering at the end of the day to say goodbye. Although I loved the place and the teachers, who interwove play and learning so cleverly and intimately that it was never a struggle to get me to my studies, by the age of ten I was chafing against the boundaries of this small safe world, and I was more than ready to move out.

High school was the biggest change of my life so far. The morning cycle was still there, but instead of turning with Phoebe down the long lane to the schoolhouse, I carried on along the road to the local transporter. There, in a bustle of noise and laughter and the usual teenage squabbling, the local kids gathered to head into Bloomington. The school

I was attending was a small charter school, covering grades seven through twelve, but it was a huge step for me. I remember that first morning piercingly: standing by myself, clutching my bag and books, staring at the gang of kids gathered, and wondering what the school itself must be like, if this was just a few of its students... Then I heard a friendly voice call my name.

"Kathryn!"

It was Aisha, the other girl from my elementary school heading up that year, and with her was her older sister, Tamara, who had gone up to high school two years earlier. I ran over to them with relief. Tamara, who must have seen my wide-eyed look and guessed what it meant, put one arm around my shoulder, one arm around Aisha's, and said, "Come on, kiddos. I'll look after you."

Aisha looked disgruntled (Who wants to rely on their big sister's good graces? Ask Phoebe!), but it did us no harm having Tamara as an ally. She was an outgoing, generous-spirited girl who kept an eye on us while we found our feet in those first few bewildering weeks, while keeping a sensible distance that let us make our own way without relying on her. I have, throughout my life, been lucky in the mentors that I have found, and, looking back now, I can see how this was the first of many of these kindly and well-judged relationships. I got back in touch with Aisha after my return from the Delta Quadrant, when those old friendships took on great importance, after having thought that I would never see any of them again. She was living on Mars, a professor of the history of space colonization at the Sojourner Truth Institute, University of Tharsis. Tamara was still living in Bloomington and had just published her eighth novel— Regency romances, if you can believe it! Some genres never die. We went out for dinner when Aisha was back on Earth and what joy that was, seeing these successful women living life to the full. Champagne and conversation flowed. I am blessed in my friends.

But let's go back to young Kathryn Janeway, arriving at high school, smallest of the small all over again, but dead set on making her mark. High school, despite my trepidation, turned out to be a good time for me. I remember that Dad, just before I set off on my first day, said to me, "Try everything once, Kitten. New sports, new hobbies, new ideas, new everything. You never know until you've tried." It's been a good rule of thumb over the years, even if it meant I ate more of Neelix's cooking than I might have risked under other circumstances. But it was the philosophy that guided me through high school (and, eventually, through the Academy). I threw myself into life there—lessons, clubs, friendships—everything I could, and I found that the more you put into something, the more you get out.

Like most children, this is the age when serious passions emerge. It is also an age when one is first able to devote energy for extended periods of time to one's object of passion, pursuing it with single-minded intensity. My first year at high school is known by my long-suffering family as "The Year of Amelia." This was the year that I discovered the life and story of Amelia Earhart during a classroom project to research a pioneer that we admired. Naturally, I chose the history of flight (Grandpa used to say I should have been born with wings), and naturally I chose a woman.

Well, I went far beyond the call of duty. I started with the data banks, and the story captivated me. I learned that she was flying in a time when women were held to be inferior to men (That took some understanding. How had anyone ever believed such nonsense?), but that within her family no such backward views prevailed. Her mother was forward-thinking, and Amelia and her sister were not held back. I didn't miss Amelia's involvement in women's rights, but it was the stories of her flying exploits that truly captivated me. The courage to conduct those flights alone, and her good humor and practicality. And then, of course, the mystery of her disappearance, with the hint of espionage about it. I knew everything. I made my family quiz me on the details of her life, built models of the planes she flew, and would have built a full-size version if Mom hadn't forbidden use of the barn. I tracked her journey around the world, and even lobbied to visit Lae, in Papua New Guinea, where she and her navigator last set out from, only to disappear on that same flight, in order to pay my final respects. This went on well past the submission date for my class project. My Aunt Martha fueled the fire by telling me stories about our ancestor, Shannon O'Donnel, whom, she said, had been a pioneering astronaut. And I got from my father a promise that when I turned sixteen, he would teach me to fly.

This intensity of mine sometimes manifested itself as a competitive streak, best shown by my tennis career. I took up tennis in my first year at high school (dropping, with some relief from all quarters, not least my teacher, my rather lackluster efforts at ballet). Grandpa, seeing how this was developing into a serious activity, quietly cleared an area of land to turn into a practice court for me. The problem then was to find a partner: Phoebe, naturally, was not in the least interested in having tennis balls whacked at her by her older sister. It was, quite unexpectedly, Grandma who turned out to be game: it transpired that she had been a keen tennis player in her youth, and she was delighted to have the chance of a game or two. I was all set to have family tournaments... Sadly, nobody else would bite, and I had to make do with competition at school and, later, as I improved, state tournaments.

This competitive streak led to one of the more notorious episodes of my high-school career. I had been participating in a tournament at our high school, and the truth was that I had overextended myself, playing not only in the doubles' tournament, but in the singles too. The doubles matches had gone well, although my partner and I had been outclassed in the semifinal by a hugely accomplished pair who later went on to represent Earth at the Federation Schools Olympiad (one of them ultimately becoming a top-ranking adult player). We took them to a third set, and felt pretty proud in those circumstances, knowing we'd acquitted ourselves well against real stars. But losing this meant I had my heart on bringing home the trophy in the singles, not least because this was a rare occasion when Dad was there to see me play. Sadly, I hadn't paced myself. I had not dropped a set in the singles tournament, and I threw everything into my singles semifinal to keep this up (a more experienced player would have conserved energy and been prepared strategically to sacrifice that). And then of course the doubles semifinal wore me out.

My opponent in the final was a good player who deserved the place but was one that I had beaten on each occasion we had met in the past— sometimes with real ease. But that day, however hard I tried, I could not get my limbs to respond to instructions. This quickly rattled me. I didn't know what was going on; I thought I was ill! But the simple fact was of course that I was tired: too many games, even for a teenager in her prime. I needed to rest, and instead I was trying to scramble together muscle strength and brain power to win a tennis match. I lost the first set and, when the break came, sat with my towel over my head, cheeks burning and limbs aching, and didn't make eye contact with my coach or with my family (most of all my parents). The second set was even worse. Thinking of it now I shiver for my younger self! I was demolished. Game, set, and match to my opponent in two sets: 6–2; 6–1. The worst game of tennis I played in my life. In a daze, I managed to take my runner-up trophy, and watch my opponent lift the winner's trophy.

If this story ended here, it would already be a fairly dispiriting one for me, but the day wasn't over yet. I showered and changed, but not even that helped. Sulking—yes, I admit it—in the changing room, I was not ready to see my family or my coach, and when they all turned up, I reached my absolute limit. When Mom said, "Poor Katy! We know how hard you worked!" I picked up my racquet, threw it at the wall, and stormed out.

Not my finest hour: but even the most hard-working teenager is surely allowed the occasional temper tantrum. This being me, it had to be the finest temper tantrum that the state of Indiana had seen in some time. Dad, chasing after me, said, "Come on, Katy, let's go home—" And I turned to him—turned to my beloved Dad—and yelled, "I am not coming home! Leave me alone! I don't need *any* of you!"

Off I marched. Oh, how I cringe to think of it now! How brattish! How unsporting! What my plan was, I'm not entirely sure, but by this point I was committed to wherever it was taking me. Backing down was not an option. I got my feet somehow onto the road out of town, but there was a danger of running into people, and I was, to my credit, starting to feel both ashamed and embarrassed, so I quickly took a turn onto one of the country lanes. After about fifteen or twenty minutes, I was starting to think that perhaps this wasn't the best decision I'd ever made (I'd just played some pretty tough tennis matches, remember), but the stiff neck of the Janeways would not allow me to give up, turn back, and either find my family or take the transporter home. Instead, I walked on. Seven kilometers home. What could possibly go wrong?

Well, the weather on the plains can be a fickle thing, as Dorothy Gale can tell you, and summer, as well as being tennis season, can also be storm season. The heat gets up there, and something has to give. Four kilometers into my walk, stewing in the heat, and aware that the sky was getting heavier and darker, I felt the first spots of rain on my face. I gritted my teeth and walked on. The rain became heavier and heavier. The sky now was very dark. I heard a distant rumble of thunder. I knew what was coming. I was out on the plains, and a lightning storm was headed my way.

I had the good sense to look for cover, but places to hide were thin and far between this far out. I had to walk on at least another kilometer and a half before I saw a barn that might do, and by now I was seriously frightened. The storm was not lessening. The lightning was truly scary. And I was very, very tired. The barn seemed so far away…

Then I heard a dog bark, and the sound of a groundcar heading my way. It was Dad, coming to look for me, with Jess. He pulled the groundcar up alongside me.

"Excuse me, miss—are you by any chance heading my way?"

Jess barked. I burst into tears. "Oh, Dad!"

"Hop in, Katy. I don't fancy being out here much longer."

I climbed in, and hugged Jess to me. Dad pointed the groundcar toward home.

Let's hear it for my family, who at no point told me what an idiot I'd been, and how I'd brought this whole thing down on my own head. Once home, I was tucked up straight into bed. Mom came and sat down next to me, and before I knew what was happening, I was *howling* on her shoulder. Exhaustion, disappointment, shame, and the fright of my life… What else do you want to do but cry on your mother's arm? She stroked my hair and said all the right things, and eventually my tears reduced to sobs, which reduced to hiccups, which reduced to laughter.

"Oh, Mom," I said. "I'm such an idiot!"

"Kate," she said, "if this is the most idiotic thing you ever do, you'll be doing all right."

Well, I've done a great many idiotic things since then. But I will note that the following year I came back and took both trophies, the doubles with my fine partner, and the singles for my very own self.

There was one last serious conversation to be had about this whole business, and that was with Dad the following day. Because I'd been making it clear for some time now that my plan was to follow him into Starfleet, and he had a few things to say about my performance the previous day. I was out on the porch, curled up on the hammock with a book, Jess snuggled beside me. He came to find me, bent to kiss me on the forehead, and said:

"Well, Kathryn. That's one hell of a stubborn streak you've got there."

I blushed beet-red. "Oh, Dad! Please don't—"

"And that's not necessarily a bad thing... except when it is. Because—as I think you might have learned from this whole escapade—a streak like that can lead to a person making bad decisions. Striking out on their own rather than looking to their team for support—"

"Dad, it was a terrible mistake, I know it was. I knew within ten minutes that it was one of the dumbest things I'd ever done—"

"But you didn't stop."

"No," I said. "I didn't."

We sat in silence. Jess, sensing my mood, gave a low whine. I stroked behind her ears.

"I'm not here to scold you," Dad said, after a little while. "But you've told me that you're set on joining Starfleet, and I want you to be very sure you understand what that means."

I looked at him, carefully. He was staring out across the beautiful countryside. This morning, you'd never have guessed there had been such a storm. The sky was clear and that fine bright shade of blue that you only see in the Midwest. The fields were green and bountiful. But my father, I thought, wasn't seeing this. He was seeing something else. For the first time, I saw him not as Dad, but as a person in his own right, a man with worries and concerns that went well beyond our family, well beyond my teenage dramas.

"You mean the Cardassians, don't you?" I said.

Turning his head to look at me, he nodded. His face was the most serious I had ever seen. I wondered, briefly, however he had concealed this from us in the past.

"Are they really that bad, Dad?" I said, quietly, just in case Phoebe was passing by. I had the sense of being initiated into something, into a graver, more sober, adult world.

"They can be," he said. "Have you heard of Setlik III, Kathryn?"

I thought. "Yes…" I said, slowly. "A colony world on the border. Wasn't there was a battle there a year or two ago?"

"Not so much a battle. A massacre."

Any reply I might have had stuck in my throat.

"The Cardassians thought the colony was the cover for a military base—"

"Starfleet wouldn't do that! Starfleet would never use civilians as shields!"

"That's one big difference between Starfleet and the Cardassian *guls*," my father said.

"*Guls*?"

"The captains in the Cardassian military," he explained. "The admirals are called legates. What do you know about how the Cardassian Union works, Kathryn?"

The truth was, very little. My interests were flying, tennis, and getting ahead in math and science. I was starting to glimpse that perhaps this wasn't going to be enough, if I was serious about Starfleet. "Not much," I admitted.

"Okay, then listen up." And he gave me a quick briefing on how the Cardassian Union worked: a government run by the military—the Central Command—for the benefit of the military, with laws rubber-stamped by a powerless civilian Detapa Council, and everyone and everything kept in their place by the shadowy, terrifying secret police—the Obsidian Order. Almost the very opposite of our Federation, with Starfleet's primary purpose of peaceful exploration, a culture that celebrated diversity and opportunity, and a Federation Council that showcased these values.

"What really happened on Setlik III?" I said.

"Cardassian Central Command sent a squad to destroy the base."

"But there wasn't a base," I said.

"No," he said, "so they destroyed the colony instead. Like I said—a massacre."

This was hard to wrap my head around at first. "Did they know there wasn't really a base?"

"I don't know. Either way around, it doesn't reflect well on the Central Command. Either they didn't know, which means they were expecting us to behave as badly as they would, or they did, which means they deliberately and ruthlessly attacked defenseless people."

He must have seen the look on my face, because he reached over to take hold of my hand.

"I don't tell you these things to frighten you," he said, "but because I think you're mature enough to understand, and because you're soon going to be making decisions that will affect the rest of your future. What Starfleet and the Federation are facing in the Cardassian Union is a cruel society that seems bent on war. You can bet your boots that our diplomats are hard at work trying to stop that from happening—but the reality is that it takes two sides to make peace. And I'm not sure that both sides want it. We do. But the Cardassians?" He shook his head. "I just don't know."

"I see," I said slowly.

"Do you, Kathryn?"

"Well, it's like you said, isn't it? If I really mean it, if I really mean to get into Starfleet and become a captain—"

He grinned at me. "Oh! *That's* the plan!"

I gave him a steely look. "Did you expect anything less?"

He patted my hand. "Not from you, Kitten."

"It's not going to be fun and games, is it? It's not going to be all exploration and new worlds. There's a hostile enemy out there—and it might mean war."

He nodded. "So that's why I want you to be sure before you decide completely that Starfleet is for you. And that's why…"

I groaned. "Don't say it!"

"That's why temper tantrums like yesterday won't be good enough."

Yesterday's performance seemed years ago, as if it had happened to an entirely different person. A child. I was older already. "I know. I understand."

"Wanting to win and strategizing to win—those are admirable traits."

"I know. But pushing when I can't win, losing *badly*… and, well, the rest."

He laughed. "And the rest!"

"If that's not good enough, it won't happen again. I want to be the best I can be."

"I know."

"And I'll work to achieve that."

He leaned over and kissed my brow. "I bet you will."

It's strange to think back on that conversation now. Exploration turned out to be a larger part of my Starfleet career than either of us could ever have guessed. As for the Cardassians—well, there were a fair few of those in my life too across the coming years, that's true, and little did any of us know that the border conflicts would not be fully resolved until the Dominion War—but fate ensured I ended up missing that whole damn thing.

✦

It did not escape my attention that after this we had many more Starfleet visitors than we ever had in the past. Dad had often brought colleagues home, so Phoebe and I weren't unused to captains and commanders and top brass. (Grandpa sometimes joked when we were small that we were in danger of seeing admiral's pips as signifying "someone who will give me a piggyback.") But often these people had come to our farm for the same reasons as Dad: to enjoy a break from command and high-level decisions. From this time on, however, there was less of a gap between the outside world and our happy home. We were getting older, and we stayed up now around the dinner table, and listened to the adult conversation, and sometimes we even joined in. I don't underestimate how much of an impact this had on my Starfleet career: I learned at fourteen and fifteen nuances about the working of Starfleet that some ensigns who have served under me were still only starting to learn.

I made these resources work for their suppers. With the single-minded intensity of the ambitious teen, I grilled these people not only about Starfleet, and contemporary thinking and strategizing about the Cardassian threat, but about how entrance to the Academy worked, what the tests were like, what the examiners were looking for. I was already specializing in sciences, and, quietly, with the guidance of my teachers,

I began to take extra classes: contemporary galactic politics, advanced astrometrics, astral cartography, and so on. One weekend, when Dad was home, I presented him and Mom with the results from these and announced to them my intention to skip a year at school and go for entry into the Academy early.

Mom was not convinced. "This is so impressive, Katy, but what's the hurry?"

Dad didn't say anything. He just let me get on with making my case.

"I'm in a hurry because I know what I want, Mom. I can do the work—no, better than that, I can *excel* at the work. Why waste time?"

"I'm worried about burnout, that's all." Mom shot Dad a worried look. "This wasn't your idea, was it?"

"Nope," he said.

"Mom! This isn't anything to do with Dad! This is what I want!"

"What can we do, Gretchen?" Dad said. "I imagine if we said no, she'd just go off and do it anyway."

I nodded in furious agreement. I hadn't, in fact, thought of this, but now that the idea was in my head... Crafty Dad, huh?

"But you're right," he said, "about burnout. Kathryn, there's no point in being accepted at the Academy early if you're not able to function by the time you get there."

This, I had to admit, was true... I remembered that awful tennis match, and how badly I'd coped with being tired...

"How about we make a deal?" said Dad. "We let you start on this, but every eight weeks we take stock, and we discuss honestly whether it's working."

"That sounds good to me," I said quickly. I was sure I could convince them.

He held up a finger. "But Mom and I have the final veto."

I frowned.

"It's a good deal, Katy," he said. "And it's what's on the table."

I guessed—rightly—that this was part of the test. Did I know when to compromise? Did I recognize that I could get most of what I wanted if I was willing to give a little here and there? I stuck out my hand to Mom. "Deal?"

Mom took my hand and shook it. "Deal, Kathryn." She looked at Dad. "I hope you know what she's setting herself up for."

I remember now how sad he looked at that. "Gretchen," he said, "I know *exactly* what she's setting herself up for."

✦

So the deal was made. I would work like I'd never worked before, and I would aim to enter the Academy a year early. But at the first sight of overwork, or stress, or burnout, my parents would nix the whole idea. Good heavens, but I worked, and I wasn't going to skimp on extracurricular activities either. Every single minute of my day was scheduled: and I'll say now that this skill at timetabling that I developed at this point in my life stood me in good stead when the unhappy task fell to me of preparing ship duty rosters. (Not to mention that I was the kind of kid that loved a full-color three-dimensional organizational chart.) Everything was there: classes, private study time, and, of course, breaks. I meant to prove that I could do this, and that it wasn't going to burn me out.

The Cardassian War took ever-increasing prominence in our lives. I mention this because I think this happened in our family much sooner than with most others. My father's work obviously meant that we were more aware of what was happening along the border, and his increased absences meant that there was a genuine, direct, and piercing, impact upon our family. Around this time, my mother, aware of the suffering of the Bajoran people under the Occupation, began to get deeply involved in raising awareness of their plight within the Federation. By this point, the Occupation was long established, and the effects on the Bajoran people were becoming devastating. I remember sitting with her and Phoebe one evening (Dad was surely away), watching holo-images of a refugee center just within Federation space. Those images were dreadful; heartbreaking. I remember feeling Mom stiffen alongside me, as if she had come to some resolution. My mother was gentle, artistic, solitary—but she was not a shrinking violet, nor was she sentimental. She saw a terrible need, and a great injustice, and she did whatever was in her power to alleviate it.

Her public profile as a children's writer gave her a platform to speak, and she used it. For a woman who preferred to be at home, among familiar faces and places, this was a great sacrifice, although it was her consciousness of her great fortune in having all this that drove her. Many of the interviews she could give from her office at home, but speeches required her to be present in the hall to have the most impact, and she began to visit schools to explain the situation to children. How would they feel, to have to leave their homes? How would they feel, to lose track of family and friends? What could they do to help? There is a generation of Federation children who first came to awareness of the Bajoran Occupation through the picture books that my mother wrote at this time. Starfleet officers, specializing in humanitarian work, have told me that reading about the little girl, Amjo Jafia, leaving Ashalla to escape the Cardassians, and her journey to the refugee center on Metekis II, was the first crucial step toward them doing the kind of work that they did. I was so proud of her. I *am* so proud of her: my brilliant, gifted, fearless mother.

It might have been easy, in these circumstances, for Phoebe and me to form the idea that Cardassians were a species without any redeeming features. This is, of course, inaccurate—not to mention an insidious kind of racism—and Mom and Dad were scrupulously careful about how they spoke about Cardassians. I recall one or two conversations with university colleagues of Granny-in-town, specialists in Cardassian history and culture, who had many glowing things to say about Cardassian art and literature, and how it survived under difficult circumstances. I even read some, but I didn't understand much, and I didn't like it. Truth be told, it was many years before I saw Cardassians as individuals, as people who might be suffering on account of their own government as much as others. It was a lesson I learned in a hard place too… but I'll come back to that at the right time and place.

✦

My hard work paid off. By age fifteen, I had passed various exams and was well on track to graduate high school a year early; I also put my head down and started a two-year program of study to prepare for entrance to the Academy. The exams were notoriously difficult, and competitive, as were the psych tests. I meant to excel.

I don't want to leave you with the impression that all I did was study, although this naturally consumed a great deal of my energy at the time. My father, knowing that the years were coming to an end when we would be a family unit, made a point of taking a month of leave over the summer, and we had some fine holidays. Surely the most memorable was our tour of Europe: we visited Geneva, where they had met all those years ago, and my mother spoke to the Interplanetary Red Cross and Crescent about her work; we went up into the mountains, were Phoebe and I learned to ski; we saw Paris, and nearly lost Phoebe in the Louvre, and London, where the same nearly happened in the National Gallery; and then we went to Florence, where my passion for the life and works and sketches of Leonardo da Vinci was born. And the summer I turned sixteen, my father made good his promise and taught me to fly. I slipped the bonds of Earth and began my journey toward the stars.

But we all sensed that childhood was nearly over, and that my decision to enter the Academy a year early was hastening the day when family life as we had known it would come to an end. Perhaps some of this fed into the difficult relationship that Phoebe and I had at the time. She has said to me subsequently how she envied me being so close to getting away and leading my own life, while at the same time she resented that I was going, breaking up the happy home. Not to mention that my father's increased absences put a strain on how the family worked. We both knew that we had more in common with one parent than the other: Mom and Phoebe shared passions for arts and activism; Dad and I were peas in a pod. With my father away so often, I sometimes felt like the odd one out, and Phoebe and I were often typical teenage siblings, quarreling and bickering at the slightest provocation. It must have driven my poor mother mad!

Eventually, our sulks and quarrels ended in an honest-to-goodness blowup on my part. I would like to point out that at the time I was midway through studying for entrance to the Academy, and so perhaps I was more than usually stressed. I had taken a break from study and come down into the kitchen to get a drink and a snack. I brought some notes with me, thinking that I might sit in the kitchen for a while for a change of scene. I put the notes on the table, and then went outside for a breath of fresh air. When I came back inside, I found Phoebe, mopping the kitchen table, a guilty look on her face.

"Don't shout at me, Kate," she said.

I saw my pile of notes. They were covered in paint. My beautiful, hard-worked notes...

Well, I blew my top. "You stupid, careless, selfish little *brat*—!"

"It was an *accident*!" yelled Phoebe. "Why did you even *bring* them down here?"

Mother had to raise her voice to get us to stop—something never heard in our house. And I would not be placated. I packed my little bag and marched off to my grandparents' house across the fields, announcing my intention to remain in their attic until I'd passed these damn exams or the damn exams killed me. My grandparents—presumably forewarned by my mother that I was on my way over—didn't even blink.

"Bed's made, Katy," said Grandma.

"Get yourself set up," said Grandpa. "I'll bring you a coffee."

And that was that: I settled into that space, and put my head down to prepare for the entrance exams, and Grandpa, bringing up regular trays of snacks and drinks to get me through all-day and late-night study sessions, helped establish my addiction to coffee. Thanks, Grandpa. It might not sound like it, but I'm supremely grateful.

This whole period culminated in a three-day assessment at the Academy: written tests, psych evaluations, group exercises, interviews with panels, and interviews with individuals. Everything—all my hard work—narrowed down to three grueling days. Mom offered to take me there, but I knew she hated being away from home, and Granddad-in-town came up with me instead. A good choice on my part: I would have fretted about Mom, but Granddad-in-town was always cheerful, and he knew the area well, and always managed to find a good place to have dinner in the evenings. By the end of the third day, I was exhausted. I had no idea how well I'd done. Some of the other candidates were in their late teens, or even their early twenties, and had come to Academy entrance after study or travels or volunteer work. I had felt achingly young in comparison. After the last day, I went back to the apartment where Granddad-in-town and I were staying, fell on the bed, and *howled* into the pillow. Granddad, bless him, had predicted this letdown, and had spent the day making the best curry I have ever eaten in my life. The next day he took me on a tour of San Francisco, showing me his student haunts.

"You'll need to know these places," he said. He at least had no doubt where I'd be the following year. I was no longer able to tell.

✦

I came back to Indiana, spent a week mostly asleep in the attic at Grandpa and Grandma's house, and then I went back home. Results were due eight weeks later, and I had no idea what to do with all this free time. I sat and watched Phoebe paint and wondered when she had got so good, and whether anyone had noticed. I took old Jess for a few walks, but from the way she sighed when she saw me and hauled herself up, I got the impression that my lovely old dog was humoring me and would much rather have been snoozing in the sunshine. I wondered what I would do, if I wasn't successful this time around, and I decided that I would get some real experience, like those confident young people that I had met. I'd go out to one of those centers on the Cardassian border and work with Bajoran refugees.

Somehow, Dad managed to get home the night before my results were expected. I tried to sleep in—I had a whole morning to fill, of course, since San Francisco was on Pacific time; Bloomington on Eastern. But I was up by eight o'clock. Everyone tiptoed around me like they were walking on eggshells. I drank a strong cup of coffee and nibbled at some toast. I sat out in the hammock and cuddled Jess. I read one of Mom's books. But at last, at 11:00 a.m., the family communicator beeped with an incoming message. The others let me go over.

To my surprise, there were two messages: one for Ms Kathryn Margaret Janeway; one for Ms Phoebe Teresa Janeway. I forwarded Phoebe's to her personal comm, stared at the Starfleet seal on my message, opened it, and read.

"Well, Kathryn?" my father said, after a minute or two.

THE HISTORY OF THE CAPTAIN WHO WENT FURTHER THAN ANY HAD BEFORE

I cleared my throat. "Dad," I said. "I'm in."

He came to read the message. "You're not just in, Katy," he said. "You've been commended on your excellent results, and on your performance in one of the group exercises." I felt his arm squeeze my shoulder. "Oh Katy," he said, his voice breaking slightly. "I'm so proud of you."

I turned to look at Mom, and that's when Phoebe said, "Holy moly. They're going to show one of my pictures at the Met."

✦

Never has thunder been so effectively stolen. Honestly, I could have strangled her! Yes, my baby sister—at *fourteen*—had placed one of her damn pictures at a damn exhibition at the damn Met and had chosen the day of my early acceptance at Starfleet to receive the damn news! Well, I bit my tongue, and bottled it up, but it was always bound to explode. We spent a day with Mom and Grandma, preparing for a big party to celebrate our successes, both of us stewing. As the family started to arrive, we both dashed upstairs to get changed. I couldn't find a necklace I wanted. I went storming into Phoebe's room, where I found the thing on her dressing table.

I snatched it up. "Phoebe, you're *impossible*!"

"Kate, you haven't worn the thing in *years*."

"You're a *damned pain in the neck*!"

"You're not such great shakes yourself, you know—"

"Honestly—"

"If you could only imagine what it's like having you as a big sister, *Kitten*!"

"If you could only imagine what it's like having you as a little sister, *Feebs*!"

And then, my word, it all came pouring out! I told her just what I thought about this latest stunt of hers; always having to steal the limelight from *any* achievement that I managed, always trying to get one over me; Mom's favorite little girl; and she told me exactly what she thought of me, oh yes, the big sister, one step ahead, the apple of Dad's eye, always game for another road trip or a night in a stupid tent... You know, we were on the verge of thumping each other. We were all ready to restage the fight from the end of *The Quiet Man* when there was a tap on the door. We both shut up.

The door swung open. There, framed in the light of the hall lamp, stood Grandma, possibly our most formidable relative. She took a good long look at us, her eyes narrowed. She knew *exactly* what was going on in here.

"Young ladies," she said, "when you're ready, the rest of the family would like to toast your successes."

She left. We stared guiltily at each other.

One of us—can't remember which one—began to laugh. That set the other off. We collapsed on each other, in fits of helpless giggles. From the stairs, Grandma called, in her sternest voice, *"Ladies!"*

That nearly set us both off again. Stifling our laughter, clutching each other's hands, we ran downstairs, where we both graciously accepted the congratulations from our aunts and uncles and all the rest, and Dad made a very nice little speech. Later, each clutching a glass of champagne, my sister and I convened out on the porch. We both looked at each other and burst out laughing.

"Did you *see* Grandma's face?"

"I thought she was going to roast us *alive!*"

We laughed on for a while, and then I said, "You know I'll always have your back, don't you, Phoebe?"

"Back atcha, sis."

I lifted my glass to her. "Cheers, Feebs," I said.

She clinked her glass against mine. "Cheers, Kitten," she said.

Phoebe, I think we agreed years ago that I was a beast and you were a brat, and that neither of us would have it any other way. Little sister, you're brilliant. You take the arts, and I'll take the sciences, and together we'll conquer the world.

CHAPTER THREE
AT EASE, CADET—2353-2357

I WENT TO THE ACADEMY AT THE TENDER AGE OF SEVENTEEN, a full year younger than most of the rest of my freshman classmates. The first couple of weeks were a blur. Everything was a rush of new names: names of the other new cadets, names of professors, names of classes... Then there was all the new information: sorting out timetables, signing up for extra credit, taking up a whole new slew of extracurricular activities, and, of course, socializing. There were so many interesting new people and more species than I had ever seen before. Sometimes it seemed that every second I encountered something new. This was why I had joined Starfleet—and this was just the Academy! Imagine what the real thing would be like.

I ended up in the lower half of the room ballot, which meant that I was sharing a room. I didn't mind: it seemed like a good way to make a friend. As I had hoped would be the case, I hit it off immediately with my roommate, a quietly dry and extremely funny Betazoid named Nexa Ochiva who was specializing in xenolinguistics, and who persuaded me along to a huge number of extra lectures that I might not otherwise have even been aware of. Nexa came from a large family and knew how to share a room with someone else: we didn't encroach on each other's space, and, after a while, even our work patterns fell into sync. Thinking back now to those days, I smile to recall her quiet sigh, the signal for one of us to stand up and make a fresh pot of coffee. We would then join each other to sit in the beaten-up armchairs in the middle of the room, and grumble about the latest set of problems in our astrometrics classes. Nexa and I remained good friends. We kept in touch during our various postings right up until *Voyager* was lost. It was one of the saddest pieces of news that I received on my return from the Delta Quadrant to learn that she had been killed during the latter stages of the Dominion War. I made it back to the Alpha Quadrant in time for our twenty-first annual reunion. There were a number of sad losses to our class, but Nexa's was the one that hit me hardest.

Back to those early days. I worked out quickly that being the junior Janeway at Starfleet could cut both ways. On the one hand, I was keenly aware that what I did—for good or ill—inevitably reflected on my father. He had made a point of saying to me that I should not consider this—but I knew that others did. I worried too, given my comparative youth, that any failure or lapse would make people assume that I had won my place through his influence, rather than on my own merit. It's a difficult situation to be in, and one that gives me some sympathy to others who are children of flag officers, following in the wake of successful and respected older relatives. My relationship with my own father was supportive, but I was still acutely conscious of his success ahead of me, and I did feel that I needed to prove that I was there because I deserved to be.

On the other hand, my familiarity with Starfleet procedure and protocol undoubtedly gave me a head start over many others. Such things were second nature: Phoebe and I had been present at many formal events from as soon as we were capable of attending without kicking up a storm. There were other benefits too, some of which I hadn't predicted but proved among the most useful. For example, Mom, Phoebe, and I had often come up to San Francisco to visit Dad, and sometimes Granddad-in-town liked to tag along to visit his old haunts, see old friends, and show us the sights. Thanks to him, I knew shortcuts, places to hang out, and, in general, campus felt like a familiar place rather than bewildering. Almost an extension of home. That kind of local knowledge is helpful in your first weeks (as long as you don't show off): it gives you confidence, and it's a genuine help to your new friends to be able to tell them how to find the seminar room they're anxiously hunting.

THE HISTORY OF THE CAPTAIN WHO WENT FURTHER THAN ANY HAD BEFORE

With Nexa as company and my first friend, I settled quickly in my room. I sometimes missed my home and family so much that I felt almost queasy with longing for them, while simultaneously luxuriating in the fact that I was an adult at last. Sure, the schedules of classes and other activities meant that the days were still thoroughly timetabled (very much like school), but otherwise my life was mine to lead as I chose: where and what I ate; whether or not to work on free days; how to spend my evenings, and who with. Nexa had a knack for one-to-one conversations, making people feel special and welcome. I was great with groups, making people feel like they were part of a great gang. The combination worked. We soon acquired a large group of friends, and a favored spot to meet for study and socializing. This was a coffee house slightly off the beaten track that Grandad-in-town had spied while we were in San Francisco for the entrance exams. It was called the Night Owl. You reached it via a shortcut behind the parrises squares courts: there was a gap in the hedge there (I assume this had been left there deliberately, out of pity for sleep-deprived cadets anxious to get their caffeine fix; the academy groundskeeper, Boothby, as you shall learn shortly, would certainly not have missed a gap in the hedge), then snuck two blocks along a back street, and there it was. Somewhat shabby, large enough for many tables where groups of cadets hunkered down to study or else irritate the life out of friends who were trying to study and didn't want to listen to your idle chatter. The Night Owl served the third-best coffee I have ever tasted. (For the record, the best was the espressos I drank on that family holiday in Italy; the second best was the cup I had on arriving back in the Alpha Quadrant. By any general standards, that was not a great cup of coffee but... Oh, the smell! The taste! Nirvana!)

Coursework was a heavy burden, but I stuck at it, and I did well in classes. In part, this was because I was playing to my strengths, specializing in the sciences, and also taking classes and lectures to help me onto the command track once I had enough experience under my belt (I have always enjoyed giving orders). In part, to give myself credit, this is because I worked damn hard! I didn't want to let myself or my father down; I wanted to be the best I possibly could be... and I also didn't want to miss out on anything. Nexa, knowing that I was fascinated with first-contact scenarios, persuaded me to come along to an advanced communications course run by Professor Hendricks, where each week was devoted to learning from scratch a nonverbal form of communication. This was my first introduction to gestural languages, including ASL, and chromolinguistics. I know that one or two of my professors looked askance at my taking yet another extra class, not least as my conversational Klingon remained something of a joke, but the principles I learned in that class turned out to be of huge benefit in the Delta Quadrant: how to grasp rapidly the fundamentals of a language, and use that knowledge to make grounded extrapolations about the culture within which that language was used. The Delta Quadrant was a baptism of fire as far as first-contact scenarios went: we were flying by the seat of our pants in so many ways. That extra class came in handy many times.

As ever, I tended to take on a great deal, probably slightly too much, often burning the candle at both ends and pulling all-nighters to get through study commitments while maintaining my social life. I did get a note from Dad, toward the end of my first year, that said: "Remember to rest. A Starfleet officer cannot survive on caffeine alone." And I had not forgotten our conversation after the dreadful tennis match, and I decided I should try to find a way to relax. The Academy grounds proved a godsend here, as I think they have for many overworked cadets, not least because being in the garden reminded me of home, and my mother. One summer afternoon, tired after a long morning's seminar on fractal calculus, and fretting about the forthcoming exam (Patterson's exams were the stuff of nightmares), I found myself sitting in the garden, simply trying to *be*…

My eyes closed, but still I couldn't rest. All I could see were those damn equations, flashing in front of me: fractals, never-ending, always getting deeper and deeper with no resolution… I was *dreading* the test… And then I heard a voice.

"Patterson," the voice said.

I opened my eyes and found myself looking at a small, white-haired man whose gnarled face and hands suggested to me that he spent a lot of time outside. A veritable garden gnome.

"I beg your pardon?" I said.

"You," said the gnome, "have the look of someone who is currently studying under Patterson."

I stared at him. "How did you guess that?"

He smiled. "I've seen a lot of cadets come and go over the years," he said. "I get used to their worries. And I know that the biggest worry for first years on the command track is passing Patterson's fractal calculus class, and I also know that the exam is coming up soon. Am I correct, Cadet Janeway?"

Maybe it was because I was still half-asleep, but I was starting to get very bewildered by this whole encounter. It was as if I'd woken up in a strange enchanted land—Narnia, perhaps, or my beloved Oz—and had found myself in conversation with a magician, who could read my mind and saw all my worries.

"Who *are* you?" I said.

"My name," he said, "is Boothby."

That broke the spell—a little. My father had mentioned Boothby, so had Granddad-in-town. Yes, I knew who this was—not a sorcerer or enchanter, but the gardener! I should clarify this—Boothby was not simply a gardener, but the head groundskeeper at the Academy and, given the size of the campus, this was a significant responsibility. How long had he been there? I don't think anyone knows for sure.

"You've heard of me, I think," he said. "And I hear your mother likes roses."

I was amazed. Dad had said that Boothby knew everything about everyone, but this was pretty specialist knowledge. "How on earth did you know that?"

"I keep my ears open," he said. He peered at me. I know that look well: it's the one given by officers when they're assessing whether you're fit for a task. It's a look I've given myself over the years. "Yes," he said. "I think you'll come in handy."

"Come in handy—?"

He started to walk away. "In the rose garden, of course," he said. "Come along, Cadet!"

Well, I did what I was told. Boothby had this way about him… Next thing I knew, I was hard at work in the rose garden. How he persuaded me of this, I'll never know: you'll recall that I wasn't much one for messing around in the mud. Still, you didn't grow up with my mother—or, indeed, on a farm—without knowing how to find your way about a garden, so

41

I daresay I did come in handy. After an hour or so, Boothby stood up, grunted in satisfaction, and said, "Good work, Cadet. You'll do very well. I'll expect you back here same time tomorrow."

And then he headed off across the garden, before I could open my mouth to protest. I looked after him in horror. I didn't have time to come and play in the garden! I had work to do; I had a goddamn fractal calculus exam with goddamn Patterson to goddamn pass! Still, the next afternoon, I didn't think of disobeying. I left my friends in the Night Owl, saying something vague about an errand, and I went and spent a quiet hour in the garden, under Boothby's watchful eye. And oh, what a blessing it turned out to be! A rest for my poor overworked brain; a real balm for the soul! Just that hour, once a day, doing nothing but using my hands and letting myself get away from my studies—it made all the difference. I found my focus got better; my concentration improved. And when the roses began to bloom, there were fresh flowers in my room every morning, courtesy of Boothby himself, as a thank you, so the man said, for my hard work. Nexa appreciated them too: she loved roses. When I finally did take the fractal calculus exam, not one of Patterson's fiendish tricks could discompose me, and I did one of the best papers he'd seen. So thank you, Boothby, for helping me, as I know you have helped thousands of stressed cadets before me, and thousands after me, to get things back into proportion, and for all the wondrous roses.

At the end of the year, my marks in general were excellent: I was hardly outside of the top one percent, even in my weaker subjects. Altogether, when I packed up my room for the summer, and headed back to Indiana for a couple weeks, I was proud of what I had achieved. I could justly feel that I was at the Academy on my own merits, and not because of favors shown to me on my father's account. But boy—was I ready for a break!

Going home that summer, even for so short a period, was an odd experience. I was glad to be back with my family, back in familiar places, but everything seemed smaller than I remembered. Messages I received from Academy friends told me that this was a common feeling, as if we had in that year outgrown our childhood homes. Still, I was glad of the rest. I was glad to enjoy Grandma's cooking once again, and Grandpa's strong black coffee. Most of all, I'm glad to say, I loved being back with

Phoebe. If our quarrel had cleared the air between us, my absence for all those months had sealed the deal: we didn't want to waste the time we had together on our old competition for attention; we wanted to be friends and counselors. Her art studies were progressing incredibly well; more and more she was exploring sculpture as her primary form, although I have to say that her watercolors and drawings of our locality—its wildlife, its landscape, not to mention its characters—were a huge joy for me. She was working on building a portfolio for entry to the Vulcan Academy of Art, with an eye on postgraduate work at an arts school on Trill. It was a pleasure to discuss her work with her, to see her increasing understanding of material form. What we both found interesting was how much my engineering interests overlapped with her hands-on approach to her artistic practice. It's easy to say that we were opposites, but the real pleasure for me—and, so Phoebe tells me, for her—was finding how much we had in common.

That short break was tinged with sadness, however, as we said goodbye to my lovely Jess. She was old now—fifteen—and she slept most of the time. When I walked through the door, she lifted her head and thumped her tail at me, saying "hello," and I had one more week with my old companion, sitting with her in the sunshine as I read and rested, and she lay beside me. I think she was waiting for me to come home again, because one morning, a week after I arrived, she didn't wake up. I cried a great deal, and together Mom and Phoebe and I buried her in the garden, near the roses. My lovely Jess. I knew that given that I was heading into Starfleet, I would be taking posts onboard ship that were going to keep me away for long periods of time. I was not likely to get another dog for many, many years, and I knew the next one would have to be special. I was right there. Saying farewell to Jess felt at the time like the end of childhood for me.

Then it was time to say goodbye to the old homestead once again. I had an internship that summer in the office of Councilor T'Lan (don't get too excited: mostly it was answering correspondence, although I did get some insight into the ongoing Bajoran refugee crisis); also a group of us were going hiking through the Andes. (My parents said, "Aren't you supposed to be having a rest?") And then, before I knew it, I was back at the Academy for my second year. More of the same—only more of it. Much more. More work, more exams, more coffee, and more fun, as much as I could possibly fit in between everything else. Time in the garden, decompressing, simply being among the roses. More and more complex equations, more and more complex command scenarios. They say about the Academy that the individual moments—as you're trying to get a piece of written work done, or you're fretting about a forthcoming test—pass extremely slowly, but that the months fly by. It's true. Before I knew it, the second year and the second summer were over, and I was heading back for the second half of my Academy career. It struck all of us, heading back for our third year, that we were on the downward slope.

In the third year at the Academy, the nature of your studies alters somewhat. The number of large lecture classes gets fewer and fewer, and the barrage of in-class tests and end-of-semester exams reduces. Instead, you find yourself in smaller seminar groups and, if you're on the command track, as I was, you do more and more practice scenarios. I did not fail to notice how many of these involved encounters with Cardassian ships. By this point, the border conflicts that we now call the Federation–Cardassian War were well established and showed no sign of slowing down. Our tutors were preparing us for this conflict. There were some practical additions, for example, field medicine and surgery courses. I have certainly used these in my later career (not to mention the memory-training techniques we were taught in H'ohk's physiology classes). This background rumble of potential conflict was something we were all keenly aware of, and I recall numerous late-night conversations among friends, as we pondered what it might be like on the battlefield.

Life was full, and busy, and we were far enough away from graduating to be able to put aside our worries for a little while. By this point, I felt that I had the right balance, combining studies and my social life, and keeping at or near the top of my classes, getting downtime in the gardens. As long as nothing happened to disrupt my equilibrium...

Naturally, this was the moment I chose to fall in love.

✦

What can I say? I was still only nineteen years old; gregarious, yes, but I was still very inexperienced when it came to romance. I concealed my tender heart beneath an outgoing demeanor and being part of the gang. I think it was inevitable that when I fell in love, I fell hard.

Let's leave names behind; that wouldn't be appropriate. Suffice to say that the object of my admiration was what Granny-in-town would call "a fine figure of a man"; a rugged sort who exuded physical confidence. I thought he was gorgeous. He was a friend of a friend of a friend who came along to the Night Owl one afternoon and found himself sitting next to me. We talked about the Grand Canyon and worked through the equations for our advanced spatial engineering class (he was taking the same course, but in a different seminar group). We agreed to meet for dinner later that week. After that, we were inseparable.

I grasped fairly quickly that Nexa was ambivalent toward him, and I have to say that I was not pleased. My first serious beau; surely my best friend should be delighted for me? About three weeks into the relationship, I remember a very unhappy conversation—no, let's call it what it was, an outright argument—between me and Nexa. She said she didn't trust him; I told her she was jealous that he was taking up all my time. It's hard to come back from that one, and things became briefly frosty between us. After a few days, we tentatively made up (you can't live in a shared room with a cold war, and, besides, she was my *friend*), but I could see that as long as I was with my beau, she was not going to be happy.

I had no intention of giving up this one. He made me feel desirable, and that was not something that Kate Janeway had felt much in her life so far. I was outgoing, a good sport, active, and more than a little tomboyish. Boys were friends, not lovers. I was beside myself with joy that I had attracted someone like this—and that made Nexa's reaction even more upsetting. But I was eager for him to meet my family, and I invited him home for a few days during the winter break. That was another huge disappointment.

The whole family was there: my father had leave, and Phoebe had managed to get back from Trill, where she was on a graduate arts fellowship that year. I was so excited to introduce my boyfriend to them. Oh dear. It was plain within a couple of hours that they did not like him, my father most of all. Oh, he made polite conversation—friendly conversation too; this was a young cadet, after all—but I could tell. After his visit was over, and he went back to his own family, I confronted my father.

"Not good enough for your darling daughter, hey, Dad?"

He didn't rise to my bait. "Katy, this is your life, and I'm not going to interfere."

I was furious. "Dad! That's not an answer!"

"I'm not going to dictate who you should and shouldn't see," he said. "But no. I don't like him."

"Why not?"

"He's a taker, Kathryn. He won't give you what you need. He won't give anyone what they need."

Just on departure he had given me a beautiful pendant. I showed this to my father. "How can you say that?"

"Oh, sure, he'll be good with gifts. He certainly puts on a good show."

"Dad, that's not fair—"

"But he's a taker. You've spent half your holiday helping him with his coursework—"

"I don't mind!"

"Well, you should. He's the kind of ensign that I would get off my ship as quickly as possible. He's the kind of ensign that I wouldn't put anywhere except behind a desk. I wouldn't put my life in his hands."

I stalked out of the room. I took my woes to Phoebe, but I could see that even my beloved sister was finding it hard to be supportive. "You know Dad," she said, rather lamely.

I was shocked. "You don't like him either, do you?"

She struggled to find the right words. "It's not me that has to like him, Kate."

What was the right response to this familial ambivalence? Naturally I dug in my heels. I went back to the Academy after the break determined to stick with this relationship through thick and thin, and I would make it a huge success. That would show them! We spent most of that year together, living in each other's pockets, and if I found that I was doing more and more of his advanced engineering papers and seeing much less of my friends, I didn't admit this to myself.

Six months to the day after our first meeting, we went out for dinner, traveling all the way to Paris. It was very romantic. A violinist came past, and my beau brought out a ring. A ruby.

Like a fool, I said, "Hey, anyone would think you were about to ask me to marry you!" I burst out laughing. I stopped when I realized he wasn't joining in.

What followed was even more painful. Because he was, of course, asking me to marry him, and I'd taken the wind out of his sails. He didn't like that, I could see. We were off to a bad start, although after a moment or two he began to get back into his groove. He had prepared a speech, you see, in which he laid out his plans for us. He wanted to marry me as soon as we graduated, and he wanted us to set up home right away. He'd had a bright idea. The idea was that I put my career on hold for a while so we could "do the family thing," and once he had his command, I could get back to my career.

I listened to him talk and I drank my glass of wine. I felt like someone waking up from a dream; not a nightmare, that wouldn't be fair, because he really was very handsome, and we really did have a good time, most of the time.

"What do you say, Kit?" He always called me that. I don't know where he'd got it from. Suddenly it struck me as deeply annoying.

I put down my wine glass. "Here's an idea," I said. "You put *your* career on hold, and when I have my command, you can get back to your career."

Oh, his face. He was outraged. He opened his mouth to reply, but before he could, I had stood up. I leaned over the table to kiss his cheek, for old times' sake, and I said, "Thank you. It's been fun." And I left and walked back through the streets of Paris to the nearest transporter, and I was back in my room at the Academy within the hour and talking to Phoebe over the comm.

"You'll never guess what just happened to me," I said.

"I hope you shoved that ruby where the sun doesn't shine," she said, when I told her. A huge cheer for my sister, my best ally. Talking it through with her that night, I realized I wasn't as upset about the whole thing as I thought I might be. I guess I'd known on some level that my friends and my family were right, and that this wasn't going anywhere. I won't deny it took a while to bounce back from the whole business: my confidence took a blow, and I found it hard to trust for a while afterward. But at least I had the good sense to get away when I did, and I'd only wasted six months. I could have wasted years. I could have wasted my career. The next morning, I caught up with Nexa, told her what had happened, and said sorry.

"Oh, Kate! There's nothing to apologize for! He was *very* handsome!"

Yes, he was; but he really wasn't right for me.

There's a side note to this which I should mention; after my conversation with my sister, and with her encouragement, I finally got around to doing what all my female friends and relatives did at some point: I had some eggs frozen. Well, a girl has got to think ahead, hasn't she?

✦

My third-year grades took only a small hit from this distraction, I am very glad to say, and I was not outside of the tenth percentile, but that wasn't good enough for me. I came back to my final year intent on getting as close to the top as possible. Our fourth and final year continued the smaller group seminars, role shadowing, and holodeck scenarios of the year before, as well as a significant amount of outdoor training. We were also assigned a mentor, and I was beyond lucky to find myself come under the wise protection of Admiral Parvati Pandey. In my final term, Pandey invited me along to her Ethics of Command sessions. If she gave you this invitation you took it: it was a sign that you were being taken very seriously for command. That final term was crammed, but whatever else you had on, you found the time to go along to these discussions.

We were a small group, half a dozen of us, and the meetings took place at Pandey's home, in a large office whose huge windows looked over her beautiful garden. A lot of that final year at the Academy passed so quickly—cadets are conscious that the clock is now ticking—but those sessions remain strong in my memory. We grappled with questions of honor, integrity, loyalty, candor; how to know when an order was a bad order; what to do about that. We talked about respecting the ethics of other civilizations while upholding our own values of diversity and openness. We discussed the ethics of war; how to comport yourself in a combat zone; how to command in a combat zone. We talked about the trolley problem, and the principle of utility, and means and ends. I am grateful to Parvati

Pandey for this space she gave us as we shifted from the protected world of the Academy to the real world of ship life. After I had my turn on the *Kobayashi Maru*, Pandey came to me and praised me for my grace under fire. "Don't forget this, Kathryn," she said. "This is a lesson about courage in the face of overwhelming odds."

She was a fine teacher. I'd like to think I learned well from her. I'd like to think I made her proud.

✦

One final memory of my time at the Academy, since I believe this episode has earned its spot in the legends of the place, and that is no mean feat when you consider the people who have passed through there as cadets. There was an informal custom—certainly not a custom sanctioned by the authorities—for the outgoing students to play some kind of grand prank to celebrate their imminent release. After many years of some very inventive young people coming up with ever more baroque ideas, it was our turn to think up something impressive. Flash mobs weren't our style; sowing wildflower seeds around companels seemed more in the line of a protest than a prank; dyeing the lake pink was an old one and far too easy. The nexus of students who formed to take up this task wanted a challenge. We wanted to do something that would never be forgotten. We succeeded.

I had, for various reasons, been reading about prisoners of war, and the kinds of schemes they came up with not only in their attempts to escape their confinement, but to fill the hours and prevent despair and boredom setting in. Digging a tunnel didn't seem much in the way of fun, so when our "escape committee" was formed to pull our stunt, I suggested something else. I'd been reading a very detailed account of some prisoners of war who had been held in central Europe, during the last big war of the pre-Atomic Age (the war that ushered in the Atomic Age, in fact). They were prisoners who had a reputation for repeated escape attempts: their captors, in exasperation, decided to lock them all up together—in a huge castle perched up on a cliff, no less! There was some wisdom to this idea—you had them all in one place, for example, where you could keep an eye on them. At the same time, you found that you had put all the most reckless, crackpot, and stubborn eccentrics in one place. They were not going to give up until they had made a home run. Reminds me of *Voyager*, now that I think about it.

These guys just kept the ideas coming—with limited success, it has to be said, but then the point was to keep everyone busy: themselves, to stave off boredom, and their guards, never entirely able to relax. There were various attempts to get out using disguises: in uniforms stolen from their captors, or else, inevitably, in drag. A smaller man hid himself in a tea chest, and, of course, there were several tunnels. The cliff beneath that castle must have been Swiss cheese by the end of that war. But I had another of their plans in mind. Two of the men held there were pilots, and they decided to build a glider. Once I read about this... Well, what else was my graduating class supposed to do? I put it to the committee, and they looked at me as if I had lost my mind, and then somebody started to laugh, and the next person began to laugh, and I saw in their eyes what I had been thinking: *We've got it!*

We used the plans that those two men had devised, and we decided to use the same tools that they had used. As a matter of principle—and bearing in mind that they somehow had to lay their hands on all this material—we decided not to replicate anything. The rummage shops of downtown San Francisco did good business that year, but do you have any idea how hard it is to find a gramophone spring? As for the prison sheets used to skin the thing, and the ration millet that those men used to seal up the pores of the sheets... Who knew porridge had so many uses?

There were times I thought we weren't going to be able to do it. As for finding a place where we could hide this thing while we built it... Let's just say in return for some extra labor, Boothby turned a blind eye on what was happening in one of the larger garden sheds. Eventually, we had it: a two-hundred-and-forty-pound, two-seater, high-wing glider. The day before our exam results were due to be announced, and in the dead of night, we hauled the beast across to the library, and up onto the roof. The next morning, as our year group gathered in the main campus square, finding solidarity in each other before learning their individual fates, my copilot and I launched our beautiful machine over their heads, landing it with perfect precision just beside the lake to rapturous applause.

It's not a final-year prank if you don't get hauled up before the president of the Academy, and indeed we were, and I took responsibility as the main architect and chief ringleader of the scheme. I looked the president in the eye and said, "And I'm proud of it, ma'am. We've shown initiative, technical skill, a substantial amount of guile, and we've fitted it all in around exam season. I think our final grades will speak for themselves."

I could see that she was having a hard time not laughing, and I knew we'd get away with it (more or less), not least because we were leaving campus the following week, and there weren't that many sanctions they could impose. Besides, we'd excelled ourselves. I'm about as proud of that glider as I am of just about anything else I did at the Academy, and given how often my father told the story afterward, I'm pretty certain he was proud of me too. All this time later, looking back on the whole escapade, I'll add that our make-do-and-mend approach to sourcing the materials we needed came in damn handy on *Voyager*.

✦

I graduated in the top four of my year (that means fourth, of course), and I was grateful for and pleased with this result. The people ahead of me were stellar students: you could see that they were going on to early commands. All three of them were decorated for valor during the Dominion War, although only two of them survived that war. Those two have gone on to great things at Starfleet Command, and one of them is surely in line to become commander-in-chief. Alongside these stars, I was content that I had shone to the very best of my ability. I had done my father and my grandfather proud; most of all, I had done myself proud. There could be no question now that I had not earned my place at the Academy. Now I had to prove myself worthy of Starfleet—and worthy of command.

The powers that be stage these last couple of weeks very well. After the officially unsanctioned prank came the exam results, and then there were a couple of days to enjoy the feeling of elation (or come to terms with the disappointment) before the graduation ceremony itself. We partied hard that year, I have to say; that's the kind of class we were. Everything got our full attention and our best effort. Besides, we knew that we weren't in for an easy ride. The Cardassian border conflicts dragged on, and our graduating class knew that it was going to see active service straight out of the door in a way that previous years had not. Exploration would have to wait.

Graduation came and went, with my whole family present (Phoebe decided not to steal my thunder this time around), and then came the serious business as we learned our first postings. This is a major rite of passage for every newly graduated cadet. We all gather in our brand-new dress uniforms, and our new assignments are formally announced. This is tough if you didn't get the grades; it's even tougher if you did well but you've not got the posting your heart was set on. I saw a few brave faces being put on that day, when assignments turned out to be station personnel or desk jobs. But I wasn't disappointed. I had been assigned a junior science officer's post on the *U.S.S. Al-Batani*, serving under one of the most respected men in Starfleet: Captain Owen Paris. He was going to be a significant presence in my life from here on, in ways I hadn't entirely anticipated.

But I'm getting ahead of myself! What about my other friends, my gang? We all ended up where we wanted to be. My copilot on the glider got a test-pilot placing out at Utopia Planitia: he was beside himself with delight. And my dear friend Nexa took up the analyst's posting she wanted with Starfleet Intelligence. We were a happy band of brothers and sisters, and the party lasted the rest of the week. After that, we all departed, with promises to stay in touch and meet again. And those of us who could—we've kept that promise, and we've never forgotten the ones who couldn't keep it.

Some of you might be wondering how that ex-boyfriend did. I didn't ask and I'm glad to say that nobody took the time or trouble to tell. I guess he graduated; I didn't hear that anyone had failed or been asked to repeat the year. I must have heard them read out his first posting, but I've forgotten what it was. Strange though; his name cropped up last year, fourth in the list of authors on a report I was reading. So I do know one thing: he never did make captain.

CHAPTER FOUR
CHILDHOOD'S END—2357–2358

"ENSIGN KATHRYN JANEWAY, REPORTING FOR DUTY, MA'AM!"

It was my first day of my first posting, and I was shaking in my shiny boots, and tugging away at the cuffs of my stiff uniform. My new direct superior, Lieutenant Commander Flora Kristopher, the *Al-Batani*'s chief science officer, was waiting in the transporter room to welcome me on board, leaning against the console. She looked at me steadily, and—bless her—did not smile at my overseriousness and formality, but simply said, "Welcome aboard, Ensign. Please don't call me 'ma'am.' Makes me sound fifty years older."

I blushed bright red. "Sorry… Commander!" (He won't thank me for this, but I can't help but recall a certain Ensign Harry Kim, so keen to make a good impression on his new captain in our first meeting that I thought he was going to strain something. Don't worry, Harry. We've all been there.)

Kristopher gave me a lopsided smile, pushed herself up from the console and nodded to me that I should follow her. I snapped to it. I was desperate to make a good impression. I trotted at her heels as she gave me a rapid tour of the ship, introducing me to various other officers, senior and junior. They were all friendly; one or two invited me to the mess hall for a drink once I was off shift. I gratefully accepted, muttering their names, ranks, and specialisms under my breath as we went on so that I wouldn't forget them. After about an hour of this, Kristopher said, "Relax, Janeway. This is home now. Keep up this level of intensity much longer and I'm going to have to go for a lie-down."

I blushed again. "Sorry, Commander. I'll try and take it a little easier."

"Good. Don't worry, Janeway. You're going to do fine."

Kristopher was a supremely talented officer, who gave the appearance of being very laid back, but who never missed a thing. She had an enviable gift for being able to come up to speed rapidly in hugely technical subjects, ideal for a chief science officer, who frequently finds herself having to offer expert advice in fields well beyond her specialisms. Kristopher's own area of study was sustainable xenoagronomy. She had grown up on Mars, on one of the terraformed colonies, and so had early experience of experimenting with crops growing under less than propitious circumstances. By this stage in her career, numerous colony worlds had benefited from various technical advances she had made in soil science. My mother, learning that I would be serving under her, was incredibly excited. I had been instructed to get advice on a new rose hybrid she was trying to grow. Kristopher, in her turn, was delighted to discover that my mother was *that* Gretchen Williams: she had, so she told me, been inspired toward her field by an early encounter with her stories for *The Adventures of Flotter*. (I have to say that I thought it would be my father's name that went before me on my first Starfleet posting, not my mother's.)

Flora Kristopher was a fine mentor to have at this stage of my career. She was patient with mistakes born from inexperience, tough on mistakes born from sloppiness, and more than usually able to spot the difference. The only way to get on her bad side was to point out the nominative determinism of her first name. My word, she hated that. She must have heard it almost every day of her adult life. I am eternally grateful that another new ensign made this mistake before I did. I've never seen a young man so thoroughly cut down to size. Under Kristopher's guidance, I flourished, and I started to gain confidence—which is, after all, exactly what a newly minted officer needs at this stage of her career. I thought about her constantly when I had junior staff of my own, when I tried to instill this same kind of confidence: trusting their judgement but always having a backup plan in case their inexperience let them down.

I was lucky too that I got on well with my commanding officer. Captain Owen Paris had a reputation for rigidity within the service, but he and I hit it off immediately. We both came from families that had been in Starfleet for generations, and this shared culture eased our relationship from the outset. I too can be rigid in my own way, and the discipline of his ship suited my nature. I know that my father respected him greatly and I took my cue from this. He lacked much of a sense of humor, but he got things done. It was a pleasure to serve under him, and I have been personally grateful to him for his many kindnesses over the years, not least in the roadblock I hit during my second year, but also in his championing of the Pathfinder Project that allowed *Voyager* to establish contact with Starfleet.

My first six months on the *Al-Batani* were, broadly speaking, a success. Half a dozen new staff had come on board at the same time, and we formed a close-knit group. One of our number—a Vulcan named T'Nat— had been captain of the Velocity team at the Academy and persuaded us to form a junior league with some of the junior lieutenants. I had not played the game at the Academy, but I was always ready for a new physical challenge, so I agreed to try it out. I took to it immediately; it filled a tennis-shaped gap in my life. The game became popular across the whole ship, leading some of the more senior officers to form their own league. Flora Kristopher was instrumental in this, and the first officer, Commander Shulie Weiss, joined too. The captain kept his lofty distance. The inevitable challenge was offered, which we junior officers accepted with alacrity: surely we would have no trouble defeating what we gleefully referred to as our "elders." Well, this is where I learned that Velocity is as much about wits and guile as it is about speed and agility. I won't say that we were trounced, but… all right, we were trounced. I have never seen a more triumphant set of senior officers. Paris came and awarded a trophy he'd organized for the occasion, and we junior officers swore to get our revenge. We never did while I was on the team.

Between this and our survey mission, which expanded my scientific knowledge and my practical skill immensely, I had a good and challenging life. I count myself lucky to have entered Starfleet during this period. The border skirmishes with the Cardassians rumbled on, but there was still time and space for us to enjoy something of the old Starfleet, when ships were dedicated chiefly to exploration, and we were able to pursue our primary purpose as individuals, devoting our energies as much to our own personal advancement as to protecting the Federation. I knew that at the back of our minds we all feared that a larger conflict was coming—even outright war—and we were intent on seizing the day. Speaking to officers younger than me, who came of age just before and during the Dominion War, I know that they had a very different experience during their first postings. They were straight into the thick of it. Even after the Dominion War was over, there was the hard work of reconstruction, and not as much time to play. I am fortunate to have been on a ship like this. I enjoyed my work; I enjoyed my downtime; I was making good friendships and I was earning praise from my superiors not only for my work, but for my handling of various situations that were intended to prepare me for command. I was pleased with my performance. The only risk was that I was starting, perhaps, to get a little cocky, but Starfleet has its own corrective measures for this kind of thing, as I was going to find out.

About six months after I joined the crew of the *Al-Batani*, I had a first meeting with an individual who was later to become extremely important in my life—and who made his presence felt from the first moment that we laid eyes upon each other. It's testament to his quality—and his judgement—that this first encounter did not put me off him for life. The *Al-Batani* had come back to Earth to allow Captain Paris to participate in a conference about the ongoing crisis on Bajor. The Occupation was now decades old, and the Cardassians showed no signs of ever intending to leave (they were gone, I'm glad to say, within the next eleven years). The situation was increasingly desperate: not only the increasing numbers of refugees, but a growing sense that Bajoran culture was in danger, and also the ecosystem of that beautiful world. The Cardassians were stripping the place of resources, and an environmental tipping point would surely soon be reached. Starfleet was constrained in what it could directly do, both by its policy of nonintervention, but also from the natural concern of embroiling the Federation in a war with a highly militarized and aggressive neighbor.

"It will take a major alliance to defeat the Cardassians," my father used to say. He was right—a bigger alliance than perhaps he had realized, but, then, he hadn't known about the Dominion, and he hadn't expected the scale of that defeat.

This conference on Earth that Captain Paris was attending was very significant, with representatives not only from Starfleet and the Federation Council, but various relief organizations (my mother ran a panel about efforts by artists and writers to raise awareness), and, of course, displaced Bajorans, coming to speak out on behalf of their people, and ask for whatever aid Starfleet and the Federation could offer. The whole event lasted a week, during which time we junior officers were left in charge of a skeleton ship. Kristopher, who was taking some shore leave, said to me, on departing, "Don't mess this one up, Janeway."

By the end of the week, we had perhaps got a little slapdash, and I'm sorry to say that I didn't pull it back together in time. On the day that the senior crew was due to return, I received an unexpected message from Captain Paris that the *Al-Batani* would be carrying three admirals from Earth to Betazed, and that since they would be arriving before the senior crew was able to return, I should receive them on board with all due ceremony and protocol. I therefore arrived in the transporter room at the right time and watched as the three admirals and their security team arrived on board. I put on my most welcoming smile and stepped forward, intending to make a good impression.

"Sirs, I'd like to welcome you aboard the *Al-Batani*—"

I was stopped midflow when the senior officer in charge of their security team, a humorless-looking Vulcan, said, "Ensign, you have not performed a weapons sweep upon us."

I turned to look at him. "Sir?"

"We gave you only four hours' notice of our intention to travel on the *Al-Batani*. Are you not aware of the regulation that requires that any passengers travelling upon a starship who are brought on board without twelve hours' notice should be subject to a weapons sweep?"

"I am, sir."

"And yet you have not conducted the sweep. Can you explain your reason, Ensign?"

There *was* a reason. The reason was that I had forgotten. (I didn't say it was a good reason.) And… Well, we were within the solar system, after all. What threat could there be? (It's not a mistake anyone entering Starfleet during the Dominion War would have made, is it? The threat of a Changeling on board ship seriously changed security procedures. But these were simpler times.) Anyway the protocol existed, and I had not followed it. I had made a mistake, and I was being dressed down— and in front of three admirals.

I raised my chin and looked squarely at the Vulcan officer. "No, sir," I said. "I cannot."

"May I ask how you intend to remedy this situation?"

It's possible that I have never loathed someone as much as I loathed this lieutenant right at that moment. By far the worst thing about it was that he was of course completely right. I'd been sloppy, and I'd been called out, and there was nothing I could do but suck it up.

"Sir," I said, "I should conduct the weapons sweep immediately."

"That's correct, Ensign."

I conducted the sweep. As expected, nobody was carrying any unauthorized weapons, these three admirals clearly having decided not to hijack Captain Paris's ship that day.

"Is everything satisfactory, Ensign?" said the officer.

"It is, sir."

"Are we cleared to board, Ensign?"

"Yes, sir, you're cleared to board."

"Anything else, Ensign?"

I sighed to myself. He really wasn't going to let this one pass without drawing blood or, possibly, while leaving me standing. "My apologies, sir. It won't happen again."

"See that it doesn't, Ensign."

He gestured toward his charges and led them out of the transporter room. One of the admirals, on his way past, winked, and said, "Don't take it too hard, Ensign. But don't do it again, huh?"

They left the room. I fell back against the transporter console. My colleague, Ensign Chang, who had been operating the transporter, said, "Wow. Kathryn. Are you okay?"

I made a show of checking myself over. "No limbs lost," I said. "Just fatal damage to my dignity."

Chang shook her head and whistled. "There's a reason I didn't go for the command track," she said. "That was *brutal*."

And I was sure that wasn't going to be the last of it, either. That security officer was bound to submit a report to my superior officers. When the summons from Captain Paris came, as was inevitable, I took a deep breath, made sure I looked as faultlessly smart as I did on my first day, and reported to his ready room, steeling myself for the dressing-down that I was sure was coming.

Bizarrely, it did not come. Captain Paris let me stand there and sweat for a while as he sat and studied me, and then said, "I hear you met Lieutenant Tuvok."

So that was the damned security officer's name. I filed that one away for future reference. I'd been keeping an eye out for it—to keep well away. "Yes, sir."

"I hear he had a few things to say to you."

"Yes, sir."

"And I hear you took them on the chin."

Cautiously, I said, "I'd like to think so, sir."

"Which suggests to me that you thought you deserved it, Ensign."

I swallowed. "Yes, sir," I said.

"Yes," he said. "I think you deserved it too."

"My apologies, sir."

"Accepted, Ensign."

"If it's any consolation, I'll have cold sweats about this for the rest of my life, sir."

"As you should, Janeway. Don't let it happen again."

"No, sir," I said, fervently, and then I was dismissed. Outside his ready room, I took a deep breath and thanked my lucky stars. I'd been expecting much worse. Had I really got off this lightly? Possibly, but just recounting this story I felt my stomach sinking, and, yes, those cold sweats breaking out. I think I got exactly what I deserved.

That, thankfully, was my worst experience during my first year on the *Al-Batani*, and once Kristopher was back from leave, up to date on the whole sorry episode, and gave me a scolding for letting her down, that was the last I heard of it. I'd made a mistake, I'd got told off, and I'd made it clear that it would never happen again. I put the experience behind me and concentrated on making my time on board a success, learning as much as I could from example and from practice. The Academy can teach you the principles of being a Starfleet officer, and it can even present you with holo-training simulations covering as many different scenarios as you can think of—but there is no substitute for learning on the job. Nothing knocks the corners off a cocky young ensign like finding yourself floundering and having your more experienced colleagues move in smoothly to help you out. Every day brought a new practical challenge; every day, I found myself muttering, "They didn't cover *that* at the Academy." (After I managed to delete a morning's worth of data analysis from readings we had taken from a nebula, Kristopher got this legend printed on a t-shirt for me, and ordered me to wear it each time I used the gym.) But I started to find my feet, and most of all, I started to enjoy myself.

Without doubt, my favorite experiences on board the *Al-Batani* at this time were when I had the privilege to observe first-contact scenarios. Surely this, at heart, is why we all joined Starfleet: to seek out not only new worlds, but new life; to learn from these encounters and thereby enrich ourselves and our own civilization, by ever increasing our knowledge and our diversity of experience. Let me note that, as such a junior officer, I was only ever allowed to observe, and then in circumstances in which we were plainly dealing with a friendly species. There were other, more complicated situations at which a probationary officer was not allowed even to be present, and these were tantalizing, since they were the cases which posed the most interesting questions of intercultural and interspecies communication. I longed to participate more actively in these meetings, and I envied my superiors their direct involvement, but protocol demanded that such delicate encounters were handled by experienced officers. (And I certainly wasn't intending to breach protocol again in a hurry.) But I read every single report of these encounters several times over, and I must have annoyed the hell out of my superior officers, demanding they recount every contact down to the very last detail. I looked forward desperately to the day when, as a captain, the privilege would be mine. And when that day finally came it was indeed my privilege to participate in these encounters (though I might wish I hadn't had to go so damn far to have them).

It strikes me as ironic that I ended up giving many junior officers on *Voyager* their first experience of first contact well before they would have ever been permitted involvement back in the Alpha Quadrant. But if material resources were thin on the ground in the Delta Quadrant, then so too were human resources. All we had was what we brought with us. Tacit knowledge, experience: these things were at a premium, and to bring my ship home again, I had to accelerate my junior officers, ask them to take on challenges well ahead of schedule. It remains a great source of pride that these young people invariably stepped up to the challenge. I surely could not have asked for a better crew.

✦

At the end of my first year on the *Al-Batani*, I joined Lieutenant Commander Kristopher and Captain Paris for my end-of-probation meeting. We had a full and frank discussion of my year on board ship (I even managed to laugh about my encounter with Tuvok). They commented on my tendency to take on slightly too much (although they had to admit they hadn't seen any effect on my performance so far), and encouraged me to consider strategies for conserving my emotional and physical resources as I took on more duties and seniority. Overall, I had to be pleased with my first appraisal:

> *"Practical and solution-orientated, hard-working and personable, Ensign Janeway's doggedness gets the job done, and only sometimes translates into stubbornness. A highly committed junior officer, who inspires trust and respect from both peers and senior officers, she is well on track for command."*

Not the flashiest of reports, I'll grant you, but who wants to burn out in a flash? I was working hard to curb my stubborn streak and turn it into something productive, and I was remembering that hard work could be overdone, and downtime was necessary. The report duly went back to Starfleet Command, and I got a holomessage from Dad the next day. He sent me an image of a glider soaring over the Grand Canyon: *That's my girl, Katy. Keep flying.*

The *Al-Batani* had taken on half a dozen new ensigns at the time I joined, and Captain Paris held a cocktail party to celebrate the end of our probation. This was the occasion where I met a young man who was going to feature significantly in later years. At twelve years old, Thomas Eugene Paris was energetic, full of mischief—and clearly already a source of some exasperation for his more straight-down-the-line father. I often wonder where Tom got his high spirits from: Owen was so steady, so upright, and his wife, Julia, very grand and sophisticated. It might simply be that Tom had found getting into scrapes was a good way of attracting his father's attention… although it was invariably not the kind of attention he might have preferred. At this party, I noticed how bored Tom was looking, and I had a sense that some trouble was about to ensue. I had a word in Kristopher's ear, and we marched him off down to the holodeck where we ran flight simulations for him for an hour, and got him back to the party in time for the speeches—none of us missed, and the youngest of us in a very good mood from getting to play pilot all afternoon. I don't know if Tom remembers this—there must have been a lot of tedious cocktail parties over the years—but I've been keeping a close eye on you from an early age, Tom, and I didn't miss a trick.

✦

Altogether, I decided to count my first year in Starfleet a success. But events were about to hit me that I hadn't prepared for and couldn't have predicted. I was about to suffer the first serious blow of my life.

Around the time that I entered the Academy, my father had been assigned to oversee a number of projects which were aimed at designing new flight technologies for use against Cardassian warships. He had,

THE HISTORY OF THE CAPTAIN WHO WENT FURTHER THAN ANY HAD BEFORE

after all, been a test pilot at the start of his Starfleet career, only retiring from this role when he married and had young children. The details were hush-hush, of course, and I am not sure of the extent to which my mother and sister were aware of the details of his work during this period, but I had an inkling of the kind of thing that he was doing. Nevertheless, he and I never discussed it. Perhaps if we had, I would have known that his involvement was more hands-on than I would ever have guessed. I knew that by this stage he was spending substantial periods of time at the Utopia Planitia shipyards; what I did not know—what none of us in the family knew—was how often he went along on test flights, and that in fact he had started flying again.

I don't know my father's reasoning behind this. Perhaps he was unwilling to ask pilots to take risks that he himself wasn't willing to take. Perhaps now that Phoebe and I were grown-ups and established, he wanted to get back to what he always thought was his real work, the work that he had given up when Phoebe was born. I don't know what was in his mind, and of course I never had the chance to ask. It's the question I most want to ask him: Dad, what the *hell* were you thinking?

I remember receiving the news of his death vividly. I'll never forget it. Traumatic experiences burn themselves into your neurons, don't they? I was on duty on the bridge. The XO, Shulie Weiss, was in the captain's chair, and we were all surprised when the captain appeared and went to have a quiet word with her. Then Weiss called over to me and asked me to go with the captain. I followed Captain Paris into his ready room, wondering what the hell I'd done wrong and whether I was about to get in trouble for a late-night gambling session with the other ensigns… I was already preparing my defense: we hadn't made any noise and we hadn't stayed up *that* late… Everyone had been bright-eyed and bushy-tailed the following morning… But of course, this was nothing to do with that.

"Please sit down, Kathryn," the captain said.

I knew from the use of my first name that this was something else, something truly serious and not simply a quiet word about the high spirits of some of his junior officers.

"Is something the matter, sir?"

For a moment, I saw that he was lost for words. He pressed his fingertips against his temple. "It's about your father. It's about Ted. Kathryn, I am so sorry to have to tell you this—"

"Injured?" I think I already knew this wasn't the case.

"I'm so sorry, Kathryn. He's been killed."

A whooshing sound rushed through my head; there was a ringing in my ears. My eyes went strange: black patches in front of my field of vision.

"Kathryn! Kathryn!"

I became aware of Captain Paris's voice, somewhat distant and muffled.

"Here, drink this."

He had found some whisky (we can always lay our hands on it from somewhere in dire need—and my need was dire), and he put the glass up to my mouth and made me drink. That helped restore me to some kind of equilibrium; sufficient to be able to ask a few questions and listen to what he was saying to me. There had been an accident, it transpired, out on Tau Ceti Prime... At first, I struggled to understand: An accident? What in God's name had he been doing all the way out there? What had taken him from the shipyards on Mars? I listened to the captain, talking clearly, and began to piece things together. Here's what happened.

Cardassian activity along the border had, in recent months, been focused on Etaris IV, a disputed world that had great strategic significance in securing supply lines between two Cardassian border systems. Starfleet had no intention of letting that happen. These barren rocks that we fight over! Etaris IV was a dead piece of ice in the middle of nowhere! Still, that was the battleground that the Cardassians had chosen, and Starfleet had no choice but to meet them there. As a result, Starfleet had been testing a ship that could operate under lower-than-average temperatures without giving off heat signatures that would allow the Cardassians to trace it. The ship needed to be able to fly not only in orbit above Etaris IV, but also within the atmosphere and, ideally, be able to dip below water. This meant it needed to be able to work beneath the ice that covered most of the planet's surface. A prototype had come off the production line at Utopia Planitia, and now was being tested under the polar ice cap on Tau Ceti Prime, where conditions came closest to the surface of Etaris IV. They had six successful runs, shifting from orbit, to atmosphere, then under the ice for over an hour, then back again. On the seventh run, my father decided to see for himself how well it was operating. That was when the damn thing broke down. Full systems failure. After a hellish couple of days, they got the ship back up again, but by that time the three-person crew was dead. Including my dad.

I had nightmares about his final moments for many years after. I have still not read the full report, in case the reality was worse than what I could imagine. Had they died on impact? Or had they lasted a while, as their air ran out? Had they escaped the ship, only to drown beneath the ice? Had they faced fire? I did not want to know. But all these images were burned into my brain; no wonder, when I was traveling home on *Voyager*, that an alien found that these were a potent means to convince me that I too had died. More than anything in life—more even, perhaps, than wanting to get home to the Alpha Quadrant—I longed to see my father again. No wonder I was nearly persuaded of the truth that I was dead and had joined him in the afterlife. No wonder I was so nearly fooled.

✦

I went directly home. Captain Paris told me to take as long as it took. By this, I assumed that he meant for as long as my family needed me. As it turned out, I was the one who needed the break.

The funeral was hard. Not just because Mom was so grief-stricken, and yet being so brave, but because there were so many *people*... Our quiet little home in the country, our haven, suddenly became the focal point for hundreds of people, all of whom wanted to pay their respects, many of whom were Starfleet top brass... I honestly don't know how Mom kept on going throughout that day. I know how much I was struggling; I know how much Phoebe was struggling. To have to listen to people tell you, over and over again, how brave he was, how well respected, how many people he had served with and supported and encouraged... Trying to find a "thank you" to everyone who took the time to come and speak to us... As the day went on, we came up with a system—the widow and the two daughters— one of us coming forward to be the point of first contact for well-wishers; another one moving in to take over when that person began to flag... All the grandparents were there too; Granny- and Granddad-in-town distraught at the death of their boy... God, it was hellish. I think what made it worst of all was that all this grief and sorrow had come to what had been such a happy home. The picture I have painted of my childhood may seem to make it too idyllic, but I was lucky and blessed in my early life. This was the first real tragedy I ever faced. I talked to more admirals and captains and councilors and ambassadors that day than I think I have in the whole time afterward. But do you know which conversations hit hardest? The ones with our neighbors. It turned out that whenever Dad was home, he never missed a meeting with the local astronomical society. I knew he was a member—he'd taken us there when we were small—but I didn't know how active he'd tried to be for a man so often away from home. They put out a newsletter every two months, and it turned out he always wrote something, however small; sometimes just a letter, sometimes as much as an article. That short but heartfelt conversation with the secretary and the president of that little society of enthusiasts was the closest that I came to breaking down completely that day. My father was a busy man, an important man, with lots of responsibilities as the border situation got worse, and still he had found the time to stay in touch with them. At heart, he remained the little boy who had looked up at the stars and wanted to fly among them.

As the afternoon wore on, and our guests began to leave, Parvati Pandey, who had known Dad well, came to speak to me. She took both my hands in hers and gave me a steady look. Remember that look? The commander's look? Checking out the reserves of her junior.

"How are you, Kathryn?" she said.

I was frank with her. "I'm... I'm not good, ma'am."

"This is going to take time, you know. Grief and shock—it can take a while to bounce back from that."

If only it had been grief... I think I would have understood that. Feeling bereft, feeling shocked... But what I couldn't understand was the *violence* of my emotions... Pandey must have seen something in my expression; she frowned and said, "What is it, Kathryn?"

"I... I don't feel sad, ma'am. I feel... *angry*."

"That's natural," she said. "When someone dies suddenly, we often feel angry with them—"

"Not with him," I replied softly. "With the Cardassians."

She looked at me in surprise. "He was nowhere near the front, Kathryn—"

"But he was still fighting that war, wasn't he? Putting himself into danger because he wouldn't ask people to take risks that he wasn't ready to take. If they weren't pushing their luck, forcing us to respond, he wouldn't have been in that damn flyer—"

"Kathryn," she said firmly. "It was an accident. Nobody was to blame. This isn't productive; it won't help."

I nodded.

"Do you understand? This won't help, Kathryn."

I let her think she had persuaded me, but she didn't. I knew who was to blame. And I knew there wasn't a damn thing I could do about it.

✦

That helpless anger: that's what lays you low. In the days and weeks that followed, I just couldn't shake off this sense of deep rage that I had. Thoughts kept whirling around my head: angry, vengeful, vicious thoughts. I would lie in bed staring up at the darkness, thinking about what had happened, and how the Cardassians were to blame. I thought about how I could get reassigned, get to the front, start paying them back for all that they had taken from me. And then at the crack of dawn I would fall into a restless sleep, and I would not be able to drag myself out of bed until late the following day. Even when I was awake, I couldn't settle. I would wander around the house (I didn't want to be outside), or I would sit in one of the big old armchairs and stare into the garden. I knew my family was worried about me, Mom and Phoebe and all the grandparents. I received a message from Captain Paris, telling me that I'd been granted indefinite leave. I thought, *But I didn't request it...* and then fell back onto the bed and into a deep and exhausted sleep. Eventually, I stopped feeling angry. I stopped feeling anything at all.

Looking back on this gray, lifeless period, I think I understand now what was happening to me. Many people lose parents young—I was still only twenty-two, remember—and aren't hit so hard. I think my problem was that so far, I'd been able to achieve pretty much everything that I put my mind to. Tennis trophies: sure, I lost them one year, but the following year I came back and won them in style. Getting into the Academy a year early: I'd checked that one off. Graduating near the top of my class: I did that and proved to everyone I was more than just my father's daughter. But this—there was nothing I could do. No action of mine, not even if I had brought my revenge fantasies to reality, could have brought Dad back. He was dead, and there was nothing that Ensign Kathryn Janeway could do about that. And that realization—of my own incapacity—was too much to bear.

If I have ever wanted proof of how much my mother loved me, it was how she cared for me during this time, when her own grief must have been overwhelming. I guess people always thought my father was the strong one—the Starfleet officer, the hero—and perhaps thought my mother's artistic, homebody personality meant that she was sensitive or easily shaken. But she proved to be the toughest of us all. She must have thought that she and Dad were going to have a long and happy retirement together—like her parents, like his parents—and instead that future was lost. But she gathered herself up, and faced that changed future, and found some strength within her to prop me up as well. Phoebe too—I don't know what I would have done without her quiet patience. She took a term's absence from art school; stayed at home; made me get up and go for walks; made me sit with her and sort out photographs. And she faced my sudden outbursts of incoherent rage with equanimity.

One night, passing her bedroom door, I heard her crying to herself. I tapped on the door and walked in. She was lying on the bed. I went over to her—my baby sister—and wrapped my arms around her and let her cry. That's when I knew I was coming through the other side of this. I felt something else again, beyond the pendulum swing of dull ache and bitter anger. I felt compassion, the need to look after my sister, the desire to care. Phoebe, you got me through this. I hope I helped you too.

Four months went by, altogether, and then someone came to see me: Parvati Pandey, dressed in civvies. "Just passing by," she said, with a sly look. Whoever would be "just passing by" our place? We were at the end of our own damn lane.

We sat on the porch and drank iced tea. She said, "Still angry, Kathryn?"

I shook my head. "No. Just tired."

"Tired?" she said. "Or bored?"

The words seemed to break a spell. I looked across the land, and suddenly it was as if I could see in color again: the green trees and fields, the bright roses, the sparkle of sunlight. I felt something surge inside me, some upswell of energy that I had started to think I would never experience again. I felt... like I could do something.

I looked at Pandey. She was smiling at me, fondly.

"I think... I'm ready," I said.

"I think you are too," she replied. "I knew you'd get there, given time."

And I was ready. Ready to start over.

After Pandey left, I contacted the *Al-Batani* and asked to speak to Captain Paris.

"Kathryn," he said. *"How are you?"*

"I'm much better, sir," I said.

"I'm glad to hear that, Kathryn. It's good of you to check in—"

"Sir," I said. "I'm ready to come back."

He gave me the commander's look, sizing me up. *"Are you sure?"*

I looked back, steely-eyed. "Surer than I've been of anything, sir. Permission to return to duty?"

I saw a gleam of pride in his eyes; perhaps I'm not going too far to say of paternal pride. *"Permission granted, Ensign. We're ready to welcome you home."*

I learned later that Owen Paris had lost his own father young, a father killed while serving in Starfleet. No wonder he understood. No wonder he was so patient with me. Looking back now on my first year in Starfleet, with its great highs and its desperate lows, I see now how easily my career could have been derailed even before it started. And I recognize—and am beyond grateful for—the good luck that I have had in my mentors. Flora Kristopher, who took me from rookie cadet to capable ensign. Owen Paris, who gave me the space to bring myself back from the worst blow of my life. Parvati Pandey, who helped me understand my grief and anger. And of course, Tuvok, who has never allowed me to let my standards slip. I am grateful to them all, and I have tried to pay it forward.

CHAPTER FIVE
MISSION ACCOMPLISHED—2359-2364

IT WAS TIME TO SAY GOODBYE TO MOM AND PHOEBE, and the grandparents: a more tearful farewell than usual. Home would never be quite the same again, but it was still home, and always would be—the place of rest and restoration; the place where I could always go, whenever I was in need. Before I left, Phoebe and I had one last walk down the country lanes which we knew so well, stopping to look at the little schoolhouse where our journeys away from home had begun as little girls, all those years ago.

"I worry about Mom," I said.

"But I'll be here for a while yet," Phoebe said. "Don't let it stop you going back."

I felt bad. Phoebe had her own career to think of. She had a studio over in Portland, and I knew there was a romance back there, someone special that she surely wanted to be around. "Shall we give it a few months?" I said. "I could come back… Take over…?"

Phoebe shook her head. "I don't think so, Katy. Now you've got the nerve back, I think you should go for it. You know, I think Mom will surprise us all."

On my way back to Starfleet Command, I stopped for a day with the Grands-in-town. That was a sad visit. Granddad-in-town had lost some of his ebullience; Granny-in-town looked gaunt. They lived long lives—happy lives, too, to the end—with many grandchildren and great-grandchildren (Granny even saw a great-great-grandson), but that loss of their child was always there. How could it not be? Feeling a decade older and wiser and sadder than I had been only a few months earlier, I made my way to San Francisco, to report, as instructed, to Starfleet Command, and my meeting with Captain Paris and Admiral Pandey.

Before the meeting, I took a little time to wander around the grounds of the Academy. How young the cadets looked! How green! The last eighteen months had changed me more than any other period in my life: not just my time on board the *Al-Batani*, but the fundamental shock of my father's death. There was no one ahead of me now, nobody clearing the path for me. We have such an expectation these days about how long our parents, and our grandparents, will live, but it isn't always the case that they survive to old age, especially if you're Starfleet. I felt strangely exposed. I know from speaking to other friends who have lost parents relatively young that they felt something similar: that some significant barrier had fallen too soon. It was both terrifying and yet, at the same time, strangely exhilarating, as if I had been initiated fully into the adult world. Still, I would have done anything—gone anywhere—if I thought it would bring Dad back home to us. But some journeys have no return.

I wandered through the garden, sitting on a bench among the roses, breathing in the deep rich scent. With that preternatural skill by which he always seems to appear when needed, I saw Boothby walking slowly down the path toward me. He seemed no different. Did he ever age? My father said he had looked exactly the same when he was a cadet. I wouldn't be surprised if he'd looked this way when Grandad-in-town was at the Academy. I wouldn't have been surprised to learn he was here when the foundations had been laid. He stopped beside me and pushed back his hat.

"Good to see you, Ensign Janeway." He sat down beside me, his face saddening. "I was sorry to hear about your father. Poor Ted."

"Thank you, Boothby."

"It's worse when they're so young."

It was strange to me to think of Dad as young, but of course Boothby was right. He had been no age at all. "I know."

"How's your mother?"

"She's amazing."

"Roses flourishing?"

"Always."

We smiled at each other. He said, "Have you got some time to help me today, or are you too busy?"

I breathed in deeply. Suddenly, more than anything, I wanted to stay in this peaceful place, quietly pottering around after Boothby, tending the garden, watching the weather and the seasons change. How strange, for one who had always wanted to get out of these chores and get back to flight. Suddenly, my mother's way of life made perfect sense. But it wasn't my way. I wanted to be out there. I wanted to be among the stars.

"I wish I could…"

"But the admiral and the captain await you." He stood up, surprisingly agile for such an old man, and offered his hand courteously to me to help me to my feet. "The garden will always be here, Kathryn. Home from home. Come back whenever you need us."

We parted company: I went to my meeting; he went back to his garden. Later that day, I found fresh roses had been sent to my quarters.

✦

Captain Paris and Admiral Pandey welcomed me into her office and put me at my ease. Tea was poured, and we took seats around her desk. She had a fine view over the harbor, the kind of view that, when the weather was fine, as it was today, lifted the heart. Looking out over that big blue sky I could feel my spirits rise. I was ready to take flight again.

Pandey eased herself into her chair. "Kathryn. Good to see you looking more like yourself again."

"Thank you, Admiral. I won't deny it's been a tough time, but the worst is definitely past. I'm ready to resume my duties." I glanced at my captain, sitting in the chair beside me. "If you're still willing to take me back on board, sir."

I saw the two senior officers exchange a look and felt worried. Was something the matter? Had they decided against my return? Had they decided I wasn't fit for duty? But I felt so well, so capable…

"Well, Kathryn," said Paris. "That's partly why we asked you here today. We want to hear from you *exactly* how you are. We want to know what you're ready for."

I spread my hands out across my knees. "Like I said, it's been a rough ride. I wasn't prepared for him to…" It was time to say it loud, way past time to speak the truth. I took a deep breath and said, "I wasn't prepared for Dad to die. And it knocked me miles off course. Like I'd been…" I searched for the right words. "Picked up by a tornado and swept into a world that didn't make sense." Like Dorothy, I thought, whisked off to Oz. I was glad that some of her nerve, her grit and determination, had come back to me.

Pandey leaned forward, chin resting on her hands, and studied me carefully. That commander's look. *Are you fit? Are you ready? Are you able?* "And now, Kathryn?"

"I'm better. Things make sense again. It was a horrible accident, and it wasn't fair. But I can't do anything about that, so I need to concentrate on the things that I *can* do, and let…" I gave a sad smile. "Let grief take its course. I want to get back to work, and I'm ready to get back to work."

Again, she and Captain Paris glanced at each other. "All right," said Paris, relaxing back in his chair. "I'm glad to hear that. Because we do have a posting for you—although we want to hear first whether you want it."

My ears pricked up. "I'm grateful for the opportunity, sir."

"You might not have heard," he said, "but Flora Kristopher is moving on."

I hadn't heard. "Oh, that's a big loss to the ship, sir!"

"I know!" he said. "But it's a fine opportunity for her, and one that will take her back to her real work."

"Where's she going?"

"Over to the *U.S.S. Cúchulainn*," Paris said. "They're heading across to some of the worlds being settled by Bajoran refugees to work there on soil reclamation projects."

I'd heard from my mother about these projects. Bajorans fleeing the Occupation hadn't had much choice about where to settle, and some of the places where they'd landed were largely barren worlds. This was a good and practical way in which Starfleet and the Federation could help them, and I was not surprised to learn that Flora had been persuaded to become involved. It was a chance for her to use her technical expertise to achieve genuine good.

"That's a great move for her, sir," I said.

"It's where her heart is," he agreed. "But, unfortunately, it does leave me without a chief science officer."

"Who do you have in mind, sir?" I said. I started running through a list of names of likely candidates, but nobody on the *Al-Batani* came to mind. Kristopher had been young for the job and had been building up a young team. I'd been part of that cohort of new cadets, serving under Paris as their first posting.

"Well, Kathryn," said Paris, "the job's yours if you want it."

I stared at him. "Me?"

"It will mean promotion, of course. To lieutenant, junior grade," he said. "But it will also mean being away from Earth for a long period of time. We have a new mission."

"Sir, I don't know what to say..." I was deeply touched by this offer. For him to show this much faith in me, after the difficult time I had been through.

"Perhaps," said Pandey, "you'd like to hear about the mission before you make your decision."

I was still reeling from the offer. "Yes please, Admiral."

Paris passed over a padd and began his briefing. "The *Al-Batani* is being sent out to the Arias system."

I had heard about the system. About a year ago, some interesting massive compact halo objects had been identified out there which required closer analysis. The problem was that the system was extremely close to the Cardassian border, and the class of ship that was generally assigned these kinds of exploratory and analysis missions was not sufficiently well equipped to defend itself against attack. I listened to Paris describe the scientific objectives of the mission for a while, but he said nothing about the proximity of the system to the border. He wrapped up his briefing.

"Any questions, Kathryn?"

"Yes, sir," I said. "Is this only a scientific mission?"

He began to laugh. "No fooling you, is there? Our other purpose is to gather intelligence about Cardassian fleet movements along the border. That part of the mission is of course classified, and you'll not discuss that outside of this room, please."

"Absolutely not, sir."

Pandey said, "There's also a strong chance of encountering hostile forces, and of direct combat. What I want to know—and what Owen here also wants to know—is, are you ready?"

I thought about this. Was I ready? "Can anyone really be ready for combat, Admiral? I'm trained for it."

"Good answer," she said. "The other thing that I want you to be clear about is that this is going to be a lengthy mission, Kathryn. Several years. Are you ready for that too? Do you need to remain near home for a while longer?"

I could see why she would ask. But throughout that day, something had been lifting from me, some burden of grief. I felt as if I had been pushing against a door that suddenly opened and I was stepping out into the light of morning.

"I know why you're asking, Admiral. I've had a serious downswing. But I'm through. It's done. I'm ready for this mission—more than that, I'm *eager* for this mission. I want to get back to work."

A third time they looked at each other. This time they were smiling.

"Told you so," said Paris.

"I didn't doubt for a second," replied Pandey. She rose from her seat, and therefore so did we, and she came around the desk and stood before me. Reaching into her pockets, she brought out my new insignia. "Congratulations, Lieutenant Janeway."

"Thank you, Admiral. Thank you, sir."

We saluted each other. I felt marvelous—buoyed up, lifted up. It was a feeling as good as flying. I'd come back from the edge, and now two of the senior officers I most respected were signaling their trust in me. I'd be damned if I would let them down.

Paris reached out to shake my hand. "I wish Ted could be here to see this," he said. His voice was surprisingly hoarse.

"Me too, sir," I said.

"He would be damn proud of you, Kathryn."

I clasped his hand more tightly. I felt the need to console him, rather than to receive consolation. "Thank you, sir."

He cleared his throat. "Well. A good morning's work. Get your gear together, Lieutenant; I expect you back on board the *Al-Batani* in thirty-six hours."

"I'll be there, sir."

Suddenly his eyes twinkled with mischief. I knew that look, and I didn't trust it.

"Something the matter, sir?"

"Only that I've saved the best surprise till last," said Paris.

"Surprise, sir?"

"I have a new chief of security."

"Oh yes, sir?" I said blithely. "Anyone I know?"

✦

"Lieutenant Janeway," said Lieutenant Commander Tuvok.

"Sir," I replied, as calmly as I could manage. *Of all the damn dirty tricks, Owen Paris*, I thought. It's not as if I would have refused the mission or the promotion, but he hadn't needed to be so gleeful about revealing the identity of his new security chief, and he didn't need to send me to the transporter room to welcome him aboard. People who said that Owen Paris didn't have a sense of humor didn't know him. He did have a sense of humor, and it was damn twisted.

"I'm delighted to report that you are clear of weapons, sir," I said, dryly. "Welcome aboard the *Al-Batani*."

Tuvok raised a puzzled eyebrow. "Lieutenant Janeway, thank you for the welcome. The regulations with regard to weapons only apply when less than twelve hours' notice has been given of arrival. I was assigned to the *Al-Batani* two months ago and confirmed my day and time of arrival immediately. The regulation therefore is not relevant in this instance. Nevertheless, I commend your diligence." He stepped off the transporter pad. "I believe I am expected in the captain's ready room. I would be grateful if you could direct me there."

Paris had asked me to bring him along. "This way, Commander Tuvok," I said with a sigh. I'd learned my first lesson of dealing with him: sarcasm would be taken at face value, and completely miss the mark. Either that, or he had forgotten me completely. Just another cocky ensign who needed teaching a lesson. Well, I could work with that. I certainly wasn't that ensign any longer. We walked along the corridors toward the bridge, Tuvok's hands clasped behind his back. I gave the usual spiel, although I was sure that he would have familiarized himself completely with the ship's specifications within twenty-four hours of receiving the assignment. Nevertheless, he listened gravely and attentively, and asked questions which showed he was taking on board everything that I said.

I delivered him to the door of the ready room in one piece. Paris was sitting behind his desk, smirking at me. I risked a small glare back. "Nice to see you two making friends," he said. "Always good to have senior staff who get along."

Tuvok turned to me. "Lieutenant Janeway," he said, "allow me to thank you for your attention this morning. I have followed your career with interest since our first meeting, and I have heard only excellent reports. I am looking forward to serving alongside you."

That took the wind out of my sails. "I... Well. Thank you, Commander. I... look forward to serving alongside you too." I nodded to Paris, who was looking too damned pleased with himself. "Dismissed, sir?"

"Yes, thank you, Janeway."

I left, and the door closed behind me. "Well," I said. Looked like Tuvok wasn't going to be such a pain in the damn neck after all.

✦

"That man," I said to Laurie Fitzgerald, the CMO on the *Al-Batani* and my closest friend on board, "is a damn pain in the neck."

He laughed. "Commander Tuvok does have a knack of rubbing you up the wrong way, Kate."

"You know what the worst thing is, Fitz? It's not reciprocated. Nothing I do annoys him. He just... always seems to find it lacking somehow."

"Kate, you run on intuition so much of the time," said Fitz. "I bet he finds you damn irritating."

"Thanks, I think." We were making light of the situation, but the truth was that my working relationship with Tuvok was troubling me. It seemed to me that he shot down every suggestion that I made—and, worse, he shot it down with logic. At heart, I am a scientist—I understand how to hypothesize, gather evidence, analyze that data, and provide measured conclusions or reasonable conjectures. But there was the other side to my personality; the side that I guessed Tuvok saw as irrational, but which I called instinct, hunch, gut feeling. Fitz was right: some of my best decisions have come from following my intuition. But Tuvok could see no place for this, and clearly seemed to think it was a fault. I knew that Paris was keeping an eye on things; for this reason, among others, I wanted to make this relationship work. But, most importantly, our mission was likely to take us into dangerous situations. We needed to function as a team. We needed to trust each other implicitly—and I wasn't sure that Tuvok entirely trusted me.

"Show him what you can do, Kate," said Fitz.

"You know, I think I will."

We had been out in the Arias system for a little over nine months. Our scientific mission was progressing well, although since this involved shifting in and out of the system regularly to examine other similar phenomena, our intelligence mission was, as a result, proving less successful. We knew there was Cardassian activity around here: we kept on picking up odd transmissions; nothing we could trace, but hint after hint that something was going on. The Cardassians denied everything, of course; any activity in this area would be a violation of agreements made about territorial expansion, but we didn't believe them. We just couldn't pin them down. At this point, however, we were all getting tired, and restive, and ready to head back to Starbase 22 for a break. But I just couldn't let the matter go, and I kept turning it over in my mind.

At the senior staff meeting before we were due to return to Starbase 22, Paris heard our reports, and then said with a sigh, "And are we any closer to working out what the Cardassians are doing out here?"

All around the table heads were shaking. I raised my hand, and said, "I have a suggestion, sir."

His interest piqued, he said, "Go on, Janeway."

"I think we should take a look at the ninth moon of the ninth world."

Now everyone around the table was looking at me as if I'd jumped up on the table to show them my Charleston. The ninth world was a barren chunk of rock that would make Pluto feel overdressed. It was something of a joke on board. As for its ninth moon...

"Another trip," Paris said, doubtfully.

I saw my colleagues agreeing. Everyone just wanted to get back to base.

"He makes a good point, Janeway," said Paris. "Any good reason we should drag all the way over there?"

"I can give a reason, sir, but I'm not sure you'll think it's a good reason."

I saw a twinge of something—Amusement? Irritation?—pass across the captain's face. "Try me," he said.

"It's the ninth moon, sir. Of the ninth world."

"How's that relevant?"

"Cardassians like to do things in threes."

There was a pause. Fitz, sitting beside me, muttered something about me dropping by later for a checkup.

"All right, Janeway," said Paris. "Explain your thinking."

"Cardassians have a tendency to do things in threes. Look at how their government is organized: Central Command, Obsidian Order, Detapa Council. Look at the design of their insignia; damn it, even the architecture of places like Terok Nor. Their music: triple harmonies. Their art: all around a principle of triples—"

"Are you a student of their culture, Lieutenant?" said Tuvok. Damn the man, I could never tell when he was sassing me.

"No, but it does no harm to understand something about your..." I hesitated at saying the word *enemy*, and ended up with "your rivals for space and resources."

"*They do things in threes...*" Paris was shaking his head. "Tuvok. What do you think?"

Tuvok shook his head. "This is not a logical reason to investigate, sir. Nor is it a logical reason to locate a base upon so remote a location—"

"That's part of my point!" I said. I was starting to enjoy myself. "It *isn't* logical. It's intuitive. It's possibly superstitious. It might even be a kind of joke. These aren't Vulcans we're dealing with. They're Cardassians! Whatever we might think of their ethics, they have a strong sense of *aesthetics*. The ninth moon of the ninth planet. We've been looking for a base. I bet it's on that moon. It can't be any moon of the third planet—because it's got no moons."

Paris had been observing our exchange with great interest. "Well," he said.

"Sir," said Tuvok. "I must advise against wasting time and effort on this. The crew is tired, we have been out here for some time, and everyone is ready for rest and relaxation."

"I know that what you're saying makes sense," said Paris. "But… *they do things in threes*. I can't pass that up. We'll set a course for that moon, and if we're wrong…" His eyes gleamed. "I'll send anyone who complains about the delay to their holiday over to you, Janeway."

"Sounds fair to me, sir," I said.

The meeting ended. "Follow me," murmured Fitz. "You need your head examined."

✦

It was nearly six weeks before we were able to return to Starbase 22, but nobody was complaining. As we drew nearer to the ninth moon, we were able to pick up a steady stream of Cardassian transmissions. It turned out that this ninth moon of the ninth world in the Arias system was home to a Cardassian communications array and deep-space freighter repair station. The existence of this outpost was directly contrary to the terms of a nonexpansion agreement signed between the Federation and the Cardassian Union the previous year, the purpose of which was precisely to prevent the militarization of this part of the border. Well, of course the Cardassians were violating that agreement with this outpost, and of course this hidden outpost was on the ninth moon.

We kept the *Al-Batani* out of reach of the outpost's sensors, but close enough to be able to monitor transmissions. The Cardassians on that outpost were arrogant, and that made them sloppy. It took me and Tuvok no time to crack their encryption codes. It wasn't long before we assembled the evidence that proved that the intention was to establish a larger base here, an outpost that would serve as spearhead for a larger Cardassian military presence to threaten Federation supply lines along this section of the border. We slipped away and were back on route to Starbase 22 just as the president was summoning the ambassador from the Cardassian Union to explain himself and his government.

I was sitting in the rec room enjoying a drink with Fitz and some of my team when Tuvok appeared.

"Lieutenant Janeway," he said.

"Commander Tuvok," I replied. "Can I help you?"

"No," he said. "I wished simply to acknowledge that you were correct in your assessment of the situation, and that I was wrong. Your analysis was... impressive."

Well, he didn't have to say this in front of other people, and that was impressive in its turn.

"Not analysis," said Fitz. "Intuition."

Tuvok tilted his head in acknowledgement. "So it seems."

"I'm just very relieved we didn't have a wasted journey," I said warmly.

"So are the rest of the crew," said Fitz.

"Sit down and join us, Tuvok," I said. "We'll be breaking out the kadis-kot board in a little while. I'd like to see your game."

"I am not familiar with the game," he said.

I stood up and pushed out a chair. "You soon will be."

He did sit down with us, if a little stiffly, and watched us play the game for a while, whereupon he proceeded to defeat us all in multiple rounds. As we talked that evening, it turned out that we were both great admirers of Parvati Pandey.

"I attended the admiral's classes," he said. "On—"

"The Ethics of Command," I finished up. "I attended those classes too."

He looked at me with interest. "Only the very best cadets were invited to those classes."

"I wasn't such a bad cadet," I said. "And I was only very briefly an arrogant ensign."

"You are neither a bad nor an arrogant officer," he said.

"Why, Tuvok!" I said. "That's almost a compliment!"

"Merely a statement of fact," he said, and proceeded to win another game.

I'm glad to say that after this, not only did we establish a cordial professional relationship, but we began to establish to a genuine rapport, a real friendship, and one that has stood me in good stead over the years. Tuvok would say, I think, that I changed his opinion of humans—although I do have a regrettable tendency to rely on intuition and insist on making decisions based on emotion and gut feeling. I take that, too, as a compliment.

✦

That mission brought us several close encounters with Cardassians. I must admit that, however irrational this was, I still bore considerable anger toward their species as a result of the circumstances of my father's death. I'd like to say that this was aimed specifically toward their government, but in all honesty at this time my antipathy had a more general focus. It was very easy to find oneself slipping into generalizations: that Cardassians were bloodthirsty, that they were duplicitous, that they were not to be trusted. Captain Paris came down hard on these sentiments whenever he heard them; such speciesism, he would say, should never be heard in the mouth of a Starfleet officer. But border wars are dirty fights: not outright hostilities, but sniping at each other, month after month, until respect is whittled away. My mother's work with Bajoran refugees, to my mind, lent support to my sense that there was something fundamentally wrong with Cardassian society. It has been a long journey away from this prejudice, which I know was shared by many of my peers after the Setlik massacre and reinforced during the Dominion War.

I did not experience the war, spending that time with my own business in another quadrant, and saw only the plight of the Cardassian Union after the murderous rampages of the Jem'Hadar. But my attitude had already undergone a substantial sea change during my time on the border on the *Al-Batani*. Strangely enough, this was during an actual firsthand encounter with the Cardassians at Outpost 936. Tuvok, myself, the second officer, Luis Martinez, and another officer had been sent down to a small outpost in the Retik system. There were only a dozen personnel there, at most, and we were providing technical assistance to upgrade their communications system. Nevertheless, we found ourselves under attack from the Cardassian Militia 29, part of the Sixth Order under the command of Gul Pa'Nak. (The Cardassians later claimed that we were the first to open fire; I will deny this until my dying day.)

Communications with the outside world were cut off within the first few minutes of the attack (one reason to assume that this was planned rather than in response to any action of ours). We were under bombardment for the next three days, struggling to reopen communications and call for backup. We made good use of our resources, our defensible position, and our knowledge of the local terrain, and, after three days, struck back hard against the Cardassian unit attacking us. After a very long twelve hours, the Cardassians fell back. We sat and listened to the sounds of the brush around us—and then we heard the unmistakable sound of someone in pain. It wasn't one of ours; it could only be one of theirs.

We listened for a while. He was in agony.

One of our ensigns was trying not to weep.

Martinez said, "I can't listen to this any longer. Janeway, take Ensign Sinclair and go get him. Bring him back."

"Luis," I said, "that's crazy! They're waiting for us to go and get him! He's *bait*!"

"Whatever else he is, he's someone in pain. Go and get him."

Well, I wasn't quite tired enough to disobey a direct order, so Sinclair and I slipped out under cover of darkness, made our way to where our enemy lay shivering and dying, and gave him a sedative. I remember his eyes—bright and feverish, staring up at me. He was very young. Younger than one of our first-year cadets, and already in battle. I took his hand.

"You'll be all right," I said. "We're here to help you."

He passed out, mercifully. Sinclair and I got him on the stretcher and carted him back. While we'd been out there, they'd got the comms link working again. Reinforcements from the *Al-Batani* were on their way. Fitz transported down and took our prisoner back up to the ship to treat him, although he wasn't in time to save the young man's left arm. Later, once the outpost was secured, we went out into the brush again, looking for the dead. We found half a dozen bodies; none of them much older than the one we had saved. Back on the *Al-Batani*, I went to see our prisoner. His name was Tret Rekheny. He was an ordinary foot soldier, not even an ensign (or a *glinn*, as the Cardassians would say), and this was his first action. He was scared of us, and scared of what his commanding officers would do once we returned him to them. "They'll think I gave them away," he said. "The Order will want to see me. I don't want to see them…" I realized that he was shaking with real terror at the thought of falling into the hands the Obsidian Order.

There was little that we could do for him: there was a long-standing agreement that we returned theirs if they returned ours, even though poor Rekheny was not much to bargain with. He was with us for no more than a few days before he was well enough to send home. I saw him most days he was on board the *Al-Batani*. I remember hearing him chanting names, three times each. It was part of the Cardassian funeral rite, he said: naming the dead to remember them. I said, didn't I, that they did things in threes. I found myself wondering about his friends, too, the lives behind those dead names. Who they were; where they'd come from; who would learn of their deaths, and whether they would be struck down by grief, the way that I had been when I heard about my father. I knew that I would never see Cardassians in the same way again. They felt pain, they grieved, they were afraid. For the first time ever, I felt compassion for the Cardassian people.

I have often wondered what happened to our prisoner after he went back, and whether the Obsidian Order did indeed finish what the Central Command had started when they sent him out there to fight us in the first place. I doubt that he survived the Dominion War or the Jem'Hadar's mass slaughter: very few of his rank did. Perhaps it was better if he did not live to see all the pain that followed. When it was time for him to leave the *Al-Batani*, an Order operative came over to collect him: a slick, supercilious man who put a possessive hand upon the young soldier's arm, and said, "We'll take care of you now." I have never loathed anyone so much in my life. They beamed back across to their freighter, and that was the last that I saw of Tret Rekheny.

The four of us—Luis Martinez, Tuvok, Anna Sinclair, and myself—were all decorated for our part in this operation. I suppose that I am proud of what I did, even though at the time I thought the order that Shulie had given us was madness. But what I took mostly from these events was what I tried to tell Seven of Nine later, that a single act of compassion can transform us. Having met Tret Rekheny, however briefly, it was not so easy, in future, for me to think of all Cardassians as cruel, as murderous, as vicious. Some of them, it seemed to me now, were as much victims of their government as the peoples they oppressed.

✦

Altogether, I served as chief science officer under Owen Paris on the *Al-Batani* for eight years. Much of that time I spent out near the Cardassian border, trying to combine scientific observation with intelligence gathering. To some degree these purposes could be made to work together; in other respects, they were completely at odds. For one thing, science does not care for borders. It does not care that the place where you need to be to make necessary observations would violate a treaty or test diplomatic sensitivities to the limit. Sometimes we found ourselves tantalizingly close to a breakthrough, an expansion in our knowledge, and we would have to pull back, away from territory we had agreed not to enter. I would have found this less frustrating, had I not known how flagrantly the Cardassians would break their word when the situation was reversed.

Altogether, I found it increasingly difficult to resolve the tension between these two objectives, and, privately, I was coming to believe that further and more serious conflict with the Cardassians was inevitable. I often found myself thinking back to a conversation I'd had with my father, when I was first making my decision to join Starfleet. He'd said: *It takes two sides to make peace. And I'm not sure that both sides want it.* The Arias expedition had taught me two things: that not all Cardassians were bloodthirsty warmongers, but that the bloodthirsty warmongers were the ones calling the shots on Cardassia Prime these days. War was coming—the question was, what could I get done before it came to me?

I knew that the *Al-Batani* would be continuing in this dual role for the foreseeable future. But I wanted my chance to experience the old Starfleet: the Starfleet of exploration and scientific study. I decided to put in for a transfer. When I told Owen Paris my decision, he did me the kindness of saying how far I had come in the years that I had served under him, and that he now considered me one of the best rising officers within Starfleet. "Whoever gets you next is a lucky captain, Kathryn," he said, and sighed. "Three requests for transfer on the same day! I must be losing my touch."

"Three, sir?"

It turned out several of his senior staff had made similar decisions. My friend Fitz was heading off to Caldik Prime, to take up a surgeon's post at the medical facility there. It was one of the leading hospitals in the Federation, with a specialty in biosynthetic prosthetics. I think Fitz's mind was on the forthcoming war too. I knew that he felt he had been ill-equipped for some of the field surgery he had been required to perform during our time on the border. And Tuvok was moving on as well, to take on a senior security role on Jupiter Station. That evening, the three of us met for supper and a game of kadis-kot, for old time's sake. We discussed our future plans, and they asked me where I was heading.

"The *U.S.S. Billings*," I said. "Captain Melita Vas. It's a big survey of the Glass Horse Nebula, and I'll be heading up a pretty large team. Which means a promotion!" I was now Lieutenant Commander Janeway, having been promoted to full lieutenant during the Arias mission.

"Overdue," said Fitz.

"I note that scientific study has won out in your affections after all," Tuvok said. "I am glad that your rational side is moving to the fore."

"I think I'm just tired of looking over my shoulder for Cardassians," I said.

"You and me both," said Fitz.

"I want to do some science, some real science! I want to feel as if I've had the chance to explore, before… Well."

"I understand that contrary to all expectations, there is hope that a treaty may well be signed between the Federation and the Cardassian Union within the next five years," said Tuvok.

"I don't see that happening," said Fitz. "Even if they did sign it—they don't keep their word, do they?"

Fitz really was very bitter about some of what he'd seen over the last few years.

"I guess we have to hope," I said.

"Hope has nothing to do with it," said Tuvok. "Peace is the rational choice."

Fitz and I glanced at each other but held our tongues. I knew what he was thinking. If only the Cardassians were as rational as our Vulcan friend.

"Well," I said, raising my glass. "Until we meet again."

Tuvok and Fitz raised their glasses in turn. And we did meet again: as captain, chief of security, and CMO of the *U.S.S. Voyager*—but only for the briefest of times.

✦

There's one last meeting I should record before bringing my account of my time on the *Al-Batani* to a close. Before we all left, Captain Paris held a lavish party for his crew at his home in Oregon. And there I met young Tom again; seventeen years old now, but not, I thought, a happy young man. Observing the interactions between father and son, I sensed a lot of regret on one side, a lot of sullen resentment on the other. He clearly didn't like having all these young officers around, the apples of his father's eye.

"I hear you're heading to Starfleet," I said.

He shrugged. "What else is there to do?"

I hid my surprise. "Plenty of things—"

"Not if I want to fly."

"Is that what you like doing, Tom?"

That shrug again. "I guess."

It wasn't the most promising of encounters, but I couldn't put young Tom Paris out of my mind. I suppose on some level, I sympathized with him. It's not easy, having a Starfleet officer as your father. It's not easy proving yourself. I often found myself wondering about him, over the next years, what he was doing, and where he was going to end up.

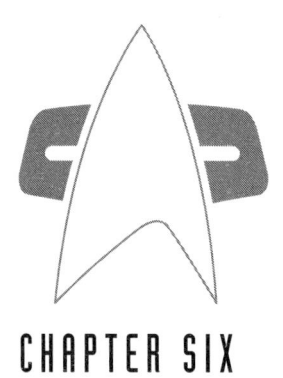

CHAPTER SIX
NEW CHALLENGES—2365-2370

BEFORE HEADING TO MY NEW POSTING ON THE *BILLINGS*, I was due a few weeks' leave. Naturally, I went home, back to Indiana, on from Bloomington, into the country and back to the farm. As ever, the place restored me to myself. Gone now was the sense that everything was smaller, that I was returning to a coop in which I no longer fit. Instead, I found peace and quiet, the chance to rest, the familiar places and patterns of childhood—although, inevitably, there was a great sense of sadness that one of our number was missing.

My mother, as brave and beautiful as ever, had made great strides in coming to terms with her widowhood. As many women do who lose their partners young, and who cannot ever imagine themselves marrying again, she had thrown herself into tasks that turned her focus outward. She was now deeply involved in the Bajoran relief effort, and it was notable that she spent a great deal of time away from the farm. My father's absence was of course a significant element in this change: even though he had spent so much time away from home, there had always been the promise of his return. Throughout their marriage, my mother had been content to wait, living the life that she loved best, waiting for the person that she loved best. It was not as if she was running away, but the house must surely have felt lonely at times. I had left; Phoebe had left; and, while her parents were still living nearby and in good health, it was not the family life that she had been used to.

This time when I came home, my mother was still coming back from a long trip to the headquarters of the Federation Bajoran relief effort in Geneva. That must have been a poignant visit for her, bringing back the time when she and my father had met, all those years ago. When I arrived at the house, late one evening, the place was dark. I believe that may well have been the first time that I had ever seen it that way: lights off, blinds up, nobody there. I went inside, listening to the unusual quiet, and then I wandered around, asking for lights, making tea, slowly bringing the place to life. Phoebe arrived about an hour later, apologizing that she hadn't made it in time to meet me, smothering me with hugs and kisses. My mother was not back until well into the evening. There was a touch more silver in her hair these days, a few more lines upon her face, but when she saw us, she threw out her arms to embrace us both.

"My girls," she said. "My two darling girls."

That was a fine vacation, one of the best. Chief among my pleasures was getting to know Phoebe's wife and children, who joined us a day or two later. Just before I set out on the Arias expedition, Phoebe had taken an artist's residency on Trill, where she had been exploring the effects of longevity upon their creative practice. How did joined Trills relate to the art produced when joined to a previous host? Where did their artistry lie? Fascinating ideas, posing fundamental questions about identity and personhood, questions that I found myself wrestling with over and over again on my voyage home. During the fourth month of Phoebe's year-long residency, she met a painter, a joined Trill named Yianem Lox. They fell deeply in love and were married by the end of the year. Yianem, always ready for adventure, had agreed to come back to Earth with Phoebe. They were currently living on the West Coast, near Portland, part of a writers' and artists' community. They also had three small daughters—one of whom, the eldest, I had met before, but as a baby. The younger two, still small, I was planning to get acquainted with during this break.

What a busy, fun, joyous leave that was! Three little girls under the age of four, full of curiosity and mischief. Their moods were ever changing:

sudden laughing sunshine followed by rapid squalls of tears, then rainbow smiles. With one aunt, one grandmother, and four great-grandparents in attendance, they now had roughly the attention which they thought was their due, and both Phoebe and Yianem could take some well-earned rest. Two grown-ups with three children are outnumbered, and not even the guile of a long-lived joined Trill is necessarily the match for the wits and speed of a toddler who has just learned to walk and is intent on wreaking havoc. These three children filled the gaps in the house. Sitting on the porch with my mother one afternoon, watching them tumbling over the grass, I said, "It's like the place has been given a second life, Mom, don't you think?"

She smiled and nodded. "I know what you mean. There were some days when I couldn't seem to bring the place alive. Some of the rooms stood empty for days on end. Nobody there. It was hard, after having you two here..." She breathed in deeply. "But these three—aren't they marvelous? I think they cause more mayhem than you and Phoebe ever did. As it should be."

I watched her, watching her grandchildren. She looked vibrant, happy, alive; and I knew then that she would be fine. Her relief work had given her purpose, but her grandchildren had given her heart. I knew that I could take up my next posting and not have to worry about her without Dad. She was strong and brave, with a huge capacity for love, and although my father's death left a hole that could never be filled, she had found a way through. I knew that when my leave was over, I could return to Starfleet with my mind at rest.

✦

After two months back at home, it was time to say goodbye again to my family, and head off to near-Earth orbit, where the *U.S.S. Billings* was waiting to take on its new crew. I could only be pleased with the ship itself: a prototype *Nova*-class exploration vessel, one of the very first of its kind, kitted out with excellent facilities for our mission. The science and data analysis team, of which I was now in charge, was well established, but made their new senior officer very welcome. Taking over a team like this can be a huge challenge, particularly when you join one that works well together, and who must be concerned about a change at the top. None of them had requested my position, I was glad to realize, so there were no resentments about my appointment. They were a grand set of people, the best of Starfleet, competent and intelligent, and well able to train a new commander overseeing her first big team. They made a huge difference to my time on the *Billings*.

Rather than their new senior officer, they were more concerned about the fact that the ship had a new captain. I too was somewhat worried about this change: I had requested this posting in part so that I could serve under Captain Melita Vas, who had such a good reputation. Unfortunately, Vas, after a sudden period of bad health, had accepted a long overdue promotion to admiral and was, in effect, retiring to teach at the Academy. I was most disappointed by this news, and sorry that I had not had the chance ever to wish her well: she had left the *Billings* a day or two before my own arrival. A new captain had been assigned: Neil Ward, who was taking up his first captaincy, and was on his way from Mars when I arrived on the *Billings*.

The captain sets the tone of any starship, and there was a great deal of anxiety about the new man. I'm sorry to say that it was not misplaced. Serving under Neil Ward was one of the most difficult periods of my life (just edged out by being flung seventy thousand light-years from home), and I came very close to leaving Starfleet as a result on several occasions. What can I say about Ward? Certainly, he had a way with admirals, all of whom seemed to like him, and spoke well of him. He was certainly ambitious, and plainly did not intend to remain captain of a comparatively small research vessel like the *Billings*. His facility with the egos of the top brass meant that he did have a knack of getting resources and equipment, but the benefits were not equally shared. Provided you were one of his favorites, you didn't struggle to get whatever you required. If you were not one of his favorites, the situation was much different—and I'm sad to report that it rapidly became clear to me that I was not one of the chosen ones. I sat through several meetings of the senior staff having my opinions passed over, taken apart, or simply ignored, while others were encouraged to speak. After one very difficult meeting, I decided that I had to say something. This situation simply could not continue; I was finding it increasingly difficult to be able to function.

"Captain," I said, as the other team heads were leaving, "may I have a word with you?"

He gave a sigh. "Is it urgent, Janeway? I'm pretty busy."

"It's not urgent, sir, but I do think it needs to be addressed."

"All right," he said, but he opened his companel and began to look at messages there. I remained standing; he hadn't invited me to sit again. Nor did he attempt to lead the conversation.

"Sir," I said, at last. "I have the distinct impression that you don't like me, and I want to understand what it is that I've done wrong, so that I can rectify that."

He closed the companel. "What makes you say that, Commander?"

"I just… It seems to me that I haven't been able to make a suggestion that you like, sir."

"Maybe you haven't made any good suggestions yet, Commander."

I was beginning to feel angry. I knew my weaknesses—but I also knew my strengths. "With respect, sir, I don't think that's true."

"*With respect…*" He eyed me thoughtfully. "You're blessed with confidence, aren't you, Janeway?"

"I beg your pardon, sir?"

"I meant—you don't often doubt your judgement, do you?"

Well, what on earth could he mean by that? I was well trained, experienced, smart, and hard-working. I'd learned good lessons early in my career about arrogance. I liked working in teams, and I tried my best to mentor junior colleagues. I was, on the whole, pleased with my performance, and a captain as good as Owen Paris had agreed. Had we all been missing something? I wasn't entirely sure what to say in response to this. Carefully, I said, "I try to give my best, sir."

"I envy that kind of confidence," he said. "Your father was a vice admiral, wasn't he?"

"Yes," I said. "Sir, I don't see how that's relevant to this conversation. My grandfather was Starfleet too. I imagine you could find a few Janeways here and there over the last century or so."

"That wouldn't surprise me in the least," he said. "I've often observed this kind of confidence in officers with a long family history with Starfleet. Like Starfleet is an extension of their family. It's not, of course."

Now, I thought, I was beginning to understand some of his antipathy toward me. He thought my success was down to me being my father's daughter. Well, it was a while since I'd come across this prejudice! There had been a few asides at the Academy, swiftly quashed when my first semester's grades arrived. Since then—a few comments here and there in my early days, but nothing much since. My work, my dedication, and my experience spoke for themselves. By this point in the conversation, I was pretty angry, as you can imagine. I had served in Starfleet for nearly a decade; I'd seen active service along the Cardassian border; I'd worked hard, and I'd earned every damn one of my promotions. I had not expected to hear this kind of thing again, and I was alarmed to hear it coming from my new commanding officer. I had committed to this mission. Had it been a mistake?

As calmly as I could manage, I said, "I'm sorry to hear that, sir, and I'm certainly sorry if I've given that impression."

"You had a leave of absence, didn't you, a few years back? And came straight back to a promotion."

Now I was furious. "It has been my good fortune, sir," I said, "that I have been shown various acts of kindness since my father's death. But I'd like to think that I didn't take any of this for granted."

He did have the good grace to look embarrassed at that. "Yes, well, just so we're all aware—everyone is equal on board this ship, Commander."

"You're the captain, sir," I said. "You set the rules."

"That's right." He turned back to his companel. "Is there anything else, Janeway?"

"Not right now, sir."

"Dismissed."

I left feeling very downhearted at this whole exchange. I'd signed on for a long trip, and it seemed that the captain, for reasons best known to himself, did not like me. Worse, it was difficult to know who to broach this with. Had I been back on the *Al-Batani*, among colleagues with whom I had served for a long time, then I would have someone to talk to. I'd have talked to Tuvok, and received good counsel; or to Fitz, if I'd wanted some cheerleading; or even to Captain Paris himself, if I thought the matter was serious enough to warrant his advice. These were people who knew me well. But here on the *Billings* I was new, trying to establish myself. I did not want to get a reputation of being someone who arrived only to complain. This was a very tricky period, and also rather lonely. Increasingly, as Ward's antipathy showed no sign of abating, I found that I was starting to second-guess myself. I started questioning whether my opinions were justified, grounded in data and good reasoning, or whether I was being overconfident. I withdrew slightly from crew activities, not realizing that I was starting to get a reputation for being standoffish. I'm not ashamed to admit that I spent some evenings alone in my quarters, shedding a few tears.

(Years later, talking to a colleague about this time, she shook her head, and said, "There's a word for this, Kate. It's called gaslighting. Make someone doubt themselves. It's a rotten, stinking trick." And I think she was right. But I do wonder now, looking back, whether I was little too sure of myself, a little too certain about my career path and its upward trajectory. In other words, I have tried to see it from Ward's perspective—although I do wonder whether he ever tried to see it from mine.)

At the time, however, all I knew was that this was the reality of serving on board the *Billings*, and that I was stuck for the foreseeable future. As I approached the end of my first year, I began to contemplate putting in for a transfer. It would mean a sideways move, perhaps even losing my seniority (I was indeed young to be in charge of such a big team), but I was wondering whether it would be worth it. I went along to an appraisal meeting with Ward and, bizarrely, he was all smiles. Pleased with my performance; pleased with the team; seemingly pleased with everything. The next day, sitting in the ready room with the other team heads, he ignored my contributions entirely. I knew I couldn't carry on like this. I needed advice, good, level-headed advice. I naturally turned to Tuvok.

I sent my old friend a long, rather rambling message, in which I outlined the events of my first year on board; minor exchanges that seemed almost ridiculous and inconsequential as I detailed them. But as I spoke, and they accumulated, I began to realize how much of a toll this was taking on me. I wrapped up the message: "I know that you of all people will look at this with a cool eye. I know you'll be able to tell me whether this is all in my imagination, or whether what I hear and see is true. I hope to hear from you soon, Tuvok."

It was a week or so before he replied. How glad I was to see his cool and sensible face upon my screen—and how far we'd come since that first meeting! As ever, his advice brought me fresh perspective.

"As you know, Kathryn, I have been able to study you across the whole of your career so far. I saw you at the very start, making elementary mistakes, and I saw you the day before you left to take up this posting. I am pleased to say that by that time you had evolved into a capable young officer. It is not possible for you to control your captain's emotions, nor is it your responsibility. I see no reason why this should have changed in the short months since we have been serving together. Therefore, I must conclude that the problem does not lie with you, but with your commanding officer. And a commanding officer who squanders such as resource as an officer like you is not acting rationally.

"Whatever irrational impulses motivate Captain Ward are his responsibility. What you are able to do is control your own response. Therefore, I would say that it is for you to determine whether this situation is tolerable for you, or whether it has become intolerable. There are clear benefits to you in remaining on the Billings. *You are young to be put in command of a large team. To ask to be transferred would, in some quarters, be seen as an admission of failure. This may affect your route to captaincy, which I suspect is not something you are prepared to sacrifice simply for the sake of avoiding Ward. One alternative, then, is to treat your relationship quite logically—as a kind of transaction. A means to an end. Do your duty to the best of your ability. Act in good faith. Take all that you require from this posting in terms of experience, and, when the time is propitious, move on."*

I took his advice to heart. When I was dealing with the captain, I thought of myself as Vulcan. I responded logically, accurately, precisely, and unemotionally. I stuck to data and evidence and kept away from conjecture. It's hard to fault someone when their facts are straight. He tried to find fault (after all, not everyone wants to act in good faith), but he was rarely able to do it, and that brought a little job satisfaction, even if it never brought much in the way of thanks or praise.

But I am not Vulcan, and I could not cut my emotions out entirely. I was too sociable to be able to sit alone in my quarters every night for another four years, and I was damned if I was going to do so. Screwing up my courage, I decided to make some friends. I started tentatively, inviting two of my lieutenants over to my quarters for dinner, then, as my confidence returned (and they began to realize I wasn't so standoffish after all), I began to get the whole team to socialize together. Soon I began to find my feet again. Invitations from people began to arrive. I joined the Velocity team—there's nothing like helping your team win a few games to make your colleagues fonder of you! I began to find my way again. I began to feel more like Kathryn Janeway.

And I began to find out that it wasn't just me with reservations about Ward. Quite a few of my team didn't like their new captain very much either. The ship had changed since Vas had left, they said. Ward's an empire builder, one said. He's only using this ship as a stepping-stone to something else, said another. He plays people against each other, said yet another. No, they didn't like him at all, and they missed their old captain immensely. We were well into my second year, and when I asked my colleagues why nobody had brought this up before, they looked embarrassed. I'd arrived at the same time, they said, and I'd got associated with him in their minds. And I'd been so damn serious! No fun at all! They thought I was part of the new regime. They weren't sure I was on their side.

Well, there's a lesson about isolating yourself. I saw that I had been failing my team in a significant way: part of my role as their commander was to act as a buffer between them and the captain, to make sure that his irrationalities didn't affect them. It wasn't an easy situation but knowing that I was actively improving my team's day-to-day life went a long way to making me feel better about being on board ship. We all wanted to see this mission through, and, part of my role, I realized now, was to make sure that my team were not affected by the maelstrom of difficult emotions swirling around and the unhappy environment in which we found ourselves. I wish things had been different on the *Billings* (not least that I had served under the previous captain), but I learned valuable lessons there which stood me in good stead on board *Voyager*.

You can learn as much from a bad captain as you can from a good captain: how not to motivate people; how not to get a team to come together; how not to build trust and loyalty. If I'm ever in doubt, I think, "What would Ward do?" and I do the opposite.

✦

The irony of all this is that Cardassian–Federation relations were the best they had been in decades. An armistice had been signed in 2367, considerably easing tensions between us, and, while there were still numerous incidents around the border, the feeling was that peace was now a real possibility, and the word was that the top brass and the diplomats were hard at work on a treaty. This became even more likely when the Cardassians announced that they were withdrawing from Bajor. I remember being in the mess hall with my team when this news came through: the sense of elation, and relief, was enormous. There were one or two Bajoran crew members, and they were in tears. I don't believe any of us had ever thought we would see that day. It gave us real hope that things had changed for the better, and for good, which seemed to be borne out with the signing, in 2370, of the Federation–Cardassian Treaty, which established the border between our territories, and created the Demilitarized Zone, a buffer zone between us. With the treaty, we all felt that peace was on its way. (Although there were complications that none of us had foreseen, when some of the colony worlds within the DMZ began to realize what the treaty meant for them.)

In general, however, the mood was positive, and this brought home how petty the situation on the *Billings* was. It was around this time I received some information from Tuvok that clarified my difficulties with Ward. Tuvok reported to me that the *U.S.S. Rotorua* had recently stopped off for refitting at Jupiter Station. Tuvok, entering a turbolift, overheard a conversation involving the ship's chief science officer. It seemed that this person had been expecting a posting on the *Billings* by the new captain, but it had gone to somebody else.

"A vice admiral's daughter," they said. "You know how it works! And it was promised to me!"

THE HISTORY OF THE CAPTAIN WHO WENT FURTHER THAN ANY HAD BEFORE

Several things clicked into place when I heard this. Ward, I guessed, knowing that he was taking on the captaincy of the *Billings,* must have known that the post of chief science officer had also become vacant, and promised it to his friend. But he was behind on the news: Vas had already assigned me, in more or less one of her last acts before taking ill. Ward arrived on the *Billings* expecting to be able to promote his crony—only to find Kathryn Janeway, the vice admiral's daughter, firmly in place, and raring to go.

This was more or less what I'd come to expect from Ward, but finally having an explanation for his behavior went a long way toward relieving any lingering sense I had that things going wrong was my fault. A further experience I had with him that year reduced any respect I had for my captain to rock bottom: not a happy situation. We had detoured into the Katexa system for a brief survey mission, where we detected some unusual volcanic activity on one of the moons of the fourth world in the system. We all agreed that this was worth closer analysis and consequently took the ship toward the moon. Around this point, having seen some preliminary analysis of the magma flows, I began to have serious misgivings about the whole idea, which I expressed in a meeting of the senior staff.

"We can get some fine readings from on board ship," I said. "Not to mention it'll be a chance to find out whether the adjustments we've been making on the forward sensors have been worth the effort."

I don't know whether it was because I was the one who had made the suggestion, but Ward wasn't having it. He insisted sending down an away team.

"Where's your sense of adventure, Janeway?" he said.

Well, my sense of adventure was fine, thank you very much; my sense of whether it was right to risk an away team in a shuttle on a volcanic moon was simply much stronger. And I'm sad to say that I was proved right: the away team's shuttle had barely entered the atmosphere when there was a massive magma eruption, badly damaging the craft. There were a couple of hours when we thought that the three crew members were lost. I was furious with Ward. He had ignored my advice—my *considered* advice, my *expert* advice—and he had, so far as I could make out, done it for no other reason than spite, risking the lives of three members of his crew. I kept these feelings bottled up while we were trying to find out what the hell had happened to my team, but I was enraged. I knew it; he knew it; and the whole damn ship knew it.

Eventually, I am glad to report, we were able to retrieve the three members of the away team, but they had some pretty serious injuries. One of them was out of action for a couple of months. The shuttle was a write-off. After everyone was safely back on board, the captain called his senior staff together for a debriefing. I imagine everyone was expecting that I was going to explode in much the same way as that volcano had, but I kept my cool, even as I watched Ward make excuse after excuse. I could see that he wanted to blame this debacle on me in some way. But he couldn't. The decision to send the away team had been his, and he had made it against the advice of his chief science officer, and in front of the whole senior staff. I let him talk, and I watched as the respect leached away from almost every single person in that room.

Eventually, he dismissed us all. I waited until the room was empty.

"Sir," I said. "Permission to speak freely?"

"Go ahead, Janeway."

"I know that you didn't want me for this post, but I'm here now, and there's nothing either of us can do about that. But I sincerely hope, sir, that you won't ignore my expert advice again. We're just lucky that nobody was killed today." I headed for the door. "One more thing," I said, before I left. "You want those damn readings? You'll get those damn readings. I'll go and get them myself—but I'll go when it's safe. And I'll be the one who decides that—based on sound scientific judgement."

He got his readings. I was able to go down the next day, by myself, and get them. And the *Billings* moved on.

✦

As well as Tuvok, I had remained in contact with my old friend Laurie Fitzgerald, CMO on the *Al-Batani*, who had taken up a surgeon's post on Caldik Prime. In one of his messages, he passed on some worrying news about our old captain, or, more accurately, his son Tom. It turned out

Tom's career in Starfleet had come to an unpleasant conclusion: he had, it seemed, been the cause of an accident which had led to the tragic death of three officers. Worse, he had tried to cover up his responsibility for the accident but had been found out. He had been cashiered out of Starfleet.

"I know you liked that kid, Kathryn, but he never impressed me. Careless, cocky—the worst. Owen Paris must be heartbroken."

I imagined he was. I sent my old captain a message, saying how sorry I was to hear about his troubles, and I received a kind note back. But I couldn't help feeling sorry for young Tom, who had always struck me as a young man who was floundering, and never felt quite good enough. This was a tragic end to his career, before it had even had a chance to start. I could only hope that this was not the start of a downward spiral for him, and that he found his way somehow.

I, meanwhile, was still considering my next move. I had found a way to work on the *Billings*, and I had earned the respect of my team, and of many of my direct colleagues. But I was never going to earn Ward's favor. and he was never going to earn my respect. I was never going to be one of his cronies and I didn't want to be. There was a wider universe out there, as my correspondence with Tuvok reminded me—but I did feel constantly on high alert, ready for the next putdown, or the next sharp word.

This made my trips back to Earth even more blissful. And one of these occasions, during my fourth year serving on the *Billings,* just after I'd been promoted to full commander, changed my life. I was visiting Phoebe and Yianem and their tribe, out in Portland, and they invited a friend of Yianem's over for dinner. "It's a sad story," Phoebe said, as we stood together in the kitchen, she busy dressing the salad and me drinking wine. "His wife was killed in a shuttle accident on Mars eighteen months ago. He's only really started to come out again. He's still very fragile. We just want him to have some cheerful evenings."

Well, I was happy to switch on my charm, such as it is, and I'm pleased to report that their friend, a handsome man of about my age named Mark Johnson, was not immune. He certainly laughed a great deal that evening, more so as my stories about my appalling captain became less and less discreet and more and more pointed. (It did me a world of good to talk about Ward like that too: all of a sudden, he felt ridiculous, rather than powerful.) While Phoebe and Yianem were busy in the kitchen organizing dessert, Mark said, "Are you back on Earth for a while yet, Kathryn?"

"A couple of months."

"That's good. Are you around Portland for most of that time?"

"A week or so. Then I'll visit my mother near Bloomington for a while. I don't intend to travel much, though. Just take it easy."

"And what does 'take it easy' mean to Kathryn Janeway? From what your sister says, I imagine you're planning to climb Everest, or hike across Mongolia—"

I laughed. "Not this time! I was thinking of getting a dog."

"A *dog*?"

I looked at him in alarm. "Do you not like dogs?" I don't trust people who don't like dogs.

"I've... I've never owned a dog. Aren't they a lot of hard work? Don't they need a lot of walking?"

"That's the general idea," I said.

"You're going to spend your leave walking the dog?"

"Precisely that. Sounds blissful, doesn't it?"

He smiled at me. "Depends on the company, I'd say."

"You can't go wrong with a dog, Mark."

"And is the dog sufficient for your purposes, company-wise?"

"What are you asking, exactly?"

"I'm asking whether you'd like some company. When you go and walk your dog."

"Depends on the company," I said, with a smile.

"How about mine?" he said.

"Then the answer's yes."

After that night, we saw a great deal of each other. He helped me choose my new dog—a very affectionate Irish setter named Mollie, whom I'd seen listed in a pound on Taris Seti IV (she was the runt of the litter, but I sensed a little fighter there, and I'd found a fine kennel for her for when I was away). As promised, he joined me on our walks. I was embarrassed at first—I'd come all this way to see my sister and her family—but she and her wife were warmly encouraging. "I've never seen you so serious about someone since the Academy, Kate," Phoebe said. "I think we all want to know where this is heading."

"Oh, Phoebe! We've only met half a dozen times!"

I saw my sister and her wife exchange knowing looks. Is there anything more annoying to a single person than their partnered family and friends? Always so very smug about the whole business, always in a hurry to pair you off! It was hardly as if I'd been living as a nun. I'd had various dalliances during my time on both the *Al-Batani* and the *Billings* (no, I won't say who). It was true, though, that this was the most serious relationship since my near-miss at the Academy.

"He's very nice though," said Phoebe.

"If he wasn't nice," I said, "I wouldn't be spending time with him."

Yianem said, "Remember to be gentle with him, Kathryn, please. He... he's had a bad time."

I hastened to reassure her. "Oh, of course I'll be gentle! That's all either of us want. A little tender loving care."

Our walks together became a daily fixture, Mollie bounding between us. And the more we walked, the more we opened our hearts to each other. I talked about the trials of serving on the *Billings*; how much my confidence had been knocked by that first year; how hard I'd worked to earn the trust of my colleagues and to make a few friends. He talked about his wife. How terrible a blow it had been; how sudden (I knew how that might feel); how he'd thought he would never get through some of the long and empty days. "I think because she was away from home when she died, when the shuttle went down," he said. "I kept expecting her to walk back through the door, complaining about missed flight connections or something... Of course, she never did."

He had moved house in the end. Tried to draw a line underneath those years. "They had been so happy—we had been so happy. But eventually you have to admit that they're finished. That you have to move on."

"Like my mother," I said. "Finding a new way to live. I think it's about the bravest thing I have ever seen."

"Brave!" He shook his head. "Surely what you do is brave!"

"What do you mean?"

"Fight Cardassians—"

"You make it sound like I'm in single combat!"

"I wouldn't put it past you, Kate!"

I laughed. Mark always made me laugh. "Well, it's all a lot less exciting than people think. Mostly I'm on board ship, tracking transmissions, analyzing data—"

"Ah, you're spoiling the magic!"

I looked into his eyes. "I hope not."

We stood there for a moment, looking steadily at each other, and then we both moved forward, and shared a kiss. "I think you're something special, Kathryn Janeway," he said.

"I second that emotion, Mark Johnson," I replied.

Later that night, when I quietly slipped back into my sister's house, Mollie asleep in my arms, Phoebe was sitting up waiting for me. She took one look at me, and said, "It's serious, then."

My head was spinning; my heart was dancing. I felt like a girl again. "Phoebe," I said, "I really think it is."

✦

I had another two weeks of leave, and I did spend most of it with Mark. (My mother was not in the least put out that I didn't come home: it seemed that Phoebe had let her know what was going on.) On the last day before I was due to head back, we went out into the woods together, and walked arm in arm under the huge trees.

"You know," he said, "I was going to suggest we go somewhere for this last day. Rome, or Paris... But then I realized I just wanted to be here."

I smiled. I'd had the same thought.

And then he said, "Kate, you do realize, don't you, that I want to marry you?"

I stopped dead in my tracks. Mollie was snuffling around my boots. "I beg your pardon?"

He smiled at me. "You must have worked that out by now!"

"Mark, we've known each other... What? Two months? Not even that! Seven weeks!"

"Long enough for me to know."

"But... You don't mean it, do you? Surely you don't mean it."

He took my hand. "Kate," he said, "I mean it absolutely. I think you're great. I haven't laughed this much... Well, you've made me feel happy again."

I felt a deep wave of affection toward him. "Oh, Mark, I'm so glad about that! But *marriage*?"

"Listen," he said. "Losing Lisa..." For a moment, his face took on a haunted look. He went on, "It brought home to me how fragile life is. How easily we can lose everything. And that if another chance comes our way, we should have the good sense to seize it. I mean it, Kate. I want to marry you."

For a moment, I wavered. He really did make me feel so special. He made me feel loved. But I was leaving on the *Billings* the next morning. "Oh, Mark, it's much too soon!"

He lifted my hand to kiss it. "All right," he said, and began to laugh. "I'm hardly going to force you, am I?"

"Can we still see each other?"

"When you're back home, you mean?"

"There is that," I admitted. "Please?"

"Oh, Kate," he said. "I'll be waiting at the docking bay to welcome you home."

So that's where we left it, for the moment. Agreeing to see each other whenever I was home... And I found that whenever I was with him, that's how it felt—like coming home. The *Billings* was close to Earth during this period, and so we saw a fair amount of each other. We found, yet again, that what made us most happy was simply being together. Lots of long walks, with Mollie, of course, but also just time at home. He was a great cook (I am not), and he would make me stop and take time away from messages and reports (once you reach a certain level at Starfleet, you're never totally on leave). Left to my own devices, I would lose myself completely in my work. But Mark made me look up from my desk, made me relax and enjoy the world around us. And did I mention how handsome he was?

I thought long and hard about his offer of marriage. I was trying to see a way through, but I couldn't yet. I didn't want to be an absentee wife—he had lost one wife already, lost the home they had together. And I guess, too, that I had been frightened by my experience with my former lover. In my mind, perhaps, I had conflated an offer of marriage with the need to give up some essential part of myself. A year after his first proposal, tucked up at home with my big silly dog snoozing between us, he asked again, "Is it still too soon, Kate?"

"It's still too soon, Mark."

"That's okay," he said. "I'm still prepared to wait."

Further discussion was interrupted as a message arrived for me.

"Damn," I said. "The kennels have cancelled—"

Mark sighed. "I'm even prepared," he said, "to take care of your dog."

And he did take very good care of my dog.

CHAPTER SEVEN
IN THE CAPTAIN'S SEAT—2371

EACH TIME THAT I SAID GOODBYE TO MARK (AND MOLLIE) WAS A WRENCH. Whenever I came home, we fell so easily back into step with each other. We picked up conversations again as if one of us had only been away for five minutes. We liked to do the same things. We liked to spend time with friends and family. We liked to sit in front of the fire, reading, sometimes sharing some piece of information that we knew the other would find interesting. We liked to be outdoors (his work, as an industrial designer, kept him at the drawing board; mine, of course, often kept me from the outdoors completely). And Mollie, of course, was growing and needed her exercise. We were often out together for hours, the three of us, walking through the woods or along the coast, Mollie running ahead. It was good just to be together. If this all sounds very sedate—I guess it was. My job brought enough in the way of adrenalin rushes. Home life I wanted to be steady and reliable.

We were fortunate that we both got on with each other's friends, and we liked each other's family members. Mark loved my nieces: partly for Yianem's sake (their friendship went back a long way) and partly because he clearly liked children. He was good with kids too. He had a great deal of patience (he needed that, given my stubborn streak). But I often wondered why he was not a father already. I wouldn't have minded if kids had been part of the package. One evening, back at his home in

Portland, curled up before the fire with mugs of hot chocolate (with a good dash of brandy), and some Debussy whirling gently around us, I decided to ask. It's one of those conversations that most partners have to have at some point. I knew how serious he was.

"Mark," I said. "You don't have to answer this if you don't want to, but was there a reason that you and Lisa didn't have children?"

He looked at me in surprise, and with a little shock. I didn't very often bring up Lisa—that was his prerogative—although I by no means minded if he wanted to talk about her. I never felt that I was in competition with a dead woman. Mark had loved her immensely, that was clear from the way he talked about her, and they had been very happy. She was a huge part of him, a part that I would never want to change or deny. And his relationship with Lisa proved to me how deeply and carefully he loved.

"That's an interesting question, Kate."

His face was turning sad. I reached over to take his hand. "Hey," I said. "I don't want to upset you. We don't have to talk about this."

"It's okay," he said. "No, it's a fair question. It's just… another one of those regrets. I guess we thought there would always be time. We were busy; we were enjoying life. We'd only been married three years, you know."

I nodded. Another late starter.

"We knew it would be a huge commitment, a huge change," he said. "We'd both seen what happened when friends had children. You have to hunker down, don't you? Focus on building a home."

I had observed this too, with my childhood friends. Knowing this was something of a weight on my mind: How did I square that with my desire to be on board ship? With my desire to be a captain? How would I be able to make this work: ship life and home life? Would I want to be away so much, like Dad had been? In my heart I knew I couldn't give up ship life. But was it fair to ask this of Mark, who had lost one home already? I started to feel very sad that I couldn't square this circle.

"But it just never happened?" I said.

"Pretty much. I guess we thought, let's store up a little more time together as just the two of us before we brought someone else into the mix. But we were nearly there. I guess there would have been a baby within eighteen months."

My heart went out to him. This was another part of his future that had been lost: a child of his and Lisa's that could only ever now remain imagined. I reached out to hold him and he accepted my embrace. We sat like that for a while, simply being together. Talking about this had made him sad, but I wasn't sorry that I had asked. I understood him better now.

"Do you not want children, Kate?"

I sighed. "I like the *idea*... You know how I love the nieces."

"Well, they're very lovable. But?"

"But it doesn't seem very practical, does it?" I said. "It's like you said, you have to hunker down. Turn inward. Build... I don't know, a nest, or something!"

"That's Phoebe and Yia, isn't it? Two momma birds running around, and three chicks, beaks upturned and squawking!"

I laughed. "That's exactly it!"

"And you don't want to build a nest, Kate?"

"I want to be a starship captain." I flushed. I sounded like a kid, saying what job they wanted when they grew up, blurting out a dream. But I was a Starfleet commander, chief science officer on a large ship, overseeing a big team. It wasn't a dream. It was within my grasp. "And I guess I struggle to see how I can do both."

He thought about that for a while. "Your father did it," he said.

"He did, didn't he." I looked Mark straight in the eye. "He also died young."

"I understand," he said. "But, you know, Kate—life is risk—"

"You need to visit my workplace, mister! Far too many Cardassians, these days!"

"But there's a treaty now, isn't there? I thought we were at peace."

And we were, more or less. Some rumbles on the border, and some very unhappy colonists.

"Anyway," he said, "I don't mean that kind of risk. I mean, risking connection. Risking what being with someone might mean. You know, don't you, that I'm ready to take that risk again."

After all he had lost. "Oh, Mark..."

He smiled at me. "I'm ready to wait, you know. And, Kate, one more word on this—if I've learned anything over the years, it's that we shouldn't meet trouble halfway. Life has a way of taking us by surprise, and we should take our chances of happiness while we can."

✦

Going back to the *Billings* that time was very hard. My conversation with Mark filled my mind, as if he had offered a glimpse to me of how I might have it all; how there needn't be this divide between ship life and home. He was right about Dad: he had kept on within Starfleet, and he would have carried on indefinitely—if it hadn't been for the Cardassians. I guess that this was what had always held me back: the thought that I might at any moment be called to action, and that this was not fair to someone outside of Starfleet. I knew how hard Dad's death had hit us all. I realized now that at the back of my mind I had always assumed that there was going to be open war with the Cardassians, and that when that happened, I would have duties to perform. But Mark was right: the treaty with the Cardassians had been signed, and the Demilitarized Zone established, and, at that time, it really did seem that war was no longer going to happen. Perhaps it really would be possible for me to combine my two loves.

Yes, I was most certainly in love with Mark, and it was like nothing I had ever experienced before. My affair at the Academy, my only other comparator, had been a children's game in comparison to this: two people who were barely adults playing at having a serious relationship. As for the affairs I'd had since, all of which had been with other officers—well, they had most certainly been a lot of fun, good company and great sex, but they had not been intended by any of the participants to be anything more than brief encounters while between postings. Being with Mark was nothing like that. With Mark, I had felt straight away that I was coming home. We had skipped the whole dating period completely; we had never felt the need to dress up and go out or spend time away in exotic and romantic locations. It was as if we didn't need these set dressings: we got the hang of each other very quickly. We were happy puttering around his home or my home; walking Mollie; reading and listening to music; cooking, talking, or even just being together. We were happy looking inward.

When I was back on the *Billings*, but still in near-Earth orbit, we spoke again briefly via the comm. "I've been thinking a lot about our conversation," I said.

"Have you changed you mind? About my offer, I mean."

"Not yet... I guess, I'm trying to see how we can make it work. When I'm on board ship so much. Away so much..."

"If that's all that's stopping you, Kate, then let's think about it. Because I don't think it needs to. What we have—it's great. It already works. We can keep on making it work. We're grown-ups." He smiled. *"Aren't you Starfleet command types meant to be tactical geniuses?"*

"We have our moments."

"Then, like the song says—we can work it out." I heard a whining noise in the background. Mollie jumped up into view and barked. Mark sighed. *"You'll have to excuse me. Your damn dog needs walking."*

✦

The treaty with the Cardassians was in place, but during the following year we were seeing how fragile it might prove to be. During this year, a new complication arose which threatened the hard-won peace with the Cardassians, and which certainly tried the consciences of everyone in Starfleet. There were numerous Federation worlds that now found themselves within the new Demilitarized Zone. Other worlds found that, with the new border that the treaty established, their worlds were suddenly transferred to Cardassian jurisdiction. Naturally, these people did not want to become subjects of the Cardassian Union. Everyone was offered the chance of resettlement—and the resources were put there to assist them— but who willingly abandons their home? How would I have felt, if I had been told that our old farm was now the property of the Cardassians, and that I could either live with it, or move on? I had a great deal of sympathy with their plight, but there were broader concerns, and a larger peace to maintain. When colonists on these worlds began to arm themselves, my sympathies lessened considerably. Terrorism is never the answer, and, ultimately, that's what the Maquis were. Suddenly, that peace we had all expected had become more precarious.

It's remarkable, looking back, to realize how many Starfleet personnel went over to the Maquis. Some went out of principle—this was why Chakotay joined them, and I respect that decision, although I do not agree with it. But some were just looking for adventure, a chance to live outside the confines of the Federation. Laurie Fitz informed me that Owen Paris's son, Tom, had gone out there. I guess I wasn't surprised—Tom's decisions now seemed to be entirely guided by what would most cause embarrassment for his father—and my heart went out to Owen. All of this, as well as my conversation with Mark, whirled around my head. What was my duty? Was there anything that I could contribute to this? I had believed that I had a duty to stay in Starfleet as long as war was coming, and although war seemed no longer imminent, the peace was still not secure. The next few years would surely see me back in combat, even if this time I was fighting people who had once been colleagues.

Life on the *Billings* had not improved. After a couple of months back on board, playing Ward's pointless games, I began to give serious consideration to resigning my commission. I was missing Mark terribly, and I was starting to think I had made a bad decision coming back. I felt that I was not being reasonable asking him to wait. I knew he wanted to marry me, and I knew he wanted children. He had lost so much when Lisa died, and I felt that maybe this delay wasn't fair on him. I felt as if I should make a decision, either way. I should commit, or I should let him move on. Increasingly, however, I was struggling to think of how I could be happy without him, and I was struggling to see how I could combine this with fighting the Maquis. This wasn't a decision to take lightly, so I turned to my mentor for advice.

Parvati Pandey was semiretired now, but was still teaching her Ethics of Command classes at the Academy. She smiled when she saw my face.

"Kathryn. Always good to see you. How's life on the Billings*?"*

"That's part of what I want to talk to you about."

"I think I can guess. Ward being his usual self?"

"It does baffle me, Parvati, how he's gotten this far."

"I've seen him in action. He knows how to flatter people."

I guess it was indiscreet of an admiral to talk this way to a commander about her captain, but I've observed that as people move closer to retirement, they start to care less and less about workplace diplomacy. I suppose they're halfway out of the game, and this is their last chance to shape how it's played after their departure. These days I sometimes find myself doing the same.

"I never did quite work out how to flatter people."

"Oh, you have your own charms, Kathryn. I've watched senior officers fall over themselves to raise a smile from you. But you said in your message that you wanted some advice?"

I took a deep breath. "I'm thinking of resigning my commission."

She looked at me in horror. *"What? Kathryn! That's a terrible idea!"*

I laughed. "Well, I guess I don't need to force you to tell me your opinion!"

"Why on Earth would you do that? Not over Neil Ward, surely!"

"No, no, it's not just that, although—damn the man, he sure does make life miserable! It infuriates me! It doesn't have to be this way! It shouldn't be this way!"

"It's not how you'd run your ship?"

"Damned right."

"So at least you've learned something from him."

"I guess…"

"And you've made sure you've got command opportunities?"

"Yes, night-shift command, all the usual boxes checked."

"So tell me the whole story."

I explained about Mark; how much I missed him and wanted to be with him. How he wanted me to marry him. How I felt I was being unfair to make him wait.

"Is he asking you to resign, Kate? To choose between him and your commission?"

"What? No! Quite the opposite—"

"I'm glad to hear that."

"I made that mistake before, Parvati. Marriage isn't sacrificing yourself, is it? It's… about each of you letting the other flourish."

"But you don't think that's possible?"

"I think it's hard."

"You never struck me as someone who would back away from a challenge. Do you think you can flourish outside of Starfleet?"

I thought about that. Haltingly, I said, "Starfleet isn't everything."

"I think it is for you, Kate. All right. Let's say you leave. What would you do instead?"

"Maybe... teach at the Academy?"

"You could, I guess... But what would you do? I guess Boothby's always in need of an extra pair of hands."

She was right, and I knew it already. What would I teach? I couldn't teach her class. I hadn't yet commanded a ship. I'd be teaching freshman science, and I'd always be looking up to the stars and wondering what kind of captain I would have been.

"I'm doubting myself, Parvati. I'm doubting that I can do it all, or, maybe, doubting I can do it all as well as I would want to."

"You don't know that," said my wise mentor, *"until you've tried."*

That was true.

"Then my advice, Kathryn, is to seize the day."

I didn't mention this conversation with Pandey to Mark. I felt oddly embarrassed, as if I'd been doing something clandestine. I simply knew that he would be upset that I was thinking of leaving Starfleet on his account. Next time we talked, it was about our usual, comfortable topics: the exploits of the redoubtable Mollie; our families and our friends; about what we planned to do next time I was back. In the meantime, my work with my team kept me busy, but I felt increasingly detached, as if I was halfway out of the door. I just didn't know where that door was leading yet... One interesting effect of this was that the captain seemed to sense that I had moved on in some way and, as a result, our working relationship was the best it was throughout the whole time I was on board ship. Well, he did already have my replacement lined up, didn't he?

About six weeks after my conversation with Pandey, she contacted me again, on a secure channel. *"Time to talk, Kathryn."*

"Go ahead."

"You have a ship—if you still want one."

Her words took a moment to sink in, and then I felt myself begin to tremble. Calmly, I said, "I'm listening, Admiral."

"It's called Voyager."

What a name! A name to make the heart soar!

"Intrepid class, brand new, just about to leave Utopia Planitia for McKinley Station. It's got everything, Kathryn—bioneural circuitry, variable

geometry warp nacelles... It's even got a mission. What it doesn't have yet is a captain."

I didn't want to get ahead of myself. "What's the mission?"

"A trip out to the Badlands. We've got a few simple missions in the area—perfect for a new captain. They all have one thing in common though."

"Maquis," I said, grimly.

"Tracking one ship in particular—the Val Jean.*"*

Named for the hero of *Les Misérables*, an underdog unfairly hounded by the authorities. That was revealing, to say the least.

"It's captained by a former Starfleet officer—a man named Chakotay. We want it infiltrated, and ideally stopped. Our plan is to put an undercover on board."

"You got someone in mind?"

"An old friend of yours—Tuvok. He's already out in the DMZ."

An old friend indeed. I was wondering why I hadn't heard from him for a while. He'd been undergoing briefing and training, presumably, and now his mission was underway.

"What do you say, Kathryn?"

"You mean—"

"The ship's yours if you want it. If you still want to be a captain, that is." She smiled at me. *"Or have you decided to quit after all?"*

Well, I could see now how ridiculous that idea had been. Pandey had known too, and I imagine Mark would have known, if I'd broached the subject with him. The little girl inside me—the one who had always wanted to fly—was leaping for joy.

"Admiral," I said, "it would be my privilege."

"Congratulations, Captain Janeway." She smiled. *"I'm so pleased for you, Kathryn. You've earned this. Now—do you want to tell your captain, or shall I?"*

"Oh, I'll tell him," I breathed. But the conversation that I wanted to have right now was with Mark.

✦

It took most of the morning to persuade Ward to fit me into his hectic schedule. I guess he thought I wanted to complain about something or other. Eventually, I finally tracked him down to his ready room. He didn't offer me a seat, so I stood to attention by the door.

"What is it, Janeway?"

"I've been offered a new post, sir," I said.

"Oh yes? What's the ship?"

"The *U.S.S. Voyager*."

"I haven't heard of that one," he said. As ever, he was looking at his companel, rather than directly at me. I was glad I wasn't going to have to put up with this nonsense for much longer.

"It's new, sir. Just out of the shipyard. *Intrepid* class."

"Very nice. You always land on your feet, Janeway, don't you? I wish I had that… knack. Who's the lucky captain?"

"I beg your pardon, sir?"

"Who are you going to be serving under?"

He was making this extremely easy for me. I smiled. "The captain? That'll be me, sir."

That got his attention. I saw his hands quickly flex into fists, and then relax again. He looked up at me. "You're going to be a captain?"

"It was always the plan."

"Of the *Voyager*?"

"That's the name of the ship."

"A brand-new, state-of-the-art starship, and you're going straight in as captain."

"That's correct."

He sat back in his seat, lost for words. For a man who liked to flatter his immediate colleagues and his superiors, he had not been bright enough to remember that sometimes juniors get promoted. We were equals now, and my first captaincy was a significant step up from his. I saw it cross his mind that he might, one day, find himself saluting me. I was watching some of his house of cards tumble, and I'm not ashamed to say that it was quite a pleasant sight.

"With your permission, I'll take a shuttle to Starbase 39. I can travel on from there to Mars. *Voyager* is waiting for me there. I've checked the duty rosters, and Lieutenant Crossman is available to pilot the shuttle to the starbase and bring it back again. I'll be off the ship within twelve hours."

I saw him starting to come up with some reason to disagree, and quickly added, "Unless there's any reason my expertise is required any longer?"

"I suppose that's acceptable..." He collected himself. "Well," he said. "I guess that'll be all—Kathryn."

"I guess so." We looked at each other coldly. "I'm sorry we couldn't get this to work, Neil. Perhaps we can both learn something from this."

✦

On board the shuttle, I sent a message to Mark. His face appeared on-screen, rumpled and sleepy. "Hell," I said. "What time is it there?"

He peered at the chronometer. *"There's a four in that number. That can't be right. That's not a real time."*

"I'm so sorry!"

I watched him start to focus on me. *"Is everything all right, Kate?"*

"I have some news," I said.

"Oh yes. You know, I have some too."

We gazed at each other.

"You go first," he said.

"I've been offered the captaincy of a ship," I said. "The *Voyager*. I'm on my way there now."

Bless his heart, his face lit up in sheer delight. He was happy for me. *"Oh, Kate! I'm so glad! After all your hard work! Sweetheart, I am so proud of you!"*

"The bad news is… We have our first mission. It's not a long trip, but it's going to be risky. I can't say more."

He nodded his understanding. Good man. There would be more of this lack of detail in our future, I suspected.

"What's your news, Mark?"

He looked sheepish. *"It's not news, not really. You know, I think it can wait…"*

"No, tell me! I've no idea when I'll get a chance to speak again—I've got a crew to get together, and a mission to get underway!"

"I feel bad now," he said. *"The last thing I want to do is steal your thunder…"*

"You can't. I promise. Go on."

"It's just that… Last week was the anniversary of me proposing for the first time, and I thought, well, third time lucky… And I was away for work, and I kind of bought a ring…"

He reached into his pocket and brought it out. Even at this distance I could see it was one *hell* of a ring… I put my head in my hands. "Oh, Mark! I'm just about to go away!"

"Look, Kate," he said quickly. *"It doesn't matter. I know what your being in Starfleet means. We've been living that life for nearly two years now—and it's a good life! I miss you, and I want to be with you—of course I do!—but while you're away I fiddle about, and I look forward to the times when you're back with me. I want to be your home, Kate, whenever you come home. Why would I want anything else?"*

I was beginning to waver. What had Parvati said? *Seize the day.* But was it fair to him?

"Mark," I said, my voice thick, "I love you, I truly do—"

"Uh-oh…" he said.

"I don't want to be the absentee wife. It's not fair on you, not after Lisa—"

His expression changed, as if something had suddenly become clear to him. *"Oh, Kate—is that's what's been on your mind? Sweetheart, you're not Lisa! You're Kathryn Janeway! That's whom I'm asking to marry me. Because she's brilliant and brave and the most incredible woman, and because even when she's not at home with me, she's changed my life so much for the better that waiting for her to come home is all I want to do. We can make it work, Kate—we already have, for two years! You can have everything you want, you know,"* he said. *"There's no reason why not. You of all people, Kathryn Janeway, can have everything. Let's give it a go."*

What can I say? He was so good, so kind, and I didn't ever want to be without him. He lifted up the ring. *"We'll make this work, Kate. Whatever it takes—we'll make this work."*

I held out my hand, and he mimicked setting the ring in place. I held up my hand and pretended to admire it. *"Hot damn!"* Mark yelled. *"I did it! The captain said yes!"*

In the background, I heard barking. We'd woken Mollie.

"Just so we're clear on one thing, Mark—love me, love my dog."

"Ain't that the truth," he muttered.

I believed then—and I still believe—that we would have made a success of things. If only life hadn't got in the way. We blew kisses and said goodbye. I sent quick messages to Mom and Phoebe, saying: *Here's my news—there's quite a lot of it.* Then I got back to work. As I drew ever closer to my new ship, I realized how happy I felt. All the burden and misery of being on the *Billings* had gone away. I was taking charge of my life once again. I had never had it so good.

✦

Now was my chance to assemble the team I had always wanted. Many of the junior staff were already in place, and a first officer had been assigned to me—John Cavit, who had been a couple of years behind me at the Academy. While we had never served together, we had many mutual friends and colleagues, and I knew he was a fine officer: dependable, with an easy manner but excellent discipline. We quickly established a rapport, and his loss is a source of great grief to me. I brought a couple of people over with me from the *Billings*, not just science officers, but a couple of others who had heard on the grapevine about my new command and wanted to serve under someone else. I was happy to offer them a lifeboat. Tuvok was already in place as my chief of security, and I sent a message to my old friend from the *Al-Batani*, Laurie Fitzgerald, asking him if he was ready to leave the Caldik Prime medical facility, and come with me. As luck would have it (or so I thought at the time), Fitz was on Earth. He got back to me within twelve hours, saying his transfer request had been put through, and he was already heading out to McKinley.

"It'll be good to have the old team together again, Kate," he said. "Owen Paris will be delighted—he's been having a bad time over Tom, and he could do with hearing some good news."

Ah, yes, the problem of Tom Paris. His career with the Maquis had been about as successful as his time in Starfleet. He had been with them for no more than a few weeks before being captured. The last I'd heard of him he had been sent to a penal colony in New Zealand for eighteen months. My heart went out to my old captain, but I couldn't help still feeling sorry for Tom. All of that promise, and he had been reduced to this. It was a damn waste. Surely there was still potential there? He had been, by all accounts, a fine pilot. My mind started working overtime. Perhaps he might come in useful. He had knowledge of the Badlands, knowledge of the Maquis, he could certainly fly a ship... I sent a message off to Starfleet Command, asking about a special assignment. Well, if you don't ask, you don't get. I knew I'd have a hard time selling this to Fitz, though. He loved the old man, as he called Owen Paris, but had very little time for his son.

My crew was coming together, and I was approaching McKinley Station, where my new ship was waiting for me. I was already fielding a vastly increased number of communications—plus messages were starting to flood in from family and friends, delighted at all my news. Phoebe had said, *"Damn, Kate—a ship and a fiancé in one day?! This time you've stolen your own thunder!"* My mother said, *"I am so proud of you, Katy. Dad's heart would be bursting for joy. And Mark is a treasure. I'm so glad. You're going to be so happy. Mark deserves it, you deserve it."* My dear family. They said everything I needed to hear, as I embarked on this new stage of my life. There was a little parcel waiting for me too; a present from Mark, beautifully wrapped. When I opened it, I found a fine copy of Dante's *The Divine Comedy*. There was a note from Mark, which said: *For my Beatrice—my love, my redemption, may we share a long life's journey.*

Just as I was arriving at McKinley, I received news that the Maquis ship on which Tuvok was undercover, the *Val Jean*, had gone missing in the Badlands. That accelerated our plans somewhat: there would be no time to take a day to catch up with Mark and my family and celebrate our news. A huge disappointment, but this was the way it had to be. Everything was coming at me all at once (to top it all, it turned out the damn dog was pregnant...). I took the time, however, to speak to Tuvok's wife, T'Pel, whom I had met on several occasions. This was not an easy conversation: I could not give her details of his mission, but of course she understood that he was in considerable danger. I assured her that I was going to do everything within my power to bring him home again, safely. I was his captain now. I had a duty of care, not just to my crew, but to their families. I kept that promise to T'Pel—even if it took a lot longer than any of us had anticipated, and led me to make decisions I had not expected.

At last I arrived at McKinley, and I beamed over to take command of my beautiful new ship. I was more than ready to fall in love, and *Voyager* did not displease. I was met on board by my old Academy instructor (and source of many a nightmare) Vice Admiral Theoderich Patterson, and he promptly set about quizzing me. I must have passed the test, since I got a bear hug and warm congratulations, and we went on a tour of my new ship. Fifteen decks, upper limit of warp 9.975, and of course the latest in bioneural circuitry: a brand-new captain, and I had been entrusted with a brand-new ship. I was planning to take good care of her. I caught up with Fitz in sickbay (he was talking about the new Emergency Medical Holographic program, which I hadn't had a chance to look at yet) and broke the news that we had an extra crew member joining us, and who it was. Fitz was not pleased.

"Tom Paris is a liability," he said. "On your own head be it, Kate."

Patterson had sent me a message to say that my unusual personnel request had been approved, and that I could proceed to New Zealand to speak to my man. I remember distinctly the moment I set eyes again on Thomas Eugene Paris. I hadn't seen him since my days serving under his father on the *Al-Batani*, when he had been something of a sullen teenager, but I still recalled that twelve-year-old boy that I'd taken to the holodeck. It was a tragedy to see all the youthful effervescence turned into bitter resentment. At the back of my mind, I was hoping that this mission might be something of a second chance for Tom; I couldn't have guessed to what extent. It wasn't going to be an easy ride for him. Fitz was not prepared to cut him any slack, and my XO, Cavit, had serious reservations about him too.

"People think he's getting an easy ride because you knew his father, Captain," Cavit admitted.

"Nobody on my ship will get an easy ride, Commander," I said. "Tom Paris will have to earn his keep. But I think he can, and I think he will."

Just before we were ready to go, I fielded a touching request from the mother of one of my new ensigns.

"Mrs. Kim," I said, "I am so sorry—but we are minutes away from setting out for Deep Space 9. I'm afraid Harry will have to manage for a little while without his clarinet."

With the news of the disappearance of the *Val Jean*, we were in such a hurry. I was so worried about Tuvok, and eager to get underway. How I wish now I had said yes.

✦

At Deep Space 9, I had time to exchange intelligence reports with the chief of station security, Odo, and spoke briefly to Commander Sisko about Maquis activity in the area. I was startled to learn that his former senior officer, Cal Hudson, had defected to the Maquis. Bearing in mind what I now knew about the crew of the *Val Jean* and its captain, Chakotay, I was starting to think that the Maquis was almost entirely run by former Starfleet officers. With the final members of the crew gathered, we proceeded toward the Badlands, and I began to ease myself into command. The Paris situation needed monitoring; otherwise I was content that my crew were well able for the mission assigned to us.

And then everything changed.

Has ever a captain had a first week on the job like mine? I was prepared for action so close to the border, whether it came from dealing with belligerent Maquis, treacherous Cardassians, or furious plasma storms. I was not prepared to be flung seventy thousand light-years away from home at the whim of an ancient and dying alien that was trying to make amends for ruining the world of a childlike species. Nor was I prepared to make enemies so quickly with the local Kazon warlords. And I was most certainly not prepared for Neelix, although I was damned grateful. Most of all, I had not been prepared to lose so many good people, so quickly. My first officer. My chief engineer. And, hell, my chief medical officer, Laurie Fitz, my dear old friend, who had come over specially to *Voyager*, because I had asked him. How I regretted that now; how I wished beyond measure that he was safe back on Caldik Prime. That was the hardest of all, and there were so many, many others, some of whom I had not even had a chance to meet properly, to hold even more than the briefest of conversations with…

But in the rush and chaos of the moment, I had to put this aside to be able to ensure the safety of my ship and crew, to work out what was happening, and to try to put a stop to it. In the end, it came down to listening to an ancient dying alien as he came to understand that he had to let his children go; that he had to accept that there was an end to all things, and that change and growth and evolution might be painful, but they are for the best. The Caretaker had done his job: now it was for the Ocampa to make their way. They were ready for it: we could see that from the ones who had been struggling to get their elders to accept the changing reality. But it was going to be hard—and without our help, their move toward self-determination would have been stopped before it had the chance. The Kazon were waiting to move in and seize the array, whatever it might cost the Ocampa. And I couldn't let that happen.

Let me lay down once and for all my reasoning behind making this choice, since I know that many have disagreed with the one that I made that day. Perhaps it would help to remember how much, throughout my career, I had longed to make first contact with an alien species, not as observer, or even as senior officer, but as captain of my own ship. Now that I had, I could see that this encounter cut both ways. Meeting the Ocampa, we acquired responsibilities toward each other. Not the suffocating love of the Caretaker, but the responsibilities that every sentient being has toward each other. The Ocampa, even after the Caretaker sealed them away, had continued to change, to develop. Despite their short lifespan, only nine years, they led full lives. They were natural telepaths. They had a rich culture, and religious beliefs. They were their own, unique species. Allowing the Kazon access to them would have been a monstrous act. I knew what they were capable of; they had brutalized Kes. But it was more than that. The Kazon would do to them and their world what the Cardassians had done to Bajor. They would strip the planet for resources and enslave its people. The Ocampa would suffer every possible indignity that a species could suffer. I knew from what I had seen—and what my mother had seen through her work— what would happen. I could not allow that. I could not condemn a whole species so that the one hundred fifty members of *Voyager* could get home. I know that many on the ship—and many in the Alpha Quadrant, when at last I was able to speak to them—disagreed. Tuvok, at the time, warned me that this decision was even in violation of the Prime Directive, altering the balance of power in this region of space. But it was too late for that. We had been flung into the whole situation against our will; we were involved by others. We didn't involve ourselves. The Ocampa would not have survived without our helping hand. If I had done anything different, I might have brought *Voyager* home at once—but I would not have been any kind of Starfleet officer.

✦

The first night of our journey home, I sat in my ready room composing letters of condolence to the families of those crew members who had been lost. I had no idea how or when I would deliver them, but it was my duty, and I knew that I should write them now, as close to the event as I could. It was a grueling task, and I found myself writing letters about some whom I had barely spoken to. It had been my intention to meet each crew member one-to-one over the coming weeks. Now some of them were dead. I never got the chance, for example, to talk properly to my conn officer, Veronica Stadi. I looked up her record that night. Only out of the Academy three years. One of the best up-and-coming navigators around. I never got a chance to quiz her about the classic of Betazed poetry, *The Shared Heart*, on which she had written a short monograph. Instead, I had to write to her mother and father—Anissina and Gwendal—that their wonderful daughter was not coming home. I finished the letter and stopped. I was done. I was tired, and sad; I felt grief-stricken over Fitz, and I was missing Mark like hell. We were seventy thousand light-years from home, and all I could do was point the ship in the right direction, and hope.

Sometimes it's not as easy as clicking your heels together three times and saying, *"There's no place like home."*

I was captain at last, of a lost ship, battered and bruised, and in charge of a wounded and divided crew. Be careful what you wish for.

I gave up on my letters. I took down the book that Mark had given me as an engagement present and looked at the inscription: *For my Beatrice— my love, my redemption, may we share a long life's journey.* Beatrice, Dante's love. She died young. I turned to the start of *Inferno,* and I read:

Midway on life's journey,
I awoke to find myself in a dark wood,
I had wandered from the straight path…

CHAPTER EIGHT
SEEK OUT NEW LIFE—2371-2372

IN THAT FIRST WEEK, WE WERE REELING FROM THE EVENTS that had left us stranded, from the shock of the sudden deaths of so many of us. At the same time, we tried to fix some of the damage to our ship, though I think most of the crew barely had time or energy to take stock. It's the captain's job, however, to think ahead, and to consider above all the wellbeing of her crew. It seemed to me that some stability and certainty would help amid all the chaos. I know that my insistence on running *Voyager* so strictly as a Starfleet vessel has attracted criticism in some quarters: believe me, I've heard it all before, mainly from the ex-Maquis on board ship. I know that people think that this was rigidity—denial, even, a failure to come to terms with our changed circumstances. But it was crucial in those first few weeks. We all needed something upon which we could depend. The uniform, the formal relationships, and the protocols of Starfleet were the closest thing that we had to a shared culture or system of values. Many of the ex-Maquis had been in Starfleet—or, at least, the Academy—and knew how it functioned. Still, it was not an easy sell. They all had their reasons for leaving, or staying away in the first place.

Somehow, we pulled it off. Somehow, we persuaded everyone to pull together, under the shared banner of Starfleet and the Federation. None of this would have happened without the support that I got right away from

Chakotay. I thank my stars that he was the one captaining the *Val Jean*, a rare stroke of good fortune for me in those days. Consider the alternatives. I could have had a fanatic, someone who would never work with Starfleet under any circumstances. I could have had a mercenary, spending the next seven years watching my back in case he took the ship and decided to make his fortune in the Delta Quadrant. Instead, I had a man of principle: dare I say it, a Starfleet officer through and through. I relied upon Chakotay completely, and, even when we had disagreements, he never let me down. Without him, the former Maquis crew members would not have integrated so successfully—and no doubt I would have had a mutiny on my hands. Handling the ex-Maquis crew was difficult enough: B'Elanna Torres seemed to be fueled entirely by fury, and only the complexities of engineering seemed to come close to soothing her, giving her a challenge that worked her intelligence without causing frustration. Still, she was what I needed right now in engineering, and I could only hope that something over the coming months and years would give her a much-needed sense of stability. I came to rely on many other former Maquis during those years: Lieutenant Ayala for one; Chell, too, more or less, despite various problems. Maybe I should have let him loose in the mess hall sooner.

But there were other members of the ex-Maquis crew who left me uneasy—the Betazoid Lon Suder, for one. Having said that, his former colleagues didn't like or trust him either and for good reason. Suder murdered Frank Darwin, and for his sake, I wish that I had taken greater heed of their concerns sooner. It seems a terrible tragedy to me that Frank died at the hands of a member of the crew. But there was so much happening in those first days, and while I had anticipated discord, possibly even mutiny, I had not anticipated having someone with such antisocial tendencies on board. As we struggled to deal with the ramifications of these events, I found myself recalling a line from the start of Hawthorne's *The Scarlet Letter*:

> The founders of a new colony, whatever Utopia of human virtue and happiness they might originally project, have invariably recognized it among their earliest practical necessities to allot a portion of the virgin soil as a cemetery, and another portion as the site of a prison.

THE HISTORY OF THE CAPTAIN WHO WENT FURTHER THAN ANY HAD BEFORE

We were a new colony, in a way; a little collection of people striving to pull together in order to make our way and survive. It saddens me beyond belief that I so quickly found myself conducting a funeral for a murdered man and ordering another man's quarters to be converted into a holding cell. Suder came good in the end, finding some kind of peace and developing a sense of right and wrong. Of course, then your previous acts become difficult to live with. I think he was always, given the chance, going to sacrifice himself in some way, and so he did, and as a result we were able to retake our ship from the Kazon who had captured it. Lon Suder saved himself. But I wish I had been able to save Frank Darwin.

Then there was Seska. In one of my earliest conversations with Chakotay, and thinking of the defection of Cal Hudson, I said to him what I had noticed before: that the Maquis seemed to be almost entirely made up of Starfleet officers, whether undercover or renegade.

"Perhaps that's something that Starfleet should start considering, Kathryn," he said gently. "Ask a few questions about why so many are choosing to leave."

"Right now," I said, "I don't care. I don't care who has been undercover or Maquis as long as you all do your job."

I wonder if he recalled this conversation later. None of us expected Seska's betrayal, and the whole series of events was a terrible shock to Chakotay, who had trusted her and loved her. The revelation that she was not Bajoran, but an undercover Cardassian agent planted on the *Val Jean* was shock enough. But that in itself would not have been enough for me to expel her from the ship. Indeed, had she revealed her identity to us, and then gone on to prove herself, I would have invited her to join the crew in her own right. We all wanted to get home to the Alpha Quadrant, and I needed experienced people to crew the ship. But it seemed that treachery was too ingrained. Almost from the beginning she had been working against us, joining forces with the Kazon, ultimately taking a Kazon warlord as a lover, and having his child. I wonder often about that child, and the life it must have led.

Seska's betrayals threw a long shadow. Almost three years into our journey, Tuvok's holodeck simulation of a Maquis insurrection was activated, causing all kinds of unexpected strife and grievances to reemerge. And Seska, long dead, turned out nonetheless to be the cause, having found the simulation and reprogrammed it to cause maximum disruption. I will never understand why, faced with the choice between carrying this distant war into the Delta Quadrant, or working alongside us to bring us all back home, Seska chose the former. But Cardassian culture, at that time, was so pernicious, so harmful, that I guess it was always going to happen. Reflecting now upon these events, I see how they worked in my favor. Seska's treachery so shocked the ex-Maquis, that in many ways it drove them into my arms. There was an idealistic streak in the ex-Maquis crew members that was revolted by her actions, Chakotay and B'Elanna in particular. I knew that once I had won the hearts of Chakotay and B'Elanna, the rest of the former Maquis would follow. So it proved. But I wish we had known who and what Seska was before she betrayed us. We made a home for so many others: Maquis, holograms, even Borg. I wish we had been able to persuade a Cardassian to join us. But there it is—there's a utopian streak in every Starfleet captain. I wouldn't want to lose that—but I would wish, with all my heart, that it did not so often lead to a prison or a cemetery.

✦

As we began to find our feet, I tried to remember that I had been given a unique privilege as a Starfleet captain, to survey a part of space where nobody had gone before. Just the presence of Neelix and Kes on board ship required us to get to know two new species (and come to terms with their cuisine). I can't fault Neelix for his enthusiasm, however, and he was right to identify that someone needed to be keeping an eye on crew morale. Kes was a wonderful addition to our crew. She had a great calm about her, a real gentleness, that I found a great balm over the years that she spent on board. To look at her, an Ocampan, was a daily reminder that I had made the right choice stranding *Voyager* in the Delta Quadrant. Her people had been saved. And nobody was better suited to handle our Emergency Medical Hologram. Did any member of the crew come on as great a journey as our ineffable Doctor? In those very early days, it was difficult to think of him as anything other than a poor replacement for my dear Fitz, and quite an arrogant one at that. His bedside manner was terrible. But life—and personality—have a way of not just surviving but thriving. And our Doctor, so it was to turn out, had *plenty* of personality. I might have wished that Fitz had survived, but I could not wish the Doctor out of existence. His presence—his capacity for growth and change—made us truly wrestle with the nature of identity and selfhood. The Doctor, at every turn, exceeded the parameters of his programming. Our voyage created a new form of life.

And, it turned out, we had brought new life with us. I cannot begin to imagine the swirl of emotions that Samantha Wildman must have gone through, realizing that she was having a baby, and so far from family. In the case of Phoebe and Yianem, both of whom have been pregnant, I observed a great need for the familiar people and places. Much as I tried to make *Voyager* seem a haven for us all in the Delta Quadrant, it was, ultimately, not home. She missed her spouse, Greskrendtregk, too, very much. I knew how much I ached for Mark; to be the mother of a new child so far away from her spouse must have made the separation acutely painful for Samantha.

And then there were the practical realities of having a baby on board ship. I had not given much thought to how we might raise a child on board *Voyager*. It had never exactly been the plan! But you have to respond to the realities of the situation. I had a new mother, more in need of support than ever before, who was also a valued crew member in a situation where everyone was needed. We had to do all that we could to support her. It takes a village to raise a child, they say, and this was a ready-made village, one which now had another incentive to return home. We all wanted to see this little family reunited, so we all pitched in. With only one child, there was no need to establish a formal day-care center, although I would have done if it had been necessary. I see the provision of excellent childcare as a marker of civilization. I have had no personal need for it over the years, but I'm capable of empathy, and capable of seeing how crucial it is for others. Samantha was one of us: we loved her as a person, and valued her contribution as a xenobiologist, and we were behind her all the way.

I had no worries about medical care—for all his (how shall I put this?) *foibles*, our EMH was a faultless medical practitioner—and Kes, our new nurse, proved a wonderful support in the early days when Samantha was establishing a routine of work and caring for her daughter. But it was Neelix who proved to be the hero. Patient, good-humored, fun, and completely reliable—he was an ideal companion and playmate for that little girl. It was one of the quiet but constant joys of life on *Voyager*, watching Naomi Wildman grow and thrive. She was quick-witted, sensible, intelligent, curious, and a gift to our ship. I hope we did well by her. I think that we did. We never expected to find ourselves taking care of children (and there were more to come). I would like to think that we rose to the challenge. I would like to think that those children felt safe among us and able to flourish.

✦

What about myself? In those early days, and, in fact, throughout our voyage home, I struggled intensely with loneliness. I was the captain: I had to give a convincing show of being in command of myself and not on the verge of cracking, but sometimes it was hard. There was no way to contact a colleague or a mentor to sound out decisions, or confirm that I had done something right, or advise about what I might have done differently. Chakotay understood, I knew, and that quiet support got me through many tough times, but not only was I alone as captain, I was alone as Kathryn Janeway. The simple fact was that I missed Mark dreadfully. I played over and over again the messages from him that I had stored. I wrote to him twice a week. I told him how much I missed him, how much I wanted to be back walking in the woods with him and Mollie, enjoying the quiet calm of his solid presence beside me. I confided all my hopes and my fears, but ridiculously, I only shed tears once: three months into our voyage, I realized that Mollie must have had her pups, and that not only had I not been there, I hadn't even been conscious of the date. I felt dreadful, as if I'd let her down. It's strange what hits you. I haven't told anyone this before. I cried my heart out for a good hour. Then I washed my face, brushed my hair, pulled on my uniform, and went down to engineering to wrestle with a recalcitrant warp coil. Later, I challenged B'Elanna to a game of Velocity, and we both burned off some excess emotion. Turned out she was pretty damn good at the game too.

Throughout those early years, the thought of eventually being reunited with Mark was what kept me going. At the same time, I went through agonies thinking about what he must be experiencing. For him to have lost Lisa was terrible enough. For him to have taken the risk of loving someone again; pinning his hopes of a future on me (and children; I do believe we would have had children together someday) only to have this chance snatched away for a second time… It was truly, awfully painful; a double anguish of my own loss compounded by imagining what he must be going through. I had no way of knowing if we were assumed to have died in the Badlands; our own initial assumption had been that the *Val Jean* had been destroyed in the plasma storms. Would that same assumption be made about us? Even as we strove to come home by the quickest way possible, were others already grieving us, believing us dead, trying to carry on with their lives? The uncertainty was terrible. I wanted to be able to get back *now*, yesterday, a week ago! I wanted to click my heels together, say the magic words, and be whisked immediately home. Instead, we had to travel home the long way.

Chief among my concerns throughout the voyage was to find ways to shorten our journey, and I set this as one of engineering's main goals. I sure as hell didn't want to be arriving back in the Alpha Quadrant in time to celebrate my centenary, and neither did anyone else. Projects like this served a multiple purpose: they kept the crew busy; they kept us focused on our main goal and kept alive hope and belief that we might achieve it; and, damn it, there was also the possibility that they might even work! Just like that glider I had built, all those years ago, from pieces of string and globs of porridge. Those prisoners of war held in the castle who had built the first one had been given hope by this project. (And I never forgot that, although they never got to try it, that damn glider *flew*.)

We integrated all kinds of tech during this period and worked on all kinds of projects. I'd say the *Delta Flyer* was by far our most successful (although I often thought sadly about how such a flyer, with its capacity to operate in multiple environments, was the kind of ship on which my father had died). I know that the subject of the technological advances we made in flight technology is one that often came up on my return, with questions about Borg tech and wormholes and time travel and even breaking the maximum warp barrier. Sounds unbelievable, doesn't it? Breaking the warp barrier. Nobody could possibly believe it. You know, a lot of what we did here is classified, and so for all of your asking questions about that, let me fall back on official secrets. I guess you'll know—in a hundred years' time. As for some of the other rumors flying around: there are a lot of crazy stories about what we encountered on our way home, or things that happened to us. I'd say you shouldn't believe everything you hear. Hell, I was *there*, and I can't believe some of it.

As well as Mark, I missed my family dreadfully. I wrote many letters to them over the years. I wrote to Mom, and I went through agonies on her account too. Having already lost her husband, what must she be feeling now, having to come to terms with the loss of a daughter? I tried to comfort her, tell her that I was doing just fine, and that I was coming home as quickly as I could. I wrote to Phoebe and Yianem, my sisters old and new. I confided in them how often I felt despair at the vastness of the distance between us and home, and how often I felt that I wasn't up to this task: an experienced officer, yes, but a new captain, learning on the job. I wrote about how much I feared that Mark would give up and move on. I hoped they were looking out for him; taking care of him—I knew they would. These were perhaps my most honest letters. I could never keep secrets from my sister. I wrote to my nieces too (and tried to imagine how they were changing): chatty stories about the curious things we had seen; an adventure tale for children that I hoped my mother might appreciate too. I wrote to the grandparents, of course, and, every new year, I wrote a big newsy letter to the whole family. I tried to focus on the positive aspects of our journey home: the strange encounters; the camaraderie of the crew, as we pulled together; the various exploits of Neelix, the Doctor, Naomi Wildman. (Let's leave aside the time I had to break the news about Shannon O'Donnel to poor Aunt Martha. At least I got to practice in this letter before dealing with the real thing.)

One letter that I wrote from the early days I recall very well, imagining how my family would have laughed and groaned on reading it, recalling, as it did, the infamous "Year of Amelia," and my childhood obsession with her. I made this letter fun, lighthearted, imagining the family reading it together and laughing that Katy's stubborn streak proved so strong that she went all that way just to stalk her childhood heroine. I started with the mystery of the ancient SOS signal, and then the amazement of discovering—of all things—a Lockheed Model 10 Electra... Then realizing we had solved one of the greatest mysteries in human aviation history, and that I was about to meet my idol... They say that you shouldn't meet your heroes, but to my relief Amelia Earhart was willing to trust us, ordering her navigator to cooperate with us. She proved willing to believe the tall tale that we told her: that she had been taken by aliens, and was now living a long way from home, and many centuries in the future. I was not disappointed at how open-minded she proved to me. I was not disappointed in her at all. What an honor, to be able to show her my ship! To let her see that a woman in command was no longer considered an exception, but how the future would be.

I may have devoted more than a few pages of this letter to my encounter with her before remembering to finish up the story: of how humans, back in the 1930s, had been abducted by aliens, and brought to this world, only to establish what was now a human colony. More than a hundred thousand of them, across three cities, all thriving. Humans can be resilient in this way. Since I was writing this letter with the nieces in mind, I glossed over some of the less pleasant aspects of the tale: how the Briori had used these kidnapped humans as slave labor, and how brutal their later rebellion must have been. You don't lightly win freedom from slavery, as human history attests over and over again. But here was this human civilization, light-years away from home, flourishing, and ready to welcome us with open arms.

That offer brought about a tough decision, not just for me, but for all of the crew. Here was an established human colony in the Delta Quadrant. Here we could end our journey; we could settle, put down roots, lead what would clearly be happy lives among our own kind. I won't deny that the temptation to remain was strong: hell, I could have been Amelia Earhart's next-door neighbor! But the truth is, I never did waver. I was committed to going home. But while that was my decision, I had to let each member of the crew choose for themselves. I had, in effect, forced them into the Delta Quadrant when I made the choice to destroy the Caretaker's array, and it seemed only fair to give each person a chance to make this decision. This was a worrying time: I simply had no idea what each person might decide. Remember that we had been traveling for over a year by this point, only a tiny fraction of the voyage that still lay ahead of us. I would not have blamed anyone for wanting to stay behind, particularly those crew members who had been part of the Maquis, and could not be sure of the reception they would get back in the Alpha Quadrant. The problem was that if enough of them decided to cut their losses and stay, I would no longer be able to crew *Voyager*. The decision would be made for us.

I don't know whether there were behind-the-scenes discussions between the ex-Maquis crew members, and I've never asked. If there were, I suspect Chakotay of having a hand in them, and persuading people that they should trust me to look after them in the event of our return to the Alpha Quadrant. In any case, nobody opted to stay. This was a deeply significant moment for me: my first confirmation that all the work we had done to bind our crew together into a coherent, supportive community, bent toward a common goal, was working. I was hugely heartened by the fact that everyone was committed to our voyage home. I felt that I could enter the next stage of our journey with renewed confidence that we could make it; that we could hold together, and travel together, and one day come home together. I did want Amelia Earhart to come with us, though; boy, did I ever! Can you imagine? The wonders she would have seen on *Voyager* alone, never mind on the journey! I remember that conversation vividly, the note of yearning in her voice at the thought of flying in our ship. But the pull of the settlement was too strong. In my letter to my family, I jokily described my failure to persuade her to come along as the greatest disappointment of my life. Surely, I wrote, we would have been the best of friends! I am still convinced of this. But it remains a source of great joy to me that I met her—my great childhood heroine. What an honor to be the one to solve this great mystery. For me to be the one to learn the fate of Amelia Earhart!

This temptation to give up, to simply accept that we were now denizens of the Delta Quadrant and to make a home there, was very strong in the early years. On one occasion, it seemed to have been forced upon me and my first officer. On an away trip, we both caught a virus that would kill us if we left the environment in which we had contracted it. We suspected from our encounters with the Vidiians, a species in the Delta Quadrant who had advanced medical technologies, that they would most likely have a cure. However, the reason for the Vidiians' expertise in this respect was that the species suffered from a pandemic, the Phage. This horrible disease, which was slowly destroying their species, had led the Vidiians to take terrible actions against other species with whom they came into contact, harvesting their organs to save their own people. I forbade contact with them. As ever, I weighed the balance of the needs of the many against the needs of the few, and it was plain to me that the danger to the rest of the crew from a species of organ harvesters took precedence over the needs of myself and Chakotay. It seemed that, for a while, at least, my journey home was at a standstill. I put Tuvok in command of *Voyager*, and, in my final order as captain, instructed him to continue the journey home to the Alpha Quadrant. Under no circumstances, I said, was he to contact the Vidiians on our behalf.

Then Chakotay and I got on with taking stock of our situation. We were both experienced at living in the wild; we both had many years of camping and hiking behind us, as well as our Starfleet survival training, and his time in the Maquis had made him used to rough conditions. We built a shelter; we built, dare I say it, a home. I knew from the outset that Chakotay would have been happy to remain here: there was a stoicism about him that made him capable of accepting his fate, and he is also, at heart, a solitary man happy to spend time in his own company. But I was set on finding a cure. I didn't care how long it would take. Ten years, twenty: I'd find it, and then we could both leave this world and continue our own journey home. I know that this part of me—always looking ahead to the next adventure—has made me miss a great deal during my life. I sometimes forget to see the gifts and the blessings that are right in front of me. But I can't change this about myself—and I don't think I want to. That sense of curiosity, of longing to push myself onward and outward, is so crucial a part of my personality that without it I simply wouldn't be myself. I knew I wouldn't be content with the pastoral harmony this world offered me; I guess, like Eve, I would always want to taste the fruit of the tree of knowledge. Then a plasma storm came and destroyed all my work.

It looked like I was going to have to be content with staying in the garden of paradise.

As it turned out, I wasn't allowed to. *Voyager* returned with a cure. As Tuvok described it to me later, my crew were not happy with the replacement that I had provided for them, and had insisted on approaching Dr. Danara Pel, with whom we had a good relationship, in order to find a cure for us.

"It seems," Tuvok said, rather dryly, "that only Captain Janeway and Commander Chakotay are acceptable."

Well, that was certainly gratifying, although once I was back on board, I had more than a few things to say to my senior staff about disobeying orders. I had expressly instructed them not to contact the Vidiians, and they had ended up fending off a Vidiian attack. This was one of my least effective group rebukes. The whole time I was talking, Tom Paris had a big self-satisfied grin plastered over his face, and even Tuvok looked about as unrepentant as it's possible for a Vulcan to be (I have a sneaking suspicion he didn't enjoy the captain's seat). I could see B'Elanna beginning to bristle; the words *"You could always say 'thank you'!"* were clearly forming on her lips.

"Nevertheless," I said, "I would like to *thank you* for your initiative, and most of all for your loyalty. If I couldn't spend the next seventy years living in the wild on a paradise planet, then there's nowhere else I'd rather be than on board *Voyager*."

"Seconded," said Chakotay, although I wasn't so sure about that.

✦

The letter writing was a crucial part of how I dealt with the realities of my unusual command. I had the best support that I could hope for from Chakotay and Tuvok, but a captain needs someone outside of her own crew. These letters, together with the occasional ones I wrote to Parvati Pandey and to Owen Paris, reflecting on some decision I had made and imagining their advice, provided me with a version of this external reality check. Of course, I couldn't send them, never mind expect a response, but I filed them all away, and I treated them as if they had been sent, and I didn't go back to them at all; I made a point of that. I have only reread them now, writing this memoir, and my heart goes out to Captain Kathryn Janeway in those very early days, thrown into these circumstances on her very first mission. I wish I could go and tell her that everything would turn out all right. I wish I could go and give her some comfort. She had a tough job. It would be good to let her know that all would be well.

Reading them back now, I see plenty of other encounters that I have long since forgotten. I recall species that we met in those early days that we left behind as we moved on through the Delta Quadrant. As well as the Vidiians, there were the Kazon—I wasn't sorry to say goodbye to either of those. And then I had my first encounter with the Q Continuum: you can be sure that I raided *Voyager*'s data banks, but nothing could truly have prepared me for the tragicomedy that unfolded. The Q we encountered—he took the name Quinn—was trapped, imprisoned, inside a comet. We released him, whereupon he immediately tried to end his own life. It transpired that Quinn was a being that had thought deeply about the nature of immortality—and wanted it to end. He was not the trickster figure, the fool, that we had assumed, or that we associated with his species. When the other, more familiar Q appeared, wanting to return Quinn to his imprisoned state, Quinn requested Federation asylum. I was duty bound to take it seriously and decided to hold a hearing to consider Quinn's request.

Well, this being the Q Continuum, a variety of most interesting witnesses were called to support Q's case that Quinn should not be allowed to die. It seems that Quinn had been pivotal at all kinds of moments in human history. But Quinn had his own argument to make, and he showed us what it was like to live as part of the Continuum. What a bleak vision that was. A dusty country road, that only came back to the place where it had started: a run-down gas station and store, a dead end where the inhabitants sat around, almost comatose from boredom. Everything done; everything said. Nobody talking to each other; nobody had in millennia. It truly was a vision of hell. I couldn't think of anything more dreadful: at least my own road was leading somewhere, took me past marvels and wonders. At least my life still held *novelty*. But living in the Q Continuum was a road to nowhere—for eternity. Quinn, having shown us this, argued that to condemn him to this unchanging life was cruelty. I was moved by this argument—and, ultimately, it was his life, and he should have the chance to choose what to do with it. I granted his request for asylum. (This was the moment when, poignantly, he chose his name.)

I had hoped, of course, that the transition to mortality might provide Quinn with sufficient novelty to persuade him that he might explore this new condition, and that this would keep him alive for at least a while longer. This was not to be the case. Q, respecting the other man's wishes, had given Quinn access to Nogatch hemlock, and he took his own life. I wish this could have turned out differently. There was still so much for Quinn to see and do. But it was not to be.

These encounters form some of the most memorable aspects of our journey home—and it was part of our mission, to seek out new life. I tried not to forget that in many ways I was lucky to be the captain of the Starfleet ship that had traveled furthest, and that I might, one day, bring information about these places and new species home. But I was fascinated at least as much by watching how my crew responded to our unique challenge. Harry Kim, struggling with homesickness and a first assignment that nobody should receive, not even the Academy's finest. B'Elanna Torres, trying to put aside her anger and find a way of life that used her passion and her intellect constructively. Tom Paris, who, with seventy thousand light-years between them, was finally able to live outside of his father's shadow and become his own man. Our Doctor, evolving every day beyond what his programming had ever anticipated. Chakotay, day by day coming back to his old life as a dedicated Starfleet officer. Even Tuvok, perhaps the most collected and stable of us all, had to find a way of living with the exigencies and irrationalities of our situation.

Damn, though—I wish Amelia had come on board.

✦

There is one series of events that preys on my mind after all these years. I still am not sure that I made the right decision: I'm not sure that there was a right decision to be made. The whole affair started in a most straightforward way: Tuvok and Neelix went down together to investigate an M-class planet which we had encountered and to collect botanical samples which we hoped to be able to use. When they—and the samples—were beamed aboard, we were confronted with a single individual. Investigations showed that the samples they had collected, when demolecularized through the transporter, acted as a symbiogenetic catalyst, merging the DNA of my two crew members into a single being. We had lost two people and replaced them with one.

Tuvix. He made his presence felt from the outset. He combined the knowledge and capabilities of both men—I had lost neither a chief security officer nor a head chef and morale officer—but I had lost Tuvok, my old friend and mentor, and Kes had lost her Neelix. I know how difficult this time was for her—Tuvix was so like Neelix in many ways, and yet so unlike. I recall the conversation that I had at this time with Kes, who was going through a kind of loss that we had all faced when we were stranded in the Delta Quadrant, not least myself, with the loss of Mark. She had been shocked that Tuvix still retained Neelix's feelings for her—while, at the same time, still loving T'Pel in the way that Tuvok had. I sympathized: this must have been deeply disconcerting. Tuvix was not Neelix. To his credit—there were many things to his credit—he did not press himself on Kes and gave her the space and the room to deal with what was, to all intents and purposes, a bereavement. And he was, in himself, a good and kind man. He had fine instincts on the bridge. He even cooked well! However, the Doctor found a way to reverse the process, enabling the transporter to separate the DNA of the two men. Most of us wanted this resolution—with one notable exception, Tuvix himself, who wanted to live.

I will not dwell on the decision that I made. I am, to this day, unsure about it. The Doctor would not perform the procedure, and therefore I took it upon myself. Tuvix died, and Tuvok and Neelix lived. Later that evening, Tuvok came to my quarters.

"An interesting decision, Captain," he said.

"What can I say, Tuvok? You know, just before we set out to look for the *Val Jean*, I told T'Pel that I would do everything in my power to bring you home."

"But at the cost of another man's life?"

"Tuvok," I said, "remember Pandey's classes at the Academy?"

"The Ethics of Command. Of course."

"Do you remember the session on the trolley problem?"

"The clash between utilitarian and deontological ethics," he said.

"Only you would phrase it that way," I replied, with a wry smile. "Yes, whether an action should be judged by its consequences, or according to a set of moral principles."

Pandey set us this thought problem, a well-known one in moral philosophy. A runaway trolley is heading toward five incapacitated people, and you are left with a choice: reroute the trolley, which will save those five people, but kill one other person, or else let the trolley take its course, and save that one life at the cost of those five. What is the ethical action? You know, we argued that problem back and forth for a couple of hours. I guess I never thought that I would have to answer it so directly.

"On the one hand, I had Tuvix, a single life," I said. "On the other, I had you and Neelix—two lives, established, with people who loved them and who were grieving for them. You know, Tuvix had your tactical skills, and he was at least as good a chef as Neelix. But you had families, Tuvok. People that I knew, people that I had met. Could I have faced them, knowing that I could have saved your life, and not done it?"

He sat for a while before replying. "The logical choice, certainly," he said. "Although I myself would have hesitated."

Maybe there is no answer. I made my choice. Can I live with it?

I will learn to live with it.

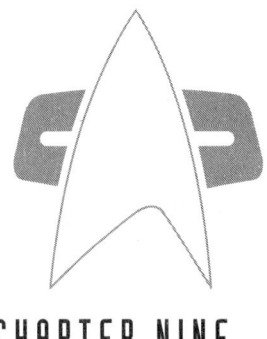

CHAPTER NINE
YEARS OF HELL—2373-2374

WE ENTERED OUR THIRD YEAR IN THE DELTA QUADRANT acclimatizing to our situation, but with the growing and sinking thought that we were indeed out here for the long haul. Day by day, week by week, our life seemed to alternate between shipboard routines and sudden, explosive encounters with the worlds and species that we met. Starfleet protocols went a long way to stabilizing our life on board ship, and my decision to enforce these was vindicated when even a few former Maquis confessed to me that these routines helped them along the way. I could see that B'Elanna, for example, for all her frustrations, was flourishing on *Voyager*: her technical expertise and creativity were vastly appreciated, and by no means taken for granted. Those of us who watched the crew carefully—by which I mean myself and Chakotay—did not miss the growing closeness of B'Elanna and Tom Paris. Chakotay explained how the attraction had been clear to him when the two had met during their time in the Maquis, although Tom's capture had prevented it progressing further. Still, it was a situation worth watching. Close relationships gave comfort to the crew but, if there were breakups, then there was the potential for resentment, which could cause excessive disruption within a crew so small. Either Tom would persuade B'Elanna that he was a good bet, or she would decide to eat him alive. Neither Chakotay nor I could call it.

I began to give serious thought to what it might mean, if we did indeed take seventy years to reach home. The crew would age; we would need people to look after us, never mind continue the ship on its journey. How would families work on board ship? How would we teach the children, care for them, bring them up? I watched Samantha Wildman closely, and how the crew supported her, and wondered how we might scale this up, when the time came. I know that others were thinking the same: we had been en route for two years now and were likely to be in the same condition for the foreseeable future. Perhaps this was how the rest of our lives would be. The urge to create stability in this transitory situation seemed catching: many of the crew, in this third year, seemed to commit to longer-standing relationships. Besides, we all knew each other very well. We were used to each other and, perhaps, more forgiving of each other. Even the Doctor experimented with a home life: an exploration of his humanity that became a tragedy when his simulated daughter died. I would not wish this on anyone, not even someone made of photons. The Doctor loved his little girl, Belle, as much as any person had loved their child, and he grieved her loss. A first, true encounter with the vicissitudes of life. It is to our Doctor's credit that he did not abandon his experiment at this point but continued to risk change and growth.

Some of us, however, were not prepared to leave the past behind, or could not. For Harry Kim, as an example, giving up on his beloved Libby would clearly be an admission that he would not get home, and Harry was never going to do this. He coped with life on *Voyager* by insisting that it was a temporary interruption to his real life, that one day he would go home, and see his parents, and pick up with Libby where they had left off. I know that Tom Paris tried to make him accept some of the realities of our situation and consider at least going on a few dates. Not the most tactful advice, but Tom Paris was proving to have a kind streak that had not been allowed to flourish in the past. You saw it with how he looked after Harry; in how he tried to take care of B'Elanna. Chakotay too frequently expressed surprise at how Tom was maturing. I had always thought that all he needed was a chance: to get out and prove himself. The Maquis must have seemed like this to him; of course, it went disastrously wrong. But now another chance had come, and Tom seemed to be pulling himself together.

For myself, I was not prepared to give up on my old life. Men like Mark Johnson don't come along every day. My chief regret was that I had not accepted that first proposal when it was made. We could have had a few years of married life behind us. I have wondered, sometimes, whether that might have made a difference to how things worked out, but some things can't be changed, and you can't live in the past. For now, I wrote my letters to him, confided in him as if he were there, and hoped beyond hope that I would see him again. There was no question of my starting a relationship with a member of my crew: as captain, I could not risk this and hope to keep the necessary distance upon which rank and, thus, authority depend. Yes, it was lonely; sometimes it was extremely lonely. Chakotay was my rock when it came to my fears about our journey home, or my worries about individual crew members. We established a long-standing routine of a weekly supper together, a time when we could both relax and put aside, if only for a few hours, the burden of our senior rank.

But it was Kes who came closest to becoming a confidante for Kate, rather than Captain, Janeway. The conversation that we had when she thought that Neelix was lost had created a closeness and warmth between us that I found a great consolation. Even if I rarely discussed with her how I felt, I knew that someone on board *Voyager* had seen this side of me and understood. Her growing psionic powers no doubt gave her increased sensitivity, and, of course, the fact that she was not Starfleet helped. But besides her gifts, there was an inherent gentleness and wisdom to Kes, a calmness about her, that inspired trust. I was grateful for her quiet and steady support. We were always conscious, with Kes, of her abbreviated life span in comparison to the rest of us, and that every moment was precious. As it turned out, we lost her sooner even than we anticipated, but not in the way that we expected.

Triggered by our encounter with Species 8472, her psionic abilities began to outstrip what her body could bear, and even began to threaten the ship itself. Kes made the decision to leave. I begged her to stay with us, to hold out until the Doctor had a cure for her condition, but she wanted to go, to find out where her powers could take her. Before she left, she sent us forward through space more than nine thousand light-years, past Borg territory, taking nearly ten years off our journey. A gift indeed. Her departure was a great blow for Neelix, even if their relationship had already concluded. It was noticeable how from this point on he began to spend more time with the Wildmans. Naomi, with her accelerated growth from her Ktarian heritage, was starting to want playmates rather than carers, and Neelix was ready and willing to fill this need. I imagine it gave him solace too. (Kes warned us, in her last days, about a species named the Krenim: one reason why we elected to avoid entering their space. I often wonder what might have happened had we chosen to go there.)

The urge to create a family seemed to be endemic, as I learned when we once again encountered the Q Continuum. Motherhood had certainly not been on my agenda at that moment in my life, and even more certainly I had not contemplated that Q would father any child of mine. Nor is there any timeline in which I would ever contemplate this. I was more interested—if alarmed—to learn that our previous encounter with the Continuum had brought about significant changes (there's a reason the Prime Directive exists), although this had, after all, been Quinn's intention when he asked us to help him die. No longer a dead-end track, the Continuum was now on the verge of civil war, which Q was trying to prevent by bringing a child into existence. I sympathized with his purposes, having seen the plight of his faction; but it's his damn methods, as ever, that I take exception to. Never has a woman been so wretchedly wooed. Fortunately, he moved on quickly enough—and I acquired a godson. I guess I've mentored all kinds of people across the years.

✦

No person has challenged me on such a fundamental level as Seven of Nine. Nobody has made me reflect so deeply upon the nature of selfhood, on our responsibilities to ourselves and to each other, as she has over the years. Living alongside Seven of Nine was not always comfortable, particularly in the early days, but I must surely count coming to know her, watching her grow and change, as one of the most rewarding experience of my life. For this all to emerge from an encounter with the Borg is all the more satisfying. No other species, in their cruelty and conformity, in their pursuit of uniform collectivity over infinite diversity in infinite combinations, stands so much in opposition to my own culture and mores. As we approached Borg space, we identified a narrow band through which we hoped we might pass without being detected. We dubbed this the Northwest Passage, and, as we drew closer, we detected fifteen Borg cubes heading our way. I am sure we all believed this was the end... and the cubes went past us, and then registered as destroyed. What the hell could destroy fifteen Borg cubes? This, we learned, after sending an away team to one of the cubes, was Species 8472, which, as we discovered from the Borg logs, had defeated them many times before. Before we beamed back, Harry Kim was struck and infected by one of the aliens, and rushed back to sickbay, where the Doctor was able to modify a Borg nanoprobe and cure him.

My enemy's enemy is my friend. Perhaps, I thought, we could strike up an alliance with the Borg, using the Doctor's cure for the infection as bargaining power. My crew were not convinced of the wisdom of this—but we came up with no other alternatives, and took *Voyager* to a Borg world, offering an alliance. An attack by Species 8472 persuaded the Borg to take my offer seriously and sent a representative drone to communicate with us. This was my first encounter with Seven of Nine.

My account, from hereon, necessarily relies on others, since I was badly injured when Species 8472's bioships attacked us. Before I was sedated, I made Chakotay promise to continue working with the Borg. I gather that what happened next was that Seven of Nine, learning that millions of Borg had been killed in the middle of the sector, asked Chakotay to take *Voyager* to help, and he refused, on the grounds that this would take us too far off our course home. His intention was to leave the Borg behind for others to collect them, but Seven circumvented this plan by opening a spatial rift. When I was able to take back command, it was to learn that all the drones apart from Seven of Nine were dead, and that *Voyager* was stranded in fluidic space. I resumed work with Seven of Nine to develop a weapon to defeat the bioships, and she returned *Voyager* from fluidic space. We defeated the alien fleet, only for Seven of Nine to turn on us and attempt to assimilate *Voyager*. We knocked her out using a neural relay and resumed our course. When she awoke, she was severed from the Collective, and in our care.

Not the most auspicious introduction of a crew member, but we were responsible for her now, and began the process of restoring her individuality. The Doctor was initially unwilling to operate on her to remove her implants against her wishes, but as she was in no condition to make the decision for herself, I persuaded him that it was a necessary course of action. These operations saved Seven's life, but they left her in a condition which she did not want: severed irreparably from the Collective, and, not incidentally, hostile toward us. I presented her with information about her past—her name, Annika Hansen, assimilated as a child— but this only enraged her.

Can you force freedom on someone? Of course not. I believed that Seven of Nine could return to some kind of humanity, but it was plain to us all that the journey was long and hard. She had to learn even the most basic of human actions, which we learn as babies: how to eat, how to chew food. She began to have hallucinations of a raven (it was the name of her parents' ship, which she was on when they were captured by the Borg). She experienced flashbacks. The Doctor diagnosed post-traumatic stress disorder. As we learned more about her experiences, that came as no surprise. A small child, captured by Borg, her parents assimilated, hiding away until she herself was taken. I would not willingly imagine such horrors. We could not bring that child back, but we could, I hoped, bring Seven forward, allow her to become fully individual once again. My relationship with Seven was, in these early days, often marked by hostility and tension. At other times, I saw her courage and determination. When we entered a region of space where subatomic radiation from a nearby nebula would have killed us, Seven agreed to remain out of stasis so that we could pass through the space in a matter of weeks, rather than adding a year to our journey to go around it. Who else could have survived this isolation? She risked not only her precarious mental state but her life to save us.

What can I say? Like a mother, I had given Seven of Nine her life as a human being; like a mother, I could not force her to live that life in the way I chose. Her life was hers to live, and she must make her own choices. But above all, I believed that she could find herself. She was—she remains—unique. She has never failed to exceed my expectations of what she could learn, of how she could come to terms with all that had been done to her, of how she might live beyond the horrors that marked her early years—transcend them, indeed—and become her fullest self.

There is one situation I recall where her desire for perfection, instilled in her by the Borg, was at odds with the fact of human imperfection. Still, she came the closest that any of us can. Much of this mission remains classified; suffice to say that there are good reasons for this. It is a situation, too, where I hope that I was able to reciprocate in some way the lessons that Seven taught us and warn her that her pursuit of knowledge was leading her into a disastrous mistake. But she did, for a moment—for 3.2 seconds, in fact—see perfection, the alpha and the omega. What can bring us to a more forceful realization of our own frail and finite humanity, than a glimpse of the numinous? I found her on the holodeck, running my Da Vinci simulation, contemplating religious imagery. Contemplating the divine.

✦

The Da Vinci simulation gave me many happy hours over the years, once in unexpected ways. I sometimes think that my time on *Voyager* made me draw on every single one of my Academy experiences. Under no circumstances, however, did I ever imagine that I would be called upon to build a glider from scratch, and certainly not in the company of the Grandfather of Flight himself. We had come under attack from an unknown species who used their transporter technology to steal weapons and equipment directly from the ship. After tracking our missing goods to a nearby world, Tuvok and I beamed down to discover that the Doctor's mobile emitter had been one of the items stolen—and that the Leonardo Da Vinci simulation had been taken too. It was up and running, and Da Vinci was hard at work under a new "patron"—a local trader named Tau, responsible for stealing from our ship. The Master and I escaped by virtue of his technical expertise (with a little guidance from me), and, of course, my ability to land a punch upon our guard. This was a minor incident, I suppose, in our journey home, but one that my adolescent self would have adored. Like meeting Amelia Earhart, I suppose. Our time in the Delta Quadrant was not all bad.

Other holodeck experiences were significantly bleaker. At this time, we had regular encounters with the Hirogen, a nomadic species whose culture was organized around notions of "the hunt." Other species, across their hunting grounds, were seen as prey, and we were no exception. A group of Hirogen hijacked *Voyager* and forced half of us to reenact hologram simulations of ever more violent and vicious hunts, and the rest to act as slave labor, treating their wounded colleagues and turning more and more of the ship over to these sickening games. Many of my memories of this experience are hazy: those of us forced into the simulations were fitted with neural interfaces that made us believe the parts we played were completely real. I still have shards of memory of my life as a Klingon warrior, of the day that Troy was set ablaze, of chasing Black and Tans down the back lanes of Ireland. Most of all I recall the simulation in which myself and others of *Voyager*'s crew became part of the French Resistance. This simulation expanded so rapidly that the integrity of the ship came under threat, and only the overloading of the hologrid brought the program to an end. It was plain, even to our Hirogen captors, that this was now a zero-sum game. Nobody could win. We had to make a truce. I gave them the ability to create holodeck technology on their own ships, a small price to pay to get them off *Voyager*.

I've talked to other crew members about this whole episode, and I know we were all shaken at the extent to which some of these memories still seem real to us. A huge shock to your sense of self, and one or two have reported that they sometimes still wonder whether or not they are inside a simulation. Well, that way lies madness, I think; you have to proceed as if what's going on around you is real. But the thought of how the ship was taken over this way gave me many sleepless nights. The holodeck was a great solace to us across the years, but also proved an Achilles heel on many occasions. Some people cannot tell the difference between fantasy and reality, and sometimes, our own daydreams worked against us. There was one occasion, however, where our encounter with a simulation led to genuine rapprochement, and this time with a species we had real reason to fear.

KATHRYN M. JANEWAY VS-982-429

STARFLEET ACADEMY
CLASS OF 2357

Kathryn Janeway's graduation photo
Image courtesy Starfleet Archives

▲ 2342: *Kathryn at the Barre*
Art by Gretchen Williams. Image courtesy K. Janeway

Dodecatheon meadia (Shooting Stars)
Art by Phoebe Janeway. Image courtesy K. Janeway ▼

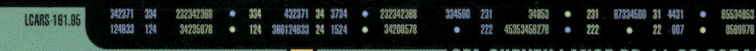

| LCARS-161.95 | 342371 334 232342368 · 334 432371 34 3734 · 232342368 334500 231 34853 · 231 97334500 31 4431 · 85534853 |
| | 124833 124 34235676 · 124 366124833 24 1524 · 34200578 · 222 4535346827G · 222 · 22 987 · 0569976 |

SFA SURVEILLANCE DD.11.06.2354

SEA.SECURITY
ONLINE

LEVEL IV

MONITOR
09: 1701

MODE SELECT

PZ: 214500.3/11.22/4

PZ: 35500.3/11.22/4

FILE ID: SFASP4412668
STARFLEET ACADEMY SURVEILLANCE TAU16D

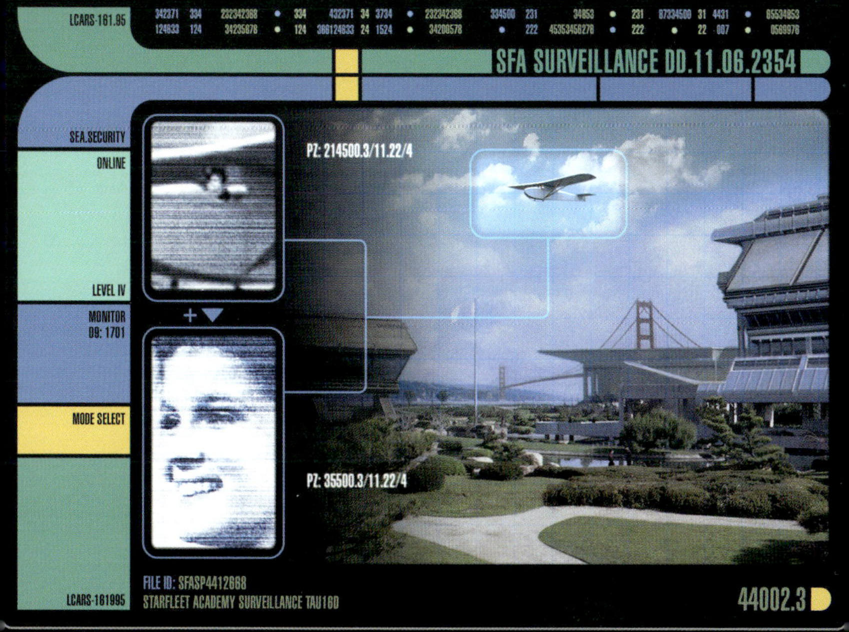

LCARS-181995

44002.3

▲ Cadet Janeway piloting the *Colditz Cock II*
Image courtesy Starfleet Archives

Starfleet Notice of Death for Edward Janeway
Image courtesy Starfleet Archives ▼

STRFLT. SEC.CD 331154880WSV

CLASSIFIED

SECURITY LEVEL 778
STARFLEET SB-SPC
FREQUENCY:
88112224P

U.S.S. AL-BATANI
CAPT. OWEN PARIS, COMMANDING
ENSIGN KATHRYN JANEWAY:

6611.2333
TAU CETI PRIME FED. O.P. 1138.0966
0907 16 JUNE 2358

DEEPLY REGRET TO INFORM YOU THAT VICE-ADMIRAL EDWARD JANEWAY
IS OFFICIALLY REPORTED AS KILLED IN THE LINE OF DUTY, 15 JUNE.
IMMEDIATE COMPASSIONATE LEAVE APPROVED.
DETAILS TO FOLLOW.

LT. DONALD DAVIS, T.C.P. ADJUTANT

▲ 2359: Newly promoted Lieutenant Janeway with her friend/mentor, Boothby
Image courtesy K. Janeway

▲ 2343: Kathryn and Jess
Art by Gretchen Williams. Image courtesy K. Janeway

Mollie
Photo by Mark Johnson. Image courtesy K. Janeway ▼

2626111.34
SECURITY LEVEL-01-A
STARFLEET COM-K1A
FREQUENCY:
OPEN CHANNEL

NON-SECURE

K —
BEST I COULD DO... [YOU KNOW HOW SHE IS ON HER WALKS]
LOVE YOU — LOVE YOUR DOG. M

STRFLT. NON. SEC. CO 517721

To Catarina: Who Gave Me Wings
Art by Leonardo Da Vinci. Image courtesy K. Janeway.

| MEDICAL | NCC-74656 |

USS VOYAGER NCC-74656 MAKES
HEROIC RETURN FROM DELTA
QUADRANT AFTER 7 YEARS

STARFLEET COMMAND REPORTS SHIP'S
COMPLIMENT INCLUDES NEW ARRIVALS

IMMEDIATE RELEASE

FREQUENCY:
GG112224P

STRFLT. PRESS 331154889WSV

▲ United Federation of Planets press-release announcing *Voyager*'s return.

Admiral Janeway with her daughter, Ensign Amelia Janeway, at Starfleet Academy Commencement, 2395
Photo credit: Yianem Lox Image courtesy K. Janeway

THE HISTORY OF THE CAPTAIN WHO WENT FURTHER THAN ANY HAD BEFORE

I cannot describe how uncanny it was to encounter, on a space station so far from home, a near perfect recreation of Starfleet Academy. Yet there it was—up to and including our beloved Boothby, friend and mentor to so many of us during our time as cadets. I sent Chakotay and Tuvok to investigate, and they learned that this was a simulation created by Species 8472. This added significantly to our alarm: what could a species so terrifying that even the Borg withdrew in the face of them, want with our Academy? I ordered Seven to prepare warheads using Borg nanoprobes; I hoped, too, for a diplomatic solution.

Chakotay's investigations were uncovered, and Species 8472 were alerted to the fact that at least some of the humans within their simulation were exactly what they appeared to be. Chakotay was captured and interrogated by an individual who appeared exactly like Boothby; he described to me later how disconcerting this was—to know that behind this familiar, beloved, trusted face lay an intelligence of which we knew so very little. He learned from this simulated Boothby that Species 8472, having encountered us, was now afraid that Starfleet intended to invade fluidic space. The simulation had been created to prepare them for further encounters with us. I, in turn, was terrified that this simulation was a prelude to invasion—a training ground for Species 8472 before they took on the Alpha Quadrant for real. For a while, this seemed a dangerous and unresolvable stalemate. I wondered, however, if there was something of the real Boothby in this simulation and tried to speak to it with some of the warmth and trust I would have extended to the real man. It seemed to work. We traded information on Borg nanoprobes for expertise that Species 8472 had on genetic modification. We moved on—the truce holding, and I for one slept a little easier in my bed that night, knowing that an understanding had been reached with a truly terrifying species.

But wishing, truly wishing, that the simulation had been real, and that somehow, we had transported all that long way back to the Academy. All that long way home. Absence makes the heart grow fonder, or so they say; I would say too that a moment of presence makes absence just a little harder to bear.

✦

As the fourth year of our time in the Delta Quadrant drew toward its end, I found myself taking stock of our situation. We had all, more or less, come to terms with our life here, even those of us, like Harry, who were still hoping that our return would be sooner rather than later. We had found ways to live with the distances and the absences; we had found solace and friendship in each other. And then, quite unexpectedly, this equilibrium was disrupted. Seven of Nine, working on our sensors, had expanded their range significantly, and discovered an extensive relay-station network. By tapping into this network, she'd been able to locate a Starfleet ship on the very edge of the Alpha Quadrant, the *U.S.S. Prometheus*. This was not a ship with which I was familiar, and no wonder: this was a secret experimental warship under development for the war against the Dominion. Who the hell were they? What the hell was this war? And what was the significance of Romulan noninvolvement? Given our position, these were hardly questions to which we could readily gain answers. What we could do—or the Doctor could do on our behalf—was send news of us to the Alpha Quadrant. We temporarily transferred the Doctor to the sickbay of the *Prometheus,* and, speaking directly to Starfleet Command, he told them that *Voyager* was still very much intact, and that her crew was trying to find their way home.

I won't forget that conversation with the Doctor in a hurry. So much news, all at once. Learning that we had been declared dead more than a year ago and thinking about how dreadful an experience that must have been for all of our friends and family. My poor Mark, thinking himself widowed a second time; my poor mother, the loss of her husband compounded by the news of the loss of their older child... No, soon they would both know. All of our families and friends would know. We were alive and well and trying our very best to come home. And more than that, we knew now that Starfleet was working on our behalf. They would be working to bring us home, however they could, as quickly as they could. Most of all, they had a message for us: *You're no longer alone.*

It was a great privilege of my life to be able to pass that message on to my crew: *You're no longer alone...* I watched as the ramifications of this sank into their faces. There were tears: of relief and joy, and a few tears at the thought of what families must have suffered, believing that we were dead. Harry was almost beside himself with worry. I think he spent much of the next week quizzing the Doctor about what he'd seen and what had been said. Poor Harry, he went through torments thinking about Libby and his parents having to come to terms with his death, and then the shock of learning we were still out there. "But will she know that I'm still on board?" he kept saying. "Will she know that I'm okay?"

I had a responsibility to keep spirits up, however, and I kept myself all smiles and laughter while I was among the crew. But I'll not deny that when I was back in my quarters that evening, I was close to shedding a few tears of my own at that message. The loneliness: that had been by far the worst thing for me. The fact that, ultimately, Kathryn Janeway was captain of *Voyager*, and that here in the Delta Quadrant the buck stopped with me. Nobody would arrive in the nick of time to pull us out of any desperate situation in which we found ourselves. But this small communication reminded me that I was part of something greater: I was part of Starfleet. Contact had been established. Whatever happened next, whatever trials they were undergoing back in the Alpha Quadrant, I knew that some small part of this fine organization, some of those brilliant minds, were now at work on behalf of me and my crew. Captain Kathryn Janeway was no longer alone. Knowing this made it truly possible for me to bring my crew and my ship back home. I took a moment to be proud of myself—to acknowledge how far we had come, how far we had brought us—and then it was back to work. Miles to go before we sleep.

✦

This contact was quickly followed by a transmission from Starfleet Command via the network, but after a tantalizing few words the transmission ended. Naturally this became our priority, although this was not without complications, given that the hostile Hirogen controlled the array via which the message was sent, and were intent on using this to hunt down our ship, and that our ship was shaken by gravimetric forces coming from the array. Nevertheless, we had to get closer, and were soon able to download the message from Starfleet Command. It was seriously degraded, but I set Seven of Nine to work to get what she could from it.

Letters from home. What we had all been longing for. Oh, be careful what you wish for...

Shock after shock. The devastating news for Chakotay and B'Elanna and others that the Maquis had been wiped out, the Cardassians and their allies from the Gamma Quadrant (that shadowy Dominion of which we'd heard) triumphant, and their friends either dead or in prison. It's a measure of how far we had all come that, as far as I know, the reaction of all the non-Maquis crew was only shock and sympathy for our friends and colleagues. Whatever our thoughts about the rights and wrongs of the Maquis, we knew that those people who had chosen to resist the terms of the treaty and fight for their worlds had on the whole done so as a matter of conscience. Their resistance had not deserved to meet such a brutal end. And it was terrifying, also, to think that the Cardassians had made an alliance that was destabilizing the fragile peace that had been constructed along the border, and were, if we understood what we were reading, on the warpath, and in the ascendancy. I tried to put these thoughts aside: much as I would have liked to have been serving alongside my fellow officers in whatever conflict now threatened the Federation, I was too far from home to be able to make any difference whatsoever. But the news was troubling, the uncertainty unhappy.

For others, the news was only good: we were able to celebrate the new addition to Tuvok's family, and all of us were glad to see how happy Harry was to have some contact with his people at last. Harry's regret was these communications were hardly likely to be a regular occurrence. There wasn't going to be a weekly mailshot, bringing his family up to date on his news, hearing from them what they had been up to. Poor Harry. For Tom Paris, meanwhile, the lack of a message was its own relief. Tom still had a way to go before he could feel free of the burden of his father.

As for me... The good news was that Mollie was thriving, and so were her pups...

But Mark was lost to me, forever. My handsome fiancé, the first man that I had been able to imagine spending my life with... As I had on some level feared, a second widowhood had been too much for him, and he made the wise choice—the choice that he had been forced to make once before—and moved on. I think what was hardest to bear was how narrowly we had missed each other. He had remarried only four months ago… But that was not a useful way to think. It was more than a year since we had been declared dead, and he would have made himself move on at that time. I did not, and could not, begrudge him this. Perhaps even if we had made contact, I would have told him to move on. Seventy years is a long time to wait for someone to come home from a work trip… He wanted to marry; he wanted a home life, and he wanted children. I knew this. I would not have made him wait for me… but pretending that he was had been solace. Now this fantasy was no longer available for me. I was alone.

"You're hardly alone," Chakotay told me, echoing that message from Starfleet that only a little while before had given me such comfort. I didn't talk to anyone beyond Chakotay, although I found that I missed Kes all over again. I would have taken some time to sit with her, I thought, to tell her how I felt. But she was gone. How much we had gained, in those few short weeks. But how much we had lost already. How many others on my crew must have gone through the same experience? There's no place like home—but even home cannot stay the same. What would we find, should we ever get there?

CHAPTER TEN
A LONG WAY FROM HOME—2375-2376

I HAVE BEEN TOLD ON MANY OCCASIONS THAT I TAKE DECISIONS on behalf of my crew that they would not take on their own behalf, and I must confess that there is some truth in this. But the fact is that while we were in the Delta Quadrant, I could not afford to lose the expertise of a single person. If the crew fell below a certain number, then *Voyager* was no longer sustainable as a working ship. I would not be able to staff her; I would not be able to bring the people remaining to me home. There are occasions, therefore, where I put the well-being of the whole above individual wishes. I know B'Elanna has a few words to say on this subject; so might the Doctor, if asked. I shall leave others to judge.

In B'Elanna's case, I made a call about saving the life of a necessary member of my crew, someone vital to the continued operation of *Voyager* and therefore the likelihood of our reaching home, rather than respecting her own wishes. We had responded to a distress call and found a ship containing a single, nonhumanoid lifeform, which we beamed directly to sickbay. This creature—which was scorpion-like in appearance—attacked B'Elanna, wrapping itself around her body, and piercing her with its "sting." The effect was to create a biochemical bond between them—but the prognosis was not good for B'Elanna, and the Doctor was not able to find a way to separate them that would not result in her death. Searching the ship's data banks, he learned about work conducted in this area by a Cardassian exobiologist, Crell Moset, and he programmed the holodeck to recreate Moset. Together, they set to work to find a cure for B'Elanna.

Nothing is ever this simple, however, and word about the Doctor's simulation of Moset passed around the ship. You will recall that I had one or two Bajoran crew on board *Voyager*, and one of these, Ensign Tabor, learning about Moset, confronted the Doctor in sickbay. Moset was notorious on Bajor; his work had involved experiments on thousands of Bajoran prisoners. Tabor wanted the work to stop—and, unfortunately, B'Elanna, overhearing the conversation, and, as a former Maquis sympathetic to the plight of Bajor, agreed with him. She did not want to be cured by any procedure developed by Moset, simulation or not. I understood her scruples, but I could not let her die. But I deliberated hard. The historical comparisons from our own human history were hard to put out of my mind—Thomas Parran and the Tuskegee experiments, or Joseph Mengele's work. I understood both Tabor's distress, and B'Elanna's scruples. But I could not let her die. We removed the alien—and were able to send it back to its own kind—but B'Elanna was very angry with me. We deleted the Moset program, and I remain uneasy about the choice I made to use the procedure that the Moset simulation and the Doctor devised together—but I do not, and I cannot, regret saving the life of B'Elanna Torres.

There were other occasions where I had cause to reverse my initial decisions. One such situation arose when the shuttle of an away team comprised of Ensign Kim, Ensign Jetal, and the Doctor came under attack. The Doctor managed to force the alien out of their craft, and fled back to *Voyager*, but by this point the unknown weapon used on them had sent Kim and Jetal into synaptic shock. Back on *Voyager*, the condition of both ensigns became critical, and the Doctor had time only to operate on one (nobody else was capable of performing the surgery). He chose Kim, and Jetal died. Nobody blamed him for this; absolutely nobody. He made a choice, and he saved a life. But the Doctor began to blame himself. He became obsessed with his choice, trying to determine why he had picked one ensign over the other. He entered what we could only call a feedback loop, with his ethical and cognitive subroutines at odds with each other. It manifested as obsessional thoughts, over and over, as he tried and failed to reconcile the decision to treat one over the other. He was in danger of breaking down completely. I made the decision to erase his memories of the circumstances of Jetal's death, and, indeed, of the ensign herself.

What can I say? I needed a functioning medic. These events in and of themselves had shown how close to the wire we were: there was nobody else—not a living flesh-and-blood person—able to perform the surgery that the Doctor had performed to save Kim's life. That alone showed how vulnerable we were in some areas of expertise. I could not afford to have my only medic out of action.

Well, the repressed invariably returns, and, after several months, after we had put the whole unhappy series of events behind us, the Doctor, conducting routine checkups, learned that Kim had undergone surgery—surgery which only he could have performed. By this time, of course, we had taken on a new crew member, Seven of Nine, and, with her customary combination of doggedness and technical acuity, she uncovered the deleted files, confronting the Doctor with memories of an ensign whom he did not know. I tried once again to delete them… but the Doctor was ahead of me. I explained, in general terms, what had happened, and that the deletions had been necessary to prevent the Doctor from a complete breakdown. To his mind, however, he had been operated on without his consent. I was prepared to do the same again—until Seven of Nine came to speak to me.

It's humbling, to say the least, to have your ethics called out by a Borg drone. But it was hard to refute Seven's arguments. If the Doctor was primarily a machine, she said, then to some extent so was she. When would I decide that I had the right to operate on her? I grasped her point immediately. Seven *had* been operated on without her consent; that little girl Annika Hansen had been transformed into a drone. How did this differ? How did I differ from the Borg who had eradicated her personhood? She left me struggling to see how. This is how Seven of Nine changed us. I had made this decision to eradicate the Doctor's memories before her arrival; with her on board, there was no question of doing the same again. It would have made a mockery of our attempts to humanize her. Seven told me that despite all the pain she had undergone, both mentally and physically, in her attempt to regain her individuality, she would not change a thing.

What course could I take, after that? I had to let the Doctor find his own way and live with the consequences. We restored his memories, and for two weeks we sat with him, as he wrestled with the choice he had made. I took on the bulk of this: this was my responsibility, after all. I listened to him repeat himself, over and over, and I despaired that he would ever find a way through. What finally drew him back was when he saw that I was ill. The solution to his pain was to see the pain of someone else and make a move to alleviate it. I guess we could call it compassion. I was sent off to bed (I had a headache and a fever), and the Doctor... I suppose he upgraded. He transcended his programming, yet again. All thanks to Seven of Nine.

I reflect often upon this decision of mine. Nothing in my Ethics of Command classes had prepared me for a Borg who had a greater sense of individual needs than I did, or a hologram that was in every meaningful sense alive. Our mission: to seek out new life. I am grateful to Seven for giving me the chance to make amends, for giving me the chance to change my mind. Recognizing our mistakes is part of what makes us human too, I guess.

Seven of Nine herself had to confront the consequences of her own actions a little while later, when we were docked at the Markonian Outpost Space Station. This interlude started out as welcome respite from our voyage: we had, for once, been made welcome, and we extended hospitality of our own, inviting people to visit and explore the ship. Seven of Nine was approached and, subsequently, attacked by three visitors, while she was regenerating in her alcove. They were attempting to inject her with Borg nanoprobes, but Seven was able to call for backup, whereupon we subdued her assailants and restrained them in sickbay. There, the Doctor was able to identify them as former Borg drones, which, on waking, they were able to confirm. Furthermore, they had been part of Seven's unimatrix. They had approached her to learn about a series of events that occurred several years ago, when their ship crashed on an uninhabited planet. Seven, who at first had no memory of these events, found her memories gradually returning.

It was not a happy awakening. After the crash, and temporarily severed from the collective, the three other drones, who had been assimilated as adults, found their individuality beginning to reestablish. But Seven, who had of course been assimilated at six years old and had much less of an established identity, fought against this change. Worse, when the others attempted to flee, she followed them, reinjected each with nanoprobes, forcing their reassimilation. It was, frankly, a horror story, made worse as we got to know these people, their lives and histories, the families from which they had been forcibly taken, not once, but twice, the last time at Seven's hands.

There was not much of a happy ending to this story. Again, we were faced with a choice: these three could not survive for long without reassimilating. In the end, a short life as themselves rather than a long life as Borg was what they preferred, and the Doctor and Seven performed the procedure to sever them permanently from the link that existed between them, the last remnants of Borg technology. Lansor, Two of Nine, remained at the space station, while P'Chan, Four of Nine, traveled on alone, to experience peace and quiet and solitude before he died. But Marika, Three of Nine, stayed with us on *Voyager*. This was a tender, sad, interlude—a few brief weeks making her acquaintance, before she was lost to us. One of the most poignant encounters of our whole time in the Delta Quadrant, and one that profoundly affected Seven.

✦

Reflecting back now on these cases where I had to make ethical decisions, all I can say is that I did the best that I could under the circumstances. I had a clear goal: to bring the ship home with minimum loss of life. I did not always get it right—but I tried always to bear this in mind, and to balance our situation as far as possible with the principles of Starfleet. I was out on a limb—a Starfleet captain without Starfleet. I could not summon up help or stop off at a starbase for extra supplies. I could not, for most of the time, even ask for advice on the decisions I had to make. Some were sound; some were less sound. Those Ethics of Command seminars could only help so far. I'm aware that the situation could, however, have been much worse. I am lucky that I arrived in the Delta Quadrant with my ship more or less intact, and enough people so that—despite some grievous losses—I was able to crew that ship. I know that this was not the case for Rudy Ransom on the *Equinox*.

Our astonishment in receiving a distress hail from another Starfleet vessel was matched only with our delight at discovering that this was no trap, but indeed another ship of ours, sent into the Delta Quadrant by the same means, at approximately the same time. They'd had a much rougher ride than us: an encounter with a power called the Krowtonan Guard had, in the space of a week, caused the death of half of Ransom's crew, and caused serious damage to the ship. I began to thank my lucky stars that our encounters—even with the Borg—had not caused so much harm. And I was curious as to how the *Equinox*, although a smaller and less powerful *Nova*-class ship, had managed to cross the same distance, and was excited to learn that Captain Ransom's people had made enhancements to their warp engines. I hoped this was a technique that we could adapt.

Alas, this was not to prove the case. Ransom, after that devastating week, had become wholly focused on the survival of his crew—at any cost. The secret of the *Equinox*'s rapid progress was revealed to be the wholesale slaughter of nucleogenic creatures, from whom they were harvesting bioenergy. This was how *Equinox* had enhanced their warp drive. They had crossed ten thousand light-years in a matter of weeks— and Ransom, and his XO, Maxwell Burke, were ready to sacrifice more to make the journey home. And I was going to do anything to stop him, particularly when we came under attack from the nucleogenic creatures, intent on a very justifiable revenge.

It's disheartening, to say the least, that it took an encounter with our own species and civilization to draw out the most mistrustful and savage behavior from us on our voyage home, as if coming face to face with our own baser selves was too much to stand. I certainly lost my bearings somewhat in this encounter—I'll admit that. Some of the decisions I made in my desire to bring down Ransom and the *Equinox* crossed the line. My interrogation of Noah Lessing went too far, as Chakotay told me at the time. I even went so far as to relieve Chakotay of his command, when he questioned my decision to fire torpedoes on the *Equinox*. The deletion of the Doctor's ethical subroutines by Ransom's crew (a flaw we quickly corrected) allowed him to explore aspects of human behavior about which I am sure he would have preferred to remain ignorant. I know his memories of his interrogation of Seven of Nine disturbed him greatly. In the end, Ransom, seeing the error of his ways, and removed by his own XO, ended up fighting back against the mutineers, and sacrificing himself—and his battered ship—to save *Voyager* from the alien assault.

I flatter myself that I would not have made the same mistakes as Rudy Ransom, but it's fair to say that I wasn't tested in the same way. I cannot and will never condone the choices he made but speaking as the only other Starfleet captain who knows a little of how he felt, I can see how his desire to protect his crew and bring them home might have brought him there. The road to hell is paved with good intentions, after all. I'm just glad I never had to set one foot upon it. Rudy made good in the end: we should not forget that. He was himself again, before he died. The five surviving crew members of the *Equinox* came on board *Voyager*: I stripped them of their ranks, put them under close supervision, and limited their privileges. And I will state here for the record that they gave exemplary service for the rest of our journey. Not everyone is beyond redemption.

Chakotay and I had some repairs to make to our relationship after these events. Truth be told, I was grateful for him—grateful to have a man of principles beside me. I should always remember that about Chakotay— it was principles that drove him to the Maquis, not profit, or vengeance. He was my true guide home. But still, as we picked up the pieces, I had to wonder—and how I wondered—what the next day might bring, and the day after, and the day after, and whether I might face a week of hell bad enough to make me cross the line for good.

✦

I have faced numerous criticisms over the years about the extent to which I allowed use of the holodeck during *Voyager*'s journey home. Let me say that critics always find something to complain about, and this seems to me another in a long list of decisions that other people are sure that they would have made differently had they been the captain. Besides, I've heard it all before. Torres and Tuvok both complained about how much time people spent on the holodeck for, as Tuvok put it, "frivolous reasons," although I suspect that B'Elanna was glad sometimes that Tom had a hobby, and I know that Tuvok used it on occasion for meditation purposes… with B'Elanna, too, now I come to think about it! But their points were fair. Nevertheless, I was the captain, and this was the decision I made. For good reason too: morale, notably in the early days, was low. In discussions with both Neelix and the Doctor, I was convinced that permitting people regular use of the holodeck was a good way for them to relieve the unusual stress and isolation of our situation. I'm sure that any inventory of holodeck programs on board *Voyager* would have revealed a high proportion of simulations simply named "Family" or "Home." We were so far away, and there was a strong possibility we would never see the people and places that we loved again. I considered this use of resources worth it in terms of the effect it had on crew well-being.

As for the other programs—damn it, they were fun! They helped people relax and unwind, and, given the precariousness of our situation at times, this was also necessary. I knew there was a risk that people might slide into holo-addiction, a well-documented phenomenon, and we did monitor use. Detractors can also be sure that I kept a close eye on what proportion of resources the holodeck was consuming. There were indeed times when I had to cut use down to almost nothing. But when the going was good, the holodeck was an important part of keeping the crew functioning. Tom Paris proved most adept at constructing scenarios which gave his colleagues great pleasure over the years: Sandrine's was a great creation and, of course, Fair Haven was a place very close to my heart. Even a captain needs time away from her responsibilities. What does the poet say? Humankind cannot bear very much reality… We all needed to take some time away from our situation. We all needed a break.

I will not deny that there were occasions when I wished I'd shut the damn thing down at the start of the voyage and never switched it on again. Let us say that I never expected my role as captain to expand into acting. You will note that my account of my childhood does not document a sparkling theatrical career, and indeed that career had more or less peaked with the dying swan. I hadn't acted since junior high—when I was a lackluster and frankly not convincing Juliet, more suited to comedy than tragedy—and was not prepared to have to extemporize the role of evil queen. (You can skip the jokes—the crew made them all at the time.) How did this all come about, you might you ask. Tom's holoprogram, *The Adventures of Captain Proton*, was a great favorite, and one which he and Harry played by preference. On this occasion, they were forced to leave the program running when *Voyager* became trapped in spatial distortions. As we tried to break free, a species of interdimensional aliens who took photonic form crossed to our dimension, entering through the *Proton* program. And so the story became real. The aliens, when attacked by Chaotica, were genuinely at threat from his photonic weaponry, which was harmless to us, but could harm them. We decided to enter the story, to help the aliens defeat Chaotica, and to free ourselves. Tom, it turned out, had a specific role in mind for me.

I defy anyone else to have brought such authenticity to the part of Arachnia, Queen of the Spider People. My task, it transpired, was to woo Chaotica so that he agreed to lower the lightning shield to allow Captain Proton to disable the death ray. I would like to think I inhabited the role convincingly. Perhaps my theatrical career is not yet over—I guess I'll need something to do in retirement. The crew rewarded me by adopting a new catchphrase, generally used after I'd issued a dressing-down. You don't want to know the number of times I heard muttered behind my back: *"Ha! You're no match for Arachnia..."* Well, they were right—they weren't.

There seems to be a subcategory of alien species unable to distinguish between fantasy and reality, and our next encounter with such gave me much more insight into the mind of our Emergency Medical Hologram than I might have preferred. The Doctor, it transpired, had been using the holodeck to daydream—all very well, I encouraged both him and Seven of Nine to explore the limits of their personhood, and the holodeck was an ideal environment for this. The Doctor's daydreams, however, tended toward the grandiose, and he had constructed a fantasy in which, as the "Emergency Command Hologram," he took charge of the ship. The Doctor might have been able to continue with this undisturbed, had not a passing ship, crewed by members of what we only knew as the Hierarchy, used a form of scan which enabled them to pick up the Doctor's program, mistaking the simulation for reality. Our knowledge of this came when a panicked junior crew member contacted us, explaining the mistake, and hoping we could save his skin.

The solution was for us to act out the deception for real, persuading the attacking Hierarchy ship of the reality of our "photonic cannon." My considerable trepidation over allowing the Doctor to use his Emergency Command routines was matched only by my sense that a small amount of rough justice was being dealt out. Nevertheless, he carried out the task with considerable aplomb, and I must admit that I was impressed at how the Doctor handled being in the hot seat. I could see some practical use to the ECH, and I reconsidered my decision not to devote formal research time to the project. I suggested that we assemble a team to explore it further. A change of heart that I am glad to say paid off in the long run.

✦

One adjustment that I had to make over these years was the extent to which my crew was now considerably more experienced than it had been at the start of the mission. Even my newest ensign, Harry Kim, by now had nearly half a decade's service behind him. In Harry's case, these years were marked by dedication, quietly getting on with the job, and being one of the most diligent crew members on board ship. I suppose at some point he was going to assert himself in the face of my authority, and the occasion arose when we made contact with the Varro. We were intrigued to learn that they had been inhabiting their generation ship for over four centuries. The ship was now in need of assistance—which we were certainly willing to give, on the principle of paying it forward; we were often in need of assistance ourselves. The situation was complicated somewhat by the mistrust of the Varro: they were, not to put too fine a point on it, a xenophobic people who would much have preferred not to have contact with us. But their need outweighed their distaste for strangers, and we were permitted access.

A generation ship was naturally of interest to me, since it was certainly one possible future for *Voyager*: if the ship's capacity diminished past a certain point, our progress might slow down to such a degree that the journey would take much longer than the life span of at least some of us. Who would crew the ship then? Naomi Wildman could hardly do this single-handedly (though that kid was determined enough that she would have given it her best shot). At the back of my mind, I was always wondering whether I needed to do more to encourage my crew to settle down, create families, treat our ship less like a place of work and more like a moving village. Not an option for the captain, of course, but a possibility for others. I was therefore interested to learn more about how the Varro's society worked. We discovered significant tensions: a dissident group had emerged, separatists who were discontent with the closed and insular life on board their ship, and who wanted to leave and follow their own path.

Usually we would not have involved ourselves; unfortunately, our hand was forced. Harry Kim, in what seemed at the time to be an unusual disregard for instructions, appeared to have fallen in love with a Varro scientist, Tal, developing some kind of physiological bond with her that was disrupting his behavior significantly, and manifested as physical symptoms. I was extremely angry with Harry over this, not least because we had no idea whether this could be a biological threat to the Varro, and because he might have disrupted our working relations with them too. Harry insisted that he had genuine feelings for Tal; I reminded him he had broken regulations, and I regretfully entered a reprimand onto his record. Poor Harry, unblemished service until then. We ended having a frank discussion about his actions: I believed he was suffering from a condition which needed treatment; Harry believed he was in love. With the unerring way in which the young know how to wound, he asked whether I would've taken a hypospray if it could have finished my feelings for Mark. I was fortunately not obliged to answer this question.

In the end, the dissident group, including Tal, were allowed to leave their ship and move on. Harry was bereft at her departure and, while the Doctor offered him a means to alleviate these emotions, he refused. I told Harry that this could not interfere with his duties, and that the reprimand stood. And I had to admit that I was surprised that it was him, of all my crew, who had behaved this way. Well, as he told me, he wasn't that fresh-faced ensign any longer. Five years is a long time—everyone changes.

I think Harry learned from this, grew from this. That's all you can ask for, in the end.

There were other examples during this time of my crew asserting themselves, and on one occasion I ended up having to dish out more than a reprimand. The ship came in range of a quite extraordinary sight: a world entirely covered with ocean. Even more remarkable, this world was inhabited. Initially its government, the Monean Maritime Sovereignty, was suspicious of us; I was able to persuade their spokesperson, Burkus, that we were not hostile, and invited a deputation to visit *Voyager*. During this visit, we learned that the Moneans knew very little about the ocean upon which they lived, and that, in fact, the Waters, as they called them, were beginning to shrink. Paris, who had attached himself to this visit, said that *Voyager* could help. I guess I should have seen we were heading for trouble, but I allowed him to take the *Delta Flyer* down to investigate the problem. Meanwhile, Chakotay reported that the rate of the reduction in the world ocean was extremely rapid, and likely to result in its dissipation within five years. I was surprised that Burkus was more concerned about the politics than the reality of this situation; perhaps I should never be surprised of the short-termism that some politicians bring to global crises.

Tom's exploration revealed that the oxygen-mining operations of the Moneans were leading directly to the dissipation of the Waters, but Burkus was clearly more concerned with the political ramifications of the news. It was plain he was unlikely to do anything with this information, leading to an angry outburst from Tom. After Burkus left, I reprimanded Tom—in hindsight, locking horns with him was probably a mistake, since it only reinforced his tendency to rail against authority. Next thing I knew, he had taken the *Delta Flyer* back down, to carry out some kind of radical act to secure the safety of the world ocean. We were able to stop this in time—who knows what could have gone wrong—and when Tom came back on board, I reduced his rank to ensign and gave him thirty days in the brig.

At the time, I was bitterly disappointed in Tom, and very angry with him. All his hard work, it seemed to me, was in danger of being thrown away; the huge strides he had made controlling his impulsive streak…

This was, so it seemed, a serious regression. I am so very glad that this turned out to be a momentary lapse. I had nothing to complain about after this incident. But I understood Tom better as a result. He would always, I had to recognize, rail against certain Starfleet strictures. The usual frustrations that we all have with the chain of command were heightened by the fact that they also represented his psychological struggle to separate from his father and to earn Owen's respect. Over the years, Tom seemed to find a working solution to this, and I guess I can forgive him his mistake. Nevertheless, I am extremely grateful that I was able to restore his lieutenancy before we were in real-time contact with home. And, in retrospect, I can see now that this marked the end of the old Tom, the last gasp, in some way, before a more mature version became fully established.

My other most impulsive crew member, B'Elanna Torres, had her own parental demons to deal with—almost literally, in this case. Returning from an away mission and hitting an ion storm, B'Elanna had a near-death experience in which she believed she was travelling on the Barge of the Dead to Gre'thor, the home of the dishonored dead, with her mother. Returning to consciousness, B'Elanna was completely convinced of the authenticity of her experience, and that her mother was on board the Barge of the Dead as a result of her actions. Against my better judgement, I authorized the Doctor to induce an artificial coma in B'Elanna, to allow her to learn more. That was a frightening time, but, when B'Elanna finally awoke, I could see from her eyes that the risk had paid off. When we talked about her experiences later, B'Elanna told me that she offered to take her mother's place on the barge and go to Gre'thor, but that this was shown to her as a version of *Voyager*—a metaphor for stasis, perhaps, of being stuck somewhere. B'Elanna needed to move on. I cannot comment on the truth or otherwise of these experiences. But they were true for B'Elanna, and whatever happened to her during those hours of unconsciousness, something had plainly been released in her. There were many more bumps along the way, but she was beginning to let go.

We had an entirely unexpected encounter with an old friend whom we had believed had long since outgrown us. Out of the blue, we were contacted by Kes—but this was someone to whom the intervening years had not been kind. She was weary, aged—and angry, stalking through the ship and attacking engineering. Many of these events are hazy to me, part of the local time distortions Kes created in her fury; suffice to say that I found memories returning to me that I did not know I had. She had come back in time, right back to her initial days on *Voyager*, and told us about her sense of loss after leaving us. That her powers were out of her control. That she had been a child when we'd allowed her to leave—and we had failed in our duty of care. As my memories returned, I remembered this encounter—and what we had done to stop it. As we came again to the moment when Kes approached us after her long absence, we evacuated engineering, and, when she arrived there, showed her the message she had left for herself. Her young self, begging her to remember what it had been like, and to leave us in peace. It helped, a little. It was sad to see Kes like that: that gifted and sensitive being that we had sent on her way with such love in our hearts. I hope that whatever happened next, she found a way back to that essential part of her: her clear sight, her curiosity, her courage.

✦

It seemed a long time now since we had received those messages from Earth, and yet it turned out that we had an ally back in the Alpha Quadrant, a man whose tendencies toward obsessive behavior could only work in our favor: Lieutenant Reginald Endicott Barclay III, Reg to his friends, and he will always have friends among the crew of *Voyager*. Barclay had become obsessed with our story, spending more and more time in holosimulation with the crew, and convincing himself that he could establish communications with us. He was working on the Pathfinder Project, which, as we were to learn, was a project spearheaded by Owen Paris trying to contact us and bring us home. It sure helps to have friends in high places—and an admiral's son on board. I knew I was right to bring Tom Paris along.

I've heard various accounts of the lengths Reg Barclay went to make his dream of communicating with us a reality; suffice to say that while I might not want to be his direct superior, I am eternally grateful for his devotion to our cause. The first we knew of his efforts was when we detected a microwormhole and then a communication signal which Seven identified as Starfleet in origin and transmitting on an official Starfleet emergency channel. Well, the speed with which we moved to clean up that signal! And then, blissfully, almost unbelievably—nearly a full minute and a half of two-way communication with home... Just time for a few words (expressing a multitude of emotions), to transmit our logs, reports, and navigational records back to Earth, and to receive some technical advice on modifying our comms to keep us in more regular contact. And Owen Paris, bless him, letting us know that they were doing everything they could to bring us home.

You can bet there were more than a few tears that day. I felt mostly joy. I'd hit rock bottom in that encounter with the *Equinox*; I'd nearly lost myself entirely. Now I knew I was going to find my way back home.

CHAPTER ELEVEN
ENDGAME—2377-2378

LOOKING BACK, ONE ASPECT OF OUR JOURNEY THAT I HAD certainly not anticipated was how many children would fall into our care. A Starfleet captain should be prepared for anything, however, and anyone who cannot manage to organize their ship to help their people with caring for their offspring is in the wrong job. Naomi Wildman, my fine assistant, had slotted right into our ship. My heart was naturally in my mouth on her behalf whenever we met with hostiles (and whatever agonies I went through were surely nothing compared to how Samantha must have felt). But her presence on board gave us perspective, and reminded us of why we kept on going; we all lightened up around her, we all wanted to bring her home to her other parent.

In the latter stages of our journey, moreover, some wholly unexpected charges fell into our care. When the *Delta Flyer* was intercepted by a Borg cube, we went to bring home our away team, and found the cube using an odd attack strategy. There was a reason for this: the entire crew consisted of five children, neonatal drones, as Seven explained, assimilated young. We found a baby too, in a maturation chamber, tiny implants on its little face… Truly our encounters with the Borg brought some terrible sights, but those lost children, wandering in the void, loyal to a Collective which, it transpired, had long since cut them loose, are among the worst. The eldest of this group, whom we only knew as First, cut off from the Collective, was now feeling the full effects of his reemerging adolescence, making him dangerous and erratic. He intended to keep our away team until we gave him *Voyager*'s navigational deflector. I was not inclined to bargain, not least as giving them the deflector would have allowed them to communicate with the Collective. I had enough Borg on my hands. I asked them to come on board *Voyager* instead, invited them to become individuals.

First was unpersuaded, and it fell to Seven to inform this little group that they were indeed completely abandoned, cut loose. The Borg do not tolerate imperfection—and they were imperfect. The shock was enough for the younger children to turn to Seven for aid; not First, though, who died insisting that the Collective would come for them. We brought the four surviving children on board, of course. The Doctor started to remove their implants, and Seven began the process of locating their real homes and families. The elder boy was Icheb, a Brunali; the younger twin Wysanti boys were Azan and Rebi; the little girl, Mezoti, was Norcadian. We put out calls to their people and their worlds, letting them know that we had found their strays. And while Seven thought that Neelix would be a better carer, I knew it had to be her. Who else could help them through these changes they were experiencing? Who else on the ship understood? I sometimes wonder what bedtime stories she told them. I should not forget that we had a baby to look after—if only for a little while. We were very quickly able to locate her home planet and return her to three relieved parents. Yet again, *Voyager* had found itself acting as a nursery in space. We might not have anticipated this extension to our responsibilities, but we carried it out with great success.

I am so proud of Icheb, and I know that Seven of Nine too became deeply attached to this unusual and gifted young man. It was therefore a significant wrench to us to discover the world from which he had originally come, and to learn that his parents were still very much alive. I could see no good reason for Icheb to remain on board: at first, he was deeply hostile toward this change in circumstances, not least when confronted with the realities of his home world. This was a rather isolated and technologically backward place where the local population had to work hard to make the land produce enough for them. Both Seven and

THE HISTORY OF THE CAPTAIN WHO WENT FURTHER THAN ANY HAD BEFORE

Icheb were concerned about the impact this would have on his ability to further his studies in astrometrics, for which he had real talent. But Icheb's people, the Brunali, turned out to have hidden depths: they had developed sophisticated techniques in genetic engineering, in part to assist their farming efforts. After some initial missteps, I watched with relief as Icheb began to move from hostility toward his parents to an acceptance and beginnings of trust. But I could only feel regret for Seven of Nine, whose attachment to Icheb had been a serious bond for her, and who was now going to have to say goodbye.

She struggled significantly with this while we were in orbit over the Brunali world, and so I must forgive myself for initially doubting her when she came to me to express misgivings about the account given us by Icheb's father, Leucon, about his son's assimilation. She told me that Mezoti had spotted discrepancies in Leucon's story, and while it seemed to me that both of them were looking for reasons to bring Icheb back to us, she argued in return that if there was the slightest chance that Icheb was in danger, we had to go back and make sure. I looked deep into the eyes of my most unusual crew member then, and I saw how much she loved this boy—and that she would not remain on board *Voyager* if I denied her the chance to find out for sure. I took the ship back.

And only in the nick of time. Seven's instincts had proven correct. The Brunali's genetic-engineering skills were not only to help their food production: they had created a weapon to infect the Borg. The problem was in the delivery mechanism—Icheb. He had been infected with a pathogen, and sent out to meet the Borg, infecting the first probe that encountered him. A truly sickening use of this boy. There was no question over whether or not we would intervene. We took Icheb back on board (it was a close shave; a near miss with a Borg cube) and learned the whole truth—his parents had not simply infected him. He had been genetically engineered to carry the pathogen, made to be a weapon, born to be a sacrifice. I remembered the old Greek tale, about the tribute sent from Athens to King Minos of Crete, of seven young men and seven young women, offered to the Minotaur to save their city. Not this time. We had Icheb back, more precious to us now than ever before, because we'd come so close to losing him. I'm glad that I was willing to listen to the instincts—the hunches, if you like—of one little girl, and one young woman, who could tell when something was not right.

Seven of Nine's educational techniques initially left something to be desired (if I never hear the words "punishment protocol" again, it won't be too soon); the children, however, took matters into their own hands, and I eventually observed a relaxation in her disciplinary strategies. She would often say that she was not suited to this task, but when the time came for Rebi and Azan to go home, taking Mezoti with them, we all felt the loss, and Seven most of all. Was there a tear? Seven insisted that her ocular implant was malfunctioning, and, indeed, this proved to be the case, and a manifestation of a very serious problem. Seven's cortical node was breaking down, causing symptoms such as dizziness and convulsions, and preventing her from being able to regenerate. In simulation after simulation, the Doctor was unable to perform a procedure that would not result in Seven's death.

My crew rallied around her, of course: Neelix came to see her in sickbay and, when she left there, I understand she had a conversation with B'Elanna Torres about the afterlife. Severed from the Collective, she could see no way that her unique experiences would live on. B'Elanna had her own wisdom to impart here. None of us would forget Seven. I was glad to think of these two women, under my command, turning to each other in friendship, at this difficult time. I myself went to speak to Seven, to assure her that we would do everything we could, and found her viewing images of Earth. I promised to take her to Bloomington when we got home—and learned that she had no expectation of surviving that long. Worse, she seemed to think that she had disappointed me, that she had failed to meet my expectations in her journey toward establishing her individuality. Oh, Seven! As if that was the case! In all ways, you have exceeded my expectations.

In the end, it was Icheb who saved her, donating his own cortical node, and relying on his comparative youth and genetic resequencing to coax his own body into surviving without the node. It was a risky gambit, and Icheb was ill for a while afterward, but it paid off, and Icheb was able to return to his studies and work toward his dream of sitting the entrance exam for the Academy. I gather there was a moment, talking to Icheb as he recovered, when Seven believed her ocular implant was malfunctioning again: this time the explanation was much simpler.

✦

Surely the most important feature of the final year of our voyage home was the establishment of regular, direct face-to-face communication with the people at the Pathfinder Project. It had been a great and continued relief to me, since our first contact with the project, to know that there were so many people back on Earth working to bring us home. And while a solution to this was, according to their reports, a long way off, they had also been working hard to establish communications with us. At first, we only had the letters: those first tiny contacts with our families and friends that so rocked our little worlds. Then we were able to receive recordings. And now—miracle of miracles!—the people at Pathfinder believed they had worked out a new method to speak to us in real time.

Again, we should acknowledge the work of Reginald Barclay, our great advocate in the Alpha Quadrant. How strange to think we had met him as a (quite inaccurate) hologram before most of us spoke to him face to face! The real Barclay was far less confident, much less a raconteur (and, not incidentally, not hijacked by Ferengi for a quick profit). Since returning to the Alpha Quadrant, I have had many conversations with Deanna Troi about Reg Barclay, and I understand a little more about the obsessive tendencies and various oddities that made him so devoted to our cause. What can I say? There's a place in Starfleet for everyone, and oddities are right at home on *Voyager*. We made him an honorary member of our crew right back when those first messages from Pathfinder arrived, and he still remains a part of the crew, as far as I am concerned. The breakthrough he made that let us all speak to each other directly for the first time in years was a hugely significant piece of work for which he has been rightly honored.

You try to be conscious, in a situation such as this, that you are participating in a historic moment. The first transgalactic two-way communication! In truth, we were all very close to being overwhelmed by our emotions. How I felt for Tom, seeing his father on-screen for the first time—seeing what was completely, undeniably, and unconditionally, sheer relief and pride on Owen's face. And how could we not have been moved by that most precious sight—those real-time images of Earth, our home, straight from McKinley Station, so white and blue and familiar. I could see North America; I could almost fancy that I saw Bloomington, my home, the country lanes and the white picket fences. So close I could almost reach out and touch… Still thirty thousand light-years away. God, that moment will remain forever in my mind. I knew without doubt that it had all been worth it: all the long years, the fears, the losses. I was bringing my ship and my people home.

With the connection made, we now found ourselves able to communicate with Earth for eleven minutes every day. Sounds like nothing, doesn't it, but it was an embarrassment of riches to us. Naturally we had to devote part of this to official communications with Starfleet Command, but I argued (and won my case) that, in particular during these early days, we should turn over the bulk of the time to letting my crew speak at last to their loved ones. Of course, that's not much time to spread across one hundred and fifty people, and Neelix organized a lottery and then the rotation. When my turn came up (of course I didn't pull rank; I was about thirtieth, which was pretty good, all things considered), I stood nervously waiting for the communication to start. I was a little conscious of Seven of Nine standing behind me, but the moment my mother's face appeared on-screen, everything around me was forgotten.

"Mom," I whispered.

"Oh Katy," she said. *"Oh, my darling girl!"*

I thought I was going to cry. Nearly seven years of keeping myself under such tight control, knowing that I was the one who always had to be strong… Well, we are all susceptible to the sight of our mother, aren't we? I'm only human, after all.

"It's so good to see you," I said. "I can't begin to say…"

She looked only a little older. Some more silver in her long hair; a few more worry lines around her eyes. *"I knew you weren't dead,"* she said. *"Owen Paris came to see me. I said to him, 'Owen, I'm not giving up, and neither should you.' He was trying to persuade me, and I ended up persuading him!"*

We both began to laugh. My mother—that was where I had gotten the stubborn streak! I could imagine her, listening to the visiting admiral, nodding politely as he spoke, and then saying: *No. This is how it is.*

"Between you and Reg Barclay, we have had some great allies back home."

"I've heard from Owen about the Redoubtable Reg. I might invite him here for dinner."

"From what I gather about him, he won't accept!"

"Well, let's not talk about Reg Barclay. Are you all right, Katy? Have you been looking after yourself?"

"Yes, Mom, fruits and vegetables at every meal."

I saw her eyes drift past me to where Seven was standing. *"I'm sorry about Mark."*

I brushed it aside. "Water under the bridge."

"Hmm." She didn't look convinced (I'm not sure I sounded convincing), but this wasn't something to discuss on a line like this. *"Your sister sends her love. Yianem too, and the girls. They want to speak to you next time around. The new one is very excited to speak to the famous family member! She's mad about Starfleet."*

Amelia: the latest addition to their family. I laughed. Sounded like she was a Janeway through and through—and she was, as you shall learn. "Three months," I said. "I hope they can all hold out that long!"

"All of us will be here. Oh, Katy. I'm so glad to speak to you again!"

"Me too, Mom."

Behind me, quietly, Seven said, "Thirty seconds, Captain."

"Not long enough," said Mom. *"Well, Katy, hurry home. We have the lamp lit, guiding you home."*

"Get the coffee pot on, for God's sake," I begged her, trying to sound cheerful. "I'm desperate for a decent cup of coffee!"

"I'll get your grandfather on it."

"Ten seconds, Captain," said Seven.

"Goodbye, Katy! We'll speak soon!"

"Goodbye, Mom," I said.

And then she was gone. I took a moment or two to collect myself and turned to see Seven contemplating me.

"Are you... all right, Captain?" she said.

"I'm fine, Seven." I took a deep breath. "You must have seen a lot of this now. Is there anyone back in the Alpha Quadrant that you're planning to speak to?"

"My father had a sister," she said, doubtfully.

"Try her," I said. "It might be worth it."

And I believe that she did. I'm not sure I can imagine how this conversation must have gone: her aunt would remember little Annika, no more than six years old. Seven of Nine was no longer that little girl. I hoped the aunt had the sense and the grace to accept her on her own terms, and not wish to have Annika back. I believe they began to communicate regularly; at least, I didn't hear of anyone accepting Seven's slots in the rotation. I wondered whether she would get in touch with her, once we were home.

This was a tumultuous time for us all: I often passed people in the corridor having a quiet cry. We had all been starved for conversations with our loved ones. The letters had been like field rations in comparison with being able to speak to them face to face, in real time. All of us were changed, of course: Harry Kim was no longer the fresh-faced new ensign who had left his clarinet at home. (I had a very nice letter from his mother about how grateful she was that I had looked out for her boy. I didn't mention this to Harry, although I did play up those night shifts, when he had been in command of the ship, for her benefit.) Even those of us with very close family ties were finding our feet again after seven years. And other relationships were starting over completely. I know that Tom always had B'Elanna with him when he spoke to his mother and father, as if to insist that this was who he was now, and that his father needed to get to know him on these terms. B'Elanna in turn had made tentative contact once again with her estranged father. How hard, to try to rebuild that relationship under these conditions! To be able to speak only every few weeks, and then for no more than a few minutes at a time! But B'Elanna was tenacious, and once she put her mind to something, she stuck to it, and she had decided that this relationship was plainly worth salvaging.

Of course, there was a very good reason for this. Our lovebirds had married at the start of our seventh year: I must say that was a typically outlandish proposal. They were participating in a race, on board the *Delta Flyer*, and the flyer's warp core had been sabotaged. I gather they thought they had about ten seconds to live when Tom popped the question. This was… very like Tom, shall we say. But he'd meant it, and they married—and before we had all got used to having this married couple in our midst, B'Elanna discovered she was pregnant. The Doctor warned us there might be emotional outbursts. Several people joked (not entirely kindly, I think; I put a stop to this) that they weren't sure how we would tell. In fact, this was a very difficult time for B'Elanna. It has been my observation that pregnancy, and imminent parenthood, make people reflect on their relationships with their own parents. I guess this is in part because they don't want to make the same mistakes—and they're worried that they won't avoid them. But at the same time, people seem to want to reconnect; they want their child to know where they came from, to know their grandparents.

For B'Elanna, this time was marked by a real coming-to-terms with what it had meant for her to be half Klingon. When she and Tom saw that their little girl was going to have the distinctive facial ridges, many unhappy childhood memories came back to her. Kids can be ghastly, after all; they'll always find something to pick on, and B'Elanna's physical differences had attracted some teasing. Worse than that, she believed that it was the Klingon part of her that had driven her father away. These emotions naturally surfaced now; she must have feared that history would repeat itself with her own daughter and husband. (As if Tom would leave her: the man was besotted with her. He'd stuck beside her through thick and thin.) She asked the Doctor to perform genetic resequencing to delete her fetus's Klingon genes and make her more fully human in appearance. The Doctor initially refused to perform such a drastic procedure on the grounds that it was not medically justified, but then later seemed to think that it was not just necessary but urgent. Tom, however, had his suspicions, and these turned out to be warranted: B'Elanna had tampered with the Doctor's program to get the diagnosis that she wanted. We stopped the procedure just in time.

I know that B'Elanna was, once she had taken a little time to think through what was happening, filled with remorse at interfering with the Doctor's programming. However, she had the means to make good. Ever since her pregnancy had been—I hesitate to say announced; *broadcast* was more like it—she and Tom had been plagued with offers from people who wanted to be godparents. (I know pregnant women often complain about finding themselves communal property: poor B'Elanna had this dialed up to the nth degree. Everyone on *Voyager* was invested in this child.) But there was only once choice after these events. I gather the Doctor takes his responsibilities in this respect extremely seriously.

Again, I must reflect on how I had never predicted the extent to which our ship would become so concerned with the nurturing of children. That last year or so, they seemed to take up more and more of our time. Not just our Naomi, whom we all loved very much. Not just our communal investment in Tom and B'Elanna's baby. Not just our Borg children, of whom we were so proud while they were with us, not least Icheb, who remained and was proving to be a most responsible, thoughtful, and careful young man. On top of all this, I found ourselves charged with looking after a recalcitrant, undisciplined, and annoying adolescent: the offspring of Q, Q Junior, unceremoniously dumped on us by his hapless father.

If ever an apple had not fallen far from the tree… Junior had no sense of the consequences of his actions. He caused havoc on the ship, even stripped of his powers, stealing the *Delta Flyer* and running into trouble with a Chokuzan vessel (or so we thought). His actions put Icheb's life in danger, and it was only then that we saw a glimpse of understanding from Junior: confronted again with the Chokuzans, he admitted that the events were down to him, and asked them to help Icheb. Of course, this was all revealed to be a situation generated by his father to teach his son a lesson. Games after games; always the same with the Q. After all the trouble those wretched Q caused us, you think they might have had the decency to send us home. No chance of that: Q provided information that took a few years off the trip, Junior gave me some roses, and with that I had to be content. I understand that I am the Starfleet captain with the most varied experience of the Q Continuum. All I can say is that I would happily have passed on this honor…

✦

THE HISTORY OF THE CAPTAIN WHO WENT FURTHER THAN ANY HAD BEFORE

There were many other ramifications of our increased contact with the Alpha Quadrant. Speaking for myself, regular contact with Starfleet Command had both pros and cons. Knowing that I was now able to speak to colleagues and superiors, to get advice and support, was a great help to me. I received regular messages from both Owen Paris and Parvati Pandey and their reflections on matters that were troubling me. Being able to share the burden of the command was a real relief. There were downsides, however. I have an independent streak at the best of times, and, for more than six years I had, in effect, been answerable to nobody. The chain of command had been severed—and now it was back. There were significant downsides arising from this, which came into sharp focus during our mission to locate the lost *Friendship 1* probe, which our superiors believed to be close to our current position.

It meant a detour, for one thing, when all we wanted to be doing was getting closer to our families and friends, and I had some misgivings about whether the crew would be happy about this. It turned out that the mystique of the missing probe was lure enough— most of us were Starfleet, after all, with curiosity in our blood. The mission itself proved to be distressing, a textbook case in the perils of sharing technology. The probe, equipped with antimatter reactors, had arrived on a world only for the antimatter technologies to be used for purposes of war. By the time we arrived, the world—and its people—were suffering from a nuclear winter, and the local population blamed us for what had happened to them. One of their leaders, Verin, taking our away team hostage, demanded that we help evacuate the population—but this would take us three years, time we could not afford. Here was my problem, then, with taking on missions such as this: we were there as representatives of Starfleet, but we could not operate as if we were Starfleet. Back in the Alpha Quadrant, I could have called in specialist ships. Here, I was operating under orders, but alone.

As it turned out, we were able to adapt photon torpedoes to explode nanoprobes in the planet's atmosphere, setting off a chain reaction that not only dissipated the nuclear winter, but neutralized the radiation. But the mission had cost a crewman's life: Lieutenant Joe Carey, part of the away team, murdered by Verin. I regretted every life lost on *Voyager*'s journey, but, looking back, this one hits hard. Had we known how close we were to getting home I would have argued against taking on this and any other mission. The priority, after all these years, had to be the safe return of all our crew. The fact that we were now in regular communication with the Alpha Quadrant gave Carey's death a bitter coda: I had to speak directly to his parents, and explain why their boy was not, after all, able to speak to them. I had some stern conversations with my superiors after this. Yes, we were Starfleet, and back within the chain of command—but the chain of command is a reciprocal relationship. It cuts both ways. We could take orders, but help could not be sent. Starfleet Command needed to remember this. We might be on the other end of the line, but we were still a long way from home.

✦

Our Doctor, now in regular contact with the Alpha Quadrant, characteristically made an immediate impact, electing to use his allotted time to speak to the publishers of his magnum opus, *Photons Be Free*. I am being a little unfair here on our estimable colleague, since he admitted that this was a first draft and, having received feedback from the rest of the crew, was willing to carry out significant revisions. You may have sampled the earlier version (I understand that a few are still out there), and so you can imagine my thoughts when I first saw Jenkins, captain of the *U.S.S. Vortex*, murdering a dying man. I do not doubt the Doctor's sincerity when he said that he did not intend the crew to represent us (although I might have a few things to say about his naivety). What was most wounding was that we couldn't help but think that this was, in some way, the Doctor's opinion of each of us. Tom Paris, I know, was very hurt: he had come a long way in the years on board *Voyager*. Well, Tom is hardly one to disappear and lick his wounds; he came back fighting, reprogramming the holonovel, and showed the Doctor exactly how it felt. This was when the Doctor agreed to revise his tome, realizing at last not only the hurt he had inadvertently caused, but how much damage could be done to our reputations, should the novel be widely circulated.

Of course, nothing can be straightforward when the Doctor is involved.

The situation rapidly escalated, and I found myself involved in a tribunal to judge whether or not our EMH was a person. Imagine having to do this across the distance of thirty thousand light-years, with only a dozen minutes a day to present arguments! His publishers, Broht & Forrester, represented by Ardon Broht himself, were arguing—and this is not to their credit—that since the Doctor was not legally a person, he had no rights over his book. Sometimes I do wonder how some people sleep at night. (They publish the Dixon Hill novels – I shall never read one again.) As ever, when faced with a legal conundrum, I turned to Tuvok, who tried to argue the case that, leaving aside his personhood, the Doctor had to be considered the author of the piece, and therefore had rights as an artist. It seems ludicrous to me that the arbitrator did not simply rule that the Doctor was a person. The legal definition of "artist" even includes that word! But no: it seemed that our arbitrator was not prepared to set a precedent that day and ruled narrowly in the Doctor's favor as to his rights over his work—but not over his rights as a person. Downright cowardice, in my opinion. What more evidence did we need to provide? The Doctor has exceeded his programming—even his creator, Lewis Zimmerman—admits that. He feels, he loves, he changes—he creates. He is as much a person as any of us—he is more of a person than some people I meet!

There's a twist in this tale. The original version of the Doctor's book got loose among a community of EMH Mark Is who had been decommissioned as medics and were working as miners. They read the book as a piece of subversive literature—a call to arms, no less—and put down their tools and went on strike, the first act in what we now call the "photon rights movement." I wait with considerable interest to see what the Federation lawyers make of this—and I hope they show a little more courage this time.

There was one more effect of our regular communications with the Alpha Quadrant that is worthy of mentioning, since it brought to the fore an issue which many of us believed resolved, but which I realized, as a result of these events, might need further thought and planning. I refer of course to the old division, which I myself no longer saw, between our Starfleet and our ex-Maquis crew members. These latter suddenly found themselves the victims of unprovoked attacks that left them comatose. It turned out that the attacks came from an entirely external source, albeit using one of my crew. A letter from Tuvok's son, Sek, sent via data stream, had, it transpired, been tampered with. Underneath the message from Sek there was another message embedded, from a fanatical Bajoran vedek, Teero Anaydis. Teero had worked with the Maquis in counterintelligence but had been forced out after experimenting with mind control. Tuvok, under Teero's influence, had carried out the attacks, and was struggling to regain control over his own mind. Put in a position where Tuvok had to choose between loyalty to his former Maquis colleagues, now themselves under Teero's influence, and his loyalty to me, I'm gratified to say that Tuvok chose his captain, and was able to mind-meld with Chakotay and the others to restore them to themselves.

Reflecting on these events afterward, I was chiefly saddened at how quickly the old suspicions had come back. I was grateful, however, to have been alerted to the fact that our increased contact with the Alpha Quadrant was causing many of them to worry about what the future held for them, and I held one-to-one conversations with all the crew who had been Maquis. These fears, it turned out, were very real. What was their reception in the Alpha Quadrant going to be? Would they face charges for their activity, even go to prison, as some of their comrades had done? To my mind, the previous half a dozen years had wiped the slate completely clear. But I could see how some back in Starfleet, still sore over the multiple defections, and without my firsthand experience of the courage and loyalty of these people, might think differently. I realized that this was something for which I needed to prepare.

✦

There is an interlude that I want to put down, because, in retrospect, I can see that when it occurred, I was so very close to home, and yet was nearly lost for good. I'll say this for Quarren labor law: the working conditions and pay were good. It was their recruitment policies that left a great deal to be desired. Their advanced industrial civilization had a chronic labor shortage, and some companies had resorted to a dubious program of systematic forced removal of aliens, giving them new memories along with their new lives. *Voyager*'s crew—or, at least, some of us, were taken.

My memories of this time remain intact—I was the same person; I simply didn't recall my true past life. I found myself a good job, and I found myself a good man, Jaffen. We moved in together. Others of my crew fitted in well too—Seven, inevitably, proved the most adaptable, slotting straight into her new role as efficiency manager at the station where we were working. Others were less successful—a shout-out for Tom Paris, who more or less got himself fired within a few days, and wound up in a bar, making conversation with a lovely woman named B'Elanna…

I would have stayed there quite happily, but part of our crew had been absent when the Quarrens took us: Chakotay, Neelix, and Kim had been on an away mission, returning to find *Voyager* empty, only the Emergency Command Hologram on board (I didn't, after all, regret allowing our Doctor to pursue this research program). Chakotay and Neelix infiltrated the plant, targeting us, and, through our conversations together, bringing our memories back. This rash of "dysphoria syndrome," among so many people of the same species, who had arrived at the plant at the same time, alerted a young doctor to our plight, and the scandal was brought to the attention of the government. We were able to depart, but not before I had to say goodbye to Jaffen.

The trouble was—he had not been kidnapped. This was his real life. He had met a woman whom he liked, and could well have loved, and he had been ready to start another chapter in his life with her. But she wasn't real. I wasn't that woman. I was *Voyager*'s captain, and I was never going to stay.

Still, I had been happy there.

✦

This whole period I recall as one of people getting to know their friends and family again. But we had one sad goodbye to say, to our dear friend and traveling companion Neelix. We were celebrating First Contact Day, Neelix-style, when we received news of a Talaxian settlement hidden within an asteroid belt nearby. I sent Paris and Tuvok, with Neelix, in the

Delta Flyer to investigate, but the shuttle was shot down and crash-landed. They were rescued by the Talaxians, who had reached the asteroid after many years of exile, and after failing to establish a home elsewhere. We welcomed visitors from the Talaxians aboard *Voyager* to demonstrate our friendship. I could see that Neelix was becoming close to one of them, Dexa, a widow with a young son, Brax, of whom Neelix was also plainly becoming very fond. I wondered, watching them, whether this might be the end of Neelix's time with us. There were numerous complications, however: a company of miners was laying claim to the asteroid belt and trying to get the Talaxians to leave. But having at last built a home there, after many false starts, they were not willing to go. And I was caught up in the Prime Directive: I could not actively involve *Voyager*.

But Neelix, of course, was not bound by the Prime Directive... as Tuvok, so it turned out, had made clear to him. This understanding between my outlandish and certainly very extroverted morale officer and my staid and utterly introverted chief tactical officer was one that I had noted on various occasions, although I think neither of them quite knew what to do about it. I have wondered whether it was some aftereffect of the merging of their DNA so early in our voyage. Neelix irritated Tuvok; Tuvok perplexed Neelix. And yet when it came down to it, Tuvok proved to be Neelix's staunchest ally on board ship, and the one who came up with the solutions that brought Neelix a very happy ending, as far as his story on *Voyager* was concerned.

Prompted by Tuvok—I learned later, much later—Neelix realized that he had, over the years, become a little more than a chef and a host. "The most resourceful person I have ever met," Tuvok said to me later. He had that right—and I daresay Neelix had learned a trick or two from us along the way, even as he taught us many things (if not, yet, managing to persuade Tuvok to dance). Neelix devised a plan for the Talaxians to defend themselves against the miners—a successful plan, with perhaps a little last-minute intervention from the *Delta Flyer*. The miners were beaten back, and the Talaxian colony left in peace.

And yet Neelix decided to stay on *Voyager*—out of loyalty to us, and not wanting to give up on his friends. I could see it was breaking his heart. He had been away from his own kind for a very long time —an exile surely at least as painful as any that the rest of the crew were going through. And, at heart, he was a family man: he loved children—and Naomi was growing up now; she didn't need a babysitter —and he wanted companionship. This was plainly the wrong decision for him: But how could he put his loyalty to us to one side?

Tuvok, in fact, came up with the idea: that methodical mind of his must have been sifting through to work out a solution. "It seems to me, Captain," he said, "that as we draw ever closer to home, and put the Delta Quadrant behind us, we might benefit from having some kind of ambassador here. Someone whom we know well, and whom we trust."

By Jove, he had it, and when I put the idea to Neelix, I could see the sheer joy and relief on his face. He could have everything: company, fatherhood, and our continued friendship through the new transgalactic communications techniques. It was a deeply moving occasion, saying goodbye to him, and I am proud of my crew, and the honor that they showed him, lining the corridors to say farewell. I saw Naomi Wildman, standing beside me, wiping away a tear, and I have to say that if I had an ocular implant, it would have been on the fritz that day. Last of all, Tuvok stepped forward, and gave the softest of soft-shoe shuffles, and said those words that his people had said in greeting to mine, all those long years ago:

"Live long—and prosper."

And so we said, not goodbye, but—till we meet again, to our first and best friend from the Delta Quadrant. Till we meet again, our dear Ambassador.

✦

Of all the pigheaded, stubborn, and downright frustrating people whom I encountered during these years, there was none to compare with my own damn self. *O wad some Pow'r the giftie gie us, To see oursels as ithers see us!* You've got to wonder about someone willing to pull rank on herself. Damn woman. But in the end, Admiral Janeway, my future self, helped bring us home—like she, like I—had promised, all those years ago.

She travelled back in time to come and offer us a route back via a Borg transwarp conduit, but it seemed to me that our priority was to destroy the transwarp network and protect the Alpha Quadrant from Borg attacks. I was not unaware that I was facing, yet again, a choice very like that which had stranded us here in the first place: to use alien technology to take us home, or to destroy it and protect others. The admiral complicated matters greatly by revealing details of her future to me: twenty-three years in the Delta Quadrant (dear god, the prospect…!), the deaths of Seven of Nine and twenty-two others, and the horrible thought of seeing my friend Tuvok's faculties decline… But the crew were prepared to take these risks, if it meant destroying the network. The future is never fixed.

In the end, there was a sacrifice—the admiral took her shuttlecraft into the transwarp hub, in search of the Unicomplex, the center of Borg operations and the lair of their queen. I can only guess at how that encounter unfolded, and what my future self must have suffered. But she was our Trojan horse: she was carrying with her a pathogen that, when released, devastated the Unicomplex, causing it to be destroyed. For a while we believed our plan had succeeded completely. We entered a transwarp corridor, and then saw we were being pursued by a Borg sphere. As we shot along the corridor, I took *Voyager* into the center of the sphere and, just as we came out—a mere light-year from my own home system—I detonated a torpedo that destroyed the sphere.

We looked out on a fleet of ships—Starfleet vessels, all. Our friends; our comrades.

We had found the straight path. We were home.

✦

The ships that had been sent to fight the Borg were now an honor guard. They took us to McKinley Station, where *Voyager* had launched all those years ago, and we docked our ship. Earth was so close I could almost touch it. We were all in a hurry to leave the ship—but first I went to sickbay, to check on the newest member of my crew: Miral Torres Paris, a fine, healthy little girl. B'Elanna was beatific, if exhausted; Tom looked blitzed. I think neither of them had entirely registered that we were home. I don't blame them. There's some question whether Miral was born in the Delta Quadrant or the Alpha Quadrant. To my mind, she's the product of both: the first truly transgalactic child. I guess if our voyage was to have a legacy, it would be this: that the time we spent there as Federation ambassadors, as representatives of Starfleet, would mean that when others visited, there would be places where we would be remembered fondly, and in friendship.

I waited until everyone had left the ship to join their families and friends, and then I sat for a little while on my bridge. It was hard now, after everything, to say goodbye. Chakotay came to find me.

"Kathryn," he said. "Your public awaits."

I stood up. I went to join him, standing in front of the dedication plaque, and we embraced.

"Thank you," I said.

"Kathryn, it's been my privilege to serve."

We left together. I had a date—with my first real cup of coffee in seven years, and with my mother, and my sisters, and the four little girls in their care.

CHAPTER TWELVE
WHAT YOU BRING BACK—2378... AND BEYOND

HOW DID WE ALL FARE, ON OUR RETURN? How did we find life back in the Alpha Quadrant, once we had achieved our hearts' desire? I've thought, many times across my life, that you should be careful what you wish for: not everything turns out to be as you expected. As a child, I wanted more than anything to visit the stars, to be whisked, like Dorothy Gale, away from the quotidian to a marvelous land, but the reality proved very different. Much more of my life among those strange new worlds turned out to be everyday worries: about resources, and maintenance and repairs; about the psychological well-being of the people toward whom I had a duty of care. Life in Oz turned out to have a lot of housekeeping! So what about the return home? Some of us settled back very quickly into our old roles and lives; for others, the adjustment proved more difficult—they had begun their lives on *Voyager*, or else come into their own there. How might the Alpha Quadrant suit them now?

The first few weeks were extremely odd. Given how limited our communication time had been, what none of us had entirely realized was the extent to which, since the Pathfinder Project had made contact with us, we had become celebrities. (The folks at Pathfinder had decided not to apprise us of this, thinking we had enough worry about making the journey home without adding the sense that the whole Federation was watching.) As a result, we came home to learn that people knew our names, our faces, and our stories. The news of our arrival home was greeted with enormous public interest. There were the usual official functions, meeting ambassadors and dignitaries, top brass and all the rest of it, but there were also ticker-tape parades, public meet and greets, invitations to speak... I was granted the key to the city of Bloomington, Indiana, a great honor. Wherever we went, even simply walking down the street to get a cup of coffee, we were stopped. People wanted to get a holo-image, explain how they felt about us, tell us where they were when they heard we were home. It was deeply touching, such as when, for example, you were told how our voyage had been an inspiration or had helped someone find hope. At the same time, it was very disconcerting. You felt strangely... *watched*. (I noticed how many of us who had the option suddenly grew beards, and there were some significant alteration in hairstyles across the board too.)

I was extremely recognizable, and I guessed that, as the captain, and the face of *Voyager*, this wasn't going to go away. I had a faint inkling of how it must have been to be Neil Armstrong, back from the moon, with everyone wanting to have a chance to speak to him. Foolish, intrusive questions, sometimes: What shirts did we wear? What food did we like? Who were we not looking forward to seeing again? It was hard sometimes to keep up one's public face: if you were just trying to get home after a long day, and someone stopped you, hoping for an inspirational moment. I tried my best, and I sincerely hope no one was ever disappointed. I increasingly found that I preferred to spend a lot of time around Starfleet facilities, and I knew that I was going to have to find a remote place to set up home—my old apartment in San Francisco had become too well known, and people would drop by at all hours "just to say hello." A shame: I liked that place, but it wasn't practical any longer. For the short term, I relocated to quarters within the Starfleet Command complex, which were quite sufficient for my immediate purposes, and kept intrusion at a minimum. I was bombarded with many requests for personal appearances, not all of which I could accept. I should note one that was a very special honor: my invitation to address the Amelia Earhart Society. What a speech to be able to give! How incredible to think that this woman was, surely, still alive and making a future with those colonists! That was an extraordinary evening, a highlight of my public career. *Voyager*'s logs changed people's perceptions a great deal.

While I negotiated the highs and lows of celebrity, I should note that my family had quite a tough time in the first couple of years: Mom was deluged by uninvited visitors at the farm, although she was quite brisk and mercenary about the whole business, using it to promote awareness of the situation on Cardassia Prime, where she had become involved in the relief effort and postwar reconstruction. Phoebe and Yianem found this period very hard, trying to protect the girls' privacy, and there were several occasions when stern words were sent from Starfleet on their account to various journalists who were hoping to make their name from catching an image of them. We got the public on our side here, and the girls were declared off limits. I think they often used Yianem's surname when they were traveling, rather than identifying as Janeways.

There was one meeting that I did manage to keep completely private: with Mark. A few messages had passed between us on our return, and I think we both hesitated as to whether this was a good idea, or whether we were simply opening old wounds that should be left to heal. In the end, we both agreed that we needed closure. We decided on an impersonal setting, one of those comfortable but anodyne lounges that are all around Starfleet Command. I was glad of the familiarity of the setting, since this was a very difficult meeting for me. I did not, and could not, and *would* not blame him for finding someone else: for God's sake, the man had been widowed once already. I will not describe the details of this meeting and keep them for me and Mark alone, but there were tears on both sides, and many regrets, but there was also, as we had both hoped, healing. In the end, neither side had meant harm. We met again afterward, and this time I met his wife, a good and lovely woman who has made him very happy, and his little boy. And I was reunited with my beautiful Mollie. Mark's son was devoted to her, which made me shed a few tears. Love me, love my dog. I took one of the pups from Mollie's next litter. I was glad to see Mark so happy, and we remain in touch. But it was hard not to feel regret for the life together that we had lost. I asked him whether he would like the copy of *The Divine Comedy* back—it had been an engagement present after all. "Oh, Kathryn," he said. "I would have followed you anywhere—if I'd only known where you were. It's yours, and always will be."

It was easiest to throw myself straight back into Starfleet. Its protocols, rules, and regulations had been such a support throughout our time in the Delta Quadrant and were a source of continuity on my return. Naturally there was an extensive debriefing, on both sides. I for one was learning about the rapidly changing situation in the Alpha Quadrant in the wake of the Dominion War. We had received detailed briefings during our latter months, after two-way communications were established, but the reality of being back, and seeing the impact of that brutal conflict not just upon Starfleet but upon the wider Federation, and beyond, took some readjustment. I found Starfleet to be a twitchier, more paranoid organization than the one I had left, and I had to realize the extent to which the (rational) fear of infiltration by Changelings had fundamentally altered the culture. As I say, nobody these days would skip a weapons' sweep when welcoming an admiral aboard. And then I would learn of the deaths of old friends and colleagues, people whom I had hoped to catch up with on my return, killed by Jem'Hadar. We have all said, at our regular crew reunions, how disorientating it has been, not to have this shared experience. The whole quadrant had changed in our absence.

On the other side, Starfleet Command was extremely keen to talk to me and my crew in detail about our time in the Delta Quadrant. I was now the Starfleet captain with more experience of both the Q Continuum and the Borg than any other, and there were hours of sessions devoted to these encounters. Our adaptations of Borg technology also formed the topic of many a discussion—and a dedicated team was put together to work on these innovations. Seven of Nine was naturally a person of great interest. There were lengthy sessions over specific incidents: the fate of the *Equinox* was a real concern, and I know that this case study now forms a significant part of an extended and compulsory course at the Academy on the Ethics of Command. I think we were all shocked at how rapidly the situation had broken down there. All cadets now attend at least two compulsory simulations which place them in environments where they find themselves with limited resources and no expectation of backup. I should note too that, following our reprogramming examples, it is no longer possible to delete the ethics subroutines on any EMH, or, indeed, any other kind of emergency hologram. I spoke privately to Ransom's family, whom I felt needed to know the full story. I am pleased to report that the five surviving crew members, who acquitted themselves faultlessly during their time on *Voyager*, have gone on to good things. Marla Gilmore was the only one to remain in Starfleet, and she has had a fine career. I am glad that this impossible situation in which she found herself, at the beginning of that career, under commanders who lost their way, has not blighted her potential in any way. We remain in regular contact, and I understand that she will be overseeing the cadet course on the *Equinox* next semester. She will, I think, be an inspiration to those students. She learned the hard way, and she has indeed learned. If anyone can teach these students to appraise themselves honestly, it will be her.

As for those of the crew who had been members of the Maquis: that war was long over as far as I was concerned. Nonetheless, a few of the top brass, predominantly those who had served out in the DMZ or who had personally been let down by Maquis defectors, were considerably more resistant. They argued that due process should be followed, and a dangerous precedent set if it was not. The matter was resolved quite simply: I threatened to resign my commission in the most public way possible if full amnesty was not granted. It's amazing how quickly that focused everyone's minds. All my field commissions were reconfirmed, and those former Maquis crew members who wanted to remain in Starfleet were able to do so without any repercussions. Many, however, were eager to return to their home worlds, to see how they had fared since the Dominion War. We see less of these people than we do others at our reunions—but they do stay in touch, and even drop by, every so often.

There were naturally debriefing sessions where my own judgement came under scrutiny, not least my decision to separate the DNA of Tuvok and Neelix at the cost of Tuvix. What can I say? I myself am unsure of the rights and wrongs of that decision, and thinking about what I might have done differently will continue to haunt me for the rest of my life. I also felt a deep and continuing responsibility toward the lives lost during our voyage home, and especially the crew members lost on that first, terrible day in the Delta Quadrant. I paid a visit to the relatives of each person that I lost, to return personal effects, and to bring home memories of them too. People like Joe Carey, Lyndsay Ballard… Even Lon Suder had a mother who'd missed him. Visiting the family of my old friend Laurie Fitz was by far one of the hardest things I have ever done. I have never stopped regretting asking him to come aboard *Voyager*. He was a fine doctor, and a good friend, and his death is one of the biggest regrets of my life.

✦

While there was no question for me that my future lay in Starfleet, this was not the case for many others that served on *Voyager*. I would say that no more than a third of the people who returned to the Alpha Quadrant continued in Starfleet, and most left within the first eighteen months of our return. Speaking to some of these at our regular reunions, they tell me that they found it hard to fit back into the old routines, and the distance between their own experiences, and those of colleagues who had come through the Dominion War, was too great to bridge. *Voyager* had been their home, but Starfleet no longer felt that way. They would have continued to serve under my command, but that was not an option. *Voyager*, my fine ship, was decommissioned shortly after our return. The wear and tear of those seven years had been too hard on her, and what had been state-of-the-art technology had fallen behind the rapid technological advances necessitated by the Dominion War. *Voyager* had served her purpose, even as she retained, in the minds of those had served on her, her status as home.

But even without a ship, and even as so many of us moved on, we have kept a kind of cohesion as a crew. We have regular reunions, and even a kind of base. Tiring of my pleasant but impersonal quarters at Starfleet Command, and realizing that it was time to have a real home once again, I have found myself a place on the Irish coast, in County Clare. A fine old Georgian country house, with plenty of bedrooms and a roaring fire, where you can "tuck up warm," as the locals say, after a day walking along the Wild Atlantic Way. (Those coastal paths are marvelous for walking the dog.) We hold all our reunions there, and of course the house is open to any of my old crew, whenever they need it, whether I am there or not. A haven—not Fair Haven, perhaps, but better, because it is real. The crew of my first command remain just that—My Crew—and I hope they know that their captain will always be there for them. Our experience was unique, and while a great deal has been written about us, or said about us, it's only we ourselves who understand what it was really like.

Some, like me, have stayed in Starfleet. Surely the most successful of these was Harry Kim, now captain of his own ship. My last act as captain of *Voyager* was to give him a long overdue promotion to lieutenant. I would have skipped a couple of ranks if I'd been able: Harry surely deserved it. (His speed of promotion since has made up for it, however.) I finally met his parents, and apologized for not picking up his clarinet, and also his fiancée, now his wife, Libby. I would say that of all of us, Harry has had the most success integrating back into his old life in the Alpha Quadrant. To some extent, I think that this was because such a substantial part of him was always still there. He was the one who had set the most store by returning home, who was young enough to keep his optimism alive, when the rest of us on some level believed we were stuck for good. But Harry's trust paid off in the end, and he's a father of four now. That keeps him out of trouble.

Tuvok too had no trouble returning to his old life, although this was for slightly different reasons from Harry. His family life and career in the Alpha Quadrant were so well established that seven years was a relatively small part of the whole. Tuvok always kept things in perspective. He had been married for many years, his children were more or less grown-up, and, while he missed the birth of his granddaughter, she was still young when he returned (I was there when he met her, and I am sure that I saw something suspiciously close to a tear in his eye). He was there for the arrival of all seven subsequent grandchildren. I am very glad to be able to report that the degenerative neurological condition that the Doctor diagnosed shortly before our return to the Alpha Quadrant was indeed cured quickly after a mind-meld with Sek, and that there have been no side effects or recurrences. Tuvok has had a long career at Starfleet Intelligence since our return, although he spends increasing amounts of time in meditation back at home on Vulcan, and I suspect that his retirement there is coming soon.

What of *Voyager*'s unlikely lovebirds, Tom Paris and B'Elanna Torres? Who would have believed that a relationship that began against the backdrop of a Maquis ship, was sparked by being flung together seventy thousand light-years from everything familiar, and was watched avidly by all their colleagues, would have had such success? And their marriage has been by any measure a tremendous success. Tom Paris was one of those who decided that Starfleet was no longer for him—or, perhaps, in his case, he no longer needed it. Tom, returning to the Alpha Quadrant, found that he had no need now to prove himself to his father. More than that, the desire was no longer there. The physical distance had been enough to establish the necessary emotional distance. He could love his father, and respect him, but he no longer had the desperate need for his attention or approval that had sent him off on such a destructive path. Tom's service on *Voyager* spoke for itself. Within six months he had resigned his commission. He and B'Elanna have a home in the south of France, near the coast, where Tom looks after the children and now has a successful second career writing holodramas (my mother was of help here), and flying whenever he can. You'll of course know him as the creator of *Captain Proton*. Altogether, it's a good way of life for Tom. He is completely content. I hear on the grapevine that he's thinking of renovating an old movie theater...

It is B'Elanna who has stayed in Starfleet, finding that her experience on *Voyager*, and the seniority and respect it earned her, has more than wiped away the disappointment of her time in the Academy. About a year after our return, she confided in me that she was self-conscious of the fact that she had not, technically, graduated from the Academy. You know, the thought hadn't even crossed my mind. If anyone has graduated from the University of Life, it's B'Elanna Torres. I put her name forward for an honorary doctorate, based on her service on *Voyager* and her exceptional work as my chief engineer, and I am glad to say that the Academy accepted the nomination with alacrity. It was a source of great pride to me to be able to give the citation, to see her in her finery accepting her degree, Tom bursting with pride alongside her, little Miral clutching their hands. This honor was the least that B'Elanna deserved. After her difficult and confusing childhood and setting herself on a course to self-destruction at nineteen, she has matured into a bold, fierce, intelligent, and capable woman, the heart of a loving family. On her return to Earth, she was able to reconnect with her father, John, and reestablish that relationship. She has found a large family back on Earth: cousins, and their children, all of whom have welcomed her.

Tom and B'Elanna have a son now too, Eugene Owen, and he is the apple of his mother's eye. Dear lord, all of those who know B'Elanna as stubborn, cranky, and entirely immune to flattery marvel at the sight of her with her son. She melts like butter when he is around. With Miral she enjoys a bond so grounded in love that even the tumults and clashes that inevitably come from putting two strong-willed women in the same household cannot shake it. It is as if B'Elanna has had the chance to revisit and rework her relationship with her own mother in a way that has allowed her to transform it. There are quarrels, of course there are, but Miral has never doubted that her mother loves her, and that makes all the difference. Besides, she has Tom wrapped around her little finger. She has a huge amount of his charm, as well as his daredevil approach, and a fine dash of his confidence. I have no doubt that whatever she chooses to do in life, she will make a huge success.

What about Owen, my old captain, now Admiral Paris? I wondered, when Tom announced his resignation from Starfleet, whether Owen was putting on a brave face about the news, but, having spoken to him about it, I know that this is not the case. He is genuinely, unconditionally proud of Tom—and completely besotted with Miral. Watching them, I see how grandchildren have the capability of transforming the bonds between parent and child: in Miral, Owen is given a chance to make good the mistakes he made with Tom. He can encourage her, and, most of all, he can *enjoy* her. She is not, ultimately, his responsibility—although she is his joy. Miral may yet choose Starfleet—although she is as stubborn as her mother and as wild as her father. I think she would make a superlative test pilot. When I see her, I remember twelve-year-old Tom Paris, having the time of his life on the flight simulators. Maybe Aunt Kate can take her out there soon. It comes in handy sometimes, having an admiral or two in the family.

What of those crew members who only existed because of *Voyager*, who would not now be living their lives had it not been for the fact that we brought them into existence? What about our Doctor, for example, who came online after the death of my dear Laurie Fitz, and who has surely exceeded whatever expectations his programmers might have had? I think the Doctor might be the one who has most embraced life after the Delta Quadrant. And why not? His mobile emitter allowed him to travel wherever he liked, and the matter of his sentience was resolved as soon as the Starfleet tech experts encountered him… I naturally hesitate to say "in the flesh," which would surely be offensive; in person surely covers it. Could anyone, meeting the Doctor, doubt his personhood? Recognized as sentient, recognized as his own person, the Doctor was able to do whatever he chose. He promptly resigned from Starfleet and has taken up the cause of photon rights (my mother, ever the activist, has been a great help, and they talk about collaborating on a children's book, explaining the issues involved). It is surely only a matter of time before the law catches up with the reality. He lives a very full and busy life, attending concerts, playing golf with Reg Barclay, driving a very fast car. Of all of us, he's the one that most embraced his celebrity status. It helps his cause, and, it must be said, he enjoys being in the limelight. I see no relationship on the horizon. (A side note here on Reg Barclay, our honorary crew member, who fought in our corner for so long. I was proud to be there to see him collect his Daystrom Prize, for his work in establishing the first two-way transgalactic communication. An honor richly deserved.)

Perhaps the person that I worried about most was Seven of Nine. Our arrival back in the Alpha Quadrant, and the subsequent disbanding of *Voyager*'s crew, meant that her "collective" was coming to an end. I was always concerned that this would be a kind of second trauma for her, the removal of support structures that had helped her in those first few tentative steps toward regaining her humanity. Her nascent relationship with my first officer, while short-lived, was crucial here, giving her some continuity with her *Voyager* days, while allowing her to make the transition to a new way of life. With Chakotay, she made a journey back out to the world where she grew up, and with his guidance, was able to lay a few ghosts of the past to rest. Although she has never discussed this with me directly, I understand obliquely from Chakotay that Seven has passed through what was surely a necessary stage of anger with her parents for their part in her assimilation into the Borg. She should never have been on that ship with them and, while she cannot change the past, she can come to terms with it.

Seven has reconnected with her family, most notably her aunt, although the gap between the memory of six-year-old Annika and the reality of Seven herself must have been a hard one for Irene to come to terms with. Seven spends a great deal of time with Samantha Wildman's family, remaining as close as ever to Naomi, who is, in effect, a much-loved younger sister. Samantha's spouse, Greskrendtregk, has accepted this extension to his family with equanimity. But where Seven has truly come into her own is through her work. She is, of course, of tremendous importance to Starfleet, not only as their special advisor and expert on the Borg, but also because of her phenomenal skills and talents. She is a key member of a significant Federation think tank, where she has access to whatever resources she requires. This is a fascinating group (I understand there are several augmented human members), although Seven does not often speak of their work in detail. And of course, there is still Icheb, whom I put in her care all those years ago, and for whom she has always come through.

And what of my first officer? What of Chakotay? How has he fared on his return to the Alpha Quadrant? I was not surprised, when the moment came, to see that it was the special circumstance of *Voyager* that allowed Chakotay to become Starfleet again. He resigned his commission after eighteen months back in the Alpha Quadrant, whereupon he and B'Elanna took a journey out to the old DMZ to pay their respects to their fallen Maquis comrades. Since then he has spent a long time traveling around North America, and also around colony worlds settled by Native Americans. He sees himself as doubly dispossessed: his ancestors forced from their lands when my ancestors arrived, and then his own family removed from their home when the DMZ was formed. He has found himself a task in life, reconnecting these places, learning about their histories and traditions, healing, perhaps, some of the wounds caused by those multiple evictions. He often drops out of communication for months at a time, suddenly turning up again, sending me a message from wherever he is, or arriving without warning at my mother's farm (my mother likes him very much). Sometimes he accepts a university post, where he will teach history for a while, before returning to his travels. When he is on Earth, we see each other every week, as we always did; he comes to my home in Ireland for dinner, and we talk about how life brought us together, and where it might take us next. My dog loves him.

✦

I am, of course, Starfleet till I die. I dreamed of captaining my own ship as a little girl, and I worked hard, kept dreaming, and turned that dream into reality. Being a Starfleet captain turned out very different from how I imagined it would be. I made many mistakes along the way, and there are some decisions to which I am still not entirely reconciled, but I did my best in unusual circumstances. I hope history won't judge me too harshly.

What of my life now? It is full, it is busy. I am an admiral, with all the responsibilities and headaches that entails. There are perhaps too many briefings in my life, and not enough ship time. Still, I would not have it any other way. When I am weary of talking to others, or listening to others, or have become tired of being inside, I walk down to the academy campus, where my career started all those years ago, and I find the rose garden. Sometimes Boothby (yes, he's still there) steals an hour or two of my time to help him, and I feel better for it, as I always did. Whenever I visit, there are roses on my desk the next day, as reward for my efforts. I go whenever I can.

I will be there later this morning, not in my capacity as undergardener, but in dress uniform, as Admiral Kathryn M. Janeway, where I shall be giving the commencement speech to this year's new crop of graduates. I have done this speech two or three times in the past: I love this task above all. What a joy to see these young people, at the very start of their careers, so full of life and hope and ambition. It reminds me that my job now, above all, is to create the conditions whereby they can flourish in Starfleet and have long and productive careers, marked chiefly by exploration rather than by conflict. I find it a great responsibility.

THE HISTORY OF THE CAPTAIN WHO WENT FURTHER THAN ANY HAD BEFORE

I shall speak to them about courage, and how life can take you around the long way, and how they might find themselves having to answer questions that they never anticipated, and that they may not like the answer that they come up with. But most of all I want to tell them that there is no better job, and no better life, and that if I had my time over, I would do the same again. Every graduating class is special, but forgive me if this one is particularly special, because this time the audience includes one Ensign Amelia Janeway.

She is, of course, my daughter. My mother and Phoebe, believing me dead, and receiving all my worldly goods, including my frozen eggs, could not help themselves, and decided to have something of me live on. Phoebe and Yianem have brought her up among their girls, although she has always known who she is, in truth. Three mothers: how lucky can one girl be! Not to forget all those others who will be looking out for her across the years, within Starfleet and without: Commanders Torres and Tuvok, Captain Kim and Admiral Paris, Tom and the Doctor and Seven and Chakotay. They would do anything for her. Later, after she has graduated, our whole family—my mother, her daughters, her granddaughters, all the grandparents—will gather together and celebrate her success. Tomorrow morning we will go flying together, and that evening she will join me and Chakotay for dinner. Life is full of surprises: you can be whisked away at a moment's notice, and then come back to treasures that you did not know you had left behind. This life of mine has been a good life—and will, I hope, long continue to be so.

EDITOR UNA'S ACKNOWLEDGMENTS

My grateful thanks to:

Cat Camacho—for fine editorial guidance, and for giving the trolley solution to the Tuvix problem.

Max Edwards—for being such a mensch.

Daniel Tostevin—for long years of *Star Trek* gossip, and most of all for Pulaski.

Dayton Ward—for niftily dodging the Warp 10 dilemma.

And, of course, all my love to Matthew and Verity—for everything.

The pop-up books described in chapter 1 are based on two beautiful books by Robert Sabuda.

ABOUT THE EDITOR

Una McCormack is the author of *The Autobiography of Mr Spock*, the *Star Trek* novels *The Lotus Flower* (part of *The Worlds of Star Trek: Deep Space Nine*), *Hollow Men*, *The Never-Ending Sacrifice*, *Brinkmanship*, *The Missing*, the *New York Times* bestseller *The Fall: The Crimson Shadow*, *Enigma Tales*, *The Way to the Stars*, and *The Last Best Hope*, and the *Doctor Who* novels *The King's Dragon*, *The Way Through the Woods*, *Royal Blood*, and *Molten Heart*. She lives in Cambridge, England, with her partner of many years, Matthew, and their daughter, Verity.

ALSO AVAILABLE FROM TITAN BOOKS

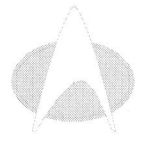

THE AUTOBIOGRAPHY OF
JAMES T. KIRK
THE STORY OF STARFLEET'S GREATEST CAPTAIN
EDITED BY DAVID A. GOODMAN

The Autobiography of James T. Kirk chronicles the greatest Starfleet captain's life (2233–2293), in his own words. From his youth spent on Tarsus IV, his time in the Starfleet Academy, his meteoric raise through the ranks of Starfleet, and his illustrious career at the helm of the *Enterprise*, this in-world memoir uncovers Captain Kirk in a way *Star Trek* fans have never seen. Kirk's singular voice rings throughout the text, giving insight into his convictions, his bravery, and his commitment to the life—in all forms—throughout this Galaxy and beyond.

TITANBOOKS.COM

ALSO AVAILABLE FROM TITAN BOOKS

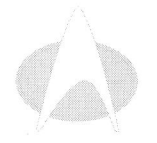

THE AUTOBIOGRAPHY OF
JEAN-LUC PICARD
THE STORY OF ONE OF STARFLEET'S MOST INSPIRATIONAL CAPTAINS
EDITED BY DAVID A. GOODMAN

The Autobiography of Jean-Luc Picard tells the story of one of the most celebrated names in Starfleet history. His extraordinary life and career makes for dramatic reading: court martials, unrequited love, his capture and torture at the hand of the Cardassians, his assimilation with the Borg and countless other encounters as captain of the celebrated Starship *Enterprise*.

TITANBOOKS.COM

ALSO AVAILABLE FROM TITAN BOOKS

THE AUTOBIOGRAPHY OF
MR. SPOCK
THE LIFE OF A FEDERATION LEGEND
EDITED BY UNA McCORMACK

One of Starfleet's finest officers and the Federation's most celebrated citizens reveals his life story. Mr Spock explores his difficult childhood on Vulcan with Michael Burnham, his controversial enrolment at Starfleet Academy, his time on the *Enterprise* with both Kirk and Pike, and his moves to his diplomatic and ambassadorial roles, including his clandestine mission to Romulus.

Brand-new details of his life on Vulcan and the *Enterprise* are revealed, along with never-before-seen insights into Spock's relationships with the most important figures in his life, including Sarek, Michael Burnham, Christopher Pike, Kirk, McCoy and more, all told in his own distinctive voice.

TITANBOOKS.COM

For more fantastic fiction, author events,
exclusive excerpts, competitions, limited editions and more

VISIT OUR WEBSITE
titanbooks.com

LIKE US ON FACEBOOK
facebook.com/titanbooks

FOLLOW US ON TWITTER AND INSTAGRAM
@TitanBooks

EMAIL US
readerfeedback@titanemail.com

THE AUTOBIOGRAPHY OF
JAMES T. KIRK

THE STORY OF STARFLEET'S GREATEST CAPTAIN

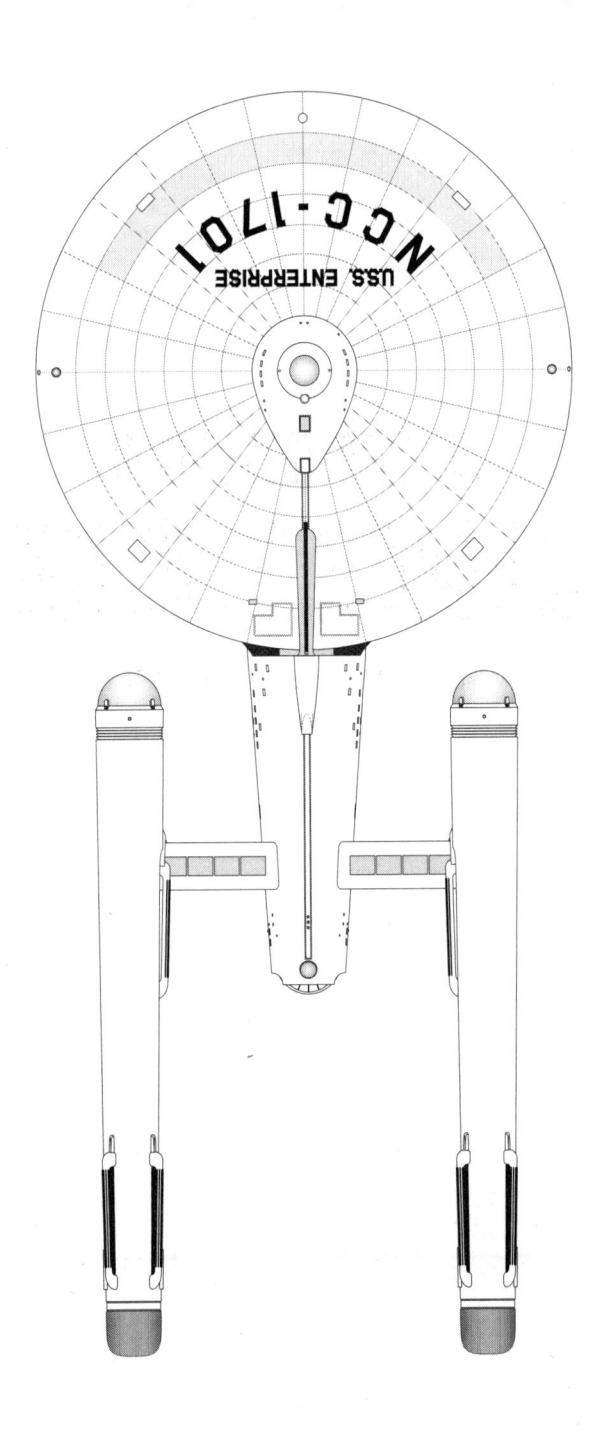

THE AUTOBIOGRAPHY OF
JAMES T. KIRK

THE STORY OF STARFLEET'S GREATEST CAPTAIN

BY
JAMES T. KIRK

EDITED BY DAVID A. GOODMAN

TITAN BOOKS

The Autobiography of James T. Kirk
Print Edition ISBN: 9781783297481
E-Book Edition ISBN: 9781783297474

Published by Titan Books
A division of Titan Publishing Group Ltd.
144 Southwark Street, London SE1 0UP

First edition: June 2016
10 9 8 7 6 5 4 3 2 1

TM ® & © 2015 by CBS Studios Inc. © 2015 Paramount Pictures Corporation. STAR TREK and related marks and logos are trademarks of CBS Studios Inc. All Rights Reserved.

All rights reserved. No part of this publication may be reproduced, stored in a retrieval system, or transmitted, in any form or by any means, electronic, mechanical, photocopying, recording, or otherwise, without prior written permission from the publisher.

The Autobiography of James T. Kirk is produced by becker&mayer! Book Producers, Bellevue, Washington.
www.beckermayer.com

Front cover design: Julia Lloyd
Illustrations: Russell Walks
Editor: Dana Youlin
Interior design: Rosanna Brockley

A CIP catalogue record for this title is available from the British Library.

Printed and bound in India by Thomson Press India Ltd.

Did you enjoy this book? We love to hear from our readers. Please e-mail us at: readerfeedback@titanemail.com or write to Reader Feedback at the above address.

To receive advance information, news, competitions, and exclusive offers online, please sign up for the Titan newsletter on our website: www.titanbooks.com.

CONTENTS

FOREWORD BY LEONARD H. MCCOY, M.D. 1

PROLOGUE 3

CHAPTER 1 7

CHAPTER 2 25

CHAPTER 3 41

CHAPTER 4 67

CHAPTER 5 95

CHAPTER 6 125

CHAPTER 7 163

CHAPTER 8 189

CHAPTER 9 215

CHAPTER 10 231

CHAPTER 11 245

CHAPTER 12 255

AFTERWORD BY SPOCK OF VULCAN 267

To Mom

THE AUTOBIOGRAPHY OF
JAMES T. KIRK

THE STORY OF STARFLEET'S GREATEST CAPTAIN

FOREWORD
BY LEONARD H. MCCOY, M.D.

FIRST LET ME JUST SAY, I'M A DOCTOR NOT A WRITER. But, having read this memoir, I've decided I do have something to add. For the most part, Jim Kirk said everything that needed to be said about himself. But he left out one important detail, for the obvious reason that he was too modest to think it, let alone say it, so I will:

He was the greatest hero who ever lived.

Now, before you assume I'm exaggerating, and before I tell you to go to hell, let's look at his life objectively. Who else in the last fifty years was at the center of so many critical events? Who else in that time made more decisions that affected the course of civilization? It seems unbelievable that so much history could be centered around one person, but the record is clear. And I don't know whether it was divine providence, luck, or the mythical Great Bird of the Galaxy that determined the man who would be in the center seat of the *Starship Enterprise*, I'm just thankful it was Jim Kirk.

Though he skips this description of himself, his memoir leaves out little else, and for that reason it is revelatory. The personal secrets in here paint an honest portrait of the man. In some ways, he was just like the rest of us: lonely, ambitious, a son, a father, a lover, never truly content. Where he set himself apart is in the way he took responsibility for his mistakes, embraced his weaknesses, and always strove to do better, to be better. It is in this way that he is a true hero; despite his successes, he knew there was always more work to be done, and he never shied away from the call of duty. His passing is a catastrophic loss; he looked after all of us.

For me, the loss is personal: I had no better friend, and I raise my glass to him one last time.

To James T. Kirk, captain of the *Enterprise*.

PROLOGUE

HIDING IN THE BASEMENT ON THE RUN FROM THE POLICE, it was difficult to see how I was going to save the Galaxy. But I had to work with what was at hand. Our hideout was neither well equipped nor comfortable. The brick room was cold and dark, smelled of ash and rodent urine, and its only source of heat against the bitter winter outside was a small coal-burning stove. All it provided in the way of equipment were thick cobwebs and a pile of damaged furniture. There were a few wooden storage boxes, stained presumably from exposed pipes that crisscrossed the low ceiling. Of course, the lack of the amenities was moot. This "headquarters" was only temporary, as it was doubtful the occupants of the building above would ignore us forever, especially if alerted by the local authorities.

And that was a concern, because though we'd been in the city, and the century, for less than ten minutes, I'd already managed to break the law. When we arrived through the time portal, I realized our uniforms made us stand out, so I stole some indigenous clothes hanging out to dry on the fire escape of a tenement building. Unfortunately, a policeman had observed my theft, so my companion had to momentarily disable him, allowing our escape. At the time, the crime didn't seem serious, but now I was having second thoughts; I had stolen the clothes from people living in poverty, who certainly couldn't afford to replace two sets of shirts and pants. This was further confirmed as I put the flannel shirt and cotton slacks on; though it presumably had been washed, the shirt still carried the strong odor of its owner's sweat. This smell was mixed with traces of diesel oil, tobacco smoke, and alcohol. The cloths' "bouquet" told a story: a primitive life of hard work, its stresses dulled by the use of cheap anesthetics. I found myself wishing for some.

"It's time we faced the unpleasant facts," I said. And they seemed endless. We didn't know where we were, only somewhere in the United States, and that we had arrived in the past *before* McCoy. That was crucial. We knew he would change the past, and thereby wipe out our future, but we didn't know exactly how. And we didn't know exactly *when* or *where* he would arrive.

"There is a theory," Spock said, when I voiced these concerns. "There could be some logic to the belief that time is fluid, like a river. With currents, eddies, backwash . . ."

So McCoy was going to surf a time current and wash up on our doorstep? If Spock hadn't been a Vulcan who had devoted his life to the pursuit of logic, I would've said it was wishful thinking. I had no choice, however, but to invest in this belief, because if McCoy were to show up somewhere else, how would we know? And even if by some miracle we found out, how would we get there? And even if we *could* get there, modes of travel were so primitive that we'd never reach another city in time to stop him. We didn't even know what he was going to do, so if any time passed before we found McCoy, he might have already changed the future. No, I was going to stick with Spock's river analogy. The alternative was too overwhelmingly bleak, and the fact that my unfailingly logical science officer believed it possible at least gave me hope.

"Frustrating," Spock said, referring to his tricorder. "Locked in here is the exact place and moment of his arrival. Even the images of what he did. If only I could tie this tricorder in with the ship's computer for just a few moments . . ."

"Couldn't you build some form of computer aid here?" I said.

"In this zinc-plated, vacuum-tubed culture?" Sometimes Spock spoke to me as though I was an idiot, and I knew most captains wouldn't put up with that from their first officers. But I accepted it as part of the package. And I had my own ways of torturing him.

"Well, it would prove to be an extremely complex problem in logic," I said, then turned to warm my hands in front of the stove. "Excuse me, I sometimes expect too much of you." The truth was, I did expect too much of him. Spock was right—the idea that he could construct a processing aid with technology 300 years out of date was ridiculous. Yet I fully expected that he'd be able to do it. And that expectation would motivate him to try. So I would leave that to him while I saw to our survival. Which seemed almost as impossible as building a computer from scratch.

We were stuck in an ancient capitalist-driven society where the *only* way to see to one's needs was by having money. We had none, and if we were going to survive, we were going to have to figure out how to earn some during a period where finding work was next to impossible. The more I thought about the situation, the more depressing it became. A lot of ancient religions relied on the concept of prayer, and in that moment I recognized the compelling power of superstition, to be able to silently ask for aid and comfort from a higher power. We would need help, and there was no one to ask, and I didn't believe in angels . . .

"Who's there?" A woman stood at the top of the stairs. I moved to intercept her to give Spock a moment to cover his ears with the wool hat I'd stolen for him. She stood in the light a few steps above me. She was in her thirties, wearing a plain blouse, skirt, and apron. Simple clothing, all somehow made elegant by its wearer.

"Excuse us, miss," I said, "we didn't mean to trespass. It's cold outside."

"A lie is a very poor way to say hello," she said. "It isn't that cold." Her light blue eyes carried a disdainful expression that immediately held sway over me. I knew at that moment either my lies were going to have to be a lot better, or that I was going to have to tell her the truth, as much of the truth as I could.

And I wanted to. I don't know why, but I didn't want to hide anything from her. And I would shortly learn that Spock's river analogy was true, and she was where it led. Because of her, I would literally save history. And I would also regret it for the rest of my life.

CHAPTER 1

WHEN MY MOTHER LEFT EARTH for a job on another planet, she said she'd be back often, and since I was nine, I took her at her word. The idea that a grown-up would not tell me the truth was beyond my experience.

I was with her and my dad on the front porch of our farm. The sun was setting and a few fireflies were out. You could see for miles; in the distance dark clouds let loose a bolt of lightning. My brother, Sam, was inside, lost in a book on his reader. Sam was twelve; he was always reading lately.

"I'm leaving in the morning," she said.

"Why do you have to go?"

My mother crouched down and met me eye-to-eye. She told me how important it was for her to go, and that it didn't mean she didn't love me. She had gotten a job as part of a colony on a planet called Tarsus IV. She said ships went back and forth all the time. I looked up at my dad, who was looking away. He watched the storm in the distance.

"When will you be back?"

"It'll be a few months," she said. "I'll definitely be back in time for your birthday."

"You don't know that," Dad snapped angrily. It was the first time he'd spoken since we had walked outside. I looked at him again, but he was still watching the storm.

"I'll be here," she said, still looking at me, determined to make it feel true. She then hugged me and lifted me up in her arms, making a big show of my weight. "God, you're so big. C'mon, let's get some dessert."

She looked over at Dad, then looked down. I desperately wanted him to make eye contact with her, and I could feel that Mom did too. But he wouldn't.

The next morning she was gone, taking my idea of home with her.

✦

Up to then I'd had a wonderful boyhood, filled with dogs, campfires, birthdays, horseback riding, snowball fights, and plenty of friends. Just like the Earth of today, there was no poverty or war or deprivation. My parents would talk about the problems in the Galaxy, but I wasn't really paying attention. Sometimes I'd look up in the sky and my brother would point out to me the satellites or a shuttle taking off, but that's as close as my mind got to outer space. Close to home felt perfect.

We lived on a farm near Riverside, Iowa, on a piece of property that had about 200 hectares of crops. We grew soybeans and corn, had chickens for eggs and cattle for milk and cheese. As far back as I can remember we were up at 4 a.m. every day to feed the chickens and milk the cows. Most of the caring of the crops was handled by automated machinery, but my father still insisted we get out in the fields for planting and harvesting. Though we were in no way dependent on the farm for our livelihood, my father still thought it important to understand the work involved in living off our land.

The house was four bedrooms, two floors, brick and wood. It was built using authentic materials and was a perfect copy of the house that had stood on the property for over 100 years in the 19th and 20th centuries. The property had belonged to seven generations of Kirks; it was family legend that my great-great-great-great-great-great-great-grandfather, Franklin Kirk, purchased the farm in 1843 from Isaac Cody, who was the father of William F. "Buffalo Bill" Cody.[*] My ancestors in the modern era let caretakers manage

---

[*]**EDITOR'S NOTE:** Though Isaac Cody was a well-known and successful developer in the region during the 19th century, there is no record of him selling a farm to Franklin Kirk.

THE STORY OF STARFLEET'S GREATEST CAPTAIN

it, until my grandparents moved back there when they retired. My father, George Kirk, also always had a strong desire to live there.

He had grown up as one of the original "Starfleet brats"; his father, Tiberius Kirk, was already in his twenties when Starfleet Academy was founded, and though he applied, he wasn't accepted. Still wanting to get out into space, Tiberius signed on in ordnance and supply, eventually serving on several of the then-new starbases. He met and married my paternal grandmother, Brunhilde Ann Milano, a nurse, on Starbase 8. My father was born there on December 13, 2206.

In those days, a child's life on a starbase was pretty spartan; there weren't a lot of families living on them, and the facilities were very limited. It was truly life on the frontier, and my father dreamed of getting back to see Earth, a dream that wouldn't be fulfilled until he arrived for his first day at Starfleet Academy. It was my grandfather's hope that his son would go to the academy, and admission had gotten even more competitive. But after rescuing five men after an explosion on the loading dock of Starbase 8, Tiberius was awarded the Starfleet Medal of Honor. And though my grandfather was still an enlisted man, the children of Medal of Honor winners are always given high priority during the admissions process.

My father graduated fifth in his class from the academy and, after serving a year as an instructor, was assigned to the *U.S.S. Los Angeles* (where he served with future captain Robert April). He was quickly promoted and eventually took the post of first officer aboard the *U.S.S. Kelvin*, when the previous first officer, Richard Robau, was promoted to captain. Over the course of six years he had moved up the ranks at record speed. If his career had continued, he might have been one of the youngest captains in the history of Starfleet, but his personal life led him in a different direction.

My mother, born Winona Davis, was also from a spacegoing family; her father, James Ogaleesha Davis (his middle name, as befit his heritage, was Native American Sioux, although I never did find out what it meant*), was in the first graduating class of Starfleet Academy; his wife, Wendy Felson, was in the third. My maternal grandfather was an engineer, my maternal grandmother a physician, and their daughter, my mother,

---

*EDITOR'S NOTE: The translation of the Sioux name "Ogaleesha" is "Wears a Red Shirt."

attended the academy and decided she wanted to be an astrobiologist. She was four years younger than my father, and had him as an instructor in her Introduction to Federation History class.

"There were strict rules about students 'fraternizing' with instructors," she told me, "and once I met your father, I wanted to break all of them."

It is hard to know how many of the rules they actually broke, as a son usually doesn't delve into those topics with his parents. However, when my father received his posting to the *Los Angeles*, the ship was still three months away from returning to Earth, so he asked for a short leave from his duties as an instructor, and immediately proposed to my mother.

"Most people assumed we'd made a terrible mistake," my mom said, "but it was impossible for us to see a possible downside then. We were crazy in love." And then, suddenly, the *Los Angeles* arrived, and my dad was off.

My mom was still in the academy and said she secretly hoped that they'd be posted together. It was over a year before she saw him next, and then almost two years after that, she graduated. She was not, however, posted to the same ship as Dad. Shortly after my mother was posted to the *U.S.S. Patton*, she discovered she was pregnant.

"Your father was aboard the *Los Angeles* then," she told me, "and by the time the subspace message reached him I was already in my second trimester."

Mom's Starfleet career came to an abrupt halt; she took a leave of absence, moving in with my dad's parents on Earth (her parents had passed away several years earlier) on the family farm. My brother, George Samuel, named for my father, was born on August 17, 2230.

The maximum amount of time my mother could stay away from Starfleet without resigning her commission was two years. For that period, she and my father were apart. She stayed on the farm and raised George with her in-laws, while she also continued her studies and completed a doctorate in astrobiology.

"It was a good time to be with George Jr.," she said, "but I missed George Sr. This was not what I expected my life to be. My own mother had resigned her commission when she had me. She had raised my brother and me by herself since Dad was off in space. I was determined not to be a single parent, yet here I found myself doing just that."

She told me she felt conflicted about leaving her two-year-old son. "Your grandparents were energetic and attentive, which made the decision a little easier, but I couldn't get past the idea that I was abandoning my baby."

Dad also missed Mom, and when the two years were up, he pulled whatever strings he could to get her posted to the *Kelvin*, where he was now the first officer. Unfortunately, soon after she arrived, she discovered she was pregnant again, this time with me.

My dad said Captain Robau was furious; even if regulations had allowed children aboard a ship, he wasn't a commander who would've wanted it. However, that wasn't really the impetus for Dad's impending decision. Shortly after determining that my mother was pregnant, Dad received word that his father, Tiberius, had passed away.

"It was a strange 'circle of life' kind of moment," my dad told me. "Though I'd grown up in space, my father had been with me the whole time. Now that he was gone, I realized I barely knew my first son, and I had a second child on the way. I wasn't going to let your mom go home and raise our children by herself." So he resigned his commission.

Over the years, I've thought a lot about the decision Dad made and how it affected me. I have told many people that my father leaving Starfleet inspired my own career, to complete the career he didn't get to finish. Though that is partially true, the rest of the story is a lot more complicated.

I was born on March 22, 2233, to a complete family: I grew up in a house with two parents, an older brother, and a grandmother. It was my own slice of heaven. I was protected, lived in a clean, safe world. But it was a façade; I just wasn't sophisticated enough to see through it.

As I look back now, I can see that my parents were not happy. They didn't fight, they didn't even disagree openly, but the moments of warmth between them were rare. Mom worked hard around the house, but the work itself wasn't what she wanted to do. I have a lot of memories of those times finding my mother off in a corner reading. My father was attentive to her, but not overly affectionate. He had strong ideas of what he wanted life on the farm to be like, and he got a lot of confirmation for this from his mother, Brunhilde, who still lived with us. Grandma Hilde had lived her whole life on the frontier of other worlds, and my memory of her was as a hardscrabble, somewhat unforgiving individual. My mother never saw herself as living on a farm, so she didn't argue with how they wanted to do things, but the situation took its toll. Eventually, she decided to pursue her career again.

"It wasn't what I wanted," my father told me much later, "but I wanted her to be happy."

✦

"Sam, can I come in?" I said. (I was the only one who called my brother by his middle name. I don't know how it started, but I kept calling him Sam well into adulthood.) I was standing outside of Sam's bedroom. He was lying on his stomach reading. It had been only a few weeks after my mother departed. It had been very quiet around the house. My father had kept up our routines of school, chores, homework. My grandmother was looking after our meals and clothing, and we were all pretending like nothing had changed.

"Yeah, you can come in," he said, without looking up. This was unusual for him to grant me permission to come into his room. It was also unusual for me to ask; normally I would just barrel in and wait for him to throw me out.

I took only a half step into the room and looked around. Sam had lots of trophies, some athletic, many academic. He always impressed me. In fact, from the minute I was aware, probably around two years old, all I wanted was my brother's approval and attention, and it seemed to me he took great pleasure in withholding both. Most of his energy directed at me went into putting up an emotional blockade to my devotion, though sometimes, if his friends weren't available, I was a stand-in playmate, or, more accurately, a fawning sidekick.

At five, I remember watching in fascination as he mixed homemade gunpowder and used it to make a cannon out of old tin cans with the bottoms cut out and soldered together. I shared the blame when his invention blew a hole in the side of the barn. Though we were given double chores for a week, I felt happy that somehow I'd been given credit for his rambunctious ingenuity. He, of course, was irritated by my delight at us being mistaken as a team.

He always seemed calm and logical, which led me to try to tease a reaction out of him with my big emotions. My dad would often have to intervene, but he seemed a little amused by my desire to get a rise out of Sam.

And as far as I could tell, both he and my father weren't the least bit affected by Mom's leaving. This didn't help me make sense of the confusion I felt. Dad was especially unapproachable; I felt an almost psychic fence around him. Sam, despite his "disdain" for me as the little brother, was somehow a little more accessible. Or maybe just a little less scary.

"What do you want?" he asked without looking up from his reader.

"Sam . . . do you know why Mom left?"

"It's because she got a job," Sam said.

"She didn't have a job before."

"She did, but she quit it to have kids," he said.

"Oh."

"She had work she always wanted to do," he said.

Sam stopped reading and looked at me. It seemed like he looked at me for a very long time. Then he spoke.

"Do you miss her?"

I don't remember if I answered; I just started crying.

Sam got off his bed and came over to me. He then awkwardly hugged me. I don't know if we'd ever hugged before that, and it didn't come naturally to him, but it was enough comfort for me. At that moment, my brother seemed like an adult, though he was only 12 years old and probably was feeling as lost as I was. I don't remember how long I cried, but eventually I stopped.

"You should probably go wash your face," he said. I left his room, but from that point on, Sam was no longer as cool to me, and eventually we became quite close.

The weeks turned into months, and then years. Mom made a sincere, dogged effort to stay in touch with us over subspace, but there was no real-time communication over that distance, so we would record messages that she would watch, and then she would record responses that we'd watch. She kept her promise to be home for my next birthday, but it was the last birthday she'd celebrate with me for several years. Over time, the jealousy I had toward my friends whose families were still whole drove me into isolation. I spent my free time after school wandering our property, trying to get lost. I was starting to feel like I wanted to get away.

My dad still did his best to create the life he wanted us to have. We spent a lot of time together and took a lot of trips. He especially enjoyed camping, and during these excursions he would share with us his knowledge of the American frontier, which our ancestors helped settle. His interest became mine, one I pursue to this day.

We took advantage of the many national parks around the country, including Yosemite and Yellowstone. He had taught me horseback riding on our farm, and on these trips he'd let me go off on my own, as long as I was back in camp by sunset. I enjoyed the independence and the sense of adventure, though there was rarely any real danger.

However, during one of these solitary horseback rides, my horse was spooked by the sound of a loud boom. Once I'd gotten the animal under control, I looked up to find the source of the noise, and saw something high in the sky, falling fast. As it got closer, it looked like it was on fire. At first it was very distant, and then suddenly it wasn't; it was growing in size and seemed like it was headed directly toward me.

I grabbed the reins tight, tapped my heels against my horse, taking off at a fast gallop. I kept looking back over my shoulder, and my error became clear. I had misjudged the angle of the approaching object, and if I had just stayed still it would have flown over me. But by riding off, I was actually putting myself more directly in its path. My panic only led me to continue to try to outrun it.

I finally looked back and saw the large metal object now only a few hundred meters behind me, flames dancing off it. It looked like it was going to hit me, and in terror I leaped off my moving horse. I hit the ground and rolled, and as I looked up, I saw the flaming belly of the craft as it flew over me, then heard it crash. There was a blast of intense heat. I smelled smoke and could hear the crackling of fire. I stood up and saw the crash, only about 30 meters from me.

There was a gash in the forest; trees on either side of the wreck were broken away and charred black. The wreck was smoking and clearly not from this planet. It was small, a two-person shuttle of some kind. My horse was gone; I was momentarily scared that it had been hit, then saw its hoof-prints heading off from the wreck. The animal had had the good sense of how to get out of danger. But now I was stranded. I wasn't even sure how far away I was from our campsite, and it was getting dark.

"You! Get in here, now!"

The voice came from inside the ship. It was a scary, guttural, accented English. I started to back away.

"Stop, or you will regret it! Now get in here!"

I froze.

"Now!"

I slowly approached the craft. The front of the ship was firmly lodged in the ground, its back end pointed up toward the sky. There was an immense amount of steam emanating from the hull as the heat from its rapid reentry dissipated. There was an open hatch, but it was too dark inside to make anything out. I looked around for any sign of an adult. Spaceships couldn't just land on Earth without being noticed; somebody had to know about this. But I didn't see anyone. I knew, or hoped, help would be there soon.

"I said get in here!"

I climbed up inside the hatch. My eyes adjusted to the dim cabin light. The whole ship was on a severe tilt, and I held on to the hatch frame in order to maintain my footing. The cabin was small, jammed with control panels and storage lockers. There were two chairs in the front, and I could make out in the dim light two figures, both large, dark. One sat unmoving in the pilot's chair, the other in the passenger seat, wedged under a fallen piece of the ship's inner superstructure. He was the one who shouted orders at me. He was humanoid, but not a human. His features, dark eyes, prominent nose, and forehead were truly frightening. At first.

"You're a child!" He said it as if I'd committed a crime.

"I'm eleven," I said.

Trying to keep my balance in the tilted room, I moved carefully toward him. As I got closer, I became more fully aware that he wasn't tall, but just wide. And his face . . . once I got a look at it, I wasn't scared anymore. He looked to me like a giant pig.

"What are you waiting for? Get me out of here! Can't you see I'm injured?!"

This was the first time I'd met a Tellarite, and to this day I'm still impressed by the ease with which they can slide into argument. I've since learned that disagreeing is actually a societal and academic tradition in their culture, a challenging of the status quo that they see as crucial to their growth and prosperity as a society. At the time, however, I accepted his disdain as an accurate judgment of my abilities.

The metal girder pinning him down had cut into his leg. There was a thick, brown liquid on his pants, which I realized was his blood. I stepped in to try to lift the girder, but it was ridiculous to try; even a grown man wouldn't have been able to lift it.

"It's too heavy," I said. "I should go get help—"

"Ridiculous! You leave me and I will die!"

It was the first time I'd seen an adult of any kind more scared than I was. I turned and was startled at the other figure in the pilot's chair. There was a piece of shrapnel lodged in his forehead. His eyes and mouth were open as if in a silent scream. This was also the first time I had seen a dead body. I was shaking as the complainer grabbed me.

"What are you waiting for?!"

"Your leg doesn't look that bad. Are you sure I shouldn't just get—"

"Idiot! Do the humans teach their children nothing?! My leg isn't what's going to kill me! The ship's reactor is leaking radiation!"

I was old enough to know that "radiation" was bad. I suppose I should've run out of there to protect myself, but somehow I felt this pissed-off Tellarite was now my responsibility. I looked around the room for some kind of solution.

"Do you have a communicator or something?"

"You are an imbecile from a race of imbeciles! It's been damaged!"

"What about . . ." I said. "What about an engineer's tool kit?"

"Oh, so you think you're going to fix my broken ship? You, the idiot human? How did I get so lucky . . ."

"No, I thought if you had a laser torch, I could cut the metal piece that's holding—"

"Do I look like an engineer? Check those storage lockers," he said. "Hurry!" He obviously quickly changed his mind about my idea. I opened the storage lockers and finally found what looked like a tool kit. Inside, the tools were unfamiliar.

"Which one's—?"

"That one, you fool! We are going to die because you are such a fool!"

He indicated something that bore only a slight resemblance to my father's laser torch. I picked it up. It was bulky and heavy. I didn't know quite what do to with it, and felt a rising flood of frustration and anguish. I was going to cry. The Tellarite's histrionics, the dead body, the dark room, and now this tool I didn't know how to use. I wanted to leave, but I had to stay. Caught in an unresolvable conflict, I just tried to keep going.

I focused on the laser torch. It was designed for a hand with two thick fingers and a thumb. After a moment, I realized I could operate it if I used both of my hands, and quickly went back to the Tellarite. I aimed it at the girder just above his chest, when he grabbed my arm.

"What are you doing?! Trying to kill me? Is it revenge you want?"

"No," I said. "If I cut the piece here, I will be able to move it so you can slide out."

"Hurry up!" I guess he was on board.

I had seen my father use a torch to cut, but he used one designed for human hands. Still, I did what I could to imitate what I'd seen. I carefully aimed the torch and turned it on. A blue-white beam hit the girder. I slowly moved it up, away from the Tellarite, and I could see it was cutting through the thick metal. I took my time and sliced through the girder. I turned the torch off, carefully put it aside, then put both of my hands on the much smaller piece I'd cut and tried to move it. It initially wouldn't budge, and I was suddenly worried that I'd missed something. I looked it over, and decided I had no choice but to try again. I pushed, and this time it gave and slid away. I chuckled involuntarily, surprised at my success. But the Tellerite wasn't interested in congratulating me.

"Move!" He pushed me aside and slid from his chair. Screaming in pain, he fell to the tilted deck. He turned on his stomach, and I watched as he tried to scramble up to the hatch. But between his weight and his injury, and the severe angle of the deck, he was helpless. I stared at this pathetic sight, unsure of what to do, until he finally stopped struggling and turned to me, breathing heavily. He said nothing.

"Can . . . can I help you?" I asked.

He was silent. I took that as a yes.

It wasn't easy getting the Tellarite out of the ship, but once I did, I got under his left arm and helped him walk as far away from the wreck as we could. We'd only gotten a few steps when a Starfleet Fire and Rescue team landed in a medical shuttle. As the medics tended to their patient, it was satisfying to watch the Tellarite treat them with the same amount of disdain he had for me.

As one of the doctors gave me an examination, another shuttle arrived, and several Starfleet officers piled out, three in red shirts, one in gold. The one in gold was in his fifties, gray haired, had a natural sense of authority. He walked over to the Tellarite, spoke to him for a moment. The Tellarite indicated me, and the gold-shirted officer turned, looked at me with surprise, then came over. I was concerned that the Tellarite had somehow gotten me in trouble.

"What's your name, son?" he said.

"James Tiberius Kirk," I said.

"Nice to meet you. I'm Captain George Mallory." He shook my hand. "The Tellarite ambassador tells me you saved his life."

"He's . . . the ambassador?" I almost missed that part because I was so surprised that the Tellarite had given me credit for pulling him out of the ship.

"Yes," Mallory said. "He was heading to San Francisco, but his pilot refused to follow our landing procedures and got into some trouble. A few more minutes exposed to the radiation in that craft and he would've died. You helped prevent an intergalactic incident, son. You're a real hero."

"Thanks," I said. I couldn't hold back my smile.

✦

"You're going to go live with your mom for a little while," Dad said. It was June of 2245, I was 12, and Grandma Hilde had just passed away. Sam, at 15, had gained early acceptance to the University of Chicago and would be starting there in a few months. Mom had made the suggestion that I come to live with her, and though Dad resisted it, I was thrilled.

Since my encounter with the Tellarite ambassador, I had definitely become more interested with everything associated with other planets. I had started to ask my father if he thought I should join Starfleet, and was always surprised at how little enthusiasm he had for it. He would tell me how competitive gaining entrance to the academy was, even for the children of graduates, and he also constantly emphasized to me the careers available to people on Earth. I could tell that he was worried that my experience with the Tellarite had filled me with delusions of heroic grandeur; and at that point, he might have been right.

On top of the adventure of moving to a new planet, I was actually going to be traveling there by myself. Dad, however, was not ready to entrust me to the crew of a ship, so he made contact with a family that was moving to Tarsus IV, and they agreed to look after me for the two-month trip. Still, to be going somewhere without a parent at the age of 12 was exciting.

A couple of months later, I was packed and ready to go. Sam had already left for school, so it was just Dad taking me to the shuttle port in Riverside in his hover car. We drove in silence on the half-hour trip along the highway that connected our farm to the city.

The port was a small one; shuttles connected to the major cities of Earth, and one made the trip each day to Earth One, the orbital facility in space. When we arrived, Dad and I went to look for the family who I was going to be traveling with.

"George!" A big bearlike man with unkempt hair barreled toward us and warmly shook Dad's hand.

"Rod, this is my son Jim," Dad said. "Jim, this is Rod Leighton." The big man looked down at me and gave me a pat on the shoulder.

"Jim! Nice to meet you! Come meet the family!"

Rod led us over to the shuttle boarding entrance, where a diminutive woman and a boy about my age were waiting.

"Hello, Barbara," Dad said to the woman. She gave him a hug, then turned and looked at me.

"Jim, it's going to be a pleasure having you with us," she said. She gave me a warm smile.

"Are you kidding, we're lucky he's letting us come with him," Rod said. He then turned to the boy. "Tom, introduce yourself. You guys are going to be spending a lot of time together."

"I'm Tom," he said. There was a little bit of sarcasm in his voice, but he put his hand out and I shook it. This less-than-auspicious beginning to my relationship with Tom Leighton was interrupted by an announcement over the public address system.

"Attention, this is the final boarding call for Orbital Flight 37 . . ."

"That's us," Rod said.

I turned to look at my dad. This was the first moment in all the months leading up to this trip that I realized I'd be leaving him.

"Don't give the Leightons any trouble," he said.

"I won't."

"I'll see you soon," he said. "Take care of your mom. Be safe out there."

I thought he would give me a hug, but instead he held out his hand for me to shake. I shook it. We then all turned to board the shuttle. I turned back and saw him standing there. He smiled at me and waved me on. I was leaving him, without Mom or Sam in the house, all alone on the farm. And I was guilty, not because I wanted to stay, but because I really wanted to go. I felt I was finally getting to say goodbye to my childhood, and in truth I was, but not in the way that I thought.

We climbed aboard the shuttle, and Rod got us seats near one of the portholes. My face stayed plastered to the window as we took off. The gravity plating and inertial dampeners on the shuttle made it almost impossible to sense you were moving at all; it made the world outside look like a movie. As the shuttle banked before heading out into space, I caught sight of my dad, standing in the port alone, watching us go. I waved, but he couldn't see me.

✦

We cleared the atmosphere in less than five minutes and were suddenly in orbit. It was my first time in space, and it was stunning to see the big blue marble of Earth below, the sky filled with spaceships and satellites, and finally Earth One, the large orbital station that serviced and supplied the ships that came into orbit. We were flying to Tarsus on the *S.S. New Rochelle*, which was in a parking orbit away from the station. It was a supply ship, an old Class-J cargo tug with an updated engine. As we approached, the ship looked huge; it had a forward command section, and a long thin hull in the back that housed modular cargo holds. It looked like an ancient railroad train in space.

The shuttle docked at an airlock near the forward command section. I grabbed my duffel bag and followed the Leightons as we entered through a docking tunnel. A crewwoman holding a tablet checked us in, then directed us aft. We passed a few open hatchways to modular cargo pods, where we could see crewmen who worked busily in the cavernous holds, stacking crates and storage containers.

We reached a hatch to the rearmost cargo hold, and Rod led us inside. As we entered, we saw that it wasn't cavernous like the others. The interior had been redesigned; walls and corridors had been inserted to create several floors of passenger quarters. We found our stateroom.

"Here it is," Rod said. "Home sweet home." It was small, with two bunk beds, two closets, and four drawers for storage. But it was clean and spare, and I found its small size and efficiency somehow exciting. Rod went over to one of the bunk beds.

"I'm on top," he said, with a wink to his wife. She looked genuinely annoyed and slapped his shoulder. Rod then turned to me and Tom.

"What say you, boys? You want to go find a porthole and watch us leave orbit?" Rod didn't even wait for a response; he was out the door and Tom and I were on his heels. We headed forward and crossed through two cargo holds and reached the entrance to the command and drive section. There was a guard posted who stopped us.

"Sorry, authorized personnel only," he said.

"Oh, apologies, the captain's son wanted to see us leave orbit," Rod said, indicating me. "I figured it wouldn't be a problem. Come on, boys, let's—"

"Wait . . . whose son?" The guard looked worried. "He's Captain Mayweather's son?"

"Don't worry about it, I understand you've got orders. Come on, boys . . ."

Rod led us back the way we came, but the guard stopped us.

"I can let you into the command section, but you have to stay where I put you . . ."

"You sure? I don't want you to get in trouble."

"It's okay, but as soon as we go to warp, you have to come back."

"Sure, fine."

The guard led us into the command section; he indicated an access ladder, and we left him behind as we climbed it. The ladder led to a forward observation deck. It was cramped, barely enough room for the three of us, but the view port filled up the whole wall. It was like we were standing in outer space, looking out on Earth and all the spaceships in orbit.

"Mr. Leighton, how did you know the captain had a son?" I said.

"I didn't," Rod said, smiling. "And you can call me Rod."

I laughed. A bluff! And it was quite a big one we found out when we later met Captain Mayweather, whose dark skin indicated a pure African ancestry. He was also well over 100.

We were only on the observation deck for a few moments before we noticed Earth and the ships in orbit slipping away. As Earth moved behind us, I noticed off to the right in the distance a metal web surrounding a large space vehicle. It was a ship in dry dock. As we got closer, I could make out small repair craft buzzing about it. The superstructure of the dry dock kept me from getting a complete look at the ship, but it had the familiar saucer and two-engine nacelle design of many Starfleet vessels. Yet somehow it seemed larger and different than any ship I'd seen before.

"Dad, what ship is that?" Tom said. I was so intent on getting a better look at the ship I hadn't noticed Tom looking as well.

"One of the new *Constitution*-class ships," Rod said.

"What's the *Constitution* class?" Tom said.

"They say it's going to be faster than any ship ever built," he said. "It's going to be able to survive in space without maintenance and resupply the way most ships have to. They have high hopes for it."

We passed the dry dock and then it and the ship were gone. It would be a number of years before I got a better look at it.

CHAPTER 2

THE TWO-MONTH TRIP TO TARSUS IV was uneventful and eventually quite dull. Tom Leighton and I were the only two kids on the voyage, and by the time it was over we knew every detail of the ship and about each other. Tom reminded me a lot of Sam; he was smart and quiet, loved to read, and wanted to be a scientist. Once he got comfortable with me, I found him to be an engaging friend. He often pulled weird facts out of his head that were always interesting and entertaining.

One night, while everyone was asleep, he woke me up, excited.

"Come on, Jim, I found out where the artificial gravity generator is." I had no idea what he was talking about, but I got dressed and joined him as we headed out to the catwalk that led to the rest of the ship. Like most ships in Starfleet, the *New Rochelle* tried to imitate Earth's conditions of day and night, so this was the late shift and most of the crew were off duty and asleep.

Tom led me to a ladder that went down to the bottom of the main hull. When we reached the deck, he indicated a hatch.

"Right behind that is the artificial generator for the entire ship," he said. "It took me a while to figure out where it was."

"Congratulations," I said. I was really tired and not a little confused.

"Come on," he said, and immediately headed off.

"Where the hell are we going?"

"You'll see."

We headed back up the ladder, and then forward again. We then snuck into a cargo hold and stopped on the catwalk. We were about 100 feet off the floor of the hold, which was partially filled with storage containers.

"According to my measurements, we're about halfway between the artificial gravity generator and the bow plate." Tom put his hands on the railing of the catwalk.

"So?"

"Watch." Tom pushed hard on the railing and suddenly was rising off the deck. He flipped over and landed, feetfirst on the ceiling. It looked like he was standing upside down.

"Holy crap," I said. "What the hell is going on?"

"I read about it," Tom said. "These cargo ships used to be run by families who learned all sorts of facts about these ships. Some of them called this 'the sweet spot.' Try it!"

I grasped the railing and pushed. At first I was just pushing up my own weight, and then suddenly I was weightless and moving through the air. I tumbled end over end. I actually hit Tom and we fell to the "floor," which was actually the ceiling. It was amazing.

"Let's do it again!"

Both of us lost in laughter, we then pushed off together and landed on the catwalk. We kept going back and forth, laughing, yelling, almost missing the catwalk a couple of times, until finally a security guard found us and dragged us back to our quarters. We spent a lot of the next two months sneaking off to this area. Eventually, I became interested in why it was happening, and I sought out a crew member who explained it to me. It was my first experience trying to understand life in outer space, and the relationship between humans and their spacecraft. It also taught me a valuable lesson on the inherent risks involved in space travel, as on one of these excursions I got careless; I missed the catwalk and landed on the cargo bay floor, breaking my wrist.

While my wrist healed, I ended up spending a lot of time with Tom's parents. They were very loving and attentive to him, and treated me like I was a member of their family. They made sure I was taken care of, and that I kept up with my studies. Barbara, a physician, always asked me lots of questions about my interests and was on me constantly about whether I was getting enough to eat. She was small, probably just over five feet tall, but she had a quiet intensity that somehow gave her authority over the three larger males in her care. She stood in great contrast to her husband, a boisterous raconteur who thrived on attention. (Rod, much to his wife's chagrin, taught Tom and me poker on that trip, where I learned more about his ability to bluff. No real money exchanged hands, but it was still instructive.) Rod was skilled in modern construction and was very excited about joining the colony, and though my mother had been on Tarsus IV for years, it wasn't until this trip that I learned about its history.

Humans settled Tarsus IV in the 22nd century after the Romulan War. Most of the settlers were veterans of the conflict who, with their families, purposely picked a planet on the other side of the Galaxy from the Romulans and the Klingons. Their goal was a society devoted to peace. So, although many of them had served on ships as soldiers, they devoted themselves to a scientifically constructed technocracy. The government was built on completely practical notions of what the individuals in the society needed and what they in turn could provide. For a century the colony had flourished as one of the most successful examples of human achievement in the Galaxy. At 13 I don't know if I fully understood the accomplishment of the people who built this world, but looking back it makes what would happen there that much more tragic.

We arrived at Tarsus IV on schedule, and the Leightons and I were among the first people to be taken down to the planet. As the pilot took the shuttle below the cloud cover, I could see huge tracts of barren, rocky land. Then in the distance there was a strip of green, and we came in on a landing field outside a small city. When we stepped off the shuttle onto my first foreign planet, I was surprised at what I saw: blue skies, rolling hills, grass, and trees. My first exposure to a Class-M planet; it wasn't foreign at all. It could easily have been mistaken for Southern California.

The spaceport was only a few kilometers outside the main town. I could see the dense sprawl of buildings, none higher than four stories. It had the feel of a late-19th-century European city, dense but not quite modern. I was trying to take it all in, when I was startled by someone calling my name.

"Jim!" I turned. It was my mother. Because of the limits of communication while in transit, I hadn't heard from her in the months since I left Earth. I had gotten so caught up with space travel and landing on a new world I'd actually forgotten about her.

She ran toward me, a giant smile on her face. She'd gotten older since I'd seen her last; in my mind she was still the young, vibrant woman who lifted me up in her arms when I was little. Now, because I'd grown, she seemed small to me. It was a difficult adjustment; she strode like a beautiful colossus in my imagination and now she was only slightly taller than me. She squeezed me in a warm hug. I could feel her tremble as she fought back tears. I felt the eyes of everyone around us as she embraced me, and though as a child I'd missed this affection, in this moment I could not return it. She felt my awkwardness and stepped back. We were almost on the same eye level.

"You've gotten so big," she said. Whether intentionally or not, that was one of the last things she said to me before she left Earth. Now, unlike then, I heard the regret in her voice. We stood in uneasy silence for a long moment; then the Leightons stepped in and introduced themselves to her. Barbara said some things about what a nice young man I was. Mom wasn't particularly warm to them; she seemed uncomfortable, anxious to get me away.

"Come on, Jim, let's go home."

I could see Rod was a little put off by her attitude, but Barbara placed a gentle hand on his forearm. Barbara said they'd see me later, she was sure, and I said goodbye and thanked them. Mom helped me with my luggage, and we headed off to a waiting hover car, a simple vehicle with four seats and an open trunk. She drove it herself into the main city.

As we glided through the streets, Mom gave me a tour. She seemed very self-conscious talking to me, and I frankly wasn't doing anything to help put her at ease. She filled the time by explaining the colony to me.

"There are 12 boulevards that radiate out from the city center," she said, as we entered the outer perimeter. The boulevard we were on was surrounded on both sides by buildings no more than three stories in height, and they looked to be made of brick and stone. It all seemed very old to me.

"All the buildings except the ones of the original settlement are made of indigenous materials," she said. I sat there quietly. "You know what indigenous means?"

"Yes," I said. I was being purposely curt. Since seeing her, I had felt an unexpected surge of anger, and it was overwhelming me.

The boulevard, simply labeled 12th Street, converged with all the boulevards in the center square. This was the site of the original settlement, and the buildings here, while in fact the oldest, looked the newest. Arranged to establish a town square, they were made from prefabricated materials designed to weather harsh environments. The square was quite large, and we drove through it and continued on to the other side of town. My mother tried to fill in as much information as she could, then asked me for details of my trip. I gave her mostly one-word answers. She was struggling to connect, and I was making sure she failed.

She pulled the hover car over near a redbrick two-story building. We got out and she led me inside to a first-floor apartment. It was simple, clean, and quaint. She had indulged in the ancient tradition of putting photographs on the wall; Sam and I were everywhere I looked, at every age. I didn't even remember some of the pictures being taken. She showed me to my room, which had a small bed, dresser, and its own window that looked out onto the street.

"I know it's not much," she said.

"It's fine," I said.

"Let me help you unpack."

"I can handle it."

"Okay," she said. There was a chime that I assumed was a doorbell. Mom left my room to head to the front door. I didn't follow, but stood and watched as she opened it. On the other side was a short, bald man in some kind of uniform coveralls. He had a badge and held a tablet with a stylus. He had a friendly, open demeanor.

"Hey Winona," he said. "Just checking to make sure you got your son okay."

"Thanks, Peter," she said. "Yes, it went fine."

"So I'll change the occupancy on your unit," he said, marking the tablet. "Can I meet him?"

"Sure," she said. "Jim?"

I pretended I hadn't been listening and came out after she called a second time.

"Jim, this is Peter Osterlund. He's an officer in the colony's security section."

"Nice to meet you, son," he said. "Now, Winona, you'll have him examined by medical—"

"In less than 24 hours, yes," she said.

"Okay, great," he said, finishing on the tablet. "See you soon!" And with that he was gone.

"What was that all about?"

"The colony keeps highly detailed records of its inhabitants. It allows for very specific planning regarding the use of resources. There are computer models that use our genetic makeup to determine accurate predictions of our consumption of food, water, medicine, everything. Even down to the wear and tear on the pavement of the sidewalks."

"Why?"

"Well, Jim, we're pretty far away from Earth and the rest of the Federation," she said. "This planet doesn't have an abundant supply of resources, so careful planning is necessary. We're self-sustaining, but just barely."

"I don't understand," I said.

"What?"

"Why does anyone want to live here?" My tone reflected a harshness that was out of proportion to the question; it belied a subtext of resentment that I'm not sure even I was aware of.

"Well, one might see it as a challenge," she said. "You can have an impact out here that you can't on Earth. But that might not be a good enough reason." I may not have been aware of my resentment, but she certainly was.

✦

Despite the initial awkwardness with my mother, it didn't take me long before I felt at home on Tarsus IV. I went to school during the day, and afterward I usually hung around with Tom Leighton. Though we were quite different boys we had formed a bond during the journey that continued. I spent a lot of time at his dwelling, which my mother initially was reticent about. Even so, she still did her best to make a home for me; she cooked us dinner every night, and though she worked a five-day week, on her free days she would take me on excursions outside of the town. The planet's small strip of arable land had been part of a limited, primitive terraforming by the original settlers; the rest of the world was what I had seen when I first arrived—rocky, unforgiving terrain. Mom, however, was an avid rock climber, and it was during this period that she taught me how to do it. It's something I still indulge in even to this day.

Mom's job on Tarsus involved research on xenobiology, the various life that was indigenous to the planet, as well as those that may have been extraterrestrial in origin. These extraterrestrial forms found their way through meteorites and asteroids that entered the atmosphere. It was one of these forms of life that ended up causing all the difficulties.

One day I came home from school to find Mom hurriedly going through some files on her computer. She seemed distraught.

"Jim, I'm going to have to go back to the lab," she said. "I've called the Leightons. You can sleep there tonight." Mom was usually restrained about all the time I spent at the Leightons', so the fact that she was facilitating the sleepover told me something was seriously wrong.

"Is there anything the matter?"

She turned and looked at me. I could see her trying to figure out whether to tell me what she knew.

"It's nothing to worry about now," she said. She then got up and gave me a kiss. "Come on, pack an overnight bag and I'll take you over to the Leightons' while I head back to work."

As we drove to the Leightons' I noticed that there was a sense of panic in the people we passed: worried looks, alarmed conversations, many of them running. At the Leightons', Mom said goodbye and I went inside. Barbara wasn't home, but Rod was there, and he wasn't his usual jovial self. He told me where I could find Tom, who was in his room reading.

"You know what's going on?" I said.

"Yeah, something to do with the food," Tom said. "Dad knows someone in the agriculture department who said it's really bad."

As history would show, that turned out to be an understatement. An alien fungus had attacked the food supply. It wasn't indigenous to Tarsus IV; the fungi lay dormant in the planet's soil for thousands of years. When a species of Earth squash was introduced into the colony's crops, it somehow caused the fungi to become active. Spores were carried in the air to every food and water storage and production facility. By the time emergency procedures were implemented, all the planet's food production capability had been decimated; half the food and water supply had been wiped out. The officials estimated that the food would run out a full month before relief could arrive. Casualties were estimated at 60 percent of the planet's population.

Tarsus IV was populated by rational technocrats, so the initial reaction wasn't nearly as panicked as it might have been on other worlds. The government was not elected; the officials were chosen based on their specific skills to carry out specific duties. The governor at the time, Arnold Kodos, was selected for his abilities to deal with the bureaucratic management of the colony. His own personal views therefore were not required to carry out his work, as he made his judgments based on computer modeling, using the detailed information about the resources available to him. It was assumed by the population that the crisis they faced would be handled in a similar manner.

School was canceled the next day, and it was sometime late the next evening when my mother came to get me from the Leightons'. As I packed my things, I heard Mom talking quietly to them in the kitchen. I approached the doorway where they were seated around the table, to listen without being noticed.

". . . the council isn't giving us any instructions," Barbara said. "The hospital management has been waiting for word about supply distribution."

"They've got to have a plan," Rod said. "They'll figure it out."

"I think you've got too much faith in them," Barbara said. She turned to Mom. "Have you heard anything?"

"They're afraid to start food production," Mom said. "The spores are still in the air. We haven't figured out how to counteract them."

"If they can't start food production—" Rod said.

"Jim, ready to go?" It was Barbara, who caught sight of me near the doorway. Mom thanked the Leightons. As we were leaving, Barbara gave my mother a hug.

"It'll be okay," Barbara said. My mother, though six inches taller, looked like a young girl next to Barbara, who had a natural maternal air about her.

As we were leaving, two security officers drove up to us in a hover car. One of them was Osterlund, the man who came to our apartment the first day I arrived. He looked different, less friendly, and he and the other security man with him now wore sidearms. He sat in the front passenger seat.

"Winona," he said. "You shouldn't be out here. Get in, I'll drive you home."

"It's okay," she said. "I've got my car—"

"Get in," he said, placing his hand on his holster. "It's for your own protection. You shouldn't be out in your own vehicle. You can retrieve it tomorrow."

Mom instinctively put her arm around me.

"Peter, what the hell is—"

"I said get in!" He now withdrew his weapon, an old pre-Starfleet phase pistol.

Mom looked at the weapon, then nodded to me. We got in the back of the hover car, and the security men drove us in silence back to our apartment. After a long beat, my mother finally spoke.

"Peter, what's going on?"

Osterlund exchanged a look with his partner, who was driving.

"You might as well tell her," the partner said. "They're going to find out soon anyway."

"Find out what?" Mom said.

Osterlund turned to us in the back.

"Governor Kodos has declared martial law."

"That doesn't make any sense," Mom said. "Why would this crisis be handled any differently than anything else—"

"The governor doesn't agree with you," Osterlund said. I didn't know this security man well, but I could see that giving him a gun and the right to use it had granted him a kind of power he was enjoying.

"So he . . . he's overthrown the council?"

The security men didn't answer. The hover car pulled over in front of our building.

"Stay inside until you receive instructions."

We got out of the hover car and Mom took me inside. She looked ashen, a vacant look in her eyes.

"Mom," I said. "What's martial law?"

"It's . . . it's when there's no more democracy. When the military takes over the government, and one man at the top of the hierarchy is making all the decisions. It's usually only in an emergency."

"Tom told me about the food," I said. "So couldn't this be a good thing?"

"Come on, it's late, you should get ready for bed." She didn't answer my question.

A few moments later, there was an official announcement. It came over the emergency public address system that was installed in all the buildings in the colony. The message just said what Mom and I already knew, that martial law had been declared, and a curfew was now in effect. The announcer said that the food emergency was being handled and that everyone should stay in their homes and await specific instructions from the government. This news didn't seem to give my mother any comfort, but it confirmed for me my faith in adults to take care of things. I went to bed as I did every night.

Several hours later, I was jostled awake. I turned to see Tom Leighton standing over my bed.

"Come on," he said. "Something big is happening."

"Tom, how did you—"

"Shh . . ." he said. "Just come on, I'll explain on the way."

Waking up for another of his late-night adventures didn't take any convincing. I quickly got dressed and we climbed out of my first-floor window, which is how Tom got in. We quietly moved through the deserted streets, hiding in alleys and behind garbage cans when security patrols drove past. We noticed several of the cars had other colonists in the backseat, and they were all headed toward the center square of the colony.

"A couple of security guys came and got my parents," he told me. "They thought I was asleep when they left, but I followed them. People have been gathering there for almost an hour now."

We were a few buildings from the square when Tom stopped me. I could see the large square was almost full now; there had to be thousands of people in there. A barricade had been erected on the boulevard to the entrance to the square, where a security man stood guard. Tom indicated a door to a nearby building that bordered the square, and we quickly slipped inside.

"We'll have a better view of what's going on from the roof," he said, as we climbed the stairs.

We got to the roof and, crouching, moved toward the end that bordered the square. We hid behind the ledge. We could see security guards on some of the other roofs, but their focus was on the people down below; we were just lucky that one wasn't posted on ours. I noticed that all the entrances to the square had been barricaded. It looked like no one could get in or out without permission.

"You see my folks?" Tom said. We scanned the crowd for a long time. The square was well lit, and I was able to find Tom's parents at the far end. Rod held Barbara in his arms. Even from as far away as we were, I could see that they were scared. I started to wonder about my mother; I had just assumed when I left our apartment she was asleep in her room, but now I realized that she might be in the square as well. I started searching for her when everyone's attention was drawn to the building at the head of the square. It was the building next to us. Two guards flanked the entrance to the roof of that building as a slight, redheaded man with a beard stepped out onto that roof and approached a lectern at the roof's edge.

"I am Governor Kodos," he said. "The Tarsus Governing Council has been dissolved." He then took a pause. "The revolution is successful."

There were audible gasps in the crowd. People seemed confused and worried. Revolution?

"What does he mean—" Tom said. I shushed him as Kodos continued.

"But survival depends on drastic measures. Your continued existence represents a threat to the well-being of society. Your lives mean slow death to the more valued members of the colony. Therefore, I have no alternative but to sentence you to death." He took out a piece of paper.

"Your execution is so ordered, signed Kodos, governor of Tarsus IV."

There was numb silence.

"Execution . . . ?" Tom said. As he did, I saw all the security men, both those on the roofs and at the barricades, take out their weapons and fire. The silence was broken by screams as high-energy weapons burned the people. I frantically scanned the crowd looking for Mom when my gaze fell on Rod and Barbara. Rod tried to protect Barbara as a blue beam of light hit them both. They screamed in pain, then turned to blackened ash before falling to dust.

"No!" It was Tom; he'd seen it as well and was already standing up. I saw that Tom's scream had gotten the attention of one of the guards near Kodos. He brought up his weapon . . .

I grabbed Tom and tackled him. He was screaming as he fell to the roof.

"Tom, be quiet. We gotta . . ." I looked at him. Half his face seemed covered with dirt. He was screaming, and I tried to brush it off, when I realized it wasn't dirt; his skin was horribly burned. When I tackled him the beam must have still glanced off his face; the whole left side was charred, the skin flapping in seared pieces. His left eye socket was a blackened hole. He wailed in pain and I could do nothing.

A guard leaped over from the other roof and aimed his weapon at us. I looked up into the barrel of the pistol, disbelieving . . .

"Stop!" The voice was from behind the guard.

Kodos. He walked over to me.

"What's your name?" he said.

"J-James Tiberius . . . Kirk."

Kodos turned to the guard who was holding the gun on us. As if obeying a silent order, he put the weapon away and took out a reader. He checked a list, turned to Kodos, and nodded.

"And who's he?" Kodos was referencing Tom, whose screams had faded to crying.

"Tom Leighton," I said.

The guard checked the list again. Another guard came over from another roof.

"Rod Leighton?" the guard with the reader said. "Rod Leighton is here on the register . . ." He was about to raise his weapon.

"It's Tom!" I shouted it. "This is Tom Leighton!"

Kodos looked over the guard's shoulder and indicated something on the reader. The guard lowered his weapon.

"Get the boy to a hospital," Kodos said.

They took Tom, and Kodos then turned to me.

"You go home," he said. "You're in violation of curfew." He then walked away.

I stood up and got a view of the square. It was filled with blackened ash in the shape of human bodies. Security men entered with a large mobile cleaner. They carved a path through the ash, sucking it up inside the machine. The people were all gone.

I wandered home in a fog and climbed into my window. I stood for a very long time in my bedroom, unable to move. I wanted to know if Mom was in the square. Her room was only a few feet away. I was afraid that I would find her gone. I don't know how long I stood there, unable to make a decision. Finally, I took a step toward the doorway of my room, then another. I went out into the hallway. The door to her room was closed. I gently slid it open a crack. The sheets and blanket were crumpled at the edge of the bed. I slid the door open a little more: I saw the bottom hem of her nightgown and her feet. She was there. Asleep. I gently slid the door closed and went back into my room. I don't remember going to sleep that night, but I did eventually, because I was awakened the next morning by the sound of my mother's crying.

✦

I never told her what happened, and when Tom came to live with us, he didn't talk about it either. I don't know why I didn't want to tell my mother; most likely because I couldn't face reliving the tragedy of what I'd witnessed. Mom couldn't get any answers out of the security force about how Tom received his injuries, and she was reluctant to press Tom himself, who was traumatized for a long time. He wore a patch over the whole left side of his face; the surgeon who would've been able to reconstruct his face had been killed in the square. That surgeon was, ironically, his mother. As an adult, he could've had his face reconstructed, but he chose not to, and would wear that patch until the day he died, as a remembrance of his lost parents.

But shortly after the tragedy, Mom's attitude changed toward me. I don't know if she saw me more as an adult, or I was acting like one, but before, she had sought to protect me from information I might not be ready for; now she shared everything with me. Looking back, I now think she needed help getting through it. She'd lost a lot of friends in the massacre, and we only had each other.

The execution was made public, and it had the desired effect on the remaining populace. No one dared question Governor Kodos's orders. Life continued on Tarsus as the remaining food and water were rationed and we awaited the relief. There was a lot of quiet discussion among the survivors about how Kodos had made his decisions about who would live and who would die. It defied logic; in some cases, whole families were killed; in others, like Tom's, one or another would be spared.

Finally, Mom introduced me to a friend, Kotaro Kimura, who worked in data analysis for the hospital. Kotaro's parents, Hoshi and Takashi, had been among the first settlers of Tarsus IV, and they were among those massacred. He told Mom that Kodos had used the medical database, plugging an algorithm into it based on his own theories about who was most useful in the colony. None of the survivors knew exactly why they were valuable in his eyes, which made everyone feel that much more insecure about their status; he could always change his mind.

But two weeks after the executions, something very strange happened. Mom was waiting for me one day when Tom and I got out of school.

"Kodos is dead," Mom told us.

"What happened?" I said.

"No one knows," she said. "The security people found his body, burned in his quarters. The governing council is re-forming, and they're appointing a new governor."

"The bastard deserves it," Tom said. "I wish it was me who'd done it."

Mom put her hand on Tom's shoulder.

"I don't understand," I said. "Who killed him?"

"It looks like suicide," Mom said.

Suddenly, there was the tingling sound of what seemed like wind chimes. It was the first time I'd ever heard, and then seen, the effect of matter transportation. I turned and saw three Starfleet officers appear.

"Bob!" Mom said. She was shouting to the leader of the three, in a gold shirt and with the most braid on his cuff. He walked over to her, and they hugged.

"Winona, what the hell's been going on down here?" the man said, after they separated.

"How did you get here so fast? The relief wasn't supposed to be here for another three weeks."

"The *Enterprise*," he said, with obvious pride. "Fastest ship in the quadrant. It was supposed to be another month before she was ready to leave spacedock, but I rushed it through. We contacted Governor Kodos a week ago . . ." He then noticed me. "Is this Jim?"

"Yes," she said. "Jim, this is Robert April. He's here to save us." I could see she meant it. And I felt saved.

CHAPTER 3

"WELCOME, CADETS, TO YOUR FIRST DAY at Starfleet Academy."

Admiral Reed, old, British, commandant of the academy, stood in front of us. It was Induction Day, I was 18, it was 5 p.m., and I was already exhausted, but knew not to show it. I was at attention with all the other first-year cadets, buttoned up in our silver cadet dress tunics, our shined black boots reflecting in the sun like spilled crude oil. We were on the Great Lawn, once part of the ancient military installation called the Presidio. I had spent the last ten hours being run ragged, yelled at by any and every upperclassman who had laid eyes on me; and it was still the greatest day of my life. It had all started five years before, when a starship captain beamed down to Tarsus IV and I decided who I wanted to be.

After the death of Kodos, life on the colony would never fully return to normal. The trauma of what happened led many of the survivors to want to leave, and the news of the horror would keep new settlers away. Mom and I, however, stayed for another year; she wanted to complete her work before she left. (The results would lead to safeguards that prevented similar food disasters on other Federation colonies.) Eventually, however, it was time to go, and we were evacuated with the remainder of the population.*

---

*EDITOR'S NOTE: The colony on Tarsus IV would be reestablished 25 years after the Kodos incident, albeit under a different form of government.

Several months earlier I had said my goodbyes to Tom Leighton, whose relatives on the Earth colony Planet Q were going to take him in. Tom and I had lived through a trauma together; we shared a bond. Though our lives went down different roads, we stayed in regular contact for the rest of his life.

Mom and I returned to Earth, and my dad met us at the shuttle station in Riverside. I had been seeing him via subspace transmissions, but in person he was a bit of a shock. He had gained weight around the middle and gray around the temples. He greeted me with a handshake and a warm pat on the shoulder. He then turned and saw Mom. They gave each other a hello kiss and hug that somehow both conveyed affection and distance. The three of us returned home to live in the same house, but things were far from what they had been. Sam was off at school and seldom came home. Mom focused on her work, which sometimes took her away, but for only short periods. She never made another declaration about leaving or staying, and Dad seemed all right with that arrangement. But I suppose the biggest change was inside me.

I'd been hardened by the events on Tarsus and couldn't trust my parents, or any adults, to look after me anymore. I had been on my own; I was looking for some way to exert control over a world that could be cruel and merciless. Seeing how that starship captain and his crew had almost single-handedly restored civilization by their mere presence had made a strong impression. I wanted to be a part of that. Or maybe I needed to. So I focused on getting accepted into Starfleet Academy.

My first goal was academics. Up to that point in my life, I hadn't taken my studies all that seriously, but for the next two years I was determined to change. I had very good role models, my brother and mother were both academics, and they taught me a lot about focus and time management. My grades soon improved greatly.

I also knew that self-defense techniques were seen as an important part of Starfleet training, so I began my own study of martial arts, including among other things karate, judo, and the Vulcan discipline of *Suus Mahna*.

As my 17th birthday approached, I started thinking seriously about my application. The competition was fierce: Starfleet Academy had deservedly earned a reputation as one of the finest academic institutions in the Galaxy. The standards for acceptance were, excuse the phrase, astronomically high.

I wasn't just competing against humans; I was also competing with applicants from other planets, including Vulcans, who had received rigorous educations well beyond what humans considered normal. In 2251, the year I enrolled, Starfleet accepted fewer than 2 percent of its applicants.

This didn't deter me. I had the advantage that my parents were both graduates of the academy, and on my mother's side I would be third generation; my maternal grandfather had been in the first graduating class and rose to the rank of captain of engineering. But none of that made me a shoo-in, and the fact that both my parents had discontinued their Starfleet careers would work against me. What I considered the tipping point of my application was that I had been vital in preventing a diplomatic incident. I just had to figure out how to make use of it.

There was no notoriety for me in saving the Tellarite ambassador's life; Starfleet kept the incident quiet out of worries that the Tellarites would be embarrassed that an Earthling boy saved one of their most important diplomats. My parents and I had been told that the matter was confidential, and that if we told anyone, Starfleet would deny it happened. However, Captain Mallory's gratitude at the time led me to hope that he'd remember me and maybe help. All I had to do was track him down.

Starfleet Headquarters would only tell me he was now a commodore, but they would give me no information on his whereabouts. I thought about sending him an electronic letter, but I was worried it wouldn't find its way to him. So I embarked on what was, in hindsight, a ridiculously dangerous plan.

In our attic we had a storage container that was filled with my dad's belongings from his time in Starfleet: various pieces of equipment, tapes containing all his work, and, most important, his uniforms. When I was little, I would put them on and traipse around the house, always a little disappointed that no matter how "big" everybody said I was getting, they still didn't fit. However, it had been a few years, and now when I tried the uniforms on, they seemed almost tailored.

I made sure I wore the uniform with the rank of ensign, then found a recording disc with a Starfleet logo on it. I took it to my computer station and recorded a message for Mallory, reminding him who I was, and asking him to write me a recommendation.

The next morning I jammed the uniform and recorded message into a rucksack and snuck out early, borrowing Dad's hover car. I had told him that I was driving to Riverside to see friends and that I'd be back by noon, so I was on a tight schedule. I drove to the transportation station in Riverside and caught a Sub Shuttle to San Francisco.*

The trip took less than two hours, and I didn't want anyone on the Sub Shuttle to notice me in the uniform, so I stayed in my civilian clothes until about five minutes before we reached San Francisco. I then got up and changed in the bathroom, and waited until we pulled into the Starfleet Headquarters stop. I then quickly exited the bathroom and immediately got off the Sub Shuttle car.

I marched through the station, found a temporary locker to store my rucksack, then took the escalator to the street level. I found myself in a shuttle port and was stunned. Shuttles and flying trams flew in and out of the port, over the bay and the Golden Gate Bridge. People of all races and species in bright gold and blue uniforms walked with purpose to their destinations. I suddenly felt like a complete fraud, but I had committed to this course of action and had to see it through. I imitated the resoluteness of the people I saw around me and walked out of the spaceport.

I had studied the mall of structures that made up Starfleet Headquarters, and immediately recognized the main building, the Archer Building, named for Jonathan Archer.**

I walked into the large reception area, and where doubt had only crept into my mind when I entered the spaceport, it now completely consumed me. The lobby of the building was filled with officers, *adult* officers, of many different species and ages. The whole place had a sense of importance and dignity, and I was a kid playing dress-up. I was only a few steps inside when

---

***EDITOR'S NOTE:** The Sub Shuttles were a subterranean rapid transit system, built in the early 22nd century, using tunnels that honeycombed the globe. They were taken out of operation in 2267 when they were made obsolete by the preponderance of matter/energy transporters.

**: Captain Kirk has made a common error: It is in fact named for Henry Archer, Jonathan's father and the inventor of the Warp Five engine. The building was constructed during Jonathan Archer's tenure as Federation president, and it was he who insisted it be named for his father.

I decided this wasn't going to work, and was about to turn around when someone blocked my way.

"May I help you?"

It was a young woman, not much older than me. She was petite, dressed in a blue uniform dress, had blond hair. Very beautiful.

"I have a message," I said, holding up the tape much too quickly. "It's for Commodore Mallory."

"Oh," she said. "Come with me."

I followed her to a reception desk, where she typed some information into the computer terminal.

"Commodore Mallory isn't here, Ensign," she said. "Were you under the impression he was?"

"Uh, no," I said. "I mean, yes, I thought he was here, but no, I didn't know for certain that he'd be here *right now*." She looked at me like she didn't know what I was talking about, which made two of us. "When do you think he'll be back?"

She laughed. "Not for several years," she said. "He's in command of Starbase 11, and they're in the middle of an extensive upgrade and remodel."

It was a testimony to the lack of forethought that went into this plan that it never occurred to me that Mallory, an officer in Starfleet, might not be on Earth anymore. My fantasy of walking into Starfleet and handing him the message had vaporized, and I just wanted to get out of there.

"Well, thanks for your help," I said, reaching for the tape.

"Don't you want to get the message to him?"

"Oh, um . . . I guess . . ."

"I'll have someone upload it to him," she said. "I'm just going to need your daily comm code."

I had no idea what that was. She was looking at me intently now.

"You know, I should double-check with my superior officer," I said. She nodded.

"Okay," she said, "and you might want to ask him what the penalty is for impersonating a Starfleet officer. I think it's five years on a penal colony." I felt all the blood drain out of my head. Up until that moment, I had no idea that what I was doing was indeed a crime. I was lucky that Mallory *wasn't* here; if he'd seen me in the uniform he probably would've made sure I never got near the academy. I was in a large amount of trouble. It was only her gentle hand on my arm that kept me from running.

"Don't worry," she said. "I'm just going to review it myself, and unless there's something objectionable, I'll make sure he gets it."

Though I'd been unaware I was holding my breath, I felt myself exhale.

"Thanks," I said. "I really appreciate it."

"Don't mention it," she said. "What's your name?"

"I'm Jim," I said, holding out my hand. She took it in both of hers. The gesture completely calmed me down.

"Nice to meet you. I'm Ruth." She looked me in the eye and I beamed like an idiot.

✦

Ruth later said she got the message to Mallory's chief of staff (and never mentioned my ludicrous "spy" mission), and since everyone I knew was pretty astounded when I was accepted to the academy, I assumed Mallory put in a good word, although at the time there was no way to know what exactly happened.

Nevertheless, a few months later, I was packed and ready to go. My parents took me to San Francisco. It was 6 a.m.; new cadets were lined up at the entry gates, waiting to go in. They were all saying goodbye to their parents, and I turned to mine. I looked at Mom and Dad. They'd both aged, but seemed happier, or at least more content than either had been in some time. Looking back, it was clear they'd found some kind of comfort in each other's presence. But I was ready to go. I took a hug from Mom and a handshake from Dad, and said I'd see them at the winter break.

"Get ready to suffer," Dad said, and Mom chuckled. I would shortly find out what he meant.

✦

There is only one military institution left in the Federation: Starfleet. Though its "brand" is one of exploration, diplomacy, and civilization, the security of the Federation and its citizens is still an important part of its charter, and to look after it requires a military chain of command. So the one not-so-secret secret of its academy is that it makes sure its graduates can be soldiers when they need to be. And that starts on Induction Day.

New cadets sign in, are handed a big empty red bag, and from that moment on they enter a maze of abuse. You're sent on an organized scavenger hunt to acquire your needed equipment in different buildings. And around every corner there's an angry upperclassman telling you *you're a stupid plebe who's walking too slow; you shouldn't be running, why aren't you at attention, why are you standing there, get moving you stupid plebe, put your bag down when I'm talking to you, who told you to drop your bag, look at me when I'm talking to you, why are you looking at me, don't you look at me!*

The bag gets heavier and heavier; you've got to carry it everywhere, and you very quickly have no idea where you're going or where you're supposed to be going, and that's the point. If you get through the day, it's because you finally realize you have no choice but to not think, just *do*, usually whatever the last thing the nearest upperclassman said. It's arduous, humiliating, and stressful, and more than a few cadets don't make it 'til sundown. I did, though just barely. I'd never been yelled at like this before, and it was only the beginning.

The first eight weeks of your first year are called "plebe summer," and they are designed to drive out those men and women who can't handle the physical and psychological stress. The survivors learn discipline and skills they need not only to get along at the academy, but more importantly in Starfleet. It is the one thing that separates it from the rest of the Federation: cadets, crewmen, and officers know the importance of following orders, because it saves lives.

At around noon, by which time I'd learned, among other things, to march in formation carrying a 50-pound bag, I was assigned to a company, the Second Cadet Corps, a barracks, and reported to my room. My section commander (there were eight of us in the section) was a cadet captain named Ben Finney. A few years older, big and fit, he commanded my attention immediately. He ordered me, two other humans, and an Andorian to stand at attention and hold our bags until further orders. We stood two on each side in front of our bunk beds for about an hour. My arms were shaking from the strain. I was looking straight ahead into the pale green eyes of the blue-skinned cadet. I'd never met an Andorian; I had dozens of questions for him, but one of the lessons I'd learned from that first day was not to speak until spoken to by an upperclassman.

"Drop your bags!" It was Finney, who finally came into our room. We dumped our bags on the floor, and before I could stop myself, I let out a "whew." Bad mistake. Finney went right up to me.

"You tired, plebe?"

"No sir!"

"Glad to hear it! Pick up your bag; you can hold on to it for a little while longer. The rest of you, unpack. I want this room shipshape." And with that, he left. While my roommates tried to navigate around me, I stood holding the bag. About an hour later, the roommates were now relaxing on their beds while I stood there, sweat pouring from me, my arms shaking.

"Atten-shun!" It was one of my roommates, who saw another upperclassman come into the room. He was a cadet lieutenant named Sean Finnegan—a big, blond, smiling Irishman.

"What's been going on in here, boyos?" I hadn't really heard an Irish accent as pronounced as this one, and felt it had to be somewhat affected. He looked at my three roommates. "You boyos should be getting down to lunch." They left, and he then turned to look at me.

"And what might you be doing?"

"Lieutenant sir, I've been ordered to hold my bag, sir!"

"What's your name, Cadet?"

"Lieutenant sir, Cadet James T. Kirk, sir!"

"Oh, well, Jimmy Boy," he said, pronouncing boy "bahy," "if you don't get unpacked, you're gonna miss chow. See you down there."

"Lieutenant sir, yes sir." I put the bag down, and Finnegan sauntered out, whistling "Danny Boy." I unpacked and made it down to lunch just in time. As I sat at the table, Finney looked up at me, stupefied.

"Kirk! You stupid plebe, what the hell do you think you're doing here?"

"Sir, I was ordered to lunch, sir!"

"Who ordered you?" Finney said, and he was bellowing. The whole room was quiet.

"Sir, Cadet Lieutenant Finney—" I said.

"There is no Cadet Lieutenant Finney!"

"Sir, sorry, sir, I meant Cadet Lieutenant Finnegan, sir." It wasn't the last time I would mix up their unfortunately similar names. Finnegan stood up.

"I gave no such order," Finnegan said. "I think the day has been too much for the boy."

I went over it in my head. He was right; Finnegan had not ordered me to put the bag down. I had read into it.

"What do you have to say to that?" Finney said.

"Sir, I was mistaken, sir!" I was also starving, but Finney sent me back up to my room and told me to repack my bag and hold it until he got there. I followed the order, and about 15 minutes later, my roommates returned from lunch, followed by Finney. My roommates stood tall as Finney inspected my living space to make sure that I'd put everything back in the bag. I felt like passing out, but held on. He smiled.

"Drop the bag, plebe." I slowly lowered the bag to the ground, then returned to attention. "Stow your gear," he said, and then left. As I started to put my gear away, I saw Finnegan standing in the doorway, smiling.

It was not a good start for me.

For the next two months we were put through a punishing regime of physical training: running with heavy packs, obstacle courses, battle simulations, survival training. The skills I had developed in my boyhood, considered primitive and unnecessary in our society, came in handy during this period: my mountain-climbing experience, my years camping with my father, and my knowledge of the Old West. Still, it was never easy, and there were always surprises.

Plebe summer was such a whirlwind that I really didn't get much downtime with my roommates. I never became close with the two humans, Jim Corrigan and Adam Castro; the Andorian, Thelin, was the first of his kind admitted to the academy, and did not always easily fit in. We shared the similarity that we tended to separate ourselves from the group.

The last weekend of plebe summer we got our first pass. I was thrilled; it was going to be my first chance to see Ruth in months. We'd seen each other several times, but not since I'd begun at the academy. The night before, as I came into my room from having washed up, I was lost in thought; she was the first girlfriend I'd ever had, and as the stress of my first few weeks at the academy relieved somewhat, she dominated my mind. I was so distracted I hadn't really noticed Castro, Corrigan, and Thelin's furtive glances to one aother as I hopped up on my bed on the top bunk. There was a splash; I'd landed in something that wasn't supposed to be there. I looked down and saw a soup bowl tipped over, my pants covered with thick, oily liquid.

"What the hell is this?" I said, totally confused, as the answer walked in.

"Atten-shun!" Finnegan said. We all leaped to our feet. In doing so, I made my situation worse as the bowl of soup followed me off the bed and spilled down my body. I now recognized the liquid as the corn chowder that had been served for lunch that day.

"Sneaking food, are we, Jimmy Boy?"

"No sir!" The congealed yellow liquid was dripping off me onto the floor.

"You know the regulations about eating in your rooms," he said. "This is a serious infraction. Twenty demerits."

"Yes sir!" I was furious. If a cadet got 100 demerits during his years at the academy, he was out. This man was carrying out some archaic practical joke that I couldn't imagine had ever been funny, *ever*, and it might cost me my future.

"Something you want to say to me, Jimmy Boy?" He was standing an inch in front of me. I held his stare.

"No sir!"

"Really? 'Cause you look like you want to lay one on me." He was right. I wanted to hit him. Which is what he wanted, because then I'd be out.

"No sir!"

"All right, then, clean up this mess, before I give you ten more demerits," Finnegan said as he swaggered through the doorway.

"Sorry, Jim," Castro said, handing me a towel. "We saw him come out of our room when we got back. He ordered us not to tell you what he'd done."

"If you report him," Thelin said, "it will be a mark on his record. If my testimony is necessary, I offer it."

THE STORY OF STARFLEET'S GREATEST CAPTAIN

The Andorian had a sense of honor, which I appreciated, but as I glanced over at Castro and Corrigan, I could see their reluctance, and I didn't blame them. Though I wanted to get Finnegan in trouble, I also knew what would happen if I went through channels. The story wouldn't be that Finnegan was abusing me unnecessarily; it would be that I couldn't take a joke.

"It's all right," I said, wiping the chowder off my pants. "I'll survive."

✦

Fortunately, I still had my pass and got to see Ruth. She still worked at Starfleet Headquarters. She had grown up in San Francisco, where Starfleet crewmen had been omnipresent, so once out of high school, looking to carve her own path, she'd enlisted, gone through the basic training in the noncommissioned officers' school, and became a clerk in the records department. She admitted to being a little lost in terms of her life goals, and she later told me that my confidence over what I wanted to do was part of what she found attractive. Though inside I was still very much a boy, I found her attention did a lot to assuage my insecurity.

We had seen each other a few times since we met the previous year, but I had had little experience with women, and the only physical contact we had up until that night was holding hands. We met in the Fisherman's Wharf section of San Francisco. It was a warm fall night, and she was wearing a lovely white-and-black lace dress. I wore my uniform, and like a crewman on a mission, I had gone into the evening having made the decision that I would kiss her. The question was when.

"Do you know why they call it Fisherman's Wharf?" she asked me as we walked along the landscaped shoreline.

"This whole area," I said, "used to be centered around the commerce of fishing. Fishermen moored their small vessels here, and early in the morning they'd leave to catch as much fish as they could, which they'd bring back here where they could sell . . ." I was about to continue when I could see she was smiling at me.

"Oh," I said, "you weren't asking. You were going to tell me . . ."

"Yeah," she said, laughing a little. "I grew up here. But you tell it well."

I laughed a little too. I felt like an idiot, but she held my arm tightly. I stopped and picked an orange and yellow sunflower and gave it to her.

"You're not supposed to pick the flowers," she said.

"I know. Let's break some rules."

I looked at her, not at all feeling the bravado I was expressing. I pushed through my fear and kissed her. She welcomed it. Mission accomplished. She parted from me and stared into my eyes. What happened next astounded me, but I tried not to show it.

"Why don't you take me home now?" she said, smiling.

✦

I had to be back at the academy by 24:00, and the guard on duty logged me in at 23:57. I was giddy, confused, happy, proud of myself at the same time I was certain I had nothing to do with causing what had just happened. So I was a little lost in my head, and I didn't notice the unusual way the door to my room was propped open. I could see the light on inside and could hear Castro and Thelin talking.

"You guys up, 'cause I got a story—" Before I could finish my sentence I was covered in ice-cold water, and a plastic bucket hit me in the head. I almost couldn't breathe the water was so frigid. I now saw Finnegan was in there talking to my roommates.

"Welcome home, Jimmy Boy," Finnegan said. "Looks like you made another mess. Twenty demerits." He strutted out. When he was gone, Castro headed toward the dresser and got me a towel.

"Th-th-anks," I said, shivering.

"How was your furlough?" Castro said.

"Great until a second ago . . ."

"This human type of humor is very confusing," Thelin said.

"I'm not laughing either," I said.

"Atten-shun!" Castro said as Ben Finney walked in. We all stood at attention. Finney took in the scene, then turned to me.

"Kirk, you want to explain this?" he said.

"Sir, I have no explanation, sir!"

Finney picked the bucket up off the floor, then went over to the door, which was dripping with water. He clearly put together what happened, and addressed my roommates.

"Did you men do this?"

"No sir!" Thelin and Castro said in unison. Undoubtedly, Finnegan had ordered them to not say anything, and Ben was smart enough to figure out that they weren't to blame. He could've asked if they knew who was responsible, but we'd been taught the academy honor code. If they said they didn't do it, Finney had to believe them. Whether he would ask them to inform on another cadet was another question, and would cause us all a lot of headaches. It was a tense moment.

"Clean this up," Finney said, "and get to bed. You have classes tomorrow." He left. Whatever we had thought about Finney up to that point, we now liked him.

✦

"So, Mr. Kirk," Professor Gill said, "your theory is Khan wasn't all that bad."

That I had expounded a theory at all was news to me. We were covering some very dense, confusing material in my History of the Federation class, and as far as I knew up to that moment, I didn't have a theory about any of it. Professor Gill was ascribing something to me I don't remember even saying. And this was the shallow end of the academic swamp I found myself in every day.

Now that plebe summer was officially over, the long slog of the academic year began, and it was much tougher than I imagined. Along with all the usual subjects of literature, history, physical sciences, there was a whole slew of other disciplines not covered in the usual college education: xenobiology, xenoanthropology, galactic law and institutions, planetary ecologies, interplanetary economics. This went hand in hand with semantics, language structure, comparative galactic ethics, epistemology, xenopsychology, and so on. And on top of all that, Starfleet Academy had to be an engineering school. Its graduates, no matter what they decided to concentrate in, needed to understand technology in a practical way for a whole slew of possible emergencies, because the situations Starfleet officers faced might require a physician to pilot a shuttlecraft or a historian to operate a transporter. The standards were rigorous because lives were at stake.

Contributing to the high standards, many of the professors were the foremost scholars in their fields, and their teaching would affect me for the rest of my life. John Gill, the professor of my history class, was no exception. The history he wrote on the Third World War won the Pulitzer and MacFarlane prizes, and was one of the texts we used in his class. It was the subject we were currently studying.

"Uh . . . I don't think I meant that," I said. "I just meant that it was amazing for one man to rule such a large part of the Earth—"

"So you admire him?" I had been in Gill's class long enough to know he was setting some kind of intellectual trap, but I couldn't figure out what.

"I guess I admire his ability, yes."

"His ability to enslave millions of people?"

"I wasn't judging the morality of what he did," I said. "Just his capacity to get it accomplished."

"But weren't his accomplishments as a leader," Gill said, "directly related to his own lack of morality? His own feeling of superiority that allowed him to oppress his subjects?"

"I guess so," I said.

"And you still admire him," Gill said. "How do you justify that?"

"I admire the railroad of the old American West," I said. "It was an amazing piece of engineering and planning for such a primitive time, and directly led to the future prosperity of the United States. Yet it could only be constructed using slave labor, and its importance to capitalists led to the near genocide of the Native Americans. But I still admire the railroad."

Gill looked at me and smiled.

"Perhaps you shouldn't. The cost sounds like it was too high." Gill was trying to make a point, one that I wouldn't fully understand until much later. Interestingly, this conversation would come back to haunt us both.

But at the time I was too under siege by work to stop to think about it. I was determined to be an academic success. I was seeing less of Ruth than I wanted; I turned down furlough passes on several weekends to focus on my studies.

THE STORY OF STARFLEET'S GREATEST CAPTAIN

On one of these nights, alone in the deserted barracks, I was so lost in trying to make sense of the Xindi Incident* that I didn't notice Ben Finney standing in my doorway.

"Sir, sorry, sir," I said, quickly standing to attention.

"At ease," he said. "No plans tonight, cadet?"

"No sir."

Finney came into my room and looked at what I was studying.

"Oh, this mess," he said. "I never could make head or tail of it. Do you want to take a break?"

Finney wasn't acting like the usual upperclassman. A few minutes later we were in his room; he gave me a chair and then pulled out a bottle. It had a long, slightly curved neck. He poured us drinks in a coffee mug and plastic cup.

"Ever tried Saurian brandy?" He gave me a wry smile. In truth, I had had little exposure to any kind of spirits and was flabbergasted that my instructor was introducing them to me now.

"Sir, isn't this against regulations?"

"It is indeed. You should report this infraction to your immediate superior." That was him.

"Sir..."

"Call me Ben," he said. "Anyone finds out about this and we're both done."

He handed me the cup, and I took a swig. That first taste was vile. It was like turpentine with a fruit taste, something like apples, and burned my throat going down. I coughed and Finney laughed.

"Give it a second," he said.

Its effects were almost immediate. A warm, relaxing cloud fell over me.

"That's amazing," I said. "Thanks."

"You're welcome. You looked like you could use it."

We spent the next couple of hours drinking and laughing, and found we had a lot in common. We were both from the American midwest, both

---

*EDITOR'S NOTE: The Xindi Incident began when that race attacked Earth in 2153 with a prototype weapon that killed seven million people. Starfleet foiled a further attack involving a much larger weapon.

our parents went to the academy, and we both had dreams of serving aboard starships. Ben asked if I had a girlfriend, then showed me a picture of his, a lovely woman named Naomi, whom he was about to marry.

"Marry?" I said. "You graduate this year. Isn't that going to be hard if you get posted to a ship?"

"I'm already an instructor in computers; they'll probably ask me to stay on at least another year after graduation," Ben said. "Then we'll just have to see what happens. Naomi understands."

Ben let on that he didn't like the role he had to play as an upperclassman. He was gregarious and friendly, and, as I would learn, had a deep-seated need to be liked. He was a popular cadet not only in his class but in the other classes as well. Looking back, I can now see that Ben's desire to not only be my friend but everybody's undermined his own ability to command respect as a senior officer. This aspect of his personality, I think, contributed to the difficulties he would face later. But at the time, I was thrilled to have a pal and confidant. It helped me get through the rest of my plebe year, which was no easy feat, as 23 percent of the first-years dropped out.

✦

A cadet's second summer was spent in outer space, at the academy Training Station in Earth orbit. There we learned zero gravity combat techniques and got our first taste of actual piloting. They were century-old shuttle pods, but to get behind the stick of any kind of spacecraft was a thrill.

When I returned to the academy for my second year, things felt very different. For one, Finnegan had graduated and been posted to a starbase. He'd been a constant irritant during my first year. The hazing was endless. His parting shot before graduating was to switch my dress pants with someone much larger than me, which led to an unfortunate incident on the final day of that year during a full-dress parade.

I've often wondered what it was that made me Finnegan's target. I think it goes back to that first day, when he saw me standing at attention in my room, holding all my belongings. In that moment, I thought he was being nice to me, telling me to go to lunch. Because of that, because of my ingenuousness, he saw me as weak, as a target. Like many bullies, he enjoyed the power he had over me. I was there to do the work, and my seriousness somehow provoked him. Ironically, his lack of seriousness led to an unremarkable Starfleet career; I never ran into him again after the academy.*

Suffice it to say, it relieved a lot of stress when he was finally gone (though it still took me a while before I would open a door or get into bed too quickly). But more important, I'd made it through my first year. Except for the demerits I'd received from Finnegan, I was near the top of my class, and I was determined to stay there.

The only thing that suffered was my relationship with Ruth. She was still in her job in the records department, her life a little bit on hold. As my workload increased, I had the sense she was always waiting for me to spare some time for her, and I didn't like the pressure. Ben Finney, now my best friend, encouraged me to not let her go. Ben had graduated, but as he predicted, was asked to stay on as an instructor in Advanced Computer Programming. He had married Naomi and moved into faculty quarters, and on our off days, they would seek Ruth and me out for dinners, drinks, and other socializing. I enjoyed these times, but I wondered whether Ben himself was getting restless waiting for a ship assignment. One day, Ruth and I were sitting at dinner with them at their home, and I asked him.

"My career can survive my staying an instructor a little longer," Ben said, turning to Naomi, who was smiling. "I want to see my son."

"Oh, that's wonderful," Ruth said. She gripped my hand under the table as she said it.

"Good job," I said, with a smile. I gently removed my hand from Ruth's to shake Ben's. Ruth got up and gave Naomi a hug.

We talked at length that night about raising a family, where they wanted to live, how Ben's career might still be flexible enough to make it possible. I did my best to be supportive, but something about the dinner made me angry. I tried not to show it, though I think Ruth could sense my distance.

---

*EDITOR'S NOTE: Kirk's assessment is somewhat inaccurate. Shortly before this book went to press, Sean Finnegan's "unremarkable" career led him to be appointed commandant of Starfleet Academy.

After a little while, she and I said our goodbyes to the Finneys, and I walked her home.

"You didn't seem happy for them," she said.

"No, I am," I said. "It's just . . . I don't know if they're being realistic."

"They're grown-ups; they can make their own decisions."

"They're making decisions that affect a child," I said, somewhat harshly. "Starfleet makes demands that can get in the way of a family. Both my parents had to give up their careers."

"And you think that was wrong, that they gave up their careers for the people they loved?" She was asking more than one question, and though I had known this conversation was coming, I didn't think it would come so soon.

"It's not wrong," I said. "It's just not for me."

We walked the rest of the way to Ruth's apartment in silence. Ruth loved me, and she was trying to make it easy for me, give me what I wanted. We kissed goodnight, and it was the last time I saw her. I often look back with regret on how I treated her. I did love Ruth; she was in fact my first love, and I don't know if I was being honest with myself about why I broke up with her. She was willing to commit to me, but for some reason I couldn't, or wouldn't, trust that. So I pushed her away.

✦

"Mr. Mitchell," I said, "next time, *think* before you throw a punch."

"Sir, yes sir," Mitchell said, with a smirk.

He was lying on the floor; I was standing over him, having just thrown him with a judo move called *koshi garuma*. I was serving as an instructor in Hand-to-Hand Combat, and Gary Mitchell, a first-year cadet, was my problem student. It didn't seem to bother him that he was going to wash out of my class. Probably because it wasn't the only class he was going to fail.

It was my third year, I'd been promoted to cadet lieutenant, and Mitchell was in my squad. He was everything I wasn't: charming, gregarious, rough, and a little reckless. I had been leaning into him, hoping to shake loose a little intellect, but I wasn't having much success. I had a feeling at that time that Mitchell wouldn't make it through.

I was at the Finneys' home one night and mentioned it to Ben.

"Let him wash out," Ben said. "Who needs another loser graduating?"

Ben was now in his second year as a postgraduate instructor, and the academy had just asked him to stay on for a third. Unlike Finney, many computer specialists could often be notoriously bad teachers, which is why he was so valuable to the academy. But he'd watched two graduating classes leave him behind, and now he would see a third; it was starting to get under his skin.

His baby, Jamie, however, seemed to do a lot to soften his mood. Ben had said he wanted a son, but didn't seem at all disappointed in having a daughter. It had come as quite a shock when he and Naomi told me that they were naming their first child after me, and it made me feel more attached to them as a family. I leaned on them during those years after I broke up with Ruth. Aside from a couple of casual relationships, Ben and Naomi became my one major social outlet, as I threw myself into my studies. (I found out later that some underclassman had dubbed me a "stack of books with legs," which I would only criticize as not being particularly clever.)

✦

In any event, it was soon time to submit Mitchell's grade. I spoke to his other instructors; though he was passing most of his classes, he was going to fail his Philosophy of Religion course. That and another failing grade from me would lead to expulsion. I weighed the decision seriously and finally decided to pass him. Maybe I had softened on him, maybe I just liked him, but whatever the reasons, I would not regret that decision.

The following summer, I was part of a flying exercise of two squadrons of five craft each; we were flying academy trainers, the century-old Starfleet surplus shuttle pods, with basic instrumentation and updated piloting software. I had rated high on piloting, so by my third year I had my own squadron, and Gary was in it. We were out near Earth's moon, learning to operate in its gravity well. I was in the second squadron; my old roommate Adam Castro led the first. Our job was to follow them, stay within ten kilometers, and imitate their maneuvers as closely as possible. Castro acted the role of hotshot pilot, so he wasn't making it easy. There was also a little bit of competition between the two squadrons, which I did my best to tamp down.

We were doing a fair job of following, until their final maneuver. They lined up wingtip to wingtip, forming a three-dimensional loop. We imitated the maneuver, when I noticed something on one of my scanners. Gary noticed it too.

"Cobra Five to Cobra Leader," he said, "they're opening their coolant interlocks. Do we follow suit?"

"Cobra Leader to Cobra Group, do not, I say again, do not follow suit," I said. I could see what Castro was up to and I didn't like it.

"But they're accelerating, pulling ahead," Gary said. "You know what they're doing, don't you?"

"Yes, I do," I said. "Cobra Leader to Cobra Group, I repeat, keep your coolant interlocks closed. Engines to all stop; we'll wait here until they finish."

The ships of the other squadron spun, moved inward on the circle, and vented plasma. As they passed each other inside the circle, the plasma ignited. The maneuver, called a Kolvoord Starburst, usually ended as the ships moved out in separate directions, creating an expanding five-point eruption of ignited plasma. It was a "top gun" piloting maneuver that cadets had been performing for decades. I, however, hadn't prepared my squadron for it, and it was too risky. My caution was justified.

As the ships moved past each other, one of them veered off its course and hit another one. It caused a domino effect; all the ships crashed into each other and were destroyed.

"Oh my god . . ." It was someone over the intercom, maybe Gary. I couldn't be sure.

"Cobra Leader to Cobra Group, stand by for rescue operations—" Before I could finish that order, however, it was rendered pointless.

There was an explosion, and not the one the pilots intended. All the ships were engulfed in the cascading conflagration, and a much more dangerous wave of energy, caused by the detonation of five engines, was heading right toward us.

"Cobra Leader to Cobra Group, 180 degrees about and scatter, go, go go!" I said, shouting. I banked my ship and watched to make sure all the shuttle pods came about. The old ships moved achingly slow, but they all turned away from the explosion and each other.

I checked my six and saw the wave about to hit . . .

"All ships, brace for impact!"

I was jolted forward by the impact of the force wave. An alarm sounded and my instrumentation panel shorted out. Smoke billowed, and coughing, I waved it away. I looked up through my view port. I'd lost sight of the other shuttle pods.

"Cobra Leader to Cobra Squadron, damage report," I said. I tried again; no answer. My communications panel was out. I then checked my helm and navigation panel; I had no instruments, no sensors. I looked up through the view ports. I still didn't see any of the shuttle pods.

I couldn't risk navigating by sight. Protocol in a situation like this was to prioritize communications and signal for help; ships flying blindly were a navigation hazard. And after witnessing the death of five cadets who weren't following the rules, I decided I had to. So I ripped open the communications panel and attempted to repair the circuits.

After about half an hour, I was having no luck and started to regret my decision. The course the shuttle pods had been on was taking us away from Earth, so it might be a while before search and rescue found us. I had a squadron out here, I didn't know their status, and because I had followed the rules, they might all be dead. I gave up on the communicator and took control of the helm. I was going to have to try to find them by sight. I started scanning the sky when I heard a loud thunk on my ceiling. I looked up as the upper hatch opened, and Gary Mitchell came through. He had docked his shuttle pod to mine.

"Permission to come aboard," he said with a smile.

"Granted," I said. "How did you find me?"

"I just started looking," he said. "I found the rest of the squadron first; everybody's alive."

"You have instrumentation?"

"Nope," he said. "I did it by sight, and when I got close to a ship, I used Morse code with my landing lights to tell them to fall behind me. Then I found you."

"You . . . that's . . ." I was dumbfounded. He'd taken so many risks, but he had brought the squadron together, and now we could safely navigate to the dock.

"I think I owe you one," I said.

"We owe you one," he said, "for not trying that maneuver."

It was a terrible day; we'd seen five comrades die needlessly. But it was not without its lessons. The academy banned the Kolvoord Starburst, which has not been performed to this day. And I learned that I could count on Gary Mitchell.

✦

"This was a labor camp," Lev said. He was a native of Axanar, humanoid, short and stout like most of his species, with reddish skin and ridges along his neck. It was the beginning of my last year at the academy. I was with a group of cadets, and we were standing in the central square of what had once been a midsize city on his planet. Some buildings had been destroyed to make room for stretches of farmland; others were converted to barracks and monstrous factories. A million Axanars had lived in this converted city, with dozens like it all over the planet, and spent a lifetime under the relentless rule of the Klingon Empire. As slaves they had no rights, and rebellion was not tolerated. Lev led us behind a wrecked building. I gagged at the sight; others gasped; a young cadet vomited.

Thousands of people, charred to their bones, in a pile two stories high. They hadn't just been burned; heads had been bashed in, arms and legs broken. The faces of the blackened skulls seemed to scream in agony. There were smaller skeletons. Children. Babies.

"What a shame," someone said. They had a mocking tone, and I turned, expecting to deliver a reprimand to one of my cadets. I was surprised, however, to see our party of had been joined by a group of Klingon soldiers, intimidating in their gold tunics with impressive sidearms packed to their waists. The one who'd spoken, their leader, wore a smile that could freeze an open flame.

"You don't sound sincere," I said.

"Oh, but I am," he said. "The rules were clearly posted. If only they'd followed them, they might still be alive." We were all about the same age, part of the same mission. A mission of peace that at the moment I wanted no part of.

Axanar was the site of a battle between the Federation starship *Constitution* and three Klingon ships. Captain Garth of the *Constitution*, in some brilliant maneuvers, defeated the Klingon birds-of-prey. (In one particular move that we would study in school, he took remote control of his enemy's weapons console. No one had thought to try that before, and it led to all Federation ships having their own combination code so no one would try it on *us*.)

Garth was a unique captain, and rather than suing for peace, he boldly claimed the system was under his protection. It was a big gamble; since the Klingons considered Axanar part of their empire, Garth's action could have started a war. But Garth knew the Klingons were embarrassed by the defeat. The Klingons relied on fear to maintain their empire, and if they took him on and he somehow defeated them again, it could undermine their authority in the entire quadrant. In addition, Axanar was no longer of value to the empire; most of its assets were depleted. For those reasons, the Klingons hesitated before taking further action.

This allowed the Federation Diplomatic Corps leverage to step in. They reached out to the Klingons, hoping for a negotiated peace. The Klingons, for the first time in history, agreed. In truth, the Klingons decided to use the negotiations as an opportunity to get more information on what they considered their greatest enemy.

Starfleet saw the same opportunity; this peace mission was a chance for our military minds to gather as much information as possible about our greatest adversary. So along with the diplomats, a contingency of Starfleet officers was selected. I was part of a group of academy cadets included since we might one day have to face the Klingons in war.

It was not out of the question; right now, I wanted to hit the one standing in front of me.

"I'm Jim Kirk," I said, extending my hand. The Klingon looked down at it with a mix of amusement and disdain. He didn't take it, so I withdrew it.

"Koloth," he said.

"A pleasure to meet you," I said.

"I don't think it will help our negotiations," Koloth said, "if we start out lying to each other." He wanted me to be open about hating him; I had no problem with it.

"You're right," I said. "Great things may come of this." Koloth ignored me and turned to Lev, who'd shrunk behind my group of cadets.

"You there," he said. "We're thirsty. Get us some wine."

"I'm sorry," I said. "He's giving us a tour. Maybe you could find your drinks on your own." Koloth looked at me. One of the men behind him reached for a knife, but Koloth noticed, and with a slight motion of his hand signaled him to stop. Koloth then turned back to me.

"Very well. I imagine this won't be the last time you and I meet," Koloth said.

"I look forward to it," I said. I gave him a smile that told him, this time, I wasn't lying. Koloth led his men away.

In the end, the mission led to negotiations with the Klingons that would keep the peace and prevent a full-scale war for 15 years. But what I saw on Axanar also cemented the negative impression I'd had about them since childhood, one that wouldn't change for another 40 years.

✦

Ben tried to talk me out of it, but I wasn't listening.

"Come on, I need you," I said. "I have to get into the program bank, and you know that computer system better than anyone . . ."

"You're spending too much time with Mitchell," Ben said. "Since when do you take this kind of risk?" Ben was right; we could get in a lot of trouble, but I could tell he was coming around.

I was a few months away from graduation and had recently been given the *Kobayashi Maru* test, relatively new to the academy at the time. We had no idea who devised it, but we'd heard rumors that a Vulcan had included the proposal for it in his application, and it was one of the reasons he was accepted. The details were a closely guarded secret, and the honor code of the academy stated that you couldn't discuss the test with anyone who hadn't taken it yet. But, as it turned out, many in the academy did not observe the honor code, and the details became public.

The test placed a cadet in command of a starship that received a distress call for a fuel ship, the *Kobayashi Maru*, which was in the Neutral Zone bordering the Klingon Empire. The cadet had to decide whether to try to rescue the ship violating the treaty and risking interplanetary war. If the cadet chose this route, his/her ship was destroyed by the Klingons. It was considered an important test of command character.

I thought the test was bullshit.

I had spent the past four years preparing to find answers to the questions I would face in the Galaxy, and up until this test, every question had an answer. There was always a way to successfully complete your mission. My old roommate Thelin agreed with me. He had taken the test multiple times; he had not even tried to rescue the ship, but instead had used it as bait to try to trap the Klingons. This agressive tactic kept him from graduating.

I decided that the central problem of *Kobayashi Maru* was really about figuring out how to beat the test. I took it very personally, felt it was an insult to all the work I'd done. I just couldn't live with the failure. So, with Ben's help, I would reprogram the simulation. Thus, the third time I took the test, I rescued the *Kobayashi Maru* and escaped the Klingons.

It caused quite a stir. I was able to keep Ben's name out of it (no one knew the reprogramming was beyond my ability), and I was called before an honor review board for cheating. It looked like I might be expelled.

"What justification can you possibly give for such duplicitousness?" Admiral Barnett said. He was the imposing head of the review board.

"Sir, with all due respect, it wasn't duplicitous. Nowhere in the rules did it state that we were not allowed to reprogram the computer."

"You violated the spirit of the test," Admiral Komack said. He was sitting next to Barnett and he was annoyed. Judging from the reaction of the admirals on the board, he wasn't alone. I didn't think I could change their minds, but I also knew that I was right. I'd been carrying a lot of demerits on my record since first year, thanks to Finnegan, and it wouldn't take much to keep me from graduating. Looking back, I don't know why I took such a risk, with all the work I'd done to get into the academy, and then all the work I did there to succeed. But I actually think all my experiences led me to make my decision, and I had to let them know.

"If I'm in command, aren't I supposed to use every scrap of knowledge and experience at my disposal to protect the lives of my crew?" Barnett smiled at this. I could see the outrage on a few of the other admirals' faces begin to flag. Except one.

"You broke the rules," Komack said.

"No, I didn't, sir," I said. "I took the test within its own parameters twice. You have those results to judge me on. By letting me take it a third time, you invalidated those parameters. So I used my experience with the test to beat it."

This argument visibly swayed Barnett and a few of the other board members. I decided to pursue my advantage.

"In fact, if I'd just let the test run its course a third time without trying to adjust its programming," I said, "I would have been guilty of negligence, as I would not have done everything in my power to save my hypothetical crew, and you would have to expel me on that basis."

"We may expel you anyway," Barnett said, though he didn't sound serious.

The admirals said they had to make a determination, and I went back to my room that night, not sure what my future was going to be.

CHAPTER 4

"THAT'S IT, THAT'S THE *REPUBLIC*," Ben Finney said.

We were in a shuttlecraft, two newly minted officers packed in with some enlisted crewmen, crammed up against the porthole trying to get a glimpse of our first assignment. Through my sliver of a window, I could see the *U.S.S. Republic*, an old *Baton Rouge*–class starship. As we passed its engines, we noticed mismatched paneling that indicated an extensive history of repair work. It was a beaten-up rust bucket, and as an ensign assigned to engineering, it was in no way a glamorous posting.

The review board had not only let me graduate, they'd given me a commendation for original thinking. Only one admiral had opposed: Komack. He stuck to his opinion that I'd violated the spirit of the test, but he'd been overruled. However, Komack had his own avenue for punishment. He was head of the committee in charge of posting cadets to their first assignments. Though I was near the top of my class and requested starship duty, he made sure I was not given an exploratory ship, which were considered the most desired postings. Instead, I was put on a 20-year-old ship that made "milk runs," delivering personnel, medicine, spare parts, other supplies from Earth to starbases and colonies and back again. I could have complained, but I felt that would be pushing my luck; I decided I was doing penance for the *Kobayashi Maru*.

I wasn't too disappointed. I was getting what I wanted: I was an officer aboard a starship. And now, as we approached the ship, I was overcome with excitement. I wish I could've said the same of my companion.

The *Republic* was not at all what Ben Finney wanted. He was hoping for a more glamorous assignment to jump-start a career that he felt had already been unfairly slowed down because he'd been an instructor for so long. However, since he was older than a lot of cadets, he was less attractive to some starship captains who wanted to mold their own kind of junior officers. His only choice was also the *Republic*. But Ben wasn't going to be passive; before we even docked, he was making plans to get himself off this ship and onto a better assignment.

The shuttle flew into the hangar, and we all stepped out into the cramped bay; it wasn't the clean, state-of-the-art facility we'd become used to at the academy. Paneling had been stripped away to make more room for shuttles, so the ship's superstructure was visible. Overhead the various small crafts were stacked in their docks, making use of all available space. Before we could take it all in, we were greeted by the ship's chief petty officer, a salt-and-pepper veteran named Tichenor.

"Welcome aboard, sirs," Tichenor said. Before we could introduce ourselves, he shouted, "Atten-shun!"

We stood at attention with the noncommissioned crew, as our new commanding officer, Captain Stephen Garrovick, entered the bay. He was stoic and imposing: well over six feet, a little gray at his temples, with a stern expression that, only with the gift of hindsight, hinted at a smile underneath. He looked us over with an air of amused disdain.

"Kirk and Finney," he said. "Chief will get you squared away." He then turned and walked off. I think I was hoping for more, maybe a "welcome to the team" speech. But we weren't getting one; we grabbed our duffels and followed Tichenor out.

The CPO led us to our "quarters." I didn't expect it to be luxurious; I figured I'd be on a quadruple bunk bed in an eight-by-eight cube, crewmen stacked like those shuttles I saw in the bay. I was overly optimistic.

We were in the primary hull's engineering deck, a crowded area packed with monitors, piping, and crewmen, many of whom were engaged in loud repair work. Tichenor pointed to a space on the floor underneath a staircase leading to the impulse engines. It had been curtained off.

"Sir, that's your berth," he said.

This had to be a joke, a hazing of the new officers. I looked at Tichenor, and then at Finney, who shrugged.

"You have a complaint, sir?" Tichenor had a smile on his face; it looked like he wanted me to complain.

"No, Chief, this'll be fine," I said.

"All right, sir, once you're squared away, regulations require you to report to sickbay for your physical," he said, then led Finney off, presumably to his makeshift quarters. I looked at the cramped space under the staircase. I wasn't even sure I could fit lying down. I tossed down my duffel, figured I was "squared away," and headed toward sickbay.

I was halfway through my physical when Finney joined me.

"They've got me sleeping in the photon torpedo bay," Ben said.

Dr. Piper, the ship's chief medical officer, stout, affable, and seasoned, chuckled.

"It won't be forever, gentlemen," he said. "Officers do their best to get off this ship."

When the *Republic* was first commissioned, it was the state of the art in exploration and research vessels. But it was a small design, and upon being superseded by the newer classes of ships, it was reclassified to tasks it wasn't initially designed for. As a result, it had to devote a large portion of what had been crew quarters to storage. Thus I would spend my first six months in Starfleet sleeping under a staircase and using the common bathroom off the engineering section.

After our physicals, we reported to our immediate commanding officer, Chief Engineer Howard Kaplan, a balding, flabby man in his fifties. I would soon discover his annoyed expression was his resting state.

"Finney, you get beta shift, Kirk, you're on gamma shift," he said. Since Starfleet ships try to duplicate Earth conditions of night and day as closely as possible, gamma shift was midnight to eight. This meant I would be trying to sleep under a staircase during the "daytime" shifts, which were always the busiest.

Kaplan checked a console chronometer.

"Finney, you're on duty in an hour, Kirk in nine. Use the time, learn the job. I don't want to be woken up unless the ship's about to blow up," he said, then turned to a member of his staff. "Lieutenant Scott! Give 'em the tour."

A lieutenant, a little older than Ben, came over and put out his hand.

"Montgomery Scott, call me Scotty," he said. He had a brogue to match his name.

"Finney, go with 'em," Kaplan said. "You'll be late to your shift, and this'll be the last time."

Scott turned quickly and we followed as he took us on a thorough tour fore and aft. It took hours and seemed like we climbed every ladder and opened every hatch on the ship. Through it all, it was hard not to become impressed with Mr. Scott. He had knowledge of engineering far beyond anything either Ben or I had experienced. He showed us repairs and makeshift constructs on everything from the transporters to the lights in the galley, all clearly completed by him. The *Republic* was held together by spit and baling wire, and Assistant Engineer Scott had provided most of the spit.

Five hours later, we had completed the tour and were well into Ben's shift. Kaplan then had me shadow Ben for his shift, since I'd be alone on gamma shift.

"And I don't want you waking me up unless the ship's about to blow up," Kaplan said again. By the time my first shift was over, I'd been up for almost 24 hours straight. My concern that I wouldn't be able to sleep under a busy staircase proved to be unfounded.

We left Earth with a cargo of supplies for the Benecia Colony, then we'd head for Starbase 9, Starbase 11, then back to Earth, to start the route again. Those first few weeks I became acquainted with one of the truths of space travel: it can be very dull. All of the major maintenance and repair operations were carried out during alpha shifts, a few minor ones and follow-ups on beta shift; the duty officer on gamma shift (me) worked alone, so it was only monitoring duty. It was crushingly tedious work, but on a ship of this age I recognized that I carried serious responsibility.

Ben, however, seemed like he was on vacation. His off-time corresponded with more of the other crew, so he quickly fell in to a social groove.

THE STORY OF STARFLEET'S GREATEST CAPTAIN

He made a lot of friends; very soon after we got there it appeared everyone knew who he was. It led to a few personal advantages; he managed to convince a personnel officer to get him an actual bed in an actual stateroom. He was sharing the room with seven other crewmen, but it was better than the staircase.

We would sometimes meet for my breakfast and his dinner (I was just waking up; he was about to go on duty for the afternoon–early evening shift). On one of these occasions, about two months into our service, he asked for my help.

"I've convinced Hardy in communications to let me call Earth," he said. This was quite an accomplishment. Use of the subspace communicator was very restricted.

"Why?"

"It's Jamie's third birthday," he said. "I don't want to miss it." I could see for the first time how heartsick Ben was. I remembered my own childhood birthdays, and my mother calling me from Tarsus. It meant a lot to me then, and I eventually grew resentful that she didn't call more often. Now that I was on a ship and understood the power involved in sending subspace communications, it's amazing to me that she called as much as she did.

"What do you need me for?"

"Hardy says she'll only do it at the end of her shift, when she's finished with the official traffic. It's also at the end of my shift, but I need you to relieve me a few minutes early so I can get over there."

"You better hope Kaplan doesn't catch you," I said.

"I don't think I have to worry. Kaplan sleeps through my shift and yours," he said, and I laughed. We'd both come to the conclusion that Montgomery Scott was the actual chief engineer, and Kaplan wasn't letting him transfer out because with Scott around, Kaplan didn't have to do any work.

A few days later, I came on shift ten minutes early. Ben was anxious to get going, and quickly brought me up to speed on the maintenance alpha and beta shifts had performed on the ship's fusion reactor.*

---

*EDITOR'S NOTE: Though the *Republic* had warp drive, its class of vessel still used a fusion reactor as an emergency backup for propulsion and internal ship's power.

After Ben left, I started my routine, which involved studying the engineering consoles and checking the status of the systems. I immediately found a vent circuit to the fusion chamber had been left open. It was contaminating the air in the engine room, and, more important, if the bridge had to shift to fusion power after another five minutes, it could've blown up the ship.

I immediately closed the circuit. Kaplan's words "I don't want you waking me up unless the ship's about to blow up" echoed in my head, so, since the ship was no longer in any danger, I decided not to alert him. But regulations stated that I had to log the incident.

I hesitated. This would get Ben in trouble; he should have noticed the open circuit during his watch. My guess was that he'd been too preoccupied about getting to speak with Jamie. I considered leaving it out of the log and just telling Finney privately what had happened. But though Finney had not noticed it being open, it wasn't necessarily his fault that it had been left open in the first place. If the responsible parties weren't found, mistakes like it could almost certainly happen again. I felt I had no choice but to log it. Looking back, I might have had a slight bit of resentment that I had had to do Finney's job for him, that he had put all our lives in danger because of his own personal needs, which may have led to my going to sleep at the end of my shift, rather than trying to find him to tell him what had happened. That was definitely a mistake.

"Wake up, you bastard!"

I'd probably been sleeping for three hours, and before I could fully register the voice that was yelling at me, I was yanked out of my makeshift quarters under the staircase. Shirtless, half-asleep, I stood in the middle of engineering as alpha shift watched in confusion. A furious Ben Finney confronted me.

"What the hell did you do?!"

"Ben, I had no choice..."

He wasn't interested in listening to me. Kaplan, as he did every morning, reviewed the engineering log from my shift and became furious. I hadn't calculated that Kaplan would be embarrassed too; the fact that one of his staff had been this negligent reflected poorly on him, and he brought the full weight of discipline down on Finney. Ben had been severely reprimanded and put at the bottom of the promotion list.

"I spent three extra years at the academy teaching idiots like you computers, and now thanks to you I'm going to stay an ensign forever!" I'd never seen him this angry.

"I did what I had to do—"

"You didn't have to do it. You could've looked after me the way I looked after you!"

"I'm sorry..."

"You're not sorry. You've been competing with me since the day we came on board, and now you've taken me down! Congratulations! Does it feel good?" He was ranting; it sounded almost paranoid. Everything I tried to say made him angrier, so I just stood quietly as he continued to yell at me. Finally, he stormed off.

I tried to process what had happened. I assumed that once some time passed, Ben would calm down and understand that, had he been in my position, he would've done the same thing. But I was wrong. In the days to come, when I would relieve him on engineering duty, he would give me a by-the-book rundown of the engineering situation. I tried on several occasions to engage him in conversation, but he wasn't interested. To make matters worse, Ben was poisoning my reputation with the rest of the crew. I never got the full story of what he said about me, but it was clear he was making a case among the other officers that the open circuit was my mistake, not his, and that I had conspired to place the blame on him. However, since no one would talk openly to me about it, there was no way for me to air my side of it.

The next few months were exceedingly lonely and depressing. The officers kept their distance from me; when I went for meals or to the few recreation areas of the ship, I could feel the coolness from the other crewmen. On top of that, Chief Engineer Kaplan wanted to make my life hell; my action had made him look bad to the captain, and though he could do nothing to reprimand me since I'd acted properly, it was also clear he wasn't going to take me off gamma shift.

One night, I was sitting alone in one of the rec rooms, a few minutes before my shift, eating dinner. Lieutenant Scott came in. I generally didn't see much of him; he was an all-work-and-no-play kind of officer, and on his off hours he spent his free time reading technical journals. He got his food from one of the dispensers and came over to me.

"Mind if I join you, Ensign?" he said.

"Not at all, sir." He sat down and immediately started eating. We both ate in silence for a moment, then he spoke.

"It might interest you to know, I told the chief engineer you might be better off in another department," he said.

"Really?" I had no idea what this was about.

"Feel free to tell me I'm wrong," he said. "I just don't know if engineering is your passion." This came as a shock to me. Scott and I hadn't spent that much time together; I wondered why he was forming this impression. I assumed it was because he bought into Ben's version of events and didn't want me around.

"I did what I had to do," I said.

"What are you talking about?" Scott said.

"When I put Ben on report," I said, "I know what the rumors are . . ."

"We're not having the same conversation," Scott said, and he looked legitimately bewildered.

"Well, I've done my work, I don't know why you'd want me transferred—"

"I don't *want* you transferred, lad. I'm thinking what's best for you. You do your work, sure," he said. "But an engineer doesn't stop there. He's always fixing, building . . . you're on a warp-driven starship, one o' the best workshops you could ever ask for. And now I hear you're sittin' around worrying about what people are saying about you." I looked at the man in awe.

"You're right, sir," I said.

"I told you the first day you got here," he said. "Call me Scotty."

It was a little better after that. During my free shifts, I decided to spend time with Scotty, helping him with repairs and upgrades. I learned more about the limits of a warp-driven ship during those months, knowledge that would come in handy in the years to come.

But the rest of the crew was still pretty unfriendly to me, and as we completed a leg of our run to Starbase 9, I was shaken awake by CPO Tichenor.

"Sir, Captain needs to see you in his quarters," Tichenor said.

I got dressed as quick as I could, and Tichenor led me to Garrovick's quarters. He was at his desk, writing something on a PADD. He dismissed Tichenor and looked up at me. I was very nervous. Except for a few brief hellos in the corridor, the only time the captain had spoken to me in the last six months was when I came on board, and this was the first time we'd ever been alone.

"Ensign Kirk," Garrovick said, "sorry we haven't had time to get to know each other, but I'm transferring you off the *Republic*."

So, even the captain wasn't immune to the rumor mill.

"Is there something you want to say, Ensign?" I felt some judgment in the question, but I wasn't going to let myself get caught up in it. If this captain had no use for my honesty, then I had no use for him.

"No sir," I said.

"All right," he said. "We'll be at Starbase 9 in a couple of hours. Be ready to leave as soon as we dock. I'll have your orders for you then. You're dismissed." He couldn't wait to be rid of me, I thought.

"Thank you, sir," I said.

I went back to my cubby and packed my things. As I did, I started to wonder, could I have been this wrong about Starfleet? I had done my duty, with honor as it was defined for me, and it had led to this. Maybe I had made a mistake.

Once I finished packing, I still had over an hour, so I thought I'd find Scotty and say goodbye. He at least had been a bright spot. I found him in the Jefferies tube leading to the port nacelle.

"You're leaving me? Who's gonna carry my toolbox?" he said with a smile.

"Thank you for all your help," I said.

"I should be thanking you," he said. "It's been a pleasure. Kind of funny, you and the captain leaving at the same time."

"The captain's leaving?" Not having many friends on the ship, I missed out on a lot of gossip.

"That's the word," he said. "Anyway, good luck to you, lad. Hope we can serve together again."

Now I was really confused. Why was the captain bothering to get rid of me if he was leaving? It didn't make any sense.

Shortly after we docked at Starbase 9, the crew was called to the shuttle bay. Garrovick was there with another captain, who I didn't recognize. I had brought my duffel with me and had it at my feet.

"Attention to orders!" Tichenor shouted, and we all stood at attention. He then handed a PADD to Captain Garrovick, who read from it.

"To Captain Stephen Garrovick, commander, *U.S.S. Republic*, you are hereby requested and required to relinquish command to Captain Ronald Tracy as of this date, and report to Captain L. T. Stone of the *U.S.S. Farragut* for duty on board as his relief in command . . ."

Wow, I thought, Garrovick was getting a *Constitution*-class ship. That was a big step up from the *Republic*. I watched as Captain Tracy, a middle-aged, fierce-looking man, relieved Captain Garrovick. I was a little anxious and confused as to what I was supposed to do; Garrovick had told me he would get me my orders, but now he looked like he was leaving right away. Tracy turned to address the crew.

"All standing orders to remain in force until further notice," he said. "The following officers will immediately depart *U.S.S. Republic*, for duty on board *U.S.S. Farragut*." There was a pause, as crewmen exchanged excited looks at the possibility of getting off this garbage scow. But Tracy only read two names.

"CMO Mark Piper, Ensign James T. Kirk," Tracy said. "Flight deck personnel, prepare shuttle bay for immediate launch. Crew dismissed." Everyone looked at me, and I couldn't believe it. I looked over at Captain Garrovick, who stood at a shuttlecraft with Dr. Piper. Piper exchanged a look with him and boarded the shuttle, and Garrovick looked at me. He was enjoying what he was seeing; he had planned this. I couldn't put it all together before he tilted his head toward the shuttle, indicating I'd better get a move on. I immediately picked up my duffel, ignoring the jealous stares of my crewmates. I passed Ben Finney on my way; I wanted to say goodbye, but his stare conveyed such a pureness of hatred it chilled me, and I just kept moving. I went over to Garrovick, who stood talking with Tracy.

"Good luck, Mr. Kirk," Tracy said. "Sorry to lose you." He shook my hand. I was in a fog; everything was moving so fast, but I followed Garrovick onto the shuttle.

Dr. Piper sat in one of the seats at the rear of the ship. I was about to sit next to him when he stopped me.

"Captain likes to have a copilot," he said, indicating the empty navigator's seat next to the captain, who was manning the helm. I hesitantly moved forward.

"Have a seat, Ensign," Garrovick said.

I put my duffel down and took the seat next to him. Through the porthole, I saw the *Republic*'s shuttle bay doors open, and Garrovick piloted the shuttle out of the bay. Out the view port I could see an orange planet blocking out the stars. We flew in silence for a long while.

"Sir," I said, finally breaking in. "May I ask you a question?"

"Yes, Ensign?"

"Why me?"

"I've read your service record. You were very close to Ensign Finney."

"Yes sir."

"Yet you logged an incident that you could've easily covered up. Why?"

"I was worried that if I didn't log it, something like it would happen again."

"Well, Ensign, I can always use a man who'd sacrifice his closest friendship for the safety of my ship," he said. "I can't control all the gossip, but I didn't appreciate how you were treated for doing the right thing."

That was what the ceremony was all about. He was taking me with him and was rubbing it in the noses of the officers who'd believed Finney.

I was both gratified and sad. Ben had once been my closest friend; he had looked after me at the academy. But as I left the *Republic*, any fond memory of him was eclipsed by his angry glare.

Garrovick switched on the communicator.

"Shuttlecraft *McAuliffe* to *Farragut*," Garrovick said. "Request permission to come aboard."

Through the view port, the *Constitution*-class ship loomed. We were approaching the underside of the saucer section. The letters spelling out the ship's name dwarfed our craft.

"Permission granted," a woman said over the communicator. "You are cleared for main hangar deck."

"No going back," Garrovick said.

"I hope not, sir," I said. And he laughed.

✦

"That, friend James," Tyree said, in a whisper, "is the scat of mugato."

We were in a small clearing in the forest, looking down at a pile of yellow dung. The primitive humanoid hunters I was with, all dressed in animal skins, put an arrow in their bows, and scanned our surroundings cautiously. I supposed the scat looked fresh to them, and that meant our prey was near. We'd been hunting the mugato for about three hours, following footprints and other spoors, but it was only now that things had become tense. I had a phaser pistol hidden in the pouch I was carrying, but I was under strict orders not to use it. These people were to have no knowledge that I was, in fact, not from their planet. And since this was my first planetary survey, violating the Prime Directive[*] was foremost on my mind.

At that point, I'd been on the *Farragut* about eight months, and life aboard a *Constitution*-class ship couldn't have been more different than the *Republic*. The big news for me was I had my own quarters. And another thing, I was no longer working gamma shift in engineering. I'd already been rotated through several different departments: security, a variety of the astrosciences, finally landing navigation. The ship itself was on a mission of exploration; we'd charted eleven solar systems since I came aboard, and within eight months I'd received my promotion to lieutenant.

I was at my post on the bridge when we entered the Zeta Boötis system. The third planet, designated Neural, had signs of intelligent life, and

---

[*] EDITOR'S NOTE: The Prime Directive is Starfleet General Order One. It prevents Starfleet officers from interfering with the societies of other worlds, whether it's the natural development of a primitive world, or the internal politics of an advanced society.

the captain put us in a standard orbit. He ordered the launch of suborbital probes and had them transmit to the bridge's main viewscreen. We got a look at the primitive structures the natives lived in, the population divided among small villages, farms, and tribes living in the wilderness.

"Technology report," Garrovick said.

"Primitive," Commander Coto said, from the science station. "Roughly corresponds to fifth-century Earth, agrarian society. Sensors detect heat signatures that suggest iron forges."

"Pretty barbaric," I said.

"Hmm," Garrovick said. "Not much we can learn from them, Mr. Kirk?"

"I'm not sure, sir," I said, though I was pretty sure.

"Well, let's be certain," Garrovick said. "Let's send a survey team. Mr. Kirk, you're in command."

"What . . . I mean, yes sir!" This was new; I'd been on a couple of surveys, but never as leader. Suddenly I had to make decisions that I had never faced before. How many people in the team? Who to take with me?

"Anytime you're ready, Mr. Kirk," the captain said. He seemed amused. I keyed the intercom.

"Uh, Ensign Black and the two on-duty security officers, report to ship's stores for landing party. Have historical computer correlate data from satellite images to determine appropriate clothing—"

"Only taking three crewmen with you?" Garrovick asked, as if it was a mistake.

"Yes sir," I said. "Population seems very sparse. A large group of new people suddenly showing up might cause undue attention." I searched his face for some clue that he agreed or disagreed with me, but got nothing. I kept going. "I thought Ensign Black could gather samples while I investigate the tribes in the mountains."

"Proceed," he said. I could see him exchange an amused look with Coto as I left the bridge.

Ensign Christine Black, the security officers Sussman and Strong, and I donned disguises that did a pretty good job of approximating the local clothing. We beamed down and found ourselves on a rocky hillside. There was plenty of green, with a warm, inviting breeze. It had an immediate soothing effect on all of us, but I tried to ignore it. I sent Black to gather biological samples with Strong, ordering her to return to the ship when she was done. Minka Sussman came with me. I was hoping to view the natives without having to make contact, but I was in for a quick disappointment, as we almost immediately found ourselves surrounded by a hunting party of Hill People.

They all carried either bows or spears. Sussman's hand moved to the pouch that held her phaser, but I gestured for her to stop. Their weapons weren't aimed at us. The leader of the hunting party came forward and spoke to me in an unknown language. The universal translators instantly deciphered the language, so we could communicate. The leader, who called himself Tyree, asked where we were from. I told him we were from another land far away (the Prime Directive prevented us from revealing our true origin to primitive people who had no knowledge of spaceflight or other worlds), and that we were only staying a short time. He indicated that we follow him. He took us back to his camp, a loose conglomeration of tents near caves and a spring.

He and his people were remarkably trusting. The leader of his tribe, an older man named Yitae, welcomed us to the village. He put Sussman in a tent with other women, me in a tent with Tyree, and welcomed us to eat and hunt with them.

I was worried about what I would see, living among these primitive people. There was certainly a chance that they believed in a superstitious religion and would engage in violent sacrifices. There was also great potential for accidentally causing an incident because we didn't understand their primitive ways. I had warned Sussman to be careful.

Over the next three days I learned that they hunted for food and clothing, and had a great knowledge of the wild roots. They had a good trade relationship with the villagers, who, more adept at forging iron, provided arrowheads and knives in exchange for food and skins. I did pick up their references to some beliefs in spirits and spells, but other than that the life they led was simple and peaceful. They killed only to feed themselves or for limited trade, and there seemed to be no conflicts or jealousies that were usually part of primitive human society. And the enthusiasm with which Tyree welcomed me into his life was affecting. One morning, he woke me up.

"Today, friend James," he said, "we hunt mugato."

The mugato were an ape-like carnivore, dangerous and deadly, that the natives hunted for food. Sussman and I joined a hunting party of four Hill People. Sussman was a tough security officer, but even she found herself relaxing while part of this community.

"The quickest way to kill it," Tyree said, "is in the eye."

I had some experience from childhood with a bow, and I gave Sussman a spear. We set out, and now that we'd found our prey's feces, the hunt was almost over. I looked over at Sussman; I could sense, as tough as she was, she was scared. Her hand was firmly in her pouch, presumably on her phaser. I had told her before that under no circumstances could we show these people our advanced technology, but the pressure of the current situation was clearly overriding my orders. I was going to move closer to her to have a quiet word when I heard the menacing shriek.

A white simian, large as a man, with a ridge of bone running along its head and down its back, leaped into the center of our party. With one arm, it knocked Tyree and one of his men aside. Two of the others, both with bows, fired arrows into the creature, hitting it squarely in the chest. They didn't slow it down.

The beast moved toward Sussman, who panicked, dropped her spear, and fumbled through her pouch for the phaser. The mugato reached her just as she got it out, but the animal knocked her down and the small phaser went flying. Tyree was now up again, joining his men in firing arrows into the creature, but it wouldn't let Sussman go. The mugato bit Sussman and she screamed.

I fired off an arrow, but I could see none were having an effect on the raging animal. I could take out my phaser and vaporize it, but my training told me to resist that urge, that it would contaminate this culture. The Prime Directive said we were expendable, but seeing Sussman in peril, I had to do something. Tyree had said hitting the eye was its weakness, but since it was bent over Sussman, we couldn't get a shot. I dropped my bow and arrow and went for a knife one of the Hill People had dropped.

"Tyree! Get ready!"

I leaped onto the mugato, wedged my foot into the bone ridge, and stabbed it in the side of the neck. I hung on to the knife as the mugato reared up, and, reaching back, tried to grab me. I saw Tyree taking aim. The creature bucked hard and I lost my grip. I flew to the ground, and the mugato quickly turned to me and roared.

And then an arrow pierced its left eye. The beast froze and fell backward, dead. Tyree had made the shot.

I got up immediately and went to Sussman. The mugato had bitten her in the neck, and she was shivering. There was some kind of poison I could see mixed in with her blood in the wound. My mind raced. I had medical supplies in my pouch, but bringing them out would expose me. I wasn't even sure any of them would help against the beast's venom. I needed help. I had to get her back to the ship. If I used my communicator, that could literally be the end of my career, but I had no choice. I couldn't let her die. As I reached into the pouch, Tyree touched my arm.

"Don't worry, friend James," Tyree said. "We will help her." I looked up at him. Could he save her? Could I trust this primitive? He seemed certain. He then turned to one of his men and told him to find a *Kahn-ut-tu*, which the universal translator didn't have a meaning for. He then quietly handed me Sussman's phaser, which one of his men had picked up from the ground.

"This was hers," he said.

"Yes," I said.

"What is it?"

"I . . . can't tell you," I said. Tyree accepted that. He ordered the remaining three men to take care of carrying the mugato back to camp, while he helped me with Sussman.

In a cave at the camp, we were met by Yitae and a young man dressed differently than any of the Hill People. He had a brownish complexion, jet-black hair, and wore different skins, from a much darker animal. Tyree had expected him; this was a *Kahn-ut-tu*. It looked like I was placing my crewman's fate in the hands of a witch doctor, and I didn't feel good about it. I longed to get her back to the ship under the care of an actual physician.

There was a beat of a drum. The *Kahn-ut-tu* man kneeled over Sussman and took out a black root. The root seemed to move like an animal. As

Yitae beat the drum, the witch doctor fell into a trance, and eventually slapped the root hard on Sussman's wound. They both heaved in pain, and then fell unconscious. I had never seen anything like it, and when I went to examine Sussman's wound, it was gone. Sussman stirred awake. She was tired but cured.

I realized that I was due to communicate with the ship, so I thanked the *Kahn-ut-tu*, who seemed completely indifferent. I then left the cave, found a private spot near the spring, and took out my communicator.

"Kirk to *Farragut*."

"Mr. Kirk, we were starting to worry." It was Garrovick. I filled him in on what had happened. I said I thought we needed another day for Sussman to recover before I could leave without raising suspicions. Garrovick agreed with my assessment, then said something I didn't expect.

"I guess you were lucky those barbarians could help you out."

"They're not barbarians, sir," I said. "This is an amazing species..."

"It's nice to know we're not the only worthwhile people in the Galaxy." Garrovick signed off, and I realized the lesson he'd taught me. I felt ashamed, embarrassed. I closed my communicator and turned to see Tyree had found me. He looked confused.

"Were you speaking to a god?"

"No," I said. I wanted to tell him the truth, but the Prime Directive was clear. Of course, if I didn't tell him the truth, his imagination might lead to a worse kind of contamination. I had gotten to know this man in the past few days, he had saved the life of my crewman, and he was my friend. I felt there was a third alternative.

"Tyree... can you keep a secret?"

It turns out he could.

✦

The experience with Tyree and the Hill People helped me grow as an officer. I had faced what was probably my most terrible experience in Starfleet up to that point—I'd almost lost someone under my command. I couldn't imagine anything worse. Fate would soon punish me for my lack of vision.

A few months later, I'd been rotated to weapons control. Though I'd been trained in space combat, in my year and a half of service in Starfleet, I'd seen none. We were in orbit around the fourth planet in the Tycho star system. A landing party had been sent to chart the planet's surface, which was devoid of life, or so we thought.

"Red alert!" The captain's voice came over the intercom. "Shields up, phaser control report status!" I was manning weapons control along with Chief Metlay and Crewman Press. They reported that all weapons were charged and ready.

"Bridge, this is phaser control. All weapons show ready." As I said this, the monitor in front of me displayed what was on the bridge viewscreen. I saw the planet, but couldn't make out anything else. Then I noticed what looked like one of the clouds in the atmosphere moving up into space. It was headed directly toward the ship. This was my target? A cloud? (I would find out later that this "cloud" had attacked and killed our landing party, but at this moment in time, I had no idea what I was even looking at.)

"Phasers, lock on target," Garrovick said. I immediately tied in the tracking system and brought the cloud into the center of my range finder. Sensors showed me the cloud was made out of dikironium. Its gaseous nature made it difficult for the computer to lock on it.

"Sir, I can't get a definite lock," I said. It was moving much faster now, growing on the screen.

"Fire phasers!" Garrovick said. I looked at the cloud. It now filled the viewscreen. It was at point-blank range. I paused for just a second, tried to figure out what the hell I was even looking at. And then it was gone. I pressed the fire button, but it was too late.

"Sir," Chief Metlay said, "something's entered the main phaser bank emitter..."

What he said was technically impossible; only forms of energy could pass through the emitter. But before I could figure out what was going on, Metlay and Press were surrounded by white gas, leaking out of their consoles. There was the distinct odor of something very sweet, like honey. And then Metlay and Press immediately fell to the floor choking.

I ran to my console.

"Weapons control to bridge! It's in the ship! Repeat, it's in the ship! I'm sealing this section."

Whatever this gas was, I knew I had to keep it from getting to the rest of the *Farragut*. I began to activate the locks on the emergency bulkheads to seal off the section. I was only about halfway done when the sweet odor got stronger.

And then it was on me. It was as though I was drowning in a vat of syrup. I couldn't breathe. I started to lose consciousness, and as I did, I heard something. It wasn't a voice. It was in my head.

"I will feed here..."

✦

I don't know how long I had been out. I had been vaguely aware of people talking, the red alert klaxon, and then quiet. But it was all distorted, a haze. And then I felt a hypo in my neck, and I slowly regained consciousness.

My vision focused, and I found I was in sickbay. First Officer Coto was standing over my bed, along with Dr. Piper. The lights were dim. There was a medical device on my arm.

"You're getting blood transfusions," Piper said to me. "But you'll be fine."

I tried to ask about the cloud, to explain what happened.

"It's off the ship," Coto said. His voice was heavy; there was no relief in it.

"It was... a creature," I said.

Coto and Piper exchanged a look.

"What do you mean?" Piper said.

"I could feel... it thinking," I said. "It wanted to feed off us..." From Coto's look, he didn't believe me. Piper, however, was considering it.

"It would explain some things," the doctor said. "It didn't just dissipate through the ship like an uncontrolled gas," he said. "It took only red corpuscles from its victims. First the landing party, then the two crewmen in weapons control, but Kirk was left alive. The attacks happened in spurts—a few people at a time were killed—for lack of a better analogy, its stomach got full."

"Wait... attacks?" I said. "How many people?"

Piper realized he had been talking too much. He gave Coto an apologetic look.

"Please tell me," I said.

"Over 200," Coto said. Half the crew.

"The captain?" I asked even though I knew the answer.

"He's dead," Coto said.

"I'm sorry..." I choked it out. "I'm so sorry..."

"It's not your fault," he said. "Staying in the weapons control room to seal off the section saved the ship..."

I couldn't hear him. All those people, and Captain Garrovick, dead because I didn't fire in time. I felt myself starting to cry and turned away.

"Get some rest, Lieutenant," Coto said, and he turned and left.

✦

The *Farragut* limped to Starbase 12 with half a crew for repairs, resupply, and restaffing. I spent two weeks in a rehabilitation facility. The creature had taken most of the red corpuscles from my body, and it took a long time before my body healed. Mental health was going to take a lot longer.

Commander Coto and Dr. Piper both came to see me during my rehabilitation. They hadn't given Coto the promotion to captain, but he was still in temporary command and, as such, was supervising the restaffing of the ship. He had gotten approval to offer me the position of chief navigator. I said yes, although I was unsure. He told me my duties would be very light for a long time; it would take weeks for such a large number of crew replacements to make their way to Starbase 12.

Once I was released from the hospital, rather than return to the ship, I took quarters on the base. It was the first time since the academy that I lived on a planet, and it was a welcome change. Starbase 12 was a state-of-the-art facility, providing storage and repair services, and surrounded by living and recreational accommodations. About 4,000 Starfleet personnel and their families lived there.

My room was in a bungalow in the single officers' living area, two-story buildings set on winding pathways among rolling grass and trees.

The apartment was efficient and clean, with its own kitchen, but I took most of my meals either in the officers' mess or one of the small restaurants and bars that civilians and interplanetary traders had set up on the base. I found myself imbibing a lot during this period; the only way I could go to sleep was drunk, and even so my sleep was fitful and disturbed by nightmares.

A particular favorite haunt of mine was called Feezal's. It was run by a friendly proprietor whose race I wasn't familiar with. He had a large skull with ridges on the sides of his cheeks and forehead, which might have seemed threatening, except for his constant joviality. He said his name was "Sim," but I suspected he wasn't telling the truth. He seemed very old and would gently deflect any attempt on my part to get him to divulge anything personal, including what planet he was from. The only thing he would tell me about himself was that the bar was named after one of his wives.

He, however, did show a lot of interest in me, asking me lots of questions about my life and history, and it was therapeutic to talk to someone. He had lost a close friend on Tarsus, which led to several discussions on whether Kodos was really dead. There were galactic rumors that he'd gotten away. Sim seemed to always know what I needed, and one evening, he amazed me by introducing me to a young woman, whom I immediately recognized.

"Hello, Jim!" she said.

I'd met Carol Marcus at the academy, where she worked as a lab assistant while she finished her doctorate in molecular biology. We had had a short, casual fling that came to an end when I graduated.

Upon seeing her I was immediately sorry it hadn't continued. She was very attractive, blond, petite—which I guess was my type—and very smart. In the intervening years, Carol had gotten her doctorate and was now part of a research project using Starfleet facilities at the base. I felt myself drawn to her immediately. She was warm and attentive, flattered by my renewed interest, and our relationship reignited.

The restaffing of the *Farragut* dragged on for weeks, and I didn't mind. I would serve a shift on the *Farragut* for eight hours a day, then return to the starbase, where Carol and I would spend the rest of our time. I moved into her apartment, and we had a rapport that was both passionate and easy. We'd spend our free time rock climbing and horseback riding, we'd cook together and read together. I stopped drinking as much, and the nightmares, though they didn't go away completely, faded. I was settled and happy. And I didn't want it to end.

"Will you marry me?" I said one morning while we were still in bed.

"Jim," she said. "Wait . . . what?"

"I want to marry you," I said. "I want to be with you."

"Jim . . . I love you . . . but I can't leave my work . . ."

"Then I'll leave mine," I said, and thought I meant it. "I'll ask for a base posting. We can make this work. I want to have a family with you."

"It's . . . what I want too," she said, and kissed me. I called the ship and asked one of the junior officers to cover my shift, and we stayed together all day.

The next morning, I arrived for my shift on the *Farragut*. The ship was busier now; as chief navigator, I also had crewmen who reported to me. I saw Commander Coto in his quarters, and told him I wanted reassignment to the starbase. He looked at me in weary acceptance. He'd known about my relationship with Carol and said he'd been expecting this.

"Look, Jim," he said, "I'm not going to try to talk you out of it. But you're an exceptional Starfleet officer. Assuming I get command, I'm going to need men like you I can rely on to help me protect the lives of this crew."

"I'm sorry, sir," I said. "I've made up my mind." But I hadn't. I had committed myself to Carol, and that's what drove me to say what I said. But Coto had an effect, and I felt a responsibility to help him and the crew. Coto asked me to at least delay my transfer until the final replacements arrived, which would still be a few weeks. I agreed.

As time went on, I became more conflicted about my decision. I was enjoying my time with Carol, but I felt the pull of life aboard the ship. And, as new crewmen reported to the *Farragut*, I became cognizant of my importance; a lot of them were fresh from the academy, and though I'd only been out less than two years, I was surprised that the experiences even in that short a time gave me a wealth of knowledge to share. I also found that, in grieving for the loss of Captain Garrovick and my shipmates, I had renewed my determination to serve, to correct the mistake I had made. I should've been talking about this to Carol, but I knew it would hurt her.

A few weeks later, *Farragut* was almost completely restaffed. As I finished up my shift, Commander Coto came over to me.

"I've received my promotion," he said. I congratulated him. He'd worked harder than anyone to get the ship back in shape, and I was glad he was rewarded. He then told me the ship would be leaving in two days, and he wondered if I'd reconsidered my decision, as he still had not filled the position of chief navigator. It was still mine if I wanted it. I said I did. I left the ship, my heart heavy with the fact that I now had to break this news to Carol. I decided I would tell her everything I'd been thinking, that I needed this to close out my grief. I knew she would be hurt, but I thought she would understand, knowing what I'd been through. I didn't get the chance; when I walked in, she met me with a smile.

"Jim, I'm pregnant," she said as she fell into my arms.

A child. I had not expected this. It was thrilling and confusing. Suddenly my self-centered arguments felt hollow. The idea of a baby was so overwhelming, so joyous, so intimidating, that I didn't know what to say. Carol, however, immediately sensed something was wrong. She stepped back and looked at me.

"I'll make it work," I said. "I promise—"

"This is exactly what you said you didn't want," she said, through tears.

"I know," I said. "But I love you—"

"You said you hated your mother going away; you didn't want that for your kids." She had been listening to me talk about the pain of my childhood. But in that moment, I thought I could do things differently. I believed I could be there as a father, and also do my job as a Starfleet officer. I would make it work. I loved her, and I wanted to have a family with her.

"Let's have this baby," I said. "I'll be there for you."

✦

"Clear the bridge!" I shouted too late. I'd been manning the *Hotspur*'s engineering station. We'd been hit several times, and the last one had shorted out the engineering console, electrocuting the crewman who was operating it. I was trying to reroute power to the shields but had been unsuccessful. Captain Sheridan took the helm and was trying to get us out of orbit.

We had been attacked by pirates on the way to deliver supplies and medicine to Altair IV, at the edge of the Federation. Aliens in unmarked ships would often attack lone Starfleet vessels in the region, in the hopes of stealing profitable cargo. We knew, in fact, that some of these ships were actually Klingon, under orders from their government to unofficially pilfer whatever they could from Federation shipping. If caught, they would deny their empire's involvement. We weren't a hundred percent sure that the ship we were currently engaged with was Klingon, but just the possibility that they were motivated me; every encounter I had with that species furthered my growing personal animosity. I watched as the stubby pirate vessel launched another torpedo, just as the captain laid in the course. The torpedo was on track to hit the primary hull and the bridge. I was a few feet from the turbolift, and just before we were hit, I shouted and leaped for it.

The torpedo obliterated what was left of our deflectors and blasted a ten-meter gaping wound in the primary hull; the bridge was open to space. I was at the door of the turbolift as the air and everything not tied down was blown out of the hole. In the millisecond before I was blown out with everything else I had grabbed the edge of the closing turbolift door. The tremendous force of the atmosphere departing the confines of the ship lifted me off the deck. I held the door with both hands; the rushing air and the sudden cold of space weakened my grip. I held my breath; I knew I wouldn't have much time.

And as suddenly as the wind started, it stopped.

I fell to the deck. The bridge was now an airless void, and I felt the unbearable cold slice through my uniform. I knew I had maybe ten seconds before I passed out. I looked up; my right hand still clutched the turbolift door. I couldn't feel it; my extremities had already gone completely numb. What had saved me so far was the ship's computer, locked in an unsolvable dilemma; it couldn't seal the turbolift as long as its sensor detected a human life-form holding the door open. As long as I didn't let go, the door wouldn't close.

I pulled myself toward the small opening and felt unbelievable pressure on my lungs. I had an overwhelming desire to exhale, but knew that would be the end of me. The lift seemed too far away. I stumbled, then dragged myself forward. Blackness surrounded me. I couldn't move anymore, tried to pull, and then had the sensation of rolling on the deck.

I'd made it into the lift and heard the doors close with a pneumatic whoosh; the sound told me there was air, so I exhaled and inhaled. I was on the floor, shivering, desperately trying to catch my breath. On the verge of blacking out, I rolled over, got to my knees, and reached for one of the lift's control handles. I grabbed it, trying to fight off the dark waiting to envelop me. I pulled myself to my feet and hit the comm panel.

"Kirk . . . to auxiliary control," I said.

"Yes sir," a voice responded.

"Captain Sheridan laid in a course—"

"I see it, sir, it's on the board—"

"Execute . . . immediately." Looking for shelter, Sheridan had set a course for a nearby gas giant. The pirate ship was too old and small to stand the pressure. The *Hotspur*, a *Baton Rouge*–class ship like the *Republic*, wouldn't be able to stand it for long either, but it would buy us some time.

I felt the deck plates shudder. The ship was moving. I turned the control handle of the turbolift, and as it moved toward auxiliary control, I took in the empty lift car and its implication: I was the only one who'd made it off the bridge. The captain and first officer were both dead. Sheridan had been a good commander. He was collaborative, encouraged my input. I learned a lot from him. I tried not to think about the fact that he was now gone.

I had only been aboard the *Hotspur* a month. It was not a desired posting because the ship was so old, but after two years of relative comfort as Captain Coto's navigator, I was looking for something different. When Coto told me his priority was protecting the lives of his crew, he wasn't exaggerating; he had become very risk averse. I really couldn't blame him given the trauma he'd been through, but the upshot was he made sure the *Farragut* always played it safe. So when the *Hotspur* needed a communications officer, who would also be fourth-in-command, I jumped at it. The ship was also on "milk runs," like the *Republic*, but in a sector of space much more dangerous.

The turbolift stopped; I got off and found my way to the auxiliary control room. It was manned by a few crewmen I didn't know well, and one that I did: the chief engineer and third-in-command, Howard Kaplan, my old superior officer from the *Republic*. He was moved to the *Hotspur* when the *Republic* was retired from service. Though he technically outranked me, I was a bridge officer, and he had not been happy to see me come aboard. The rest of the crewmen were among the least experienced on the ship; they were reserve crewmen sent to man the auxiliary control room during a red alert. When the bridge was declared uninhabitable, any and every senior officer available was supposed to report here and take over. Kaplan and I were the only ones who showed up.

"Are you all right, sir?" asked the crewman manning the helm. She was a beautiful young woman named Uhura who'd just gotten out of the academy.

"Report," I said, ignoring her question, because I was far from all right. I was freezing, my legs were weak, and my vision was blurry. But I wasn't going to let them know that, especially Kaplan.

"We're inside the gas giant, sir," Uhura said.

"Warp drive is out and we're not going to be able to stay here for long," Kaplan snapped.

He wasn't offering a solution; I looked around the room at the other faces, all of them younger than me, all of them looking for guidance. I wasn't going to get any ideas from them either, so I had to figure something out.

The pirates were better armed than we were and had caught us by surprise. I couldn't go back out there and engage in a conventional battle. They'd damaged our weapon targeting control—in a pounding match, they'd have a distinct advantage.

"Ensign," I said to Uhura, "bring up what we have on our opponent." Uhura threw a few switches, and a schematic of the pirate ship appeared on the viewscreen. I immediately looked at its mass; it was about a third of *Hotspur's*. I did a quick calculation in my head and smiled to myself. I had a plan, and I was sure it would work.

I glanced again at Kaplan. He was technically in command, so I should run my idea by him, but there was no use to that. He'd spent his career in engineering. He had no experience commanding a ship. He looked at me, worried, angry, scared. He wasn't in any position to judge my idea, and I was past hesitating where the safety of the ship was concerned.

"Stand by on tractor beam," I said. I had checked and it was still operational. "We're going to come out of the gas giant, lock on to that ship, then we're going to drag it back into the gas giant with us..."

"We won't have a lot of thrust—" Kaplan said.

"We won't need it," I said. "We're deeper in the gravity well than they are, and we're three times their mass. That'll do most of the work for us. They'll either overload their engines trying to pull away, or get crushed by the gas giant."

Uhura and the other crewmen look relieved, pleased by the confidence I had expressed. We might get out of this. Kaplan just scowled at me, embarrassed but contrite.

"Execute my orders," I said, then turned to Kaplan. "Start your repairs on the warp drive."

"Aye sir," Kaplan said, as he left.

I was 27, and I was now a captain.

And I hadn't seen my child in two years.

CHAPTER 5

"**I'M A DOCTOR, NOT A BABYSITTER,**" McCoy said. I wanted to hit him.

I'd known Leonard McCoy for over a year, since I came aboard the *Hotspur*. We did not have a lot in common; he was older than me, and though he was at the academy for a short time when I was there, we hadn't met. On the ship, he seemed competent though always a little put out. Things only got worse when I took command; he made it clear on more than one occasion that he thought I wasn't ready for the job. I suppose I couldn't blame him; at 29 I was the youngest captain in the history of Starfleet. Usually, I'd ignore his attitude as long as he followed my orders. In this case, however, I needed his help.

"I'm not asking you to babysit," I said. "The boy is going to be on board for three weeks; we're cramped for space. I want to make sure it's safe."

"It'd be safer if he didn't come on board," McCoy said.

"McCoy—" I said. He could see that I was annoyed.

"Look, Commander, what do you want me to say? This ship is barely safe for adults, let alone a two-year-old. Why the hell are they coming aboard anyway?"

I wasn't going to let McCoy or anyone else know why we were transporting Carol and little David back to Earth, or their connection to me, at least not yet. When I came to see him in sickbay, I suppose I thought he might have sympathy for a mother and child being stuck on a starship, but I could see that was too much to hope for.

"First of all, he's three years old," I said, dodging his question. "And second of all, the health and well-being of everyone aboard is your responsibility. That goes for all our passengers. I want facilities set up for the care of a three-year-old. That's an order."

"Yes sir," he said, and as I left he gave me a curious look.

I headed back to the bridge. As I walked the corridors, I was reminded that McCoy was an exception; most of the crew went out of their way to show me deference and respect. But, paradoxically, this deference thrust me into a specific kind of loneliness. This was not the friendless solitude I'd faced on the *Republic*. My responsibility to the people I was now in command of was a burden; my actions could and would literally affect their lives. And I experienced a strange sensation as captain, a shrinking of my personal identity, as if my nerve endings had been extended to the physical limits of *Hotspur*. I never quite slept, not in the way I had before; I was like a young parent, my ears listening apprehensively even in my sleep. The crew were my children; I was looking after all of them, so I could be a friend to none of them.

And yet, ironically, I hadn't experienced that with my own child. I was going to try to change that. The last leg of our current run took us to Starbase 12, where Carol had been now for four years. I hadn't seen very much of her and David during that time. We had spoken frequently by subspace, and when David was a baby she would hold him up to the screen. However, recently, she would speak to me alone, always having a reason why David wasn't there. During our last conversation, she had told me her project was finished and she was heading back to Earth. Conventional transport wouldn't be able to take her for another month, so I arranged for a scheduled layover at Starbase 12 under the guise of some minor ship maintenance that I'd been putting off, and we would transport Carol and David home.

I was very excited about them coming on board. I knew that I'd been neglecting them because of my work, but now with my position I felt I could exert some control over my life. There were starship captains who were married and had children; why couldn't I be one of them? Which is why I had also decided to make it official and marry Carol on this voyage, although since I was in command, I wasn't sure who was going to perform the service.

I arrived on the bridge; my first officer turned and got out of the command chair.

"Captain on the bridge," Gary Mitchell said. Gary knew I hated this formality; though I was "captain of the ship," I had not received the official rank of captain.

"Status," I said, as Gary went back to the helm station.

"We've assumed standard orbit of Starbase 12," he said.

"Very well, begin transport of passengers and cargo," I said.

Gary had been serving on the *U.S.S. Constitution* as a relief helmsman when I was promoted. I immediately asked Starfleet personnel to transfer him as my first officer. He was probably a little young for the job too, which is one of the reasons why I wanted him. I was 27, and all of the senior officers on the ship were older than me; having a contemporary (and a friend) as my exec buttressed my confidence. My only criticism of him was he tended to be too loose regarding the rules of fraternization with the female crew members.

We began the complicated unloading of cargo from the ship. About two hours in, Ensign Uhura, the relief communications officer, relayed a message from ground control.

"Sir," Uhura said, "a request for permission for a Dr. Carol Marcus to beam up."

"Guess she can't wait," Gary said, a little too salaciously. Gary didn't know the full story; he knew Carol and I had been involved, but not how far it went. I gave him an annoyed look.

"Permission granted," I said. "I'll be in the transporter room."

As I left the bridge, I found myself smiling; my enthusiasm about seeing David began to overtake me. I remembered my own excitement to see my father or mother after any kind of absence, and also remembered fantasizing about what it must be like aboard a spaceship. Now I would be able to show my ship to my son, who I was sure had the same thoughts. I was indulging myself, looking forward to being proud, to walking down the corridor of my ship, while my crew showed deference to me in front of my child, and the pride he would feel at being my son. I was looking forward to that admiration and unconditional love.

I arrived in the transporter room. The technician on duty informed me that one person was standing by to beam up.

"One?" I didn't know what to make of it. "Very well, energize."

The image on the transporter pad shimmered into the recognizable form of Carol. She had no luggage. I could tell immediately she didn't want to be there.

"Hello, Carol," I said.

"Commander," she said. I realized she wasn't going to talk openly in front of a stranger. I turned to the transporter technician and relieved him of his post. Once he left, however, Carol showed no sign of being more comfortable.

"Where's David?" I said.

"With a sitter," she said.

"The ship needs to leave orbit in a few hours. I thought you'd want the time to settle him in on board—"

"We're not coming with you," she said. "I don't think it would be good for him."

"You don't think it would be good for him to see his father?" I was a little indignant.

"Right now, he doesn't know he has a father," she said.

I was stunned. I didn't know how to respond, so I got angry.

"Bring my son to me now," I said. It sounded ridiculous even to me, and Carol laughed, but without mirth.

"I'm not one of your crew," she said. "I'd like to go back now."

"No, wait," I said. "Carol, I'm sorry. I just—"

"He's a little boy," she said. "He wouldn't understand why his father doesn't love him enough to be with him."

"But I can now," I said. "Give me a chance—"

"I've given you several chances. Years of chances. I kept hoping..." She was welling up. I hadn't realized up to that moment just how much my absence had hurt Carol. I kept rationalizing that at some future date I would figure out how to be together, to be a family. But I'd taken too long. "So... I can't see him..."

"I think it would be better if you stayed away," Carol said. It was hard for me to hear, but I could also see it was hard for her to say. She took a pause, finally stepped down off the transporter pad. She took my hand. "Jim, there is no easy answer. Neither one of us is going to give up our work. And that means only one of us can be there for David, and it's going to be me."

I could see there was no changing her mind. And I knew, from my own history with my mother, that in one sense, she was right: David wouldn't understand.

"All right," I said. "But one day, when he's old enough . . ."

"One day," she said. She kissed me on the cheek, then turned and got back onto the transporter. I went to the controls, signaled the starbase, and, without another word, beamed her down. In a moment, she was gone, and I was alone.

✦

A short time later, I was on the bridge, making final preparations to leave orbit, when Dr. McCoy came to see me.

"Commander, I've got a play area set up," he said.

"What?"

"I had some crates moved out of a small storage locker off the gymnasium. I've put in some age-appropriate games, and taken out anything that might be harmful. I've also set up a schedule for the nursing staff to take turns—"

"We don't need it," I said, cutting him off. I'd completely forgotten about this task I'd given McCoy.

"What do you mean? What about the child?"

"There's no child on board," I said. "The passengers made other arrangements."

Gary looked back at me from the helm, surprised.

"Mind your helm, Mr. Mitchell," I said. My curtness told Gary I wasn't going to give him any information, at least not now, so he turned back to his console. McCoy, however, wasn't letting it go.

"I've spent the last three hours on this," he said.

"Look, Doctor—"

"I'm the chief medical officer aboard this ship. I'm responsible for the health of 300 crewmen, and you're wasting my time on some kind of horseshit practical joke—"

"That's enough," I said.

"It's not enough—"

"Dismissed, Doctor," I said. McCoy still stood there, glaring at me, and I didn't like it. "Get the hell off the bridge."

"I'm putting this into my medical log," he said. "This isn't the end of it." He stormed off into the turbolift. I noticed the bridge crew glancing over at me, trying to figure what it was all about.

"Show's over, folks," I said. "Let's get out of here."

Leaving orbit and getting under way gave me a little while to cool down. I realized that I probably did owe McCoy an apology, but his attitude really didn't make me want to give him one. Still, I wasn't sure I wanted him entering this in his medical log either. I was already probably under scrutiny at Command because of my age, and I had a feeling it might not be the first time McCoy put something in his log that would undermine me in the eyes of Starfleet. Once we were under way, I left the bridge and went down to see him in his office.

"Captain," he said. "Please come in. I was just going to come see you . . ." His affect was much less confrontational than I expected. And he'd called me captain, as did many of the crew, in deference to naval tradition. But some of the older crewmen used my actual rank of commander, which I always took as a sign they didn't fully respect my position. Up until this moment, McCoy had been one of them.

"Look, McCoy, I owe you an apology . . ."

"No sir, it's unnecessary," he said. "I was way out of line." Any trace of his anger and resentment was gone.

"I'd still like to say I'm sorry," I said.

"Well, apology accepted," he said. We stood in awkward silence for a moment, and when I turned to leave, he stopped me and went over to a cabinet on the wall. "I was about to have a drink . . ."

He opened the cabinet and inside were a variety of bottles in different colors and shapes. His sudden cordiality didn't make any sense to me. He didn't seem like the same man.

"Quite a collection," I said.

"A doctor needs to be prepared for all medical contingencies." He took out a bottle of Saurian brandy and poured us two glasses. I sat down and took one.

"So, half an hour ago you were ready to rip my head off; now you're sharing the good liquor with me."

"Maybe I just realized we have more in common than I thought," he said, then activated his computer viewscreen, and turned it toward me. On it was a picture of a young girl, maybe eleven, dark hair, blue eyes. She was standing against the post of what I assumed was a porch, overlooking a grand green yard.

"She's lovely. Who is it?"

"My daughter, Joanna," McCoy said. "She lives with her mother." There was remorse in the way he said this.

This caught me by surprise. I hadn't told anyone, not even Gary, that David was my son. How could he have figured it out?

"They were coming aboard, and then suddenly they weren't," he said, obviously reading my bafflement. "It had a familiar emotional tinge to it."

It was my first exposure to McCoy's emotional perceptiveness, which I would eventually count on, but at the moment it caught me off guard. It took me a moment to realize that I also felt relief; someone knew the guilt I was carrying, someone who understood. I finished the drink in my glass, looked at the picture again.

"When was the last time you saw her?"

"It's been a while," he said, then held out the bottle. "Another?"

✦

"We're down to our last crystal," Kaplan said. "And it's fracturing. I don't know how much longer it's going to last." I had gathered my officers in the ship's small briefing room. McCoy, Kaplan, and Gary joined me at the table. Standing against the wall were Communications Officer Chen and Cargo Officer Griffin. I was very annoyed; Kaplan was a terrible choice for this ship. He went by the book, so I could never officially fault him, but the *Hotspur* was so old that it needed a lot more creative thinking than he was capable of. His regular maintenance schedule for the dilithium chamber was too lax, and had caused us to go through our crystals abnormally fast. Without them, we'd have no warp power, and he'd waited until the last minute to alert me to the situation. When the last crystal burned out, we could be stuck in the middle of nowhere.

I remember my years on the *Hotspur* with more nostalgia than they probably deserve. All we did was travel back and forth between the same planets, carrying the same supplies, and it didn't take long for me to figure out how to avoid the traps of the pirates who were looking to get our cargo. There was no real exploration, and the ship itself was never easy to run. But I often long for the simplicity of that period, my first command, when we were frequently risking our lives for no great cause other than cargo.

"Suggestions," I said. I looked at Kaplan, who sat quietly, scowling.

"I think we've got to find some dilithium," Gary said.

"That's a big help, Science Officer," I said. The ship did not have a crewman specifically trained as "science officer"; I had assigned it to Gary because he was the best choice of a bad lot.

"The Tellarites used to have a dilithium operation on Dimorous," Griffin said. "I remember the captain of my old ship, the *Rhode Island*, bought some crystals from them. Not cheap, is all I want to say, and those suckers love to argue . . ." Griffin, a breezy, rotund officer, had gotten a commission from my predecessor, for reasons that were never made clear to me.

Gary programmed some information on the computer console in front of him.

"He's right, sir," Gary said. "The Tellarites abandoned the mining facility about five years ago. It looks like they left a fair amount of gear."

"Don't expect me to operate Tellarite mining equipment," Kaplan said.

"Noted," I said. "Do we know why the Tellarites left?"

"They reported the operation was quote," Gary said, reading off his screen, "'No longer a profitable enterprise,' end quote."

"That sounds fishy," McCoy said, and I agreed with him. But I didn't see we had much of a choice.

"Any intelligent life on the planet?" I said.

"Various indigenous animals, but nothing to worry about . . ." Gary said.

✦

We achieved orbit of Dimorous and detected two compounds on the planet. One was clearly the dilithium mine, but the other, about 20 miles away, was a mystery. From orbit we detected what looked like some kind of laboratory facilities, as well as what appeared to be animal pens. There was also a large density of animal life surrounding that facility. It was tantalizingly peculiar, but there was no time to satisfy my curiosity.

I beamed down to the mining facility with Gary, McCoy, Assistant Engineer Lee Kelso, and Security Chief Christine Black. (I left Kaplan in command, since dragging him planetside was always an ordeal.) The Tellarite mining facility was housed in a bunker-like building, set in an arid area of rock and sand dunes. Inside the building, there was a control station set up next to a huge chasm, leading deep under the planet's surface. A mining laser hung over the chasm, set up to cut through the ground, down to the dilithium vein; the crystals would be brought up with tractor beams. It was state-of-the-art equipment, and the reactor that powered the station, though deactivated, was still nominal. It made little sense that the Tellarites would just leave it there, along with an abundantly rich vein of dilithium. The only explanation was that they left in a hurry.

"Jim," McCoy said, looking at his tricorder, "life-forms approaching. A lot of them." While Kelso quickly got to work, Gary, McCoy, Black, and I went outside. A wall, creating a fort-like structure, bordered the Tellarite facility. The four of us went up to the parapet and were unprepared for what we saw next.

"Jesus," McCoy said.

A moving mass of brown and gray rolled toward us. It was hard to make out distinct shapes in the mass, but there were hundreds, thousands of eyes and fangs. As it got closer, I could see the individual creatures moved on all fours, thick hind legs and small upper limbs, like rats. But huge; each was four or five feet long. They were scrambling over each other, biting, clawing, but moving fast over the terrain. As they approached, the cacophony of their piercing shrills grew in intensity.

"I think we know why the Tellarites left..." Gary said.

"There's no record of a life-form like this on Dimorous—" McCoy said.

"There is now," I said, taking out my communicator. "Kirk to Kelso, what's your status?"

"Kelso here. I'm bringing up the first sample now—"

"One sample's all you're going to get," I said. It would've been nice to have a little in reserve, but it was not to be. "On the double, we've got to get out of here." I then switched channels. "Kirk to *Hotspur*, stand by for emergency transport." I was prepared to leave even the one crystal behind, except I quickly found out that wasn't an option.

"Commander, this is *Hotspur*," Kaplan said. "Our power levels have dropped too low, transporter is out."

"Send a shuttle," I said. I looked out at the furry, noxious mass getting closer. I was angry; somehow I blamed this whole situation on Kaplan.

"Already launched, sir. They'll be there in minutes." At least he'd done that right.

The animals' shrieking was making it difficult to hear. I instinctively drew my phaser, but as Gary and Black followed suit, I was reminded of my responsibility.

"On stun," I said.

"Really?" Gary had already set his phaser to full power. "Is this the time to get sentimental?" I could see from Black's expression that she agreed with the first officer, but was respectful enough not to offer her opinion.

"Mr. Mitchell," McCoy said, "our mission is about the preservation of life."

"Yeah, I always figured that included us," Gary said.

"McCoy, go give Kelso a hand," I said. Having McCoy there harping on our duty to other life-forms wasn't helping; I knew the right thing to do, but I was also scared, and his somewhat self-righteous tone made me want to disagree with him.

"Let's see if we can scare them off," I said. "Take out a few in the front."

We fired and hit about a dozen of the creatures in front. It did not slow the mass down; the creatures climbed over their unconscious brethren without pause. The brown and gray wave now separated into more distinct shapes, spreading out in the plain surrounding the mining facility. They were moving on us from a broader front; their line was thinner, but we wouldn't be able to cover that wide an area.

"Sir, that was a tactical move," Black said. She was right; though fierce and relentless, it was a sign of intelligence. These were not wild animals. And then, just as I noticed something else, Gary did too.

"Jim, are some of them . . . armed?" Above their hind legs on a large portion of the creatures' backs were something that looked like bandoleers; each held several pointed projectiles.

"Gary, take the left wall, Black, the right. Don't let them flank us," I said.

"Can we kill them now?" Gary said.

"No, it'll drain our phasers too fast. And make your shots count. Short bursts." As Black and Gary moved to their positions, I fired my phaser. They soon joined me as our beams stunned creature after creature. It was only a temporary solution; the creatures didn't stay unconscious for very long. We weren't holding the line; there was just too many of them. Slowly they inched forward. As they did, some of the creatures gripped the dart-like projectiles strapped to their backs with one of their hind feet and threw them. They were thankfully still out of range, the darts falling a few feet short of the wall. I took out my communicator.

"Kirk to McCoy, status!" I said, now yelling to be heard over the din.

"Kelso's finished, we're on our way out," McCoy said. I then looked up and saw a shuttle break through an orange cloud. At the same time, I heard repeated thunks against the wall. The rodent creatures were in throwing range. I watched the shuttle approach. The landing pad was outside the walls of the mining facility, which, for obvious reasons, was not going to work, and there wasn't room inside the walls for the shuttle to land.

"Kirk to shuttle," I said.

"Uhura here, sir." I was pleased it was her. Uhura was a dedicated officer, and though she specialized in communications, she was a very good pilot.

"Uhura, we're not going to be able to make the landing pad—"

"I can see that, sir," she said. "I can land on the bunker, but I don't think it will hold the shuttle's weight for long . . ."

"Do it," I said.

I took a quick glance to my left. Gary was holding off his creatures' advance, but he was firing a little wildly, missing often; they were closing in. I then looked to my right and could see that Black's shooting was much more efficient; the creatures on that side were farther back. The shuttle zoomed over us, heading toward the bunker, where McCoy and Kelso were now waiting, holding a canister with the dilithium inside.

"Black, move back to the bunker," I said. I gambled that it would take a little longer for the creatures to reach her side of the wall. A few darts now hit just below where I was standing. "Stand by to give us cover."

Black leaped off the walkway of her wall and ran back to the bunker. The shuttle rested on the bunker, and I turned to Gary.

"Go!" We both turned and leaped. Darts cleared the wall just as we jumped. As I ran toward her, Black, having reached the bunker, aimed her phaser directly at me and fired. The beam missed me but presumably hit the creatures, which were now crawling up over the wall behind me.

"Get in the shuttle!" I yelled. McCoy and Kelso were already climbing up onto the roof of the bunker. Black then quickly scaled the wall, and immediately knelt and continued to fire. I turned and saw the horde of rodent-like monsters scramble over the barrier. I fired several shots as Gary reached the bunker with me. I continued to fire as he gave me a quick leg up onto the bunker. I then grabbed him and pulled him up. I looked down and saw cracks were spreading on the bunker's roof; the shuttle's weight was too much. We moved to the hatch and I motioned Black inside. I was following her in when I was suddenly shoved into the craft, onto its deck. I turned to see Gary was prone on the bunker. He'd pushed me inside and taken a dart in the upper right arm. The shuttle shifted; the roof of the bunker was giving way.

"Black, cover me!"

I dove out of the shuttle and saw the angry, empty eyes clear the roof. Black fired from the shuttle's entrance, shooting the creatures closest to me, giving me time to throw Gary over my shoulder and turn back to the shuttle. There were too many for Black to shoot, and she had to move back to let me on board. I could hear the skittering creatures inches behind me as I fell back into the shuttle. There was hot breath on my neck as the shuttle hatch slammed shut. Uhura, at the helm, screamed.

I turned; when the hatch closed, it had severed a creature's head and one of its paws. The face stared at us from the deck, its mouth open, revealing unnaturally sharp razor fangs, oozing yellow blood. I heard the thumping of the rodents outside against the hull.

The shuttle jarred, and we were all thrown against the starboard bulkhead; the roof was collapsing.

"Uhura!" I shouted, but she'd already regained her composure and grabbled the controls. She jammed the throttles forward, the engines groaned, and the shuttle righted itself as we lifted off.

McCoy had already moved to examine Gary. He ripped Gary's shirtsleeve to reveal the wound. A black stain was visibly spreading from the entry of the dart. McCoy took out his scanner. Gary looked up at me and forced a smile through his pain.

"What the hell were you thinking?" I said to him.

"Wasn't," Gary said, in pain. "Been . . . a problem . . . since the acad—"

"Gary, I have to knock you out," McCoy said. He took out the hypo from the medkit on his hip and injected it into Gary, who immediately passed out. McCoy turned to Black.

"Give me your phaser," McCoy said, as she handed him the weapon. "And everybody stand back."

"What are you doing?" I said. McCoy was adjusting the setting on the weapon.

"I don't know what this poison is. I need to buy some time." He moved Gary's injured arm out away from his body, carefully aimed the phaser, and *sliced off his arm* above the wound. The heat from the phaser cauterized the cut.

We all sat there in stunned silence for a moment. I looked around at my crew, scared, tired. There was the severed head and paw of a giant rat, as well as the amputated arm of my first officer and best friend.

"Well . . ." I said, "everybody, good work today." And after a moment, I laughed out of exhaustion. And everyone joined me.

"The DNA is a 61 percent match to the animal native to Dimorous," McCoy said. "But someone made some additions."

On the viewscreen at McCoy's desk floated a double helix. Part of the strand was highlighted.

"Genetic engineering," I said. "Outlawed for a hundred years. You think the Tellarites—"

"I don't have any proof of who was doing what," McCoy said. "But someone was up to something. Even the poison on those darts wasn't completely indigenous."

An out-of-control genetic experiment would explain why the Tellarites had abandoned a rich dilithium vein as well as some state-of-the-art equipment. But it left a lot of unanswered questions. I wouldn't get the answers for a long time.

"How's Gary?" I said.

"Recovering," McCoy said. "I was able to clean out all the poison in his arm and reattach it. That poison was naturally occurring on the planet, but it had been weaponized. It was particularly malicious. Another few seconds would've been too late."

"Good job, Sawbones."

"What?" I was surprised that McCoy had never heard this piece of ancient Earth slang.

"It's what they called surgeons in the Old West," I said. "Often men of your profession only had one option to cure their patients. Cutting off limbs to prevent the spread of infection."

"I knew about the practice; never heard that nickname," McCoy said. "Gruesome. Please don't use it again."

He probably regretted saying that.

✦

After the incident on Dimorous, I was looking forward to my shore leave. I was still wounded by my experience with Carol, but I sought comfort with another woman. Janet Lebow was a young endocrinologist completing her

THE STORY OF STARFLEET'S GREATEST CAPTAIN

doctorate on Benecia, one of the *Hotspur*'s stops, and she was part of a team that was tasked with examining the samples of the rodents from Dimorous. Janet seemed almost immediately familiar to me; in hindsight I can see that she reminded me of Carol: dedicated, beautiful, brilliant, a serious intellectual with a passionate devotion to her career. This devotion would allow me to rationalize my own emotional distance, and our fervent romance didn't last.*

But while there was a persistent emptiness in my personal life, my professional life was solidifying. I had dispensed with a lot of my early insecurities in managing a crew, and formed my command style. I knew, or thought I knew, what kind of captain I was. I was itching to get a step up, to gain more responsibility and respectability. As the years went by, I'd put together a good crew; I had a lot of bright young men and women who I thought would develop along with me and form a great team. I was counting on not losing them to better opportunities before I had a chance to take them with me wherever I would go. It was too much to hope for.

One night, I was awakened by the intercom. It was Uhura, who was on the bridge nightwatch.

"Sorry to wake you, sir," she said. "Priority message from Starfleet."

"Read it to me," I said, yawning, sitting up in bed.

"To Kirk, commanding *U.S.S. Hotspur*. From Komack, admiral, Starfleet Command. You are hereby ordered to make best possible speed to Utopia Planitia, Mars, Sol System, for decommissioning."

"Thank you, Ensign," I said. Now I was awake. "Have navigation alter our course for Sol System, best possible safe speed. Kirk out." I switched off the communicator. I'd heard that several of the *Baton Rouge*–class ships had already been decommissioned; they were all well out of their prime. Better-designed vessels specifically constructed for their tasks were taking their places. This was not good news.

I was losing my command, and since I hadn't received word of a transfer, it meant there were no other captaincies available. I could be sitting on

---

*EDITOR'S NOTE: Janet Lebow became Janet Wallace after marrying Dr. Theodore Wallace, also an endocrinologist, several decades her senior. They were only married a few years before he passed away. She continued her distinguished career until 2283, when she was on a mission aboard the *U.S.S. Vengeance*, which disappeared with all hands.

a shore posting for a long time waiting for a position to open up. It was risky; it was well-known the longer you were on a planet, the greater the chances Starfleet would leave you there. And since I had received a battlefield promotion to command of *Hotspur*, I was concerned I would be in competition with more senior commanders and captains for an open ship.

I informed the crew the next morning, but by then many had already heard. Over the next two weeks, most of them received their transfer orders; Starfleet was cannibalizing my crew, and it was painful. Many were given great opportunities: Kelso and Uhura were both posted to the *U.S.S. Enterprise*, though with no promotion. Black was made security chief of the *U.S.S. Excalibur*. I assumed McCoy would move up to a *Constitution* class as well, but no offer included a chief medical officer position, so he turned them all down. The biggest surprise, however, was Gary.

"Do you know Ron Tracy?" Gary said to me one day over breakfast.

"Met him for five seconds when he took over the *Republic*," I said.

"He's taking command of the *Exeter*. Offered me helmsman."

"I thought Mendez offered you exec on the *Astral Queen*."

"So?" Gary said.

"So the word is he's going to make commodore soon. You'd be in position to get command."

"No guarantee of that," Gary said, "and if you offer me exec somewhere, I can leave the *Exeter* without burning any bridges."

I was surprised and touched. Gary was putting his career on hold on the off chance we could continue to work together.

"Don't you want a ship of your own?"

"Me with absolute power?" he said, with a smirk. "Don't you think that'd be a little dangerous?"

✦

The Utopia Planitia shipyard, both on the surface and in orbit of Mars, was, even back then, a grand sight. There were ten dry dock superstructures that hung above the red planet, many filled with spaceships in various states of overhaul or construction, while repair crews in space suits and piloting small "worker bee" shuttles floated around them, building and mending.

We brought *Hotspur* into one of the dry docks in low orbit, and most of the crew disembarked, while a skeleton staff from engineering coordinated with the dock crews to begin shutting down the systems and inventorying what was salvageable. The day before we reached Mars, I was given my next assignment: department of strategic planning and studies, Starfleet Headquarters in San Francisco. It was the epitome of a desk job.

On the trip back, I had made sure to have a personal exit interview with every member of the crew. I told many I hoped I would serve with them again and meant it (except maybe when I said it to Kaplan). So when we docked at Mars, I didn't see any need to say goodbye to anyone again. I packed up my things in my duffel and headed for the shuttle bay; I had requisitioned one of the ship's shuttlecraft so I could pilot myself back to Earth.

As I walked through the corridors of the *Hotspur*, I was surprised at how deserted it already was. I realized that I had been looking forward to a few casual goodbyes on my way off the ship, and was disappointed that I passed literally *no one* on my way to the bay. I suppose that should've been a clue.

"Atten-shun!" I heard the words as the doors to the bay slid open, and tried to conceal my astonishment. It was Gary who shouted it, and 300 crew members immediately stood at attention. They formed up on both sides of the bay, with a clear path to the hatch of the shuttlecraft. I smiled and, duffel over my shoulder, walked by them. Kelso, Black, and Uhura (who had tears in her eyes) all stood at attention as I passed. Gary and McCoy waited at the end. McCoy was coming with me to Earth, but this was the last time I would be seeing Gary for a while. I turned and faced the crew. I looked at all the faces of my first command, many of whom I hadn't chosen, but to all of whom I'd felt connected.

"Dismiss all hands," I said.

"Company, dismissed!" Gary said, sounding as sincere as he ever had. "Prepare shuttle bay for immediate launch."

"Thanks for this," I said quietly to Gary, as I shook his hand.

"Stay in touch," he said, and followed the crew out of the bay. I then helped McCoy with his luggage onto the shuttle. He had a duffel as well as a very heavy crate.

"Are those your 'special contingencies'?" I said, as I heaved it onto the craft.

"They would be dangerous in the hands of someone less experienced," McCoy said. He sat down, and I took the helm controls. I could see through the view port that the bay had been cleared. I keyed the intercom.

"Shuttlecraft *Gates* to launch control," I said. "Request permission to depart."

"Launch control to shuttlecraft, permission granted," Gary said, now in the bay's launch center. "Uh, Jim, we're getting a request from traffic control for you to take another passenger to Earth with you. He's Starfleet."

"All right, transmit his coordinates," I said.

A moment later, I piloted the shuttle out of the bay, leaving *Hotspur* behind. I entered a maze of other ships in dock, old and new, and none of them were mine. I felt a longing to turn around, head back to *Hotspur*, but the ship wouldn't be there for much longer.

My extra passenger was in a dock in a higher orbit. As we moved toward it, we got a good look at the majestic craft inside it.

"What ship is that?" McCoy said.

"That's the *Enterprise*." Unlike the *Hotspur*, it was sleek and clean.

"She's a beauty," McCoy said. "Who's her captain?"

"Chris Pike," I said. Pike was well-known among Starfleet as a wildly successful officer. He'd been in command of a *Constitution*-class ship for ten years, made dozens of first contacts, and charted many new worlds. The sector of space he was assigned to explore also put him into several skirmishes with the Klingons. The rest of us were envious of his accomplishments.

The yard command directed me to a port not on the ship, but on the webbed superstructure surrounding it. I docked the shuttle, and the hatch opened. On the other side stood a Starfleet lieutenant commander from an immediately recognizable species.

"Request permission to come aboard," he said. I was surprised by his formality.

"Uh, permission granted, Mr. . . . ?"

"Lieutenant Commander Spock." He calmly came aboard the shuttlecraft with his small suitcase. He stood near the helm station and looked down at me. Though I'd seen plenty of Vulcans in my life, I'd never gotten used to their ominous, almost frightening, appearance. The pointed ears, slanted eyebrows, and yellowish skin, however, always stood in stark contrast to their ultra-civilized, stoic demeanor.

"Will you need any assistance in piloting? I am rated for this craft."

"Uh, no, thanks, have a seat." He quietly took the seat in the cabin next to McCoy, who rolled his eyes at me. Spock seemed quite comfortable not learning our names.

"I'm Jim Kirk," I said, then indicated McCoy. "This is Dr. Leonard McCoy."

"I was aware of your identities before I came aboard."

"Common courtesy would usually require asking our names anyway," McCoy said.

"I unfortunately have not made a study of the redundancies involved in human etiquette," Spock said. He said it very dryly; had he been human, I would've assumed he was being sarcastic, but in a Vulcan it was impossible to tell.

"Well, this is going to be a fun trip," McCoy said.

"No offense taken, Mr. Spock," I said, obviously not speaking for McCoy. "Strap yourselves in, we're leaving." I turned to the helm, and received clearance from the yard command as McCoy opened his crate.

"Anybody for a drink?"

"The consumption of inebriating beverages aboard shuttlecraft is forbidden under regulations," Spock said.

"I bet you're really good at making friends," McCoy said.

"Friendship is a classification humans use to define emotional relationships," Spock said. "It is not logical."

"Yeah, well, obviously not for you," McCoy said.

"Bones," I said, my tone telling him to cut it out. The shuttle pulled away from the dock, and I took it out of orbit. We left Mars behind and began our three-hour voyage to Earth. For a long while it was silent, until that was broken by the sound of McCoy pouring himself another drink.

"Mr. Spock, are you posted aboard the *Enterprise*?" I said.

"Yes sir," Spock said. "I am the science officer."

"I see. How long have you served with Captain Pike?"

"Nine years, ten months, sixteen days," Spock said. Vulcans didn't make it easy to carry on light conversation.

"What a coincidence," McCoy said. "That's going to be the same length as this shuttle ride."

"What brings you to Earth?" I said, ignoring McCoy. Whatever he was drinking was quickly making him impervious to authority.

"I'm visiting relatives on the North American continent, in a small town on the eastern coast called Grover's Mill," Spock said. That was strange; I wasn't aware of a Vulcan population center on Earth in that area.

"Oh. Are they stationed there?" I said.

"No, they're from there," Spock said. It was then that I remembered that I'd heard of a half-human, half-Vulcan at the academy; we'd overlapped but never met. He must have been quite a student; Spock had already distinguished himself serving aboard a *Constitution*-class ship for a decade.

"So, you're visiting your human relatives," I said.

"Yes. The *Enterprise* will be in dry dock for some time," Spock said. "It was at my mother's request I visit her sister and niece." He was a dutiful son. I wondered whether that was the Vulcan or human half.

"Wait," McCoy said, speech slightly slurring. "You've got human relatives?"

"As I implied previously," Spock said. "My mother is human."

"And yet you're still a rude son of a bitch," McCoy said.

"If I am, Doctor," Spock said, "it is a trait I share with billions of human beings."

I thought about putting a stop to it, but it seemed quite clear that Spock didn't need my help. And I was frankly starting to enjoy it.

They bickered for a while longer, but McCoy eventually settled into a nap, and Spock and I talked about the *Enterprise*'s refit. I was impressed by the amount of resources they were putting into the ship. The *Constitution*-class vessels got all the attention; ships like the *Hotspur* had to make do, until they were finally driven to the glue factory. I then asked the real question that was on my mind.

"Do you think Captain Pike is going to take her out for another five years?" An opening on a *Constitution*-class ship was rare.

"Such a mission would be beneficial to Starfleet and the Federation," he said.

He hadn't really answered my question. Maybe he knew something, maybe he didn't, but he wasn't going to help me. I had turned back to look at him for my next question, and thought I caught some emotion in his face, but it immediately evaporated.

"You like Captain Pike?"

"He's an efficient commander," he said. Served with him a decade, and showed no trace of any kind of sentiment. I moved back to the controls, suddenly jealous; Pike had been Spock's commanding officer since he got out of the academy. Garrovick had died within a couple of years.

I then started asking him about some of the scientific discoveries the *Enterprise* had been a part of, and I had the sense that he was downplaying his own role in many of the missions. It was talking about this that we stumbled upon a surprising mutual "acquaintance."

". . . but that was due mostly to what Dr. Marcus and her department had made in the area of subatomic engineering—"

"Wait," I said. "Carol Marcus? She was aboard the *Enterprise*?"

"For a short period," Spock said. "Are you familiar with her work?"

"Somewhat," I said.

I was almost unable to speak. Just the mention of Carol brought back the feelings for her and David. I was strangely jealous of this alien, just because he'd gotten to see her, to spend time with her.

"A capable scientist," Spock said. I nodded and focused on the controls. Since I was no longer keeping the conversation going, we both fell into silence. I silently castigated myself; it was ridiculous to be bitter because Spock had gotten to work with Carol.

Earth appeared in the center of my view port, and we received reentry instructions. I brought us into a landing at Starfleet Headquarters, and I shook McCoy awake. He had slept off some of the effects of his drinking.

Spock thanked me for the ride and said a curt goodbye to the two of us.

"There's a fun guy," McCoy said, as we watched him walk off. I didn't respond. I regretted my petulance over Carol, even though Spock hadn't picked up on it. I didn't know quite what to make of Spock then, but there was something compelling; he gave the impression of a man with a lot of character.

"Well, Jim," McCoy said, "hard to say when we may see each other again."

"It's been a pleasure, Bones," I said, as we shook hands. "Stay in touch." He smiled, yet also looked mildly irritated.

"You're determined to make that nickname stick, aren't you?"

I laughed. We promised to get together again while we were both on Earth, and then I headed to the Sub Shuttle station.

✦

I hadn't been home in quite some time. The house seemed very small to me; I guess it loomed large in my memory, even though I'd grown to my full height while still living there. I had decided to walk from the Riverside transportation station; they knew I was coming, but I hadn't given anyone a specific time when to expect me.

Sitting on the porch was a boy, about ten years old. He was the spitting image of my brother, Sam, at that age. He sat with his legs crossed, holding a magnifying glass. There were a couple of small insects on the porch in front of him.

"Any luck?" I said. He looked up at me.

"With what?"

"Burning them," I said. He looked annoyed.

"I wasn't burning them," he said. "I was examining them."

"I stand corrected," I said. A scientist, just like his father. "You must be Peter. I'm Jim."

"Oh, sorry," he said, standing up and holding out his hand. "Nice to meet you, Uncle Jim." The last time I'd seen Sam was shortly after he'd met Aurelan, whom he would marry. My missions in space had caused me to miss their wedding, as well as the birth of their son over ten years before. And now, here he was, in the flesh, healthy, curious. Before I could really take him in, everyone else was out on the porch, giving me warm hellos.

Sam was looking older, wearing a hearty mustache, though Aurelan was still stunning and youthful despite being the mother of a ten-year-old. But it was Dad and Mom that I really wasn't ready for. I'd really been gone a long time; they were both gray. Dad had put on more weight, and Mom had taken some off; she still looked energetic, though slightly frail. She gave me a fierce hug, and Dad grabbed my shoulder.

"Welcome home, Captain," he said, with a proud smile.

"Not a full captain yet, Dad," I said, somewhat self-consciously.

"It'll come," he said. They all but pulled me inside the house.

We sat down to dinner, and I was peppered with questions about my time on the *Hotspur*. I did my best to appear relaxed, but it was difficult; I'd spent the last several years in a command position, never fully letting my guard down, and now it wasn't coming easily. I had experienced a lot of stress that I hadn't quite worked through yet, and I wasn't willing to share stories that might bring it to the surface. I did my best to turn the attention to Sam and his family. Sam had continued work as a research biologist at the University of Chicago but was probably going to be transferred to a colony that specialized in research, either Earth Colony II or Deneva. Peter seemed excited about the idea of going into space. I found him the easiest to engage with for most of the evening.

"Do you stay in touch with Carol?" Mom said, later in the meal. She and Dad knew Carol and I had been serious, but I had never told them about David. Sam, however, did know, and I could feel him watching me as I answered. I'm sure he wasn't comfortable keeping a secret from them.

"Not really," I said. "I think we've both moved on." I could sense Mom's disappointment, though she didn't express it. She'd met Carol briefly when I was at the academy, and they'd hit it off. Coincidentally, their work paths had crossed later. They had a lot in common and I think Mom had some hopes for a lasting relationship for me. Peter then came over with a large box.

"Uncle Jim," Peter said, "Dad says you're good at three-dimensional chess. You want to play me?"

I looked at the young boy, the image of my brother. Peter was eager, pleasant, and solicitous of my attention. I thought of another boy, who I didn't know, who might by now be the image of me, and who would want the same things Peter wanted. I felt horrible, guilty.

"I'm sorry, pal," I said, "I'm really beat. We'll play tomorrow." I tousled his hair, said a quick goodnight to everyone, and headed off to my room.

✦

The next day I requisitioned quarters at Starfleet; I felt it would be too emotionally draining to stay at the farm, though I promised Mom and Dad I'd come back on the weekends, which I did.

The department of strategic planning and studies was housed, ironically, in the Archer Building, where about a decade before I'd impersonated a Starfleet officer. When I walked into the lobby now I was overcome with the feeling that I was still a fraud. I found my way to the offices on the tenth floor and reported to my commanding officer.

"Reporting for duty, Admiral," I said. Behind the desk was Heihachiro Nogura, a man of Japanese descent, white-haired, diminutive but with a quiet authority.

"At ease," Nogura said. "I hope you don't mind a little time at a desk, Commander. I like to have officers in the department who have extensive field experience."

"My pleasure, sir," I said, lying.

"We've got a lot going on here, Kirk. I'm afraid you're going to have to jump into the deep end." He indicated a small stack of tapes on his desk. "Take those. I'm going to need a report as soon as possible."

I was a little thrown. He wasn't telling me what he wanted the report *on*, and that was obviously on purpose. It felt like I was back in the academy again, being tested. I picked up the tapes.

"Yes sir," I said. "I'll need someplace to work."

Nogura had a yeoman show me to a cubicle with a desk, a simple setup with a computer and viewscreen. I sat down and started going through the tapes. They were excerpts from log entries of the commanders and officers on starships and starbases. A quick glance at the first few indicated encounters with Klingon ships and personnel. As I went through, I could see that the incidents were all in the past month. Not quite knowing what Nogura was looking for, I started collating the information, first on a graph of where the encounters took place, what the results of the encounters were, and what snippets of information the officers involved relayed about the Klingons' attitudes and intentions. A lot of the entries were from Christopher Pike's log; the sector of space the *Enterprise* was assigned covered a good portion of the border with the Klingons, and Pike had accumulated a lot of experience dealing with them. He had successfully survived several skirmishes with Klingon ships, but had lost multiple crew members in the battles.

The work was interesting enough that the days passed quickly. I got to know my colleagues in the department. Lance Cartwright, a few years my senior, was a full captain, having joined Nogura as his chief of staff after several years as captain of the *Exeter*. He was friendly and sharp, and was probably a few short years away from joining the Admiralty. Harry Morrow and William Smillie were commanders like me, and they considered this desk job one that they wanted. Though I was consumed with the assignment, I still felt the itch to get back on a bridge.

About a week in, I finished my report, and Nogura had me present it to the staff in his office. I went over the data that I pulled from the logs, and then summarized my conclusions.

"Within the time frame of the logs I reviewed, the Klingons appeared to be testing our response with aggressive moves in the disputed area of space that serves as the border between the Federation and their empire."

"Do you have any theories as to the purpose of these tests?" Nogura said. From the way he asked it, I felt that he thought there was only one possible answer.

"Without any actual proof," I said, "I would think it's a prelude to invasion."

"If that's the case," Cartwright said, "without the *Enterprise* on patrol in that sector, we are leaving ourselves wide open."

"The *Enterprise* is in desperate need of a refit that will take at least eight months," Morrow said. "The ship is 20 years old . . ."

"Then we need to reassign another starship to that sector," Cartwright said.

"Uh, sir," I said to Nogura, "I think there's another solution. I've examined the *Enterprise*'s refit schedule, and it could be split into a two-month period and a six-month period. The components necessary for the second period could be sent to Starbase 11."

"Why would we do that?" Cartwright said. "The *Enterprise* would still be out of action for those eight months."

"Yes, but if we are careful to keep the shipment of the upgrade components as well as the personnel transfers a secret, it would appear to the Klingons that Starfleet has a shipbuilding capacity well outside the Sol System. If they were planning to invade, it would give them pause, forcing them to take it into consideration as part of their strategy."

No one argued this point, which made me think it had landed. Nogura assigned me the task of determining how long it would take to ship the necessary components. I found out pretty quickly it was a much more difficult task than I originally thought; it would take over a year using the standard shipping routes to get all the material and personnel that far out. I presented my findings to Nogura but didn't think it would go any further.

As the days passed, it became clear to me that this department was doing a lot more than studying strategy. Nogura was an influential admiral, and he was using his department to gently guide Starfleet and Federation policy, to great effect. Resources were being moved around, officers transferred and promoted as a result of recommendations coming out of the department. One day, Nogura brought me into his office. There was a captain there and a younger man in a cadet uniform.

"Jim Kirk, this is Matt Decker," Nogura said, referencing the older man. I had heard of him; as a young lieutenant commander he'd fought a superior Klingon force to a standstill at Donatu V. Decker was shorter than me, but he had a rough presence, a force of personality that I felt immediately.

"Pleasure to meet you, Captain Decker," I said.

"It's commodore now," Decker said. "I haven't had a chance to change my braid." Decker's ship, the *Constellation*, had recently returned to Earth at the end of its five-year mission. I knew that Nogura had recommended Decker for promotion to commodore. He would keep command of his ship, but in case of a war with the Klingons, Decker's flag rank would put him in immediate command of all the ships in his sector. It was a strategic promotion where Nogura put a like-minded officer in charge of resources on the projected front lines.

Decker then indicated the younger man. "This is my son, Will." The young man seemed nothing like his father; where Matt was coarse and unrefined, Will appeared friendly and polished, although somewhat nervous around all the senior officers. I must have shown my surprise, because Decker added, "He takes after his mother."

"Cadet," I said, shaking his hand. "Fourth year?"

"Yes sir," Will said.

"Since he doesn't look like me, I want to make sure everyone knows he's my son," Decker said, then turned to Nogura. "Don't dump him on a starbase."

"I'll see what I can do," Nogura said, with a rare smile. Decker then turned to me.

"Wait, are you the Kirk who commanded the *Hotspur*?" he said.

"Yes sir," I said.

"I heard about that gas giant move," he said. "Well done. And call me Matt." Decker turned back to Nogura, referencing me. "Put this guy on a bridge too. He could come in handy." I was hopeful that Nogura would take Decker's suggestion, but I saw no sign of it.

A few days later, I walked into Cartwright's office, while he was meeting with another officer I didn't know.

"Jim, this is Major Oliver West," Cartwright said. We shook hands; he was much taller than me and had a stare that I could only describe as "mean." I noticed he had the rank of major and was part of the small contingent of Starfleet officers whose focus was infantry operations. Cartwright had brought me in because West wanted to ask me some questions about the incident on Dimorous. He seemed very familiar with my logs on the subject.

"How long do you think you could've held out?" he asked.

"Not very long," I said. "There were too many of them, and they were fearless."

"I was curious," West said, "why you didn't kill them, instead of using stun?"

"The Prime Directive," I said. "As far as I know, they were indigenous."

"Even though your lives were at stake?" West said.

"Isn't that the point?"

"So you can't imagine a situation where you'd violate the Prime Directive in order to protect the lives of Federation citizens?" West said. It felt like a trick question. Because in my mind, there was only one response.

"I think it's my duty not to," I said. West and Cartwright exchanged a look.

"Thanks for your time, Jim. I'll see you later," Cartwright said, getting up and leading me out.

I left feeling like I'd taken some kind of test and failed.

✦

"Pike is getting promoted to fleet captain," Nogura said. He had called me into his office, alone. Pike's promotion wasn't a complete surprise; our department had been discussing how his tactical knowledge of the Klingons was invaluable to Starfleet, and had to be part of overall mission planning. The revelation was what came next.

"You're receiving a promotion to full captain, and you're to assume command of the *Enterprise*," Nogura said.

"Thank you, sir," I said. I could barely get it out; I was thunderstruck.

"No need to thank me," he said. "You were on top of the promotion list. Your years on the *Hotspur* are well regarded by the Admiralty. You were assigned a dangerous area of space, completed all your missions without any loss of life." He made it sound very reasonable, but since joining the department, I had made a study of all the available command-grade officers. I was among the youngest, and there were several with years more experience than me as shipmasters.

"We are also implementing your plan to complete the *Enterprise*'s refit on Starbase 11," Nogura said.

"Sir, a conservative estimate has the components reaching Starbase 11 in ten months," I said.

"The ship should still function properly," Nogura said. "You're used to less-than-up-to-the-minute technology. Pike will bring the *Enterprise* to Earth tomorrow. We'll transfer command then. Start going over personnel; see what spots you can fill in 24 hours. I think, if my recollection's correct, you're going to need a first officer." He then stood up and shook my hand.

THE STORY OF STARFLEET'S GREATEST CAPTAIN

"Congratulations, Jim."

"Thank you, sir," I said. My head was mush; this was what I wanted, and yet I wasn't sure why at this moment I was getting it. I felt it was somehow connected to the conversation I had had with Cartwright and West the week before, but I couldn't figure out why.

Whatever doubts I had, I chose to put out of my mind. I went back to my desk, double-checked the *Enterprise*'s files to make sure the first officer position was open, and put a call in to Starfleet Personnel to requisition Gary Mitchell. His new captain wouldn't like it, but I would figure out some way to pay him back.

I then opened the rest of the personnel files and started scanning them, then decided to call my parents while I did it. I opened a call on the screen. Dad answered.

"Hey, Captain," he said. He took great pride in calling me that. "What's going on?"

"Dad," I said, "I really am a captain. I've got a ship. It's the *Enterprise*."

"Oh my god," he said. "Bob April's ship?"

"Yeah, but it hasn't been his in ten years," I said. "And anyway, it's Jim Kirk's ship now." My dad laughed, and I could see he was welling up.

"I'm so proud of you," he said. "You're 29, that's got to be some kind of record . . ." I hadn't realized it until Dad brought it up, but I did a quick record search, and he was right. I was the youngest person to receive the rank of full captain in Starfleet's history; the record, interestingly enough, had been held by Matt Decker, who achieved the rank at 31.

I'd been absently scrolling through the personnel records while we spoke, but stopped. I could see that Dad wanted to say something else to me, but I didn't know what. I felt like he needed me to either prod him or change the subject.

"Where's Mom?" I said. I chose the latter.

"She went to a conference this morning in London," he said. "She should be back a little later."

"Well, tell her the good news," I said. "I'll try to come home for a bit before I leave."

"Do what you need to; you've got a big job," he said. "Take care of yourself. I hope it's everything you want it to be."

"Thanks, Dad," I said. "I think it will be." We said goodbye and I shut off the communication. I could sense that he was proud, but there was something else, too. And then I thought about Carol and David. Dad didn't know about them specifically, but now, looking back, I think he wanted to tell me what I was giving up. He didn't know that I already knew.

I was soon distracted by all the work I had to do. I had to finish getting through the personnel records, to try to fill my open spots; I also had to see about a new uniform with the proper braid, and make any other last-minute arrangements before I shipped out. Busy with these tasks, I was happy. This was the fulfillment of my dreams. And just as I was thinking I was leaving all the struggles of my past behind, I noticed something in the personnel records that told me it wasn't going to be all that easy.

The *Enterprise*'s records officer was Ben Finney.

CHAPTER 6

"WELCOME TO THE *ENTERPRISE*, CAPTAIN," Christopher Pike said. I stepped off the transporter and shook his hand. I was struck by how tall he was, much taller than me. He greeted me with a friendly smile, and there was camaraderie about the way he said "Captain." I felt like I was joining a very exclusive club.

"I think you know our transporter operator," Pike said, and I saw a familiar face at the console.

"Mr. Scott," I said. "Need someone to carry your tool kit?" We shook hands warmly. I knew Scott had been transferred to the ship as an engineer, and I was thrilled. This was one bit of luck I would never take for granted, and I would make sure he was permanent.

"Thanks for the offer, sir," Scott said. "But I've got plenty of help here already." He gave me a weary smile. I noticed his eyes were a little bloodshot.

"Rough night?" I said.

"My going-away party," Pike said. "Come on, we've got a lot to cover."

Pike took me on a tour of the ship, giving me a rundown of the areas of the refit that weren't finished yet. It had been a while since I'd been on a *Constitution*-class ship, and its comfort was inviting. When we got to the bridge, it was twice the size of the *Hotspur*'s; it felt like a living room.

There were several familiar faces there: Lee Kelso was at navigation, Scotty had come up from the transporter room and was monitoring the engineering console. And Mr. Spock was at the science station, looking into his viewer. Pike took me over to him.

"Mr. Spock," Pike said, "this is Captain Kirk." Spock stood up from his viewer, at attention.

"We've had the pleasure. At ease," I said.

"He is," Pike said, smiling.

"Your record is very impressive, Mr. Spock," I said. "I look forward to serving with you."

"Thank you, Captain," Spock said. "Please let me know if there is any way I can be of service." It sounded as though he memorized it off a flash card. At that moment, I wasn't sure I was ever going to be completely comfortable with this guy.

Pike then continued on the tour; Scotty came with us to engineering. While down there, Pike took me over to a small hatch near the rear of the engineering section on the secondary hull. "The sensor pod?" I said. Pike nodded and opened the hatch. Inside was a plastic bubble, clear to space, crowded with various scientific instruments. One of the many scientific missions a ship has is to get radiation readings in abnormal conditions. Ion storms, quasars, etc. This can only be done by direct exposure of the necessary instruments in a plastic pod on the skin of the ship. It was particularly important if the ship was caught inside one of the phenomena; the borders and structures could change rapidly, so the sensor pod was often necessary to navigate out of it.

I climbed up inside the pod. There was only room for one person in the cramped space. But as I looked "up" it was as if I was standing on the outside of the ship; I could stare out at Earth and the various shuttles and ships in orbit. The pods were dangerous. In an ion storm, it picks up a charge of its own very quickly; since it's connected to the ship, if the charge is big enough, excess current could flow through whatever circuitry it could find, potentially blowing out vital ship's systems in the middle of an emergency. The captain has to make a determination how long to let that crewman stay in, acquiring as much information as he or she can without threatening the ship; if the crewman delays too long to get out, the captain might have to jettison the pod with the crewman still in it. On the *Hotspur*

I had a senior officer stand by at the hatch to jettison, but Pike told me he had the control moved up to his chair on the bridge.

"If someone has to die," Pike said, "I don't want anyone else to carry the burden."

As I stepped out of the pod, I saw that Pike had waved over another officer to introduce to me. I guess he didn't know we'd already met. It was Ben Finney. I politely cut off Pike's introduction by extending my hand to Finney.

"Good to see you, Ben," I said. I wasn't going to assume bad feeling. To my surprise, Ben smiled and shook my hand, albeit somewhat formally.

"Congratulations, sir," Ben said. "It's nice seeing you again."

We talked briefly about Jamie and then he excused himself to return to his post. It was difficult to tell how he was feeling about me; Ben had acted properly, was even friendly. I hoped this indicated my concern about serving with him was unfounded.

Pike and I continued on, finally ending in Pike's quarters, which it took me a minute to realize would soon be mine. I'd forgotten how much larger a captain's quarters were on a *Constitution*-class ship. I had gotten used to my stateroom on the *Hotspur*, which wasn't much more than a bed and a closet.

Pike and I sat on opposite sides of the desk and went over specific members of the crew. He had recommended Spock for my first officer, but I wasn't comfortable enough with him to give him that position. I wanted to keep him on as science officer, and asked Pike if Spock would care if someone was brought in over him.

"If he did," Pike said, "he'd rather die than let you know. He's all about the work." We then went through a few more. Pike's chief engineer was retiring, and I was determined to give Scotty that position. Mark Piper from the *Republic* had replaced Pike's chief medical officer, Philip Boyce, who died about a year before the end of Pike's mission. I could see that the loss had affected him. Pike said that the death of Boyce was the first sign that maybe he stayed in space too long. I changed the subject by congratulating Pike on the promotion, but he only laughed, somewhat derisively. I didn't realize until this moment how political promotions could be in Starfleet.

"Fleet captain is a desk job," Pike said. "They wanted me out of the way."

Decker and Pike were contemporaries and had different schools of thought about their roles as starship captains. Decker was more focused on defense and protection, while Pike saw himself as an explorer. Nogura favored Decker, who would now be in field command of all ships in the sector that bordered the Klingons if there was an incursion. Since Decker didn't like Pike, Pike felt he had played some role in getting the *Enterprise* away from him.

"I probably need a break," Pike said, although it sounded like a weak rationale. He started talking about the ship and how much it meant to him, but that the mission itself was much more trying than he ever expected. The *Constitution*-class ships were designed to operate without a net; you were really on your own. He'd lost a lot of friends during the ten years he'd been on the *Enterprise*.

"This job will rip the guts out of you," he said. "You have no choice but to lean on people. This crew will become your friends."

He took another long pause.

"And then they'll die."

We sat in silence for a long moment. I didn't quite know what to make of this advice. I'd faced the death of crewmen for my whole career, but I felt like answering would only make me appear weak, self-justifying. So I sat in silence until he was ready to move on. He then decided it was time to transfer command, and he ordered the ship's crew to report to the hangar deck.

A few minutes later, I was part of a ceremony I'd witnessed only once. Pike and I stood at a podium near the bay doors, facing the 400 faces of the crew. Spock stood by, and Pike gave him a nod.

"Attention to orders," Spock said, shouting. I'd never seen a Vulcan raise his voice; it was unnerving. But I supposed it was necessary serving aboard a starship. I stepped up to the podium, placed the tape of orders in the portable viewer that was set there, and read them.

"To Captain Christopher Pike, commander, *U.S.S. Enterprise*, you are hereby promoted to fleet captain, and requested and required to relinquish command to Captain James T. Kirk as of this date, signed Heihachiro Nogura, admiral, Starfleet Command." I then turned to Pike. "I relieve you, sir."

"I stand relieved," Pike said. We shook hands, and I turned and took in the faces; a familiar few: Scotty, Kelso, Mark Piper from the *Republic*, Uhura. But they were quickly lost in an ocean of strangers. I had never taken over a ship like this before; I had been serving on the *Hotspur* when I was given command, so I had already been working with everyone on that ship, and there had been no need for a ceremony. Now, I could see a lot of the crew members weren't looking at me; they looked at Pike. It was easy to read affection and admiration in their expressions.

I was envious; it was ridiculous for me to expect anything from these people. It would be the hardest job in my life to win them over, since being a good captain meant doing nothing that was designed to win them over. I had to count on them to do their jobs, and do my best to protect their lives, which, despite what Pike had said, meant I couldn't let anyone be my friend. Thrust into command of the *Hotspur*, I had felt alone, but not quite as alone as this.

And then I saw an unexpected face in the crowd. Gary Mitchell was in the back; he must have just come aboard, his duffel still over his shoulder. He gave me a conspiratorial grin and nodded. I smiled.

"All standing orders to remain in force until further notice," I said. "Crew dismissed." Captain Pike came over one last time and shook my hand.

"Hope to see you again," he said. "Good luck."

"To you too," I said.

I went back to the cabin, which only a little while ago had been Pike's. Now everything of his was gone; my clothing had arrived and had been magically put away. I decided to start going through the ship's status reports, which took me late into the evening, and fell asleep.

The next morning, I woke early, dressed, and left my cabin. As I walked along the corridors I received friendly but reserved hellos from the crew I passed. I reached the turbolift and noticed a lieutenant, who was obviously heading toward it, make a last-minute decision to turn in the other direction and take a ladder; whoever he was, he wasn't comfortable riding with his new captain. I didn't mind; I think I liked the fact that he was nervous.

I rode the lift alone and stepped out onto the bridge. The viewscreen was off; the night shift was still on duty. To my right, Uhura was at communications.

"Nice to see you again, Ensign," I said. "Have the department heads report to me on the bridge as soon as they come on duty."

"Yes sir," she said. "Oh, and congratulations." I smiled as I headed to the command chair, where Spock sat in command. He worked the night shift, Pike had told me, by his own request, as well as his day shift as science officer.

"You're relieved, Mr. Spock."

"You are 15 minutes and 44.3 seconds early for your shift, Captain," he said, as he got out of the chair.

"Captain's prerogative," I said. I sat down in the chair. It was a lot more comfortable than the one on the *Hotspur*. I took in the bridge, simultaneously busy and quiet. My nervousness was fading. I was now eager to get under way. I was lost in my reverie and didn't notice a zealous ensign in his twenties approach my chair. I was a little startled when he was suddenly standing beside it.

"Ensign Morgan Bateson reporting for duty," he said. I nodded. I had no idea who this kid was and what he was waiting for.

"Very well, Ensign," I said, "assume your post."

He looked at me, confused.

"Um, Captain Pike liked to have me on the bridge," he said. "If you prefer me to wait somewhere else . . ." I had no idea what he was talking about, and I guess he could tell from my expression.

"Sir," he said, in a low voice, "I'm your yeoman." I felt like an idiot, and somehow had forgotten that captains had yeomen; there wasn't room for that kind of luxury aboard the *Hotspur*. He must have been the one who magically put away all my clothes. I asked him for the morning status reports and a cup of coffee. He seemed pleased to be given something to do, and was off.

A few moments later, as I drank my coffee and scanned the reports, the day shift came onto the bridge. I caught the glances of a few officers who were somewhat worried that I made it there ahead of them. Lieutenant

Lloyd Alden relieved Uhura at communications; Gary took over the helm position and was joined by Kelso at navigation. After a few minutes, the department heads had gathered behind me.

Dr. Piper, chief medical officer, and Hikaru Sulu, the head of astrosciences, whom I had not met yet, stood with Scotty, who leaned forward as I joined them.

"Just want to thank you, sir," Scotty said. He'd gotten his official promotion to chief engineer. "I won't let you down."

"I'm sure you won't," I said. I then turned to the others and we had an impromptu conference. They all reported the status of their departments, and that they were ready for departure. I ordered communications to get clearance from the dockmaster for departure, and had Kelso plot a course for our patrol sector. Once we had clearance, I stepped back to my chair.

"Mr. Mitchell," I said, "take us out."

"Aye, sir." Gary keyed the console, and I watched the viewscreen as Earth quickly fell away.

As I think back on that moment, Pike's last advice would prove to be correct: everybody on that bridge would change or die. And I'd have the guts ripped out of me, a lot sooner than I could've imagined.

✦

"We're leaving the Galaxy, Mr. Mitchell. Ahead warp factor one," I said.

The *Enterprise* sat motionless, less than five light-minutes from the Galaxy's "edge." On my order, Gary keyed the controls, and I heard the now familiar rumble of the ship's engines. I'd been in the command chair of the *Enterprise* for almost two years and had done nothing of note. I had underestimated the *Enterprise*'s need for a refit, and rather than risk the crew in an unreliable vessel, we spent most of our time waiting at Starbase 11 for the parts to arrive. Unfortunately, the wrong nacelle domes were delivered, and parts for the new internal communications system were somehow left off the manifest, so we would have to go back at some point. I then had a shakedown cruise that lasted another month. We finally began our patrol of the Earth colonies and starbases in the sector, over a year after we left Earth.

Despite the delays, my plan to refit the *Enterprise* seemed to have the desired effect; there wasn't a peep out of the Klingons, and in fact they'd agreed to negotiation regarding the disputed area between their territory and the Federation. Everything was peaceful enough that Starfleet gave us a mission of pure research, and all the scientists on board were as excited as I was. A true history-making venture; even if we discovered nothing, that too would be memorable. But that had changed just a few moments before.

We'd found an old-style ship recorder from the *S.S. Valiant*, a 200-year-old ship that had somehow also reached this far. The burnt-out tapes indicated the ship had encountered a "magnetic space storm"* that had thrown them out of the Galaxy, and in returning they'd encountered some unknown force that had caused the captain to order the destruction of his own ship.

Now, suddenly, our mission of pure research had a hint of danger. We were studying an area of space no one had ever been to before, and I was reminded that my responsibility included determining whether it was safe for future travel.

Suddenly, on the viewscreen ahead, a violent, crimson barrier appeared.

"Force field of some kind," Spock said. A force field? *There's a force field around the Galaxy?* It made no scientific sense.**

"Deflectors say there's something there, sensors say there isn't," Spock said. "Density, negative. Radiation, negative. Energy . . . negative." I looked over Kelso's shoulder and saw that our deflector screens were reading the wall of negative energy in infinite directions. There was no way around it. It literally surrounded the Galaxy, and we were heading right for it. This must have been the unknown force the *Valiant* encountered.

I watched the viewscreen as the force field grew, blocking out the rest of space. Just as I silently questioned whether our deflector shield would protect us from it, surges of energy went through the ship's instruments.

---

*EDITOR'S NOTE: It has been a generally accepted theory that the "magnetic space storm" the *Valiant* encountered was in fact an unstable wormhole that the scientists on the ship were unfamiliar with.

**To this day, there is no widely accepted scientific explanation for the origin of the field of negative energy that completely surrounds the Galaxy.

Control panels all over the bridge shorted out and exploded. Kelso frantically tried to fan out the smoke. We weren't going to make it through this thing. I ordered the helmsman, Gary, to turn us around.

But as Gary keyed the controls, his body suddenly flared with a torrent of energy. He fell to the deck. Spock took over the helm, navigating us out of that strange barrier.

Our engines were burnt out, and nine of my crew had been killed. I went over to Gary. He was okay. I was relieved, until I saw his eyes: they were silver orbs. Gary had been changed.

✦

About a week later, we were in orbit of Delta Vega. It had taken several days to get here without warp engines, and we then spent a few more days while the very talented engineering staff repaired the ship using components from an automated station on the planet's surface. We were finally ready to leave orbit. In that time, we'd lost three more crewmen. One of them was Gary Mitchell.

And I killed him.

It's hard to explain what happened, the series of events that led me to take the life of my first officer and best friend. That barrier at the edge of the Galaxy imbued Gary with a kind of almost magical power, giving him telepathy and telekinesis. As the ship moved away from the barrier, the powers grew, and as they did, Gary lost touch with the person he had been. He started using his abilities to adjust controls throughout the ship. He was making it very clear he could take over whenever he wanted. Spock was the only member of the crew trying to get me to face the truth that Gary would eventually destroy us without giving it a second thought.

"Kill Mitchell while you still can," he said to me.

I didn't want to hear it, so rather than kill him, I brought the ship to Delta Vega and had Gary imprisoned on the planet. My intention was to leave him there. But Gary was able to escape.

And then he killed Lee Kelso.

Kelso had been a good friend of Gary's, and Gary had killed him without blinking. Spock was right; I realized that this was a problem I couldn't just leave behind. It was impossible to know how powerful Gary would become. He had to be stopped.

I pursued Gary into the wilderness of Delta Vega. I didn't stand a chance against him. Either I got lucky or he was just too overconfident. He slipped, and I phasered a giant boulder that crushed him.

It was the first person I'd killed face-to-face. I never saw the faces of the beings who lost their lives battling me ship-to-ship. This face, Gary's face, is one I still see every day. He had been looking after me for almost ten years, and in a few short days he was turned into some kind of monster. Yet in my nightmares about that day I still see the face of the man who was my friend.

On the bridge, about to leave orbit, I recorded in my log that Gary had died in the line of duty. I noticed Spock listening in.

"He didn't ask for what happened to him," I said. Spock decided at that moment to surprise me.

"I felt for him too," he said. I didn't know what to make of that. Spock had never openly revealed an emotional side. But in that moment of despair, of loss, of losing the best friend I'd ever had, his decision to show me empathy was one I wouldn't forget.

"There may be hope for you yet, Mr. Spock," I said. It was probably the first time I'd smiled in a month.

✦

Though we'd been able to repair the warp drive on Delta Vega, the ship had still suffered extensive damage. We had to return to Starbase 11 for repairs. The final components for the refit had arrived by then, so the refit could finally be completed. It would also allow the crew a little time to recover from what we'd been through, and I could try to replace the people we'd lost. But in our damaged state, it would still take three weeks to get there.

A few days after Gary's death, I was sitting on the bridge, lost in thought, when Lieutenant Hong came off the turbolift and approached me.

"I'm sorry, sir," she said. "I know this has been a difficult period, but may I have a moment of your time, in private?" I nodded and led her off the bridge and to a conference room on Deck 5. She got right down to business.

Kirk's graduation photo from the academy yearbook.

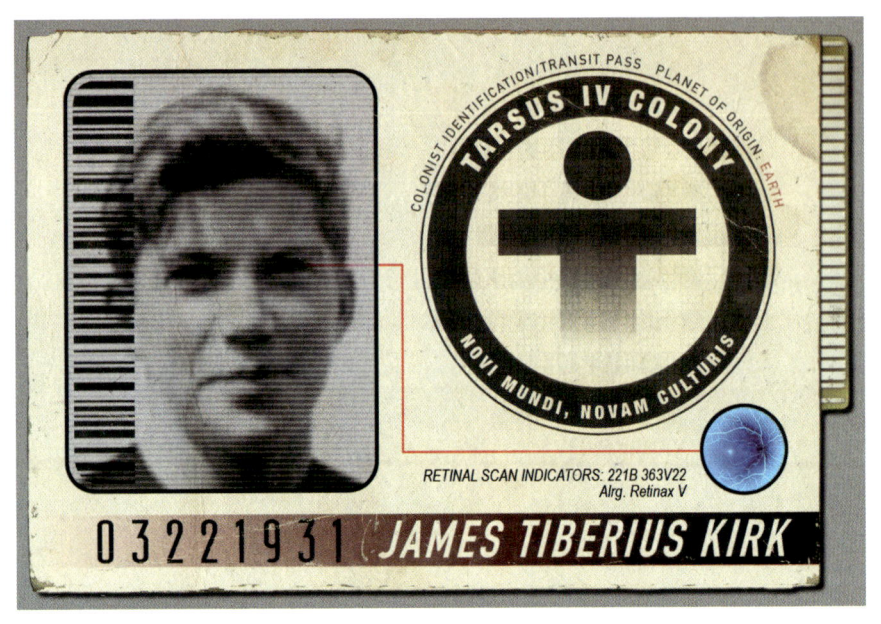

The travel pass issued to young Kirk for his journey to Tarsus IV.

James Kirk with his friend Gary Mitchell taken aboard the *U.S.S. Hotspur*.

STARFLEET ACADEMY

Be it known that *Cadet James Tiberius Kirk*
of the *Planet Earth*
having been carefully examined on all the Branches of the
Arts, Sciences, History, Literature and Engineering
taught at Starfleet Academy
has been judged worthy to graduate
with the rank of

ENSIGN

In testimony of and by virtue of authority vested in the
Academic Board
We confer upon him this rank.
This day,
The Eighteenth Day of June
Twenty-Two Hundred & Fifty-Four

Richard Barnett
─────────────────────────────
Admiral, Chairman Academic Board of Starfleet Academy

Kirk's diploma from Starfleet Academy.

Kirk, Spock, and Yeoman Janice Rand taken around 2266.

A painting from the Starfleet Museum that commemorates the meeting of James Kirk and Christopher Pike. (The illustration favors Kirk; in reality, Pike was several inches taller.)

Photos and artifacts from Kirk's journey to the 1930s found among his belongings after his death. Edith Keeler is seen in the photo strip, a common souvenir in 20th-century Earth.

Dear David,

How are you? I'm sorry I haven't ~~written to you in a long~~ written until now, but I'm always thinking about you. If you get this letter and want to write back, I would love to hear from you. Tell me about where you live. Do you have a lot of friends? Where do you go to school? Do you like your teachers? Do you read a lot? I hope so — I read a lot when I was your age.

~~I don't know how much your mom has told you about me, but~~ I wanted to tell you a little bit about me and my work. I'm a starship captain. That means I'm in charge of a ship with a lot of people on it. I think it's a pretty important job, and I'm very proud ~~and lucky~~ that I ~~have it~~ earned it. The ship is called the Enterprise, and it's part of Starfleet. Its job is to protect the people of the Federation, explore new planets and meet new people. Sometimes it's dangerous, but most of the time people are happy to meet me.

Yesterday I visited a planet where everybody acted like a gangster from ancient Earth. It was very strange because they weren't play acting. I met a little boy on that planet who was probably around your age. He helped me with my mission, and we had to pretend for a minute that I was his father. It made me think of you.

I hope I can see you one day soon, ask your mother if you can come visit me on my ship.

Hope to be in touch with you soon!

~~Love~~ Best

~~Love Dad~~ ~~your father,~~ ~~Dad~~ Jim

This handwritten draft of a message to his son David, whom he had not met, was among Kirk's effects. From the events described, it's estimated to have been written in 2268 when David Marcus was around seven. It appears the message was never sent.

Dr. Carol Marcus and her son David, at age two.

Kirk, Spock, and Dr. Leonard McCoy on a camping trip to Yosemite National Park in 2287.

Kirk and Spock during Kirk's first year as commander of the *U.S.S. Enterprise*.

THE STORY OF STARFLEET'S GREATEST CAPTAIN

"I'm sorry to bother you with this, sir," Lieutenant Hong said, "but we have to fill three positions immediately." Lieutenant Hong was the ship's personnel officer; one of her jobs was to make sure any open spots in the duty roster were filled appropriately, so as to prevent extra strain falling on any particular crewman. Given the deaths we'd had recently, this was a difficult subject to bring up, but necessary for her job. She put a tape in the slot and a list of available crewmen appeared on the viewscreen.

"There are three positions that need your immediate attention. We need a new chief navigator," she said.

"Bailey was on beta shift," I said. "Put him on alpha shift." Bailey was a competent young officer, a few years out of the academy. He'd served a few shifts with me on the bridge; he was a little eager to please, but he knew the job.

"Sir, Ensign Bailey is only two years out of the academy. Usually chief navigators have a minimum of four years shipboard service."

"He'll be fine. I'd been planning on promoting him," I said. It wasn't true; I was making a rash decision, I admit, partially because I found the process and Hong's officiousness at that moment annoying, and wanted to get it over with.

"Very well, sir. We also . . . need a new helmsman," she said. I could see that Hong had tears in her eyes. Gary as first officer had dealt with all the personnel issues; I'd seen him joke and flirt with Hong, as he did with most women. This was a loss for her too. I decided to cut her a little slack.

"What about Alden?" Alden was communications, but we had other officers qualified in that department, and Alden had often served as a helmsman when needed. Good, qualified officer.

"Mr. Alden has requested not to be considered for the position," she said. That was strange; I would have to look into it, but I wasn't going to assign Alden to a vital position if he didn't want it. Hong continued to scan through the files.

"Mr. Sulu has actually a lot of experience from his last assignment."

"Okay, I'll talk to him," I said. "And the third position?"

"First officer," she said. Gary again. Replacing the helmsman was one thing; a difficult job, but one that could be executed by someone with the proper training. First officer was something else; it was the person who took command when I wasn't available, whose advice I relied on the most. There wasn't anyone in the crew I had as much faith in as Gary.

"Who's next in line?" Since it was only three weeks to get to Starbase 11, maybe I could let whoever had the highest rank have the job, at least until then.

"Let's see . . ." she said, looking over the list. "Lieutenant Commander Benjamin Finney."

"No," I said, a little too quickly. I felt terrible, but that would never work. Finney, it turned out, still hated me. Gary had told me a few weeks before that he'd had a bit of a row with him when he'd heard Finney complaining to a few dinner companions that I had ruined his career, that I was holding him back. (Gary didn't specifically tell me what he'd done to get Finney to shut up, but I imagine it was more than just a stern talking-to.) Finney, early on, had requested transfer, but there were no open spots on other *Constitution*-class ships, and he didn't want a lesser class so he stayed on the *Enterprise*. And now, his one opportunity to move up, and I *was* holding him back.

No, I thought, it was his own fault; his attitude with me had affected my opinion of him. But I had to be careful; I couldn't pick someone obviously less qualified. Finney could complain about me, but I couldn't give the rest of the crew a reason to give his criticism legitimacy. And then I realized the answer was right in front of me.

"Spock," I said. "I'll give it to Spock." It made perfect sense; Spock was already a bridge officer, which, although not a requirement, was at least efficient. Pike had recommended him for the job; a lot of the crew would know that. They maybe weren't friends with him, but everybody respected him. Especially me; I'd just been through one of the toughest series of decisions I'd faced as a captain, and Spock's advice was correct at every stage. I was so lost in the satisfaction of my choice, I hadn't noticed Hong's expression. She didn't look happy.

"Yes sir," she said. "And I assume you would like me to continue regular personnel meetings with Mr. Spock, as I did with Mr. Mitchell?" There was a little subtext to her question, and I understood. Spock was not an easy person to deal with; his Vulcan demeanor could be very off-putting, if not a little scary. And he certainly wasn't going to try to make her laugh.

"Yes, Lieutenant," I said. We all had our assigned duties.

THE STORY OF STARFLEET'S GREATEST CAPTAIN

✦

"We've entered standard orbit," Sulu said, as the familiar image of Starbase 11 spun on our forward viewscreen. He, at least, was pleased to get the job of helmsman. When I spoke to him, he thought I was going to fire him; most ships needed a department head for astrosciences, but not the *Enterprise*. Spock, as science officer, was more than capable of handling that job as well, and Sulu had felt extraneous. He had ambition to command, and being a bridge officer was the faster route.

Spock had shown no emotion when he got the news that he was first officer. He said only that he would "endeavor to fulfill the job requirements satisfactorily." And Bailey was doing fine as navigator. Those positions were filled, but by the time we got to Starbase 11, there were two more openings.

Alden, my communications officer, was leaving the ship. He wasn't sleeping or eating, and Dr. Piper determined that he was suffering from a stress disorder caused by trauma. Gary had relieved him on the helm about ten minutes before we'd gone through the barrier. Piper thought that Alden somehow blamed himself for what happened to Gary, that if he'd stayed at the helm, it would've been him who'd been changed, even though there was no basis for believing that. I approved Piper's recommendation to give Alden a medical rest leave. It was a loss, but Uhura had already been filling a lot of Alden's shifts, and it was reasonable to promote her to the position. Alden's leave wasn't the only bad news Piper was going to give me.

"Jim, I've decided it's time to retire," he said. Piper was a veteran, which is what made him valuable in one sense, but was often at a disadvantage when dealing with the unknown. He said the experience with Gary had hit him hard; he had been focused on the physical health of his patient, but had offered no prognosis on his mental health. I'm not sure that any of us could've changed the outcome, but Piper especially felt that the situation had gotten away from him. I wished him the best, and felt a little bad about how quickly I moved to get his replacement.

As luck would have it, McCoy wasn't far away; he'd been posted to a planet, Capella IV. It was a primitive society that was, however, aware of the Federation. As such, under the Federation Charter, Starfleet was permitted to provide limited aid. McCoy had been stationed there to offer medical assistance. It wasn't long before I was facing his crabby expression on my viewscreen.

"I'll take it," he said. I laughed.

"I haven't offered anything yet," I said.

"I don't care. The Capellans are warriors, have very little technology, and even less medicine. They think the sick should die. They want nothing to do with doctors. So if you can get me out of here, I'll happily clean bedpans."

I was able to extricate McCoy from Capella, and he would end up joining us well before the refit was finished. I was thrilled; McCoy felt like a security blanket. Though I neglected to tell him that my new first officer was the Vulcan we had shared a ride to Earth with several years before. I knew he wouldn't like it, which is why I brought Spock with me to greet McCoy when he arrived on Starbase 11. Upon being reintroduced, McCoy turned to me and said:

"I should've stayed on Capella."

I laughed and took them both to a cafe on the base. I noticed in the same restaurant Ben Finney was sitting with a woman who I first took to be his wife, Naomi. I got up excitedly to go say hello to her, but as I approached, I realized the woman was far too young. I was a few feet away when she looked up at me and smiled in recognition.

"Uncle Jim!" She stood and hugged me.

"My god, Jamie," I said, "I didn't recognize you." I noticed that Ben had stood up too. He wore a smile that felt false and forced. I kept my focus on her. "What are you doing here? Shouldn't you be in school?"

"I graduated early," she said. "I'm taking a year off before I go to college. Dad arranged a job for me here so we could be a little closer." There was too much for me to process.

"You must be very proud of her," I said to Ben.

"Yes, Captain," he said, a little too formally. Jamie picked up on the awkwardness.

"I'm lucky the *Enterprise* is here for so long," she said. "I don't think Dad and I have had this much time together since he was at the academy."

"Well, I'll let you get back to your meal," I said. "It was great seeing you, Jamie." Upon saying her name, I could see Ben scowl; it hurt him that he'd named her after me. As I walked back to join Spock and McCoy, I realized that this was still an open wound.

✦

"The imposter's back where he belongs. Let's forget him," I said. But I couldn't forget him. He was back inside me, and I had all his memories. And they were monstrous. And I was beginning to understand what Pike had been talking about.

I'd been the victim of a transporter accident and been split into two people. But these weren't two evenly split halves. I had never ascribed human intelligence to a machine before, but I couldn't help but feel that the transporter itself decided to have some "fun" with the idea of good and evil. To use Freudian terminology, one half got both the id and the ego; he was brutal, savage, but also clever and resourceful. The other half had the morality, the superego. They were both me, and neither could live without the other.

We'd managed to keep what happened to me from most of the ship's population; Spock rightly pointed out that if the crew saw me as this vulnerable and human, I'd lose the almost inpenetrable image of perfection that allowed a captain to command. We just referred to the savage half as "the imposter," implying that some human or alien had taken on my form. The crew was familiar with the legend of the shape-shifting Chameloids, and now many believed they'd met one. But he was not an imposter. He was a part of myself.

Scotty and Spock had repaired the transporter, and my two halves were thrust back together. I was in command again, walking to my chair, when Yeoman Rand intercepted me.

My old yeoman, Bateson, had been promoted and transferred, and I hadn't been happy when I'd been assigned an attractive female yeoman; McCoy joked that I didn't trust myself. He was right; she was a compelling distraction. But whatever my personal attraction to her, I knew there was no hope for us; I was her commanding officer, and when one person wields that much power professionally over the other, it can't lead to a real relationship.

But my savage half had no need to abide by this wisdom, or show Janice any respect. He tried to use the power of his position, and when she refused, he'd assaulted her, or tried to. And his memories were now mine. As I stood looking at her, I remembered what he, or rather, what I, had done to her; her screams, struggling in my grip. I was nauseous, angry. I wanted to go back in time and stop that monster, but I was the monster.

"Sir, the imposter told me what happened," Rand said, quietly. I remember him telling her that I'd been split in half. She knew he *wasn't* an imposter. She knew.

"I just want to say..." she said. "Well, I just want you to know..." She didn't know what to say, but she wanted to make me feel better. I realized that she thought she understood, but she'd gotten it wrong; she thought the transporter *made* an evil Kirk. She really didn't understand that the evil Kirk was always there in me. It was making me feel worse; I could barely look at her. But I smiled.

"Thank you, Yeoman." I went to my command chair. I would try to face it, to accept it, but it was impossible.

✦

"Lieutenant Robert Tomlinson and Ensign Angela Martine have requested a marriage ceremony," Spock said, "and they would like you to perform it." I laughed reflexively, then remembered Spock wouldn't come all the way to my quarters to do a comedic bit. Once I realized he was serious, I had a different response.

"How wonderful," I said, unable to control my sarcasm. I suppose I should've been touched, but for reasons I couldn't quite identify, I found the whole thing annoying.

"We will have to schedule a time. Also, Ensign Martine is a Catholic," Spock said, "and she wishes to have the ceremony reflect the traditions of that religion." I knew nothing about the practices of ancient Earth religions.

"How different is Catholic than Christian?"

"They both come from the same root religion, but there are specific details of the wedding service—"

"Never mind," I said. "Just have somebody write up what I'm supposed to say, and I'll say it." Tomlinson was currently the officer in charge of weapons control, and Martine was doing a tour in that department. I had specifically recruited Martine less than two years before; she graduated second in her class at the academy, had a wide range of specialties. I saw a lot of potential for her as a member of my crew. I didn't initially understand why I had such a negative reaction to the idea of the two of them getting married, but I was silently determined to put a stop to it. "Have them report to me, immediately."

"Yes sir," Spock said, and left. A few minutes later, the door chime sounded, and Tomlinson and Martine came in. I had them sit opposite me on the other side of my desk. Tomlinson was boyish, friendly, and in my estimation wasn't Martine's equal. I wanted to talk them out of this.

"So, first, congratulations," I said.

"Thank you, sir," they both said, unintentionally in unison. Then they looked at each other and giggled.

"This is a big step. How long have you two . . ." I let the implication hang in the air for a moment. Tomlinson jumped right in.

"Not very long, sir," he said. "I've strictly obeyed the rules regarding fraternization with subordinates."

"Then forgive me, how do you know you want to get married?" It was a harsh thing to say, and Tomlinson wasn't ready for it. He looked like I'd just killed his pet dog.

"We're in love, sir," Martine said.

"You have no doubts," I said. "Because you will have to make sacrifices."

"That is what love is about," she said. And as a show of solidarity and love, she took Tomlinson's hand.

And I felt like a fool. What was I trying to do? Break up a couple, because I was unconvinced of their love? I looked at these two young people and remembered the intensity of affection and desire. I realized I was jealous; I was envious that they'd found each other.

"Yes," I said, chastised, "that is what love is about." I took a pause, then added that I was honored to perform the service. As they thanked me and left my quarters, hand in hand, these two people reminded me of my parents. They bore no physical resemblance, but something about their feeling for each other evoked Mom and Dad.

Six days later, the wedding ceremony was interrupted by the Romulans.

A hundred years before, Earth engaged in a war with the enigmatic species. It was a war fought in space, on ships; no ground troops, no captives, against an enemy we never met face-to-face. The peace treaty was negotiated by subspace radio. Earth had defeated the Romulans and put them behind a Neutral Zone, cut off from the rest of the Galaxy. Outposts constructed on asteroids monitored the border, making sure the Romulans never crossed it. For a century we'd heard nothing from them, and then they came across with two new weapons: a working invisibility cloak for their ship and a catasrophically destructive plasma weapon, which they used to destroy our outposts. They were testing our resolve, looking for an easy victim. We'd engage them, and along the way, would discover a secret that would affect politics in the quadrant for decades to come.

"I believe I can get a look at their bridge," Spock said, early on in our engagement with the invisible ship. He had intercepted a communication and was using his creative technical wizardry to follow the transmission back to its source. On our viewscreen, we got a look at the cramped control room of the Romulan ship and the face of its commander.

Pointed ears, slanted eyebrows, he could've been Spock's father.

It was a revelation: the Vulcans and the Romulans were the same species—the Romulans an offshoot, a lost colony. It was fascinating to think about; when the war with the Romulans occurred, we had only known the Vulcans for a few decades. Would Earthmen and Vulcans been able to form a lasting friendship if this connection were known? It made me think that perhaps if it had been known, Starfleet Command might have kept it a secret all this time because of the negative connotations the war had for so many on Earth.*

I didn't think it would matter a century later, though I was quickly proven wrong. My navigator, Lieutenant Stiles, whose ancestors had fought

---

***EDITOR'S NOTE:** Captain Kirk's instincts were correct. Shortly before publication of this work, Starfleet declassified a trove of documents from the Romulan War revealing, for the first time, that Starfleet Command and the leaders of Earth were aware of the Vulcan-Romulan connection during the war and kept it a secret to protect the Vulcan-Earth relationship.

in that war, immediately decided upon seeing the Romulans that Spock was a spy.

I wasn't having a lot of luck with navigators. Bailey had left after it became clear he wasn't ready for the position. I'd tried a few others who weren't up to snuff, and now here was Stiles, who showed the terrible judgment to openly insult his superior officer based on his looks. To Spock's credit, he didn't let it affect him. Or at least he said it didn't. But I wasn't going to have it; it was ridiculous, raw, and obvious bigotry, and as soon as I could replace Stiles, I would. But not in the middle of a crisis.

I was facing an invisible ship with a weapon that could pulverize large asteroids. I had to make sure the ship didn't get home, or we'd be facing an all-out war. But I couldn't cross the border without also risking a war that could be blamed on us. The *Enterprise* and the Romulan ship played a game of cat-and-mouse for hours. The commander of the enemy craft was clever, but his ship wasn't the juggernaut it pretended to be; we learned that its power was drained by its invisibility field, and its weapon had a limited range. The *Enterprise* could beat it: we could outrun its weapon. But during the engagement I'd failed to stop them before they returned to their space; they'd made it to the other side of the border, a border I'd been ordered not to cross. I had to draw them back.

I decided on a risky strategy. We'd suffered damage at the hands of the enemy ship, so it wasn't difficult to appear vulnerable. And though they'd made it into the Neutral Zone, I gambled that they wouldn't resist the opportunity to finish us off. So I ordered us to play dead.

If they fell for it, we'd have little time to fire. They couldn't fire their weapon while they were invisible, and we couldn't fire until we could see them. I had to make sure we fired before they got off a shot. As a precaution I sent Stiles to help Tomlinson, who was manning the forward phaser control room by himself.

I sat looking at the viewscreen, waiting for the ship to appear. My shields were down, engine power at minimum. If that ship fired first, we wouldn't be able to escape their plasma weapon. As I waited, I thought about the *Enterprise* and its 400 crewmen. They could all be dead in a moment, and it would be my fault. The seconds passed, and I became less sure of myself. I had a last-minute thought that maybe I should power up and warp away. That was the safer course. I was about to give that order when Sulu spoke up.

"Enemy vessel becoming visible," he said. I was committed. I told the phaser control room to fire.

And nothing happened.

The enemy ship was getting closer. For some reason, Stiles and Tomlinson weren't following my orders. I tamped down my panic, keyed in the public address system, and shouted for Stiles to fire. No response.

I looked up at the Romulan ship. It was so close now. I had the thought that I'd killed us all.

And then the phasers fired; the Romulan was hit.

What I didn't know at the time was there had been an accident in the phaser control room, reactor coolant was leaking in and suffocating Stiles and Tomlinson. Fortunately, Spock was nearby, went into the control room, and fired the phasers. He then pulled Stiles out in time to save his life. I'd always thought Spock might have been overcompensating by choosing to get Stiles first. His choice had further ramifications.

Because Spock chose Stiles first, Tomlison died.

I later found Angela Martine in the chapel, praying. It was surprising to me that in this day and age people still found comfort from this. But I was in no position to criticize how this woman chose to grieve. She turned and saw me, then came to embrace me.

"It never makes any sense," I said. "But you have to know there was a reason." This seemed empty; to appeal to her patriotism, her service, but I really didn't know what to say. Neither did she, and she soon left me alone in the chapel.

I looked up at the podium. I thought of the traditions of so many religions, where clergy, preaching from a similar podium, would offer comfort, protection, or motivation. And those clergy were required to sacrifice their personal lives to provide that comfort and motivation. They could help others achieve happiness and contentment, and the clergy's only reward was that service. There was really no rest for them.

I understood that job. I left the room and got back to work.

THE STORY OF STARFLEET'S GREATEST CAPTAIN

✦

"We have a request from Dr. Tom Leighton that we divert to Planet Q," Spock said, at our morning meeting. "He reports it's urgent."

I hadn't seen Tom since his wedding, five years before. He had grown into the image of his father, a bear of a man, but without the light touch. He still carried the burden of what had happened on Tarsus IV, even into adulthood. It had influenced his career path; he became an astroagricultural scientist, specifically devoting himself to the development of synthetic foods for Earth colonies. And he still wore the patch on half his face. But his career success and his marriage to a lovely, supportive woman had softened him somewhat. The wedding had been celebratory, and I saw some hope for happiness for my old friend.

"Planet Q is three light-years off our course," I said.

"He reports he has discovered the formula for a synthetic food that could avert famine on Cygnia Minor," Spock said.

This was a strange coincidence. Cygnia Minor was an Earth colony whose population growth had gone unchecked, and its arable land had been diminished because of uncontrolled development. It was off the major shipping routes, so a food crisis could develop there quickly, though it hadn't yet; Starfleet and Federation colonies had been placed on alert to the situation less than a month before. The fact that Leighton already had a solution to the problem was unbelievable. But I had to follow it up.

"Inform Starfleet Command, and set course for Planet Q," I said, and Spock left. I was always a little ambivalent about seeing Tom; it brought up a lot of memories that I'd pushed away, but I also felt a kinship and a responsibility to him.

When we arrived at the planet, I received a message for me to meet him at a theater in the capital city of Yu. I didn't know what to make of it, but I beamed down. The city was modern and sprawling, with a large distinctive arch at the city's entrance. I found my way to the theater, shaped like a giant silver chicken egg that lay on its side. There was a ticket waiting for me at the box office, and I went inside.

On the stage, the Acturian version of Shakespeare's *Macbeth* was being performed. As I found my way to the empty seat, I gathered I'd missed a good portion of it, as Macbeth was already about to kill King Duncan.

Tom was already there, sitting in the seat next to me. He did not give me a warm greeting; he was concentrating on the stage. This whole thing seemed very strange. I was here to get a food synthetic, but he was going to make me sit through a three-hour play.

And then he told me to pay attention to the voice of the actor playing Macbeth.

"That's Kodos the Executioner," he said, his voice intense and angry. I was baffled. Was he saying Macbeth reminded him of Kodos? I looked at the actor. It had been almost a quarter century, and the man playing the part did bear a small resemblance. But it was unbelievable that Tom thought it actually *was* him. I started to think Tom brought me here under false pretenses.

At the intermission, I told Tom I didn't have time to sit through a play. He took me back to his home where he told me the truth. There was no food synthetic; he had made it up to get me to Planet Q. Tom had seen this actor, Anton Karidian, and was sure he was Kodos. It made no sense. His theory was Governor Kodos had escaped death and was now traveling around the Galaxy acting in plays? My old friend, who I'd been through so much with, sounded insane.

Until Tom ended up dead. Murdered.

✦

"Are you Kodos?" I was a few feet from Anton Karidian. He did evoke Kodos in some way. But my memory still wasn't clear. I had only seen him the one time; he had towered over me, and I had been scared, in shock, crying. I didn't fully remember what he looked like. But Tom was dead, and Tom had been sure.

"Do you believe that I am?" he said. I said that I did, but I still wasn't sure. Circumstantial evidence had piled up. Karidian's history began almost to the day that Kodos's ended. And there had been deaths, seven people, all of whom had seen Kodos and knew what he looked like, each of whom died just when the Karidian players were nearby.

But I still wasn't sure.

If this was Kodos, I thought, what a monster; what an ego. He killed thousands of people, escaped punishment, but rather than going into hiding, he *performs on a stage*; his need for attention outweighed all other considerations.

Tom had been murdered after telling me he was sure Karidian was Kodos. I'd found him, stabbed to death out near his home. I'd felt guilty for not believing him immediately, and I had become obsessed. I engineered the situation so Karidian and his players would travel on the *Enterprise*. I was going to find out if Tom was right, and if this was his killer, and his parents' killer, and the killer of all those people I'd known as a child, I would have my revenge.

It was all coming back, the horror of Tarsus, of that night. I was confronted again with my helplessness in the face of evil.

So I became evil, and I went after Karidian in what I thought must be a weak spot.

I tried to seduce his 19-year-old daughter, Lenore.

She was lovely, smart, and she seemed easily dazzled by me. We had long walks together, both on Planet Q and then the ship. We talked about acting, Shakespeare, commanding a ship, her life in the space lanes. One night aboard the ship, I took her to the softly lit observation deck and kissed her. And then I took her back to my quarters.

She was lonely, as I was, and I began to feel guilty, because I felt a real connection to her. But my whole purpose had been to shake her father's identity from the shadows. She was of no help. She told me she'd never known her mother, who died in childbirth, so her father had been everything.

"He is a great man," she said that night we were together in my cabin. "He has given me so much, I'll never be able to repay him for this wonderful life and career he's given me." Though she was an adult, she was also a child, and I was trying to take away her only parent, as Tom's parents had been taken away. I decided I had to challenge him directly and leave this poor girl out of it.

So I went to see him in his quarters, and made him read the speech he gave when he killed all those people. I had written it out from memory, and made him record it.

"The revolution is successful . . ." I always remembered that phrase. He'd said it back then with confidence, with arrogance, as if the crazed rationale for killing all those people was somehow a cause. Now, an older man said it wearily, with some bitterness. He got through the whole speech.

I still didn't know.

✦

"I know how to use this, Captain," Lenore said, aiming a phaser at me.

She was an actress, and she had been acting, pretending to be enthralled by me. She was the one who had killed Tom, along with the six other people. The whole time, she wanted me dead, because I was one of the people who she thought could hurt her father. It was ironic that she wanted to kill me, because I still couldn't remember. I had to be told by Karidian that he was Kodos. I was a fool, almost as big a fool as Karidian, the narcissist, who didn't realize how he had damaged his daughter until it was far too late.

We were standing on the set of *Hamlet* in the *Enterprise*'s theater, where the Karidian players had been performing. Lenore raised the weapon and pulled the trigger.

And her father stepped in front of it, saving my life. It was again his own vanity that led him to do it. He'd destroyed so many lives, which mattered to him not at all, but when he'd discovered that his own daughter was a murderer, that moved him to regret, to self-sacrifice.

Kodos the Executioner was dead, by his own child, by his own actions. His whole life he had never taken responsibility for his crimes, and it killed him in the end. I was reminded of Shakespeare's King Lear: "We make guilty of our disasters the sun, the moon, and the stars: as if we were villains by necessity."

The quote also applied to me. Catching him had been my "necessity," and I became a villain.

THE STORY OF STARFLEET'S GREATEST CAPTAIN

✦

The *Enterprise* was falling into Psi 2000, an ancient, ice-covered planet in its death throes. We'd originally been sent to pick up a scientific party and watch the planet break up from a safe distance. Things didn't go according to plan. The scientific party had all succumbed to a strange disease that made them lose their self-control. One of them, a crewman named Rossi, had turned off the life-support system, and then gotten in the shower with his clothes on, while they'd all frozen to death. When we got there, everyone had been dead for over a day, and our landing party brought the disease back to the *Enterprise*.

The ship had quickly become, for lack of a better term, a nuthouse. A half-naked Sulu tried to stab me with a sword, and my new navigator, Kevin Reilly, literally turned off the engines. McCoy eventually found a cure, but not before we began to spiral into the planet's atmosphere. There wasn't enough time to turn the engines back on through the usual process. Our only hope was Spock: Could my brilliant science officer come up with a formula to "cold start" the engines? It was our last chance.

Spock, despite succumbing to the disease, came through. With Scotty's help, they manually combined matter and antimatter, creating a controlled implosion that jump-started our engines. We pulled away from the dying world.

And the immense power sent us into a time warp. We travelled backward in time over seventy hours.

The importance of the discovery was initially lost on me, because I had also succumbed to the disease. It was a little like being drunk—it removed the perimeter I kept around myself. It had also brought to the front of my mind just how attached I'd become to the *Enterprise*. I had found something I was willing to commit everything to, but because it was an inanimate object, the ship could give nothing in return. It was a dark psychological moment: I loved something that couldn't love me back. My science officer, however, was trying to make me see that we'd discovered something much more important than the heart of my relationship problems.

"This does open some intriguing prospects, Captain," Spock said. He pointed out we could go back in time to any planet in any era.

"We may risk it someday, Mr. Spock," I said, but I wasn't really processing it. I told Sulu to lay in the course for our next destination. As he did, however, I thought of something.

"Wait a minute," I said. "Spock, it's three days ago. That means Psi 2000 hasn't broken up yet."

"Yes," he said. And then he understood what I was getting at. "The scientific party might still be alive—"

"Mr. Sulu, reverse course! Get us back to Psi 2000, maximum warp!"

We made it back and beamed down. They were all succumbing to the disease, but we found Rossi as he was turning off the life-support systems. I had to stun him with my phaser, but we stopped him, and saved them all. McCoy gave them the cure, and we got them back up to the ship, where we watched the breakup of Psi 2000 again, this time from a safe distance.

Some days we'd had our losses, but some days we had our wins.

✦

The ship jerked violently. I checked the navigation sensors; we hadn't even reached the center of the ion storm; it was going to get much worse. I became concerned that the eddies of the storm would pull us off course if the helm didn't compensate.

"Hold on course, Mr. Hanson," I said.

"Aye sir," he said. "Natural vibration force two . . . force three . . ." Hanson, the beta shift helmsman, compensated for the force of the storm by reversing the starboard engine. He was not the man I wanted at the helm in the middle of an ion storm. He lacked confidence and experience, but I couldn't relieve him now.

No one fully understood what caused ion storms, the magnetic conflagrations of ionic particles traveling at thousands of kilometers an hour. Their mystery was part of their sway. They caused terror in a starship crew and its captain; they felt malevolent. You would move the ship, and it felt like the storm was countering your moves, trying to swallow you whole.

And its greatest power was this fear it caused, fear that might lead a captain to make a wrong decision.

I checked the board, then ordered engineering to increase thrust, and called the ion pod.

"Ion pod," Ben Finney said. He sounded calm and confident. He'd been in the sensor pod during an ion storm before; he knew the orders were to gather as much sensor data as possible, but to get out before the pod itself gained a charge. It was a delicate balance, since navigating an ion storm without some data from the pod was almost impossible. Ion storms had been known to change their size by several million kilometers in a matter of minutes. The more data a ship had, the quicker it could find its way through.

"Stand by to get out of there, Ben," I said. I looked down at the panel by my right hand. The yellow alert light flashed; when I hit red alert, that would be Ben's signal to get out of the pod. I looked up, saw from the navigational sensors we were a third of the way through the storm.

"Steady as we go, Mr. Hanson," I said.

"Outer hull pressure increasing," Spock said.

"Natural vibration now force five," Hanson said. "Force six . . ." The ship could take this increased vibration, but the faster we could get through the storm, the better. I checked the telemetry from the sensor pod; it was giving me a three-dimensional view of the storm on the navigational console. The *Enterprise* was a little blip; the computer projected our course forward. I made a quick calculation; we'd be through in less than three minutes on our current heading, but it was going to be a rough ride.

The ship jolted; now the shuddering became continuous.

"Natural vibration now force seven," Hanson said, yelling above the din.

I looked down at my control pad and signaled red alert. Ben would know to get out of the pod.

The red alert klaxon was almost lost in the sound of the ship's vibrations; it was being buffeted now like an empty tin cup on a tidal wave, the inertial dampeners straining to keep us all upright. I watched the board near Hanson; he wasn't compensating enough.

"Helm, come right two degrees," I said.

"Aye sir," Hanson said. He initiated the change just before the ship was knocked hard. The inertial dampeners couldn't work fast enough, and the ship lurched to the starboard. I was thrown from my chair. I saw Spock had tumbled near the helm. He clawed his way up to the control, and diverted more power to the dampeners so that the ship turned upright again. I helped Hanson back to his chair, then checked our course: still a few minutes from the edge of the storm. The whole bridge was shuddering. I felt a tide of panic, but regained control; my decisions were the right ones.

And then my mind went back to the pod. In a storm of this magnitude, if we lost any of our control circuits to a burnout, the ship would be dead. Seconds had passed; Finney had had plenty of time to get out. Everyone on the bridge was caught up in their work, eyes on their consoles, doing their jobs to keep the ship safe. And I did mine. I went back to my chair and pressed the jettison button. It flashed green. The pod was away.

Soon, the vibration began to subside, and the ship began to calm.

"Natural vibration force five . . . force four . . ." Hanson said, his voice cooling with each lower number.

"Sir," Uhura said, "Mr. Finney has not reported in." It was standard procedure for the officer manning the pod to check in immediately after he'd gotten out.

"Inform security, he could be injured," I said, and got back to paying attention to getting the ship through the storm.

After a full day of searching, they didn't find Finney. It was determined that he must have still been on the pod when I jettisoned it. It made no sense; he knew the risks, he knew once the red alert had sounded, he had to get out of there.

The truth of what happened made even less sense. A few weeks later, I watched playback from the ship's log on a viewscreen. There was a close-up of my right hand, pressing the jettison button, but during the yellow alert, well before the ship was being torn apart.

And I was being court-martialed for it.

I sat facing Commodore Stone and three other command-grade officers in full dress, in the courtroom on Starbase 11. Their contention was that either I had some kind of mental lapse and panicked, jettisoning the pod earlier than I had to, or something far worse. The prosecution made the case that I'd grown to resent Ben Finney, and I used the opportunity to get rid of him.

But watching that viewscreen, looking at my hand jettisoning the pod much earlier than I remembered, I had to question my own memory. I knew how I felt about Ben: he was a pain in the ass, but he was also a good, reliable officer. The idea that I would kill him for such a petty reason was simply untrue and insulting. The theory that I had panicked was a little easier to take; I'd come close to panicking during the storm, but I held it together. I'd made the right decisions.

Except the playback of the log excerpt said otherwise. I looked guilty.

I wasn't alone; I had a lawyer named Samuel Cogley. He was an older man, tough and well-read. He was obsessed with books, the old, bound kind. He seemed quaint to me, and during the trial there wasn't much he could do in the face of the computer record. But it turned out his passion for the written word would end up saving my career.

Cogley had rested our case, just when Spock came into the courtroom with new evidence. Spock discovered that someone had tampered with the *Enterprise's* computer. But because we'd rested our case already, the court didn't have to hear it. That's when Cogley showed his true value.

He made an impassioned speech about man fading in the shadow of the machine, losing our individual rights as our computer technology takes over our way of life. It was a speech that I imagine was relevant to humans of many ages, going all the way back those people who succumbed to the primitive Internet of the early 21st century. And it moved the court to hear the evidence.

The court reconvened on the *Enterprise*. Spock testified that the modification made to the computer was so subtle, only a programming expert could pull it off. There were only three people qualified in Spock's view: him, me, and Ben Finney. It was then Cogley who made the seemingly outrageous assertion that Ben Finney had altered the log, after he supposedly died, to make it look like I'd killed him.

Which meant he had faked his death and was still hiding somewhere aboard the ship. With the ship's sensors, we were able to prove that he was still alive.

Finney had lost his senses. He'd become obsessed with taking revenge on me for ruining his career. He was truly sick, and I had to find him myself. He was hiding in the ship's engineering spaces. His twisted plan revealed, we fought, and he desperately tried to kill me, but was in no condition to take me on. In the end, he was on the deck, beaten and sobbing.

"Ben," I said. "Why? You have a daughter and wife who love you."

"No they don't," he said. "They don't."

He was ill, truly ill. I'd never seen it until now. I didn't know if he'd been born with it, or if the circumstances of his life had created it, but either way, Ben was lost.

✦

A young ensign had been recommended to me by the commandant of Starfleet Academy, and he joined the ship at Starbase 11. He had just graduated from the academy, and had exceptional grades in the sciences and navigation. I always introduced myself to new crewmen when they first came aboard; I remembered that Garrovick had done that for me, and I routinely followed his example. I also had established a practice of either Spock or myself mentoring the new crewmen, at least for a little while. So when the young man beamed aboard, I was in the transporter room.

"Ensign Chekov, reporting for duty, Keptin," he said, standing at attention upon seeing me. I was surprised at the thickness of his Russian accent; 23rd-century language education had for the most part done away with them. Except when the individual didn't want to get rid of it. I would quickly become convinced that Chekov fell into this category.

"At ease," I said. "Welcome aboard, Ensign." I shook his hand.

"A pleasure to meet you, sir," Chekov said. "I believe our ancestors are from the same region."

"I'm sorry?" I said, genuinely confused, but he kept going.

"Perhaps they served the now-forgotten Communist Party of the ancient USSR..."

"Ensign," I said. "What are you talking about?"

"Your ancestors were from Kirkovo, Bulgaria, yes? Though I was born in St. Petersburg, my mother's father was born in Odessa, which is just across the Black Sea . . ."

"Sorry to disappoint you, Ensign," I said, cutting him off, "but my ancestors are not from Bulgaria. And I don't believe any of them were ever communists." Chekov could not hide his disappointment, and I couldn't hide my amusement. I told him to report to sickbay for his physical. I decided I'd let Spock mentor this one.

✦

"Our last item, sir. Commodore Wesley has made a crew transfer request," Spock said. It was our morning briefing, in my quarters. McCoy was there, having stopped in for coffee before going on duty. "It struck me as rather odd."

"Who does he want?" I already knew the answer. Commodore Wesley was requesting Janice Rand be transferred to his ship, the *Lexington*, to fill an opening in his communications department. Bob Wesley had been an instructor for a short time when I was at the academy. We'd then met several times when I was captain of the *Hotspur*, and struck up a friendship. I asked him this favor, and he happily obliged me.

"He is offering her a promotion to lieutenant," Spock said.

"What's so odd about that?" McCoy said. "It sounds like a good opportunity."

"It is odd, Doctor, because Yeoman Rand has not requested a transfer," he said. There wasn't anything that got by Spock, which was usually a good thing. However, in this case, I'd hoped to keep anyone from being aware of my hand in this.

"Does Janice want to go?" I said, specifically avoiding the question Spock was implying. If he asked me directly, I wouldn't lie to him. He looked at me and seemed to sense I was avoiding the subject.

"I have kept Lieutenant Hong from presenting it to Yeoman Rand," he said, "awaiting your approval." I told him he should take it to her, and Spock nodded and left. Once he was gone, however, McCoy didn't waste any time getting to the heart of the matter.

"Commodore Wesley is a friend of yours, isn't he?" I nodded. "I don't think she wants to leave," McCoy said. "And as your doctor, I'm not sure this is the best way to deal with the situation." McCoy was the only one who knew about my guilt regarding Janice, and that it continued to afflict me. It had faded a little; I thought I could deal with it. But recent events made me reconsider.

"Bones, it's just better if she's not here. It's how I should've dealt with Finney. Maybe if I'd gotten him away from here, away from me—"

"It's not the same thing at all," McCoy said. "Ben Finney was sick. Paranoids are clever; they can seem normal most of the time. I gave him six quarterly physicals and I missed it."

"Maybe I should get you transferred," I said. McCoy could see that I was closing the subject.

"You can't transfer your troubles, Jim," McCoy said. "This is a personal problem, not a personnel problem." He was right, again, but I didn't have to listen.

✦

"This may be my last entry," I said into the recorder the Metrons had given me. I was on a bleak, hot, uninhabited planetoid, sitting on an outcropping of minerals, exhausted. The pain in my right leg was blinding. I thought I was done. I looked down at the minerals at my feet. There were diamonds and sulfur. Something lit in my memory, but it was faint. I was looking for weapons, something that could kill a formidable, deadly creature. I struggled to remember the connection between sulfur and weapons. I pulled myself up and kept going.

The Federation colony on Cestus III had been destroyed by a race known as the Gorn. The *Enterprise* had chased the culprits into an uncharted section of space. Another race, who called themselves the Metrons, had astonishingly reached out from their planet and stopped both vessels, plucked me and the Gorn captain off of our bridges, dropped us onto this desolate, rocky place, and told us to fight it out.

From the beginning, I'd underestimated my opponent. He was a seven-foot reptilian, dressed in a gold tunic, and despite his staggering strength, moved much slower than me; I misinterpreted this as an indication he might not be as clever. But he'd lured me into a trap, and I was barely able to slip away with an injured leg. I had no food, no water; in a short time I'd be too exhausted to stay ahead of him.

When the Metrons put us on the planet, they said there'd be weapons, yet I had not found any that could kill my opponent. But I couldn't give up. They had also said that if I lost the battle, my ship would be destroyed.

I stumbled onto a large rock and slipped to the ground. My hand landed in a white substance, a granular powder. It looked familiar. I tasted it. Salty. The memory connected to the sulfur now finally came forward.

Sam.

I'm five years old and watching my brother, Sam, build a cannon in our barn. He had soldered old tin cans with the bottoms cut out, and then he spread out three piles of chemicals onto an old table.

"What's that stuff?"

"That's sulfur," he said, pointing to a pile of yellow powder, "the black powder is charcoal, and the white is saltpeter." Before he could stop me, I had tasted the saltpeter.

"Spit that out!" I immediately did what he told me.

"You said it was salt."

"Salt*peter*. You don't eat it."

"What's it for?"

"Gunpowder."

I then watched as he confidently and carefully mixed the chemicals in the right amounts, then ground them together. I remembered that taste, and on Cestus III, I tasted the white powder on my hands and spit it out. It was the same. I smiled at the memory. Sam's cannon was going to save me.

History records that I defeated the Gorn with a bamboo cannon loaded with diamonds for cannonballs. Amazingly, the blast of diamonds coming out of a cannon only stunned the strange creature. But I had the advantage and could've killed him; I spared his life, however, and because of that the Gorn and the Federation now live in peace. I owed it all to Sam.

But I never got to tell him.

✦

Spock, McCoy, Scotty, and I sat across from Khan Noonien Singh. I had found him and his followers in suspended animation in an ancient spaceship. The product of controlled genetics, he was the superman whose rule of over a quarter of the planet Earth in the 1990s I'd studied at the academy in John Gill's class. And now, he was here in the present—the day before, he had taken over my ship and tried to kill me. He'd done this with the help of one of my officers, ship's historian Lieutenant Marla McGivers. She'd mutinied because she'd fallen in love with Khan. With her help, he'd revived the 72 followers still in suspended animation on his primitive ship. They quickly had taken over the *Enterprise*. But Khan couldn't run the ship without my crew, and they wouldn't follow him. When he tried to kill me, McGivers had a change of heart and intervened to save my life. I was able to retake the ship.

Now, we were all cleaned up in our dress uniforms at a hearing to determine what to do with Khan and McGivers. Despite her last-minute change of heart, I still couldn't forgive her act of mutiny. I looked at Khan, under guard, but still a leader. In that moment, I somehow forgot who he was, that he was a murderer, a dictator responsible for the death and oppression of millions. Instead, I fell in love with the idea that I would make a civilized decision.

"I declare all charges and specifications in this matter have been dropped," I said. McCoy was the only one who protested, but I cut him off and turned to Spock. He and I had already had a conversation regarding Ceti Alpha V, a planet that wasn't too far off our current course. It was a world of mostly jungle, with a variety of indigenous predators. The offer I made to Khan was he and his people could live there. It was arrogant on my part, but I didn't see it. I thought I was making the humane choice. These people had so much potential, it would be such a waste to confine them to a reorientation center, where they'd probably spend most of their time trying to escape. Instead, I gave Khan a world that was his to tame. He answered the offer with a smile.

"Have you ever read Milton, Captain?" He was referencing Lucifer's comment as he fell into the pit: better to rule in hell than serve in heaven.

His response was educated, rarefied, civilized. I was admiring him, and he was playing me for a fool.

I turned to my mutinous historian. Did she want a court-martial or a life on this unforgiving world with the man she loved? She of course chose the latter; no one was going to get in the way of the romantic, heroic ending to this story that I'd helped to engineer.

The prisoners left the room, and Spock ruminated on what we'd just done.

"It would be interesting, Captain, to return to that world in a hundred years and to learn what crop had sprung from the seed you planted today." It was a wonderful, hopeful thought, exactly what I was thinking when I'd proposed it.

Of course, we would be going back a lot sooner, to face the consequences of the biggest mistake of my career. But for the moment, I was confident and happy in my ignorant hubris.

It would take about a week to reach Ceti Alpha V. During the trip, I had confined Khan and his followers to one of the ship's cargo bays, and had a force field established around it. I had the bay filled with enough food and supplies so we wouldn't have need to bring the force field down; I didn't trust that they wouldn't try to take the ship again. When we reached Ceti Alpha V, I would have them beamed out of the cargo bay and directly down to the planet. During the trip, I had Scotty rig up some cargo carriers on the hangar deck to be used as temporary living quarters on the planet, which I would drop there once we arrived. I was inspecting his work when Spock came to see me.

"We've had another request for you to perform a marriage ceremony." I looked at him, incredulous. Why would he bring this up now?

"Can't it wait until after we drop Khan off?"

"I do not think so, sir. The request comes from Khan." I exchanged a look with Scotty.

"Here's one reason I never want to be captain . . ." Scotty said.

I told Spock we couldn't do it, that having 72 genetically engineered wedding guests was too big a risk. He countered that Khan had already offered to wait until we arrived at Ceti Alpha V, and that his followers could be beamed down to the planet. The only people required at the wedding were he and McGivers. I felt it had to be some sort of trick, but Spock didn't agree.

"I have given it a fair amount of consideration, Captain," he said. "Khan is a primitive man from a primitive time. He may take some comfort in ancient Sikh rituals."

"Wait," I said. "He wants a Sikh wedding?"

Spock was ready for this, too. He had assigned Ensign Chekov to research the customs for such a ritual, in the event I approved it. But the whole thing seemed unbelievable. I had to question Khan myself, so I went back to my quarters and communicated with him through the viewscreen on my desk.

"Khan, forgive me, but is this a joke?"

"I think you have known me long enough, Captain, to appreciate I have no sense of humor." He had me there. "I do not know what my situation will be once we arrive on that planet, and I want Marla to have the honor of being my wife from the moment we set foot on that new world. We are going to conquer it together."

"Then I guess . . . we're going to have a wedding."

We arrived at Ceti Alpha V. I had the cargo pods brought down to the surface, then had Khan's people beamed down, leaving only Khan and McGivers on board. I put on my dress uniform again and went to the chapel. Khan and McGivers sat on pillows that Ensign Chekov had procured from Lieutenant Uhura's quarters. The only guests, also on pillows, were Spock and McCoy. Five security guards lined the walls. I came in and sat on the one empty pillow, obviously reserved for me.

It was as close to a traditional Sikh wedding as we could approximate; Chekov gently prodded me through the ceremonies of the "Anand Karaj," which translates into "Blissful Union." The bride and groom announced their love for each other and detailed their roles in the equal partnership. It managed to be both quaint and progressive. The tradition ended with the groom taking the bride away from her own family, which in this situation had its own significance.

We escorted them to the transporter room, and as they stepped on the pad I saw a happy, contented, proud couple. Even Khan was not going to be denied marital bliss. I beamed them down.

THE STORY OF STARFLEET'S GREATEST CAPTAIN

✦

"So you're telling me," Matt Decker said, "it was all an illusion."

I was in the conference room aboard Decker's ship, the *U.S.S. Constellation*. A few days before, war had been declared between the Federation and the Klingon Empire. It had lasted for two days (and hence became known as the Two-Day War). I had been at the center of it, knew the most about it, so Commodore Decker, who was commander of the main force that was about to face off against the Klingons before the war was abruptly cut short, wanted a debrief. Admiral Nogura was also present via subspace and stared at us through the viewscreen in the center of the table.

"Not exactly an illusion," I said. "I should probably start from the beginning." I could see the doubt in Decker's expression, and I couldn't blame him. It had been a difficult truth to accept. When war had been declared the *Enterprise* had been sent to Organia, a centrally located Class-M world, to secure an agreement with the local populace for Starfleet to use the planet as a base of operations. We'd found a primitive people who didn't seem impressed with us, or the coming danger. They refused our help, and shortly thereafter the Klingons arrived.

Spock and I were stuck on the planet, in disguise, surrounded by hundreds of Klingon soldiers. All I could think about was Axanar. I was about to watch an innocent, peaceful society shattered by a Klingon occupation. The military governor, Kor, was everything I'd come to loathe about his species: arrogant, ruthless, proud of his society's glorification of war. It gave him a disgusting sense of entitlement that legitimized his atrocities on the weak.

But the Organians weren't powerless innocents. They only gave the illusion of being humanoid, and were in fact beings of pure energy, many millions of years more advanced than us. They put a stop to our war, deactivated our ships in space and our weapons on the ground. I was initially infuriated; I thought of myself as a man of peace, but my hatred for the Klingons had blinded me. I wanted a war, and the Organians weren't going to let me have my way. Because I had dealt directly with them, I had more time to accept the situation; after I finished my report to Decker, I could see he hadn't.

"We can't just let these beings tell us what to do," he said. Decker was having the struggle I'd just experienced, facing that humanity wasn't the most advanced civilization in the Galaxy, that we weren't even close. "We're not going to just sit by helplessly—"

"The Klingons are as helpless as we are," I said. They'd handed both the president of the Federation and the Klingon Chancellor a finished treaty, with an implied threat they'd disable our ships wherever they were if either side violated it.

"They'll figure some way out of this," Decker said. "We have to assume we're still at war and go forward with our plans. I could drop the bundle on Qo'noS* in two days . . ." This last comment was directed at Nogura, who held up his hand and shook his head. It was clear that Decker was referencing something that I wasn't cleared for. Nogura told Decker they had their orders, that the president of the Federation Council, the Andorian Bormenus, told Starfleet Command that we would abide by the treaty. Decker didn't look happy, and I wondered whether he would ever accept the situation.

And I also wondered what "the bundle" was.

But there would be no war, at least not for a while. It was the third war I'd been a part of stopping since taking command of the *Enterprise*. I felt I was making a difference; I was a part of history.

I was soon going to have to figure out how to save it.

---

*EDITOR'S NOTE: Pronounced like the English word "Kronos," this is the Klingon Homeworld.

CHAPTER 7

THE ANGEL WHO CAME DOWN THE STAIRS of the basement immediately saw to our needs and gave Spock and me a job.

"Fifteen cents an hour for ten hours a day," she said. "What are your names?"

"Mine's Jim Kirk," I said. "He's . . . Spock." What I knew of America in this period of the 1930s was a general lack in interest or education of the public in other cultures. I figured Spock would pass as some generalized Asian.

"I'm Edith Keeler. You can start by cleaning up down here," she said, and headed back upstairs. I really didn't want her to go.

"Miss," I said. "Where are we?"

"You're in the 21st Street Mission," she said. It had a religious ring to it. I found myself hoping she wasn't a nun.

"Do you run this place?"

"Indeed I do, Mr. Kirk." She left us to the messy basement. Spock and I immediately got to work cleaning it up. This is not where I expected to find myself a week ago, when the *Enterprise* was patrolling the [REDACTED] sector, and we'd started getting the strange readings on the chronometers. Spock had noticed that, every few hours, they were "skipping" a millisecond. He traced the source to an unknown particle wave, and the *Enterprise*

THE AUTOBIOGRAPHY OF JAMES T. KIRK

tracked it back to its source: a planet, in the star system [REDACTED], over [REDACTED] light-years from the nearest world of the Federation.*

As we approached the strange old world, the particle wave's effect became much stronger, and the *Enterprise* was buffeted by what Spock described as "ripples in time." One of these ripples caused McCoy to accidentally inject himself with the dangerous stimulant Cordrazine. He left the ship a raving madman; Spock and I took a landing party down to the surface to find him.

On the world, a relic of a long-dead civilization, what could only be described as a glowing donut three meters in diameter announced:

"I am the Guardian of Forever."

A time portal. Without even asking, it showed us Earth's past in the hole of the donut. McCoy, before we could stop him, leaped into the portal.

We lost contact with the *Enterprise* immediately. McCoy had somehow changed the past. Spock and I then used the portal to follow him back in time in the hopes of stopping further damage. We couldn't be exact in our calculations; we only knew we arrived sometime before McCoy. We didn't know how much time we had.

For now, we had to clean a basement. The tools we had to work with were primitive and inefficient; the brooms were old and constructed of straw. They pushed the dirt on the floor around, but left residue behind. There was also a lot of irreparable furniture and other refuse that didn't look worth saving.

"Assuming a seven-day workweek," Spock said, "ten dollars and fifty cents a week for each of us in ancient U.S. currency." I had no idea how much money that was, relative to the time we were in. Spock pointed out

---

*EDITOR'S NOTE: Captain Kirk wanted to play a small trick on his readers; he told me that the star system he listed in his memoirs was not the true location, was in fact several thousand light-years from the actual world. He knew that news of this discovery he'd made had become public in the intervening decades, and he was doing his duty to try to keep its location a secret. After his death, Starfleet Command reviewed the manuscript, and discovered that Kirk had unwittingly left a subconscious clue to the location of the real place, so Starfleet redacted the false references. They would not tell me what the clue was, but had no problem with me revealing his original intentions.

that it wasn't necessarily the limit of our earning potential, as it left 14 hours in a 24-hour cycle to find other gainful employment. I was incredulous.

"We need to sleep," I said.

"I do not need to sleep," Spock said.

I couldn't argue with that, but said we wouldn't have time to find any work if we didn't figure out how to clean the basement. Spock suggested a phaser locked on a minimal disintegration setting would allow us to dispense with the dirt without harming the structure. This struck me as cheating.

"I was unaware that we were engaged in a competition," Spock said. I reconsidered all the work we had to do, and decided the time stream wouldn't mind if we took a shortcut.

"Set your phaser. I'll watch the door," I said.

Even with the help of our 23rd-century tools, it still took a couple of hours to clean the room. As we were finishing, the smell of cooking wafted down to us. It was a combination of meat and onions, which I found intoxicating. I realized we'd not eaten in hours, so I hurried us to finish, and we went upstairs to the mission.

It was a small place with a kitchen, a cafeteria-style eating area with an upright piano, another room with about 15 cots with a common bathroom and shower. The smell of the food became stronger, but it was now mixed with the other powerful scents of coffee, rotting wood, and body odor.

The dining area was filled with bearded, raggedy men in frayed, soiled clothes, many with a glassy-eyed hopelessness. They stood in line for a bowl of soup, a cup of coffee, and a hunk of bread. Spock and I did the same, and we sat down among them. I was starting to feel as hopeless as those around me. If I couldn't stop McCoy, would this world ever change? Is this where I would spend the rest of my days?

And then Edith Keeler got up to speak. She spoke of the years to come, weirdly prescient on the subject of space travel, and about the people of the future who would solve the problems of hunger and disease.

"Prepare for tomorrow," she said. "Get ready, don't give up. You can't control the hardship, but you can control its effect. The hunger might not abate, but the sadness is yours. The cold bites through your blanket, but you don't need to let the hopelessness in with it. It is your decision what kind of person you will be, how you will respond to the challenges you face.

Keep your promises, forgo your grudges, apologize when necessary, speak your love, and speak it again." It was as if she was talking to me, telling me to trust in myself. I found her calming and captivating. I looked around the room and could see I wasn't the only one. She was giving these people life. Afterward she came and found me.

"Mr. Kirk, you are uncommon workmen. That basement looks like it's been scrubbed and polished." I felt guilty getting this compliment, but I took it with a smile. She told us of a room in her building, which Spock and I could rent, that sounded affordable given our new wages. She walked us there.

It took us a long time to reach her apartment building, but not because it was far away. The streets of New York City were cold and unforgiving. As we walked, we came upon people huddled in doorways or on park benches, under tattered blankets and newspapers, trying to keep warm. Edith stopped at each one, told them where the mission was, that they could rest there and stay warm. Many were hostile to her, some intoxicated, but it didn't deter her; she knew many of them personally, and we helped some return to the mission. Her selflessness was astounding.

Finally, we made it back to her apartment, and she introduced us to her landlord, a hulking, wheezy man in a stained undershirt named Altman. He scowled at us.

"I'm not lettin' no slant eye live here," he said. I looked at him, confused. "The Chinaman's gotta go somewhere else." It took me a moment to understand what he was saying, and then I realized it was directed at Spock. I had never seen such unapologetic racism before. It was frightening in its casualness and acceptability. Edith, however, seemed ready for it.

"They're employees of mine," she said. "I'd consider it a personal favor."

"You're not the only one who lives in this building," Altman said. "People'll get upset."

"Father Cawley will also appreciate it, I'm sure." The mention of the clergy swayed him. She then pulled out two slips of paper that took me a moment to remember were money. She was paying him our rent a week in advance.

"He has to use the back entrance," he said. "And I catch him talking to any white women or kids, he's out."

"That sounds reasonable," Edith said. In fact, it sounded ridiculous, but it was clearly the practical course.

She left us with Altman, who took us to the room. Like everything else we'd seen so far, it was drab and depressing. A sagging bed, sooty curtains, and a wooden table and chair, scratched and stained. The room smelled of ashes; the habit of inhaling the smoke of burning tobacco was an epidemic in this world. I knew this was going to be a difficult time to navigate, but somehow this woman had given me hope.

The days filled up quickly. There was a lot of work to be done at the mission. Spock and I learned how to make coffee in a device called a "percolator," wash dishes, and cook food using other ancient appliances. We also went with Edith to scrounge food donations from the open markets all over the city. New York was in the grip of an economic downturn of massive proportions. People all over were in lines for soup or bread; despondent men stood on street corners, with wooden buckets filled with mostly rotten apples that they offered to sell for a penny. Yet Edith bullied her way into the kitchens of the upscale hotels and restaurants, getting discarded bones and bruised vegetables for soup, and three-day-old bread with mold that Spock and I would have to cut off.

I learned more about her. The daughter of a minister, she was raised in London, England. She came to America in the 1920s and worked in the church. She was doing the same work then she did now; there were always poor people who needed help, she said. Now there was just more of them, and some had once been rich.

We worked at the mission from 7 a.m. to 5 p.m. on that first day, and then we tried to find other work, which was very difficult. I found some day work at the loading docks. I also picked up ideas from the other men in the mission; you could go to one of the upscale parts of the city in the morning, gather up discarded newspapers, and resell them downtown. I was scrounging for pennies, but we needed whatever we could.

Spock discovered Chinatown in the lower part of the city. He passed for Chinese, and thanks to the universal translator in his pocket, it appeared that he could speak it. As such, he was able to acquire work, first washing dishes in the local restaurants, then repairing broken machinery.

Once our money started to come in, we began to acquire the bits of primitive electronic equipment Spock needed to build his memory circuit. He had to figure out some way to slow down the recording on his tricorder so we could see how history had been changed. We didn't know how much time we had; Spock estimated that McCoy might not arrive for a month.

Despite how hard I was working, I found myself more relaxed than I'd ever been. The work was physically exhausting, but all the responsibility for our mission lay with Spock; I could only wait for his machine to work. I began to feel differently; the emotional connection to the men and women of the future began to fade in my mind. I became this regular workingman on primitive Earth. It was a strange vacation: I was mistreated by employers, usually smelled terrible, and was always hungry.

And I was drawn to Edith, and she to me.

We'd take walks in the evening, I would talk honestly about the future, and she would laugh as if I was joking. But she was no primitive; she had an advanced view of people that would have made her quickly at home in the 23rd century. She seemed to know that rich industrialists were holding on to their money, and could end the suffering of the world in a heartbeat, but that they wouldn't.

"They'll only open their purses," she said, "to make some war."

She was disgusted by her era's priorities. I found her fervor appealing and enchanting. Our physical relationship was both passionate and chaste; she was a religious woman and this was a primitive time. But I spent many evenings in her apartment, where she would cook me something she called shepherd's pie and we'd talk and laugh and comfort each other. And I'd go back to my room in a bit of a romantic haze to find Spock, working on an ever-growing contraption of wires and radio tubes. One night, about a week and a half after we'd been there, I walked in, and he had something to show me. On the small screen of his tricorder, an image appeared of Edith in a newspaper article six years in the future. I read the opening sentence in proud astonishment.

"The president and Edith Keeler conferred for some time today—"

Suddenly, Spock's invention exploded in a shower of sparks and smoke.

"How bad?"

"Bad enough," Spock said. But I was lost in my delight in what I thought to be Edith's future.

"The president and Edith Keeler—"

"It would seem unlikely, Jim . . ." Spock said. "A few moments ago, I read a 1930 newspaper article . . ." I wasn't listening, or I would've heard that he called me "Jim," usually a bad sign.

"We know her future. In six years she'll be very important, nationally famous—"

"Or, Captain, Edith Keeler will die. This year. I saw her obituary. Some sort of traffic accident."

"They can't both be true," I said. It was stunning. What was he talking about? But even as I asked the question, I knew what the answer was.

"Edith Keeler is the focal point in time we've been looking for, the point both we and Dr. McCoy have been drawn to." Spock's theory about time rivers ended up being true. But it didn't seem possible that all of history could turn on one person. McCoy does something when he shows up.

"In his condition, what does he do? Does he kill her?" I felt terrible after I said it; I was actually *hoping* that McCoy had killed her, so that I could stop it, so that she could live.

"Or perhaps he prevents her from being killed, we don't know which."

I told him to fix his machine so we would. He then said it would take him weeks.

"We should stay as close to Miss Keeler as we possibly can," Spock said. "This will provide us with the best chance of stopping Dr. McCoy before he commits whatever act changes history."

"That shouldn't be a problem," I said.

"If you find it difficult, I will be willing—"

"I'll be all right, Spock." I then left the room and took a walk.

Days passed into weeks, and there was no sign of McCoy. I gave up my other jobs and escorted Edith to and from work. I spent every waking moment with her, and sometimes perched myself on the roof across the street from her apartment until she turned out the light and went to bed. Some nights she would let me stay in her apartment, as long as I slept on the floor. I was keeping her safe, but the truth was I felt safe next to her. I think, for the first time in years, free of the responsibilities of command, I let myself fall in love.

It was only bad luck that we missed McCoy arriving at the mission. He was exhausted and paranoid. Edith greeted him; he begged her not to tell anyone he was there. She took him to an upstairs room in the back, cared for him and kept the secret, even from me. Around this time, Spock completed the repairs to his machine. It told us that Edith started a pacifist movement that delayed the United States' entry into World War II, allowing Germany to win. It was clear how history was supposed to play out. Edith had to die.

But I wasn't going to let her. I didn't tell Spock, but I wouldn't let the woman I loved die. I couldn't. All those people whose lives would be changed weren't real to me anymore. I would stay in the past, live my life with Edith. I indulged in a delusion we could change the future together. With what I knew, with the knowledge I had, I could make sure Germany *didn't* win, and Edith could still live. I think Spock suspected my plan, but he said only that if I did what my heart told me to do, millions would die who didn't die before.

One night, I left work with Edith. I had a little money in my pocket now; we didn't need to spend it on radio tubes anymore. I was going to take her out to dinner; she, however, had a different suggestion.

"If we hurry, maybe we can catch the Clark Gable movie—"

"What?"

"You know, Dr. McCoy said the same thing . . ." I stopped and grabbed her.

"McCoy! Leonard McCoy?" McCoy was here . . .

"Yes, he's in the mission . . ." How long had he been here? Had he already saved her life? Had we missed it? I truly hoped that we had.

"Stay here. Stay right here," I said, then turned. "Spock!" I ran across the street. Spock was still working in the mission, and he heard my shouting. He came out, and seconds later, McCoy did too. I couldn't believe it. I grabbed him in a hug. And stepped back.

He was in his Starfleet uniform. I hadn't seen mine in over a month; it was in a bag at the bottom of the closet in our room. Suddenly I was back on the ship, back in my head as captain. I felt guilty at what I'd been doing, about what I'd been thinking. I turned and saw Edith. She was crossing the street. And a truck was barreling toward her.

"Go, Jim!" McCoy yelled. It almost drowned out Spock's shout.

"No, Jim!" I stared at Edith, frozen. The uniform blazed in my mind.

I felt McCoy try to push past me to grab her, so I grabbed him. I heard Edith's cry as the truck's horn honked and the terrible rending of metal and flesh. I held McCoy a long moment, as Edith's painful scream seemed to echo in my mind.

"Did you deliberately stop me, Jim?" McCoy was incredulous, angry. I pushed him away. And then we were soon back in the 23rd century, on that dead world.

After a week back on the *Enterprise*, I was more sure of my mistake. My mind wasn't on my job; I could only think of Edith. When I was in the past, the future faded in my mind. But now that I was back in my own time, Edith was right there. I should've saved her. I let her die. The millions that were saved still weren't real to me, even though they were with me every day. I didn't know how I was going to live with it. In some ways, her memory has faded now, but I find I still regret it emotionally. I was a content man; I discovered what life was without duty and honor—just a job and love. It is horrible and self-centered that I regret it, and I suppose I paid for that selfishness, because I would never experience that contentedness again.

✦

"I've got the receiver you requested, sir," Uhura said, over the intercom. I was in my quarters, lying down. I hadn't slept in days, but I couldn't put this off. I sat up on the bed and activated the small viewscreen.

"Thank you, Lieutenant, put it through." On the viewscreen, Uhura's face was replaced by Mom and Dad. They were looking particularly haggard.

"Jim, this is a nice surprise," Dad said, but Mom looked worried.

"I don't think it's a social call, George." Since she had seen through it so quickly, I knew there was no point holding off.

"Mom, Dad, Sam's dead." Mom immediately burst into tears. Dad put his arm around her. I had to keep going. "Aurelan too."

"What . . . about Peter?" It was Mom who asked. Though he wasn't crying, Dad stood in stunned silence.

"He's fine," I said. "I've got him here with me." That was only technically true; since his parents' death I'd had various members of the crew keep him occupied, though I made sure to see him for evening meals.

"What happened?" Mom asked.

"It was some kind of space parasite. It infected a lot of people on Deneva," I said. "A lot of people died."

"But you stopped it," Dad said, finally speaking.

"I stopped it," I said.

"Was it . . . painful?" Mom said. I had watched Aurelan die in unimaginable pain, and Sam had to have gone in much the same way.

"No," I said, "it was quick." The circumstances of what happened on Deneva would not become public, so I thought it was a useful lie. "How're the twins?"

"They keep us up a lot," Dad said, "but they're healthy." Aurelan had given birth to twins two months before Sam was transferred to Deneva. The babies were deemed too young for space travel, so Mom and Dad offered to care for them until they'd reached six months, when it was safe for them to go. Now, though . . .

"I'm going to take Peter to Starbase 10," I said. "He'll get quick passage back to Earth from there."

"You can't . . ." Mom said, pausing. "Can't you bring him—"

"I'm sorry, Mom," I said. I had known that the appropriate thing to do was to bring Peter home, but I just couldn't. First Edith, and now Sam. It was all I could do not to crumble. If I went home, I felt like I might not ever leave. But I could see the hurt in Mom's expression. She needed me.

"It'll be fine," Dad said. "How is he?"

"He's a trooper," I said. It was the truth. Peter, though sad, was holding up well. He seemed curious about the workings of a starship, and the crew had stepped in nicely as caregivers. While we talked, Sam's two babies, Joshua and Steven, woke up and began crying.

"You take care of yourself . . ." Dad said, his voice cracking. I could see he was about to cry. "We love you."

I smiled and turned off the viewer.

I felt guilty; I hadn't seen Peter all day. I left my quarters and went to the rec room. Peter was there, playing three-dimensional chess with Spock. The ship's quartermaster had fitted him into a gold command uniform. I went to the food dispenser, got a cup of coffee, and joined them. I asked how the game was going.

"Mr. Kirk has your predilection for unpredictability," Spock said.

"My dad taught me to play," Peter said.

"Then you and I had the same chess teacher," I said. "I hope he let you win every once in a while."

"Not really," Peter said. "Dad said I would never learn anything that way. I did beat him once, though." I watched them play for a little while. Spock eventually beat him, but it wasn't easy. Then Spock excused himself. I really didn't want him to leave; when I was alone with Peter, the pressure to connect with him was overwhelming.

"Should I set up another game?" he asked. I said sure. I watched Peter as he put the pieces in place. He reminded me of Sam; same color hair and eyes, same intensity. He was focused on setting up the game, but I could see the sadness. I didn't know what to do for him. And then I remembered when Mom had left, what Sam did for me.

"Peter, do you miss them?" He stopped putting the pieces on the board. "It's okay to miss them."

I hugged him for a while.

✦

"He's kind, and he wants what's best for us," Carolyn Palamas said. "And he's so lonely. What you ask would break his heart. Now how can I . . ."

I was on Pollux IV, otherwise known as planet Mount Olympus, and I was the prisoner of a man calling himself Apollo. This was one of my most fantastic encounters; a being who claimed to actually be a Greek god. He was from an advanced race who had visited Earth in the distant past and had seemed like gods to the primitive humans of prehistory. It wasn't hard to understand why, even to me: he controlled an incredible power source that he could channel through his body. When we first arrived, he had reached out with a force field like a giant hand that "grabbed" the *Enterprise*.

Spock stayed on the bridge, while I took a landing party down to meet him. He stood in front of his temple, the source of his power, and told us he expected we'd become his worshippers again. And then, like any accomplished Greek god, he seduced a human woman, who happened to be one of my crewmen.

Lieutenant Carolyn Palamas was an expert in archaeology, anthropology, and ancient civilizations. She was stunning, intelligent, and had fallen head over heels in love with a guy in a toga. He'd "magically" put her in a pink dress before taking her off alone. She had been a consummate professional for the year or so she'd been on the ship, but now she was willing to give it all up. And it was making me ill. Not because I looked down on it, but because I understood it.

The double tragedy of the deaths of both Edith and Sam in my own life forced me to retreat from the emotional world. I avoided connection with others, and I was critical of it in my crew. So now, I'd asked her to spurn him. My hope was that if he lost her, he'd be weakened and vulnerable. She initially refused. She'd forgotten her duty for love. I had to remind her.

"Give me your hand," I said. She gave it to me and I grasped it firmly. I appealed to her sense of loyalty. I gave her a long speech about how we were tied together beyond any untying, that all we had was humanity. She said she understood, and stood up. I wasn't sure I'd gotten through. I could tell her that I was speaking from experience, that I'd given up my love for duty. But I didn't want to. I wanted her to give me what I wanted without question.

She would. She walked off, and soon after, the storm clouds brewed, lightning cracked, and in the distance Carolyn screamed. Apollo had shown us that he had powers that conceivably could control the weather on this planet, and I had assumed this meant she'd done what I asked. Spock, still on the *Enterprise*, had figured out a way to penetrate the force field holding the ship, and fired phasers at Apollo's temple. The god alien returned, but too late; we'd destroyed the source of his power. We found Palamas bruised and beaten. He'd attacked her. Apollo, devastated, weakened, literally faded away. We'd won. But it didn't feel like a win.

Back on the ship a few days later, I was on the bridge. McCoy walked in. He told me that Carolyn Palamas had come to see him, not feeling well.

I asked if she brought some kind of infection back from the planet. McCoy smiled, ruefully.

"You could say that," McCoy said. "She's pregnant." I was stunned. I saw Spock turn from his scanner. It seemed impossible; they were different species.

"Interesting," Spock said. "There are many ramifications about having an infant born on the *Enterprise* who may have inherited some or all of his father's abilities." I was determined that this child was *not* going to be born on my ship. I told Chekov and Sulu to set course for Starbase 12 at our maximum safe speed, and then left the bridge for sickbay.

Palamas was in a diagnostic bed. Scotty stood by her; before Apollo had come into the picture, he had been pursuing a relationship with her, albeit unsuccessfully. He looked affectionate and concerned, and she seemed comforted by his presence.

"Mr. Scott, I believe it's still your shift," I said.

"Yes, Captain, I was just looking in on Carolyn."

"I believe the medical staff is well equipped for that," I said. Scotty nodded and repressed his annoyance before turning to Palamas.

"I'll stop in later," he said, then left us. She looked at me with a smile that I could only describe as chilly. I asked her how she was feeling, and she said she was experiencing a little nausea. I told her we were on our way to Starbase 12, which would have the necessary facilities to deal with the birth of a child with both human and alien blood, and that I would happily grant her the traditional two-year leave of absence.

"That won't be necessary," she said. "I'll be resigning my commission."

"You don't have to decide that now—"

"It had nothing to do with the pregnancy," she said. "I decided on Pollux IV." She didn't elaborate, and she didn't have to. I'd pushed her too hard. At the time, I didn't think I had a choice; in retrospect, however, once I found out Spock could destroy the temple, I probably didn't need her to spurn Apollo for the mission. Maybe just for myself.

"If you'll excuse me, Captain, I'm very tired," she said, as she turned away from me on the bed.

"Of course," I said. "Let me know if there's anything you need." She wouldn't; I lost touch with her as soon as she left the ship.*

✦

During this period, the only personal connections I relied on were with Spock and McCoy. McCoy and I went back far enough that our friendship was like old leather. Spock's friendship was different; because of his devotion to Vulcan principles, it never felt close, and he never required emotional support from me. But I could always count on him to be there. So the one time he was in emotional distress, I knew I had to be there for him.

Spock was the one member of the crew that I never had to worry about losing to romance. He didn't seem the least bit interested in women (despite the many romantic overtures made by the ship's head nurse, Christine Chapel). Which is why the events that transpired involving Spock's wedding came as a complete shock.

It began with Spock throwing a bowl of soup against a wall and heatedly asking for a shore leave to his home planet.

I had no idea what the hell was going on. I soon found out that if I didn't get Spock to Vulcan, he would die.

I learned something that, at that time, few other non-Vulcans knew. Spock was going through the "*Pon farr*," a kind of crazed sexual fever that men on his planet went through every seven years. The Vulcans were barbarians in the ancient past, and though they were among the most civilized races in the Galaxy now, their people had to let their inner barbarian out once in a while to allow them to mate. This mating rage was caused by a biochemical imbalance that, if not heeded, would eventually kill him. It explained a lot, and though in the last 20 years, the Vulcans have become more open about their mating practices, at the time, this was a well-guarded secret.

---

*EDITOR'S NOTE: Carolyn Palamas did have a child she named Troilus, and in 2271, she became part of an expedition that established a colony on Pollux IV.

So I had to get him to Vulcan, and I violated orders to do it. I wasn't going to let my friend die.

When we arrived, Spock asked me and McCoy to join him on the surface for a ceremony. I'd never been to Vulcan before; the sky was red, the breeze was hot, and the air was thin.

The ceremony was very primitive, held in an ancient outdoor stone arena with a gong in the center. It was astounding to find out how important Spock's family was. The wedding was officiated by T'Pau, who'd been a leader on Vulcan for over a century.

Spock's betrothed was a beautiful woman named T'Pring. The ceremony began; it was, to use Spock's favorite term, "fascinating."

And then everything went to hell. T'Pring referenced an ancient law that allowed her to choose a champion to fight for her. Spock was going to have to engage in a battle to win his bride. And no one, especially me, expected that the champion T'Pring chose would be *me*.

I would find out later that T'Pring had devised a strategy to get out of marrying Spock, as she had her eye on another Vulcan. By choosing me, she all but guaranteed that neither Spock nor her "champion" would want to marry her, thereby leaving her available.

I agreed to fight Spock, but I hadn't read the fine print; the battle was to the death. We were handed *lirpas*, ancient staffs with a blade on one end and a weighted cudgel on the other. Spock, lost in his fevered stupor, was clearly out to kill me, and he knew how to use the weapon. He sliced open my chest, knocked me on the ground. I was able to get a few shots in, but I was losing.

McCoy stepped in, told the Vulcans that the air was too thin for me, and said I needed a shot to help me breathe. He gave it to me, but it didn't feel like it was helping that much. We were given new weapons: *ahn woon*, similar to bolos. Spock had me on the ground right away; his *ahn woon* bands were tightly wrapped around my neck, and Spock wasn't letting up. Everything went black.

"How do you feel?" It was McCoy. He was standing over me in sickbay.

"My throat," I said. And then I remembered Spock choking me with the *ahn woon*. I put it all together. "That shot you gave me—"

"Neural paralyzer," McCoy said. "Very low dosage, so it took a minute to knock you out." I sat up in the bed.

"What about Spock?"

"He'll be beaming up soon," McCoy said. "His fever seemed to have broken. I think he wanted to say goodbye to everybody. So, am I going to get a thank-you?"

I told him it might have been simpler to let me die. He was confused, until I pointed out that it was a "battle to the death," and that we'd just committed fraud on Vulcan's most revered leader. Something that I didn't think the Vulcan government was going to appreciate.

"I have a solution," McCoy said. "Don't tell them."

"Bones, this isn't a joke—"

"I'm not joking," he said. "T'Pau's never going to see you again, and I don't think she's following the comings and goings of Starfleet captains." He made a fair point. It did seem unlikely that T'Pau would ever run into me again. At least at that moment. And there really wasn't anything I could do about it anyway.

Shortly, Spock came back aboard and couldn't control his emotions upon seeing me. He burst out with a big smile and bellowed "Jim!" as he grabbed me. He then immediately went back to his normal controlled self. It was a rare moment of affection that I will always remember.

✦

I watched Matt Decker die.

His murderer was a robot planet killer. It was several miles long, constructed of neutronium, with an anti-proton beam that allowed it to destroy planets and use the debris for fuel. It was an ancient machine from another galaxy, perhaps millions of years old. It had already destroyed three solar systems and was working on the fourth when Matt Decker's ship, the *Constellation*, tried to stop it. The result was a wrecked ship and a dead crew.

We found the *Constellation*, drifting, burnt, and broken. It was like looking at the *Enterprise* in a cracked mirror. Matt was the only one aboard; he

THE STORY OF STARFLEET'S GREATEST CAPTAIN

had tried to save his crew by beaming them down to a planet, which the planet killer quickly destroyed. He was catatonic, weak, unshaven, on the verge of hysteria. He in no way resembled the confident, hardscrabble shipmaster I'd come to know. He was overcome with his failure. That would lead him to escape and commit suicide by taking a shuttlecraft into the maw of the machine.

His death was not completely in vain. The shuttle's explosion caused minor damage inside the planet killer, which I took advantage of and aimed the wrecked *Constellation* inside the giant construct. Once it entered the machine, I blew its engines up. The planet killer was defeated.

From the bridge of the *Enterprise*, I looked at the dead hulk of neutronium on the viewscreen. And I thought about the first time I'd met Matt Decker; he was with his son. When Matt decided to commit suicide, had he forgotten about him? But perhaps he didn't want to face his child after the disgrace of losing his ship. His son must now be serving on a starship somewhere. It made me think of my son, whom I hadn't spoken to in so many years. I hoped if he knew about me, I had been painted favorably. With that in mind, later that night I recorded my log.

"Captain's log, 4229.7, we have successfully deactivated the planet killer that destroyed the solar systems previously reported. Commodore Matt Decker was in the *Enterprise*'s shuttlecraft *Columbus* making his way back to the *Constellation* to lend me assistance when he was caught in the planet killer's tractor beam. Knowing he couldn't escape, he set his engines to overload. This selfless act provided necessary data on the possible weaknesses of the device that allowed me to use the *Constellation*'s engines in a similar way to deactivate the machine. Recommend highest posthumous honors for Commodore Decker."

It was the truth, with a sprinkling of fiction, for his son.*

---

*EDITOR'S NOTE: I questioned whether to include this, as Captain Kirk is admitting to falsifying records. His response to me: "They want to lock me up for that? Good luck to them." He seemed both determined to be as honest as possible in his account, as well as being confident that Starfleet wouldn't prosecute a hero whose success as an officer was often due to a loose interpretation of the regulations. In any event, the circumstances of the book's publication made the point moot.

Dilithium crystals are a necessary component of warp engines. The unique properties of the crystals allow for precise control of the matter/antimatter reactions that propel starships faster than light. Unfortunately, the crystals don't exist everywhere, so when sensors detected them on the planet Halkan, the Federation dispatched the *Enterprise* to try to make a mining treaty.

The Halkans were a race that had already been to space and decided it wasn't for them. They had a peaceful, thriving society, and they greeted us with friendship. But they weren't interested in letting us mine dilithium on their planet. They had a dogmatic code and would prefer to die as a race than let their dilithium be used in the taking of one life. McCoy, Scotty, Uhura, and I did our best to make the case for the peacefulness of the Federation, but to no avail. And while we were on the planet, an ion storm moved in, engulfing the *Enterprise* as well. Since my ship was getting damaged, and I didn't seem to be getting anywhere with the Halkans, I called a temporary end to negotiations and had my landing party beamed up.

Like a hundred transports I'd been on, I started to see the *Enterprise*'s transporter fade in around me, but then it faded out again. I felt dizzy, and when we finally materialized, everything was different.

The room was darker. Spock and Transporter Chief Kyle gave us a strange salute. Their uniforms were more ornate.

And Spock had a beard.

I instinctively knew that we were in danger. I decided to play things close to my vest. (And I looked down and saw I was actually wearing a vest, a gold one.) I soon discovered that "standard procedure" was to destroy the Halkans if they didn't give us the dilithium crystals. I then watched as Spock *tortured* Lieutenant Kyle for some minor mistake during our beam-up with a small device called an agonizer. This was an insane world, and I had to get some time alone with the landing party to try to figure this out.

I made an excuse, and the four of us went to McCoy's lab for some privacy. I theorized that beaming up in an ion storm had disrupted the transporter circuits, and we were beamed to a parallel universe, transposing with our counterparts in this alternate reality. Another Kirk, McCoy, Scotty, and Uhura were now on our *Enterprise*. And where my mission had been to arrange a mining treaty with the Halkans, I now had to figure out how to save them, while also arranging to get back where we belonged.

We were in for quite an experience. The Chekov in this reality tried to kill me so he could move up in rank. I also discovered that the Captain Kirk on this ship had a "kept woman." She was a lieutenant, but it was clear that her duties on the ship weren't just in the service of Starfleet. (Since the woman's parallel counterpart in our universe is still a member of Starfleet, I have decided not to include her name.) This was a universe of ids, and since I'd previously seen my "id" in the flesh, I knew how to pass as one of them.

The parallel Spock was as clever as our own; he figured out who we were, and eventually helped us to return to our universe. He was also the only person on the ship with an ounce of integrity. I knew that as soon as I left, the Halkans would die. It seemed like such a waste, so I took a shot. I made a plea to Spock to get rid of the "me" in that universe, and save the Halkans, to change his world. As we beamed away, it sounded like he was going to try. I've never gone back, and I never want to, but my hope is that he made a difference.

✦

"I want more of these," Tyree said. He was holding a flintlock rifle. He was enraged, frightening. "Many more!"

I hadn't seen Tyree in thirteen years, and two days before, when I came back to his world on a routine survey, he had seemed the peaceful, friendly man who'd taken such good care of me when we were both much younger. But the Villagers, who'd lived in peace with the Hill People, now had weapons far too advanced for the technology of this world. I had discovered that the Klingons were providing these flintlock rifles to the Villagers in exchange for their obedience and access to the riches of the planet. They wanted to make it part of their empire, and the way they seduced the Villagers into being their slaves was by giving them their own slaves, in this case the Hill People.

Now, standing in a clearing, I was with Tyree as he saw his wife brutally attacked and killed in front of us by a group of Villagers. It changed him.

"I will kill them," he said to me, regarding the men who'd done it.

I couldn't let Tyree's people become slaves, so I'd decided to give them flintlocks as well with the idea that as the Klingons gave the Villagers improved weapons, the Federation would do the same for the Hill People, creating a balance of power. I went back to the ship, and contacted Admiral Nogura at Starfleet Headquarters. He didn't like my plan.

"It doesn't make sense," Nogura said. "For it to work, we'd have to know exactly what improvements the Klingons are giving the Villagers, and exactly when they were giving them." I suggested a Starfleet adviser be permanently posted on the planet to relay that information, to which Nogura laughed. That would be a flagrant violation of the Prime Directive.

"Admiral, if we don't do something, the Hill People will become subservient to the Villagers. And once the Hill People become conquered, there will be one government that will happily join the Klingon Empire. This will follow the letter of the Organian Peace Treaty, and the Klingons will have a planet well inside our borders." I could see this worried Nogura.

"You say you have the proof that the Klingons were providing the weapons? We will present it to the Klingons," Nogura said. "Under the terms of the treaty, they will have no choice but to withdraw." That had been my thinking when I acquired the proof, but now it wasn't what I wanted.

"But sir," I said, "the damage has been done. The Villagers will still have flintlocks."

"The damage was not done by *us*," Nogura said. "In fact, you may have violated the Prime Directive by getting us into this situation."

"The Klingons had already interfered," I said.

"They can't break the Prime Directive because they don't have one," he said, mockingly. "We do, so no matter what they've done, it's no excuse." Nogura felt with the evidence I'd gathered, the Klingons would no longer be providing upgrades and new materials. The cost to the planet would be temporary, and it would eventually find its own path again.

"The only victims will be the Hill People," I said.

Nogura wasn't interested in continuing the conversation, and signed off. Tyree would be on his own; the Villagers would continue to kill his people and take their land. It wouldn't go on forever, but I doubted my friend would survive it. At that moment, the door buzzed. Scotty entered, holding a flintlock rifle. I had forgotten that I'd already asked him to make some for the Hill People. He was very proud of his handiwork. I then had a thought.

"Scotty, did you log that you made them?"

"No sir. I was waiting for you to tell me what they were for."

"Well, it turns out you *didn't* make them," I said, and Scotty smiled. They wouldn't solve the problem that had been created down there, but I wouldn't be completely abandoning my friend either. The Admiralty was wrong, we can't be absolutists where the Prime Directive is concerned and stand by while the Klingons destroy something beautiful. Given what was to come, it would be ironic that the admiral I had this argument with was Nogura.

✦

About a week later, I was telling the whole story of Neural again. I was reminiscing, or more accurately orating, about life aboard the *Republic* and *Farragut* under the command of Stephen Garrovick. I was in my quarters, sharing a bottle of Saurian brandy, my drink of choice, and holding my audience of one in rapt attention; it was Captain Garrovick's son, David, who was now, coincidentally, my chief of security.

Garrovick was 12 years old when his father died, and he seemed hungry for information about his father. I told him everything I could remember, but most of the stories were from my point of view, and I really had not spent that much personal time with Captain Garrovick. Still, there seemed to be some entertainment value, especially the story of how I found out I was going over to the *Farragut*.

"He just waited until he was about to leave and told you to get on board the shuttle?" Garrovick was incredulous. It seemed almost impish to the young man, who thought of his father as serious and responsible.

I came to know the younger Garrovick during one of those freak coincidences that made primitive people believe in a higher power. The *Enterprise* accidentally stumbled on the cloud creature that had killed so many of the *Farragut*'s crew. It went on to kill some of mine, and in doing so, I discovered that Ensign Garrovick, the son of my former captain, was actually aboard my ship. We would eventually destroy the creature together, but not without cost.

Over the years, I'd had nightmares about the cloud creature. In the dream, I'm in phaser control, and I don't hesitate; I fire and the creature is destroyed. It was always a nightmare because I'd wake up to discover it wasn't true. Sometimes in the dream, Captain Garrovick is standing next to me.

I got to live the dream, because a few days earlier I was on the bridge, the creature was approaching the ship, and the image of Garrovick was standing next to me, in the form of his son. Like in the dream, I felt triumphant as I ordered Chekov to fire the phasers.

They did nothing.

And like the nightmare I'd already lived through, the creature came aboard my ship and started killing again. I was able to get it off the ship, and Garrovick and I had destroyed it using an antimatter bomb.

I had invited the young man for a drink. He evoked his father, and we had a far-ranging discussion. I learned that he had joined the academy searching for an identity, hoping to reconnect with his father by imitating his career. When I first met him, I was guilty over the fact that my own hesitancy had cost this son his father. I then learned my hesitancy made no difference; our phasers were useless against the creature, both now and eleven years ago.

It didn't make me feel better. As I talked to this young man, something about our discussion made me feel guilty. I didn't realize why until we finished our conversation and he got up to leave.

"Goodnight, David," I said. I had had a few drinks, but wasn't too drunk to realize he had the same name as my son.

✦

"Most efficient state Earth ever knew," John Gill said.

I was dressed as a Nazi, I was on a planet of Nazis, and I was staring at the Führer.

John Gill, my old academy history professor.

He was in a chair, drugged by a native named Melakon, his deputy Führer, who was now running the planet. Gill had come to Ekos, a world of unsophisticated, crude people as a cultural observer. They had a technology that corresponded with mid-20th-century Earth. Gill had stopped transmitting reports, so we'd been sent to find out what happened to him. Somewhere along the way, Gill had decided to start his own Nazi movement and take over the planet as the Führer. It made no sense.

"Perhaps Gill felt such a state," Spock said, "run benignly, could accomplish its efficiency without sadism." It was hard to take him seriously, since he too was dressed as a Nazi. Also, it didn't explain it.

John Gill was the greatest historian of his generation. He'd studied history his whole life and taught generations of students what he learned. He'd had a great effect on me as a student at the academy. He taught me to look at the causes and motivations of people to determine why history happens, and how to fight those trends that lead to large-scale suffering and conflict. I felt that any of the good I did in Starfleet was due in no small part to the teachings he gave me. I especially remembered my conversation with him about Khan, when he told me I couldn't separate admiration for accomplishments from the morals behind those accomplishments. It was a truth that would soon rear its head in my own life.

But I still didn't understand him, and what he had done on Ekos, and he would not survive to explain himself. After we corrected the damage he caused as best we could, we returned to the *Enterprise* without Gill, who'd been killed. McCoy and I talked at length about why a peaceful man would indulge himself in this way. As usual, McCoy was able to boil it down.

"All those years teaching history," McCoy said. "Maybe he just wanted to go out and make some."

✦

Something began to happen to me toward the end of my first five years on the *Enterprise*. I had many successes, made so many discoveries. I'd stopped wars, sometimes single-handedly; I had a record number of successful first contacts. I'd escaped death on numerous occasions, not just for myself but also for my crew.

I feel now that the problems began when I started to "believe my own press." I got arrogant, confident in the belief there was nothing I couldn't do. I was losing touch with who I was and buying into the prestige that went with being a starship captain. And since there was little else to my life than serving on the *Enterprise*, I began to think I needed more. I wanted promotion. I started taking unnecessary risks to get even more attention from my superiors.

One mission in particular comes to mind. I had received coded orders from Starfleet regarding intelligence on a new Romulan cloaking device. This new upgrade rendered our tracking sensors useless; the previous cloak was invisibility only and allowed Federation ships to detect movement. Now, however, the Romulans had solved that problem. It was a grave threat to our security; the Romulans had tried to start a war a couple of years before, and now, with this new weapon, they would do it again. It was too big an advantage, and we had to nullify it.

My orders were simply "acquire intelligence, specifications, and, if possible, procure a working example." That was it; whoever cut the orders knew that "procure a working example" was basically asking the impossible. At that time, however, I was convinced I could *do* the impossible. I came up with a plan and presented it to Spock, who would be the only crew member I would initially include. I briefed him on the intelligence, and then told him my intention.

"We're going to steal one," I said. I was looking for a reaction, and Spock gave me none.

"Indeed," Spock said. "That will prove difficult."

"I have a couple of ideas," I said. My plan involved both of us getting aboard a Romulan ship. For this to work, I needed to speak fluent Romulan. The shortcut I had in mind for this language course was for Spock to mind-meld with me.

I had had the experience of a mind-meld before with him. It is difficult to describe what it's like. It was a stripping away of all my mental armor. Your thoughts are there for the Vulcan to peruse; Spock picks up my memories and thoughts like they are books on the shelves of a library. You try to protect the secrets, but the Vulcan is in there and pushes you aside. Your most embarrassing memories and thoughts are his; yet his logical demeanor makes you trust him as he reads your intimate desires and fears. I was willing to go through it, however, because it could efficiently teach me a language that Spock already knew.

"How do you propose, Captain," Spock said, "that we then get aboard a Romulan ship?"

This part was far riskier. I was going to spend several weeks as a difficult captain on my own ship, convincing the crew I'd become irrational, someone who was craving success. Ironically, I was playing only a less affable version of the person I was turning into. This glory hound captain would take the *Enterprise* across the Neutral Zone into Romulan space.

"It is likely we will be captured relatively quickly," Spock said.

"Yes," I said, "and when we do, you're going to say it's my fault and defect to your Romulan brothers. And to prove your loyalty, you're going to kill me. Then, after I'm dead, I'm going to disguise myself as a Romulan, beam back aboard the Romulan ship, and steal the device. Then the *Enterprise* will beam us both back, and we'll get away."

Spock raised an eyebrow. *There* was my reaction.

The plan was audacious, dangerous, and in hindsight, ridiculous. And it also happened to work. Upon reflection, the only reason we succeeded was we encountered a Romulan commander who was so blinded by the possibility of capturing a functioning starship, she ignored some pretty obvious warning signs she was being manipulated. In any event, I delivered a new cloaking device to the Admiralty, and, in doing so, prevented another war. And in less than a year, it got me what I thought I wanted.

CHAPTER 8

"NOGURA SAYS THEY'RE GOING TO MAKE ME AN ADMIRAL," I said. I was sitting with McCoy and Spock in my quarters. McCoy had a drink and sat across from me; Spock stood by the door. He carried a data pad, clearly expecting this was a work meeting.

There were about six months left in our five-year mission. I should've had the meeting with Spock alone, but I'd become so used to the three of us together that I broke protocol. Upon hearing the news, they congratulated me, though McCoy said it wasn't really news; there'd been subspace chatter about it for weeks.

"It is, however, a logical choice, Captain," Spock said. "A gratifying recognition of your service and abilities."

"Don't get all mushy on us, Spock," McCoy said.

I brought up the fact that it left open the question of who would replace me. I let the implication hang there for a moment and looked at Spock with a smile.

"Captain Spock," McCoy said. "That's going to take some getting used to."

Spock didn't seem to take the bait, so I explicitly told him that Nogura said the "big chair" was his if he wanted it.

"I am honored by your faith in me," Spock said, "but I must respectfully decline."

I was somewhat taken aback. I wanted Spock to take over; it was a way for me to maintain connection with the ship and the crew. I found myself getting annoyed; this had hurt my feelings. I asked him why. He told me he had decided to resign his commission and return to Vulcan at the end of our tour.

It was really too much for me to take. I asked him to reconsider. He thanked me and said he appreciated it, but that his decision had been made. We hung in the awkward silence for a few moments, and then he excused himself. After he left I turned to McCoy.

"Did you know that was coming?"

"No idea," McCoy said. "But I'm not surprised."

"Why not?" I said. McCoy laughed and took another sip of his drink. He reminded me of how much Spock had changed in the years since we served together.

"Would you have ever thought that stick-in-the-mud we took that shuttle ride with would become your best friend?" I had to laugh at that too. When Spock first began serving with me, he'd been cold, distant, and harsh. As time went on, he seemed more confident revealing his human side; he once said prolonged exposure to humans caused "contamination," which had to be a joke, further proof he was okay with letting his human half peek through. I take some credit for this since I spent a lot of time teasing it out of him. Over time, however, I began to feel his friendship even though he couldn't express it. And though I was his commander, we were equals, partners.

"Friendship was the furthest thing from my mind," I said.

"Well, imagine how *he* feels," McCoy said. "He probably never thought he'd ever have *any* friends. Then scuttlebutt starts that the person he's closest to in the world is leaving him. How does he deal with that pain? The way his forefathers did, with logic."

This was insight that was exceptional, even by McCoy's standards. It never would have occurred to me that Spock would be hurt.

"He'll become the president of logic, if there is such a thing," McCoy said.

I suppose I understood. When I'd received news of the promotion I was ambivalent. I wanted to be an admiral; I wanted to get involved in Starfleet policy on a macro level. But I also didn't want to leave the *Enterprise*.

THE STORY OF STARFLEET'S GREATEST CAPTAIN

Two months later, we'd received orders to move our patrol. Starfleet wanted to bring the *Enterprise* to Earth when we were done with our mission, so the Admiralty put us on a leg that brought us closer to the inner systems of the Federation. There had been twelve *Constitution*-class ships in the fleet, and half of them had been lost.[*] It meant something to the Admiralty to bring the *Enterprise* home intact. The plan, as I understood it, would be for the ship then to undergo a major refit, much larger than it had undergone before. They wanted essentially a new ship, but still make it seem like it was connected to the *Enterprise*; the survival and continuity of this vessel was in Starfleet's view a powerful piece of propaganda.

So we would finish our five years, but maybe in less wild territory and on less hazardous duty. As it happened, our new patrol course put us only a few days away from Vulcan, and Spock came to me with a request.

"I would like to return to Vulcan," he said. "And use my accumulated leave." This was unusual; as far as I could remember, Spock had only asked for a leave once. As a result he had accumulated over four months of leave time. It didn't take me long to figure out what he was doing. The leave period would end just around the time he would be mustering out of the service. When we returned the ship to Earth, there would be wide-ranging ceremonies and baldly emotional goodbyes. He was trying to avoid it all by essentially going on vacation until the end of his term of enlistment.

"You're a complicated person, Spock," I said. I was torn. I wanted Spock at my side when we brought the *Enterprise* home, not only was he my friend; he was objectively responsible for so much of the success of this mission. But I also respected his wishes. I granted his leave. We set course for Vulcan.

When we arrived, McCoy and I waited for Spock in the transporter room. Spock entered, carrying his own duffel. I relieved the technician on duty.

"Well, Spock," McCoy said. "This is it."

"What 'is it,' Doctor?"

"It's goodbye," McCoy said.

"Goodbye," Spock said. McCoy shook his head.

---

[*] EDITOR'S NOTE: *U.S.S. Constellation*, *U.S.S. Defiant*, *U.S.S. Excalibur*, *U.S.S. Exeter*, *U.S.S. Intrepid*, and *U.S.S. Valiant*.

"The least you can do is shake my damn hand," McCoy said. He extended his hand and Spock took it. "I'm going to miss you."

"Yes," Spock said.

"You just can't make it easy," McCoy said.

"As I have perceived that you enjoy complaining," Spock said, "that is undoubtedly what you will miss about me." I laughed, and McCoy joined in. Spock turned to me. I took his hand. There was a lot to say. Too much, in fact, so we said nothing.

"Request permission to disembark," Spock said.

"Permission granted," I said. Spock stepped up onto the transporter pad. I moved to the control panel.

"Say hello to T'Pau," McCoy said.

"If you wish, Doctor," Spock said.

"Not for me," I said. "She thinks I'm dead."

And as I energized the transporter, I watched Spock dematerialize. And as he disappeared, I thought I caught the hint of a smile.

✦

About a month later we were on Delta IV. I had never been to the planet before; Starfleet maintained a base there, and the world itself was a curiosity to many of the other species of the Federation. The Deltans, humanoid but all bald, had a "sexually advanced" society, but what that meant hardly anyone knew, since they had strict rules about who they mingled with.

Will Decker, who was stationed there, looked very much the same as I remembered him; lanky and boyish, he was pleasant and friendly. We shared a bottle of Tellarite beer at a bar situated on a cliff, below us, the starbase, three-quarters surrounded by blue mountain foothills and facing a green sea. In the distance, the shiny metal spires of a city on an island (which the Deltans simply called "City Island"). The air was filled with the scent of flowers I didn't recognize but that was nevertheless very soothing.

Will seemed happy that I'd looked him up. We'd only met that one time, now over five years before. Since his father's death about a year ago, I had started to keep tabs on him. He had served on several ships, eventually on the scout ship *Revere*, where he rose to the rank of commander. He then stepped down from the center seat to join a program he had had a hand in devising.

"Emergency transporters for shuttlecraft," he said, after I'd asked what led him to give up his command. "I coauthored the proposal with several engineers I'd gone to the academy with. Delta IV was the natural place to experiment because the Deltans have designed and manufactured small transporters for replicating plants from stored patterns."

"How's it been going?" I said.

"Well, if failure is the mother of innovation," Will said, "then I guess we're innovators." I smiled at his little joke, as he continued. "We're definitely a few decades away from them being standard equipment, but if at some point in the future we can save the life of someone in Dad's situation, it'll be worth it." I nodded, trying to disguise my discomfort at the mention of Matt Decker's death. He was doing work that, if successful, would be an incredible boon for Starfleet and possibly save hundreds of lives.

All inspired by a lie I had recorded in my log. I hoped he'd never find out that Matt Decker would not have used an emergency transporter to beam out of his shuttlecraft, even if he'd had one. I decided to change the conversation to the topic I'd made the trip to discuss.

"You've had a taste of command, don't you miss it?"

"I don't know," Decker said. "I'm a scientist first, an officer second. And I'm pretty happy here." I read something into this and took a gamble.

"What's her name?" I said. In my experience the only thing that competes with commanding a ship is a woman. Decker smiled, and I knew I was right. He told me about a Deltan woman named Ilia who he'd started a relationship with.

"There's a lot of misconceptions about them," Decker said, a little defensively.

"I make no judgments," I said. That was a bit of a lie; I was judging him, but not in the way he thought. He was choosing a settled life, and I had other plans for him. "To get to the point, Will, I need a new first officer, and I think you're the man for the job."

"Um . . . what?" Will said. I could understand his surprise. He didn't know that I'd lost Spock, and that Scotty, who I'd made first officer, didn't enjoy many of the administrative requirements of the job. I had looked at other members of my command crew: Sulu, Chekov, Uhura, all great officers, but I thought there was something missing with all of them. In truth, I now think any of them would've been a terrific choice in their own way, but I wasn't just choosing my first officer for the next four months.

"It's a great opportunity, sir," Decker said, "but you're almost done with your tour. I don't know that I'd want to leave this project just for a few months as your exec."

"I understand. I'm taking the *Enterprise* back to Earth, where it's going to undergo a major refit," I said. "I think it would be good if the next captain spent a little time on her with me."

Decker was momentarily staggered, for good reason. I'd gone from offering him executive officer for a few months to offering him a *Constitution*-class ship for however long he could succeed at the job. Finally, he opened his mouth.

"Why me?"

"It's a special ship," I said. "It needs a captain with a solid background in engineering to supervise the refit. I've looked at your record; I want it to be you." This explanation sounded a little thin, even to me. And I was being a little arrogant; I was going to have to convince the rest of the Admiralty of it, but since I was going to be one of them, I was confident I'd get my way.

"Captain Kirk," Decker said, "I'm floored. It's just so sudden."

"Opportunities like this come along once in a lifetime," I said. "Don't let it pass you by." I finished my beer and got up from the table, which I think startled him even more. I told him I'd be in orbit for two more days. The implication was clear; he had that time to decide whether to take the job. It was a brutal negotiating move, but it worked.

Decker showed up on the *Enterprise* the next day and accepted. He seemed a little discombobulated; I wondered if he had difficulty wrapping up his personal life that quickly. We left orbit, and I have to admit the next few weeks on the *Enterprise* were a little strange. The crew was guarded with the new first officer; I think many of them had hurt feelings that I didn't choose them (although Scotty was relieved to wash his hands of the clerical duties). But Will worked hard to win them over. He was initially nervous and a little taciturn, but we soon developed an easy friendship and he fell into the role quickly. It was McCoy who decided, however, that I wasn't seeing the truth in the relationship.

"Are you going to stay aboard?" I asked while we were having drinks. I was curious what McCoy's plans were.

"I'm going to move on," he said. "I've got a lot of medical experience that I can share with a new generation of doctors. It's time to pass the torch. Besides, I can't take orders from Decker." That caught me off guard. He had given me no clue before then that he didn't think Decker was up to the job. More important, I thought Decker was working out nicely. I asked him what his problem was.

"I don't have a problem with Decker," McCoy said. "I have a problem with how he got the job. You picked him because you felt guilty."

"Guilty? What am I guilty about? I barely knew Decker when I gave him the job."

"You've defined yourself by this job, and now that it's coming to an end and you're going home, you're trying to fill a hole in your life you've been ignoring." We sat there in silence for a while. I didn't want to hear what he was saying, but I couldn't ignore it.

"Go on," I said.

"You picked a man like yourself, who doesn't have a father, who you could mentor, help in his career," McCoy said. "Do I have to spell it out? You don't want a replacement; you want your son."

"I don't know if I agree with you," I said. "But if you're right, what's the harm?"

"The harm is, there's no real relationship there," he said. "Someone could end up being very disappointed." We finished our drink in silence. What McCoy said cut deep, but I didn't let it get in the way of my plans. In hindsight, he of course was completely right; I was using Decker, and though he went on to something truly extraordinary, to this day I'm ashamed of the life I deprived him of because of my actions.

✦

The rest of our tour of duty was routine; with Sulu's and Chekov's help, I was able to time our return to Earth five years to the second after we left.

Admiral Nogura, now commander in chief of Starfleet, came aboard with Federation president Bormenus. In a grand ceremony, the entire crew was given medals, I was promoted to admiral, and Decker promoted to captain. We then had a reception on the shuttle bay hangar deck.

My parents were there, too. Both in their seventies now, they were fit, energetic, and happy to see me. They brought with them Sam's sons, Peter, now fifteen, and his twin brothers, Joshua and Steven, now three. The young boys all seemed awed by what they saw; Peter was friendly to the crew and delighted that they all remembered him. During the reception, I was surprised to find my father talking with Admiral Nogura very casually; I didn't know they'd served together. The three of us chatted for a while, and then Nogura made his excuses and left.

"Heihachiro was Robau's yeoman on the *Kelvin*," Dad said.

"Was he good at it?" I asked. It was hard to picture Nogura getting coffee.

"Depends how you define the job," Dad said. "He was ruthless. Unusual in a yeoman."

I left the party before it began to break up. I realized that I understood why Spock had not wanted to be here; saying goodbye to this crew was too much for me to handle. I think, also, I was sure I would be back in one way or another.

The next day, I put on my new admiral's uniform and reported for duty.

It was in the penthouse of the Archer Building, and I was greeted by a yeoman who showed me to my office. It was along a hallway with several other admirals, all of whom I knew: Cartwright, Harry Morrow, and Bill Smillie, and at the end of the hall was Nogura. He had successfully transferred his department of strategic planning and studies to the Admiralty, and had a group of relatively young admirals to help him make policy.

I reported to Nogura, who gave me my assignment: I was chief of Starfleet Operations. It sounded like a more important title than it was. I was responsible for a lot of the scut work of maintenance and supply the other more senior admirals didn't want to deal with. However, I was still in their ranks and would participate in the daily meetings of the Admiralty to decide on policy and planning. But on that first day there was a lot to catch up on, so I went back to my office to dive in.

THE STORY OF STARFLEET'S GREATEST CAPTAIN

I sat at my desk; behind me, the wall was transparent, and I had a view of the Golden Gate Bridge. In the distance, I could see the old prison island of Alcatraz.

I was 36, I was an admiral, and this lovely office would also turn out to be a prison cell.

I'm not sure I fully comprehended the endless but efficient bureaucracy I was a part of before becoming an admiral. Starfleet Command had the herculean task of maintaining its fleet, training its personnel, supplying and protecting the starbases and Earth colonies, monitoring trade between Federation members and nonmembers, law enforcement, emergency medical and disaster assistance, as well as implementing the political policies of the Federation Council. And that was when there wasn't even a war on.

And as a member of the Admiralty, every day was a pile of orders I had to cut so that tasks big and small could be completed across Federation space. On just one day: the starship *Obama* was running behind schedule and over budget at Utopia Planitia, so I had to call of meeting of the yard's officers to try to get them back on schedule; Starbase 10's commander, Commodore Colt, died unexpectedly, so I had to find her replacement; an intelligence report came across my desk that indicated increased activity of Tholian ships along their border with the Gorn, so I ordered a freighter, equipped with the latest surveillance equipment, to move near that area of space to surreptitiously gather more information; and I approved the budget for the building of three new cargo vessels, the *Waldron*, the *Kuhlman*, and the *Asaad*.

And then there was the politics. It seemed all the admirals had their own priorities and pet projects that they lobbied for. Everyone got along, though I sensed there was a subgroup who saw the Klingons as a growing threat. Diplomatic efforts with the Klingons had fallen away in recent years; admirals, especially Cartwright, were pushing for increased expenditures on defenses along the border. It was a two-tiered strategy: it guaranteed a little more security, but it also had the effect of pushing the Klingons to do the same, with the intent of straining their resources to defend the border. The theory was this would weaken them over time; it might also provoke an attack, which Cartwright felt we'd be ready for. This was obviously a continuation of the work Nogura had been pushing in the department of strategic planning and studies, though then it was much more discreet.

I had help in my new job; Uhura became my chief of staff, and I brought on Sulu and Chekov as well. This had the double advantage of keeping them from getting new assignments on other ships so I could put them back on the *Enterprise* when the time came, as well as providing me with a group of officers I was already comfortable with.

Even though I was busy, I found myself looking inward, trying to figure out if this was what I wanted. My last few years on the *Enterprise* had begun to feel empty, and I thought a promotion would be the solution; I found, however, it just left me with more questions about who I was and who I wanted to be. I began this self-examination during one of my first meetings of the Admiralty. I was approached by a colleague, one who I hadn't seen in over 20 years.

"Admiral Mallory," I said.

"Captain," he said. "I just wanted to thank you for that lovely note." This was the man who I'd met as a child when I saved the Tellarite ambassador, and who'd recommended me for entrance to the academy. But now he was a reminder that, though people considered my mission a success, a lot of good people lost their lives because of my decisions. I came to the *Enterprise* having never lost a crewman under my command; soon, I was responsible for eleven deaths on average for every year for my five years. This wasn't even counting Gary, whose death I thought about almost every day. This was what Pike had been talking about all those years ago—it had ripped the guts out of me, and left me now a little hollow. One of these losses was the son of Admiral Mallory, this man who'd changed my life by getting me into the academy.

"It was the least I could do," I said, referring to the note. "He was a fine crewman. And I felt I owed you." I smiled, but he looked confused.

"Have we met before?" Now I was confused. He wasn't that old. I reminded him about the incident with the Tellarite when I was a child. He laughed delightedly at the story.

"That was you?" he said. "I'm sorry I didn't remember, it was so long ago . . ."

"But," I said, "you helped me get into the academy." I then told him the story, that Ruth sent my message asking for his help.

"I'm sorry," he said. "I never got it." Ruth said she had given it to his chief of staff, and I was sure she hadn't lied. The only conclusion was the chief of staff hadn't passed it on, and that I somehow got into the academy on my own merits. It left me a little confused.

✦

"There's a planet called Dimorous, which has been off-limits for a number of years," I said. I had gathered Sulu, Chekov, and Uhura in my office. I had resources at my command, and I decided to make use of them. I showed them my log entries from the *Hotspur*, specifically the details of the attack of those mysterious rodent-like creatures. I then told them to see what they could find out about the Tellarite facilities on the planet. They were an efficient group; they had a report for me later that week. Uhura was convinced that, though the dilithium mining facility belonged to the Tellarites, the other facility did not. Sulu had contacts in the Tellarite embassy, and though they had very detailed records of the dilithium facility, they had no records of the other one.

"If it involved illegal genetic experiments, they might have kept them a secret," I said.

"Yes," Chekov said, "except their records clearly state that the dilithium facility had to be abandoned when they also were attacked by the creatures. If they were keeping the genetic experiments a secret, would they be so open about this fact?" That was a good point. I asked if they found any indication of who the facility belonged to.

"In one entry of the Tellarite manager's record," Uhura said, "he details an accident that led to some of his workers being severely injured. He reports receiving medical aid, but doesn't say from where." They had already personally tracked down the manager, who said he remembered that the aid was provided by the Federation starship *Constellation*. Even back then, it was Matt Decker's ship, and Nogura was his immediate superior.

They had checked the logs, which showed no record of the ship visiting Dimorous during that period, though there were gaps where the ship could have. It was starting to look like a conspiracy. Uhura asked if they should keep investigating, but I told them not to, at least not yet. It felt like a hornet's nest in our own backyard, and I wasn't sure how to proceed. But I thanked them and pointed out that they were fortunate the Tellarite manager they tracked down was so forthcoming. Uhura, Sulu, and Chekov exchanged looks that were simultaneously guilty, pleased, and conspiratorial.

"Well, sir," Chekov said, "I may have not been completely honest about who I worked for." Then he added, "Or what my rank was . . ."

"I think I've heard enough," I said.

✦

I did my work, and the time passed, but I never fully invested in the world of the Admiralty; I spent a disproportionate amount of time focused on the *Enterprise*'s refit. I consulted for a year with Decker and Scotty and all the designers and technicians who were working on the new *Enterprise*. The designs used for the refit were based on technologies and construction techniques of the many new classes of ships that were now flying. Scotty and I would help vet and refine the designs based on our practical experience from our five-year mission. Then it was another 15 months as they oversaw all the engineering work. I had a feeling they thought I was getting in the way. At the time I didn't care; the ship was somehow still mine. A few months before her scheduled launch, I became very hands-on in helping find the new crew.

One of my main focuses was trying to find a science officer. My experience told me that, no matter how brilliant or well trained a human officer was, there was no comparison with a Vulcan. The rigorous education and training they received from the time they were children made them invaluable in that position; it was like having a living computer with you at all times. I had to find one for the *Enterprise*.

My first thought was to go to Spock. Not to offer him the job, but to see if he had any recommendations. Of course, it was all an excuse to talk to him again; I hadn't seen him in over two years, and I missed him. I had

Uhura patch me through to his home on Vulcan. He wasn't there, but his mother took my call.

"Admiral Kirk," Amanda said. "It's a pleasure to see you again." I had met Spock's mother several years before on the *Enterprise*. She was human, and like many human mothers, completely maternal, protective, and loving of her son.

"The pleasure is mine, Amanda," I said. "I was hoping to talk to Spock."

"He's not here. In fact, he hasn't been for over a year," she said. "He's undergoing the *Kolinahr*." Her expression saddened a little. I didn't know what she was referring to.

"What is the *Kolinahr*?"

"It's the discipline where a Vulcan sheds his emotions completely. It is rigorous and unforgiving." I could see now why she was sad. The big misconception about Vulcans was that they didn't have emotions. That wasn't true; they just chose not to listen to them, to instead obey the philosophy of logic. But the emotions were still there, and a human mother like Amanda could still believe her son loved her, even if he couldn't show it. However, this was different.

"So, he will actually have *no* emotions?"

"That's his intention," she said. "He's in seclusion, at the *Kolinahr* temple, where he will stay."

"For how long?"

"Captain, *Kolinahr* is a . . ." Amanda said. She got choked up at the thought, then forced her way through. "He will be there for the rest of his life. Communication with the individual members of the temple is forbidden." It seemed that the practitioners of the *Kolinahr* acted as a kind of logic "think tank," working with each other, providing help to the Vulcan society through only occasional contact.

I thanked her and ended the communication. I now understood. She had lost her son completely. She would never see him again, and neither would I.

✦

"There was a Vulcan in my graduating class at the academy," Chekov said later, while we were going over candidates. "His name is Sonak. He's currently second-in-command of the science vessel *Okuda*." I looked at his record; it was impressive. I then looked at his photo. He even looked a little like Spock.

A week later, the young Vulcan was sitting across from me in my office.

"Do you like serving aboard the *Okuda*?" I said.

"The question, sir," Sonak said, "is irrelevant."

"So serving aboard the *Enterprise* as science officer is something you're interested in?"

"Again, sir, that is irrelevant," Sonak said. "I am interested in serving in Starfleet. Where I should serve is up to you and those in command." I smiled. I think one of the things I like about Vulcans is their lack of fear when addressing superior officers. After he left, I convened my staff and told them to pass him along to Decker with my highest recommendation. It was at this meeting that Uhura asked for special consideration of a "friend of hers" for transporter chief. She showed me the file on the viewscreen.

It was Janice Rand.

I hadn't seen her in four years, and as I looked over her record, she'd accomplished a lot. She'd aged a little, lovely but now a mature woman. I guess enough time had passed that the guilt and discomfort over what had happened had faded. And I wasn't going to be aboard the ship anyway. I told Uhura to make sure Will knew about her.

I also informed them that I wanted them to return to the *Enterprise*. Chekov requested to be put in charge of security; I wasn't completely comfortable with this, as I had hoped to have everyone back in his or her old jobs. (The fact was, this was really Decker's call, and I had no rational explanation for this desire. In a few weeks I would figure out what was behind it.) Chekov had also broken my bad luck streak with navigators, excelling in the position. But I didn't want to hold him back, so I recommended it. Uhura wondered if I didn't want to keep one of them around to help train whoever my new staff would be, but I told her I felt the *Enterprise* wouldn't be the same without them.

"It won't be the same without *you*, sir," she said. I appreciated the compliment, and I realized what was behind all my efforts regarding crewing the ship; I was literally trying to re-create a moment in time, the high point of my career, of my life. But I was re-creating it without me.

As the day approached for the refitted *Enterprise*'s launch, I found myself growing despondent. I'd look out and see the shuttle and trams flying everywhere, and I felt trapped, cheated that I wasn't on my old ship. Finally, three days before she was to begin her shakedown cruise, I decided to take a vacation.

My mother's brother had a farm in Idaho. He'd passed away several years before and left it to Mom. She didn't have any use for it, but hadn't gotten around to selling it either. Caretakers looked after it; my uncle had had a couple of horses and a fair amount of land. I decided this was the perfect chance to take a family vacation. I invited Mom and Dad to join me, and they brought my nephews. I thought a little time with my family might just be what I needed, since my other family was about to leave the Solar System without me.

It was a lovely couple of days and brought back some fond memories of childhood to be out with the boys and my parents. I had the sense right away upon seeing Mom that there was something on her mind, but she wanted to talk about it in private. When Dad had taken the boys off to fish in the creek, Mom stayed to talk to me alone.

"I ran into Carol Marcus," she said.

"Oh?" When I had returned to Earth, I had thought of looking up Carol. Something always prevented me from following through.

"It was at a conference in Bejing," she said. "Did you know she had a son?"

My mother was clever. She either knew or had guessed. I wasn't going to make it easy. I said I had heard she had a child.

"Cute kid," she said. "Reminded me of you when you were little." She wanted me to tell her. But I couldn't. I was a little raw now; the *Enterprise* was leaving without me, and the idea of facing the son I hadn't seen since he was a toddler was too much for me to handle. At first, I thought she understood, since she seemingly changed the subject.

"Are you sorry not to be on board the *Enterprise*?"

"Yes," I said. "I didn't think it would be this hard to let it go."

"Sometimes we think we know what we want, and we ignore other possibilities around us," she said. "I regret the time I missed as your mother..."

"I know how hard you tried to make up for it," I said. "But don't you wish you'd had a little more time in Starfleet?" She laughed.

"What I wish is that we'd been more careful," she said. "But I know now a few more years in Starfleet wouldn't have satisfied me. I was a little lost, never really clear on what I wanted to do, who I wanted to be. I blamed your father because I was envious at the clarity of his decision making. I compounded one bad decision with another, and missed some wonderful years with my sons that I'll never get back." She teared up at this; she was thinking of Sam. I took her hand. She smiled and went on.

"There's no rule book on how to be a parent and have a career. Man or woman, you end up sacrificing something. But whatever age your child is, there's always time to fix things."

She was telling me to try. She made me remember that I was a father. David would be ten. I could try now. I could reach out to him. Maybe Carol would be open to that, especially since I wasn't tethered to a ship. I had stability, I was only 38. But what if Carol had moved on? What if she was with someone else? The thoughts flew through my head. Whatever her situation, there was still David, my son. Mom wanted me to see it wasn't too late. I could reach out to them. I would reach out to them.

As I decided that this is what I needed to do, my wrist communicator suddenly signaled.

"Kirk here." It was my new chief of staff on the other end, Morgan Bateson, my first yeoman all those years ago. He informed me there was a Code One Emergency, which signaled a possible invasion or disaster code. He told me he'd already sent a tram to my location. I signed off.

"What is it?" Mom asked.

"I don't know," I said. I saw the white tram in the sky coming toward us. "Please make my apologies to Dad and the boys." I gave her a hug. "And thank you for giving me so much to think about."

Once I was aboard the tram, a yeoman provided me with a clean uniform, and I then watched a recording from the Epsilon IX Station, located near the Neutral Zone with the Klingon Empire. Commander Branch, the station's commander, dictated a report.

On my screen, a luminescent cloud of energy, immense, moving at warp speed through the Galaxy. Since nothing organic could move faster than the speed of light, this meant it was not a natural phenomenon. I watched as the cloud destroyed three Klingon *K'Tinga*-class cruisers and kept on coming. Branch then closed his report.

"The cloud, whatever it is, is on a precise path heading for Earth."

I immediately checked on the availability of starships that could intercept it. Given the speed it was traveling, and the course it was on, only one starship was in interception range. And it had a new captain who'd never dealt with a crisis like this before.

I don't know exactly at what point I decided I had to be the one to take over. I think my certainty might have come from the thoughts I had been having about David. Figuring out how to get back the *Enterprise* was a simpler task than figuring out how to be a father after all these years. Racing off to deal with a threat that had erased three powerful Klingon warships without slowing down was easier for me than facing possible rejection from Carol.

By the time I landed in San Francisco, I was determined to take over command of the *Enterprise* for this mission. I ran into Commander Sonak and was so sure of myself that I told him to report to *me* on the ship. Nogura, however, wasn't going to make that easy.

"Out of the question," he said, sitting at his desk. "I need you here." He raised a good point that if I felt Decker wasn't ready, why did I recommend him so enthusiastically? He also said I'd stacked the ship with the most experienced crew on any starship, many of whom could be captains themselves. The only argument I could make was that, as good as Decker was, I'd be better.

"Admirals don't command starships," Nogura said.

"Then make me a captain," I said.

"You're being ridiculous," Nogura said. "Request denied." Nogura wanted to go through a list of crew positions that hadn't been filled to make sure the ship was as fully staffed as possible before it left, but I wasn't listening. I couldn't let this go. It was too important; couldn't he see that he was putting Earth in danger? I had inflated my own abilities to such a degree that I was under the delusion that I alone could save the situation. I decided to play a card he didn't know I had.

"Admiral," I said, "before we continue, there is another matter I wanted to bring to your attention. It's regarding the planet Dimorous. I've uncovered some disturbing information about it."

Nogura looked at me. A heavy silence followed. He had no idea what I knew, and in fact I didn't really know what I was implying, but from his reaction, it was something dangerous to him and his reputation.

"I see," he said. "Well, whatever it is, can it wait until after the current crisis has passed?"

"I think so, sir," I said. "I can put it on the agenda for the next meeting of the Admiralty Operations Committee." Nogura knew what I was doing. If I were no longer in the Admiralty at the next meeting, it wouldn't be on the agenda.

"Very well." Nogura went on to say he had reconsidered my recommendation regarding command of the *Enterprise*. I'd made a bargain with the devil; whatever Dimourous was really about, it was serious, and I'd just blackmailed not only an admiral, but the man who was probably the biggest supporter of my career. There would be payment for this. But right now, I had the *Enterprise*.

✦

"You're what?" Will said. A second before, he'd been his usual affable self, but his demeanor transformed as soon as I told him I was taking over, and that he would stay on as my first officer.

We were standing in the *Enterprise*'s new engineering section. Crewmen buzzed about, hurrying to get the *Enterprise* ready to leave orbit in 12 hours. I'd found Decker with Scotty working on a problem with the transporter system. I looked at him; he was too young, and it was a mistake putting him in command. He wasn't ready. This was for the best, I thought. I was very convincing, to myself at least.

THE STORY OF STARFLEET'S GREATEST CAPTAIN

Will was furious, and I couldn't really blame him. He'd been working for two and a half years as captain of the *Enterprise*, yet had not spent one day in actual command of the ship. All his work had been in rebuilding it, almost from the ground up. And now, hours away from reaping the rewards of his hard work, I was taking it away from him.

"I'm sorry, Will," I said.

"No, Admiral, I don't think you're sorry," he said. "Not one damn bit." He knew me better than I thought. He was right; I wasn't sorry. I was getting exactly what I wanted. I'd given him the impression of being his mentor, that I would look after him. So he dismantled his life to take this job, putting his trust in me, and now I'd betrayed him. Will left, and I got an admonishing look from Scotty.

And then a console blew up.

The transporter system was malfunctioning, right in the middle of a beam-up. Scotty and I ran to the transporter room. Rand was on duty; she was trying to fix the problem, but it was out of her control. The faulty circuit was in engineering. Scotty and I took over the console.

On the transporter pad, two figures started to materialize. And then started to deform. I tried my best to pull them through, but it was too late. The figures on the pad screamed in agony. I recognized one of them; it was Sonak. The images faded from the pad, their screams with them. We would find out shortly that both died as a result.

I then noticed Rand. I hadn't seen her since she'd received her posting on the ship. This was one of her first days on duty, and these were the *first people she tried to beam up*. And they were dead.

"There was nothing you could've done, Rand," I said. "It wasn't your fault." I may not have sounded that comforting, as I was devastated myself. Because I'd been in command for five minutes and already lost two of my crew. The faces of the 55 who'd died when I last commanded this ship started to flood back. Had I done the right thing? Was I really the right man for the job? Doubt crept in.

✦

"That's all we know about it, except that it is 53.4 hours away from Earth."

I stood in front of the crew on the recreation deck, who I'd gathered to show the transmission I had received from Epsilon IX. I knew they needed to see that, despite the destructive power of that cloud, I was still confident. In the middle of my laying out our orders to intercept it, we received another communication from Epsilon IX. I had it relayed to the viewscreen, and the crew watched with me as Commander Branch appeared.

It was not a good idea. Commander Branch did his best to hold it together as the cloud, an advanced energy field, attacked his station. We went to an external view, saw the power field engulf it. Then suddenly the station was gone, and all that remained was the cloud.

I looked at the crew. Whatever confidence I had instilled in them was spent; we were going out to face something that would probably kill us. I tried to redirect their focus on their work.

"Prelaunch countdown will commence in 40 minutes," I said, and then left. I went to my quarters. It was clean and large, much larger than my old quarters on this ship. I changed out of my admiral's uniform and into one of the captain's uniforms hanging in the closet. I looked at myself in the mirror. I felt younger, better. And then again I thought of the two dead crewmen, one of them Commander Sonak, whom I'd just spoken to an hour ago. I tried to push the guilt away as I strode from my quarters and headed for the turbolift.

I walked onto the bridge and sat in the command seat. The bridge was different; darker, not as warm as it used to be. But the chair felt good; I'd missed it.

"Transporter personnel reports the navigator, Lieutenant Ilia, is already aboard and en route to the bridge," Uhura said. This was the last-minute replacement for the navigator who died in the transporter accident. I'd sent word to Nogura to get me someone as soon as possible who could fly this ship, so I assumed this must be the most qualified person available. The name sounded familiar to me, and I suddenly remembered where I'd heard it, as Uhura continued. "She's a Deltan captain."

The turbolift doors opened, and a bald woman stepped onto the bridge.

"Lieutenant Ilia, reporting for duty, sir," she said. She had a heavy Deltan accent. Despite her baldness, or perhaps because of it, she was exquisite.

THE STORY OF STARFLEET'S GREATEST CAPTAIN

I welcomed her aboard and saw Will Decker get up from his chair. They exchanged a greeting that immediately told me that this was the Ilia that Decker had left to join me on the *Enterprise*. He'd abandoned a comfortable life with her for the promise of command, which I'd just stolen. I could feel the resentment in both their tones as she realized what had happened.

"Captain Kirk has the utmost confidence in me," Decker said. Earth was in danger; I would have to live with the sarcasm.

✦

"In simpler language, Captain, they drafted me!" McCoy said, as he stepped off the transporter pad. He'd grown a thick beard and seemed even more cantankerous than I'd remembered. But I was thrilled. I'd seen very little of him over the past few years. He'd gone on a one-man medical teaching crusade, sharing his knowledge of "frontier medicine" with any doctors who'd listen. I'd arranged for Nogura to implement his reserve activation clause, forcing him to join me; McCoy quickly picked up on the fact that I didn't share his indignation about being brought back against his will.

I told him I needed him. He stared at me, surprised at the vulnerability I was showing. But I was alone; I'd forced my way back onto the ship, convinced everybody I was the person for the job, and I'd already presided over the death of two crewmen. The ship itself wasn't dependable, had a lot of new, untested equipment, and my first officer hated me. I needed the pieces of the *Enterprise* that I knew I could depend on, like my old crew. And now I needed the emotional support of a friend who I could count on to be honest, to tell me when I was wrong. I threw my hand out, silently begging McCoy to take it; it was a lifeline, not for him, but for me. He took it and smiled.

✦

"Wormhole! Get us back on impulse, full reverse!" I had pushed Scotty and the crew to get the warp engines operational too quickly; as a result, an imbalance had thrown us into an artificially created wormhole. Now we were spinning through a tunnel in the fabric of space, out of control, headed toward an asteroid. There was no way to stop, and at our speed if we hit it, we'd literally disintegrate.

I ordered Chekov to destroy it with phasers, but Decker countermanded me. We had no time, so I couldn't stop to have an argument with Decker; he had to have his reason for belaying my order. He helped Chekov fire a photon torpedo, which vaporized the asteroid before we hit it. We were soon out of the wormhole, a fair distance from where we started.

I was embarrassed; it was my fault that we'd just gone through that ordeal. On top of that, Decker had made it worse by countermanding my order. I asked to see him in my quarters and found out just how badly I screwed up. Engine power had been cut off when we entered the wormhole, and the phasers with it. If Decker hadn't intervened, the ship would've been destroyed. I suddenly started to doubt the confidence that had gotten me here. Decker left me alone with McCoy, who decided he'd had enough.

"You rammed getting this command down Starfleet's throat. You've used this emergency to get the *Enterprise* back." I was aware of this before, but only when McCoy brought it up did the plan come to the surface of my conscious mind. I intended to keep her. That's why I wanted my old crew in their old jobs; I had always planned on getting her back and keeping her.

I went back to the bridge. I felt disconnected, self-conscious, and scared. I was now fully doubting myself. In the interim, Mr. Chekov had informed me that a warp-drive shuttlecraft had wanted to rendezvous with us, but I was so lost in my own emotional state that I'd forgotten about it.

So I was shocked when, like magic, Spock walked onto the bridge.

He was dressed in black robes and looked as severe as I'd ever seen him. The shuttlecraft had delivered him from Vulcan. He was back, just when I needed him most.

He stated that he'd been monitoring our communications, and thought he could help with the engines. I immediately reinstated him as science officer. I watched as several of his old comrades reached out to him, welcoming him back, but he gave them nothing. He was different. I was initially touched upon seeing him; now I was confused.

But his help was invaluable; in no time at all, the ship was at warp. I remembered what his mother had told me about the *Kolinahr*; it was a lifelong discipline. That meant he broke it to join the *Enterprise* on this mission.

I had Spock join me and McCoy in the officers' lounge to find out what was going on. For a brief moment, it felt like old times, thanks to McCoy.

"Spock, you haven't changed a bit," McCoy said, obviously looking to restart their old relationship. "You're just as warm and sociable as ever." In falling back into old patterns, Spock obliged him.

"Nor have you, Doctor, as your continued predilection for irrelevancy demonstrates."

I pressed Spock on why he was there.

"On Vulcan I began to sense a consciousness from a source more powerful than any I had ever encountered," Spock said. It was remarkable; he had been in telepathic contact with whatever was in that cloud. He would be an amazing resource. But Spock made it clear that he was looking for personal answers, and, for the first time, I wondered if I could trust him to look after the ship's needs over his own.

I was disappointed, maybe a little hurt. Spock hadn't come back to participate in the mission and walk down memory lane with me. He had entered the *Kolinahr* discipline to purge his emotions, yet he broke that discipline to use the *Enterprise* to pursue his own self-centered goals. It was uncharacteristically *human*.

Despite my disappointment, I couldn't blame him. I was doing the same thing.

We were able to intercept the cloud a full day before it reached the Solar System. It filled the viewscreen; its deep blue plumes of energy were arresting, incomprehensible in size and power. Spock theorized that there was an object in the heart of it generating the field, so I ordered a course to take us inside. Decker objected, but I dismissed him out of hand. I had something to prove, that I could take on whatever was in that cloud and stop it. It was rash and bold decision making, which I felt were what I brought to the table as a captain.

We soon found a spaceship in the heart of the cloud, more massive than anything any of us had ever seen. It launched a probe that entered the bridge, a column of plasma energy. It attacked Ilia. She screamed, then disappeared. And then the probe was gone.

I could feel Decker's anger, but I couldn't meet his gaze. I'd just lost another crewman, and still knew nothing about how to stop this thing that was undoubtedly on its way to destroy Earth. My "rash and bold" decision making was causing deaths. I was failing, and for the first time I wondered if the mission would've gone better if I'd just left it to Decker.

✦

"Jim . . . I should have known."

Spock was lying on a diagnostic bed in sickbay. Something calling itself "V'Ger" was on the ship, and it had literally swallowed the *Enterprise* whole. Spock, against my orders, had left the ship and tried to make contact with this "V'Ger." He had mind-melded with something, and it had caused him neurological trauma. He was different, but not as cold as he had been when he returned to me.

"I saw V'Ger's home planet, a planet populated by living machines. Unbelievable technology. V'Ger has knowledge that spans this universe. And yet, with all this pure logic . . . V'Ger is barren, cold, no mystery, no beauty. I should have known." He then closed his eyes. I had no idea what the hell he was talking about. The mysterious spaceship had reached Earth, and I was no further along in stopping it than when we first encountered it. I shook Spock.

"Known? Known what? Spock, what should you have known?!" I was desperate, so lost. I'd been going through the motions of being a captain, but I'd done nothing to get us closer to completing the mission.

Spock opened his eyes and took my hand.

"This simple feeling," Spock said, "is beyond V'Ger's comprehension." And Spock smiled. Looking back, this was a pivotal moment in my friend's life. From this point on, he was no longer hiding his emotions; he found a way to integrate them into his life and character. He would later tell me that V'Ger showed him the *Kolinahr* was in itself illogical; knowledge of one's emotions provided answers.

But the more important moment for me was when he took my hand. I had my friend, my partner. I was no closer to finding the truth of how to get out of this situation, but with Spock returned to the fold, I had no doubts anymore. We'd beat this thing.

THE STORY OF STARFLEET'S GREATEST CAPTAIN

✦

"As much as you wanted the *Enterprise*, I want this!"

We were in the center of the strange ship, a concave amphitheater, pulsating with light and sound. The most advanced technological construction I had ever seen; a literal living machine. And in control of all of it, a 20th-century space probe called *Voyager*.

We had solved the puzzle. V'Ger was *Voyager*. This ancient NASA probe had disappeared into a wormhole and ended up on the other side of the Galaxy, where a planet of living machines had built an advanced ship for it to carry out its primitive programming to "learn all that is learnable." It then traveled the universe, amassing so much knowledge, the machine achieved consciousness itself. It had come back to Earth to find the "god" who created it, and join with it.

Decker was going to give it its wish. Branches of energy reached out to him from the floor, transforming him. I stared at this young man, whose life I'd changed. I'd taken him away from the woman he loved; I'd given him a ship then appropriated it out from under him, all for my own selfish reasons.

And I watched as he left our reality.

Decker was totally engulfed in energy; he was gone, and the energy started to spread, to engulf the entire spaceship. I was captivated, but Spock and McCoy pulled me away. We ran back to the *Enterprise*, as a torrent of light consumed the giant ship around us. In an explosion of energy, V'Ger's ship and the threat to Earth were gone, leaving only the *Enterprise*.

Back on the bridge, I looked around; the room was different, but the people were the same. I thought about Decker, who now existed on a higher plane; the knowledge of the universe was his. Despite what I'd done to him, he had gained something wonderful. And I had too. I had my ship back.

And of course the cliché is right: you can't go home again.

CHAPTER 9

"I DON'T THINK THEY'RE INTERESTED IN US, JIM," McCoy said.

Spock, McCoy, and I were in environment suits, standing at the edge of a pink and green "ocean," though it wasn't strictly water, more of an ooze of chemicals natural to this planet. Staring up at us from the ooze were three natives. They were all about three feet long, with blue skin that was like a flexible shell, no eyes that I could detect, and claws that resembled lobsters'. The liquid they were swimming in was abnormally hot, something on the order of 150 degrees centigrade. We all stood there, with the creatures vaguely clicking their claws. It was an unusual first contact.

We were about a year into my second five-year mission. Nogura, after my little bit of blackmail, had been in no rush to have me back in the Admiralty, and so, after some cursory congratulations for stopping V'Ger and saving the planet, he sent us out again. Once the technical issues of the refitted *Enterprise* were worked out, it became a very smooth-running ship. There were obvious advantages to having so much of my old crew back, as they could train the new crew in what I deemed priorities. We did a lot of what we'd always been good at: carried diplomats, resolved conflicts, and made first contacts.

We were on a routine mapping expedition when we detected something unexpected.

"The planet closest to the sun," Spock said, "has artificial satellites." The planet was not a Class-M world; it was much hotter than any celestial body we'd found life on before. But the artificial satellites indicated an advanced civilization.

"The planet has no cities on the surface. Its oceans are not water; they seem to be a swirling mixture of elements in a liquid state," Spock said. "I'm detecting abundant life-form readings beneath the surface." Though Starfleet didn't approve of a captain and a first officer being in a landing party, I was always nostalgic for the way we had done things during my first tour on the *Enterprise*. So I almost always went, and almost always took Spock and McCoy with me. As I stood face-to-face with some of the natives, however, I wasn't sure I was the best person for the job.

"These are the creatures I detected, Captain," Spock said. "There's over seven billion living in these oceans." Most of my first contacts were with humanoids. This usually made communication a little easier. In this case, these life-forms were unlike any I'd encountered, and I probably should've brought an expert in astrobiology. But at this stage I was still trying to recapture old glory, so I walked over to talk to them.

"I'm Captain James Kirk, of the *Starship Enterprise*," I said. "Representing the United Federation of Planets." The creatures continued to click their claws.

"I feel like this used to be easier," McCoy said, reading my mind. I was hoping the universal translator would work as it usually did, but we got no response. At least not initially. So Spock started to make adjustments on the translator in our communicators. It wasn't necessary.

"We understood you." The voice came out of our communicators. It was the creatures. "You have not observed the proper protocol." I couldn't tell which creature was speaking, so I decided it was the one whose claws had been clicking the most. I addressed it and asked what the proper protocol was.

"It violates *Legaran* protocol to ask," the creature said. Then, without another word, they all slipped under the ooze and were gone. *Legaran.* That must be the name they call themselves, or at least what the universal translator heard them call themselves.

I now was more determined to make contact with these creatures; they were clearly an advanced society. Spock pointed out that, with no knowledge of their customs, there was no clear way to proceed. But I didn't want to give up so easily. This was a fascinating discovery; I thought it was worth another shot.

"Let's go to them," I said, then called the *Enterprise* and asked for the new aqua shuttle. Scotty had successfully renovated one of our shuttlecraft to be able to effectively operate as a submarine. Sulu piloted the craft down to the surface; the three of us got on board and removed our environment suits.

"The natives may not react well to us invading their living environment," Spock said.

"I agree with Spock," McCoy said. "Let's get out of here."

"What happened to the hearty explorers I used to know?" I said.

"You're thinking of someone else," McCoy said. But we were going to go ahead. I told Sulu to first land on the ooze. The craft bobbed on the surface while Spock took readings. He served as navigator as Sulu piloted, we submerged, and they set a course toward the center of the population. As we moved deeper, I saw what appeared to be lights in the distance.

"Phosphorescence?" I said to Spock. He checked his scanner.

"No sir," he said, "electricity."

As we got closer, we saw the blue creatures moving in and out of openings in what at first appeared to be underwater caves in a cliffside. Upon further inspection, we saw that this "cliff" was in fact an artificial structure, one among many. It was a city, and it went on for miles. Thousands of the creatures swam about, engaged in various activities.

"Spock, are you picking up any transmissions?" I said. "We need to try to talk to them again."

"We can hear you," a voice said over our communication speaker. I turned to Spock.

"Were we transmitting?" Spock shook his head no. They could hear us; I wasn't sure how. I decided to take advantage of it. I told them we came in peace, and the voice responded and said they knew that, but that we had not observed protocol. This was frustrating, and I was single-minded about opening a dialogue. But it wasn't in the cards.

Sulu reported that several dozen of the creatures were closing in on the aqua shuttle.

"Take us out of here, Mr. Sulu . . ." But before Sulu could execute my order, the shuttle was suddenly jolted. Spock reported that about 40 of the creatures had latched on to our craft, pulling us down.

We were at a depth of 1,000 meters, and the shuttle could withstand 4,000. But that was in water. The liquid on this planet was a lot more dense. If these creatures brought us too deep, we'd be crushed. I spoke to the voice.

"If you just let us go, we will leave you alone," I said.

"You will leave us alone," the voice said.

"Depth now 2,000 meters," Sulu said.

"Killing us won't solve anything," I said. "And I don't want to have to hurt you by increasing my engine thrust."

"Depth now 2,500 meters," Sulu said, then checked the air pressure gauge. "Outer pressure 500 GSC and climbing." My eardrums started to hurt; the pressure was building. I went to the communications panel.

"Kirk to *Enterprise*," I said. All I got was static in response.

"I think we've been nice enough," McCoy said. I agreed. This trip had gone bad very quickly. Sulu tried to activate the engines, but they didn't work. The shuttle was going down, with no way to stop it. Just then, Spock detected tachyon emissions underneath us.[*]

On the viewscreen, directly below us, appeared some kind of pentagonal hole in the seafloor. There was a silvery glow in the center. The creatures were bringing us directly toward it.

"They're letting go of the shuttle," Spock said. "But it is too late . . ." Our momentum downward carried us into the hole. The shuttle shook violently, and then suddenly was still. The air pressure was back to normal. Sulu reported that outside pressure was now at zero, but we still had no engine power.

"Jim, look . . ." McCoy said.

Out of the view port, outer space and the *Enterprise* in orbit. The pentagonal hole was some kind of portal. The Legarans had sent us back to our ship, and Scotty tractored us on board. I suppose making contact with the

---

[*]**EDITOR'S NOTE:** Tachyons are particles that move faster than light.

Legarans was historic, and though I'd managed to do absolutely nothing, I take some pride in the fact that to this day, despite years of efforts, no Federation diplomat has managed to get in a room with them. But it was also the first sign that the Galaxy might be different, and not as easy for me as it used to be.

✦

"Sir, I'm picking up a group of strange readings," Chekov said from his security station. "Some kind of subspace displacement."

"Location?" I said.

"I can't pinpoint it," he said. "But it's definitely on the other side of the Klingon Neutral Zone." I got up out of my chair and went over to Spock at the science station. He wasn't detecting any ships, and I wondered whether the displacement was caused by cloaking devices.

"If so," Spock said, "in order for us to read the subspace displacement, it would have to be a large number of ships." Up to this point, the Klingons, as far as we knew, didn't use cloaking devices. But several years earlier, they had either shared or sold their ships and ship design to the Romulans. It made sense that, in trade, they had acquired the Romulans' cloaking technology.

I ordered Sulu to execute a course near where the readings were, but staying on our side of the zone. We hadn't had any specific trouble from the Klingons in a while, but if they had use of cloaking technology, they would have a tactical advantage, and they might decide to violate the treaty.

We reached the closest coordinates to the reading we could without crossing the Neutral Zone, and could detect that the displacements were following a straight course moving along the border but not crossing it. I ordered a parallel course at the same speed. If the ships were cloaked, I wanted them to know that we knew they were there. I had to admit the possibility of engaging the Klingons excited me. It was dangerous, but I was confident in my ability to deal with them.

After a few tense hours tracking the course of the displacements, Uhura turned to me. We were being hailed, but from an unknown source. I turned to Spock.

"I think we got their attention," I said. "Put them on, Uhura."

On the viewscreen, the stars were replaced by Kor. He was on the bridge of his ship. I hadn't seen him since our encounter on Organia. He looked somewhat older, had put on a little weight. His hair was longer and thicker, as the Klingons were now wearing it, and was mostly gray. He still looked dangerous, intimidating; he gave me his greasiest smile.

"Captain Kirk," he said.

"Commander Kor," I said.

"Oh, I wouldn't expect you to know this," he said, "but I'm a general now." He looked me over carefully, then gave me a look of insincere sympathy. "Sorry to see your superiors don't value you to the same degree."

I smiled and decided not to give in to this by explaining I'd already been an admiral. Instead I inquired about where he was calling from and told him that we weren't detecting a ship in the area. He said that it wasn't important where he was, then made an unusual pledge.

"Captain," he said, "you have my word of honor as a Klingon warrior that, wherever I am, it does not concern you or the Federation. I would encourage you to move away from the Neutral Zone, however, as it may provoke a reaction you do not intend." I looked at him. He was trying to tell me something. I signaled Uhura to cut off the transmission, and turned to Spock.

"Duplicity is not outside the Klingon code of behavior," he said. "But I do not think he's involved in an action against the Federation."

"I agree, sir," Sulu said. "He wouldn't have given himself away."

I decided that *we* might be giving him away. He was worried that, by tracking his course, we were calling attention to his position to whoever his intended target was. I had Spock plot a possible destination based on the course information we already had.

"It would seem, Captain," Spock said, "that they are headed for Romulus."

Were the Klingons starting a war with the Romulans? Is that what we'd stumbled onto? A surprise attack? It would make sense. The Organian Peace Treaty had tied the Klingons' hands as far as the Federation was concerned, and the policy of containment by Starfleet had worked. The Klingons needed resources, and the Romulans had a lot of valuable worlds.

I reopened communications and told Kor we were leaving the area. I then told Uhura to get Admiral Nogura on the line, and went to my quarters to talk to him in private.

✦

"We had intelligence that the Klingons were building new ships," Nogura said on the viewscreen. "This, however, is a complete surprise."

"Do you think this is a result of them straining their resources to keep up with our defenses on the border?" I said.

"Who knows?" he said. "And who cares? This doesn't concern us." I felt, however, that it did. I suggested that there was an opportunity here. The Klingons wouldn't reach Romulus for another 24 hours. They were about to engage in a war that could cost millions, or even billions, of lives. It seemed like this gave us leverage with both parties. But Nogura wasn't interested.

"It's a moot point," he said. "The Prime Directive says we can't interfere with the internal politics of another government." I could see from his expression that he was using this as a dodge, hiding behind principles to serve a less than noble end. I could also see he had no patience for my suggestions. The relationship between us had become very strained; what I'd done to get the *Enterprise* back had created a serious rift. But I still tried to do my job and pushed a little harder, suggesting he take it to the Federation Council, who might have success if they pursued a quiet and careful diplomacy that would serve the entire quadrant.

"I think what would serve the quadrant," he said, "is if they wiped each other out. The matter is closed. Nogura out." This was worrisome; Nogura had always had hawkish instincts, but sitting by and letting our enemies kill each other indicated a cold-bloodedness that I didn't expect. I had no love for the Klingons or the Romulans, but war didn't serve anyone. Yet there was nothing I could do about it.

I went about my work, and a few days later on the bridge, Uhura said she was receiving battle transmissions.

"They're Romulan, sir," she said. "Romulus is under attack."

Everyone on the bridge looked at me. My orders were clear; we couldn't interfere. And I didn't know what I would even do if we could. I could see, though, the crew expected me to do something.

"Very well," I said. "Inform Starfleet Command, and continue to monitor those frequencies. We'll continue on course to Starbase 10." I sat in my chair. There was a war going on, and we weren't invited. It was good news that the Federation wasn't involved, but it also gave me a sense of helplessness. I convinced myself I was angry that Starfleet was no longer the instrument of peace and civilization I believed it to be. In fact, upon reflection, I was craving action, but the Galaxy had changed. I wasn't sure I belonged out there anymore.

✦

"Mr. Chekov would like a transfer," Spock said. It was during our morning meeting.

"What? Why?"

"There is an opening on the *U.S.S. Reliant* that he would like to pursue."

I'd had Chekov as a member of the *Enterprise* crew for now almost ten years. He'd grown from an eager, hardworking navigator to a very capable head of security and weapons control. He'd received his promotions through the ranks from ensign to lieutenant commander at a little better than the average pace, so I couldn't begin to understand why he'd want to leave. Spock called for him, and he quickly arrived. The position he was seeking on *Reliant* was first officer, definitely a step up. I couldn't match it, but still wanted to make a pitch for him to stay. Maybe we could give him more responsibilities, different duties. But Chekov smiled and cut me off.

"Sir," he said, "please don't misunderstand me. I have cherished my time serving with you, but I feel that my career is standing still. I'm not embarrassed to admit to some ambition, and I think I am being honest when I say I will never be captain of this ship, or even first officer. There are too many people ahead of me." I was about to jump in and disagree with him, when I noticed Spock and the acknowledgment in his expression. And I had to accept the truth of what Chekov was saying.

THE STORY OF STARFLEET'S GREATEST CAPTAIN

For an ambitious officer, the *Enterprise* was a dead-end job. I wasn't going anywhere, and as long as I was here, Spock was staying, Scotty wasn't leaving, and Sulu and Uhura were more senior than Chekov.

"Fair enough, Mr. Chekov," I said. "I'll approve the transfer."

It started me thinking about what I was accomplishing on the *Enterprise*. There were a lot of people aboard who were qualified to command. And I was keeping them all here, all to keep myself comfortable.

It turned out Chekov got off the *Enterprise* just in time.

✦

We finished our second five-year mission with a lot less fanfare than the first. On our way back to Earth, I did what I could for the crew. I felt both Spock and Sulu should make the captains' list and get ships of their own. I put Uhura and McCoy in for promotions and told them both that they were free to leave if they wanted to. I didn't quite know what was next for me, but I planned on staying with the *Enterprise*.

When we reached Earth, I was called into Nogura's office. Cartwright and Morrow were there. It might've been a friendly reunion, but Nogura got right to business.

"I'm giving Spock the *Enterprise*," he said. I could see the other two admirals avoiding eye contact with me. I wasn't sure what that meant.

"Sir, I'd still like to stay in command," I said.

"We need you here," Nogura said. "I'm making you fleet captain. Congratulations." Fleet captain. I remembered when they gave that rank to Pike, he said it was a desk job, one without influence. Nogura was mocking me and wasn't trying to hide it.

He was done with me; I'd played his game and lost. He'd used my five-year mission to keep me out of the way while he undoubtedly scrubbed any evidence of wrongdoing involving the incident on Dimorous. Now, he was sticking me at a desk, where I would stay for the remainder of my career, influencing nothing. I only saw one way out.

✦

"You resigned? You let him win?" I wasn't sure I'd ever seen McCoy this angry.

"Bones, I'd already lost," I said. We were at an outdoor cafe in the Embarcadero. Nogura, I found out, wasn't just putting me out to pasture; he wasn't accepting the transfers of any officers off the *Enterprise*. They would all have to stay there, or resign their commissions. He'd made Spock captain, which was the only way he could justify taking the ship away from me. Scotty's, Sulu's, and Uhura's careers would advance no further, at least as long as Nogura was in charge. He understood revenge; it pained me to admit that my political posturing had cost not just me but the people closest to me.

McCoy asked me what I was going to do. I was 43, there was plenty I could still do. I was going to start by taking over my uncle's farm. He scoffed at the prospect.

"You're not going to be happy on a farm."

"What are you talking about? I grew up on a farm, remember?"

"No you didn't," he said. "You grew up in outer space. I was there." I laughed, but it was a little joyless.

✦

I moved to the farm and life quickly got quiet. My parents visited a lot, with Sam's youngest sons, who were now rambunctious nine-year-olds. Peter had gone off to the academy, now the fourth generation in our family to make it. I spent a lot of time working in the fields like I did as a boy, then rode horses for recreation. I supposed I'd earned a vacation, and I took it.

But I was a little lost. I'd been in Starfleet since I was 17; I had not experienced adult life without the organization determining how I was going to spend every day.

I got restless on the farm pretty quickly and decided to travel. I acquired a shuttlecraft and took an extended tour of the Solar System, visiting sites I had never seen. But several months later I found myself in an environment suit exploring an impact crater on Jupiter's moon Ganymede, and all I could think was how bored I was. This wasn't exploration; it was tourism and couldn't match the excitement of discovering new worlds. So I went home.

I thought a lot about Carol and David, and made a small effort to track them down. Unfortunately, I couldn't find them; Carol was involved with some kind of confidential project, and my contacts couldn't (or wouldn't) tell me where she was.

I eventually found a rhythm. I did farm work, some teaching at the academy, and a little consulting to the ship builders on Utopia Planitia. Before I knew it, four years had passed. I knew I would need to find some kind of replacement for the discipline of the service, or I would slip into old age very quickly. One day while on a horseback ride, I inadvertently found it.

I saw another rider up on a hill. It was a woman. I rode up to her.

"I'm sorry," she said. "I'm a little lost. I hope I'm not trespassing." She was striking, tall and thin, with long brown hair and dark brown eyes to go with an olive complexion. She was also a fair amount younger than me.

"We like to share," I said. "I'm Jim Kirk."

"Antonia Slavotori," she said. She asked me to show her the way out of there. I asked if she'd mind joining me for lunch first. She smiled.

"I've already eaten," she said. "If you could just give me directions." She was shutting me down. I told her I would happily lead her out. I rode with her for a while.

She wasn't from Idaho; she was only visiting, buying a horse from one of my neighbors, who'd let her take it out for a ride. She lived somewhere in California, but withheld details of exactly where. As we rode together, I realized she had no idea who I was; that was unusual, as my exploits had gained me some notoriety. I somehow found this compelling, and I stayed with her far longer than I had to. When we reached the farm where she'd picked up the horse, I asked if I could see her again. Again, she smiled.

"Probably not," she said, and then rode off.

However, I was not deterred. She'd given me her name, and finding out more about her gave me a goal, albeit a short-term and lighthearted one. I took her as kind of a mission, and I decided to try to see her again. If she rejected me again, I would move on.

Her name was somewhat unusual, and the fact that she mentioned California made her easy to track down. I thought showing up at her home would be somewhat unnerving, but I saw that a designer with her name had a studio in somewhere called Lone Pine. About two weeks after I met her, I took a trip.

I beamed into the sleepy little town at the base of Mt. Whitney, beautiful, as even in April snow covered the nearby peaks. I found Antonia's studio attached to an ancient building called the Old Lone Pine Hotel. It was spartan and clean, with modern furniture that had a rustic touch. She sat at a drafting computer in the back, and when I walked in she looked up. It took her a minute to place me, and then she was incredulous.

"What the hell are you doing here?"

"I was interested in buying some furniture." She laughed. I asked her to show me her work. It wasn't really my area of expertise, but her designs intrigued me, and I was fascinated hearing her talk about her techniques and influences. After a while, I asked if she would finally join me for lunch.

"Look, Jim, I'm flattered," she said. "But I don't want to mislead you. I'm with someone." I felt like an idiot; for some reason, that had never occurred to me. I realized I'd given it everything I had, and decided to leave, but this time she stopped me. She invited me to join her and her boyfriend at their house for lunch. At this point, I figured why not.

She contacted her beau to let him know she was bringing company, then drove me up to a large cabin set up on the mountain. Set against the hillside, surrounded by trees, it was a lovely, peaceful setting. Her boyfriend met us at the door, with no shirt, holding the leash of a handsome Great Dane. I think he meant to present a picture that would mark his territory and intimidate me, but it really didn't work. I introduced myself, and once I said my name, his entire demeanor changed.

"Wait a second," he said. "You're Captain James Kirk!" This came as a surprise to both Antonia and me. Whatever slightly threatening persona he'd tried to affect was now history. He turned to her and sounded like a screeching teenager. "You didn't tell me you knew him!"

"I *don't* know him!" she said. But he wasn't interested in talking to her anymore.

"I'm sorry, I didn't introduce myself, Captain. Lieutenant Commander J. T. Esteban."

Esteban hurriedly ushered me in, leaving a bemused Antonia in his wake. I turned, and she and I shared a quiet laugh at the absurdity of it.

Three months later, Esteban had gotten a plum posting, so I bought his house. He also gave me the dog, whose name was Butler. Antonia, however, immediately moved out.

Four months after that, she moved back in.

She wasn't like the women I'd become involved with over the years. The "swagger" I tended to employ with other women didn't seem to interest her, and it took a long time before she would agree to see me romantically. She was 34 and had never gone into space; she paid no attention to Starfleet, and didn't seem interested in it. The only thing she found appealing about other worlds was the food that got exported to Earth. There was something about the relationship that reminded me of the one I had with Edith: I wasn't a starship captain to Antonia, I was just Jim.

We stayed in Lone Pine for almost two years together. I had lost touch with almost everyone at Starfleet, though Bones made a consistent effort to call. I thought I might marry Antonia; I didn't know whether I was truly in love with her the way I was with Edith or Carol, but I was very comfortable. Pursuing a romantic relationship over everything else was a new experience for me, and it gave my life the purpose it was lacking.

On a day in July, while Antonia was out at her studio, I was about to walk Butler, when I was surprised to see Harry Morrow walking up the path. He was wearing civilian clothes.

"Harry," I said. "I don't remember the last time I saw you out of uniform."

"I didn't want to draw attention," he said. "Admirals tend to attract junior officers." He was friendly but had a grave air about him. I took him back to the house and poured us some coffee while we engaged in a little small talk. Finally, he got to the point.

"Nogura is gone," Morrow said. "Resigned." I felt an unabashed pleasure at this news; Nogura had fouled my memories of serving in Starfleet. I asked what happened.

"Before the Organians forced peace on us," Morrow said, "Nogura was making contingency plans for an invasion of Klingon space." When I discovered the truth about the genetically engineered creatures on Dimorous, I thought it involved a possible invasion tactic. But I had also assumed that he'd gotten rid of all the evidence. Morrow confirmed that he had, but he made the mistake of trying to do it again. He'd moved a lot of Starfleet resources to the border with the Klingons, with the expressed purpose of pursuing his containment strategy, forcing them to spend and build to defend the border. But then Nogura started drawing up plans for an incursion.

"I took it over his head to the Federation Council," Morrow said. "They forced him to resign. I'm the new Starfleet commander."

"Congratulations," I said, but I wasn't sure it was good news for Morrow. Nogura had a lot of allies in the Admiralty: Cartwright, Smillie. I wondered how they felt about this. And I still didn't know what he was doing here.

"I didn't like what he did to you, Jim," Morrow said. "You're one of the best officers in the fleet, if not the best. We need you back."

The sad thing is, the minute I saw him on the path, this is what I was hoping he'd say.

✦

"Did you really think making me eggs was going to 'soften the blow'?" She was sitting in bed in an undershirt, her hair up, the breakfast tray in front of her. I'd made Ktarian eggs, her favorite, and brought it up to her. Then I told her I was going back to Starfleet.

"I guess that was kind of stupid," I said.

"I'm kind of relieved," she said. "I thought you were going to propose."

"You didn't want to marry me?" I was stunned.

"You're insulted I'd turn down a proposal you had no intention of making?"

"Well . . . yeah." We laughed. She often reminded me how "screwed up" I was where women were concerned, and this seemed more confirmation. I told her I was sorry to lose her.

"I'm not sure you ever had me," she said. "You're always a bit in outer space." She kissed me, then offered to share her eggs.

Antonia moved into her studio; I left the house and got an apartment near Starfleet Headquarters. Morrow reinstated me as an admiral; I got a new uniform and began assembling my staff. Angela Martine, now a commander, became my chief of staff. Garrovick and Reilly also joined me; though they weren't friends necessarily, I felt at ease having old crew around who understood me.

Most of the people I thought of as friends were on the *Enterprise*, but it was off on a mission, so I threw myself into my work. The politics of the Admiralty were still just as uncomfortable to me, and I found myself going home to an empty apartment at night. The hollow feeling started to return. I began to examine my decision. Had it been too rash? Morrow had asked me to come back, and I'd thrown a happy life away with a beautiful woman for what?

One morning in my office, Martine gave me a tape. It was a project that needed a starship assigned to it for extended duty. I put the tape in the viewer. It was top secret, so I told Martine to leave. The computer scanned my retina as a security precaution, and as the recording began, I literally gasped.

"Project Genesis. A proposal to the Federation," Carol Marcus said. I hadn't seen her in over 20 years. I couldn't even listen to what she was saying, I was so lost in a reverie of memories. She was still so beautiful.

David. What had happened to David? I wanted to talk to her, to call her. She ended the proposal with "Thank you for your attention." And a little smile. I watched it three times just to see the smile.

I was overcome with a feeling of loss. There she was, everything I could've had. I caught my reflection in my glass desktop. For the first time I saw the lines on my face. I was old and alone.

CHAPTER 10

"WELL, MR. SAAVIK, ARE YOU GOING TO STAY WITH THE SINKING SHIP?"
Spock's trainee crew had made a mess of the Starfleet Academy simulator, which was not at all unusual. As I walked through the replica of the bridge, I remembered doing the same thing 30 years before. I still thought the *Kobayashi Maru* test was a load of crap, but, like every officer before me, I took perverse pleasure watching young cadets struggle with it.

The young officer Saavik was Vulcan but had more obvious emotional responses than I was used to seeing in her species. She didn't maintain her composure as confidently. And she complained that the test wasn't fair. She fell right into the trap I'd fallen into. I went on to tell her that a no-win situation was a possibility every commander might face, which is exactly what Commandant Barnett said to me when I put up a fuss. I actually imitated his condescending arrogance. I then strode out of the simulator, not quite sure what I had accomplished, except perhaps continuing a tradition I didn't believe in.

About ten months before, when the *Enterprise* had returned from its five-year mission, this time with Spock as captain, I'd had meetings with him and some of the crew. I wanted them to know I would do everything to help them in whatever career path they chose. The *Enterprise*, which was going to need another refit soon, had become a training vessel for Starfleet Academy, and I was surprised that Spock, Scotty, McCoy, and Uhura wanted to stay with the ship. The lighter duty of training cadets appealed to all of them. Sulu, however, had wanted his own ship for a while, so I put him on the captains' list. He decided to pursue the new ship *Excelsior*, which was still on the assembly line, and in the mean time joined his *Enterprise* friends in teaching as well. This group of cadets who'd just participated in the *Kobayashi Maru*, and were under Spock's tutelage, would be going on a training cruise, with support from some of the older officers. Out of a sense of nostalgia, I arranged to conduct the inspection.

As I exited the simulator, I was pleased to run into Spock. In the intervening years he'd become much more comfortable in his own skin; he balanced his human and Vulcan halves with much more ease and conveyed a kind of judicial wisdom. He was a pleasure for me to be around: he was captain to everyone else, but for me he fell right back into being a first officer.

We joked about what his trainees had done to the simulator, and he reminded me the only way I beat the test was by cheating. Before we parted, I took a moment to thank him for the present that he'd left in my office and I'd been carrying all day. A first edition of *A Tale of Two Cities* by Charles Dickens. I would take great pleasure in reading the book. Its themes of self-sacrifice and rebirth would end up having unique meaning for me. He went back to the ship to prepare for my inspection, and I went home. The ennui that had set in when I returned to Starfleet the previous year had not abated.

It was my 50th birthday. I decided to spend the evening alone, though Bones had other plans. He showed up uninvited, with a bottle of Romulan ale and a pair of reading spectacles to fix farsightedness. He didn't waste time getting to the crux of my problems. He told me the solution to my depression was getting back my command. I thought about it. I wasn't sure; I thought that my foray into space had shown me that my day was over. And I felt like I was lost in an endless cycle.

"What do you mean?" McCoy said.

"I go out in space, I get promoted, I give up the promotion and go back to a ship," I said. "I did that already. I can't do it again. I'll look like an idiot."

McCoy and I talked about the pursuit of happiness, and that some of us just didn't have the tools to achieve it.

"You're not going to find contentment outside of yourself," he said. "It's got to come from within." I then wondered why he thought I needed a command to make me happy. He said it was as close as I was going to get. And he was getting tired of taking orders from Spock.

We drank a few more glasses of Romulan ale, and McCoy staggered out. The intoxicating effects were a little hard to shake off the next morning.

"Admiral," Uhura said. "Are you all right?" She was in uniform, standing over my bed. I had arranged to travel with her, McCoy, and Sulu to the *Enterprise*. She gave me a warm smile; I wasn't sure how she'd gotten into my apartment, but when I checked the clock and saw how late it was, I was thankful she had.

We beamed up to the maintenance satellite, where we met Sulu. McCoy joined us, also looking a little worse for wear. Sulu piloted us over to the *Enterprise* in a travel pod. It was always nice to see my old ship from the outside. It was majestic, comforting.

We docked and entered through the port torpedo room, greeted by Spock, Saavik, and a phalanx of crew and cadets. This wasn't the first time I'd seen these trainees, but I still couldn't get over how young they were. They looked like children. But among the young faces standing at attention, an old one: Scotty, now gray, still with the bloodshot eyes, just like that first day I'd come on board, still enjoying his shore leave too much. I decided to talk with one cadet.

"Midshipman First Class Peter Preston, engineer's mate, sir!" He looked like he was 12. I couldn't imagine I was that young when I had served, and then I remembered myself sleeping under a staircase on the *Republic*, and smiled. Whatever ambivalence I had toward this inspection, it began as a paean to nostalgia. It would soon become a requiem.

✦

"Who the hell even knows about Genesis?" Morrow said. "It's a top secret project."

"It's not the first time that's happened, Harry," I said. I knew the Klingons and Romulans had extensive spy networks. And they'd all love to have it. The Genesis Project was a device that could theoretically reorganize inanimate matter on a subatomic level to create life on a planetary scale. It was Carol's project. I was very worried because she had just called me from her lab on the space station Regula I. We hadn't spoken in years, and she was angry. She was accusing me of "taking Genesis away." I didn't know what she was talking about, and the communication was quickly cut off. Someone was jamming it; she was in danger. I was worried, and I could see Morrow was worried too. The Genesis Project would be a powerful weapon; it would destroy all life on a world to make room for the new life it created.

"You've got to get a ship to Regula I right away," I said.

"Okay, get going," he said.

I hadn't meant me. I wanted to go; I was concerned about Carol, but I didn't have the support I needed. This ship and crew weren't cut out for it.

"You have to make do," Morrow said. "Except for some freighters and a science vessel, you're the only ship in the quadrant."

"But I'm going to spend the whole trip changing diapers." Morrow laughed, but he didn't care.

"Report progress. Morrow out."

I went to see Spock. I told him the situation and my concern that his crew would crumble at the first sign of trouble. They were kids. Spock, however, had faith in them. And he instinctually knew what I needed.

He gave me back the *Enterprise*. He could see that I wanted to take control of the situation, that I didn't want to be second-guessing him or anyone else. He made the right decision for me; I'm not sure it was the right decision for everybody else.

We soon ran into the *Reliant*. It cut into us with full phasers.

Reliant was the ship I'd assigned to assist Carol and her team in the search for a lifeless planet to test the Genesis Device. The last I'd heard it was several hundred light-years away; now it was intercepting us. That should have been my first clue that something was wrong; Morrow said the *Enterprise* was the only ship in the quadrant. If *Reliant* had been reassigned, it had come from the direction of Regula I. Morrow would've assigned it to investigate.

I had trouble believing a Federation starship would be an enemy, especially one where Chekov was the first officer. That was my mistake. They knocked out our shield generators and warp drive with their first shots.

The impulse engines came next. I hadn't been in a battle in years, and my instincts were slow. My crew consisted of a few adults trying to manage a screaming, crying nursery. A lot of people died in that attack; I felt responsible, and that was even before I saw who was firing at us.

The *Reliant* called for our surrender, and I had no choice. On the screen, a face I hadn't seen in 15 years. Long gray hair where it was jet black before, strange clothing, but it was him.

"Khan."

I couldn't believe it. I'd left Khan a hundred light-years away, but somehow he'd hijacked the *Reliant*. He said he wanted vengeance on me. At first I didn't know why. But I didn't see McGivers with him. I soon found out his wife was dead. He blamed me. And now everyone on the *Enterprise* was at risk. I offered myself in exchange for the crew.

"I'll agree to your terms if . . ." he said. "If in addition to yourself, you hand over all data and materials regarding the project called Genesis." Oh my god, how did he know about it? That weapon, in his hands. Had he already been to Regula I? Had he hurt Carol? David?

This was all my fault. I'd let this murderer live. I had to get us out of this. I remembered Garth at Axanar taking remote control of his enemy's weapons consoles. Federation ships had combination codes, but Khan might not know about it. It was all I had.

It worked; I lowered Khan's shields and damaged his ship so he had to withdraw. But I'd done nothing clever; my only advantage was I knew more about our ships than he did. As I watched the young cadet Peter Preston, whom I'd met only a couple of days before, die in sickbay, I realized it was no victory, and it would only get worse.

✦

We limped to Regula I, a lonely space station around a desolate asteroid. It was a chamber of horrors: bloody corpses hanging from the rafters; Carol's team had been tortured to death. Chekov and his commanding officer were locked up in a storage cabinet. They were not quite themselves after having been abused and forced to do Khan's bidding. More suffering caused by my hubris.

I had left Khan alive, and now he was leaving a trail of devastation across the Galaxy. I had to find Carol and David.

McCoy, Saavik, and I had beamed down into the Regulan asteroid with Terrell and Chekov. We found constructed tunnels, and we also found the Genesis Device. Carol had hidden it from Khan.

And then someone hit me in the back. He then jabbed a knife at me, but I easily disarmed him.

"Where's Dr. Marcus?" I asked. He was at least 30 years younger than I was, but he couldn't fight. I was going to hit him again, when he spoke:

"I'm Dr. Marcus!" I looked at him. Oh my god. He was a little baby the last time I saw him.

"Jim!" Carol came running into the tunnel. It was my family reunion. And I'd just greeted my son with a punch to the gut.

There was no time to catch up.

As I watched, Khan beamed Genesis up to his ship. The most evil man I ever met now had the greatest weapon man had ever created.

✦

"It's the Genesis wave," David said. Khan had set it off, and if we didn't get out of range, we'd be caught inside it, our lives wiped away by its life-creating effect.

We were on the bridge of the *Enterprise*. We'd defeated the *Reliant* in ship-to-ship combat in the Mutara Nebula. I had noticed that David came onto the bridge during the battle, and had allowed myself a moment of pride that my son was getting to see me in action. But it was short-lived. David was the one who recognized that the Genesis Device was going to detonate. He said we had only four minutes. We couldn't get away; we didn't have warp drive. We were going to die.

I don't know how I lost track of what happened next. We were only a few thousand kilometers away from *Reliant*, and then suddenly the cadet at the engineering station said we had warp power. I ordered Sulu to take us to light-speed, a second before the Genesis Device exploded.

We watched an amazing metamorphosis as it condensed all the matter in the Mutara Nebula into a new world. Khan was dead. I thought I'd won and cheated death for myself and the *Enterprise* once more.

I didn't know how Scotty had fixed the engines. Then McCoy called me from engineering. And then I noticed Spock wasn't in his chair.

I flew down there. I saw him in the reactor room, cut off from the rest of the engineering section, flooded with radiation. He was the reason we'd gotten our warp drive when we needed it. He had literally opened the warp reactor and repaired it *by hand*.

I hadn't cheated death, I was looking at it. The first officer who'd looked after me for so many years, my partner in so many adventures. He defined me with his friendship and loyalty; he taught me with his knowledge, honor, and dignity. And he sacrificed himself so that we, so that I, could survive.

He said goodbye, and I watched him die.

✦

We had a funeral, and I put his body in a torpedo casing. My best friend was dead, and I couldn't save him. I had experienced loss before. Gary, Edith, Sam, but this one seemed worse. He had been a part of my adult life like no one else. He himself had escaped death many times, and I assumed he would be immortal.

When I fired his coffin out to land on the new Genesis Planet, I cried, feeling selfish at what I'd lost.

The battle had wrecked the *Enterprise*, so while Scotty led the trainees in the needed repairs to get us home, I mourned. I finished the book Spock gave me. I read as the main character sacrificed himself for the greater good. It was as if Spock were speaking to me from the grave.

David came to see me. I was sad, but my son was reaching out to me. He was a brilliant young man, a little headstrong, certain in his point of view. Carol said he was a lot like me, but I didn't see it; I saw a man, whose life I hadn't been a part of, but who was welcoming me into it now. Maybe we could become friends. We spoke about Khan, who he was. David was a smart man; he seemed to understand Khan's ambition. I remembered when I was in school, talking to my professor John Gill about Khan, about how I admired him. And that conversation was a straight line to Spock's death; I admired Khan, and because of that he survived to try to kill us all. I'd been a fool; we so often hold up as heroes men who achieve great things, ignoring the sacrifices they force others to make in order to succeed.

David took what I said personally; he thought Genesis wasn't that kind of achievement. I smiled and nodded, and decided I wouldn't point out that we all almost died for it.

Scotty got us up and running, and we set out for Ceti Alpha V, where Khan had marooned the crew of the *Reliant*. It was an interesting voyage. Saavik and David started some kind of relationship, though the rest of us could only guess at exactly what was going on. McCoy went into seclusion; I'd wondered if the death of Spock had hit him harder than he wanted to let on.

And I had some time alone with Carol. She too was going through a difficult period of mourning. Khan had tortured and killed her entire staff. She spent a lot of her days reaching out to their families, and I could see it was taking a toll. In bereavement, we found some comfort together.

One night, we were sitting in my quarters, sharing a drink. She told me about David as a boy, as a young man, and the difficulties of raising him by herself.

"He was lucky, though," I said. "He always had his mother." After a while, I could see she had something she wanted to ask me, but was hesitating. I forced it out of her.

"Did you ever get married?" she said. I told her I hadn't, but she could tell that there was another story I wasn't sharing. She pressed, wanted me to tell her about this mystery woman. I realized I had never really talked about it with anyone.

"Her name was Edith Keeler . . ."

✦

We rescued the crew of the *Reliant*, all of whom survived, though they were in pretty rough shape, and took them all to Starbase 12. Carol had spent many years there, and she proceeded to set up a base of operations from which to coordinate the study of the Genesis Planet. She lobbied Starfleet Command to assign several science ships right away, but the Admiralty, for some reason, wasn't cooperating. I tried to intervene, but they said they couldn't spare any vessel. I volunteered the *Enterprise*, but Morrow pressed me on the damage that she had undergone, and I had to admit she needed more work before I could take her out again.

However, I had to help Carol and David. It was somehow related to Spock's death. They were helping to fill a hole, and I wouldn't give up. There was a new science vessel in orbit of Starbase 12, *U.S.S. Grissom*. It was finishing up some minor maintenance, and it turned out I knew its new captain. I decided to pay him a visit aboard his ship. I beamed up and walked onto the clean, bright bridge of the small vessel.

"Admiral Kirk," J. T. Esteban said, "great to see you again."

The *Grissom* was on a general patrol in this quadrant, but with Esteban's help, we were able to get it assigned to this project. I again was kind of proud that I could do something to impress my son.

The news on the *Enterprise*, however, wasn't so good.

"I cannot fix the damage without a spacedock," Scotty said. "She'll run at warp, but that's about all. I've got to get her home." The commanding officer of Starbase 12, Commodore Jim Corrigan, my old roommate from the academy, was very interested in my trainee crew.

"There's going to be a lot of ships coming through here needing replacements," Corrigan said. "It'd be a shame to make all those kids go all the way home just to come out here again." So I talked it over with Scotty, Sulu, and Uhura, who agreed we could run the ship to Earth with a skeleton crew, and I let the trainees be reassigned. I wanted to stay longer at Starbase 12, squeezing every bit of time I could with Carol and David, when Uhura came to see me in my quarters.

"Sulu was only supposed to be with us for three weeks," she said. "His ship is waiting for him back in Earth orbit." I'd forgotten. I was torn, but I had an obligation to him. I told her to prep the *Enterprise* to leave orbit immediately. I went to say goodbye to Carol.

She was in her office with David, going over some of the data on the Genesis Planet. David and Saavik would be going on to begin studying the new world, while Carol would stay behind on Starbase 12 to find more ships. I promised her I was coming back with a fixed *Enterprise* to help on this mission. She smiled.

"You'll forgive me if I take that with a grain of salt," she said. As sure as I was that I was coming back, I decided not to argue with her. We had reconnected after all these years, and now I wanted to be with her again. I knew it was what she wanted too. My promise was real; for the first time, I saw the future.

I then turned to David.

"It's been a pleasure, sir," he said. I shook his hand.

"Call me . . . Dad," I said. After a moment, we all laughed. It sounded ridiculous. "All right, don't call me that."

✦

"You left him on Genesis!" Spock's father, the Vulcan ambassador to the Federation, was in my apartment. I hadn't seen him in a long time, and he wasn't sounding logical. He was sounding angry.

I'd come home to a lot of bad news. The Genesis Project was a galactic controversy. No one was allowed to talk about it, and we were all going to be extensively debriefed. This meant Sulu wasn't getting his ship; they'd already given it to someone else. The *Enterprise* was going to be decommissioned, and I wasn't getting another ship, not until the Federation came up with a policy on Genesis. But the worst of it was Bones.

I found him in Spock's quarters on the *Enterprise*, babbling about having to go home to Vulcan. Spock's death had wrecked him; he had had some kind of nervous breakdown. I remember thinking that I had always taken McCoy's durability for granted: this reminded me he was only human.

And now Sarek, Spock's father, whom I'd first met almost 20 years before, was *shouting* at me. He said I hadn't carried out Spock's last wish. I didn't know what he was talking about. He asked to mind-meld with me.

Sarek's thoughts reached into my head, opening the door to memories I had no desire to relive. I was back in engineering; Spock was saying goodbye. And he was dead again. Sarek broke the meld.

"It is not here," Sarek said. He told me that Vulcans transferred their living spirit, called the *katra*, to someone or something when they died. But Spock hadn't been able to meld with me. And then I put it together.

It was Bones. It wasn't a nervous breakdown. Spock had melded with him, and somehow, McCoy had some bit of Spock in his brain. It was surreal, difficult to conceive, but Sarek's assuredness that this was true drove me to act. Sarek said I had to get Spock's body off of Genesis, and take it and McCoy to Mount Seleya on Vulcan. It was not going to be easy; Genesis was off-limits to everybody.

Morrow turned me down flat, so I went to my friends.

✦

"I've asked for transporter duty in Old City Station," Uhura said. It was the closest Starfleet transporter to the Starfleet security facility where McCoy was being kept. McCoy had gotten himself in trouble trying to hire a ship to take him to Genesis (clearly, on some level, he also knew what needed to be done), so we were going to have to break him out of prison. Uhura was a commander, and choosing this duty station would probably raise some red flags, but it would be too late before anyone noticed.

We were in my apartment: Scotty, Uhura, Sulu, and Chekov. Breaking McCoy out wasn't the biggest crime we were planning; we were also going to steal the *Enterprise*.

"There's at least two guards on McCoy at all times," Sulu said. "Visiting hours are over at 9 p.m., and the shift reduces to two people at 8:30." Sulu and I would be going in to rescue McCoy. We would then make our way to the Old City Station transporter room, and Uhura would beam us to the *Enterprise*, where Scotty and Chekov would be.

"Scotty," I said, "what about the *Enterprise*?"

"Chekov checked the automated systems this morning," Scotty said. "My new captain has been keeping me pretty busy on *Excelsior*." Scotty unhappily had been transferred to the new ship when we got back. But it would turn out to be our best bit of luck.

"Admiral," Uhura said, "if we do this, what guarantee do we have that it will help Dr. McCoy?"

"Or Mr. Spock?" Sulu said.

I realized at that moment that I'd been risking not just my life and career on Sarek's word, but theirs as well. I looked at my compatriots; they were willing to follow me without question, but I still owed them an explanation.

"I think the people on Vulcan will be able to help McCoy," I said, "but I'm taking it on Sarek's word that somehow Spock will rest easier. But I really don't know. You all have to make your own decision."

"We've learned a lot about Vulcan over the years through Spock," Scotty said. "It always seemed to me that his people had a little bit of magic."

"Nothing could ever stop him," Sulu said.

I looked over at Chekov. He was the only one not saying anything. He'd been first officer aboard the *Reliant* for a long time, and he'd lost his ship and his captain. I asked him for his opinion.

"Spock taught me how to be an officer," Chekov said, "how to be a man. I think it's worth the risk to try to get him to the Vulcan afterlife."

✦

"It is not I who will surrender, it is you!" The Klingon captain was calling my bluff, and I was out of moves.

We had stolen the *Enterprise*; Scotty had sabotaged the *Excelsior* so it couldn't follow us, and we'd gotten ourselves to Genesis. A Klingon bird-of-prey was waiting for us. It was small, but menacing, and the *Enterprise* was in no shape for a fight. We got in one good shot, but the Klingons knocked out our automation system. There were only five of us on board; there was no way to make repairs. We were dead in space. The Klingons had us. They'd destroyed the *Grissom*, and had hostages on the planet. They wanted the "secret of Genesis." They didn't seem to realize that their hostages, Saavik and David, were more likely to have it.

Saavik said someone else was with them. "A Vulcan scientist of your acquaintance," she said. *Vulcan scientist.* Spock. He was alive.

She also let me know something was wrong with the Genesis Planet, the thing the whole Galaxy was in an uproar about, but I didn't care. Spock was alive. Spock was *alive*.

I was going to get him back.

And then the Klingons killed David.

The Klingon commander, Kruge, wanted my ship, so the goddamn Klingon killed my son. I stood by on my dead ship on my dead bridge and couldn't do anything. My son, who I'd abandoned, who I'd only just gotten to know. Who was a wonderful, sweet, brilliant man. They killed him, because Kruge wanted me to surrender the *Enterprise*. He wanted to prove how serious he was about threatening the hostages. So I, in turn, showed him how serious I was.

I tricked most of the Klingon crew into boarding the *Enterprise*, and blew it up. McCoy, Scotty, Sulu, Chekov, and I watched from the surface of the Genesis Planet as it burned up in the atmosphere. I've thought back to this moment many times over the years. That ship meant a lot to me; the happiest moments of my life were when I was sitting on that bridge, and when I'd lost my command of it, I fought hard to get it back. How could I destroy it? Yes, Kruge was threatening to kill the others, and I had to stop him. But did I really have no other option? The *Enterprise* was a dead ship, with outdated technology. I could've erased every bit of computer information; the Klingons would've gotten nothing if I'd given to them. My career was already over; wasn't it worth our lives? I could've let myself be taken prisoner of the Klingons, trading myself for the hostages, and said I would tell them nothing if they didn't let them go. And my plan of beaming the Klingon crew onto the doomed *Enterprise* was a huge risk; Kruge could've immediately ordered the hostages killed.

The truth was, I wanted blood. And as soon as David died, all the emotions I'd invested in the *Enterprise* seemed hollow; it was a ship, a technological marvel, but still a piece of machinery. At that moment, it was nothing but a trophy to my accomplishments, and I purposely threw it away as penance for my son's death.

And now we didn't have much time—the planet we were on was breaking up. We found Spock; the energies that had created the Genesis Planet had regenerated him. It was, as Scotty said, a little bit of magic. His mind, however, was in McCoy's head, and if I could get them both to Vulcan, there was a real possibility we could get him back.

Nothing was going to stop me. I killed Kruge, and rescued Spock literally as the ground crumbled beneath my feet.

CHAPTER 11

THERE WAS NO COFFEE ON VULCAN.

The second day there, that was the least of my troubles, but I really wanted a cup of coffee. The Vulcans had strict rules about chemical stimulants, so none of their food replicators were programmed for it. Scotty found something on the Klingon ship called *raktajino*, but it really wasn't what I wanted. There was also no alcohol, which I thought was also going to be a problem.

When we had arrived on Vulcan, as I expected, its people were able to put whatever was in McCoy's head back into Spock's. He wasn't completely whole; he had some of his memory, but his mind would have to be retrained. Still, it was truly awe inspiring: he'd risen from the dead.

But it had come at a cost. We stole the *Enterprise*, Scotty sabotaged the *Excelsior*, I then destroyed the *Enterprise*, and we stole a Klingon ship after I killed most of its crew. Both the Federation and the Klingons wanted our heads on a platter (the Klingons, literally).

"We're intergalactic criminals," Chekov said.

"Scourges of the Galaxy," Sulu added. Now, we were on Vulcan, near Mount Seleya, at the edge of the Forge, the great tract of wasteland that was home to so much Vulcan history. I wasn't sure what to do next, so I asked Sarek if he could arrange for us to stay. Scotty, Chekov, Uhura, and Sulu could work on the bird-of-prey. If we could bring that ship home to

Starfleet, maybe it would do a little to smooth over the trouble we'd caused. Maybe.

But my real reason for wanting to stay was Spock. He still wasn't himself; they would have to retrain him. I wanted to see if he would come all the way back. It wouldn't make up for what I'd lost, but it might make my life easier.

But my first duty was I had to call Carol to tell her of David's death. She unleashed a rage that was frightening and justified. Her love and attachment to him was something I envied. She was also, like me, mad at herself.

And though David was investigating a planet that he helped create, the fact that he'd been killed in space by Klingons assigned responsibility for his death, in Carol's mind, to me. She knew it was irrational; she was grieving for her lost child. I wanted to grieve with her, but I could feel that there was no real chance at reconciliation. The Klingons were my mortal enemies, and they'd killed her son. Rational or not, she would always blame me for his death. I said I would be in touch with her soon, but I never spoke to her again.

✦

Sarek came to me on that second day. I assumed he was going to tell me we were going to be extradited immediately back to Earth; there were inviolable treaties guaranteeing that criminals could not find safe harbor on any Federation world. But Sarek said that was not the case, at least not right away. I was incredulous.

"Starfleet Commander Morrow's going to want my head on the chopping block," I said.

"Morrow is no longer the Starfleet Commander," he said. Morrow, it turns out, was another victim of my crimes. He was the one who brought me back into the Admiralty, and as his reward, I stole a ship, wrecked another one, and stirred up a mess with the Klingons. He resigned in disgrace. One more life I ruined.

"Who took his place?" I said.

"Admiral Cartwright," Sarek said. Cartwright had told Sarek that the Klingons were not yet aware that we'd stolen their bird-of-prey. There were a lot of secrets aboard her that would be tactically useful to Starfleet. Cartwright implied he would suggest to the Federation president we not be extradited. We may be tried in absentia, but with the help of the Vulcans my crew would find out all we could about the ship, before the Klingons tried to steal it back.

"Did he say we had a choice?" I said.

"He did not propose an alternative," Sarek said. Cartwright hated the Klingons more than I did, and was looking for any advantage. He was appealing to my sense of loyalty, and really offering nothing definite in return, though there was an implicit suggestion that it would help us at trial.

I decided, initially at least, that it was better than going home to immediate imprisonment.

"In the meantime," Sarek said, "my wife has invited you to join us for an evening meal." This came as a surprise, but I of course took him up on it.

Sarek maintained his home in the city of ShiKar, whose spires rose out of the surrounding rocks and sands like enchanted crystal. Their house was one level, bright, airy, and modern, filled with sculptures, paintings, and other works of art. Amanda met us at the door.

"Admiral, it is wonderful to see you," she said. Her warmth was infectious, and stood out to the aloofness of everyone else I'd been in contact with since arriving.

"Please call me Jim," I said. Sarek led us inside, and we sat down to a meal that, though vegetarian, was more human than Vulcan. It was a lovely supper. I discovered that Sarek had taken on opening diplomatic talks with the Legarans, the lobster-like species I had encountered several years before. I told him of our initial difficulties.

"You were ill-equipped to handle such a delicate first contact," Sarek said. "Humans lack the patience necessary to construct even a structure for diplomacy with this species." Amanda gave him an admonishing look, and I took a little umbrage at the insult; I'd made dozens of successful first contacts.

"How much patience would I need?"

"I estimate it will take seventy years before an agreement is reached to begin negotiations." I looked to see if he was joking, then remembered that

Spock was the only Vulcan who did that. I decided then, in this case, he was right, I did not have the patience.

When I got ready to leave for the evening, Amanda took my arm.

"You brought me back my son," she said. "I know what you lost, and I'm so, so sorry." In that moment, for the first time, I understood the wisdom of Vulcan society. I remembered David. The feelings of anger, despair, frustration invaded. I had no control of them, and I wished I had the discipline of a philosophy that would allow me not to feel.

Months passed and we worked on the Klingon ship, and I learned that though I had obviously spent a lot of time with Spock, that hadn't prepared me for life on Vulcan. For starters, there was no small talk. People only spoke for a specific purpose; if they didn't have one, they didn't speak. Initially, it was unnerving; it was like a planet of awkward silence. But over time I came to appreciate it. And eventually all the logic began to seep in, and some of my emotions seemed to fall away. I was "going native," and I think it helped me through a difficult period.

One day, we had a visitor at our camp. An elderly Vulcan woman in a hover chair floated toward me, escorted by several aides. Though she was much older, I recognized her immediately.

"You are not dead," T'Pau said.

"No ma'am," I said. I don't know how she heard that I was on the planet, but when she did, she obviously felt a need come see me. For what purpose, I couldn't even guess.

"You disrespected our traditions," T'Pau said.

"I did not mean to," I said. I suppose I could've blamed McCoy for what happened at Spock's wedding, but that didn't seem logical. "I apologize if that was the result."

"It was," T'Pau said. We stood in silence for a long moment. I knew there was nothing more to say. She then looked at me. "You have increased your weight. It is not healthful." She then turned and floated away with her entourage.

Did she come all that way to tell me I had gotten fat?

✦

THE STORY OF STARFLEET'S GREATEST CAPTAIN

"The Federation Council has finished their deliberations," Sarek said. It was about three months after we'd arrived, and upon hearing that the council was going to try us in absentia, Sarek had gone to Earth to speak in our defense. He was on the viewscreen of the Klingon bird-of-prey. McCoy and I spoke to him from the bridge, which Scotty and his team were almost finished refitting for human operation.

"You have all been found guilty of nine violations of Starfleet regulations," Sarek said, "which carry a combined penalty of sixteen years in a penal colony." I had no idea if our work on the Klingon vessel would gain us any leniency, or if that sentence had already taken that into account.

"In addition," Sarek went on, "the Klingons have threatened war if you are not executed."

"Everybody or just me?" I said.

"Just you," he said.

Even my time among the Vulcans had not tempered my rage against the Klingons. I was hoping to bump into them again. I could have easily killed some more.

Sarek asked what we intended to do. Prison waited for all of us. I suppose we could've taken the bird-of-prey and become pirates on the run.

But the truth was we wanted to go home, whatever the consequences. We couldn't hide on Vulcan forever.

On the day we left, Saavik came to see me. She was staying behind. The rumor was she was pregnant. I wondered whether it was David's, but it seemed inappropriate to ask.

"Sir, I have not had the opportunity to tell you about your son. David died most bravely. He saved Spock. He saved us all. I thought you should know." I nodded. I don't know if it was a comfort. He died a hero, but like many parents, I think I would've preferred if he'd been a coward and lived.

After Saavik left, Spock came on board. It was the first time I'd seen him since we'd been back. He had been undergoing a reeducation and seemed a kind of childlike version of himself. But he was just as brilliant and just as loyal. He was coming with us to offer testimony in our defense. We, and the entire population of Earth, were lucky he decided to do that.

✦

"Save yourselves . . . avoid the planet Earth at all costs." It was Federation president Hiram Roth, sending a planetary distress call. A mysterious probe had come into Earth orbit and had sent transmissions that were ionizing the atmosphere, blocking out the sun, and had caused all power systems to fail. We were in the bird-of-prey, approaching the Sol System, when we received the message. It was dire; Earth would die.

I had to do something, but it was hard for me to believe that we'd make a difference in our little alien ship, when all of Starfleet had been paralyzed. But we were the only ones who had Spock.

He listened to the probe's transmissions and determined that they were meant for something that lived underwater. The life-forms were trying to communicate with humpback whales, a species that had long been extinct on Earth.

If we got close to the probe, our power would fail too. So, the only way to talk to the probe was to find some humpback whales.

I told Spock to start computations for time warp. It had been almost 20 years since we'd attempted time travel in a ship. We were in a different kind of vessel, but the theory was the same. We would "slingshot" around Earth's sun, and it would send us back in time. I was on a mission to save my world.

✦

"Watch where you're going, you dumbass!"

San Francisco in the 1980s was a lot different than it was in the 2280s: loud, polluted, angry, but also intense, energetic, and more colorful. The person who called me a "dumbass" had almost just run me over with his automobile, yet somehow blamed me for it.

Spock had chosen the era based on accessibility of humpback whales as well as available power; the Klingon ship wasn't built for time travel, and going back in time had already weakened the reactor. So fixing the ship became part of our mission.

THE STORY OF STARFLEET'S GREATEST CAPTAIN

Finding the humpbacks ended up being relatively easy; they were at the Cetacean Institute outside the city. Spock and I went to investigate, while the others dealt with building a whale tank in the bird-of-prey and making sure our engines had the power necessary for the return trip.

Walking the streets of San Francisco with Spock brought back a lot of memories, especially of our trip to 1930. Stuck in the primitive past, we had a mission to save the future. It took me out of the darkness I'd experienced recently, and I had my best friend and companion back at my side.

And, just like in 1930, we met an angel who would help us.

Her name was Gillian Taylor. She was the guardian of the two whales in captivity at the Cetacean Institute. She was a guide and a scientist, young, pretty, and passionate about whales. The whales, named George and Gracie, were male and female, which fit in perfectly with our plan to repopulate them in the future. I assumed they were named for great leaders of the time, but I never found out.*

Spock and I had a lot more trouble seeming like we belonged in this era than we did in the 1930s. We looked out of place and a little incompetent. This ended up having the unintentional effect of gaining Gillian's sympathy.

She took me out to dinner for something called a "large mushroom with pepperoni." I also had a drink, which was remarkably similar to Tellarite beer.

During the meal, she revealed to me that she worried that the whales were going to be released into the ocean and be killed by whalers. I told her I could take the whales somewhere they would never be hunted.

"Where can you take them?" she asked. She was hopeful.

I was hinting around, and finally just came out and told her I was from the future. I somehow didn't worry that revealing it would change history. Given her reaction, I was right not to be concerned.

"Well, why didn't you tell me to begin with? Why all the coy disguises?"

---

*EDITOR'S NOTE: The whales appear to have been named for comedian George Burns and his partner and wife, Gracie Allen, although it is unclear what their relationship was to marine biology.

I didn't have to be concerned, because she clearly didn't believe me. I was frustrated because I needed her help to take the whales, and it initially didn't look like I was going to get it.

Later that night, I was back aboard the bird-of-prey. Gillian had dropped me off, with the food I'd ordered. It was in a square box and had an intoxicating smell. Spock and I opened it. There was a disc inside made of bread, with pieces of meat and vegetables mixed on top with cheese.

"This is a pizza," Spock said. I had heard of it. It looked delicious, but given what T'Pau had said to me, I decided to forgo it. Spock couldn't eat it because it had meat, so Scotty ate most of it.

I didn't know what we were going to do; without Gillian's help, I didn't think we'd find the whales.

The bird-of-prey sat in Golden Gate Park, but the cloaking device was activated, so it was transparent. Gillian was "banging" on the invisible hull the next morning. She must have seen me beam inside the night before, and this led her to begin to consider the possibility that we were telling the truth. She found herself in a quandary: believe someone she thought was crazy, or let her whales be hunted and killed. She decided on the former, and with her help, we rescued George and Gracie, beaming them into our ship to take to the 23rd century.

She didn't want to stay in her own time. And I didn't care. This time, I got to take the angel from the past home with me.

✦

"Because of certain mitigating circumstances, all charges but one are summarily dismissed," President Roth said. I stood with Spock, McCoy, Scotty, Uhura, Chekov, and Sulu in front of the Federation Council. The "mitigating circumstance" was that we saved the planet.

We dropped the whales off in San Francisco Bay, and they immediately started talking to the probe. And the probe left, just like that. And everything was fixed.

The remaining charge was disobeying orders, which they directed solely at me. They could kick me out of Starfleet for that. I thought of myself as a civilian again; I hadn't been able to make it work before, and now I was even older. I was scared at the prospect; the idea of prison seemed easier.

"James T. Kirk," Roth said. "It is the judgment of this council that you be reduced in rank to captain, and that as a consequence of your new rank, you be given the duties for which you have repeatedly demonstrated unswerving ability. The command of a starship." I smiled. I was completing the cycle again, going back to a ship after getting a promotion. Starfleet had decided to enable me.

I went to find Gillian. I was excited at the prospect of showing her my world. But I had barely said hello and she was already saying goodbye.

She was already assigned to a science vessel and was anxious to get started. She was a lot younger than I was; she really didn't need me in this world. She could make it on her own. She kissed me and ran off. I smiled and thought about Edith. I felt like I'd just rewritten some history: a young, selfless woman who saw the future but didn't belong to her time was now in a place where she could shine. A hole in me had filled.

I went back with my family. We went up to our new ship. The travel pod approached. It had been a *Constitution*-class ship called the *Ti-Ho*, but they had renamed it the *Enterprise*. We had come home for the last time.

CHAPTER 12

"I THINK YOU GOT DRUSILLA PREGNANT," McCoy said.

"There's no proof—" I said.

"Yes there is. We're looking at it," he said.

"Shhh!" said a stranger sitting behind us.

We were in a cinema, on Planet IV of System 892, watching people on the screen playing, well, *us*, the crew of the *Enterprise*. It was a strange experience; the actors on the screen vaguely resembled me, Spock, and McCoy. The movie got a lot of the details about Starfleet and the Federation right, which seemed impossible. Spock's doppelganger even had pointed ears and slanted eyebrows.

The world we were on was a startling example of Hodgkin's Law of Parallel Planet Development.[*]

We had originally visited the planet almost 30 years before and found a Roman Empire that had survived into the 20th century, finally struggling with the spread of Christianity. My landing party and I barely escaped with our lives, and the planet was marked "off-limits" by Starfleet. Enough time

---

[*] **EDITOR'S NOTE:** Hodgkin's Law of Parallel Planet Development was from a theory first proposed by the 21st-century biologist A. E. Hodgkin. He showed that if two planets had a similar biology, this could translate over time to similar societal developments. His theory was proven after his death when parallel humanoid societies were discovered across the Galaxy.

had passed, and it was determined by someone in the Admiralty (a young admiral named John Van Robbins whom I'd never met) that we should take another look at it to determine if there'd been any residual contamination from our visit.

We entered orbit and monitored their radio and television transmissions. Nothing seemed out of the ordinary. With knowledge of the society, I decided a landing party in disguise was worth the risk. McCoy, Chekov, and I donned clothing roughly corresponding to the Earth year 1990, and we beamed down to a midsize city.

Rome had not fallen, though the current emperor had allowed Christianity to flourish; it was already the dominant religion of the empire. We saw several examples of Christian churches nestled between homes and businesses, and religious iconography was prevalent. We gathered what information we could and were preparing to beam back to the ship, when McCoy noticed an advertisement on the side of a public transportation vehicle with an internal combustion engine that I believed was called a "bus." We barely got to read it before the bus pulled away from us, but among the images on it, there was a clear photo of a Vulcan. I turned to Chekov.

"Did you catch what it said?"

"'The Final Frontier,'" Chekov said. "It was a title."

"I think that's how they used to advertise movies," McCoy said.

"Contamination?" Chekov said.

"When we were here the last time, the government had a pretty tight lock on information," I said. Our mission to this planet back then was to find a missing merchant ship, the *S.S. Beagle.* The ship had been destroyed, but some of the crew of the *Beagle* had survived on the planet and had become part of the Roman society. The movie advertisement suggested we needed to do a little more research.

"Captain," Chekov said, "we might be able to find something in here." He indicated a bookstore, Cicero's Tomes. We went inside and quickly found a section on popular culture. McCoy pulled out a book on the topic.

"*The Making of 'The Final Frontier,'*" I said, reading the cover. The first chapter had a short biography of the filmmaker, whose name was Eugenio. He was born a slave, and from a very young age, his mother, whose name was Drusilla, had told him stories about his father.

"Uh-oh," McCoy said. He was reading over my shoulder. He recognized the name as well. Drusilla had been a slave to the proconsul who'd captured us on our first visit. She and I had been intimate.

"But it doesn't make any sense," I said. "It wasn't like I told her anything."

"I think we should go see the movie," Chekov said. So we did. (I also bought the book.) When we saw the movie, we noticed that a few people in the audience seemed to be wearing homemade Starfleet uniforms. McCoy had a theory about that.

"Those are fans," he said. "Dressing up like you."

Back on the *Enterprise*, we relayed what we found to Spock in the briefing room. The film had gotten a lot right about Starfleet and the Federation, and its portrayal of me, Spock, and McCoy was dead-on. Spock theorized that Drusilla must have been paying more attention when she served the three of us.

"I'm pretty sure she only served one of us," McCoy said, and I gave him an annoyed look. I still wasn't clear how they had gotten the details of Starfleet and the rest of the Galaxy.

"I think I know the answer to that," Chekov said. He had the book in front of him turned open to a page at the end. Under a title head called "Credits," there was a list of people who had been involved in the making of the film. Chekov had done some cross-checking in our data banks. Three of the names listed under "Consultants" matched the names of members of the crew of the *Beagle*.

"So this slave, Eugenio," I said, "hearing some details from his mother, searches out the surviving members of the *Beagle*, and they fill in the rest."

"What was the nature of the film?" Spock said.

"This Eugenio was obviously using this film to say something about religion," Chekov said. "The *Enterprise* went on a mission to the center of the Galaxy to find God."

"That is not possible," Spock said. "The center of the Galaxy is a black hole."

"I thought you were going to say," McCoy said, "that there's no such thing as God."

"I have no evidence on that subject," Spock said, then brought up the question of whether this constituted a violation of the Prime Directive.

"It's just a movie, Spock," McCoy said. "I doubt it will come to anything."
I hoped McCoy was right.

✦

"Do you know Uhura's 54?" I said to McCoy. We were in my quarters enjoying a drink, as we were wont to do.

"The *Enterprise* now has the oldest senior officers of any ship in the fleet," McCoy said.

"How do you know that?"

"I looked it up," he said. "We've got three captains. Do we really need three captains?" Scotty had the rank of captain, along with Spock and myself. It was definitely a top-heavy ship, but no one wanted to leave. The last person who'd left was Sulu, who'd finally gotten command of the *Excelsior* three years before.

"We're doing our jobs, aren't we?" I said.

"Who's a little defensive?" he said, with a smirk.

I guess I was. We were on our last legs; our tour was over in four months, and the senior officers and much of the crew had decided to "stand down" and not seek reenlistment. It was just as well. In the last few months our missions had not been vital; we'd become a showpiece. I had a reputation that Starfleet used for security reasons. The Klingons still didn't like me, because they were also a little scared of me, which frankly pleased me. The work wasn't arduous, and the ship itself was a lot like us. They phased out the *Baton Rouge* class 40 years before, and now the *Constitution* class had seen her day. The *Excelsior*-class ships were taking over, and there was already one designated for the name "Enterprise" being assembled. They would be decommissioning this ship probably right after we walked off it.

The door chime rang. It was Spock.

"I request an extended leave of absence," Spock said. "I'm needed on Vulcan."

"Has it been seven years? You need to get someone pregnant?" McCoy said. He reached for the Saurian brandy but I grabbed the bottle first.

"I'm cutting you off," I said.

THE STORY OF STARFLEET'S GREATEST CAPTAIN

"When Vulcans reach a certain age, Doctor, they are spared the turbulence of the *Pon farr*," Spock said, then he turned back to me. "I have been requested to return."

I asked if everything was all right, and Spock said he didn't know; the reason he was being called back was something of a mystery. So I ordered the helm to set a course for Vulcan and told McCoy we would be down to two captains for a while.

"How will we survive?" he said with a chuckle.

We dropped Spock off at Vulcan and were then soon ordered to Earth. It looked like we would spend our last three months in dry dock. It was strange to think it was all coming to an end. I went back to my old apartment. It overlooked Starfleet Academy, and my mind often wandered back to those days. I felt a specific memory gnawing at me and decided I needed some closure.

On one of my leave days, I took a trip to the New Zealand Penal Settlement. Criminals from all over the planet lived and worked there, under guard, and were given carefully guided lives. It was punishment because it wasn't freedom, but it wasn't cruel either. I beamed into an administration building. The clerk behind a desk checked my security clearance and approved my request to visit an inmate. A guard took me out onto the grounds.

There were rolling green hills where inmates worked on a variety of building projects. The guard took me to a technical facility, where inside several men and women labored over an antique computer. One of them immediately recognized me.

Ben Finney was much older and thinner. When he saw me walk in, he immediately excused himself from the group, came over, and quietly said hello. He was not unfriendly, just reserved. I asked him if we could go for a walk. We took a stroll on the lush grounds.

"You'll be getting out soon," I said. "Do you have any plans?"

"Jamie and her wife live on Benecia; they've offered to let me live there with them." Ben's wife, Naomi, had passed away several years before. I didn't bring her up, but I gathered they had not stayed in touch.

"If there's anything you need," I said, "please let me know." Ben stopped.

"Jim," he said, "I appreciate you coming. I appreciate your forgiveness. I have a sickness, and it led me to hurt a lot of people. But I guess what I'm saying is, it would be easier if I didn't see you again."

"Okay," I said. "But I just wanted you to know, I don't think I would've been the person I've become without your help. I wanted to thank you."

Ben nodded. I think the pain of his own actions kept him from being able to embrace my appreciation. We shook hands and said goodbye.

I was glad I took the time to do it. My life as I knew it was about to come to an end.

A few weeks later, I was alone in the dark. I wasn't sure how long I'd been locked in the cell of the Klingon ship. There was no light, no bed, no toilet. Time would pass, I'd sleep for a while, then wake up in a panic, trying to find the walls, or a door, or a hatch. They didn't feed me or give me water. I was weak, disoriented. I sat in the dark, hungry, and I was sure that I was on my way to my execution. I had a lot of time to think about how I'd gotten there.

The chancellor of the Klingon High Council was dead. Apparently by two Starfleet soldiers who beamed aboard a Klingon ship from the *Enterprise* and shot him. We were escorting him to Earth for a historic peace conference. The Klingons had asked for the conference; they were desperate. Their moon, Praxis, had exploded. I remembered when I was part of the DSPS, Cartwright had done extensive studies on the Klingon Homeworld Qo'noS and its single natural satellite Praxis. Despite the widespread nature of the Klingon Empire, it was still highly centralized around their Homeworld; the overwhelming majority of the Klingon population lived there. The only moon, Praxis, had been discovered centuries ago, when the Klingons first went into space. Its rich mineral wealth had been considered a gift from the Klingon gods. According to the strategic studies I had read, without the moon providing energy, they would lose almost 80 percent of their available power.

This had been part of Nogura's plan all those years ago, one which Cartwright enthusiastically pursued: fortify our borders, forcing the Klingons to fortify theirs, spending capital we knew they didn't have. It looked like it had worked; now they didn't have the resources to combat this catastrophe. If they couldn't build air shelters for their population,

Qo'noS would be uninhabitable in less than 50 years, and most of the population dead well before then. When I heard this, I thought, our greatest enemy was about to be defeated. The Galaxy would be safe.

But I hadn't known about the peace mission. That was why Spock had been called home to Vulcan. His father had asked him to act as a special envoy, and he had begun negotiations with the Klingon leader Gorkon to dismantle the defenses on our borders and help the Klingons integrate into the Federation. And then Spock informed me at a meeting of the Admiralty that he had volunteered the *Enterprise* to bring Gorkon to Earth.

"There is an ancient Vulcan proverb: Only Nixon could go to China," Spock said, by way of explanation. I had no idea what that meant.*

I was furious. He knew how I felt about the Klingons, what they'd done to me, to David. I had no interest in helping them, or bringing them into Federation space.

"They're dying," Spock said.

"Let them die," I said. And I meant it. I wouldn't miss them, and, as far as I was concerned, neither would the Galaxy.

But then I met Gorkon.

We rendezvoused with his ship and had him over for dinner. He was a bit of a surprise. He didn't seem like the usual Klingon. A man about my age, he was cultured, civilized, and with a beard and manner that evoked the ancient American president Abraham Lincoln. Before we parted, he quietly said to me that our generation was going to have the hardest time living in a postwar society. His wisdom was lost on me at the time, but not now.

Less than an hour later he was dead. McCoy and I had beamed over to help, but the doctor was either too drunk or too inexperienced with Klingon anatomy or both to prevent Gorkon's death. We were placed under arrest,

---

*EDITOR'S NOTE: This is a well-known Vulcan proverb, but its origin is unclear. It derives from the events of 20th-century Earth, when President of the United States Richard Nixon opened diplomatic relations with Communist China. The meaning of the proverb refers to the fact that it was considered a political success because of Nixon's career history of being a virulent anti-Communist; as such, none of his opponents could accuse him of being "soft" on Communism. It is unclear, however, what Vulcan was a student of Earth history to the extent that they created a proverb. And it couldn't be "ancient," as the events it referred to were only 300 years old.

put into shackles, and shoved into these dark, separate cells. I knew I was being framed for the murder. And the problem was, I was a great suspect: I had means, motive, and opportunity.

Time passed. The darkness made me hallucinate. I thought I was beginning to see glowing orbs or bubbles, but then I'd put my hand in front of my face and it wouldn't block the light; it was true darkness. I began to think I was already dead; I had the urge to scream, just so I'd know I was still alive. But I wouldn't; I didn't want to give my jailers the satisfaction. I slammed my hand against the wall 'til it bled, then put it in my mouth. I could taste the blood. I was losing a sense of time and myself. Maybe the war had already started. Billions were dying because of me. They'd open the door and shoot me. There was no hope.

And then I felt it on my back. My thoughts were foggy. What was it, an insect? No, it didn't move. Then I remembered. Spock had put his hand on my shoulder before I left the bridge of the *Enterprise* for the Klingon ship. I thought he was uncharacteristically patting me on the back, wishing me good luck, but instead he had placed something there. I knew immediately what it was: a viridian patch. A little technological marvel that would allow the *Enterprise*'s sensors to locate me over 20 light-years away. As angry as I'd been at Spock for dragging me into this, he was still looking after me. I gently rubbed the patch. I smiled; it felt like he was in the room with me. He was going to save me.

Shortly thereafter, the door opened and light flooded in. I squinted as two guards grabbed me. I forced my eyes open in the glare and saw McCoy being dragged along with me.

"Bones," I said. "Are you all right?"

"Not at all," he said.

They brought us to the transporter and beamed us down to another prison. (We were on Qo'noS, but we didn't get a tour.) The guards threw us into a cell, this time together. This one at least had a toilet, and they gave us the leg of some dead Klingon animal, which we both tore apart. I was going to tell McCoy about the viridian patch, and then thought better of it; the cell could be bugged.

A few hours later, a younger Klingon, dressed in military robes, came in. He introduced himself as Colonel Worf, who'd been assigned to represent us at our trial.

"I am familiar with the facts of your case," he said, "but we should go over them to be certain nothing important was left out. First, why did you kill the chancellor?" (It reminded me of the famous example of the "loaded question" of ancient Earth, "Have you stopped beating your wife?") We were emphatic that we had not killed Gorkon. We went into great detail about what had happened from our point of view. Worf was another Klingon who surprised me; he believed us. He said he didn't think humans would carefully plan an assassination and then beam themselves into custody.

The trial was in a grand hall, with hundreds of Klingons yelling for our heads. The evidence was piled high against us, and my reputation for hating Klingons was well known. But in case the judge wasn't convinced, they played an excerpt from my log.

"I've never trusted Klingons, and I never will. I'll never forgive them for the death of my boy." I couldn't deny that those were my words. But I knew in that moment that it wasn't only the Klingons who were framing me. I'd recorded that a few days before; only a member of Starfleet, a crewman on my ship, could've gotten that log excerpt.

My own people were part of this. As angry as I was at the Klingons, it had blinded me to much closer enemies. And I had been an unintended coconspirator.

I had assumed Gorkon was lying, that he didn't want peace; I couldn't imagine a Klingon who'd seek the same things I did. And I would have let all them die rather than help. David's death festered, and I didn't want it to heal. It was easier to hate and blame. I understood the conspirators.

McCoy and I were of course found guilty, but due to Worf's spirited defense our death sentence was commuted to life imprisonment on Rura Penthe, the frozen prison planet in Klingon space. Thanks to the viridian patch, Spock was able to rescue us from there, and then we rooted out the conspirators.

Their leader was Cartwright.

I arrested him and put him in the brig on the *Enterprise*. I was personally going to take him back home to stand trial. I also wanted to talk to him. As we began our trip to Earth, I went to see him in his cell. He looked me straight in the eye; he was not sorry for what he'd done.

"I was trying to protect us," he said. He used the excuse men had relied on for centuries: war is necessary for security. I wanted details of the conspiracy. I knew it had involved several highly placed Klingons as well as the Romulan ambassador. All of them wanted the same thing: the same balance of power and the same borders that kept the Galaxy the way it was. Cartwright wouldn't give me too many details, and he apologized for having put me in prison. But he felt the consequences were too great.

"They're animals," he said. "We can't live with them." A few days before, I might have agreed with him. But now, I took great pleasure in pointing out something he'd missed.

"Lance, don't you see? You proved that we *can* live with them. You hate Klingons more than anyone, and yet your conspiracy proved that, when Klingons and humans have a common goal, they work together just fine."

I'll remember the look on his face for the rest of my life.

I went back to the bridge and looked around at my old friends. Spock, McCoy, Uhura, Chekov. We had all been brought to the brink of a holocaust that would've cost billions of lives, by a bunch of old men whose fear of death made them seek an unobtainable measure of security. Men like me, who'd grown up hating Klingons, and didn't know there was another choice. Men who'd gotten used to being the inner circle of a democracy's military, thinking they knew best, and depriving the rest of us of our right to make decisions. I'd seen it firsthand working with Nogura. And now, my contemporaries and I in the upper ranks at Starfleet had almost missed it. "The price of liberty," the American patriot Thomas Jefferson wrote, "is eternal vigilance." We needed the next generation to start keeping watch.

It was time for me to go.

We brought the *Enterprise* home, again. Or maybe the *Enterprise* brought us home, it's hard to know which. As we pulled into Earth orbit, we passed a space dry dock, where the next *Enterprise* sat, almost completed. This was truly the end of my era as captain of the starship; I didn't even know who would be taking over. I said goodbye to my friends, certain I would see them all again soon.

As I usually did after a long trip in space, I went back to Iowa. My father was there, and we sat on the porch on a pair of antique rocking chairs. Mom had taken off again to a conference, this time on Andoria. Dad was in his eighties; he was big and stocky, and still vital. He asked me what I was going to do now. I said I wasn't sure. I thought about the fact that I had nothing to come back to, no wife, no children, no home that I'd built myself. I looked over at my dad and saw myself, but also my opposite. He had all the things I didn't, and I had much of what he'd given up.

"Dad," I said, "did you regret giving up your career?" He took a long pause.

"I don't know," he said. "I made a decision. My dad was never home; I wanted you and Sam to know I would always be here. I don't know if it was a good choice, or the right choice; it was just my choice." We sat and talked a while longer, and then noticed a Starfleet officer walking up the path to our house. It was Peter, now in his thirties. Dad said he heard I was coming and decided to take a quick shore leave. He'd gotten a new assignment, commanding the *Starship Challenger*. I stood up to greet him, and he grabbed me in a hug.

"Great to see you, Uncle Jim," he said. I stood back and took in his new rank insignia.

"Great to see you too, Captain Kirk," I said.

✦

That was several months ago. When I announced my retirement from Starfleet, a historian at Memory Alpha contacted me. He requested if he could collaborate with me on my autobiography. With no other projects on the horizon, I agreed. I sit now, having finished it.

Tomorrow, they are christening that new *Enterprise*. I will be there, but there will be another captain in the command chair. I suppose the journey back through my memories has made me realize that perhaps I had retired too soon, because as long as I sat in that chair, I felt relevant. I have some regret that I could never figure out how to break the cycle of my life, finding relevancy in something besides Starfleet. I suppose that makes me like a lot of other people, who don't really know how to change.

My collaborator, upon reading an early draft, noted that he was surprised I didn't mention any of the commendations I received from Starfleet, and I had to examine that. I realized that the medals I have do remind me of my victories, and that's the problem. The Duke of Wellington said, "Nothing except a battle lost can be half so melancholy as a battle won." Too many people died for me to win those medals. And all those victories I suppose made it hard for me to connect, to foster relationships and a life. I just kept going back to being a captain. In that chair, I felt like I accomplished a lot; it felt like I helped more people than I hurt. I hope that's true.

Even as I sit here, this doesn't feel like an end. I realize 60 is not all that old. Starfleet may not want me, but maybe I can get a decommissioned ship. I could fill it with people like myself, who still want to help but have been mustered out. We could set our own missions, help where we can, try to stay out of trouble. But also get into some trouble.

I laugh. The cycle, it's starting again. I'm not finished with the Galaxy, not ready to walk away from command. I want more.

But then, who doesn't?

AFTERWORD

BY SPOCK OF VULCAN

JAMES T. KIRK WAS REPORTED KILLED IN ACTION shortly after completing this manuscript. He was aboard the new *Enterprise*, and helped save it from destruction. The report said he was blown out of the ship when the hull was ruptured. His body was never recovered.

But he is not dead.

I will justify that statement in a moment. First, I take fault with some of the logic in his manuscript. He wonders whether he helped more people than he hurt. But it is a matter of objective fact that due to his efforts, four major interspecies wars were avoided. The innocent billions whose lives were saved by his actions far outnumber those who fell by his hand. This does not even include all the discoveries the ships under his command made, which have gone on to improve the quality of life for all the citizens of the Galaxy.

He has many regrets about not having a family of his own. From my own perspective, James Kirk pushed me toward an acceptance of my humanity, and by extension, an acceptance of myself as a whole. I learned from him many things, especially how to joke, and always felt his watchful eye over me. I know that I was not the only crew member to feel this way. He was our father, and though it violates my philosophy to say so, we loved him for it. His children are the crew members who revered him and carry his legacy now to the limits of known space. His family lives on.

In addition, his work and accomplishments make him one of the greatest men who ever lived. That is objective fact; as a Vulcan, I am incapable of hyperbole.

But his story is not over, because, as I said earlier, he is not dead.

This is not the first time I have said this, and many individuals believe that I have no proof, and that I am indulging my human half's need for "wishful thinking."

But it is not. I know this logically; it is actually my Vulcan half that has the proof.

One of the effects of my people's ability to mind-meld is a permanent connection between the mind of the Vulcan initiating the meld and that of the subject. From moment to moment, I am only vaguely aware of these connections; our mental disciplines keep them compartmentalized and away from our daily thought processes.

But one thing we are always certain of is when a connection is lost when someone dies.

Over the years, I have experienced the death of the Horta on Janus IV, and of Dr. Simon Van Gelder, and of Gracie the whale. The experience was akin to a building at night with its windows lit. And then one light goes out. You know whose light it is; you feel them gone.

I had mind-melded with James T. Kirk on several instances over his lifetime. His light still burns. He lurks in the recesses of my mind. Sometimes, I try to focus on him, to try to determine where he is. I do not believe he knows, but I can sense his emotional state. Wherever he is, he is happy.

I do not believe in an afterlife, but I will let my human half indulge in some wishful thinking.

He will return.

ABOUT THE EDITOR

David A. Goodman was born in New Rochelle, New York. After graduating from the University of Chicago, he moved to Los Angeles in 1988 to write on the television sitcom *The Golden Girls*. Since then Goodman has written for over fifteen television series, including *Wings, Dream On, Star Trek: Enterprise*, and *Futurama* (for which he wrote the Nebula Award–nominated *Star Trek* homage "Where No Fan Has Gone Before"). But he is probably best known for his work on *Family Guy*, for which he served as head writer and executive producer for six years and over one hundred episodes. He is the author of *Star Trek Federation: The First 150 Years*. He lives in Pacific Palisades, California, with his family.

EDITOR GOODMAN'S ACKNOWLEDGMENTS

First and foremost, I'm incredibly indebted to Dave Rossi, who came up with the idea for this book, and who, along with John Van Citters, made me an author. Both also made huge contributions to the manuscript. Thanks also to Andre Bormanis who pointed out what really could have happened on Psi 2000, as well as giving me an indispensible email lecture on ion pods; Mike and Denise Okuda for all their work providing the timeline and then giving their permission for me to depart from it; Richard Doctorow for the Wellington quote; John Scalzi for writing "Redshirts"; Simon Ward, my editor at Titan; Rosanna Brockley at becker&mayer!; Russell Walks for his amazing illustrations; and endless appreciation to my editor at becker&mayer!, Dana Youlin, for her hard work, guidance, and considerable talent at both writing and intimidation.

To my friends Mark Altman, Chris Black, Adam-Troy Castro, Manny Coto, Howie Kaplan, Dan Milano, Peter Osterlund, Mike Sussman, and Austin Tichenor because they read my work; Seth MacFarlane, whose professional patronage allows me this sideline. Thanks to the writers and directors of the canon, especially Brannon Braga and Rick Berman for admitting me to the club; and to William Shatner, for obvious reasons. And to my two cousins Michael Kaufman and Mike Metlay, whose example jump-started this interest in me.

To my sisters Ann Goodman and Naomi Press, my brother Rafael, my nieces Julia and Emma, my nephews Josh and Steven, my sister-in-law Crystal, my brothers-in-law Steve Press and Jason Felson, my in-laws

Phyllis and Bill Lowe, and my father-in-law Fred Felson (who holds the record for buying copies of my last book to give as a gift). Thank you all for your love and support. To my mother, Brunhilde Goodman, for her inspirational life, and her guidance in mine. And finally to my delightful and astounding children Talia and Jacob, and my lovely and loving wife Wendy, who are probably only going to read the acknowledgments and that's okay.